Praise for
AMERICAN RE

"This is amazing storytelling. In *American Red*, David Marlett expertly creates a time and place so real that you can't help but be taken in and enthralled by this most American of stories; the legal thriller. Add in the politics and the people — a deeply drawn cast of characters from lawmen to lawyers — and you have a page turner that holds you until the last train out."

— Michael Connelly, multiple *New York Times* bestselling author

"A cracking good tale! Part love story, part espionage thriller."

— Jacquelyn Mitchard, *New York Times* bestselling author of *The Deep End of the Ocean*

"Vivid, well-researched, and told bare-knuckled across a tapestry that is both broad and nuanced. *American Red* brings to life the 1907 West and the actual war that raged there between mine owners and their assassins, and labor leaders and their bomb makers. David Marlett's characters are outsized and real, from Chief Detective James McParland of the Pinkerton Agency — to ruthless union boss Big Bill Haywood and his polio-stricken wife — to famous attorney Clarence Darrow, who lies down with murderers and thieves, and defends the bombers, to realize a life-long dream. This is a historical novel to get lost in."

— Mark Sullivan, international bestselling author of *Beneath a Scarlet Sky*

"A stellar novel of intrigue, adventure, engaging characters, and a fascinating backdrop. A historical legal thriller that will take you back to another time — bringing that world into pristine focus — when American justice was loaded with mischief and mayhem. A true gem of a story."

— Steve Berry, multiple *New York Times* bestselling author

"With a gripping story and unforgettable characters, David Marlett breathes new life into one of the most fascinating chapters in American history. A country in transition, lurching into modernity, as its heroes and villains — lawyers, hitmen, spies, politicians, union bosses, and captains of industry — battle for the upper hand."

— Adam Benforado, *New York Times* bestselling author

Praise for

David Marlett's national bestseller

FORTUNATE SON

"A masterful blend of historical fact and detail, of adventure and peril and courtroom drama. This rousing murder-mystery adventure that was the life of James Annesley and his battle to reclaim his stolen heritage in the precedent setting case of *Annesley v Anglesea*, also gives us the story of the first Kennedys in America."

– Vincent Bugliosi, #1 *New York Times* bestselling author of *Helter Skelter*

"David Marlett sets a wonderful historical novel against beautiful descriptions of Ireland in telling the story of a disputed earldom. *Fortunate Son* offers rich history, well-developed characters, and a unique conclusion."

– *Christian Science Monitor*

"I'll be recommending this book far and wide to anyone who loves historical novels and characters who stay in the reader's mind long after the last page."

– *Views from the Countryside*

"I could tell that Mr. Marlett knew his subject inside and out and I truly believe that this is what made this book so very readable.... The blood, sweat and tears, of the characters and the author are ever-present in this book. I really recommend this book to adventure fans, historical fans, and legal fans. It's a great book and I thoroughly enjoyed it!"

– *Tales of a Book Addict*

"If every book I read were as textured and well-written as *Fortunate Son* by David Marlett, I would need to live a lot longer just to read. I was enthralled from the first sentence."

– *Bags & Books*

AMERICAN RED

ALSO BY DAVID MARLETT

Fortunate Son

AMERICAN RED

A NOVEL

DAVID MARLETT

Though based on a true story and real characters, this novel is a work of fiction. Names, characters, places, and incidents either are the product of the author's imagination or are used fictitiously. Any resemblance to actual events, locales, organizations, or persons living or dead is entirely coincidental and beyond the intent of either the author or the publisher.

Studio Digital CT, LLC
P.O. Box 4331
Stamford, CT 06907

Story Plant Paperback ISBN-13: 978-1-61188-178-3
Fiction Studio Books E-book ISBN-13: 978-1-945839-30-6

Visit our website at www.TheStoryPlant.com

Cover and map design by BlueRun Media

First Story Plant printing: July 2019
Printed in the United States of America

0 9 8 7 6 5 4 3 2 1

UNITED STATES
1906
Railroads (some)
100 mi.
Washington
SEATTLE
SPOKANE
COEUR D'ALENE
Bunker Hi Mine
WALLA
MISSOULA
WALLA WALLA
PORTLAND
PENDLETON
Montana
North Dakota
Minnesota
Idaho
Oregon
CALDWELL
BOISE
SILVER CITY
CORRAL
PO ATELLO
Wyoming
South Dakota
Wisconsin
BATTLE MOUNTAIN
OGDEN
GREEN RIVER
Iowa
BLUE TENT
TRUCKEE
RENO
AUSTIN
SALT LAKE CITY
PARK CITY
LARAMIE
CHEYENNE
Nebraska
CHICAGO
SACRAMENTO
FORT COLLINS
GREELEY
SAN FRANCISCO
Nevada
DENVER
Illinois
CASTLE ROCK
Uta
CRIPPLE CREEK
Stratton Mine
Kansas
Missouri
California
Colorado

For my mother

★

OVERTURE

Nature is loath to swallow us whole, flesh and soul,
Rather the raptor rips, devouring us in bits.
Yet we resist, with scythe cut and hammer bang,
with bomb, bullet, and bitter blade.
And for a measured time we thrive,
Tearing loose Her elements for our design,
Shaping expressions into mechanical lives.
But all man's measures are artifice contrived,
For Nature triumphs when we transcend,
returning us to our granular end,
tumbling our existence into Her shadows,
from where we once went and will again

But in that imagined land where man is alive,
What centers his weight is fire inscribed.
Where conflict is duty and pugilists survive.
In peace he kills, in war saves, but only in living does he die.
For man finds right in strain from tribe.
Nature wove it in his grain, particles entwined.
Thus in snarling fits and clashing plight,
Are not some more honorable, more right?
Some gain—some kill—some turn the key.
The blood-red feathers of a cardinal in keep,
at war with itself, with justice to find,
the sirening of splendor and peril aligned.

Yet woman reflects and in silence goes.
She sings with their Mother of grace bestowed,
Her womb, Her heart, Her plumes aglow,
Yet with falcon talons and eyes of crow.
She rules man's summit, the Empress plateau.
Though too in her time her grain falls fallow,
She remains chosen—and all men know.
Thus he strips to knight and burro, star and stone.
Vined he beats cattails, while she in willows weeps.
Blind he digs diamonds, while she in meadows sleeps.
Thus does her warmth make his failings flow.
Thus do her wings raise him from below.

PROLOGUE

In the early 1900s, across the Rocky Mountains, what the bears didn't maul, the sun didn't burn, or the snows didn't freeze, the silver and gold mines consumed, gorging themselves on the bones, sinews, bowels and lungs of those who entered the gaping jowls of earth. And as the mine consumed their bodies, the mine's masters destroyed their spirits. Those owners, many gluttonous and detached persons and corporations alike, often saw working men as mere commodities covered in sweat and blast chalk whose need for breath and sustenance was a bothersome necessity, a fuel cost of production. Miners were walking machines to be used, lost, replaced, ignored—to treat them as such was apt capitalism, utilitarian mastery, superior economics. And when the virtue of American business required teeth, the Pinkerton Detective Agency was there to engage on its behalf, even if it paled civility. The system paid, bloating the owners' wealth and political power while fattening the pockets of their shareholders. And why should it not? The corporation was the creator of society, the engine of progress, the queen bee of the quivering hive. The working class existed to serve her and her leaders—for she alone provided life, liberty and the pursuit of happiness. Thus when those owners saw paths to colossal profits, though they be paved by cruel measures and inhumane conditions, they seized them in both fists, defending them vigorously—and they declared themselves just.

But mired in the wretchedness of the mine owners' creation, men were lost to the endurance, the sixteen-hour shifts, the pittance wages, the searing heat and broken bones, the unsafe reaches, the suffocating air where only their hatred found breath. Still they came by the thousands, replenishing the ranks, clamoring for work—no man's dream of the American West. Where was their promised land, their adventure and plenty? Where was their hope of providing for their wives and little ones? Where was their dream of independence and honor? By the late 1800s, those were mostly vaporous ideas for the working men who migrated west of the prairie expanse. When they finally saw the mirage for what it was, and no other work possible, they turned to the mines for work, supplicating themselves for the rudimentary resources of life, lowering themselves into the sweltering darkness where only the tommyknockers dwelled. There those ghosts of miners killed in the deep would tick and tap, knock and pop, sometimes saving a life, sometimes heralding their living comrade's doom—not that those outcomes were much different. When the owners brought in industrial inventions and bigger machinery, deaths rose, and the miners felt the chill of human weakness—tears to rivers to seas that never fill. Thus they federated into a labor union, the Western Federation of Miners. They found strength in numbers, in their collective force. Nevertheless, whether unioner or not, the men descended into the choking holes each dawn carrying their pick, lunch, helmet and the steadfast hope of returning to the surface by nightfall, preferably on their feet. But tens of thousands did not, and when enough men died in the course of provisioning other men's avarice; when sufficient blood was spilled without recourse or remorse, the leaders of the Federation reached for the only weapon they saw remaining: murderous revolt—and they declared themselves just.

★

– 1 –

WEDNESDAY
July 18, 1906

The lawyer lobbed a verbal spear across the courtroom, piercing the young man, pinning him to the creaky witness chair and tilting the twelve jurymen forward. Their brows rose in anticipation of a gore-laden response from the witness as he clutched his bowler, his face vacant toward the wood floor beyond his shoddy boots. When the judge cleared his throat, the plaintiff's attorney, Clarence Darrow, repeated the question. "Mr. Bullock, I know this is a strain upon you to recount that tragic day when fifteen of your brothers perished at the hands of the Stratton—"

"Your Honor! Point in question," barked the flint-faced defense attorney representing the Stratton Independence Mine, a non-union gold operation near Cripple Creek, Colorado. On this warm summer afternoon in Denver, he and Darrow were the best dressed there, each wearing a three-button, vested suit over a white shirt and dull tie.

The robed judge gave a long blink, then peered at Darrow. With a chin waggle, his ruling on the objection was clear.

"Yes, certainly. My apologies, Your Honor," feigned Darrow, glancing toward the plaintiff's table where two widows sat in somber regard. Though his wheat-blonde hair and sharp, pale eyes defied his age of forty-nine, his reputation for cunning brilliance and oratory sorcery mitigated the power of his youthful appearance: it was no longer the disarming weapon it had once been. No attorney in the United States would ever presume nascence upon Clarence Darrow. Certainly not in this, his twenty-sixth trial. He continued at the witness. "Though as just a mere man, one among all ..." He turned to the jury. "The emotion of this event strains even the most resolute of procedural decorum. I am, as are we all, hard-pressed to—"

"Whole strides, shall we, Mr. Darrow?" grumbled the judge.

"Yes," Darrow said, turning once again to James Bullock who seemed locked in the block ice of tragedy, having not moved a fraction since first taking the witness seat. "Mr. Bullock, we must rally ourselves, muster our strength, and for the memory of your brothers, share with these jurymen the events of that dark day. You said the ride up from the stope, the mine floor, was a swift one, and there were the sixteen of you in the cage made to hold no more than nine—is that correct?"

"Yes, Sir," Bullock replied, his voice a faint warble.

"Please continue," Darrow urged.

Bullock looked up. "We kept going, right along, but it kept slipping. We'd go a ways and slip again."

"Slipping? It was dropping?"

"Yes, Sir. Dropping down sudden like, then stopping. Cappy was yelling at us to get to the center, but there was no room. We was in tight."

"By Cappy you mean Mr. Capone, the foreman?"

"Yes, Sir. Our shift boss that day." The witness sucked his bottom lip. "He was in the cage 'long with us." He sniffed in a breath then added, "And his boy, Tony. Friend of mine. No better fella."

"My condolences," said Darrow. "What do you think was the aid in getting the men to the middle of the cage?"

"Keep it centered in the shaft, I reckon. We was all yelling." Bullock took a slow breath before continuing, "Cappy was trying to keep the men quiet, but it wasn't making much a difference. Had his arms around Tony."

A muscle in Darrow's cheek shuddered. "Please continue."

"So we was slipping, going up. Then the operator, he took us up about six feet above the collar of the shaft, then back down again."

"Which is not the usual—"

"Not rightly. No, Sir. We should've stopped at the collar and no more. But later they said the brakes failed on the control wheel."

"Mr. Bullock, let's return to what *you* experienced. You were near the top of the shaft, the vertical shaft that we've established was 1,631 feet deep, containing, at that time, about twenty feet of water in its base, below the lowest stope, correct?"

"Yes, Sir. Before they pumped that water to get to em."

"By 'them' you mean the bodies of your dead companions?"

"Yes, Sir."

"Ok, you were being hoisted at over 900 feet per minute by an operator working alone on the surface—near the top of the shaft, when the platform began to slip and jump. Is that your testimony?"

"Yes, Sir."

"That must have been terrifying."

"Yes, Sir, it was. We'd come off a tenner too."

"A ten-hour shift?"

"Yes, Sir."

Darrow rounded on the jury, throwing the next question over his shoulder. "Oh, but Sir, how could it have been a ten-hour work day when the eight-hour day is now the law of this state?"

The defense lawyer's chair squeaked as he stood. "Objection, Your Honor."

"I'll allow it," barked the judge, adding, "But gentlemen ..."

The witness shook his head. "The Stratton is a non-union, gold ore mine. Supposed to be non-union anyway. Superintendent said owners weren't obliged to that socialist law."

"Hearsay, Your—"

"Keep your seat, Counsel. You're going to wear this jury thin."

Darrow stepped closer to the witness. "Mr. Bullock, as I said, let's steer clear from what you heard others say. The facts speak for themselves: you and your friends were compelled to work an illegal ten-hour shift. Let's continue. You were near the top, but unable to get off the contraption, and it began to—"

"Yes. We'd gone shooting up, then he stopped it for a second."

"By 'he,' you mean the lift operator?"

"Yes, Sir. He stopped it but then it must have gotten beyond his control, cause we dropped sixty, seventy feet all the sudden. We were going quick. We said to each other we're all gone. Then he raised us about ten feet and stopped us. But then, it started again, and this time it was going fast up and we went into the sheave wheel as fast as we could go."

"To be sure we all follow, Mr. Bullock, the lift is the sole apparatus that hoisted you from the Stratton Mine, where you work?"

"Yes, Sir."

"And the sheave wheel is the giant wheel above the surface, driven by a large, thirty-year-old steam engine, run by an operator. That sheave wheel coils in the cable"—he pantomimed the motion—"pulling up the 1,500-pound-load platform, or lift, carrying its limit of nine men. And it coils *out* the cable when the lift is lowered. But that day the lift carried sixteen men—you and fifteen others. Probably over 3,000 pounds. Twice its load limit. Correct?"

"Yes, Sir. But, to be clear, I ain't at the Stratton no more."

"No?" asked Darrow, pleased the man had bit the lure.

"No. Seeing how I was one of Cappy's men. Federation. And, now 'cause this." His voice faded.

Darrow frowned, walked a few paces toward the jury, clapped once and rubbed his hands together. "The mine owners, a thousand miles away, won't let you work because you're here—a member of the Western Federation of Miners, a union man giving his honest testimony. Is that right?"

"Yes, Sir."

Again, the defense counsel came to his feet. "Your Honor, Mr. Darrow knows Mr. Bullock's discharge wasn't—"

The judge raised a hand, took a deep breath and cocked his head toward the seasoned attorney before him. "Swift to your point, Mr. Darrow."

"Yes, Your Honor." Darrow's blue eyes returned to the witness. "Mr. Bullock, you were telling us about the sheave wheel."

"Yes. It's a big thing up there, out over the top of the shaft. You see it on your way up. We all think on it—if we was to not stop and slam right up into it—which we did that day. We all knew it'd happen. I crouched to save myself from the hard blow I knew was coming. I seen a piece of timber about one foot wide there underside the sheave, and soon as we rammed, I grabbed hold and held myself up there, and pretty soon the cage dropped from below me, and I began to holler for a ladder to get down."

"Must have been distressing, up there, holding fast to a timber, dangling 1,631 feet over an open shaft, watching your fifteen brothers fall."

Bullock choked back tears. "Yes, Sir. That's what I saw." He paused. When he resumed, his tone was empty, as if the voice of his shadow. "I heard em. Heard em go. They was screaming. They knew their end had come. I heard em till I heard em no more."

Round-headed, forty-year-old Harry Orchard sat motionless in the Eagle Head Saloon of the tiny mining town of Wallace, Idaho, about a hundred miles up the track from Missoula, Montana, and about the same crow-flight south of the Canadian border. It was July and the mountain air carried a chill, though not enough for his bear coat—so it was in his trunk at the boarding house. Instead, he was in his clay-colored coat that bore a bullet hole in the back. (Though Orchard put the hole there moments before assuming the coat, he'd forgotten the prior inhabitant's name, or why he'd killed the man.) He fingered his pucey-black homburg hat on the planked bar. He knew what was about to happen and wanted to be ready. His partner, the younger, ferret-faced, infallibly ignorant Steve Addis, was about to spray a broth of blood and brain across the bar. The mess, once splattered, will have belonged to the quivering man standing beside Orchard: the vice president of the Bunker Hill Silver Mine and Concentrator, the largest of its kind in the world, located ten miles further up the Northern Pacific rail line.

"Hold on there!" protested the man, eyes bulging.

Addis gave a scurvy smile from under his green plaid cap and pressed the Colt against the man's forehead, indenting a circle there. Addis's other hand held a Bowie knife to the man's throat. "Which you rather? You're gonna die, so dealer's choice: bullet or blade? I pick blade. But I'm sportin, so you decide."

"You don't need to do this," the man cried, his face clammy and flushed. "I'll leave. I swear."

Orchard knew he needed to move, otherwise he'd have to pay a dollar to have blood cleaned from this coat, again. He lifted his drink and stood, muttering to Addis, "Outside."

"Please mister. I did nothing. My boys. My wife ..." He wept.

Addis clucked his tongue. "Family's everything, ain't it?"

"I'm begging you—"

"Take him outside," Orchard tried again.

"Tired of this talk," barked Addis, sticking out his chin.

"Do it in the street. Less mess."

Addis leaned, his pointy nose almost touching Orchard. "He might talk me confused if I go out."

Orchard paused on that. At least the weaselly fellow knew his weakness. He had to give him that. When they'd been introduced a month gone, the man gave his name as Steve Addis. Maybe it was. Maybe wasn't. Didn't much matter. These loose-gun killers were never around long. Like the men seizing the owners' train down at Missoula. Orchard knew nothing about them—only that they'd load it as he'd asked, then bring it there in an hour or so. He glanced at his pocket-watch and shrugged. "I'll finish my drink."

The man plead again, "I had nothing to do with busting that meet. I get on with Federation fellas. You tell em. You tell Bill." Another shuddering breath before he continued. "Oh, you think I'm a Pink! Well, Sir, I'm not! Most decidedly not! I'm a Wobbly, a union man, if anything. Can prove it, so you let me be. I ain't one of them snollygoster Pink spies!"

"Snollygoster?" mused Orchard.

The man began to tremble visibly.

"Bullet or blade?" Addis asked. "You gotta choose, friend."

"Or dynamite," Orchard added.

When Addis grinned toward Orchard, the mine vice-president attempted to swat the gun, but Addis reacted too quickly, leaving the man hitting air. Addis popped him on the forehead with the flat of the knife. The man recoiled, exclaiming, "Goddamnit! Leave me alone. You've got the wrong man."

"Bullet or blade?" Again Addis brought the pistol up and returned the knife to the man's throat.

The man didn't know—or perhaps he did—that Addis was hired to kill him. In fact, Addis had no knowledge of what the man had or hadn't done. It simply didn't matter. It was all for union gelt: twenty dollars a head.

The man sobbed uncontrollably.

"Bullet or blade? Pick your way. Or I'll let this sombitch decide," said Addis, indicating Orchard. "He'll strap a bomb to you."

The man bit his lip, urine streaming his trousers. "I don't want to die."

"Bullet or blade!" Addis screamed.

"Bul—"

Addis returned his Colt to the man's face and pulled the trigger. Sure enough, bloody brain tissue exploded, covering the bar and its mirror, with some spattering Orchard's hat and coat.

"Well, shit on a cracker!" Orchard exclaimed, jumping back though not losing hold of his glass. Addis stood motionless, watching the body crumple and convulse. He holstered his pistol, sheathed the Bowie, repositioned his cap, and walked out the front door calmly, as if leaving church on a brisk Sunday afternoon. Orchard saw his glass and the whiskey in it were blood-misted. He pondered it for a second, wiped the rim with his sleeve, then downed the reddish drink as he left. In his wake, the saloon remained pin-drop silent though it held fifteen stunned miners and one unhappy barkeep, all of whom heard Orchard yell outside, "Addis! You owe me a dollar!"

The gruesome scene held its viewers in a paralytic grip. No one wanted to approach the dead man. Finally, the barkeep, a man named Clement, murmured, "One of you fetch Sutherland." Fetching the sheriff would do no good. Everyone knew it. The man missing a quarter of his head was mine management. The killers were identifiable by most everyone in the saloon, though not likely by their real names. Regardless, they were untouchable. A murder this bold was sanctioned by Big Bill Haywood in Denver, the dead-eyed union boss of the Western Federation of Miners—known simply as the Federation. It had been ordered and paid for, and no man who wished to again earn a miner's wage, however slight, wanted the attention of Big Bill. Neither his bad attention nor his good. Indeed, anyone who appeared to support the killing may find himself being conscripted to do similar work—a request not to be declined. Communicate disapproval of such blood-spillage and you risked having to flee to the other side: non-union scab lines under the protection of the Pinkerton Detective Agency—or the Pinks—the bitter enemy of the Federation. Or worse, one day it might be you being asked, "Bullet or blade?"

So the men shuffled from the saloon in almost single file, their rhythmic boots plodding, their gaze to the back of the man ahead. Don't talk. Just leave. Don't look at the dead man. Step over the expanding pool of blood. Don't bother to pay your tab. And, most certainly, do not fetch Sheriff Sutherland.

★

– 2 –

The warm afternoon brought more testimony from a number of miners, operators, foremen, and laborers, as well as representatives of the owners of the Stratton Independence Mine. Darrow felt certain he had the jury. As the attorney for the Federation, Darrow had shown that the owners had allowed the lift to be overburdened by twice its designed load. That alone should be sufficient negligence to shift liability to the owners, regardless of the mine workers' presumed "assumption of the risk of death." The jury should go his way, especially as he was seeking an insultingly small sum from the owners: three-thousand dollars per miner killed. He needed only to close his case with the strongest witness he had: the lift operator, now squirming in the witness chair. Darrow approached him.

"Mr. Simmons, you're the operator of the—"

"The hoisting engineer," retorted the thin-faced, mustached man in his best sack suit and narrow tie.

"The hoisting engineer, yes. The hoisting *engineer*." Darrow slowed the word engineer so the jury could get a whiff of its importance. "You're much more than a mere operator. Please accept my apologies. You're a hoisting engineer. You're trained to operate the lift. The Stratton mine must have educated you for two weeks or more to perform your duties as the hoisting *engineer*."

"No, Sir. I'd been on that job for two days."

"Two days! Surely you'd operated, I mean *engineered*, a similar hoist at other lode mines before the Stratton?"

"No, Sir."

"No? Two days to become a hoisting engineer. Two days and the owners of the Stratton put you in sole control of the lives of the four hundred and sixty-three men who rode that shaft down to the stopes each morning. All right, Engineer Simmons, tell us: you had that platform coming up. What happened?"

The witness bounced his gaze off the jury then back to the floor before clearing his throat. "I seen the cage was at the collar of the shaft and moving quickly. I tried the brakes but they weren't slowing it none, so I went to—"

"Might the brakes failed owing to twice the load tolerance?"

The defense counsel's attempt to object was straightaway squashed by the judge's almost imperceptible shake of his nose.

"Might have. Might. But I wasn't aware sixteen had gotten on. Least not then. But it wasn't right in its working."

"Continue, please."

"I immediately reversed the engine and sent the cage down a hundred feet. Again I tried the brakes, reversed the engine again, and brought the cage back to the surface. Then the brake just stuck. Froze up and I couldn't move it none. I again reversed the engine and sent the cage back about the same distance and stepped over to the other side and took hold of the other brake, and it was in the same condition. The second time ..." Simmons's voice cracked. He sniffed a few times, his neck and cheeks reddening. "That second time the cage came up, I called three times for the shift boss, 'For godsakes come and help me put on the brakes.' Meantime I was reversing the engine backwards and forwards. Mr. McDonald, he came and tried to help me, but this time when the cage came up it was going quick above the collar." He cleared his throat once more, then, swaying his slumped head, spoke just above a whisper. "I reversed the engine, but it was too late. The cage hit the housing fast and went to pieces and ..." The hoisting engineer began to tremble, then a series of sobs overcame him with such force that it required both bailiffs to assist him from the courtroom

Unaware that his second-in-command had just been murdered a hundred miles up the track in Wallace, the superintendent of the Bunker Hill Mine, James Branson III, climbed the steps of a well-appointed, private Pullman Special train car of the Northern Pacific, resting at the Missoula, Montana station. The engine hissed steam, but otherwise remained idle. Branson was in wholesome spirits, with reason to be ebullient: production was up, shutdowns at an all-time low. And only twenty-three miners had been killed in the Coeur d'Alene Mining District during the first three months of the year—a twelve percent drop from the previous year's first quarter, and of those only nine died at Bunker Hill.

Surely the owners' representatives had summoned him for extollation, to pin praise upon him like ribbons upon his chest. He was so certain of it that he had splurged on a pair of Sorosis, patent-leather cap-toes that now clicked up the Pullman's metal stairs to its rear platform. The gentlemen in this train car, gods of capitalism, will appreciate his shoes—here in the wildlands of silver country where working folks don't know a Sorosis from a squaw's sandal. These Chicago chaps will see his shoes and recognize him as one of them: owner-stock not labor-stock. Of course they won't say anything—that would be too obvious. But they'll think, why is this Sorosis-wearing fine fellow stuck in this godforsaken place? Let's bring him back with us to Chicago. Or, let's move him to San Francisco where he has family. All right, not San Francisco, thought Branson, not after its quake and fire devastation three months earlier. But any other city. Anyplace but here.

In the last decades of the nineteenth century and the first few years of the twentieth, the Coeur d'Alene Mining District in far-northern Idaho was prime for the extraction of silver. Among the rolling elevations between Coeur d'Alene, Idaho, and Missoula, Montana, and north to the Canadian border, the great barons of American wealth, the denizens of privilege and power, bought and built a scattering of profitable silver mines. Offering their workers all the comforts of a Russian gulag, the mines served their masters well—making them exponentially richer year upon year, decade upon decade. Of course, where wealth is highly concentrated, governing oversight limited, and the need for work broad and urgent, abuse of the working class abounds. The mines of northern Idaho were no exception, especially the one Branson supervised, the Bunker Hill.

Mine owners professed two self-exonerations for each miner killed: First, men freely chose to toil in the deadly mines, assuming all risks, working conditions, and requirements—therefore it would be entirely un-American to stand in the way of such a freely made individual choice. Second, whatever happened in an old wilderness to enrich a new-century, city-dwelling shareholder was sanctioned by the progress of humanity, by an unwritten, capitalist decree. It was ordained as the rightful exercise of the owners' patriotic duty. And whatever suffering ensued was warranted against the frightening rise of godless socialism, especially in places like Wyoming, Idaho, and Colorado.

At the top of the stairs, the Sorosis shoes paused, and the westerly wind blew with a bite. Something was amiss. At least one Pinkerton guard should be at this door, yet it was vacant. Branson narrowed his gaze through a slight window, but found it obscured by an interior curtain. He inhaled, turned the door handle and entered. Void of people, the car held only well-appointed benches, tables, curtains, and candelabras. Silence. He removed his tall bowler and surveyed the interior. Crystal glasses were put away. Cigar boxes were in their humidors. Not just empty, it was tidy, as if it had carried no one at all on its journey west from Chicago.

As much chilled as puzzled, Branson turned, looking out the windows. Perhaps he would recognize someone on the depot landing. No—just strangers, and only a few at that. Had he forgotten the meeting place? Perhaps the time? He retrieved the telegraph from the pocket of his suit (another recent mail-order from Chicago). After his eyes twitched across it, he stuffed it back. Monkeys' asses were testing him. Maybe they were squeaking beds at Jane's boarding house again. He placed his hat on a peg as he had many times before, then took a seat in view of the door. He had no choice. He had to wait. Sorry sons of whores.

Darrow had been modestly confident of a victory. Evidence had poured forth on the lack of commonly used stops in the vertical shaft, the negligence of not having another man on duty at the collar, the incompetence of hiring a hoisting engineer with no qualifications, the carelessness of allowing sixteen men on the lift, and the overall failure of the mine's owners to ensure the brake system was properly inspected. Thus, the jury's verdict rattled him. They found in favor of the mine's owners, holding the men's deaths to be within the risks taken in the performance of their labors. The dead were nothing and their widows were entitled to nothing. Their children nothing either. Nothing.

Walking from the courthouse, Darrow's embarrassment was assuaged only by his outrage, his fury at the obvious judicial bias in the Colorado courts. Though he had won the battle of evidence, had even been buttressed by the judge's sympathies, Darrow had lost the jury to the artifice of an inherently corrupt system. He reasoned and rationalized—the jury must have felt trapped, like birds in a cage, unable to exercise their natural abilities. The law (written by politicians bought wholesale by the mine owners) encouraged juries away from their principles, their private, moral sense of justice. Clearly the mine owners were responsible, but they would not be forced to pay.

He fumed as he walked, feeling flat footed and fraught. The horrific deaths of those men, flesh and blood fathers, husbands, brothers and sons, were just ledger-sheet costs. And the cost of this trial but a pittance plucked from those shareholders' ripe asses. "Damnation," he muttered aloud as he crossed Larimore Street.

Corporations were a duplicitous class of self-proscribed "citizens" able to fly the gold *laissez-faire* flag when it served them, when it was needed for profits. But then they would shuttle up the red flag of socialistic sanctuary to shield themselves from losses, like a semaphore in a hurricane. And the voters were too ignorant to see it. Too lazy to pay attention. Too comfortable. Too miserable in their personal failures to identify their true oppressors.

He felt his cheeks flush, then heard his wife, Ruby, faintly admonishing him. *Darling, no man tries harder to right things,* she would say. *But your wax wings will take you only so far. You can flap and fly, and try, but sooner or later the flames of other men's stupidity will get you.* She was aggravatingly right, even if her analogy was wanting.

He took a breath and checked the creases in his hat. He would deliver the bad news to his client, William "Big Bill" Haywood, the leader of the Western Federation of Miners. He would tell him in person, man to man—ignoring what was probable, that Haywood would've already learned of the verdict from one of his spies and minions. They were everywhere in these streets. Along with their counterparts—Pinkerton operatives. Darrow grimaced. Haywood might fire him. Maybe not. Probably not.

The one consolation: thirteen of the fifteen dead had been Federation, thus they had received ceremonial funeral cartages:

shiny black carriages pulled by teams of equally black horses, trailed by hundreds of miners in solemn procession. Haywood had instructed that the other two dead men, neither being union, be left where they fell, to rot at the bottom of the shaft.

Nearing the Federation's offices (and his own office nearby), Darrow passed under sycamore trees whose disconsolate shadows matched the gray of his cynicism. And in that gloom, Haywood's favorite rubric (and polemic alike) came to Darrow's mind—the four boxes of change: the soap box, ballot box, jury box, and cartridge box. Certainly, the soap box could be commanding—it had led to the formation of the Federation, the most powerful labor union in the United States. And with the ballot box, the Federation had forced laws for an eight-hour workday, wage protections, and prohibitions against child labor. But those laws were useless without enforcement, without the power of the jury box, Darrow's domain—or so it was supposed to be. But when he failed, like today—when juries brought back verdicts such as this one, unwilling to hold owners liable—what was left? Perhaps Haywood was right: the moment was at hand for the fourth and final box: the cartridge box. Regretful but true. Maybe it was time for violence to bear its inexorable teeth, to exact what it had proven throughout history to be singularly capable of achieving: authentic and proximate change. One thing was certain, thought Darrow as he stepped around bird droppings towards the granite-arched portico of the Pioneer Building: by any means, by any box, it was time for real change.

★

– 3 –

That same afternoon, a thousand miles northwest of Denver, Sheriff Sutherland was managing the aftermath at the Eagle Head Saloon in Wallace, Idaho. The body, now covered in course burlap, was in a wagon bed through which blood dripped to the axle beneath. Inside the saloon, the barkeep (who had fetched the sheriff on his own) and two deputies were sweeping up brain and skull bits, along with dirt and shards of glass—a menagerie of earth, elements, and man.

Outside, Sutherland lit his cigar and looked down at the crimson-splotched sack over the dead head. With a "humph" and a sway of his large gray-white mustache and unshaven chin, he turned and walked back toward his office, two blocks away. Behind him, a tall, spry, ginger deputy approached. Both sheriff and deputy were in canvas trousers and floppy jackets, and both under Montana-style, wide-brimmed hats.

"Fellow named Addis done it," said the deputy. "Big knife and a pistol."

"He's long gone," said Sutherland, keeping his pace. "Addis?"

The deputy continued. "One fella, the taller one, called the other Addis—the one that did the shootin."

The sheriff turned. "Frankie, son ... then his real name's probably anything but 'Addis.'"

"Oh ... alright," said Frankie.

"His partner planted it in the ears of the bystander folk."

"Oh."

"Then again," said Sutherland as he resumed his stride, "we don't know that there isn't a man out there somewhere named Addis, someone who did the Federation wrong, and Big Bill is marionetting us as his instruments of vengeance." As they reached the office, he stepped to the porch. "Or maybe the taller one was betraying the Addis fellow by saying his name aloud." He paused just inside the office to unbuckle his gun belt. When Frankie was also inside, the sheriff continued, "If that's how it is, then Addis *is* the killer's name." He strolled to a window, staring out blankly. "So what should be done, son?"

Frankie removed his hat and peered into it as if that's where he kept his ideas.

Sutherland turned to the young man. "Son, I know you want to be treated like any other deputy. It's not easy."

"If you'd give me something—"

"Your mother—" Sutherland sucked air through his teeth and rubbed his forehead. "Alright, take two men. See if you can find this 'Addis' about town. And his partner."

"Thank you, Pop. You'll see."

"Mind you, these animals are killers. They'll turn without a moment's reflection. Understand? If God Almighty puts an opportunity in your hands, you're obliged to gun em down."

Frankie's face fell. "Shouldn't I at least—"

"You want to try these bastards in a courtroom? They get some fast lawyer in front of a scared judge? You think they'd ever hang? Here in Idaho? You think any witness will say a word?"

"I don't know."

"You find em, you shoot em. No hanging." The sheriff noted his son's troubled squint. "My pop used to say: 'Every man deserves justice: The good, long lives—the bad, short uns.' He was right, but it's not our duty to help the good. You're a lawman now. You're to dispense God's revenge on the bad. You're obliged to give them the short lives they deserve. So don't get yourself hurt on account of the law. If we arrest Addis, he'll get himself a fancy, city lawyer and be free, killing again, fast as whistling Dixie. But if you kill him, I'll back you. Every US Marshall from here to St. Louis will support you. Hell, Governor Steunenberg wouldn't look twice. No, some debts don't need a jury to tally."

"How about I bring him here and *you* shoot him?"

Sutherland's mustached lips straightened as he saw his son's eyes dart about. "Alright, Frankie. Alright. If you see him, just keep your distance and send for me."

Down the line in Missoula, James Branson remained alone, sunk plush in a lounge chair of the luxurious Pullman. The sun was streaming in acutely, particles afloat in its warmth, Branson's head bobbing in half-slumber. Suddenly the train rocked forward. "Whoa!" he exclaimed, jumping to his feet. There had been no whistle, no notice of departure, just an abrupt jolt in the undercarriage. The train rolled slowly, squealing and creaking. Branson hurried to leave but a grizzled man was chaining the door from the outside. He saw Branson and shouted, "God speed to Bunker!"

"Wait!" Branson yelled, running to the car's windows. As the train picked up speed, the man hopped from the car's platform. Branson tried window after window, but all were nailed. He considered breaking one, but the vision of a long fall to moving tracks dissuaded him. The train was chuffing, rolling, leaving the Missoula station with him on board, and there was nothing he could do about it. They were just trying to scare him. It would be all right. Just a prank. Just an annoyance. He took a seat by the window and watched the accelerating forest beyond, broken occasionally by rock outcroppings and grassy foothills.

As he began to gnaw on what he knew, his calm evaporated. That man must've been union. So this train had been hijacked. It was probably carrying a swarm of Federation men to the Bunker Hill Mine, where he was superintendent. So, the Federation was scheming for a bloody battle—a battle against the sixty-seven strike breakers that he had brought in under Pinkerton guard several weeks earlier. He needed to telegraph ahead. Or telephone, perhaps—a device he was not entirely comfortable with. Regardless, he needed to warn his men at the Bunker. But how?

He had ridden this two-hour route over a hundred times in the three years since he had arrived from Pennsylvania to assume leadership of the Bunker. He had moved at the behest of the mine's owners—as imposing and impatient of men as Branson had ever known. In those three years, he had come to know every bend in this track, every switch and siding, every telegraph box, every trestle and river crossing. And he knew that twenty minutes before arriving at the Bunker Hill Mine, this train would go through the little town of Wallace, Idaho. That would give him an opportunity to get off and signal ahead.

As the first hour passed, Branson attempted to juggle the variables in his mind, to force them into recognizable patterns. Federation men, union thugs, had this train. He was confident of that. They had done things like this before: the Federation would fill a train with labor boys scrapping for a fight, then take the train to the mine's depot. There they would lay siege to the industrial machinery while brutally removing all scabs and strike breakers. And the Bunker Hill was ripe for that kind of action. They were in the midst of the third Federation strike this year. This one, just as with the other two, was guised under the demand for eight-hour workdays—something Branson knew the mine's owners would never agree to. To them, an arbitrary work limit such as the eight-hour workday affronted the decency of the free market. But still the union struck for it, time and again. Branson may have admired the Federation's tenacity were it not for the vicious undertone of this latest, third strike—one that was occurring in Colorado as well as in northern Idaho.

At the outset of the current strike, the Federation had discovered a Pinkerton among their ranks, the man having infiltrated a union meeting in Denver. Within the hour of the discovery, the man was so severely beaten and tarred that he fell blind in one eye and would likely not walk again. When some management remarked that the Pink was lucky to be alive, Superintendent Branson had agreed, knowingly. As the mine owners had Pinkertons ingrained in their strategies for breaking the Federation's hold, the discovery and loss of an agent was unfortunate, but not uncommon. An acceptable cost. In fact, such discovery and retribution usually re-established balance between the two warring sides. But this recent time, even after tarring the Pinkerton, the Federation seemed dissatisfied. Rumblings of additional reprisals against mine owners and their Pinkerton militia had been adrift for weeks. A new level of violence was stirring. Tensions were so palpable as to have a smell, a taste in the air.

Therefore Branson reasoned that the Federation was using this commandeered train to transport a small army of union men to his Bunker mine, with a fight certain to erupt upon arrival. But never to Branson's knowledge had a hijacked train included a Pullman, an owners' car. It was a big prize for the Federation. And they had locked him in it. But, why? Why force him to return to the mine he managed? At this hour and in this manner? And what had become of the mine owners he'd expected to meet? And where was the usual Pinkerton protection detail? This was wrong.

As the second hour of the journey wound down, he began to suspect the union men were going to kill him. Could the Federation murder the superintendent of a mine in broad daylight? No, they wouldn't. Yes, of course they might. His pulse quickened, skin prickling, his breath shallow and fast. Death was ahead. His blood iced. Standing quickly, he removed his suit coat and prayed aloud, "Lord, get me off this train."

In front of the Pullman, just beyond the tender, was the engine where the conductor lay dead on the steel floor. The coal man and brakeman were nowhere to be seen. Beside the conductor's bloody face were the muddy boots of his killer and replacement, a man deftly operating the train as it puffed through the wild, the Wallace depot coming into view.

From the windows of the Pullman, Branson saw the advent of Wallace. If the train stopped there, as it was supposed to, he could break a window and shout for help. But that would draw the attention of unioners who might shoot him. Best to just slip off, undetected. Then he could scuttle whatever plans these devils had for him and the Bunker. But how to get out? His eyes lit on a fire ax mounted in a corner.

The Wallace stationmaster stood resolute on the platform, noting the approaching train in the far valley was not simply off schedule, but it would arrive almost an hour before due. He turned to an assistant and barked, "Go around to the Eagle Head. Tell Sheriff Sutherland to get here right away."

Holding the ax, Branson first thought to bust down the rear door, but he hesitated. Federation men in the car behind him would stop him. He looked around. How to get out unseen? He considered the ceiling, then the floor. That was it. He rolled back the carpet to reveal the wood below. Swinging the ax, Branson began to tear through the floor of the Pullman Special. Albeit slowly. Swing after swing. First the planking, then the under-floor; bits of daylight, then the push of air and the blur of rail ties below. Wood splintered wildly with each swift chop. Soon the hole approached a size he could reach through. He kept swinging.

What Branson didn't realize was that the two passenger cars behind the Pullman were, in fact, empty; as was the caboose behind them. They were not carrying union men bucking for a fight, as he had presumed. It was just him and the rough in the engine compartment chugging steadily into Wallace.

Sheriff Sutherland joined the stationmaster on the Wallace platform. "Lester. What's on your mind?"

The man popped his watch open. "Doesn't make sense."

"I see that. It's not stopping. Just slow-rolling." Behind Sutherland, three deputies appeared, including his son, Frankie. All watched expectantly as the engine hove into sight. In an instant, Sutherland realized what would happen next. He spun, shouting to his deputies, "They must be here! Addis and that other fellow are somewhere near. They mean to board that train! Find them!" He motioned to the men, ordering two to search along the near side of the track, and one to search the station. They complied, shotguns ready. A hundred yards away, with its black smoke pillaring into the sky, the train continued steadily—not speeding, but not slowing either. Seeing the opportunity closing, Sutherland motioned for Frankie to cross the track, to look over there. The young man complied just in time. The loud train passed by. First the engine—the silhouette of a conductor making no eye contact—followed by the tender, and then the Pullman with a man in the window, the two empty second-class cars, and then the caboose. Then it was gone.

Sutherland turned to the stationmaster. "That man in the special—did you see him?"

"Yeah. Superintendent Branson. Looked to me."

"Un-huh," said Sutherland. "But why would he—"

"Sheriff, nothing here," said one of the two deputies who had been assigned to search for Addis along the near side of the tracks. Sutherland spun on his heel and surveyed the far side of the tracks, beneath the lodgepole pines. The toe of a boot rising from the grass caught his attention. He leapt from the platform, crossed the tracks, and ran to it. There was his son, supine, gawking, silently pleading, throat slit to a gurgle, blood spurting, sopping his shirt and the earth below. Sutherland collapsed.

Orchard clung to the railing of the rear stairs of the last passenger car as it accelerated toward the Bunker Hill Mine. Behind him was the caboose, and just ahead, Addis was already up the stairs and disappearing inside. Orchard followed quickly and saw Addis plopped onto a seat. "We gotta do the rigging," said Orchard. "Ten minutes. Get up."

"Mn-huh," said Addis, smearing blood from his knife onto the damask seat cushion. He then rose and sheathed the blade.

Orchard slid a trunk from the back of the car and opened it. "Here we are," he breathed. From within he removed a long role of blasting fuse.

Meanwhile Addis strolled to the front of the car, opened the connecting door, stepped over the noisy gap, entered the first passenger car and proceeded down its length to its front wall. There he stood and whistled. "Ain't that a thing of beauty!" In front of him was a stack of crates, five high by ten wide and at least two deep, all marked DYNAMITE! DANGER!

Behind Addis, Orchard approached, unspooling several feet of fuse from a roll. "You needn'ta killed that boy."

"He was the law," mused Addis, watching Orchard with the fuse. "They already done most of it." He pointed to the network of fuses and blasting caps protruding from the boxes. "Wonder why."

"Damnifino," said Orchard, contemplated the rigging. He used his hand to measure the length of the master fuse stemming from the center of the web. Then he glanced at the roll and grumbled to himself, "No reason to give us all this, then. Just need the main."

"Case these caps don't full do it," said Addis.

Orchard snorted. "You reckon if only half this shit blows, we can just fuse it all over again? That right?"

"Can't leave it half blown."

"Goddamned if you ain't stupid, Addis."

Addis looked out the window, folding his bony fingers into the palm of his hand. "That ain't my fucking name."

"Didn't figure it was," said Orchard, unrolling a length of fuse.

In the car ahead of them, the luxurious Pullman Special, the hole in the center of the floor was now a gaping breech through which rushed a whir of sound, wind, and light. Lying on his stomach, head dangling through, Branson studied his options below—options which, under there, were not favoring his survival were he to drop while the train was in motion. He lifted himself and sat on the Persian rug covering a portion of the Pullman's floor, proud for having created such an impressive hole. He'd wait until the train stopped at the mine, then jump through the hole and be gone before anyone knew better.

Standing, he looked out a side window, surveying the passing landscape. Just then the train entered a sharp curve, giving him an opportunity to see through the windows of the passenger car behind him. To his surprise, he saw no one—no silhouettes of heads on the bench seats. No one standing. No one at all. No army of Federation men hell-bent on a fight. He moved to the back of the Pullman and tried the door again. It was futile. He pulled back the curtain and looked at the front door of the trailing passenger car, just beyond the coupling gap. Some boxes or crates obscured the door window of that passenger car. He studied them. The train hit a loose rail tie and the jolt caused one of those boxes to turn slightly, revealing the first two letters of a word stenciled in bold red: DY. Branson paled. *Dynamite.* He turned and saw smoke rising from the massive mine buildings ahead. His veins ran cold. His breath caught. He had to get off. Immediately.

For a moment, he stared at the hole, then hurried to it, sat, stared some more, then slowly lowered himself until his new Sorosis shoes were sailing just above the flashing rail ties. Triceps trembling, he gripped the undercarriage, lowering himself until he swung suspended beneath the hole, head toward the rear of the train. He lifted his feet, hooking them into cross braces, and studied the tenuous situation. The wind whipped his pant cuffs, shirt sleeves, his hair. Looking between his knees at the approaching track, he searched for an opportunity to drop. *Wait. Wait,* he thought. *Just wait. Not on a curve. That'd kill you.* His mind was a whir of probabilities and prayers. He had to stay very flat when he landed, but protect his head. This was going to hurt. Then came a long straight section. He braced, took a breath, and let go, slamming into the speeding rail bed below, feeling the rock rip into his back as his body shuttled forward, his shoes digging through the gravel, his back across the rail ties, all while desperate to turtle-in his head and all appendages. He finally stopped sliding just as the last passenger car rushed over him. Suddenly a dangling piece of metal smacked his left hand, knocking it outward onto the rail, where the last wheel of the caboose severed it. In the next instant, Branson found himself looking straight up into the blue sky with the sound of the train disappearing below his cap-toes. He rolled to his right, managed to sit, feet spread, staring in shock at the halved shirt sleeve, white turned red, arterial blood squirting onto the rail bed.

The depot at the Bunker Hill Silver Mine and Concentrator did not resemble a train depot in the traditional sense. It was more an industrial shipping dock surrounded by the mine's maintenance buildings, supply sheds, shower cabins, offices, and the back wall of the cacophonous concentrator where silver findings were processed from the ore. That massive wood-and-iron building ran fifty yards along the track, with the main entrance having its own rail landing accompanied by assorted cranes and loading equipment. It was a dirty, bleak place, covered in rock dust, attended at the time by twenty-six men, all strike breakers, clustered around the main office. Alongside them were three Pinkerton guards in their employer-prescribed attire: clean dark suit, trim vest, white shirt capped with dog-eared collars, black silk tie, and a small bulge mid-coat betraying the revolver holstered beneath. Hearing the train approach, the Pinkertons, along with the group of workers, turned to the sound. A leader of the non-union workers spoke up.

"Boys, that's it—what we were called for! Thanks to the alert from the Pinks." He turned to acknowledge the three Pinkerton men but couldn't find them. He continued, lifting his voice over the concentrator's din. "There's a hoard of labor dogs on that train, all looking to deny you the right to work!" A chorus of grumblings and threats ensued. The man continued, "We ain't scabs! We're honest, God-fearing Americans who'll not bow to the wicked Federation. We're free men, damnit. We gotta stand our ground. We mustn't let em deny us our rights!" That caused cheering, grunts, and general clamoring among the men, each holding an ax handle, candle pike, or some other makeshift weapon. They moved in solidarity onto the grimy landing. Again the leader looked for the Pinkerton guards, but again couldn't find them.

The train eased its way into the mine's depot. The hissing engine squeaked loudly as it passed slowly, followed by the tender. Then it all came to a creaking, shuddering, shushing stop just as the Pullman passed, leaving the front of the first passenger car aligned with the landing. Had the strike breakers noticed, they would have seen a man disembark on the far side of the engine, mount a horse and gallop away. But no one saw him. One of them did take note of two men—one tall, one short—on the far side of the track, behind the train, hurrying away. Others took notice of the cars being empty, devoid of the expected brood of Federation men. Alarm came to some, but too late to matter.

The white-hot detonation occurred in such an instantaneous fury and force that none nearby stood a chance of surviving. It leveled most every structure, including the lift buildings at the mouth of the mine and the entirety of the massive concentrator, sending missiles of wood, iron, and humanity hundreds of yards in all directions. When the debris began to settle, only the caboose, the rear of the last passenger car, a bit of the tender, and the hulk of the engine were recognizable. The first passenger car and the Pullman Special seemed to have never existed at all. In a deafening instant all the noise of production had been eliminated. Dust billowed angrily over everything. Silence cut by distant cries of agony, the finishing moans of life. Gory heaps missing limbs, heads, impaled or crushed. Bare bones and bright blood. Men writhing in wounds. Men docile in death.

★

– 4 –

MONDAY
October 22, 1906

For Nevada Jane Haywood (Neva to everyone who didn't address her as Mrs. Haywood), late autumn was the best stretch of year—the golden trees mixed with pine spicing the brusque air while early snow dusted into the shadowed eaves, ready to stay the course for months to come. And before polio had withered her leg, Fall had meant crisp walks through foothill leas, through streams gurgling with the cold water of recent rains. Now walking was gone and her rolling invalid chair was her throne—on good days. But on days like this, when clumps of melancholy filled her like stones, the chair was her judicial bench and the world her accused. Still wearing her cream dressing sacque, she rolled herself closer to her bedroom's wide window, midway up the five-story Pioneer Building in downtown Denver. From there she took pleasure in the birds fussing on the electric wires, fluttering between street lights—finches and scrub jays, doves and a cardinal—all squirting droppings on the walking, running, standing people below them. Or so she hoped. Her thoughts flew likewise, flitting here, landing there, remaining but a moment till startling up to settle again.

She knew her prior years of pain—stabs from her contorted leg to the top of her spine, along with the accompanying crumples and creases of discomfort—had advanced her appearance a decade beyond her thirty-two. She would never walk again, she knew that, at least not without contortions, crutches, and a dependent gait. And though in the last year she had begun to have weeks when the pain abated, she knew she would never be fully liberated from it, from the piercing agonies that arose on their mysterious schedules. She would never stroll freely with the man she loved. Never dance. Never satisfy her murderous husband—but that was a different matter. And she knew it was unlikely she would see her fiftieth birthday. Perhaps not her fortieth.

Still, a soft smile came to her. Whether it was earned, a reflection of an emotion she deserved to feel, or just an accidental spasm, she tried not to consider. But she couldn't help herself. It was probably due to this beautiful autumn day. Or maybe it came from her habit that most annoyed her: reflexively reminding herself how blessed she was. In his most recent letter, Reverend Sanders had recapped the blessings of faith. But that wasn't it. It was earthlier. She was blessed to be in this city, ennobled, empowered, and in the center of all that was important, all that mattered. And the truth was that she (George would be cross at her for thinking this) owed that blessing to being married to William D. Haywood, or Big Bill, the President of the Western Federation of Miners, the most powerful, most influential man in the United States—ceding only to President Roosevelt, but none other. Yes, Bill was a killer. Of hundreds probably. But not by his own hand. And he had saved ten times as many. Benefited the families of thousands more. So, yes, his words slit her throat on occasion. But sometimes he could be charming. Neva could remember eras of balance some distance ago when Bill had been as often kind as cold. But for the past year, he merely drifted by, knifing her with dull indifference. Regardless, he was her husband. She his wife. Thus a life. So to speak.

When a fleet of sparrows flurried up from their Fifteenth Street tree, she returned her scrutiny to the little people navigating both Fifteenth and Larimer Streets. Though she knew only a few of their names, she could surmise their status relative to her husband. For example, the two bristle-bearded gunhands slouching in front of the Pinion Hotel were Federation guards. They were betrayed by their shotguns and their attentiveness toward the building she was in, the Pioneer Building, which housed the headquarters of the Federation on its second floor, one below these living suites. The men could also be identified as gunhands because of their frayed pant legs and muddy boots. She squinted at them—pants and shoes receiving her most strict assessment. If a person has two good legs and feet, they are obliged to clothe them correctly. She noted that one of the gunhands, the one in a black hat, kept glancing up. Did he just look at her? Maybe they were undercover Pinkertons, but what did it matter? If they were Pinks, they were wasting their time—they couldn't touch her husband. There, that guard looked again. He was certainly a handsome fellow. Due to the broad brim of his hat, the gesture was pronounced: he couldn't simply raise his eyes. He seemed younger than the other, and more square shouldered. But something was amiss. What she could see of his short beard seemed too recent, too intentional. Yes, a Pink. Then the old cigarist passed in front of her view, and behind him toddled the butcher. Then came the cigarist's even fatter brother.

She glanced up the street to an argument that appeared to about a dusty-black Victoria bicycle. Then she recognized a man and lowered her chin reflexively. Reverend Sanders, the Seventh-day Adventist minister, had rounded from Fifteenth. She watched him bisect a cluster of men working on the tram line, then pass the two fussing over the bicycle, before he disappeared through a door adjacent to A. M. Morton Furniture. He was heading to see her husband's attorney, Clarence Darrow, whom she had requested handle the church's Fort Collins land claim. She knew Sanders had arrived in Denver the day before, having come down from Walla Walla, Washington. What might've he done with his evening? Perhaps he had visited the women of California Street. No, not him. Of course not him. She was glad he'd come. He bolstered her power. The church needed her. They needed her donations—money from the Federation. And she alone could provide them with America's Lawyer at no charge. No one else could do that.

She surveyed the busy swarms. Those disapproving people. When she was down among them, she saw their askance glances from the tails of their eyes, heard their whispered intrigues. They didn't like her. Well, hell's bells—if she wasn't Mrs. Haywood, if she didn't maintain that status at all costs, then they wouldn't get funding for their petty causes. If she didn't do as she felt she must, how would they receive their spoils? They were just a flock of ugly sparrows bathing in the largesse of her sins.

Her sins. Her one big sin. No different than any other sin. Not in the eyes of the Lord. That afternoon, Reverend Sanders would cross the street to call on her. He would avoid the Federation headquarters on the second floor, praying he might avoid her husband. But should *she* see the reverend? No. She would say she was ill, or some such thing. He had come to Denver. He was receiving Mr. Darrow's services. Wasn't that enough? Was he also entitled to sit in her parlor, sipping her tea, judging her? He was kind. But he was a reverend—he was supposed to be kind. But no. No. If she let him in, he would want to talk about Bill and might bring up her sister, Winnie. No, Reverend Sanders didn't know about all that mess with them. Probably he didn't. And certainly not about her friendship with George. Thank God. But all the same, he would spout his opinions about the Federation and its violence, without a speck of deference to how the church profited from it all, from her sins. She was the one who suffered, who had given up so much. She was a martyr, damnit. She was the one God saw fit to strike lame. Not them. The one who would die early. Whose children were far away. Reverend Sanders had no right making her feel things like regret and shame. No inquisition today, Reverend. She had endured enough on behalf of the world.

All those people down there. Just look at them. They came and went, arrived and departed, crossed and stood, a cotillion of canary yellows and junco browns, deep greens, and occasional blues, all in motion—whirligigs and skate beetles skittering over water, all in motion as if they might drown were they to stop. Interwoven in the male movement were the women and children—the outliers and inliers of the world—the companions and offspring of shopkeepers, saloon managers, hoteliers, and the like. Noting Neva's third-story perch, one of the women gave a demure smile followed by a disingenuous wave, both of which Neva pretended not to see. Another woman, walking beside the first, leaned in for a conversation that Neva knew featured her at its excoriated center.

She surprised herself by the bite of her bristle that afternoon—but she let her mind run, wallowing in her own opinions while holding no concern for theirs. Their husbands may be strike breakers and non-union pigs for all she knew, or cared, but all women appreciated the sacrifice Bill made for their working men: their husbands and their lovers, their sons, fathers, and their brothers. Of that Neva was certain. Why else would they call on her, full of servile gestures worthy of any courtier? And why in their toadying conversations would they implore her to pass along good tidings to her husband? She saw their love for him and pitied them for it. They loved him more than they loved their own men. But they couldn't have him. And they certainly wouldn't get his love. No one got that. No one. Winnie was a fool to believe otherwise. Neva wiped at a tear. She had paid the highest of prices to be there, rolling chair-bound in their city lodgings, extending gestures and loaning out people, such as Mr. Darrow to her church. She could withstand those women's accusations. What had they ever sacrificed? She may have sold her dignity, but she had no intention of squandering it.

It was not just the wives who worshiped Bill, but their men too. And not just union men. Anyone, so long as they didn't feel their greed threatened by him. If that was the case—if they perceived Big Bill Haywood was in their way—then they despised him. It was one or the other. Sycophants or cynics. Bootlickers or backbiters. The haters were capitalists—money men, bankers, company men—with their Pinkerton hounds. But what of it? The masses loved him. The thousand-fold flocks who lauded Bill for his struggle on their behalf; fighting for their eight-hour workday, decent wages, medical care for them and their families. She had seen their adulation for his greatness, his selfless leadership of the largest labor union in the United States. And they loved her for being his wife. How could they not? Sure, some of the bitch-wives had taken exception to her decisions. They were just dogs nosing at the butcher's windowsill. *God, what was this fury in my blood?*

Nosy hags—it shouldn't be their concern that she'd given her sister Winnie to her husband. Her sister, his mistress. If she thought he'd earned that privilege, then they should approve as well. She saw one of them being drawn into the banter of Soapy Smith and his faultless cure for sore feet. *Tell her it'll work on her sore box*, thought Neva. *That's where she needs it.* Yes, they had no right to opine about her sins. They had their own. It was just fornication. She remembered the morning when, as she sat in her invalid chair, Bill had tried but failed to please her the French way. He had become so frustrated. But at least he had tried. Of course he had learned the technique with Winnie's young thighs at his ears—but better Winnie than one of those women down there.

Feeling a twinge of arousal—no, it was just hunger—she thought to ring for the servant to dress her for dinner. No, she'd wait. She'd rather be attended by Winnie. They'd be finished soon, and Winnie would wash up and come report that day's hubbub.

And she'd report on Bill, how he felt, and— Was that a moan in the distance, through the plaster walls? Was that Bill groaning in his completion? She hoped so. That would mean he'd be pleasant at dinner, not snarling at her discussion of birds and other things of interest to her. They'd dine, she and Winnie would discuss, then the three would end the evening with Veuve Cliquot. Yes, that would be ideal.

When a motor-carriage honked at a slow horse cart, Neva watched it, the automobile, seeing if it was a taxi from the train station. Who might alight from its shadowy interior? When it stopped at the corner of Fifteenth, a man exited, shut the door quickly, and stepped to the sidewalk beneath her. She stretched her neck to peer down. The man let two bicyclists rush by and held his bowler, his gaze fixed on the Pioneer Building, as if preparing himself to enter. He was a round-headed, nervous union man. Two reasons she knew he was union: One, the Federation controlled the Denver taxis, and this man didn't appear to have paid a fare. And two, because she believed she knew him. Bill had introduced him once, as she recalled. The man had a curious name, something to do with a tree. Apple? No. Oak? No. Limb? (She smiled at the silly thought of someone being named Limb.) Forest? Maybe. Orchard? Yes, that was it: Orchard.

The obsequious Harry Orchard was being followed by several men stationed along Fifteenth Street: Pinkertons disguised in the blatancy of the common. One was Operative 21, the young man who had drawn Neva's attention. He sat across from the Pioneer, an undercover Pinkerton charading as a Federation gunhand. He held a shotgun across his lap, had a week's worth of chin growth, and wore a low-crowned, Texas-steer-style black hat with a black silk band bearing a silver star on each side. From the shadows of its wide brim, his fair blue eyes watched the street. Beside him was an authentic Federation regular who would try to arrest him, if not kill him, if his true identity was discovered. Operative 21 stood and stretched, pulling at the back seam of his drab workman's coat, aware that Haywood's invalid wife was watching from the high window across the street. He then walked to the door of the Pinion Hotel behind him. "To the jake," he said, declaring his destination as if the other guard had asked.

"Must as you must," muttered the regular, wet-gnawing a cigar.

Operative 21 walked through the lobby, nodded at the hotel's crisp clerk, and continued down the back hall to a door marked GENTLEMEN. He entered, flipped the latch, and withdrew a small log book and pencil from his breast pocket. By the light of the curtained window he wrote with a scratching sound: ORCH PB 11AM TAXI. (ORCH for Orchard. PB for Pioneer Building.) Through the door, he heard the lobby telephone clang, then the clerk speak briefly and hang up. Operative 21 stuffed both the log and the pencil into his pocket. A knock brought his sharp attention.

"Irish," came the voice of the clerk, followed by receding steps. Operative 21 waited a moment, then left the men's room, turning away from the lobby. He exited the back of the hotel into a rancid alleyway, then entered another building through a door bearing the word "Ladies"—a portal to fleshly pleasures. He walked steadily through the curtained alcoves and latched doors to arrive in a front lobby attended by six women in various states of under-dress, all admiring him as he passed. He re-entered the sunlight on Lawrence Street and there jumped aboard a passing electric streetcar that would carry him three blocks to the Tabor Opera House at Sixteenth Street and Curtis Avenue. Midway, the tram passed the colossal granite Mine Exchange Building, home of the Mine Owner's Association—the group who employed the Pinkertons (including him) to infiltrate, investigate, spy upon and confound the mine workers' union, the Western Federation of Miners. Craning his neck to peer up at the building's three-story clock tower (then tolling 11:00), Operative 21 could see the head of the twelve-foot copper statue of an "Old Prospector" far atop the tower—the highest honor for the lowest man.

Once in the Tabor, he came to a set of stairs and climbed to the floors above the dilapidated theater. On the fourth floor, he entered a hallway and was greeted by two gunhands who bore a mix of congeniality and glares. Operative 21 ignored them and proceeded, moving with the stride of a man who had trodden that path several times every day for three months without fail. Down the hall he entered a nondescript door and approached a woman sitting at a desk. "He called for me?" he asked.

"Yes, but he's not available at this moment," she replied. "Please sit."

He found a chair. From behind the interior door came the sound of an angry Irishman: "Morris, you've been trusted! And this pulp nonsense is a violation of that trust. If you get a man of mine killed, a vast tonnage of shite will rain upon your head."

Then came another voice carrying a thick Russian accent. "People should know, Sir. I'm reporting—"

"Goddamnit," yelled the first voice, causing the woman in the outer office to wince. Then things grew quieter, and Operative 21 could only make out occasional words: something about a book, correspondences, secrets, Mr. Pinkerton, and loyalty.

When the office door flew open, a young, black-haired man exited, shutting the door behind himself. He donned his bowler as if it were the sum of his composure now put right, then adjusted his thick glasses before stopping at the desk to give a collection of papers to the woman. She accepted them, saying, "Thank you, Mr. Friedman. I'm sorry."
"Me too, Margret. You should be careful," admonished the Russian as he left.

The Irish voice yelled through the door: "Nine minutes!"

After the elapsed time, Margaret stood and held the interior door for Operative 21. The office within was well appointed with leather couches, side tables, and vases under tall windows that cast light across a massive green wool rug. Near the door hung a wood telephone box which Operative 21 noted, bemused, though he had seen it several times since its installation a month prior. Pipe smoke swirled under unlit chandeliers dangling from the vaulted ceiling. Before him was a series of tall-backed chairs. In one sat the source of the smoke, a white-haired, bespectacled man reading a newspaper. The man looked up. With a tone approaching reverence, Operative 21 said, "Good day, Chief. Mr. McParland."

"You were four minutes late to your post this morning," barked the man. "The reason for your tardiness?"

Operative 21 blanched, his mouth open to reply. He needed a moment to marshal his defenses. "I was ... I'm not sure. But—"

Through round lenses, the draped, gray-blue eyes of Chief Detective James McParland, Director of the Western Division of the Pinkerton Detective Agency, watched his operative fumble for words. McParland set aside the newspaper and stood to address the young man directly. "I've observed you to be a steady man, but for you to assume leadership, you must maintain a seriousness of mind." His Galway brogue was as bushy as his mustache. "I'll tolerate no wavering of loyalty from any of my men."

Operative 21 glanced down, his breath slight as if to not disrupt the air. Once McParland turned away, the operative returned his gaze to the man. As was his custom, McParland wore as nice a wool suit as he could afford: three-buttoned, single-breasted, with steam-creased, cuffed and pleated trousers. Across his modestly round middle draped a woven-gold chain (a gift from his wife, Mary) leading to a vest pocket holding a gold pocket-watch (a gift from Mr. Pinkerton). Above the vest, the knot of his black silk tie formed a tight shield winged by the crisp tabs of his shirt collar—Pinkerton white (meaning unforgivingly free of blemishes). His polished shoes never varied from cap-toed Florsheims with Goodyear welting. When outside, he wore a gray homburg with an unassuming band. And when walking more than twenty feet or so, he relied lightly on a brass-knobbed, walnut cane (pressed into service a decade prior by the kick of a horse). In truth the cane was as much strut as support, as much countenance as cudgel.

"You hear me, Twenty-One?" resumed the detective. "Absolute loyalty. Otherwise, none at all."

"Yes, Chief," said Jack Garrett, otherwise known as Operative 21. He was anxious for McParland to call him Agent Garrett, not the unaccredited, replaceable blankness of Operative. Though agent came next, even then it wouldn't be good enough. Not for Jack. He had his sights higher: detective—what Old Man Pinkerton called the seasoned men in the agency. Someday he would be Detective Jack Garrett, a seasoned man. Even better, he'd have an office like this one. Maybe better than this one. But, right now, in this moment, the warmth of that bright future was fading under McParland's scrutiny and squint. Jack scanned his memory for something he might've done to deserve this rebuke. "Have I—"

"Intoxicated?" asked McParland, watch in hand.

"This morning?" Jack gave a chuckle. "No, just smokin oap." Smirking came naturally to Jack, but he quickly suppressed it now.

McParland's stare burned: Jack's opium humor was unwelcome.

"No, Sir," Jack corrected.

"When was your last drink?"

Jack shook his head slightly. "Not since I swore my oath. But as an operative, I understood we—"

McParland nodded. "I'd hate to find you tarred and feathered by those Wobblies, or hanging from a tree ... like Baxter met his end in Boulder."

"He's alive, Sir."

McParland peaked his eyebrows and squeezed his lips, as if Baxter's state of being alive or dead was in question. "Not to the agency. To me, when Baxter let himself be discovered, he met his end." He knew it was a cruel business hurling such a thing in the face of a friend of Baxter, the Pinkerton operative whom the Federation nearly killed. But discipline is not discipline without discipline, and he could ill afford William Haywood discovering yet another Pinkerton spy within Federation ranks. (Chief Detective McParland would never refer to that murderer with such insouciance as to call him 'Big Bill'.) Though it was true that the other operative would likely live, the young man would carry scars from his tarring and be of no further service to the Pinkerton Detective Agency—at least not west of the Mississippi, the territory McParland commanded from this Denver office.

So, McParland was loath to also lose Operative 21. And the next Pinkerton operative to be exposed would receive a more "conclusive" beating by the Federation, making matters all the more difficult for the Pinkertons' campaign against them. Besides, these mountain and range recruits were a whisker's breadth from being Federation gunhands themselves. The only thing holding many of them from switching horses was the extra pay from Chicago's Ward Building (Pinkerton headquarters): a dollar a day more than was given from Denver's Pioneer Building (Federation headquarters). In fact, some operatives had been with the Federation for months, if not years, before taking the Pinkerton oath. Thus, word of yet another vicious beating, tarring, or even killing by the Federation of a Pinkerton operative, and McParland could see a wholesale bolt of thirty men across that disguised divide, over to the Federation. If that happened, the turncoats would not only expose Pinkerton secrets—like that son-of-a-bitch Russian Yid, Morris Friedman, had done—but they could destroy McParland's reputation: his most-prized lore.

"Return to your post, Twenty-One," McParland said, smoothing his mustache. "Stay on the Pioneer."

"Like skunk on a birddog."

McParland grunted, adding a rueful smile. "Be careful."

With a "Yes, Sir," Jack turned and left.

★

– 5 –

While Jack was in his boss's office, a few blocks away, Harry Orchard was alone on the second floor of the Pioneer Building, about to face his own boss, William Haywood. He remained standing, alone in Haywood's office, among a scattering of mismatched wooden and upholstered chairs. He fidgeted, wandered, glanced at the main door and then at the one leading to the inner vestibule. He was in his only suit: a two-piece sandy sack over a dull shirt and brown tie worn loose. Muffled, raucous voices rose through the floor from the Gassell Saloon below. He stopped pacing. Pulling a deep breath, he attempted calm, picturing the Trivoli-Union beer he would have down there, just after this meeting.

He moved to the window, rubbed his thinly forested head, then turned again to the room, giving passing mind to the feminine furnishings cluttered among the matters of men: a vase sporting pink silk flowers; three floral-upholstered, cherrywood chairs; a mahogany humidor; two deep-tufted brown settees; a black candlestick telephone; a mediocre painting of a Russian Orlov Trotter; fourteen crates of ammunition; a Venetian red Bunco table concealed by maps, papers, and an electric brass lamp; and an array of shotguns and rifles leaning in one corner. He approached the room's most prominent feature: a bulky, ornate Italian desk. On it he saw a number of papers askew, an English-to-Russian dictionary, a Russian language book, protest flyers, a bottle of ink, a cup of pens, and a rectangular porcelain ashtray.

Then he saw it, the only thing that mattered in the seconds before Haywood would return: a piece of paper—Crane's linen with a distinctive yellowish hue. It was conspicuous, as if meant to be found, to be read. By him. On it, written in a hand he recognized as Haywood's, was a list of names. But not just a list. Names on that specific type of paper, scrawled in that handwriting, made it a kill list. And the fourth name was his, Harry Orchard.

An icicle slid down his back. He moved the ashtray and spun the paper to reconfirm his horror. Of the other nine, he or Addis had killed seven. That left two: Martin Baxter (a Pinkerton spy who hadn't yet died from being tarred), and Steve Adams (a name Orchard didn't recognize). He stared again at his own name, willing the letters to disassemble and reform into another, into any other name—for Harry Orchard to become someone else. His cheeks burned. His brows widened. His breath transformed into a faint moan of deflation, then a whisper of "My God."

In that moment, William "Big Bill" Haywood burst into the room, march-striding straight for his desk, giving Orchard little time to react other than to step aside, retreating backwards, plopping into a settee before popping up again to attention. Behind Haywood came a dense bulldog, nails clicking on the wood floor as it sniffed. Then it jumped on the settee, circled twice, and lay its drooping chin on its stubby front legs.

Orchard watched Haywood. The enormous stature with a round pate the size of a gold pan was searching for something on the desk. For a moment Orchard convinced himself that Haywood had not seen him at all—as if his boss was unaware that a sweaty pale man was no more than eight feet away. The rummaging stopped, and Haywood gave an "Ah," holding up the kill list. He then placed it carefully on the corner of the desk nearest Orchard, smoothing its buttery fibers as if it were a winning trifecta ticket on display. Orchard watched this formality without breathing. Then, looking up, his gaze was met by Haywood's dead orb of an eye. The other eye scorched a hole in Orchard's forehead.

"Do you know what you've done?" asked Haywood, his subterranean voice rumbling through puffy jowls. He clapped a thick hand on Orchard's shoulder, pressing his thumb into the hollow of Orchard's collarbone. "You failed."

He then turned, took a seat in his tall-backed, bison-hide chair and pulled at his shirt cuffs, bringing them visible from under his suit sleeves. Though he claimed his attire was Bolshevik (common colors, fabrics, shoes), as if he were but a working man, it was a crafted ruse. A theater of persuasion. In truth, he was enthused about clothing—knew its power and use. For the masses, from afar, from eulogies to rallies, from platforms to stages, from balconies to union halls, he was one of them. But for those sitting or standing near, small groups and individuals, politicians and patricians, lawyers and women, minions and enemies alike, it was unmistakably clear: no common miner wore a suit tailored at Daniels & Fisher's department store. Adjusting his silver star cuff links, he asked, "Do you know how you failed at Bunker Hill?"

Orchard swallowed, surprised that the act had been acknowledged aloud, much less the name of the place. Considering the kill list, he began what he estimated to be his life's final plea. "Mr. Haywood, Sir, if I've disappointed you ..." He paused, gauging the big man's response. But it was useless—nothing was forthcoming but that damnable stare. "I beg your pardon," he almost quivered, "but was me and that Addis fella not put to that task?"

"What task was that, Harry?"

Orchard hesitated. Task orders were never stated aloud—there were too many Pinkerton spies within Federation ranks. And none of those Pinks should be afforded the opportunity to testify without perjuring himself—perjury being a corruption in the Pinkerton's single, unblinking, "private eye" ethos. Thus, the most serious operational tasks for the Federation were relayed in writing, to be read silently with only the writer and reader present. Then the paper was burned while the two men were still alone, still quiet. It was a simple and efficient rule that Orchard knew well. Just as he knew the only man not obliged to the rule was the mass of righteous vengeance glaring at him from across the desk.

"Your task?" Haywood growled again.

Orchard continued to pause, his eyes flitting about. Was this a test? Might a witness suddenly materialize, like some apparition? "I ain't sure of your meaning, Mr. Haywood."

"It's all right." Haywood gave a wry smile. "No protocol. Tell me: what was your understanding of the task put to you?"

In a near whisper, Orchard began, "To bring the mine down. Concentrator too. And its super. Its managers and scabs. To the ground. To ruin."

Haywood snorted a laugh. "To ruin? You certainly accomplished *ruin*."

"Thank you, Sir."

"Take a seat," Haywood instructed, waving at the chair behind Orchard, then watching the man do as he was told. Yes, thought Haywood, according to newspaper accounts "to ruin" would seem an appropriate description of what had occurred in northern Idaho. Not only was he proud of the outcome, the leveling of the buildings of the Bunker Hill Mine, he was delighted the bombing set a new record for non-war destruction. He might even say that publicly. But pride in the killing? He'd keep that to himself.

To Haywood, there was something glorious about a good explosion. He didn't just like them, or simply enjoy them, as one might a firework. No, he loved the power of a blast. Craved it like the squint-eyes did their opium. A well-planned, executed, and effective bomb was a feat of divine beauty: terminal art manifest in a fraction of a second. He didn't know when that admiration had first arisen. Perhaps it was at the age of nine when, while hauling water to his father and other men deep in Idaho's Silver City Mine, a fierce explosion became the last thing he remembered. He woke to find his sight halved, his face scarred, and his fate set before him.

The blast meant he never had to go into a mine again—something he had begun at the age of five. His father believed: "If you's old enough for solid food, you's old enough to mine." So, for four years of his early youth he'd pushed carts bigger than him, carried supplies, shoveled and dug—whatever his father and the other men decided his little hands could muster. But then the blast came, and little Billy Haywood was saved. In that instant he became half blind but fully free.

Now, thirty years later, the intensity of a detonation was erotic. The unrivaled nature of each explosion, like perfect snowflakes, each masterfully unique unto itself. The variables were too vast for recurrence. Perhaps the fuse was faster. The dynamite placed just this way or that. The time of day. The nearby material that would become killing projectiles. Even the barometric pressure mattered. It was a killing method far superior to a gun—which was tedious and repeatable. Though the wind might differ one day to the next, pulling a bullet this way or that, that paled compared to the matchless, unpredictable beauty of a bomb: divine destruction and creation in one exquisite instant.

Haywood wished he'd been the one to light the Bunker fuse. Not just figuratively, as he had done, but literally. But he was too recognizable. Yet would he have had the nerve? It was a question he refused to ask himself. Or, better put, a question he refused to honestly answer. But he found pride knowing he'd put this man Orchard to the task, along with the other man—Addis, Adams, or whatever was the man's real name. Their orders had been written, and then burned. And the lovely act was complete. Almost.

"Did I do something to dissatisfy—" began Orchard carefully.

"The superintendent of the Bunker Hill, Mr. Branson?"

"Dead. He was in that Pullman there. We'd locked him in."

"Dead?" Haywood asked, thrumming his fingers, then stopping. The room fell silent, save the buzz of a horsefly sluggishly dying on the window ledge. "Superintendent Branson and his family were observed in Spokane just yesterday. I'll give you, he's missing a hand now; but otherwise, he's most decidedly not dead. How do you figure that happened?"

Orchard was stone. This was the reason he was on the kill list. He didn't care how Branson might've cheated death, he was trying to figure how *he* might.

Haywood continued, "Steve Adams—you know him as Addis—has been tasked to complete your original task. It seems the now-one-handed Mr. Branson has fled to San Francisco—apparently more afraid of me than he is of fires and earthquakes." He paused, observing Orchard, this dreary-faced man who could do only one thing correctly: devise and implement an effective bomb. For that, Haywood admired him. A man with such unflinching talents was indispensable in this fight with the mine owners and their Pinkertons—this glorious crusade for the common American man. In fact, skilled and willing artisans such as Orchard were in rare supply. Thus, adding Orchard to the kill list was good theatrics. Formidable inducement. Nothing more. Fear being a most effective tactic for the control of one man by another. Haywood selected a pen, placed a short stack of the cream paper in the center of his desk, and began to write. When he finished, he slid the note to one side and wrote on the next blank page.

Upon seeing his boss writing this way, Orchard relaxed—he was being tasked again, not killed. At least not at this time. He paused mid-thought. They still might kill him. Maybe he wasn't supposed to have seen his name on that list. No, he was—of course it was meant for him to see. Meant to scare him. But why? He didn't need to be threatened to take a task, to do a job. So, why the additional lean on him? What task could possibly need such inducement behind it?

When Haywood finished writing, he stood, leaving the remaining blank paper on the desk before him, and handed the two notes to Orchard. Orchard read the first one:

Adams - once SF done

Orchard might have expected it: the order to kill Adams. Adams (as he now knew to be Addis's real name) was a dumb weapon whose time had come. The only thing special about Adams was his unflinching knack of killing another human directly, face to face. Orchard read the other note and froze:

Gov Steunenberg – bomb

He looked up at Haywood, silently seeking an explanation, then whispered, "This is a horse of a different color."

"He's a traitor. After the Bunker thing, arresting every union man—violating the Constitution he swore to uphold," groused Haywood. "He is a lapdog of the goddamned capitalist. Betrayed every vote I got him." He resumed his seat. "Betray me, you betray all of labor, the whole union, the Federation, the workers. You betray every American. You become a criminal against the United States Constitution." He mindlessly arranged a few things on his desk. "No, the federal government won't protect the rights of individuals, so we must. We must cause change in America."

"With this," muttered Orchard, making it more statement than question.

"Do you know how they accomplish change in Russia?"

"No, Sir."

"Looting, burning, blowing things up, Harry," replied Haywood. "Firing squads. The only way to get justice. Big strikes are good, but they're not enough. Everyone knows that. It takes socialist revolutionaries, leaders like that fellow Trotsky over there. Bolsheviks, they call themselves. Brave men. Bold men. It wasn't until they proved themselves willing to do violence, to assassinate government officials, that they brought change to the Russian working man and his family. That's how it is. They made that clear. Same here. Last year, the Russians made the necessary sacrifices—killed who needed to be killed. So now they've got a new government, a constitution, and their goddamned czar has been nutted. The Russian people have their power back. Why? Because they showed their mettle." He lowered his gaze toward the paper in Orchard's hand. "We're doing the same here. I'm the American Trotsky. You're the tip of the spear. I need you. We need you. This country needs you, Harry. Needs you to do what you were born to do." He held his hands up, palms out, and whispered, "Boom."

Orchard gave a wide-eyed nod.

Haywood matched Orchard's response with his own conclusive nod and reached for a matchbox from his desk drawer. But, in so doing, the matches spilled, cascading to the wood floor. "Damn," he muttered, leaning to pick them up. When Haywood returned upright in his chair, Orchard was presenting two pieces of cream paper, ready to receive the flame—the Adams kill note on top. Haywood struck a match and held it to the papers' edges. Orchard flinched as the notes flushed ablaze. "Here," said Haywood, touching the porcelain ashtray. Orchard dropped the blazing papers there. Then Haywood picked up the first kill list, the one with Orchard's name on it, and added it to the conflagration. It too burst and was gone. For a moment, neither man looked at the other, only at the ashtray, watching the flames turn to embers then to gray.

"I know of a ranch near Fort Collins," said Haywood. "Four hundred and fifty acres. Water. Decent buildings. A man could start a family there."

Orchard dipped his nose. "Sounds fine."

Haywood leveled a hard stare at Orchard—the equivalent of a kick. Orchard saw it and turned for the door, donning his dirty bowler. Nothing else needed to be said about his payment for the two murders ahead: Adams and Steunenberg. His payment would be that ranch. Plus some money would appear in his account at the First State Bank of Boise, Idaho—the state presided over by its governor, Frank Steunenberg—the man soon to be no more.

"This is difficult," murmured Winnifred Minor, known as Winnie, Neva's twenty-six-year-old kid sister. Winnie—her blonde hair tied up in a loose poof—leaned into the invalid chair to attach a lightly boned under-bodice around Neva's waist. She was helping dress Neva for the evening, but thus far had only managed Neva's muslin, knee-length drawers and half-camisole. On the bed was a high-collar, teal tea gown consisting of an outer-bodice and gored skirt. Winnie flashed her chirpy blue eyes at her older sister's cutting green ones. "I don't think ..." Winnie began.

Neva scooted forward. "Just hook it."

"I don't see the point in you having them separate—"

"To make it easier."

"Well, bravo," snarked Winnie. "Can you stand up again?"

Neva winced. "It hurts, Sissy."

"There's really no point, right?"

"To what?" snapped Neva.

Winnie gave a plaintive smile. "I understand a corset when you're standing ... with your crutches. But this?" She tugged at the under-bodice. "Why the shaping when you'll be seated?"

Neva whipped her head around. "You have a corset!" She patted Winnie's waist. "And you'll sit tonight. So why shouldn't I at least have this?"

"Don't get that way."

"What way?"

"Sissy," Winnie began with stifled amusement.

"Don't call me that."

"You just called— Why are you—"

"Are you finished yet?"

"No," said Winnie, still struggling anew with the garment. "If you'd stand back up—"

"If, if, if! You don't know."

"You should use your crutches," said Winnie, motioning toward a pair of plain crutches with bare-wood arm supports. They appeared to have been thrown in a corner.

"You use them!" snapped Neva, her neck reddening. "Stick em up your cock-catcher."

Winnie giggled. "You're in a horrid mood, Mrs. Haywood."

Neva flutter-slapped Winnie's hands away. "I'll do it. I'll do it."

"Sissy!"

"You think I'm helpless, but I'm not. I tell you, I'm not." Neva twisted in the chair, struggling get the under-bodice in position.

Winnie stepped back and sat on Neva's bed. "Why are you so angry at me? I mean, why *today?*"

"Did I disturb the princess?" Neva rejoined. "You sit there. Not a concern. Look at you. Your skin, perfect. Your hair. Nothing but blue skies for you. And a good poke at that"—tears coursed her cheeks—"from my husband." She gave up on the under-bodice and hurled it at Winnie—but being soft cloth, its impact was of no consequence. Neva's hooded eyes peered at the dresser.

Winnie saw where Neva was focused. "Want me to roll you over there so you can throw that candlestick at me?"

"Yes, please," said Neva faintly.

Winnie smiled as she watched Neva stare at herself in the cheval mirror. Then she rose from the bed and knelt before Neva, wiping the tears from her older sister's cheeks. "Crutches in my crock-cratcher ... cock-cratcher ... cock-catcher? That's hard to say." There it was—what Winnie hoped to see—Neva pressing her lips together yet failing to hide a growing grin. "Ready for your dress now?" asked Winnie.

"Yes. Crock-cratcher."

Once Orchard reached Market Street, he realized he'd forgotten to stop at the Gassell for that Trivoli-Union beer. But it didn't matter. The time had come to assess his prize. He turned, watching passersby, checking to be certain no eyes were on him. Just then a pretty young woman rounded the corner, shapely green skirt gliding, long dark hair flitting behind. Though he flashed at her what he considered to be his most alluring smile, she was too far away to see it. Not that it would've mattered, he knew. She crossed the street and walked by him, forty feet away, cold—a typical response from women he tried to engage, especially Italian sorts like this one. Moving on, he stepped between two buildings, leaned close to one wall and tilted his hat. From under it he pulled a folded piece of soft yellow paper. Opening it, he read Haywood's inscription:

Gov Steunenberg – bomb

With a faint smile, he refolded it carefully, then tucked the little life insurance policy into his bowler's inside band, and then snugged it down on his head.

What Orchard had not noticed was that, after passing him, the Italian beauty had doubled back. Now she was across Market Street, watching him between the flats, seeing him in shadows, stowing a note within his hat.

★

– 6 –

The altitude of Clarence Darrow's Denver office kept him swaying in and out of a headache. He had been there for two days, over from Chicago, and though the throbbing was no longer sharp, it had settled into a drumming of which he had grown woefully accustomed. Big Bill's summonses had doubled in the three months since the Stratton Mine trial and the Bunker Hill Mine bombing. And with all his coming and going, Darrow's body had acclimated to the higher stresses and urgencies—but it seemed unyielding to the lower air pressure of Denver, at least for the first few days following each arrival. Now he lay prone on the pine bench in his Fifteenth Street office, a wet cloth molded across his face, his fingertips flitting across his temples.

He wished his wife was already there, but it would be another week—if Ruby came at all. Every time he left their Chicago home for Denver, she would kiss him and promise she'd join him—just as soon as her editorial and writing work allowed. Sometimes she came, but usually not. Though he chose to believe her pledges, he knew that in truth they were no more than wistful expressions of best wishes she felt no obligation to fulfill. All the same, there were times he questioned why he remained married to her—a number of women vied for his attention. But those doubts were snub wicks, bright but short lived. Ruby was brilliant. And a young, terrific writer—thus to be allowed some degree of narcissism. In any case, he loved her, so he tried to temper his expectations.

But it was difficult on this particular afternoon. Having not won a case in the months since losing the Stratton, and with this altitude headache, he wished she was there. His next-best option for feminine sympathy was his secretary, Miss Carlotta Capone.

"Miss Capone?" he moaned. Hearing no reply from the front parlor, he tried again. "Miss Capone, are you out there?" He could hear the street-cacophony of hooves, boots, and the familiar call of Soapy Smith, but not a sound from his new secretary, the one Haywood had recently assigned him. Once more he began, "Miss

Cap—", but a low rumbling from the front parlor interrupted him. Or was that a growl? Perhaps a snore?

The front parlor held a small desk at which Miss Capone would normally be seated, her lithe fingers flying across an Underwood #5, transcribing Darrow's volumes of handwritten letters, motions, pleas, contracts, orders, and sundry other affairs. Across from the desk was a set of four similar chairs, all with modest upholstery and tall backs. In one sat the black-suited, Seventh-day Adventist minister, a leading figure in the church's college at Walla Walla, Washington. The man's head, crowned in a clerical-style black bowler, was flopped against one of the chair's wings, and from his drooped-open mouth came an occasional snort and gravel snore.

In the inner office, Darrow remained cloth covered and listening. When the snore came again, he pulled the cloth from his face and lifted himself to a sitting position. Then he brought himself to the open doorway between the rooms. From there he saw the minister, sighed, and moved toward him. "Reverend Samuel Sanders," Darrow said, measuring out the man's name. He touched the man's shoulder. "Reverend Sanders?" The minister roused. At that moment, the bell over the office's door tinged and Miss Capone entered wearing a high-collared, white cotton blouse under an olive jacket flower-stitched to match her figure-fitting green skirt. Below that: stockings and black, patent varsity boots.

"Mr. Darrow, you're awake," she said, brushing past him, her Italian complexion glowing.

"Am I?" Darrow quipped. "Then you must be as well, Reverend."

"My apologies," the man said, rousing.

Darrow squinted as the young woman returned to her desk. "Did you abandon us to our naps, Miss Capone?"

"I took the opportunity to fetch some of Soapy's cure. You'll be in want about now," she said with a smirk that made her dimples crease. She set a midnight-blue glass apothecary bottle beside the typewriter.

"Then you're an angel sent from the Creator herself," said Darrow. "Or from Beelzebub. I'm grateful either way." He shook the bottle, unscrewed the metal top and took a swig. "Reverend?" he asked, offering the elixir.

"No thank you, Mr. Darrow. No nostrums. No demon tonics."

Darrow chuckled. "These headaches are the devil's handiwork. Best to seek the cure from the source."

"Mr. Darrow, may I—" Carla began.

Darrow remained focused on the minister. "You've come regarding the Fort Collins land claim?" he asked. "I'm afraid I must repeat my telegraph of last week: I don't work for *Mrs.* Haywood."

"Yes, but I come at the request of—"

"I'm aware of—"

"At Mr. Haywood's request," the reverend interjected, giving the room a momentary suspension so that he might proceed. "He said you'd helped him purchase an adjoining ranch. Said you'd assist on this as well, seeing how our land is next to the other. If I'm mistaken, I'll offer my apologies and return to speak with Mr. Haywood."

"No. No. That's fine," said Darrow, giving a nodding assent seasoned with a dash of bile and a touch of surrender. He took another drink from the blue bottle, then capped the lid. He had chosen to be there, at the ready, at the call of Mr. Haywood and the Western Federation of Miners. He told himself the Federation's cause was righteous, a purpose and effort to which he was eager to ply his legal talents. But in truth, after the mass killing at the Bunker Hill Mine, his remaining loyalty was constructed squarely on the belief that this one outrageous and reprehensible client might someday be of such a notorious nature as to give him a chance to grasp the law's most golden chalice: to argue before the United States Supreme Court.

Over the years, Darrow had waited and watched, seeking an opportunity to bring himself into the Federation's graces. Fortuity came in 1904 when he was forty-seven. That year, an upstanding, albeit stumbling-drunk, Federation man was mercilessly (according to Darrow's argument) attacked outside Chicago while on his long walk home to his hungry children and sick wife (again, according to Darrow's argument). He'd been accosted by a degenerate sheriff, without probable cause or legal provocation. His client, the good family man, was then put on trial for having defended himself—albeit thirty-six hours after the sheriff's attack and through the use of an iron bar exercised deftly across the sheriff's skull eleven times, effectively dispensing with the lawman's head.

Once Darrow's flowery oratory secured the union man's acquittal on grounds of self-defense (a victory Darrow hadn't expected), a summons arrived from Bill Haywood: Darrow's skills were needed in Colorado. Now, a little more than two years since that first train ride to altitude sickness, Darrow was still returning, still serving the Federation and Bill personally, still awaiting the exigent event that would take him to the Supreme Court. He had hoped Governor Steunenberg's arrest of all labor union men in Idaho (in response to the Bunker Hill bombing) would've sparked the case that elevated him—but, though it was still ongoing, it looked to soon resolve itself without his legal acumen.

Regardless, this request today, by Reverend Sanders, was different. This was intolerable. Never before had Darrow been treated like one of the Haywood servants, asked to take orders for base transactions for whomever Bill dispatched to Darrow's office. Not for Federation lackeys. Not for pocketed legislators nor judges. Not for the one-eyed boss's polio-stricken wife. And certainly not on behalf of her irrational, self-absorbed religion that even Haywood loathed. Nevertheless, Darrow inhaled a breath of servility and muttered, "Let's talk in my office, Reverend."

"Mr. Darrow," Carla implored again, just shy of stamping her foot. "I need to speak with you. If I may. Now." Darrow motioned Reverend Sanders toward the interior office and pulled the door shut behind the man. He turned to Carla. "My goodness, girl, what is it?"

"When I was getting your remedy, I saw Mr. Orchard."

"Haywood's bulldog? His human one. What of it?"

"Mr. Haywood asked me to report anything I might see—"

"Yes, report those things to him. Not to me."

"He was between buildings, reading. He was being mysterious."

"Reading? No! That *is* so mysterious," quipped Darrow. "You should try it sometime. Is there more?"

She scowled at him. "Yesterday, when we were going through Mr. Haywood's correspondence, you told me to remove anything written on his personal paper, the yellow kind."

"What of it?"

"You said it was never to be outside of Mr. Haywood's office."

"Can this recitation—"

"It was that sort. Yellow," she added. "What Mr. Orchard was reading in the alleyway."

Darrow froze like a hunter hearing the distant crack of a stick. "Hmm," he said, his brow furrowing. He moved to the window and looked toward the Pioneer Building. "You saw him just now?"

"Yes, Sir. He was reading it like he didn't want to be seen. Then he put it inside his hat."

"Thank you, Miss Capone." He crossed to his office door. "It was probably nothing, but you should tell Mr. Haywood."

"All right."

Darrow turned the knob to his office and swung the door, rapping the head of the minister who had been listening.

Four hours later, near the back of the Gassell Saloon, Haywood's stout hand was under the table, spread across Carla's leg, his groomed fingertips feeling her knee through her skirt. "You should be working with me," he whispered in her ear. He had her on his left side, so his dead eye was less visible to her. "Why am I wasting such a beauty on my dullard lawyer? You should be in this building. You could work here, bringing beers up to me. We'd have fun."

"Mr. Darrow is nice," Carla managed, scooting away, disgust tightening her shoulders.

"Oh now, Carlotta, you'd rather work here. This is the center of everything. Everyone wants to work near me. You can come work in my office. I wasn't serious about you working in *this* place. No, work upstairs. You're smart. Your talents would be wasted in a saloon. You need to be up with me."

"That's nice of you to say, but if I wasn't working for Mr. Darrow, I'd want to work undercover—to be an agent for the Federation."

"*Under the covers*! Slow down there."

With a disingenuous smile, she looked at the door. "I meant—"

"I know what you meant. You want to do something exciting." He grinned broadly. "Something dangerous."

She stood. "I want to help with the workers' struggle."

"Where are you going? he whined. "Stay with me awhile."

She hesitated. Any desire to tell him about the paper hidden in Orchard's hat had vanished. She only wanted to leave, to be gone from his clawing fingers and lecherous sneer.

"Sit," he commanded.

She sighed and did so, though angling herself at the edge of her chair like a squirrel on a park bench, poised to jump.

"The workers' struggle?" he asked, quoting her. "You're a bricky Bolshevik now? Good for you."

"I don't know," she muttered. "Mr. Darrow is an inspiration."

"Clarence? He's my lawyer. I hire and fire lawyers all the time."

"Ok," she said, unsure how else to respond. "I must get back."

"Wait. Wait. Have a drink with me."

"It's not ... It's too early for me."

He considered her for a moment, then snorted. "Fine. I surrender. You drive a tough bargain, Miss Capone. I'll tell you what—you want an assignment? Something dangerous?"

"Doing what?"

"Be a spy for me. I've got an eye for talent—but just one." He laughed at his joke, but she didn't. "A man of mine is going to Boise, day after tomorrow. You go too. Take the same train. Follow him, but don't let him know who you are or what you're doing."

"Who is he?"

"Harry Orchard."

Her brow furrowed. "All right. What do I do in Boise?"

"Get a job at the Saratoga Hotel. Then wait. We'll contact you."

"You're sending me away?" she asked, processing it all.

"You want to help the Federation, right? So be more than Clarence's secretary. Nothing dangerous happens in a law office."

"Of course, Sir."

"Talk to Winnie. She'll tell you the details. You'll be good."

"That's quite a distance from here."

"Are you worried you'll miss me?"

"No. I mean—"

"I'll visit you. It's been awhile since I've been to Boise."

She hesitated. "Of course."

"In fact, there's a play performed there, called *Sapho*. Heard of it? You'd like it. I'll come take you."

"No, Sir," she said. "I mean, I've not heard of it."

"It's scandalous. About women and desire. Says you women have the same desires as us men. What do you think about that?"

"I don't know."

"It was a success on Broadway, in New York City. They called it 'concupiscent.' Do you know what that means?"

She shook her head.

"Means lustful. Sensual. Why it's now in Boise, Idaho, of all places, I don't know, but everyone's talking about it. You'll like it, I can tell."

Carla sniffed, looked away, one hand fumbling with a utensil.

He patted her knee again and said, "You can go now."

"Thank you." She got to her feet quickly.

He stood and kissed her cheek. "My little *concupiscent* fighter for the workers' struggle." He slipped a hand around her waist. "Do this and I'll forget you refused me."

She froze.

"Refused to work in my office," he grumbled.

"Oh."

"I'm just teasing you. Go now."

"Yes," she said, forcing her cheeks to smile. "Thank you."

★

– 7 –

WEDNESDAY
October 24, 1906

By the time Harry Orchard was on the Union Pacific heading north from Denver, he knew he was being followed by at least two undercover Pinkertons, but he gave them little mind. There was nothing for them to discover, nothing new for them to see. Even if they followed him all the way to Boise, before he undertook any action he would see to it they were put off his trail, or otherwise killed.

He settled in for the eighteen-hour journey in a second-class passenger car. Though he planned to read some, he hoped to sleep, rolling across the grasslands, up into Wyoming, then west past Green River, then up and across to Boise. He had made this rail trip many times before. He was prepared. He had two cigars in one pocket of his coat (the coyote-brown one with the bullet hole in the back), five dollars in the other pocket, and his small Smith & Wesson revolver in his pants. All a man needed. He only wished he had brought a *Denver Post* to read along the way. He could have stolen one easily enough at the station. After making a mental note to disembark in Laramie to buy (if he must) a paper, he commenced studying his fellow passengers. Some were already sleeping though the train had yet to cross the Platte. Most were men. The few women were wives, he figured. Most of them. All lumbering along. One woman was alone, her back to him: a mother in a blue dress holding her child. A whore perhaps. If so, then she was the holy trinity: Mother, daughter, and whorey ghost—three in one. He chuckled at the thought.

He turned his attention to the train car itself, especially the wood-slatted, curved ceiling. He remembered the similar passenger car in northern Idaho, months ago, coming into the Bunker Hill Mine, right before he and Addis jumped off. No, Steve Adams. He now knew that rat-face's real name. He envisioned this car packed with a similar load of dynamite. He glanced around, wondering if anyone would survive if he placed even half of that here. Of course not. He imagined the destructive impact of just one dynamite stick in this car. If placed there, under those three men across the aisle and two sections forward, it would kill them, including the two Pinks. Certainly. But how many others? What if the explosives were placed outside, on top of the car? The blast would shatter the roof, but would those slats still kill? Yes. And the holy young woman would die. At that moment she turned. He could see her clearly now, across the aisle—a young brunette in a blue dress. A dimpled smile. Holding her swaddled baby. Too beautiful to be a whore. Thus not the trinity. Damn. The more he studied her, the more familiar she seemed. He waited, hoping she might make eye contact with him. But no. She was just another woman to whom he was invisible. It was him who was the ghost.

"Goddamned nigger soldiers!" spewed from a man ahead, followed by "Wobbly scum!" from another, and the two got to their feet, one throwing a wild swing at the other. Then came the other man's crushing riposte—ferocious fist meeting jaw. The first man was already unconscious before his head slammed into the young woman nearby, knocking her baby free such that it hit the floor, the blankets opening on impact, revealing the swaddled content was not an infant, but rather, was a collection of tightly rolled newspapers.

Curious, thought Orchard, remaining motionless, observing. She's not a mother either. Only pretended to be. Other men stood, moving forward with equal parts desire to calm the situation as to impress the beauty scrambling to retrieve her flailed *Denver Post* child from being boot-scattered down the aisle. When part of it came alongside Orchard, he leaned and retrieved it and stared at the headlines:

IDAHO GOVERNOR ARRESTS
TWO-THOUSANDTH UNION MAN!
Four Hundred Held in Barns Without Trial

Orchard gave a breathy chuckle. Now he knew why that governor's name was on the paper folded into the brim of his hat. He read further:

> Boise, Idaho. On Wednesday last, Victor McDarment became the two-thousandth man arrested and his arms confiscated by Pinkerton agents upon the martial law orders of Governor Steunenberg following the bombing of the Bunker Hill Mine and Concentrator last July. Beginning August 20, 1906, the governor ordered the arrests of all men suspected to be members of, or otherwise directly affiliated with, the Western Federation of Miners. The arrests have continued from that date to this, with the two-thousandth occurring Wednesday last. Many non-union men have been arrested as well, including, by way of example, John Venerable, an itinerant dentist for the miners. The men are being held in confined quarters without bail until such time as the governor deems the crisis to be resolved, and the perpetrators of the calamitous deed are arrested. President Roosevelt has ordered a regiment of soldiers to take up guard posts surrounding the confined union men, and to manage the captives' orderly release on a date yet determined.

Yes, the governor of Idaho was a traitor, just as Mr. Haywood had said. Ordering the arrests of all labor union men in the state—a true son of a bitch if ever there was one, thought Orchard. It would be a pleasure to kill the man—not just the man, but the elected governor. That meant it would be an assassination. He smiled. It would be his first assassination. It needed to be done right. Something special, if he could muster it. So how? By bomb certainly, as Mr. Haywood had instructed. But the governor would have extra security. Orchard couldn't rush it. This might take a couple of months. He needed to settle into Boise, look around, create a new identity, be patient, plan, then execute. Assassinate. It might be his best bombing yet. But for now, one problem remained—two, to be precise. He focused on the two Pinks until they were forced to look away. He had a task to do in Boise, assigned by Mr. Haywood, and he would get it done. A great task. A noble task. A pleasure. And those two worms would not impede him.

Three rows away in the same car, Carla cursed herself. How could she have been so clumsy as to drop the bundle? It was reckless to pretend to have a baby in the first place. It had been a notion she conjured in Denver's Union Station—a rashly enacted idea that her caring for a child might mask the true purpose of her journey: the undercover, Boise assignment Mr. Haywood had given her, with details having been provided by Winnie.

Winnie Minor was her best friend. Or, better put, Winnie had been her best friend during their younger years in Spokane. Now Carla wasn't sure. In the years immediately following their schooling, they had lost touch. Winnie had moved to Denver to help her sister, Neva, who was suffering with polio. It was later that Carla learned Neva had married the president of the Federation of Western Miners, William Haywood.

Then, last year, when Carla's father and brother were killed in the Stratton Mine collapse, Carla found herself needing to do something, to somehow strike back, to join the workers' struggle, to fight for what she believed in, to do what she could as a woman. She joined the Socialist Party of the Northwestern Range, but found it feeble—a gathering of lonely, castrated male wolves baying at an empty sky, a thousand miles from being heard. Besides, she preferred to work with women, as the men were too horny to hear even her base opinions. The east coast suffragettes were women, as were the members of the garment unions. And women led the temperance movement. But those were thinly active in eastern Washington State, and none offered the justice she sought, the revenge she needed. It was the greed of the Mine Owners Association that had killed her father and brother. Those owners were responsible. They were her enemy. Not just any capitalists—but mine owners. Not just any men denying women the vote—but mine owners. Not just any men who boozed away their family's money—but mine owners. And all who supported and served those owners, including the Pinkertons. Thus she realized that her recourse could only come through aiding the enemies of the mine owners. Actually, their single enemy: the mine workers union, the Western Federation of Miners.

So, two months prior to this train ride, Carla had set out to get herself ingratiated with the Federation. To become a Wobbly. But how? At that time, she knew only two people associated with a labor union: her childhood friend, Winnie Minor, sister of the Federation president's wife; and Clarence Darrow, the Federation's lead attorney. She didn't know Mr. Darrow at that time, had never met him, but she felt a bond with him. Though he had lost their trial against the Stratton mine owners, to her, Clarence Darrow was extraordinary. In fact, it was while reading the transcript of his Stratton trial arguments that she decided to become a lawyer herself. Or a politician. Neither were tenable ideas for a young woman. Not really. But Mr. Darrow's eloquence had spurred her, clapping to flight the birds of her youthful exuberance.

In September, she left Spokane for Denver. There she rekindled a semblance of friendship with Winnie and made her wishes clear: First, she wanted to help the Federation, however she could. Second, she wanted to meet Clarence Darrow. From there, events took a quick pace. Within hours, Winnie introduced Carla to Mr. Haywood (whose lecherous behavior Winnie seemed to ignore). The next morning, Carla met Mr. Darrow. During that brief conversation, Mr. Darrow made known his need for a secretary. Carla quickly obtained Mr. Haywood's approval and reported to work that afternoon. Now, seven weeks later, Mr. Haywood had assigned her the covert task that placed her here, on this train, going back north. Not all the way to Spokane, but close: Boise.

Perhaps she had ruined everything with the dumb idea of pretending to carry a baby, hoping it would conceal her purpose. No, that was not the main reason she had performed the ruse—not if she was honest. She had hoped the faux-baby would give her physical distance from men, would buffer their taunts and advances. And perhaps would give her a bit of imagined comfort in this scary endeavor for which she felt woefully unprepared.

But it hadn't worked. Instead, in the male tussle, she had lost hold of the ploy. And now that moon-faced man, Harry Orchard—the very man she was assigned to follow, the man who was not supposed to notice her—that same man was surmising her, aware of her clumsy attempt at deceit. And it wasn't all in his eyes. It was the way he examined her, undressing her in his mind. She knew that invasive look too well.

Snap to your senses, she scolded herself. *Do better!* She steeled herself and made a new decision. The bad idea of the paper baby had been born from anxiety—a means to hold men at arm's length until she wanted them near. But that wasn't going to work. She would fail if she acted from a position of weakness, in reaction to fear. Instead of shielding herself from men, she needed to embrace the most powerful man-mastering tool she possessed: her sexuality. Perhaps it was second, with her wit being first. Regardless, she would employ them both. She had a task to do in Boise. She would get it done. And if she was lucky and chose well, she might have fun doing it—though not with the likes of Harry Orchard.

She sat up straight, pretended to have never been holding a baby or bundle of newspapers, and looked out the window. Keeping her coat about her, she tightened the tuck of her silk waistshirt into her narrow skirt, then lifted her breasts above her corset beneath, making them more pronounced under her now-tighter shirt. Then she removed her coat, placing it on the empty seat beside her. She cocked her deep-crowned hat, perching it at a slant, and feigned an absent-minded poke at her pile of brown curls where they had fallen about her ears. She wiped her teeth with her tongue, sniffed, and raised an eyebrow at her reflection in the glass, her resolute face flying across the grasslands beyond.

A man slid in beside her and introduced himself.

"Miss Carla Capone," she replied, unaware that he was an undercover Pinkerton. *Yes*, she told herself, *you'll manage these men, and it'll be a song*.

When the train stopped in Laramie, Wyoming for water, coal, and to substitute engines, Orchard took a stretch-n-piss stroll. In the small depot, he noted the two Pinkerton agents were still watching him. Idiots, he thought. Clowns on patrol. He moved to the window and sipped the coffee he'd bought at a concession stand. The rail crew were uncoupling the engine. He watched them until his focus shifted to the glass before him, and to the dark-haired girl in the blue dress—now "childless"—behind him. She was watching him. That was curious. Women didn't notice him—a fact to which he'd grown gloomily accustomed. Why her? And, curiouser still, why were the two Pinks unaware that the beauty was also trailing their mark: him? Old man Pinkerton wouldn't employ a women agent, undercover or not. Who did she work for? He moved. She moved. He scanned her way. She turned. He believed he recognized her. Had he seen her in Denver?

"You a Wobbly?" asked a big man sidling alongside Orchard. Orchard considered him, realizing he was asking if Orchard was in the union, then noted the questioner was the same passenger who had landed the devastating upper cut.

"Why you askin?" Orchard replied, keeping an eye on the man's hands.

"Heard that mess?" the man continued. "Steunenberg's barns?"

"Read on it."

"Governor was forced to let em out today."

"Oh?"

"What do you think bout it?"

"Keep my own counsel," Orchard began. "Recommend same."

The man shrugged. "Just makin conversation."

The two men stood shoulder to shoulder, silent, looking outside as the rail crew continued their noisy, arduous work. Orchard thought to move away from the man, but curiosity compelled him to stay a moment longer. "That governor is a damned buffoon," Orchard offered quietly, his fishing line touching the water. He remained facing the windows onto the platform, anticipating any quick movement from the man, while watching the young woman in the reflection. He gave the line a tug: "Foolish, sending in a Negro regiment."

"Union dogs, all of them!" the man exclaimed, taking the bait. "After that Bunker Mine bombing, I say lock em all up. Was horrific. Nothing but animals. Terrorists, I tell you. Every goddamned one of them. They don't deserve trials. Hang em on sight. Easier still, line em up and shoot em down. Any man with a labor card." He paused as if awaiting applause or an amen salute. When none came, he continued, "They were lucky to get let out of those barns after just two weeks. And who cares the color of the soldiers that kept em there. Even if they're niggers. What do you say to that?"

"A bunch of others care," Orchard said.

"You're wrong that the governor's foolish. What he is, is a yellow coward for backing down. Should've put a torch to those barns while the blackies had em surrounded. That's what he shoulda done. We'd be done with the whole lot of em. Goddamned, un-Christian reds. Bunch of socialists."

"Socialists?" asked Orchard, unwilling to further restrain himself. "For fighting for fair wages?"

"They're lazy anarchists. Rats. Reds. Malcontents, what-have-you. Un-American is what they are, I tell you. But it don't matter one goddamned bean what I call em—what anyone calls em."

Sixteen minutes after the train resumed, chugging into the sunset under the power of its new engine, the body of the fast-fisted, outspoken man was found in the men's room of the Laramie depot—a small caliber bullet hole in the back of his head.

★

– 8 –

THURSDAY
October 25, 1906

The next morning, William Borah strolled Boise's Main Street, tipping his hat to passersby, particularly the admiring women. In one week, he was to be elected to the United States Senate representing the state of Idaho. As he was the Republican candidate, the election was a mere formality. In the sixteen years since Idaho's statehood, it had been fairly evenly divided between Republicans and Democrats. But, with the recent uproar over the union bombs in the Coeur d'Alene Mining District, and Borah's Democratic opponent supporting the governor's inflammatory incarceration of all union men, Democrat voters were fleeing the polls, if not the state.

He pulled his black overcoat about him. Beneath it, he wore what was everyday for him but extravagant for most men—unless they were San Francisco shippers, Chicago railroad trustees, Philadelphia steel magnates, Boston mine owners, or New York bankers. Custom tailored in Chicago, Borah's jacket was a navy-blue morning coat. With it he wore bespoke cuffs and collar, a paisley bow tie, striped trousers, and patent-leather cap-toes. And on his head—a black derby from Harrods.

As he reached Tenth Street, he fell into the morning shadow of the Idanha Hotel, a new, large, well-appointed hotel dominating the center of Boise. It was garish in its conspicuousness, built like a red box cornered with white castle turrets climbing five stories, each capped with exaggeratedly tall conical spires. And it was entirely Republican. Another hotel, the Saratoga, two blocks west on Main Street, stood in contrast, primarily in opulence (though the Saratoga was not sub-par by any means). The Saratoga was known to host labor union leaders and Democrats. It had even hosted a Socialist Party rally the prior year at which the radical Eugene Debs spoke. Therefore, soon-to-be Republican Senator

Borah's appointment on this chilly October morning was in the lobby of the Idanha Hotel, and decidedly not at the Saratoga.

Waiting to cross Main Street, Borah watched a passing, noisy automobile. He wanted one, an Oldsmobile, but was unsure what others might say. Surely they'd admire him for being brave enough to manage a buzz cart. He wondered how many other senators drove them. It didn't matter. He'd get one and drive it around Washington, honking at Democrats. But not black. He wanted a burgundy red one, a Model B with a curved dash, like one he'd seen in Chicago.

He entered the arched stone portico, climbed the granite steps, and passed through the Idanha's tall oak-and-glass doors. Inside, he slowed his pace and removed his derby while scanning the room. A moment later he saw his objective: a disheveled man on a velvet couch, reading the newspaper, sucking an unlit cigar. A small traveling bag was on the seat next to the man. As Borah approached, the man noticed but kept the paper up, making no effort to clear the couch. Borah stood still for a second, then turned and dragged a chair noisily across the hardwood floor. When he had it close enough, he sat. "Captain Swain," Borah began. Noting the bag, he added, "Catching the early to Spokane?"

"Senator," replied the lanky, dark haired detective wearing an olive sack suit, black tie, and workman's boots. His toothbrush mustache was narrow with vertical edges. He clenched his cigar in his exposed teeth while folding the paper with a dramatic flourish, then set the paper on his bag.

Borah flipped his pocket-watch. "Should be in from Laramie."

Captain W. S. Swain nodded while adjusting the paper so it wouldn't fall, then pulled the cigar from his mouth. "Senator, don't ever ask me to this gilded pigsty again. I only work in the Saratoga."

Borah squinted at the demand but otherwise ignored it. "Your Thiel men were not very helpful."

Swain stiffened his neck, smoothed his mustache with the flat of his thumb and met the senator's eyes. "Anyone get killed?"

"Is that the Thiel Agency's measure of success—anyone killed?"

"Sometimes."

"Governor Steunenberg was thankful the prisoners left the barns without incident," said Borah.

"Then we did our job. Believe you me, a right large number of those union men had killing in their eyes, ready to exact vengeance on the governor and his Negro guards. But, yes, they dispersed peaceably, after their guns were returned to them. And the army withdrew to its train."

"Yes, but I'm left to wonder," Borah said. "Perhaps it would've happened the same without your agency's efforts? I say this because your agents were nowhere to be seen." When Swain nodded again, Borah added, "I'm not sure they were even—"

"What were you hoping for?" Swain pounced. "You and Steunenberg." His brows lifted as if an answer might be forthcoming from the senator. "If the governor wanted virtuous dandies in white shirts and pressed collars, hell, he should've hired himself some Pink ladies. Same ones he hired to arrest all those innocent men firstly. I'll tell you—there was a fellow there named Baxter who had worked for me, and while in my employ he was safe. But then that fool went over to Sherlock McParland and he got himself found out down in Denver. Got burned alive. Might as well have been killed. No, I don't let my men get known. Not to Big Bill or anyone in the Federation. Not to your bosses, the mine owners. Not to anyone. And certainly not to any godforsaken dictator governor. Or womanizing senator."

Borah nodded slightly, giving a no-teeth smile combined with a slow blink that unmistakably said, *You're an ass*. He rubbed his nose before speaking again—his tone now even and measured. "So, Governor Steunenberg is paying you two thousand dollars for services for which I have no evidence were ever rendered."

"That's correct."

"All right." Borah withdrew a bank draft from his breast pocket and held it for Captain Swain to take. But Swain just looked at it dangling midair at the end of Borah's fingers. Borah sighed, laid it on the brass-edged coffee table and stood.

Swain's eyes narrowed. "Instructions were for cash."

"Well," said Borah, pointing at the check, "that's what you get."

When Harry Orchard stepped from the train that morning in Boise, he hurried for a handsome cab pulled by a black horse standing at the depot's curb. But before approaching, he paused, reversed course, and sat on a bench. That made the trailing Pinkertons adjust their stride and return inside the depot. Orchard stood, his tactic accomplished, and resumed walking to the cab. But before he could get there, the young lady who'd been holding the paper-baby reached the cab first—a bellman freighting her bags in tow. Orchard stopped and observed. She boarded the cab without the slightest notice of him, though they were only eight feet apart. Once her bags were loaded, and the bellman told the driver, "Saratoga," the dark horse went into motion and the cab was away. *So she wasn't following me*, thought Orchard. He grinned at his dumb, wishful thinking. At least it'd been nice to imagine.

From the far side of the depot, came a bellowing call: "All aboard for Caldwell, Pendleton, Walla Walla, and points west! Fifteen minutes for departure! All aboard!"

Orchard tossed his bag in the next cab and said, "The Saratoga Hotel, please." He climbed aboard, snapping the door shut.

Behind him, just as his cab clip-clopped away, yet another cab arrived, and from it stepped the boots of Captain Swain. The tall man paid the fare, retrieved his bag, surveyed the area, then strolled into the depot—all the while being watched by the two Pinkerton agents inside—both peering like bird dogs on a fresh scent.

McParland was in his shirtsleeves and vest, alone in his Denver office, standing at the wood-boxed telephone on the wall, the receiver to his ear, hearing nothing. As he waited, he began to softly sing the Irish ballad, "Red is the Rose":

Red is the rose by yonder garden grows.
And fair is the lily of the valley.
Clear is the water that flows from the Boyne.
But my love is fairer than any.

Hearing something, he shouted into the mouthpiece, "Can you hear me, Robert?" But still no sound came from the earpiece. "Damnit," he muttered and hung it up. As he walked back to his desk, the bells in the telephone box began ringing. He returned and picked up the receiver. "Robert?"

Jim? came the crackled voice through the wires.

"Aye. This damn telephone. Can you hear me?"

Barely, said Robert Pinkerton.

"All right. Morris Friedman is going to publish."

The Jew?

"Aye."

Are you certain?

"Aye."

Can you stop him?

McParland paused. "I tried."

Send someone. Try harder.

"I don't know."

What about "whatever it takes"?

"We can only do so much with Friedman," said McParland.

Do more than "so much," Pinkerton grumbled.

"He's a stubborn fellow. Could sharpen an ax on his head."

More stubborn than you or me? I doubt that.

"Maybe so. But we don't want to cause bigger troubles with—"

Nothing bigger than a book he might write.

"I can think of a few things," said McParland.

The little socialist Christ-killer is your problem. Don't make him mine.

"Aye," said McParland. The line died. He hung up, leaned against the wall, and huffed air toward his feet.

– 9 –

WEDNESDAY
December 12, 1906

The plain, brown-suited towering mass of Bill Haywood was just getting started—his words drubbing down, anvil blow after anvil blow. "While your brothers, your fellow union men, good and family men, were languishing in that miserable barn by order of that tyrant, the governor of Idaho—while they were there, unable to defend themselves—it was US Army soldiers, Americans who are supposed to be protecting the workers—who went to the workers' homes, insulting, outraging, ravishing their wives, mothers, sisters and sweethearts!" Six feet over his head and nailed to the back wall was a round board painted white with the blue seal of the labor union. The white words WESTERN FEDERATION OF MINERS arched across the top, and ORGANIZED MAY 15, 1893 arched across the bottom. In the middle were the union's three resonant symbols: a hammer, a pick, and a sheaf of wheat, along with three stars, each bearing one of the initials: W, F, and M.

The Colorado Federation rally was underway in a Denver meeting hall on Arapahoe Street. Their hulking leader stood at the podium, his most beloved residence. He thundered on, "Those soldiers were there to incite disorder, not to prevent it. You know it. I know it. The world knows it. We all do." On the last sentence, he swept his outstretched hand across the audience with such vigor that he felt his snub-nosed Colt Army .38 slide inside his coat pocket, as if it might tumble out. He removed it and placed it on the podium, his right hand covering it. As he continued the speech, he occasionally rapped it against the podium's top—its nickel-plated steel against the wood making echoing punctuations across the dimly lit, white-washed room teeming with men in various shades of brown.

"The Western Federation of Miners, our Federation, our most beloved union [*gun rapped on wood*] is now over forty thousand strong. Two hundred locals spread across Colorado [*gun again*], Nevada [*gun*], Idaho [*gun*], and Arizona [*gun*]. Hell, we're even in Canada! And we're advancing into five more states right now, including California. At next January's gathering of the locals, we'll have representatives from every western state *and* Canada. In this past year we've become bonded—fused into a single, irrefutable iron force for freedom!"

Rapturous applause and stomping erupted.

Haywood continued, "We have arms depots and hidden caches across our territory, rivaling any country in the world. And, most important, we've trained disciplined men with the courage to use those arms whenever and wherever they're required—for the effective defense of the US Constitution and the advancement of the working class of America. For you! And if that most unfortunate of occasions arises, if the time comes, I know you can be called upon as well. You'll rise up as one magnificent fist and join our armed men in that most noble of battles for the preservation of your freedoms—to strike a fatal blow against those corporations and collective trusts that would scheme against us, against you, would buy your government, would deny you life [*gun on podium*], liberty [*gun again*] and the pursuit of happiness! [*gun raised high*] We are the future of this country. *You* are the future!"

The audience was already on its feet, clapping wildly.

Awaiting the cessation of the noise, Haywood gave a kind glimpse toward Winnie—the spirited blonde minx with an upturned nose and winsome eyes in the front row. She was also on her feet. He noted her youthful cheeks framing her sensuous grin, her smooth cleavage alive as she clapped. In the aisle beside Winnie, Haywood's wife, Neva, looked up at him and gave a small nod while tapping a minuscule half-clap against the wooden arm of her invalid chair. Her pained face bore an almost imperceptible upturn of the lips, something placating. Or was that bristling condescension, wondered Haywood. Nevertheless, as a product of performed impulse, he kept his focus longer on her than on her sister. Finally, Neva dipped her chin, releasing him.

Were he a different man, Haywood might've persuaded himself that the extra attention he gave Neva was born from appropriateness, social custom, and conciliation to her being his wife. But he couldn't dupe himself by his own stratagems. Others, yes, but not himself. The truth was that he kept Neva happy so his life-affirming, manhood-ratifying romance with young Winnie could remain unguarded, undefended, and that it shouldn't be threatened as only Neva could. Besides, he loved the women—both of them. He was good to them. He was necessary for them. But they were far from equal in his mind. If his relationship with Winnie was his coat of luxury, his devotion to Neva, with her shriveled leg and early-wrinkled face, was his penitent hair shirt.

Beyond those auspices of love, he knew he needed both women. Not only for the privilege of his morning release—Winnie's pouch being the eighth wonder of the world—but for the preservation of his honorable image: an upstanding man duteous to his frail, religious wife while not chasing whores, others' wives, temptresses all—though they were blatantly available to him. While Neva provided him the latter: the good husband persona, Winnie gave him the former: a clear mind and invigorated body. Indeed, it was the touch of his wife's sister that kept him loyal to his wife. How could either have cause to complain?

Certainly, there were rumors among the union men and their wives, between the judges and the attorneys, whispered by shopkeepers, policemen, dancing girls, and barkeeps alike, about Haywood's peculiar relationship with the two women. But the idea of the Federation leader bedding his wife's sister was too scandalous to not yield its own width of doubt. And it was in that qualm that Haywood found safe passage, the opportunity to exist, to be satisfied. The very audaciousness of the act cloaked its existence.

As the applause faded and the three hundred men returned to their chairs, a face caught Haywood's eye and he returned to it, finding it again in the middle of the crowd. With slow deliberation, Haywood smoothed his eyebrows. Then he repeated the motion. Most of these men were miners—rough faces and worn hands with temperaments to match. And they were his men. The women up front may be his private reward in this world, but his muscle mass, the red of his blood, his power beyond even the constraints of life, came from the men beyond. They would defend him. They would die for him. Most would kill for him. A few already had.

As Haywood rapped the pistol and resumed his speech, a slender man in a green jacket stood at attention near the back of the room. Upon seeing his leader's brow-smoothing, he strode to a young, disheveled man in the middle of the room and signaled him up before ushering him outside.

In the street, the young man was delivered to three roughs in their shirt sleeves, their coats draped across a boardwalk bench. The three shoved the wide-eyed man around the corner and proceeded to beat and kick him, blow after blow. In the street nearby, Denver's Sheriff Tetter, shotgun at the ready, stood bemused, murmuring with the green-jacketed man. The what and why of it all was understood: undercover Pinkerton spies were not welcome at Federation meetings, even public rallies like this one—a point being smashed into the young man unequivocally.

From inside the hall came the muffled thunder of Haywood's oration. The sheriff turned and declared, "Alright, that'll do, boys." The three men donned their coats before re-entering the building. Having only a few teeth scattered, and ribs cracked, the Pinkerton knew he was lucky. He'd known it since he too saw Big Bill's eyebrow signal. Had the man sneezed into a pocket-square three times instead, the young Pinkerton would have made a run for it, and probably failed. Then, instead of his current slow stagger into the dark of Imperial Street, he would be sliding to the dark of death's door. It wouldn't have mattered to Sheriff Tetter. Either way, Tetter would still be standing in the street, holding his favorite shotgun, watching the Pinkerton disappear.

"Look at your Federation cards," Haywood commanded, now standing in front of the podium. "Yes, pull them out. Read with me those most precious words found there." He took a moment, and then began the recitation. "Labor prod—" He paused as only a handful had started with him. Then he smiled at the group of clumsy men, all floundering for their union cards. His reaction caused others to grin, and soon a chortle the size of the room rose and then faded. A wave of merriment. Haywood took the resultant silence as an opportunity to spike a point. "Any worker who cannot produce such a membership card is an enemy to us, to himself, and to the community at large. But if you can't read it, that's all right. You good men know the words."

After another chuckle rippled through the crowd—now with their cards in hand—Haywood started anew, and this time a low-rolling chorus of male voices joined him. "Labor produces all wealth. Wealth belongs to the producer thereof." He paused. "Once more: Labor produces all wealth. Wealth belongs to the producer thereof." Again, the men recited it with him. "As we know, there are only two classes of people in the world: One is men like you, who produce all. The other is those who produce nothing, but are content to live in luxury, to grow fat on the wealth you produce."

He let the expected chorus of boos and curses shake the windows before he resumed. "We'll never forget what they did to our brothers in Idaho. We'll never forget their disregard for the laws of these United States." He paused for a drink of whiskey from a crystal glass on the podium. "Thank you, fine gentlemen. You may put your cards away."

This speech was nothing new. The words little changed since they were last hurled upon an almost identical audience. Once every six months or so, Federation men would gather in this hall and a boisterous murmuring (deigned union business) got underway. Most came as an act of union loyalty, tolerating it fine, enjoying the brotherhood, the tradition of gathering—before slipping across Arapahoe Street to The Antelope for cheap whiskey and drafts. But some were there for the unmatched exultation, bathing in the emotional lift. Matters of business were not for them. In fact, they found such particulars a nuisance. They were there to have their passions filled, their opinions validated, their sweat and anger justified. And no one could do that quite like their union boss, Big Bill. His bluster, the fullness of his bearing, his unhidden mining injury, the fearlessness behind his demands and threats, lifted them from their misery, empowered them to resume their labors for yet another season. He saw them. His good eye saw their honor, his dead eye their hatred.

Everyone suspected Big Bill Haywood had orchestrated the killings, the beatings, the bombings. Some new it to be fact. Where some chose to indulge their doubts—so they may justify their continued engagement with the labor union cause—others embraced the knowledge. Celebrated it. Through an unspoken covenant, they had collectively abolished any moral ambiguities within themselves, allowing only a resolute worship of the man. Where he led, they would go freely and without question or hesitation, including to their deaths if so required.

The only price they demanded, all that was required of Haywood, was loyalty in return—to not steal from them, not to rob them of their hope, their anger, their money. Haywood need only be true to them—or a semblance of truth—to give them something that appeared solid in which to believe. In that, they could find cause to surrender, to give themselves over to that shimmering mirage of glory such men stumble toward—each a cane to another's imbalance—lest they fall alone and, from the dirt, be forced to reconcile their fragility.

Haywood was still going. "Not but three years ago the Colorado legislature passed our long-fought law for the eight-hour workday." General applause. "You, the great torchbearers, the guardians for all working men, you made that law come to pass. You made the sacrifices necessary. You should congratulate yourselves! Yes. But still we wait for it to be obliged upon the greedy mine owners!"

He pushed on before the crowd's roar might drown the coming point. I ask you, is this state of Colorado in the United States?" He turned to a fifteen-foot wide American flag nailed to the wall. "Does any one of those white stars stand for Colorado? I wonder. And you wonder too: Is this not a land of laws and justice? Can a man here behave any way he sees fit? May there be no fairness or justice in this state? Or even now in Idaho? Where else but these mining states can the rich ignore, outright disregard, the laws established by the government—your government—your laws—your will? You, the working men of America. Where else? It's an outrage that we will not stand for! I will not stand for! You will not stand for! Eight hours of work, eight hours of play, eight hours of sleep—even for only eight goddamned dollars a day!"

After the by-then-weary audience settled, Haywood cleared his throat for his peroration. "I ask that we not forget the other color on that flag." He pointed again to the massive American flag. "Besides those white stars and bars, and the blue, there is another color on that flag. The most important color: Red! The workers' color. The blood of patriots spilt for this nation—for their families and yours. For your freedoms. For your future. And it is the blood of tyrants, spilt to refresh the tree of liberty—in the past and in days to come. For this nation we hold so dear. It is the red of *your* blood—American blood—American red—American bled!"

★

– 10 –

MONDAY
December 24, 1906

"Help me up, Bill, please," said Neva. Tired of being low in her invalid chair at their Christmas gathering, she had rolled herself into the drawing room, and then to Bill standing by the fire where he was talking with other officers of the Western Federation of Miners. Beside him, the thick, oak mantel was adorned with pine boughs and fairy-light candles. Neva glanced again at the man-cluster, all in various sack suits and jackets. Among them was her private friend, George Pennington, wearing the jacket she liked so much: midnight blue, worsted with faint chevrons. Was that why he wore it again, for her, so soon after she had complimented it the week prior? She would have preferred George helping her up, feeling his hands under her arms, lifting her. But here, in this group, actually in any assembly of people, decorum required her to behave as if she barely knew George. It was a pretense that made her chagrin all the more acute. Especially as Bill was still ignoring her. She ran her wheeled chair into his leg and growled, "Bill."

He looked down. His instant expression was a grimace wrapped in bother, as if she was a peculiar dog sniffing his leg. In fact, had she been Claus, his bulldog, humping his leg, he would have regarded her with more warmth. Snapping his countenance from scowl to careless little smile, he said, "Oh, my dear, what can I do for you?"

"I said, help me up. Get my crutches, please."

"Now?"

"Yes. Before the girls arrive."

"Where are they?"

"My crutches?"

"Yes of course, your crutches."

"In our bedroom," she said.

"I was in the middle of ... but—" He sighed, walking away.

George approached. "Merry Christmas," he said with a wink.

"Merry Christmas to you, Mr. Pennington," she replied, beaming. "There's that jacket again. Very dapper."

"Thank you. It's my Neva-coat," he said, making her blush. He leaned close. "I have a present for you."

"And I have one for you," she whispered, and touched his arm. "But not here. Later." She could smell him, oaky and warm.

"Not tonight," said George. "I'll come to Park Hill soon."

"I'll bring a mistletoe," she said, peeping at the one dangling from the chandelier above them.

"Good," he said. "But tonight, I expect you to dance with me."

"You think so?"

"Yes," he said, grinning. "The Viennese."

She laughed and began to speak, but swallowed her words seeing Bill returning with two hefty, worn crutches. They were man sized but sawn down for her, with wooden arm supports, and cloth tied at their bottoms to protect the floor. She hated them, but Bill had long declared them "good enough." She held them as Bill moved behind her, helping her up to where she could put all her weight on her right leg. As she tucked the crutches under her arms, the left one caught the white-lace trim of her gown's sleeve cap. She looked to Bill, hoping he would extricate her from the snag, but he had already returned to the men. Then George's hands came in, and, as he eased the lace free with his right hand, his left brushed her breast. "Why, thank you, gallant knight," she whispered, feeling her cheeks warm, wondering why he smelled so good.

"My pleasure. That dress is beautiful."

"Thank you."

Noting the gown's scarlet color, he remarked, "If you had green crutches, you'd be a Christmas present." He turned, rolled her chair out of the way, then rejoined the circle of resonant male voices mulling profound things of little consequence. He glimpsed back at Neva, eyes smiling.

She crutched through the front entry, glanced toward the closed door, and then into the large parlor from which "Joy to the World" was underway from musicians at one end of the room—a guitar, violin, cello, and the Haywood's Chickering parlor-grand piano. Just as in the drawing room, the parlor's large fireplace was also in full blaze; and though most of the parlor's furniture and rugs had been removed in preparation for a waltz, twelve chairs stood near the edges; and along one wall was a buffet offering champagne, port, and slices of holiday cake adorned with almonds, mince pie, and plum pudding in a basin covered with embroidered linen bearing rosy-cheeked Father Christmas. Opposite the quartet was the Christmas tree, adorned with strings of beads and popcorn, paper angels, silver yarn, gold satin bows, seventy-two small red stars, eight golden glass balls from Germany, and twelve white pen-candles waiting to be lit. Beneath it was a scattering of butcher-paper-wrapped presents tied with burgundy ribbons.

Other people were milling about, some in knots, some in pairs, all with courteous nods, convivial smiles, Christmas wishes, praises to Neva for the festive décor, and a few women gushing over her new pearl teardrop, 1.9 carat diamond earrings, courtesy of her husband. "Why, thank you," Neva would say. "Bill was very generous this year."

Then the front door opened, and a scamper of buttoned boots, high voices, and happiness hurried into the parlor and rushed to Neva. "Mommy!" exclaimed ten-year-old Henrietta.

"Merry Christmas, Mommy," said Vernie, twelve.

Behind them, while Haywood assisted Winnie out of her black sable coat, Winnie quietly instructed him to put on his eye patch.

"Girls!" Neva exclaimed, welling up, dropping one of her crutches as she clung to her daughters. "Henrietta! Vernie! Oh my! Oh my!" She looked up at Winnie who was standing in a chartreuse embroidered gown, smiling from the entrance. "Thank you, Sissy," said Neva. "My Christmas is now complete."

"Do we have presents?" asked Henrietta, adding, "Vernie has a boyfriend."

"Shush," snapped Vernie.

"Of course you have presents." Neva's grin and tears were irrepressible. "Oh my, let me look at you. I love how this fits. I was worried," she said, as Vernie spun in her white linen dress and high-buttoned boots. "You're growing so quickly. And you"—she looked at Henrietta's crimson-over-cream bib and tucker—"you're so beautiful in that. Go now, find your presents!"

As the girls went to the tree, Winnie approached Neva and picked up the dropped crutch.

"Thank you," said Neva. Winnie also wore new diamond earrings—though smaller than Neva's. She touched one of Winnie's ears. "Whoever chooses them for him certainly has good taste."

"I think it's that woman at Parker's Jewelers," said Winnie. "The round one with the scar." She gestured a slash on her cheek.

"Probably," murmured Neva. "Thank God for her, then."

"Worker's 'Marseillaise'!" boomed Haywood, entering the parlor chest first, sporting his eye patch and leading a train of men behind him.

"Oh Bear," exclaimed Winnie. "Perfect! Worker's 'Marseillaise'!"

Others were gathering as Haywood loomed toward the musicians. They stopped playing "The Mistletoe." "'La Marseillaise?'" asked the Englishman at the piano.

"The Russian version," shouted Haywood. *"'The Worker's!'"*

The violinist frowned. "The French —"

"No, no!" barked Haywood.

"Aye, we know it," said the pianist. He turned to the other musicians and said softly, "It's the same."

"No," said Haywood. "The Russian 'Marseillaise,' damn you."

The pianist gave a dutiful nod and commenced playing the French "La Marseillaise"—to Haywood's unaware delight. Most were silent, though a few began singing in French:

> *Allons, enfants de la Patrie,*
> *le jour de gloire est arrivé!*
> *Contre nous de la tyrannie—*
> (Arise, children of the Fatherland,
> the day of glory has arrived!
> Against us tyranny's—)

Meanwhile Haywood was alone belting in Russian:

> *Otrechemsya ot starogo mira!*
> *Otryakhem yego prakh s nashikh nog!*
> *Nam vrazhdebny ziatyye kumiry.*
> (Let us denounce the old world!
> Let us shake its dust from our feet!
> We are enemies to the golden idols.)

When the others sang:

> *Aux armes, citoyens, formez vos bataillons!*
> (To arms, citizens, form your battalions!)

Haywood sang:

> *Vstavay, podymaysya, rabochniy narod!*
> (Stand, rise up, working people!)

And when they sang:

> *Qu'un sang impur abreuve nos sillons!*
> (Let an impure blood soak our fields!)

Haywood stood on the hearth, booming:

> *Vperyod! Vperyod! Vperyod! Vperyod! Vperyod!*
> (Forward! Forward! Forward! Forward! Forward!)

Thirty minutes later, when the quartet played "Blue Danube," a quick-step Viennese waltz, Haywood danced with Winnie, and then for a few bars with his daughters. Afterwards, he stood near Neva and George while continuing to engage with others.

George whispered a few things with Neva before turning to Haywood. "Bill, Neva would like to dance, and—"

"Ah, no. I'm tuckered."

"In that case, may I have the honor?"

"God speed," Haywood snorted. "I like two good legs."

Neva whipped her face away, refusing the blow's impact, and muttered under her breath, "How about two good eyes?"

"Watch her crutches don't crush you," Haywood added.

"Yes," muttered George before going to the musicians. "Sirs, do you know the new waltz—a slow one, 'The Merry Widow?'"

"Aye," replied the pianist.

Moments later, at the edge of people on swirling display, including Winnie and Haywood, George and Neva smiled and turned, wobbled and swayed, his hand at her waist, her nose to his chest. They stumbled some, laughed, whispered, and silently yearned.

– 11 –

SATURDAY
December 29, 1906

The winter of 1906 was not unlike others on the bleak, wind-thrashed landscape of Idaho: it was hellaciously cold. And Saturday, December 29, was likewise unremarkable. The leaden sky had been dropping snow since before dawn, and by early afternoon a fresh four inches lay silent across the broad flats toward the Shake River, west and south of Boise; and almost erased the low mountain range to the north and northeast of what was perhaps the most banal of America's state capitals. This vast covering also buried the frozen streets of Caldwell, a somnolent cluster of homes and businesses thirty miles west of Boise. And it was there along Caldwell's longest boardwalk, reaching three quarters of a mile from the town's center to its upscale neighborhood, that death came plodding in a bear coat tugged tight against the wind.

The stout farmer-newspaperman-banker-governor of Idaho, Frank Steunenberg (forty-four, six foot two, two hundred and thirty-five pounds) was standing by the window of his home study, wearing a smoking jacket, when his lanky young daughter bounded in. Pretending to be a butler, she stood at attention, announcing the man at the front door, Mr. O'Malley, was an insurance man seeking an audience with the governor—not at the house, but at the governor's bank office, at 3:00 that afternoon. Frank grinned at her.

Just before his precocious "butler" had made her entrance, Frank had been watching from the window—observing the pointy-beaked, satchel-clasping Mr. O'Malley open the front gate and approach the house. Though Frank hadn't seen the man before, he knew who he was. Frank's $4,500 life insurance policy would expire at the end of the year—in two days. Thus, three weeks prior, Frank had gone to the Saratoga Hotel and left a message for the New York Life Insurance Company salesman who he knew was staying there. The message requested the man call on Frank before the expiration of both the year and the policy.

But today Frank was in no mood for a salesman. Least of all a salesman whose profession anticipated his death. It made his stomach gurgle with malaise, with melancholy—though in truth that grayness had draped him since Christmas day—the day an unfamiliar voice phoned Frank, warning him of some non-specific yet pending mortal danger.

Two months had passed since his mass arrests had ended. The Bunker Hill attack had been a horrific bombing, but— He winced at his decision to declare martial law in the aftermath, to have Pinkertons make the arrests. The papers had quoted him saying, "We have taken the monster by the throat and we are going to choke the life out of it. No halfway measures will be adopted. It is a plain case of the state or the union winning, and we do not propose that the state shall be defeated." It was not just pretension, but trite obfuscation. He knew that. And yes, the incarcerations had been wrong—but he had promptly turned the men loose, hadn't he? He hadn't taken further actions. He didn't hire the Pinkertons to release the men, but instead used men from the Thiel Agency, friendly to the Federation. His friend Senator William Borah had seen to that.

He understood campaign donations from the Western Federation of Miners, and from Bill Haywood individually, had played an important role in his election two years prior. Perhaps even the deciding element. And he was not so foolish or naïve as to fail to acknowledge his unwritten, post-election obligation to assist the Federation where he might—at least in Idaho. But that didn't mean the Federation could indiscriminately run wild and murderous in his state, blowing up mines and killing dozens of innocent men. No. But perhaps he had overreacted ordering the arrest of thousands, holding them without trial, letting them be guarded by Negro soldiers. But he had needed to send a message. Hadn't he?

Then, of course, the newspapers pounced, saying the captive union men were being held under the most brutal and tyrannical of conditions; and those same editors would further claim that he, the governor, had violated the free rights of every Idahoan. Well, that simply was not true, and Frank had said so, in writing:

"The inhabitants themselves deprive themselves of a republican form of government by insurrection and rebellion." It was a bit of prevarication, but it spawned a flood of poorly written, enraged letters, many from Colorado, threatening his death, declaring him a marked man. But surely Big Bill, a thousand miles away in Denver, would understand that it wasn't all Steunenberg's fault. In fact, Haywood must have understood that, Steunenberg reasoned, because the death threats had subsided. In fact, there hadn't been one since Thanksgiving. It had reached its denouement, he had told himself. Then the telephone rang on Christmas Day. Another threat—not really—more of a warning.

In a few days Steunenberg would talk with the Federation's Idaho representative. They would smooth things over. No, he would have that meeting in a few weeks. Maybe. He wanted the whole affair to be done with, for it to have never happened. Damn them, those capricious terrorists. Why couldn't they leave him alone? 1907 was just a couple of days away. It held promise. Maybe in the new year he would go to Denver and meet directly with Big Bill. They would make peace.

But for now, not only would he not let his life insurance lapse, he would increase it to $10,000—requiring a lengthy conversation with the salesman who was now stamping for warmth downstairs on the front stoop. Yes, going to his office was best. There was no reason to risk his wife overhearing the conversation, thus increasing her anxiety. The German grandfather clock began to chime 2:00. He looked at his thirteen-year-old charmer. "Tell him 'Yes,' darling. I'll meet him at my office at three."

"Can't you stay, Papa?" she implored. "Momma and I are making cherry pies."

"I smell them! Don't worry. I won't be gone long."

After she left, Frank went to the window and again peered at the stony man below. "Why didn't you telephone?" he whispered as if the man might hear him, then added, "And on such a bitter day?" Then the thought came to him: perhaps the salesman didn't know if the governor's residence had a telephone. Yes, maybe that was it.

In a one-nag cart half a block away, on the same side of the street as the Steunenberg house (so as to be unseen from the house's front windows), Harry Orchard shivered. He could see Steve Adams standing on the front step of the governor's house, an empty clutch satchel in one hand, Orchard's heavy bear coat around his shoulders. Adams's other hand was hidden beneath the coat's flap, and Orchard knew what it held: Adams's damn Bowie knife. *That imbecile had better stick to the goddamned plan,* thought Orchard.

Upon his arrival in Boise two months prior, Orchard had commenced pursuing two objectives: One was to conduct a thus-far-unsuccessful courtship with the paper-baby woman from the train, Miss Carla Capone. When he learned she'd come to Boise to serve as a waitress for the Saratoga Hotel, not only had he lodged himself there, but he dined at the Saratoga each evening. For the first week, Carla hadn't stood still long enough for even a pleasantry. She'd flit to his table in her deep-red, narrow skirt that made his limbs turn jelly, receive his order in even tones, then turn on her heel before he could muster the slightest introduction. During the second week, when she gave him a convivial "good morning," he took it for significant interest. In the fourth week, she lingered just long enough for him to learn her name and her opinion of the weather. He wanted to ask about the *Denver Post* child but lost his nerve. That was no way to woo a woman, he told himself, to interrogate her over something so private as a baby, real or not.

Then came the conversation last week when she sat briefly at his table, resting herself, smiling at him. She asked about his business in Boise—to which he spoke of being in the sheep trade, scouting for land, and how he might have doings with Governor Steunenberg. But then her ebullient dark eyes looked toward people at another table—her expression implacable, unimpressed. As best he could tell, she seemed to anticipate something else from him, perhaps some higher occupation. The gall, from a waitress. He ached to tell her that he was a master bomb maker—the best in the nation. Probably the world. That would excite her. Maybe. Women were unfathomable creatures, impossible to cipher.

Of course his primary objective in Boise was to bomb the life out of Governor Steunenberg. After following the governor for weeks, Orchard became familiar with the man's paths, his preferences, even his peculiarities about pipe tobacco and paper bills. He knew the man's brothers and friends (one being Senator Borah), and Orchard had seen the governor's wife and children. Meanwhile he quietly gathered the necessary supplies to kill the man. His plan was underway.

Then, to his severe disappointment, he discovered that the vermin Steve Adams was still in Boise. Big Bill had been clear: Adams was supposed to be in San Francisco killing the fairly-recently-one-handed Bunker Hill Mine superintendent. And Orchard, after assassinating the governor, was to kill Adams upon Adams's return. Those were his orders—orders inked in the boss's hand. Though the one to kill Adams had been reduced to ash in Big Bill's office, the one to kill the governor was still fast in Orchard's hat.

At first, Orchard managed to deflect Adams's questions as to why Orchard was there. But one night, after they'd put away enough whiskey to marinate a buffalo, Orchard mumbled out the assassination plans. In response, Adams further delayed his trip to San Francisco, insisting instead that he be made part of the assassination plot. So Orchard reluctantly included him—Adams being an exceedingly dangerous man to refuse. Of course Orchard would still be the only one designing, making, planting, and using the bomb. But Adams could cause confusion. He might lead the Pinkertons away from Orchard's scent.

Throughout December, while searching for a new plan, one possibility lingered in Orchard's mind—in fact it tormented him: Adams might go off and kill the governor himself. This thought ripened as Adams vented growing jealousy over Orchard getting the task in the first place. Adams even suggested that he might warn the governor so as to spoil Orchard's plan, thus leaving the governor to Adams's blade. If anything like that happened, well, it would be bad. Adams would be breaking Haywood's express instructions. Worse, it would rob Orchard of the chance to use the bomb he had so vigilantly devised. And, worse still, Adams would probably kill the governor's entire family. That was not acceptable to Orchard. The innocent should pass unharmed. Killing should have limits, goddamnit.

One solution was for Orchard to kill Adams then and there, before any attack on the governor. After all, Orchard had been ordered to kill Adams eventually, so perhaps he should do it sooner than later. But that would be contrary to Haywood's instructions.

Moreover, then Orchard would have to go to San Francisco himself, and kill the one-armed superintendent. No, Sir! Not after that recent earthquake and devil's fire killed everybody there. No, he wouldn't be going to California anytime soon. That was entirely too dangerous.

So Steve Adams would be the feint, the cover, the distraction. He should be observed near Governor Steunenberg's home a few hours before the bomb. Then, once the governor was a ghost, Adams should be seen hurriedly embarking a train east to Cheyenne, but with ticketing that including going west to San Francisco. That would draw the Pinks after Adams, and might confuse them, leaving Orchard time to slip from Boise securely—perhaps even with the charming Miss Capone on his arm. But under what pretense could Adams be seen near the governor's home, in Caldwell, just beyond Boise?

A week before Christmas, the solution presented itself. Orchard overheard Governor Steunenberg at the Saratoga Hotel's front desk dictating a message for one of the hotel guests: a life insurance salesman named Thomas O'Malley whom Steunenberg had yet to meet. (The message asked Mr. O'Malley to call on the governor before the year was up.) Orchard and Adams then tracked O'Malley, and on Christmas Eve they killed him beside Dickason's Livery and Machines. That allowed Adams, posing as O'Malley, to walk to the governor's house, making himself seen along the way. At the house, Adams would request the governor come to a meeting at 3:00. Orchard would be in position by 2:00. Then, when the governor walked out his front door, down his porch steps, along his walk, and opened his front gate—he would be blown into oblivion.

Now the plan was underway. Orchard was watching from the distant cart as Adams stood on the governor's porch—waiting for something or someone to return. Doubt swamped Orchard's mind. The plan was off to a bad start duc to the weather. All the way down the boardwalk, Adams had covered his face with Orchard's bear coat, protecting himself from the howling wind. That meant no one would be able to testify to having seen Adams in the neighborhood. Regardless, Adams was now on the governor's porch, having just spoken with the governor's daughter. The daughter,

Orchard thought—yes—Adams had in fact been seen by her. This might still work.

But in the next few seconds, there in that quiet, snowy neighborhood, it might also go entirely wrong—Adams might reach for his knife. Orchard cursed himself for making the plan too complicated, for making it require him to trust Adams, of all people. What a fool he'd been. Adams would cut the eyes from an angel only to piss in her sockets. So why trust Adams to show restraint? Even in the cold, Orchard found himself in a clammy sweat. "Don't do it," he whispered. "Don't kill him before I do."

When the Steunenberg's door opened, Adams flexed, preparing to spring into deadly action if necessary. But instead of the governor, there stood the same young girl with whom he had first spoken.

"Yes, he'll meet you at his office at three." She shut the door.

Adams stood for a moment, then turned and walked down the step and crunched across the snow-packed walk to the white-picket gate set in the matching fence that circumscribed the front yard—the fence's peaks and posts standing sentinel over the snow. As Adams opened the gate, he paused to touch the latch post, then knelt as if tying his shoe. From that perspective, he could see a portion of a white cord in the snow, one end disappearing along the walk path, the other dipping into a mixture of ice and fresh dirt near the gate. He then rose and strolled toward the horse cart.

As Adams approached, he groused to Orchard, "Bastard's all yours." Then he climbed aboard while the snow-dusted horse roused in its traces.

"Good," said Orchard, stepping down from the box. He checked his watch and waggled his hand in the air. "My coat."

Adams grumbled while removing it.

"Train to Cheyenne is leaving on the hour. But say you're going to San Francisco. Be seen," said Orchard, donning his coat. "But don't board till you hear about the blast."

"I know."

Orchard looked squarely at Adams. "I'm obliged that you didn't kill the governor's girl. We need her to identify you."

"I don't kill no kids," snapped Adams, but clucked his tongue. "Unless I gotta." After a beat he added, "Saw your trigger wire."

Another pause, and then, "He's coming out shortly. Going to his office at three. You remember I made this happen for you. Might oughta thank me."

"I said I'm obliged. Get gone."

"Hup!" barked Adams. The horse clomped and soon the grinding sloosh of the iron-banded wheels faded away. Orchard slipped between houses to wait.

At 5:30 that evening, Frank Steunenberg smiled in remembrance, the image of his children engulfing him. Earlier, around 2:30, having left his home through his kitchen door so as to avoid his son following him out, Frank had walked the snowy mile to his office for the appointed 3:00 meeting. But when the insurance man never arrived, Frank finished some light paperwork, then rose to make the thirty-minute walk home. Though it was after dark, if he left now, the children might still be awake for a wrestle to the bemusement of his wife. He put his arms through his coat, snuffed the oil lamps, locked the bank office doors, and left.

The near-black starless sky had resumed dropping its silent snow. Frank's shoes crunched; and, as he felt the moisture against his ankles, he wondered why he had not worn his boots. He made the turn from the boulevard onto his street's long boardwalk, and there he saw his home at the end, the warm glow from the windows. As he approached, he saw the silhouette of his daughter watching for him in the window. *Good, they are still up*, he thought. With two more houses to go, Frank passed a row of holly bushes, their black-green leaves almost buried in the dark-gray white of the evening snow. Noting the small silhouette of his son had joined that of his daughter in the window, he failed to see the figure of a man crouching low in the blackness of the hedge row.

Orchard held the fishing line in his bare, shivering hand. It was taut, disappearing into the sharp-leaved bushes and beyond, across a small roadway, then spanning another yard, and then along the governor's fence to its terminus at the gate. He had gauged this would be a sufficient distance from the blast, but now was worried.

His hand shook so much that he loosened his grip on the line, fearing he might pull it prematurely.

Just then, "Good evening, Gov," broke the silence from the roadway, just beyond the hedges. Orchard clenched every muscle, pulling himself into an even tighter ball. But in so doing he pitched ever so slightly forward to where his cheek met the sharp tips of the holly leaves. He reflexed a minuscule "mngh" sound before fixing himself again motionless, breath held.

Frank had just replied, "Good evening to you, Zeb," when both men heard a sound from the dark shrubs, but discounted it as some critter. "How was your Christmas celebration?" Frank asked flatly.

"Splendid, Governor," replied the man. "I hope you and yours have a happy new year, my friend."

"And you," Frank offered over his shoulder, having resumed his walk, unwilling to linger to talk with this Republican who was anything but a friend. Once in front of his house, he saw his children had called for their mother to join them at the window. They waved and grinned. Waving back and noting the snow was falling harder, Frank was glad to be home. He opened his front gate.

The explosion was heard and felt over ten miles away. It shook cognac snifters from cabinets, decorative plates off brass displays, and cracked glass windows for blocks around. At the Steunenberg home, the concussive blast blew out every window along the front and side of the house, shards slicing the faces of the family inside. It loosened the front porch from its piers, flattened most of the fence, leaving only a few posts, obliterating the gate entirely, and turned the cold whiteness to warm red—a massive ruddy daisy thrown onto the snowy yard, its ten-foot bloody petals shooting in all directions from a gaping black center.

– 12 –

TUESDAY
January 1, 1907

Three days later, Chief Detective James McParland stood in the transformed lobby of Boise's Idanha Hotel, having just arrived from Denver and having already assumed effective control of the entire building, staff included. Before him stood an assemblage of thirty-three agents and operatives. The agents, standing in a semi-circle closest to McParland, were in their regimental Pinkerton white shirts and dark coats. Beyond them were the operatives in various attires of working men, including some appearing to not be there for the gathering at all. Among the latter group was Operative 21, Jack Garrett, who stood near the main doors, holding his black, wide-brimmed, flat-topped hat in front of him. He and four others had been brought from Denver at the request of McParland. The other agents and operatives had come from various places in the west, and a few from Chicago and St. Louis. Each was armed with a pistol, and some clasped rifles or shotguns. At the door and windows, several faced out, attentive to the street beyond.

"We cannot fail in this endeavor," McParland said softly. "I'll not. And you'll not either." A few words were soggy with his Irish lilt. "We'll never sleep, we won't. Why? Because Pinkertons never sleep. Aye?"

A chorus of aye's responded.

"We're always watching. And you, my boys, you're my eyes. You'll not fail me. You'll not fail Mr. Pinkerton. You'll not fail your families or your country. You'll not fail yourselves."

Polite nods and mutterings of agreement spread, then slowed. Each man wore his own version of a grim expression, uniformity in resolved obedience, a mirrored dedication to the task set to them: Find the murderers. Quickly. At all costs. Spare nothing. Do not concern yourself with the law.

McParland continued low, "It's been two days since this nation suffered the first assassination of a high-ranking elected official by means of an explosion. And it happened in my region, on my watch. Not in Chicago or Boston. Not in New York City, but right the hell here: Boise, Idaho. In the heart of the American West. Our home." His voice rose. "Make no mistake. They're not men, these Wobbly terrorists. They're insurgents set upon the destruction of this free nation, this country given to us by God." He went silent for a full thirty seconds, barely blinking but moving about, staring into the eyes of the men before him, his broad gray mustache leading the way.

A man entered, knocking snow from his boots, and spoke to Jack, the nearest man he found.

McParland had resumed with a snarl. "These rats are worse than the Molly Maguires. Those men deserved the justice of their trials and hangings. This sort, I tell you, deserve a death commensurate with what they've dispensed: cruel and without consideration. And so they'll receive. Make no mistake, these ungodly anarchists will stop at nothing ... as they've proven in this most unspeakable murder. They aim to eliminate your communities, your friends, and rip the very life from your women and your children." Another pause, and then, "Arrest them, if you're able. If you must. But do not allow them to escape this territory. They must be brought to trial *here*. They must die *here*. Do I make myself clear?"

"Aye, Chief!" responded the baritone chorus, loudly echoing McParland's word for yes. Though "aye" was a natural response for some, mainly the Brits, Micks, and Scots of the group, it had become tradition for everyone to say it in gatherings like this. Far from toadying, it was respect, a verbal salute unique to McParland, their famous and fearless Hibernian chief.

McParland gave a nod. Though he didn't let his face show it, the "Aye" gesture from his men carried deep meaning for him, especially at that moment—the launch of the most important manhunt of his career.

Jack came to McParland's side, relaying the message from the man who had entered. "Sir, you're asked to return to the governor's house. They think they know where the killer was hidden."

“Very well,” McParland muttered as he turned, before looking back at Jack. “Come with me, Twenty-One.”

“Yes, sir,” said Jack, brightening at the personal summons.

At that moment, two blocks away in the Saratoga Hotel, Carla stood at a table, clearing the used glasses and plates. She was in her waitress uniform: high-collar white waistshirt and crimson skirt, beneath an apron piped in matching red, above stockings and black pumps. She listened to the dark chatter around her. The governor had been assassinated. It was the only subject. It was as if the bomb’s blast had set off an angry storm with the rain and thunder relentlessly stabbing and pounding the city.

In one cluster, they were certain the killer was a lone anarchist. Some had seen a posse of darkies, probably a group from that damn army unit. Some swore it was the union. Some even gave the bomber a name: Haywood. Though she was certain Mr. Haywood wasn’t in Boise, she had no doubts he had ordered it. Moreover, she was beginning to see how she was involved, how her assignment fit into things, which man needed to be blamed for the killing, and how she would spark that blame. But she didn’t kill the governor. She had nothing to do with it, not directly. She was just helping the cause. She was on the side of right, a fighter in the virtuous struggle for the oppressed, the workers of America. And those owners, and their Pinks, they ... well, they ... Her thoughts trailed away as she snuffed her doubts, returning them to the recesses of her mind. After placing the tray of dishes in the wash area, she detoured into the dry storage room. On a back shelf, she found a glass jar that appeared full of a whitish powder. She touched its wire-bail sealer, reassuring herself it hadn’t been opened. Then she turned the jar and silently read its label:

HIBBS PLASTER OF PARIS
Fine Grade Medical Quality

Five stories above her, ensconced in a warm bath, Harry Orchard blew soap bubbles away from his face. His work was done. He had seen the swarm of Pinkertons entering the Idanha Hotel—even the legendary McParland himself. So many people in despair for the damn dead man. So much alarm, and oh the newspapermen—he had never seen such fuss. The lobby and dining room of the Saratoga were filled with long faces, though Carla seemed nonplussed. Earlier, he'd given her his best smile, careful to keep his lips over his crooked teeth, and asked her what had happened. She said she didn't know and walked away. A lie to be sure. Everyone knew. But who could blame a girl for just wanting to stay out of the mess? She was a keeper. So, now a bath, and then down to dinner and more conversation with his love. Maybe he'd get to touch her silky hair.

The Pinkerton investigation would be in full force, but what would they find? Nothing. He replayed it all, over and over, every step. He had taken no chances. Though the bomb could've been a crude blasting cap and dynamite, set off by the gate latch, he had crafted it with watchmaker care, packed it in plaster so it was safe from the elements, and embedded a trigger activated by pulling a fishing line—once he saw the governor was in the right spot. Or the wrong spot, for the governor. (He waggled his head at the thought.) After the blast, he withdrew what remained of the line and disappeared into the dark. It had been perfect. He wished he could tell Carla the details. He had been brilliant, but no one knew.

Just as planned, the only man of suspicion was someone described as looking like Steve Adams (who Orchard figured was already halfway to San Francisco). All that remained, Orchard reasoned, was time and patience, and then to slip from Boise in the midst of the flurry and crowds. He grinned, soap bubbles still on his chin, and whispered, "My God," re-visioning the beauty of that yellow blast in the black night.

McParland was crouched behind a bank of holly shrubs in front of a little house two away from the governor's house. Behind him, four agents and two operatives, including Jack, watched. Removing his hat, McParland inclined forward, peering through an opening in the bushes, and then pantomimed pulling a cord. Finally he stood, returned his hat to his head while sucking on his bottom lip. "He was right here. What is this, sixty feet away? Seventy? Pulled a string or wire. Fishing line probably, so the snow wouldn't interfere. Wire would've been trouble spooling in flight. Ran off there, probably." He pivoted, still reeling the imagined line as he tramped away. His men remained where they were, watching their boss disappear around a corner. Soon he returned, asking one of them, "Did you talk to the neighbors on the next street over?"

"Not yet, Sir."

"Get on it. They might've seen the fellow running off ... or coming earlier."

"Yes, Sir," said the agent as he hurried away.

McParland took deliberate steps toward the governor's destroyed front yard, his shoes crunching snow. Along the way, he pointed to where he imagined the trigger cord had run. At one point he stopped and kneeled, leaning close to ground. Then he pulled back, motioning Jack to come look. When Jack's face was inches from the ice and slush, McParland pointed to a small tunnel through an odd bit of snow not yet trampled. "Right there. Came through right there." After McParland and Jack stood, the four other Pinkertons gave Jack scrutinizing looks that asked, Why you?

McParland picked up what appeared to be a small, cream-colored, jagged rock. Laying it flat in his left palm, he flicked at it, rolled it a bit, then spit on it. The others watched. As he began to walk away, he handed the rock to Jack and grumbled, "Gypsum. He packed the sticks in builder's gypsum."

Catching up to the cluster, one of the agents asked what the detective had said. "Gypsum," said Jack, handing over the shard. "Held the bomb together. Plaster of Paris." The agent studied it, then dropped it in the dirty snow.

"Get that, Twenty-One," barked McParland. "That's evidence."

Jack retrieved the plaster rock, and soon all seven men were knotted in Governor Steunenberg's yard, their shoes and boots further trampling the blood, dirt, and near-frozen slush into a muddy gunk. Behind McParland, the last of the blown-out windows was being boarded, the sound of the hammering ricocheting off the other homes like echoes of the bomb itself. "Your assessment, Twenty-One?" asked McParland, taking back the plaster piece. All eyes narrowed at Jack.

Jack cleared his throat, wondering why he alone was being grilled. "A man pulled a trigger cord from over there."

"That wasn't the first contact. What was the first?" asked McParland. "What do we know?"

A convivial, big-eyed agent named Peter Polk spoke up. "Someone warned Governor Steunenberg on Christmas day."

"Aye, good," said McParland. "You're thinking like a detective. Someone called the governor and warned him. So, gentlemen, someone in this city knows who the killer is, and knew the killer's plans. We must find that person. What next?"

Jack tried again. "A man came to the door at one o'clock, on the twenty-ninth, saying he was the governor's life insurance salesman."

McParland stood square to the taller Jack. "Continue."

"He asked to meet the governor at the governor's office, at his bank, about a mile from here, at three o'clock. But we know the actual life insurance salesman—" he checked his notes before continuing "—Thomas O'Malley, was already dead. Had his throat cut in an alley near the Saratoga Hotel, where he was lodged."

"Yep," McParland said, taking over impatiently. "The killer pretended he was an insurance man. He came here, walked up there in broad daylight. The governor's daughter got a good look at him. But he didn't come to kill the governor right then. He wanted to get the governor out. He needed him to come out front to be blown up. So he waited, over there in the bushes. But the governor went out his kitchen door to avoid his children seeing him go to his office that day. That meant the killer had to adjust his plan. He had to wait until the governor returned that evening. Then—boom."

The other plain-clothes operative spoke up. "Why not go to his office and kill him there, at the appointed time?"

McParland stopped and stared at the inquiring man, holding his gaze till the man began to fidget. "What's your name?"

"Forty-Two, Sir. Wade Farrington."

McParland's mustache lifted at the ends. "Forty-Two? So you're twice the operative as Twenty-One here?"

"No, Sir."

McParland continued, "Why not kill the governor at the office? Logical, if just killing the man was the objective. Would've been better. Easier. No one would've seen it." McParland squinted down the street, then back to the shattered porch. "No. There was two of them—one to lure him out, the other to wait and detonate it. Wouldn't have been the same man. No, it was *supposed* to be a bomb, an explosion in front of his family. This gruesome carnage is what they wanted. Wanted it in papers across the country." He stopped, his eyes alive and flitting. "But, no. *They* didn't want that. Not these two. They didn't care. They'd just as soon've shot him at his office. Or cut his throat. No, somebody else. Someone wanted to send a message to every politician ... every governor, senator ... the president. Killing the governor in his office might be mistook as robbery. This was supposed to be big, its message clear." His enunciation swelled with each realization, each invective. "This was no lone anarchist. This was planned, coordinated, and executed by two men, two animals who knew what they were doing. One's good with explosives. Look for blasting caps, pieces of cords." He held up the plaster piece. "Plaster. Hell, maybe one of them is injured. We can hope. Those hedges aren't far." He walked into the street with the men in tow like ducklings, then turned and studied the neighborhood. "Mind you, gentlemen, this was ordered. Two did it, but one ordered it. One goddamned man." McParland watched a carpenter at another house descend his ladder, having completed boarding a window. "One man sent two. One coward, and I know who—that vulgarian in Denver, shagging his wife's sister ... while the good governor here is blasted to bits in front of his children and wife." The chief detective's cheeks reddened. "He made a mistake. Now we must take advantage of it. Find the two dogs. Bring them in alive." He gave a big nod indicating his approaching conclusion. "If we get them both, we'll hang William Haywood."

– 13 –

SATURDAY
January 5, 1907

Every January, Big Bill Haywood was king when sixty to one hundred locally elected chapter officers of the Western Federation of Miners came together in Park City, Utah. They arrived from mining towns across the Rocky Mountains—the Monitor, Sierra Nevada, and Cascade Ranges to the west; the Bitterroot, Absaroka, and Bighorn Ranges to the north; the Laramie and Sangre de Cristo to the east; and the San Juan and Zuni south. They would meet for two days at the limestone Washington School House which was idle for the winter, and bunk in the Ontario Silver Mine's barracks. The mountain town of Park City was chosen because it was winter accessible (at the end of a well-maintained Union Pacific branch line) and small enough to provide a sense of freedom and privacy. Women of loose morals were railed in and put up at boarding houses, and the three saloons were stocked with whiskey and poker chips. It also provided a sense of security for the gathering. A Pinkerton spy would be more easily identified there than if the meeting was in Denver, or even in Salt Lake City thirty miles away. The citizens and merchants of Park City embraced them—the exception being Thomas Kearns, President of the Silver King Consolidated Mining Company, who would barricade himself in his Temple Street mansion, certain of a mob insurrection that never came.

Each year, the discussion topics were the same: improving the lives of miners and their families, being more persuasive against mine owners and more damaging to the Mine Owners Association, how to grow the Federation, and how to improve ties with other national labor unions. In addition, it provided an opportunity for local chapter presidents to register complaints with the Federation's central leadership. Haywood enjoyed it all, save the last. Usually he had the Federation treasurer, George Pennington, handle the chapter complaints, especially as most gripes concerned money.

The exception was this year—George wasn't there on account of a family illness that kept him in Denver. Thus Haywood, along with his staff, planned to manage it all, complaints included.

This year, one matter loomed central in the minds of the seventy-eight local officers in attendance: the recent assassination of the governor of Idaho, Frank Steunenberg. Not only had the horrific event empowered the Mine Owners Association to unprecedented action, but it might destroy the Federation *en masse*. Haywood couldn't disagree more. It was merely a lone assassin, not unlike the terrorist who shot President McKinley a few years earlier. The man, or men, whoever they were, acted alone. In fact, the Federation risked greater damage by reacting as if it bore some guilt-by-association. But few of the chapter leaders bought it. Obviously the Federation would be blamed: it was their Idaho men who had been illegally arrested and detained by Steunenberg—a reaction to the bombing of the Bunker Hill Mine last summer—which was of course also blamed on the Federation. The Federation must be seen assisting the investigation now—helping the government bring the assassin to justice. That was the only way. Haywood assured them that he was doing just that. In fact, he already had people in Boise helping. That led to a laugh-inducing quip from the president of a Wyoming chapter: "You're aiding the Pinks now? Pray tell us how that turns out, will you, Big Bill?"

On the first evening, Haywood used his annual speech to address the issue. The schoolhouse's largest room, with its desks cleared, had been filled with cloth-draped tables and chairs, and dining service was brought in on trays. Most of the attendees wore dark sack coats, though a few were in Norfolk-style hunting jackets. Haywood stood beneath two Federation banners and a sign reading:

> IN THE WORLD'S BROAD FIELD OF BATTLE,
> IN THE BIVOUAC OF LIFE,
> BE NOT LIKE DUMB DRIVEN CATTLE,
> BE A HERO IN THE STRIFE.
> —Gravestone of John Barthell, Telluride, Colorado

He was finishing his prepared remarks. "As you know, the corruption of the low wage system is slavery in another form. Corporations have monopolized the necessities of society and the means of a decent life. Change will only come when intelligence masters ignorance, when workingmen stop bowing at the shrine of wealth and begging for the crumbs that fall from the masters' tables. There can be no lasting harmony between organized capitalists of such extreme greed, and organized labor—nor between employer and employee, or millionaire and working man."

After settling the men from their rigorous applause, he added, "Before I finish, let me say—" He leaned and picked up a rifle. "Thank you all for this most wonderful gift." He lifted it and read the etched words: "Springfield Armory. M1903. It is a fine weapon. Thank you all." He set it down, then stood erect again. "Now we turn to the annual tradition of questions, though I'm more inclined to call it The Hour of Brutus." General laughter erupted, and then one hand went up in the crowd, and Haywood motioned to it. "Yes, Henry. Or rather: *Et tu*, Henry?"

After more laughter from the group, the elderly man began. "I'm hearing a lot of grumbling, from—"

"Didn't your wife pass, Henry?" chirped one, drawing laughs.

The man smiled ruefully, revealing a barren upper gum, then continued. "Men are concerned about that red fellow, Eugene Debs. If we get seen as socialist, what with the newspapers and all, we'll lose more members than we got."

"Do you have a question?" asked Haywood.

"What are you gonna do bout it?"

"We'll stay true to our ideals. The Western Federation of Miners is not socialist, but we're about the *business* of socialism. Socialism with its working clothes on."

"Don't know the hell that means," mumbled Henry, taking his seat. "Doubt you do neither, Bill." More laughter.

Haywood waited for the room to quieten. "It's about the treachery of capitalism. Gentlemen, I've never read Marx's *Capital*, but I have the marks of capitalism all over me." He pointed to his dead eye. "And I know you do too. Your wives do. Your children too. Same for all your chapter members and their families—marks of injury, hardship, hunger, disease, betrayal, anger. No, our fight is not the Socialist Party's fight. We don't seek revolution. We may be miners, but we're about the business of *leveling* the ground. We want fairness, humanity, our lives to be valued at the same elevation as that of the rich man who prospers by our labor. We don't seek to lower him, but to raise ourselves. Socialism? If it's socialism to uplift the fellow who's down in the gutter—realizing society can be no better than its most miserable—then I'll accept that name. But that's not the socialism Mr. Debs preaches. And I won't let the Federation be tarred as he's railed from the national stage."

A forest of hands and Haywood pointed to another man. "Yes, Henry ... Henry the Younger."

Laughter, and then a middle-aged man stood. "Thank you. I can only hope to live as long as Henry the Elder."

"Old whiskey and young women," blurted the aging Henry.

"I'm Mormon," said the younger.

Another popped, "No whiskey and a bunch of wives—that's an early grave."

Smiling, Haywood said, "You had a question, Mormon Henry?"

"Yes, Sir. Some of my men, those who are on injury wages, money coming through you, I mean through Federation headquarters—well, they've been getting their pay late ... and often missing ten, twenty percent. They get pretty hot at me, Sir."

Haywood took a noisy breath. "As you can see, George Pennington, our national treasurer, couldn't be here. But if you'll give one of my assistants your information, along with the credentials of your men who've had this problem, I'll have George look into it. Just soon as I get back. Fair?"

"Yes, Sir. Fair. Thank you."

Others added their agreement, saying they too had recovery pay arriving late and missing dollars. Haywood asked them all to do similarly: report to his assistants. Seeking to move on, he pointed to a raised hand near the back. "Tony, I see you back there."

An Italian man with a face like overcooked bacon stood. "I'm alarmed. And I know my feelings are shared by many here ... about the assassination of Governor Steunenberg."

"Mr. Sabini," Haywood began, "we've discussed that for—"

"Yes, you have ... you have," said the man. "But I was there"—he motioned toward his burned face—"at the Independence Mine in '04. We all know some members of this union—some say you included—believe violence has a place in the—"

"Not me, Mr. Sabini," Haywood snarled, squaring his dead eye on the man. "Not me. I'll not tolerate violence, and I don't appreciate the accusation that I might. At this moment, our people in Boise are searching for those responsible for the governor's death."

With bent elbows, Mr. Sabini raised the flat of his hands, the flesh there also fire-scarred. Though it was a gesture of surrendering the argument, no one believed the matter was put to rest.

The Haywoods' official home was a four-gabled house surrounded by low picket fencing, two miles east of downtown Denver. It sat on Bellaire Street, at the edge of Park Hill Heights (the new residential development just beyond the massive open green that was unimaginatively named City Park). Bill didn't prefer the Park Hill house. He found its domesticity overpowering, its temperament banal compared to the buzz of the city center with its opera district, saloons, trolleys, all-night cafés—the daring-do of real life with him as its most notorious citizen.

Neva couldn't fault him his preference. She understood the allure, the aroma of entitlement that oozed up through the floorboards of their expansive Pioneer Building suites. She savored the feeling. It absolved her. It was a commiserative pillow. With it she snuffed breath from her recurrent doubts about her own morality, her guilt for overlooking the deeds that provisioned her, her sins of association, her complicity.

Bill craved the electricity and danger of downtown, rubbing shoulders with his mortal enemies—the mine owners—just two blocks from the Pioneer. He needed that knife edge. That snap. It was in that crucible that he was most alive, most himself, the only person he wished to be, wished to see. But out in Park Hill Heights, his hair was cut—Samson became a resident, a neighbor, a homeowner, just a man.

Why Winnie equally eschewed the Park Hill house, Neva could only guess. Perhaps in that neighborhood of picket-fenced homes, Winnie felt out of place. A home was meant for one man and one woman, and Neva was clearly that one woman, at least at Park Hill—or so Neva convinced herself. Neva surmised that was why when Bill was out of town, and Neva went to Park Hill, Winnie stayed in the Pioneer suites by herself.

Neva found a different self in the Park Hill house. One she was beginning to prefer. Kinder. Easier. The sentiment was aided by the physicality of the structure: all on the ground level, meaning she could roll her invalid chair wherever she wished. It also had her garden, her roses, her trees, her birds. And silence. Too much silence, but at least it had enough. (Especially when Bill was gone on one of his many trips—the current one being his annual to Park City, Utah.) The gardener would come, as would the maid and cook, and they would talk about the planting depth of paper-white bulbs, the selections of electric chandeliers for the parlor, and the best way to prepare a mutton pie. They would wheel her, attend to her, and she could stay in a day dress from dawn to dusk. There she could even receive friends, were she to have any. Real friends, that is. Other than George. The house was good for receiving George when Bill was out of town. No need for the Metropole Hotel.

George was an unassuming man, though she wished he would assume more. When he arrived that morning with a new pair of green crutches, she couldn't stop smiling. "Merry Christmas," he said, standing in the drawing room, holding them out.

She covered her gaping mouth. "My dear George, how did you know I dislike the others?"

"To start with, you rarely use them," he said, adding, "except for dancing, and undressing ... sometimes." With that and a wink, he had her blushing.

"But those ... look at them, they have such soft arm pads."

"Lamb's wool," he said.

"And they're green! How did you find green ones?"

"Your favorite color."

"You're an angel," Neva gushed. "Did Denver Dry have them in green? Or Sears? Did you order them from Sears?"

"I had a chair maker paint them and add the wool."

She held them across the arms of her invalid chair, stroking and examining them. "Oh, you are my dear George, aren't you? Come, let me kiss you."

He glanced about.

"No one is in, except Maria."

"All right," he said, "but how about you stand?"

As he helped her, she said, "Yes, I'll certainly stand for *that*." Once up, she tucked the padded tops of the new crutches under her arms and straightened the pleats in the blue skirt of her sailor-styled shirtwaist dress. (She knew he liked it for its plunging neckline featuring a gauzy insert.) "Perfect," she said. "Now for the best part."

He held her face, kissed her, and she returned it. As he moved a hand to her waist, she reached for the back of his neck. The right crutch fell against the invalid chair before clattering to the rug.

"Oops," she whispered.

"Terrific," he breathed. "I'll have to bring new crutches every day ... and night."

"Well, get to it, Mr. Pennington. Every color of the rainbow."

He snorted a laugh, kissing her again.

★

– 14 –

WEDNESDAY
January 9, 1907

When the distant boom of the governor's death reached the rear, boots, and ears of Steve Adams, he had been waiting at the dark Boise station. He had then left on the next train to Cheyenne, Wyoming, just ahead of the first Pinkertons to arrive and start interrogating every person coming and going through the station.

By the time the train had switched engines at Pocatello, Idaho, Adams had heard the first babbles about the assassination of the governor. Apparently, the telegraph lines had glowed from the heated messages zipping from Boise, or so they said. The killer was known—had been spotted—was already dead—was unknown—was on the run. He was an Italian anarchist hiding with the Blackfeet—he blew himself up at the scene—he was an Irishman on his way to Canada. It amused Adams, though he was a touch irritated. He should have slit the governor's throat that afternoon at the man's house. But no, glory had gone to the goat-fucker Orchard.

Now, a little over a week later, shafts of sunlight found Adams in benched sleep aboard a rattler as it whistled, braked, and belled to a stop at the Ogden Union Station. He sat up, checked his Bowie was still booted, and began to pick his nose and stretch his mouth—all while being observed from the facing bench by two boys each no more than six years old. They snickered at his finger up his buzzard beak until a parent yanked them to leave. He stayed put—would exit later. His next train, the Southern Pacific Overland to San Francisco, wouldn't depart until 9:10 the next morning.

He slid against the window, lowered the brim of his cap, closed his eyes, bit on a yellow fingernail, then pulled his black coat around him, popping up the collar. Orchard was just a coward pulling on blasting caps. But he, Steve Adams, was Death. Death used a scythe—a blade—not explosives. Death should be intimate, up close. Death felt the knife enter the body. Felt the life leave. And

Death was coming for Mr. James Branson III, the unfortunately still-alive superintendent of the Bunker Hill Mine.

Someone had informed Big Bill of last summer's incomplete operation at the Bunker—apparently the one-handed Branson had been seen in Spokane afterwards. Adams, holed up in Boise, had received a short telegram from an unidentifiable Denver source: JB IN SF. Adams had then intended to leave Boise, but Governor Steunenberg's mass arrests had begun, and all Idaho depots were under tight guard. So, he hunkered in the Saratoga Hotel. Then Orchard arrived in Boise in desperate need of Adams's help with the bombing. The no-good Orchard couldn't just do things on his own. But he sure took the credit. Damn him.

Adams even tried to sabotage Orchard's plan by warning the governor on Christmas Day—hoping the governor would remain alive, leaving Adams to kill both the governor and Orchard. But Adams lost his nerve when Steunenberg answered the phone. Rather than giving a detailed warning, Adams just mumbled about being careful and hung up. He was never good at talking and hated those damn telephones. So, Orchard got to use his bomb.

Having done his part, Adams lit out for Cheyenne before this journey west to San Francisco where he hoped the edge of the country wouldn't fall into the goddamned ocean. He'd be fast, once there—in and out. Like a quick, lethal stab. Kill the superintendent and go. No earthquake would get him. Afterwards, maybe he'd visit his uncle in Nevada. He took a deep breath through his now-clear nose. He could rest. Tomorrow, Death would board the 9:10 to San Francisco.

Haywood moved through their Park Hill Heights home, coffee in hand, dressed for the day, save his jacket and tie. In the privacy of his home, this was comfortable. But it wouldn't do in public, not even in his office in the Pioneer Building. This rule wasn't out of some desire to always appear well attired—it was because he needed the coat to conceal his shoulder holster. And, though he wouldn't admit it, it was because he felt high-buttoned vests accented his girth. Without the span of his jacket's foliage, the circumference of his trunk was too apparent. So, he always wore his jacket in public—emphasizing the largess of his presence, not its largeness. More importantly, he would never be seen sitting coatless outside this house or the Pioneer suites—sitting only made the tree trunk wider. He regarded himself in the hall mirror. Seeing Neva's new green crutches behind him in the reflection, he turned to examine them. "Hmmph," he grunted softly, feeling the fluffy woolen pads. He entered the kitchen, walked to Neva at the table, and leaned and kissed her on the forehead. She was in her invalid chair, flanked by two empty regular chairs. "Do this for me," he said, continuing a request he had launched minutes earlier while urinating.

Neva rolled her green eyes at him, watching him sit to her left. She didn't prefer that arrangement as it placed his gray-white, dead eye nearer to her. But she said nothing. She knew the other side of him was reserved—something to which she had long acquiesced.

She adjusted the sleeves of her sporting shirt, not wanting it to get stained. Then she touched his leg and gave a measured smile, the wrinkles about her eyes spreading into view. "You cannot be serious," she said. "Claus is a bulldog." The winter sun spilled across their fried eggs, tomato slices, and bacon strips. Out the window behind them, silvery hills rolled and turned under their snow-blue quilt, their jagged sentinel parents looming in the distance.

"So is Sheriff Tetter. He's a bulldog," offered Haywood, his mouth mushy with eggs. "His wife'll tell him to do it, if *you* ask her. It needs to be his idea. I don't want anyone knowing I want Claus deputized. Tetter's got to suggest it."

"Don't be ridiculous," she whispered, turning to watch cardinals alight on the tin birdfeeder just beyond the window seat. She was disappointed Bill had come to the Park Hill house upon returning from his Utah trip. But at least when he did, Winnie did too, which Neva had difficulty minding.

"Oh, what's the harm?" he continued. "Claus will enjoy it. Hell, all the men will have a laugh." Getting no response, he relaxed his voice and touched the back of her head. "You asked for my help with your reverend and that Fort Collins mess."

"It wasn't a mess. The college wants—"

"What'd I do? Laugh and fuss, or did I get Clarence on it?"

"You laughed and fussed, actually. But when you finally did get him to help, I was grateful. You know that."

"Do this for me."

"It's not the same." She pointed at the window with her fork. "Is that a junco?"

"Let's say we each find the other's interests ... a bit ridiculous."

Neva grimaced. "You're comparing my faith with your dog? That's insulting. And you're having your dog made sheriff."

"Deputy."

She returned her eyes to him. "Oh, excuse me, deputy sheriff. That's—" She couldn't help but snicker.

He scrunched his nose and shoved his lips out to frame his front teeth. "Howdy, Ma'am. I'm Deputy Claus. At your service!"

"That's awful, Bill," she said between closed-lip giggles. "Stop."

"Not till you agree."

"Fine, you win, I'll say something, but—"

"Good morning," Winnie interrupted as she entering the room, still in her loosely tied, lilac dressing gown.

"Sister," acknowledged Neva. Her rare moment of merriment with her husband halted midair, leaving only ticks from the nearby grandfather clock.

"Good morning, dear," said Bill, standing.

"Bear," Winnie said.

He embraced her, gave her a kiss on the lips, then drew her chair on his left. The house servant brought a plate of eggs and biscuits and set it before the young woman whose corn-blue eyes glimmered. A spasm shot through Neva's cheek as she looked away.

The palliative smiles Winnie offered both Neva and Bill were genuine. Winnie loved them both. Neva was her only sibling—her only family still above ground. Of course she loved her. And Bill? She had grown to love him. In the first year of his advances, when she was twenty and had moved in to help Neva and the girls, she found Bill repulsive. Not just for their approximately twenty-year age difference, and not just because he was her sister's husband; nor because he was whoring on his sick wife. If she was honest, what repulsed her most was that dreadful dead eye. Regardless of her private reasons, she rebuffed him at every turn, every hand around her was pulled away, every expensive gift ignored.

Then Winnie's nieces, Henrietta and Vernie (Bill and Neva's daughters), were sent to boarding school to protect them from Neva's polio. That meant trips to visit them. Just she and Bill. (Neva wasn't allowed to go. According to Bill, it was too risky for the girls.) Winnie began enjoying these trips. Bill would buy her special trinkets at Mays Department store, a block from the boarding school. Other times, Winnie felt uncomfortable: Bill would stop the carriage and crowd her, speaking to her about his needs. And there was the time he felt her breasts, and she let him, even enjoyed it a bit. But afterward, she had felt terrible for having even allowed it.

Then came Neva's accident—the cut to her wrist. The result of a silly fall, Neva said. Winnie accepted that explanation, the alternative being too awful to consider. Yet its undertow pulled at Winnie. Was her behavior responsible for her sister's melancholy? No, it was Bill's doing. It was his fault for being fresh. And Bill's fault for sending Neva's girls away. Though, maybe that was best for the girls. Regardless, Neva seemed despondent. The important thing, Winnie assured herself, was that she, Winnie, had done nothing wrong. Yes, she enjoyed Bill's presents ... and began to enjoy her time with him ... and perhaps his occasional touch. But she knew what would come next. Sex with the man would destroy her sister. Winnie couldn't do that to Neva. She needed to stop imagining it. She might keep the trinkets, but— She could think of only one lasting solution: convince Neva to make Bill stop.

Finally, Winnie took the matter to Neva: Though she appreciated the gifts and living with them, Bill made her uncomfortable. Would Neva please talk to him? She didn't want to cause trouble, just to put some distance there. Nothing more. What Winnie didn't reveal was her own fears: that as a result of this, she and Neva might have to leave. She didn't want that. By then, Neva was dependent on an invalid chair or crutches. It would be too much work for Winnie. And the gifts would stop too. And she wouldn't see Bill anymore. No, the solution was for Bill's advances to end. And yet, to Winnie's astonishment, Neva kissed her cheek and whispered, "Give him a chance, Sissy. I need you both."

So the courtship continued. The flowers stayed in their vases. The dresses hung in the wardrobe—dresses Neva joined Winnie in selecting, the fabrics and styles. Bill stopped his whore house forays—stopped checking his traps, as Neva called it. Instead he stayed home in the evenings. Even sat for pinochle once. The three moved into the Pioneer Building suites; then Bill bought this house. A month later, when Winnie was twenty-one, she let Bill come to her bed. But, of course, he had to wear an eye patch—something he still did, including the night before this breakfast.

When the *Denver Post* was brought for Haywood, he snapped the fold open. Across the top it read:

ASSASSIN SOUGHT!
Governor's murder investigation intensifies
President Roosevelt alarmed

He read with the same consumptive vigor he'd employed on his breakfast: his lips moving a little with only an occasional "Mmmph," or the suck of air through his teeth.

Both women took to discussing the junco on the feeder, questioning whether it was male or female. Then their talk turned to two cardinals which had alighted there. Months prior, Neva had named the pair Cardinal and Lady Dedlock, which made Winnie laugh. Winnie hadn't read Charles Dickens' *Bleak House*, so the reference was lost on her, but still she found it funny. Haywood popped the *Post* wide to read inside. After a moment, he let the paper sag and stared at the wall. The women noticed and exchanged a questioning look.

"What's troubling you?" asked Neva.

Haywood addressed Winnie. "Have Clarence in my office tomorrow at nine. You be there too."

Winnie gave a modest acknowledgment and watched Haywood rise. He dabbed his napkin to his lips, excused himself and left.

Neva touched Winnie's arm. "Tell me later—whatever this is."

"Ok."

"And if this is something bad, tell me right away."

Winnie gave a barely visible nod. "I will, Sissy."

★

– 15 –

THURSDAY
January 10, 1907

"Clarence, have you read the new Russian constitution?" asked Haywood, pacing his own office. "Have you? It's brilliant. Power in the hands of workers, the people."

Clarence Darrow, in an olive coat with a round-collar shirt, peered over his glasses. "I think we invented: We the People."

"No, it's not the same!" boomed Haywood. "Ours is not truly We the People, and you know it. It's we the corporations. It's we the wealthy few. It'll take a bloody revolution here, just as they—"

"They still have a czar."

"We'll see. We'll see. If the czar can respect the new Russian constitution and the Duma, then he can stay."

"Is that what you told him?" Darrow asked, chancing sarcasm.

Haywood wheeled around. "I'm the standard bearer for the working man of this nation. Must I be theirs as well?"

Darrow nodded, unsure of his client's sincerity. "All right, Bill. All right." He watched as Haywood's pacing slowed. Finally, Haywood took a seat in a winged-back chair at the end of the settee where Darrow waited. Behind them both, Winnie observed from a chair against the wall, her peacock-feathered hat in her lap.

"You're the legal genius," Haywood began, "though I probably know more about the law of the working man."

"Perhaps."

"So," Haywood pressed, "what do we do?"

"Regarding what?" Darrow asked. "The Steunenberg thing?" He saw Haywood nod before continuing. "Of what concern is it to you? A radical, unevolved anarchist killed the poor man. You and the Federation should keep to ground. Say nothing. Do nothing. Don't offer your opinion. I know that's a tall order for you, but you need to refrain. Even a congratulatory inference could be wildly unpopular. Could direct their arrows right here."

"Unpopular with whom?" Haywood asked. "Unionists are happy the man received his just deserts ... for his treason."

Darrow raised his hand. "I don't want to hear that. I truly don't. That elected official was blown to shreds in front of his children. Save all that for ... for your rallies. Better yet, as I said, don't talk about it at all. Don't share your opinion, and you should discourage others from doing so. The Federation has nothing but sympathy for the family, for the people of Idaho, and so forth."

"It was an act of revolution, inspired by our Russian brothers—"

"No, Bill," barked Darrow. "Now, as I said, I won't hear that."

Haywood glared at his attorney, giving him the full front of his face, dead eye included, but Darrow didn't flinch. "When the Pinks start looking here in Denver," Haywood said, "—and they will, mind you, you need to have a plan."

"You were here. The assassin was in Boise. You don't know who he is or where he is now."

Haywood shrugged. "How would I know such a thing?"

"That's correct and shouldn't change. Understand?" Darrow waited until Haywood nodded before continuing, "The state of Idaho has no jurisdiction in Colorado. The federal government either—least none to involve you. You had no knowledge of the events prior to their occurrence. And if the terrorist—"

"He's not a terrorist. A fanatic perhaps, but terrorist is not—"

"Bill. My God."

"All right."

Darrow took a breath. "The killer is likely to be a Federation member. We know that. The press will call him a terrorist. Certainly the government will. Senator Borah cannot restrain himself from the abuse of that word. Unless you denounce the killer—whoever he turns out to be—and his actions, the moniker terrorist will be attached to the union as well, including to you."

Haywood moved to the window. "Been called it many times."

Darrow rose and came to Haywood's side, whispering so Winnie couldn't hear. "I trust there's nothing written, no witness or other evidence, that could in any way be misconstrued as to somehow implicate the Federation or yourself."

"No. Absolutely not."

"Then let the chips fall where they may. *There.* Up in Boise. But here, say nothing. Do nothing."

Haywood nodded, but otherwise remained stoic at the window.

"I wish you a good day. I must return to my office." At the door, Darrow gathered his hat and coat and nodded at Winnie. "Ma'am."

"Mr. Darrow," she replied.

Walking from the office, Darrow's thoughts whirled. He knew now what, truly, he'd already known: his client ordered the assassination of the governor of Idaho. He'd contained his anxiety in Haywood's office, but now it began to gurgle up, getting away from him. On the first floor, he entered the Gassell Saloon and ordered a whiskey. His nerves settled. After ordering another, he began to open his mind's windows, letting its curtains blow. What was done to Governor Steunenberg was grotesque. Horrid, certainly. No, of course it was. It was a reprehensible crime. A beastly murder. But ... He became still and closed his eyes, letting the skittish demon come to him. He could feel its chill before seeing its form, feel its breath before hearing its whisper. Then the forbidden thought was full upon him: Might this be the one matter, the one case, that he had dreamed of? If Bill was arrested, was charged, if it all blew up (he snorted at the word), then yes, perhaps—it may be precisely what he'd hoped for, waited for, the reason he'd tolerated Bill for so long. Besides, the demon assured him, Darrow was just the lawyer. So, as his client's actions justified his patience, so now may his own actions be justified. A little curl came to one end of Darrow's mouth. Yes, this assassination was horrendous, but it just might take him all the way to the United States Supreme Court.

Up in Haywood's office, the big man strolled to Winnie, and she rose. "My dear, the time's come. Telephone Miss Capone."

"All right," began Winnie. "Do you want me to go too?"

He wrapped his arms around her. "No, stay."

"Are you worried?"

"Why should I be? I'm here in Colorado. All of that mess will stay up in Idaho." After a kiss, he continued, "To think on it, message her by telegraph. No one can eavesdrop."

"Eavesdrop? I wouldn't say anything that might—"

"No, of course not, but she might. Send the message." He gave her a perfunctory smile. "Use the code words you told her."

Sensing his tension, she pulled close. "You *are* worried."

"Not if you leave now," he said, glancing away.

Thirty minutes later, Winnie was in the telegraph office, standing before a raised desk, behind which stood a young male attendant, wide-eying the beauty penciling a message in front of him. "Yes, the Saratoga Hotel, in Boise," she said, replying to his question. She knew he was watching her as all men did, whether they were her age, like this man, or much older, like Bill. When men unknown to her leered, she wasn't sure if it was because they were imagining bedding her, imagining introducing her to their mother, or just flummoxed knowing she was both Big Bill's mistress and his wife's sister. Regardless, the look carried a consistency, as did her practiced instinct to ignore it. Or not ignore it. The choice was hers. This was her power. Once they locked on her, she had them. She could then pretend to not see them, thus frustrating their approach. Or she could flit her eyes, touch her hair, and ensnare them. This young man's eyes were too sweet. He was too serious in his stare. Clearly, he was sizing her up for his mother. So, she handed him the completed paper without meeting his gaze.

He read it and looked up, puzzled.

She asked, "Can you not make out my writing?"

"No, Ma'am. I mean, yes, I can, Miss Minor. You want this to go to Miss Carlotta Capone at the Saratoga Hotel in Boise?"

"Yes."

"And the message is: PARIS IN THE SPRING. Correct?"

"Precisely."

"Are you sure Miss Capone will understand the—"

"I'm certain," she replied, now meeting his eyes. "Can you not send such a short message?"

"Oh yes, you're fine. I mean, that's fine. This is fine. We can send just one word, if you wish. Even one letter. Like just an A. Or just a B." He chuckled at himself. "I heard someone did that once—just sent one letter. I think it was an M."

"All right," Winnie tried.

"If you're concerned for the cost, it's the same for ten words as for one letter. Even an M. But for Mr. Haywood, there's no—"

"It's not for Mr. Haywood," she snapped. "You should mind yourself and not assume."

"I apologize." His face fell. "I didn't intend—"

"Just tell me the fee."

The young man adjusted his glasses while consulting the pricing book. "Yes, of course. To Boise. That's nine hundred miles. Five bits, please, Miss."

"Five bits?"

"Yes."

"Five," she repeated. She glanced outside, then back to the cheerful attendant. "Fine, charge it to the Federation."

"Certainly. Whatever you—"

"Thank you," Winnie said, wheeling about. But before she reached the door, she turned back. "When will it arrive?"

"A few minutes after it's sent. I think."

"Good," she said, and left.

★

– 16 –

FRIDAY
January 11, 1907

By 1907, Denver's Broadway Theater had not only driven the nearby Tabor Opera House out of business, but it had become the most prestigious theater between St. Louis and San Francisco. Outside, its Romanesque masonry bulged in viscous proportions, adorned with animal and floral motifs. Inside, in one of twenty-five onion-domed boxes, a pair of green crutches were leaning against an ornate metal rack bearing an assortment of furs, muffs, woolen coats, and men's silk top hats. In that box's first row, on the far-left seat, Neva sat smiling, her golden curls massed in the Gibson Girl style around her glittering drop-earrings; her long, pale neck bearing a sterling silver necklace supporting a brooch consisting of a rhombus of emeralds and diamonds, surrounded by her smooth skin, the beginning of her cleavage, and the white-lace and apple-green trim of her gown—a shade of green chosen for how it matched her eyes.

Below her, hundreds of Denver's well dressed were finding their seats in front of the enormous curtain painted with an exotic, East Indian panorama. She scrutinized the women down there, many popinjays wearing extravagantly ribboned feathered hats—to the theater! Could they not imagine how they were obstructing the view of others? Or did they know, but simply didn't care? Who were they? Were they more likely aligned with the Federation—perhaps wives, sisters, girlfriends of sub-bosses or the merchants that supplied the labor union? Or more likely associated with fat capitalists, like mine owners? Though she knew a few by sight, most were either unknown, or she couldn't see their faces due to the monstrosities on their heads. So, she devised a method to study the question: sooner or later the women below would nonchalantly survey the room—as Neva was doing. Who was there? Wearing what? With whom? Eventually they would look up at the boxes, and, when their gazes fell on Neva, she would produce the affect of congeniality for them. Those who responded in kind were Federation women, or at least sympathetic to the workers' cause. Those whose eyes slung abuse at her were otherwise. The orchestra pit was still coming to life, tuning in fits and starts, when Neva had her answer. Most of the thoughtless ones—those wearing garish hats in a theater—had glowered at her. No great wonder, she grumbled silently—greed, judgmentalism, and inconsiderateness being the best friends that they are.

Sitting to her right, George was dressed to the nines: tailed, black tuxedo, silk bow tie, mirror-shined patent shoes, what hair he had trimmed sharp and oiled. She nudged him to look at the women below. "Priscilla would never have approved any of them for you," she said, referring to his much-adored wife who had passed three years prior, leaving George to be a childless widower, and leaving Neva friendless. "Especially the strumpets."

He chuckled. "How do you know who's a strumpet?"

"Wearing their hats in here. Completely rude."

"That makes them strumpets?"

"If that's the kind you're after, you can pick one out. They make it easy."

"How thoughtful," he mused, leaning to peer down. "Let me take a look."

She pulled him back. "I'm afraid you'll have to stay a widower."

"That's all right, no other woman would survive around you."

"True," she replied, adding an assured nod. To George's right, the three additional first-row seats were empty, but the two rows behind them were filling with Federation associates and their guests, some of whom tilted stiffly to whisper matters of business to George, the Federation treasurer, or to greet Neva. Further back, near the box's door, a tuxedo-clad armed guard stood sentry.

Looking down again, Neva gazed with curious interest at the orchestra tuning up in its pit, and then returned to watching people scooting toward their seats. She was reminded of her third-story window, watching similar people on the street in front of the Pioneer Building. Here they were again, but different. And not just different due to the setting—interior, fine clothes, better classes—but because she felt different, not so antagonistic, not so alone—a pleasantry she attributed to the man beside her. "Everyone can see us," she said. "Should you scoot down a seat?"

"If you wish," George said, his voice having grown stony.

She tapped his leg and whispered, "Don't."

"I should when Winnie and Bill get here."

"They can sit at the end," she said.

Neva was about to inquire about George's mood change when a woman behind them inclined forward, gushing, "I am so excited, Mrs. Haywood. Please tell your husband how grateful Mr. Rutherford and I are."

"Yes of course," replied Neva.

"Ethel Barrymore, here in Denver," the woman continued. "I'm beside myself."

"Yes, it's wonderful," said Neva. She looked at her playbill:

CAPTAIN JINKS OF THE HORSE MARINES
Starring
ETHEL BARRYMORE
as Madame Trentoni

"I hope Bill hurries," said Neva, glancing back. As she pivoted to the front, she caught George's faraway stare. "What is it?"

"It's nothing, dear," he lied, flashing a quick-fading grin.

"You've had hang-dog morbs since we sat down. Out with it."

He started to speak, but swallowed it. Beginning again, he whispered, "There's money missing."

"What? From where?" she whispered back.

He glanced behind them, assuring himself they weren't being overheard. "From the Federation."

"You're the treasurer. You'll sort it. Right?"

"If it was missing from, well, from below me, then yes."

Seeing him raise his eyebrows, she asked, "Doesn't Bill have an account, or something?"

He nodded. "It's supposed to be limited."

They heard talking behind them and turned. Winnie was entering, removing her coat to reveal a winter-rose shawl and muff over a magenta, pearl-accented gown with matching long gloves. While others were praising the dress, calling it stunning and dazzling, George glanced at Neva and muttered, "I didn't see *that* in the account." Then he stood and turned around.

Neva put on a proud grin. "Beautiful Sissy. Come sit."

Winnie beamed back and moved to the front of the box.

"Good evening, Miss Minor," said George, getting to the end of the row. "You're a delight to the eyes. Is that a new gown?"

"Thank you, George. Bill insisted, so—" She stopped herself. "But look at you, the picture of handsomeness. You should be covered in women."

"Oh, I don't think so," he stuttered.

Winnie glanced at Neva. "At least one."

"Is Bill behind you?" asked George.

"No," said Winnie. "He's staying at the office. Sends his apologies. All the usual." Then to Neva directly: "He told me to say he'll see you after—at the suites."

"I'll be at the house," Neva replied, touching her handkerchief to her nose.

George motioned to the empty front row. "Winnie, after you."

"No," instructed Neva, "come back to where you were, George." She motioned to Winnie. "Take the middle seat, Sissy. George and I will continue our conversation."

Returning to his seat, he spoke to Winnie, who scooted in after him. "We can switch at intermission, if you wish."

But Winnie didn't respond. She had already re-donned her puckish smile for the dress admirers behind them.

★

– 17 –

SATURDAY
January 12, 1907

In the afternoon of the prior Thursday, a message on a desk in one of Boise's three telegraph offices had been transcribed from Morse Code to type:

Date: January 10, 1907
From: WFM, Denver, Colorado
To: Carlotta Capone, Saratoga Hotel, Boise, Idaho
Msge: SPRING IN PARIS

Then the telegram had been placed in an envelope and handed to a message boy with instructions to run it to the Saratoga. As this telegraph office was in the city block between the Idanha and the Saratoga, ordinarily it would've taken only moments for the boy to get to the Saratoga and deliver it at the grand hotel's front desk. But with the clamorous aftermath of the assassination—the onslaught of carts, buggies, armed detectives, press men, barkers and onlookers giving the street a fair-days stir—all deliveries were slowed, whether they were of liquor, bullets, flour, or cryptic telegraphs. And they got mixed up, as with the telegram to Carla. When the boy went first to the Idanha Hotel, delivering other telegrams there, he accidentally included the one for Carlotta Capone in that batch. When he got to the Saratoga, he found no message in his pouch for a guest there, so he scurried back to the wire office and said nothing about it.

It wasn't until two days later, on Saturday, that the error was discovered, and the Idanha sent one of their bellboys with the telegram to the Saratoga. There he found a sea of people queued before the front desk. Not wishing to wait, he turned to a bellman and asked for help, but was rebuffed. Then he spotted a young woman in a waitress cap and approached her, asking for her help to get the telegram to the front desk. Carla took it and was about to get a coin for the boy from the cashier, but then stopped upon seeing it was addressed to her. She flashed the boy a smile before tipping him herself. Once he was away, she thumbed open the envelope and read the message within. She read it again, took a deep breath, then strolled quickly through the dining room, into the kitchen and directly to the dry goods closet at the back. Inside, she tucked the jar of plaster into a burlap sack and hurried out with it.

Senator William Borah was in his shirt sleeves, pulling on a rope, then bowline-tying it to a tree in the yard of a large, Boise home. Several men were in the yard nearby, each well armed, most with repeating rifles. "I need to get back inside," Borah groused to one of the young guards. From the front steps of the house, he instructed another, "I'm telling you again: keep those horses out of Ms. Morgan's flower bed." He knocked muddy-snow-slush from his boots and entered the front door. Once inside he returned to the library, and to the company of seven men: the appointed governor of Idaho, two Idaho legislators, two representatives of the Mine Owners Association, Chief Detective James McParland, and the aging, sickly local sheriff of Ada County. Borah warmed himself at the fire. The others were sitting about the well-appointed room, cigars lit, single-malt scotch in glasses, the exception being the bespectacled McParland who stood surveying the books.

"Her husband died last year? No children?" McParland asked Borah. "Do you know what she'll do with these books?"

"No, Jim," said Senator Borah. "I'm not certain of her plans ... beyond whatever she has in store for me tonight."

The others chuckled uncomfortably, but not McParland. He continued, "It's a fine collection, William. If she's not in need of it, I know a broker."

Borah groaned. "When she sees what your damn horses did to her yard, I don't know."

McParland turned to the window. "It's hooves, not dynamite."

Borah frowned. "May we proceed?"

McParland returned to his chair. "Certainly."

"Lance?" Borah indicated for one of the legislators to continue. "You were reviewing the terms of the memorandum."

The young man resumed, "Yes, Senator. The Pinkerton Agency will take primary authority for the investigation—"

"I need authority to go beyond just investigating. I need to be authorized to arrest and detain, and interrogate," said McParland, staring at the new governor until the man gave a nod. "And that includes all the protections of the sheriff's office, in the event anyone is killed."

The Ada County sheriff's assent was buried in a heavy cough.

Borah took a deep breath. "You cannot let this get out of hand."

"No intentions otherwise," began the detective. "We'll apply for the correct *habeas*—"

"Enh, *habeas corpus* be damned!" said the new governor. "We'll give em all *post mortems*."

Borah shook his head and waved at the legislator who was still on his feet. "Continue."

"President Roosevelt is not sending additional troops or arms. Not unless formally requested by you, Governor. And not unless the mine owners wish to add that to their bill."

To that the new governor said softly, "No. There will be no federal troops. Not now. Not after— It'll be left to the Pinkertons to provide the protection force."

When the legislator felt the governor was finished, he continued, "The central headquarters for the investigation and prosecution will be the Idanha Hotel. The state has it leased for the duration, but the Mine Owners Association will be receiving all invoices." He glanced at the two association representatives.

They whispered to each other, then one said, "Agreed."

The standing man resumed speaking while referencing the document in his hands. "It's known there are spies and hired guns in this city, with more arriving daily. Therefore, as the governor said, since there will be no request for federal troops, the Pinkerton Detective Agency will be empowered to manage all matters concerning the Idanha Hotel, the security of any witnesses and suspects, and the security of the prosecution. That includes the protection of yourself, Senator Borah."

McParland whistled. "This will be the largest single bill in the history of the Pinkerton Agency." He regarded the Mine Owner Association men. "I hope you know that."

One nodded. The other scratched an eyebrow.

The legislator spoke on. "Regarding detective agencies, we anticipate the Thiel Detective Agency, more specifically Captain Swain, will be hired by the Wobblies ... the Federation."

"Swain? Detective?" scoffed McParland. "A possum calling itself a mountain lion, you ask me."

"Thc Federation?" the enfeebled sheriff scowled. "You've decided they're responsible?"

"Not exactly," began Borah.

"Aye, exactly," said McParland.

"There are other possibilities than the Federation," said Borah.

"Sure," said McParland. "I suppose all things are possible—though not equally. For this, be certain of it: we'll soon find the man who triggered the bomb, *and* his accomplice. But, gentlemen, the defendant in this case will be William Haywood of the Western Federation of Miners. I assure you."

"We have no evidence Haywood was here at the time, Jim. You know that," said Borah. "We don't have extradition grounds. Just find the bomber. Let's hang *him*. That's all we can do."

McParland's eyes narrowed. "That's not *all* we can do, Senator."

"All within the law," sniffed Borah.

"As was just said," McParland replied, "*we* are the law on this."

"No, now—" Borah had had enough. "I'm the special prosecutor here. I'll be telling *you*, Mr. McParland, what we can and cannot do in the court of law."

After a beat, McParland spoke, his voice level. "Senator, the law has fences round you, I know. So, I'll bring in the killers and put them inside those fences ... for you. But out beyond that, beyond those fences, beyond the courts, there's a broad range. And out there, out there is where we'll get Haywood. Whatever it takes."

Though he was in Boise, far from Denver, the young Pinkerton, Jack Garrett, maintained his working-man appearance as Operative

21: that of a liveryman or miner, not in the uniformed propriety of the many Pinkerton regulars there. He had never seen so many white-shirted men in one place. But his scruffy appearance had its limitations. Though it afforded him the inference of displacement, of uncertain ties useful to his work, it also sequestered him beyond the banter and percolation of information within Pinkerton circles. Except, of course, when Detective McParland had him engaged, as he had more and more lately, including out at the crime scene.

On this day, Jack found it best to sit outside a saloon that was two buildings from the Idanha Hotel. To go inside invited an alcoholic drink that was frowned upon, or a sarsaparilla for which he may as well be wearing a white shirt. Thus, sitting out front was best, as he had often done in Denver. It furnished the image of a man who had been in the saloon and might soon return, while also being a good roost for watching the comings and goings at the telegraph office next door, as well as scrutinizing the Saratoga Hotel one block west, on the far side of Main Street—Boise's wide thoroughfare cluttered with the commotion of carriages, cart drivers, and casket wagons.

Perhaps it didn't matter, the ruse. With the assassination, the town was swarming with people of all sorts, streaming off trains primarily. Some arriving by horse-drawn coach. Even fewer by automobile. Some were there to write about the events. Some were engaged in the investigation, like the Pinkertons. Some were government sorts. Others were lawyers, gunhands, or prostitutes—all purveyors of a similar profession, the way Jack saw it. All in motion before him. And among the throng was a host of invisible spies—any one of whom may have seen Jack with Detective McParland, thus obliterating the point of this working-man getup and rendering pointless his isolation from the center of the investigation.

As he contemplated petitioning McParland for a return to agent status, he saw a dark-haired beauty exit the Saratoga Hotel. She wore a pleated waistshirt, green skirt to the ground, and a wide-brimmed straw hat. Her narrow skirt constrained her clip to short steps as she dodged diagonally across Main Street toward the telegraph office, toward him. Before he knew it, he was standing, watching this ethereal vision approach.

They sidestepped each other. “Pardon me,” they said simultaneously, their eyes saying more.

He tipped his broad, black hat and was still looking down when he saw her laced Oxfords turn toward him.

“Miss Carla Capone,” she said, offering her gloved hand.

Momentary shock overtook him: the deep-golden eyes, the dimples, the smell of her. He removed his hat. “Pleasure to make your acquaint—”

“You’re either a Pinkerton or a Thiel, I’m certain,” said Carla. “I’m just not sure which.”

“Neither,” he lied, feeling a prickle of recognition and his face grow warm. Had he seen her before?

“Oh?” She squinted and gave a playful huff. “How unfortunate.”

“How so?”

She retreated a few steps into the street, toward the Saratoga. “I came to tell you something, thinking you were a Pink.”

“Nope. Not me.”

“That outfit isn’t fooling anyone,” she said, before turning to walk away. “Not that dumb hat either.”

“Hey, I like my hat,” he said, then muttered to himself, “What’s wrong with it?” Watching her navigate the street, he hollered, “You’re wearing a straw hat in the winter,” before mumbling quietly, “Yours is the dumb hat.” She had passed two horses and almost regained the far sidewalk before he snapped to his senses and ran after her.

In a first-floor bedroom of the Idanha Hotel—a room with a desk where a four-posted bed had been—the oak floor planks creaked as Wade Farrington, Operative 42, tilted forward onto the balls of his feet, then settled back onto his dirty boots’ heels. Detective McParland, reading at his desk, had heard enough. “Cease your pitching. You’re fidgeting.” Farrington complied, but soon the detective noted Farrington’s new twiddle: fingering his lapels. “For godsakes, man,” barked McParland. “Take a seat. What is it?”

“I believe our suspect left Boise on the night of the murder.”

“Why do you think that?”

"A man by his description left on the 7:15 to Cheyenne."

"Which man?" McParland barked. Over the decades of his rise through the Pinkertons, he had assumed a Gatling-gun manner of questioning subordinates. With it, he could extract not only what they wanted to say, but often what they didn't. This was in sharp contrast to his other manner—desultory and dawdling—that he began thirty years earlier while an undercover operative in Pennsylvania's anthracite coal mining region. There he learned that a leisurely cadence relaxed the murderous Irish gangs, the Molly Maguires, resulting in his infiltration of their ranks and leading many of them to the gallows. With a four-second count held before speaking, it had both lulling and maddening effects, causing targets to fill the gaps with unnecessary, but often revealing, words. And when he was openly interrogating a suspect, the truncated style gave time for paranoia to percolate in their minds. But with his men, like this operative before him, he preferred his fast style—no four-second holds. This tended to separate them from their prepared answers, revealing truths that might pop loose, while also allowing him to evaluate their mental acuity.

"Which man?" Farrington repeated McParland's question.

"Aye. Which one left on the train?"

"The murderer."

"Which one?"

Farrington paused. "I thought there was only one."

"You did?"

"Yes, Sir. The man who called on the governor that afternoon, summoning him to his office. The man—"

"The supposed insurance man?"

"Yes, Sir. Him."

"Were you not listening at the scene?"

"I was." Farrington's brows tightened.

"I said clearly: two men."

"Perhaps there was just one."

"Why are you questioning this?"

"I wouldn't, Sir."

"Two men— Two confessions."

"I thought—"

"Good," said McParland. "Do more of that."

"Yes, Sir."

"So, one of them ... You *know* he left? He was observed?"

"He was seen—"

"The man who pulled the fishing line?"

"I don't know, Sir, but—"

"But what?"

"The description provided by the girl, and the wife—"

"Mrs. Steunenberg."

"Yes, Sir, Mrs. Steunenberg's description of the man she saw on the porch, talking with their daughter. And the drawing you requisitioned. This one." Farrington nervously unfolded the drawing of a bird-beaked man who slightly resembled Adams. "We have three witnesses, including the ticket agent, who attest this man left—"

McParland poked at the drawing. "We have witnesses saying this false life-insurance salesman boarded a train?"

"Yes, Sir."

"He *boarded* a train?"

"He bought—"

"Operative Forty-Two, did anyone see that big nose actually get on board the 7:15? Or did he just buy a ticket?"

"Board, no. But he purchased the ticket. Thus, I assumed he—"

"Yes, you did." McParland smoothed his colossal gray mustache while locking eyes on the man. "Steve Adams."

"Who, Sir?"

"Your man here." McParland held up the drawing. "Steve Adams is his name. Goes by others too. A more murderous son of a bitch I've not known. Makes pussycats of the Molly Maguires. Two days ago, in Ogden, he boarded the Overland to San Francisco."

"Are we certain—"

"Of course. We have men trailing him. We'll see where he goes, see where he leads us. He'll be our second confession, I believe. So, now, find me the real killer."

Farrington huffed. "If you already knew that, why'd I waste my time tracking down the depot witness?"

"If I assign you something, Forty-Two, by definition it is not a waste of time," snapped McParland, noting the young man's pluck.

Farrington frowned. "We might be letting the killer go while we chase a phantom."

McParland's eyes narrowed. This pretense was not pluck, it was hubris. Perhaps insolence. He had finally pushed this fidgety operative into revealing something of himself. Exactly what, McParland wasn't sure, but there was more to Wade Farrington than met the eye. A double? Perhaps. He would take Farrington off operative status and back into Pinkerton dress code. That would make it easier to observe him. And no assignments out of Boise. He would keep this young man close. Put another man on him.

"May I go?" asked Farrington, pacing agitatedly.

McParland nodded. "Sure."

Farrington moved to leave.

"It's good to keep things running in parallel," said McParland, his voice looping across the office to snag Farrington back. "That way you shake things up, see if the two investigations come to the same conclusion." *And a good shaking also helps sift out spies*—but he didn't say that out loud.

"Yes, Sir," said Farrington as he left.

Experience had taught McParland to be wary of agents and operatives who show impatience for certain outcomes—those who are too quick to assume and hold indefensible positions. In their fragility, two dangers lurk—one born from their fear, the other from their resolve. Where facts are thin and fissures spread between knowledge, fragile men become frightened and pour into those gaps half-truths, expedient plaster filling uncomfortable crevasses. Especially in this profession—one of lies and curiosity, where a man trusts to his peril. The other danger arises from the strength of their ignorance and zealous ambitions—the overconfidence of the insecure. That kind of fragility can birth false intelligence, leading an investigation into dead-end alleys, wasting time and money, threatening success. And when false resolve solidifies into beliefs, devils can use the man, reaffirming his underlying lies, birthing the insidious danger of an effective counter-intelligence operation—a spy within Pinkerton ranks. McParland knew Haywood was good at manipulating weak Pinkertons—just as he, McParland, had done with weak Federation men. So, now that he knew Farrington was fragile, he needed to discover which danger the man represented—one from fear or from resolve. He suspected from both.

★

– 18 –

SUNDAY
January 13, 1907

The road from Denver to Castle Rock was well worn, and not only because of the hundreds of wagons and horses stirring it up every week, but recently due to the addition of a few go-like-hell machines. Haywood loved them. The joy of bumping along without a team of horses to contend with, flying at thirty miles an hour in his personal train car, free from the constraints of time tables and tracks. A year earlier, $2,750 from Federation coffers bought him this four-cylinder touring beauty—a midnight-blue Packard Model S with a collapsible black cloth top, two leather club chairs up front, two broad rear seats, smooth fenders over Continental tires around spoked wheels, a mahogany dash, and right-hand steering wheel. He also loved the loud, gurgling, *pourt-pourt* sound from its four-cylinder, forty horsepower engine. Plus the smell, the feel, the cool wind, the passing snowy landscape. George Pennington and the accountant were wrong to suggest it an impropriety of expenditure. Goddamn them. There was nothing wrong with this automobile, and no one deserved it more than he did.

Haywood drove wearing a green cap, goggles, and driving gloves, his fur coat tight to his neck, while puffing a Romeo y Julieta cigar and listening to the occasional banter of his equally goggled passenger: Captain Swain, the leader of the Thiel Detective Agency. Behind them rode an expressionless soul, shotgun at the ready; and beside that man was Haywood's recently deputized bulldog, Claus, sporting his own goggles.

"What does that lawyer of yours think?" asked Captain Swain.

"Clarence?"

"I heard a Mr. Darrow. Same fella?"

"Yeah," replied Haywood, downshifting for an embankment. "Chicago man."

"Damn."

"Do you hate everything from Chicago?" Haywood shouted over the wind and engine. "Maybe you're right ... except for the heroes of the Haymarket."

"Brave men."

"Brave men," repeated Haywood. "I led their cry for an eight-hour workday. That's all they wanted. Shot in the streets like dogs."

"You were there?" asked Swain.

Haywood focused on the rough road before replying. "The bomb those men used, defending themselves from the murderous police, where do you think it came from?"

Swain watched the passing landscape. "I didn't know that."

"Only killed seven of those company men, those hired guns in police uniforms. Should have killed more. And the *Tribune* had the goddamned audacity to call the labor men anarchists. Good men only wanting a fair wage for an eight-hour day. So, yes, there are some good men in Chicago, including my lawyer."

"It's the Pinks I don't—"

"Vermin," said Haywood. "You met Robert during your year with them?"

"No."

"Clarence admires their 'collective force of will,' as he says."

Swain frowned. "He saying I've got none?"

"No. Not at all." Haywood pulled the hand brake for a contingent of mule-deer ambling across the road, thirty feet ahead.

"Too many indecent little shits in the Pinks," stewed Swain.

Letting the car idle, Haywood turned. "All depends, I suppose."

"You think so?"

"Captain, I don't need a virtuous detective."

Swain pulled a breath. "I do what's necessary for my clients."

Haywood resumed the cleared road. "I wonder if you know something. Did you know that we, the Western Federation of Miners, far exceed in headcount any other organization, including the Pinks? Ten times the men and guns, west of the Mississippi. Everybody knows we've got a special responsibility. And not just to our members, but to every American. And one of those responsibilities is to keep the Pinks under control. Tar and rail, ax handle ... lead when it gets to that. Unless I can buy em, like at the Bunker."

"No agency can help you more than Thiel," said Swain.

"Oh, I don't know, Captain. We're mighty powerful without a small outfit like yours from ... where? Seattle?"

"Spokane. Right in the blame-middle of all this coming maf-fickin. I know the whole northwest. Better'n any Pinkerton."

"But you're here in Colorado."

"This coming thing is gonna be in Idaho. You're gonna need me. And your Chicago man, the lawyer, he's gonna need me too. Mightily so. No doubt the Federation can Sherman over the Pinks in open battle, but this is gonna be an alley war."

"Don't oversell your position." Haywood glanced at him. "I'll give you the contract."

"Mighty obl—"

"But only week to week. If I'm pleased, another week. I don't need your muscle and guns, Captain. I need information. Information. Understand?"

"Yes. Thank you."

Haywood hoisted his dead eye's brow. "I already have people in Boise. All over Idaho, Washington, Utah. Get me better information than they can."

"I'm confident—"

"Any turncoat against us will be dealt with as such. Whether he's a governor, judge, lawyer, Pink ... or a Thiel man. Are we of common mind?"

"We are," said Swain, grasping the dash as the Packard found a gully.

"I don't like that you hired your men out to that rat-governor for his imprisonment scheme—the very goddamned thing that got him killed."

"I was hired by Senator Borah, but—"

Haywood blustered a laugh. "The sagebrush dandy?"

"We saw your men, the union men, home peaceably."

Haywood downshifted. "How do you feel bout killing a man?"

"I don't lose sleep, if that's your meaning."

"Steve Adams. Know him? Big, parish-pickax nose. Goes by Addis some."

"Might've heard of him."

In Denver, Neva's bare left leg was exposed from under sheets embroidered with the words: METROPOLE HOTEL. The limb was a twisted piece of mushy driftwood, atrophied and shorter than the other. She could feel it, but not tell it what to do. It ached, but not with the arthritic pain that occasionally shot up her right leg, the one that did all the work. George, wearing just trousers, was on the bed's edge. He lifted her left leg to rub liniment into her squishy thigh.

"Noodle is so cold," he said, referring to her gimp leg by the nickname they'd given it.

"She feels normal to me," said Neva. "Just achy." She snuggled the duvet higher, covering her bare breasts.

"Hey, I was looking at those."

She laughed. "They were looking at you too."

"I noticed," he said.

She snorted a drowsy laugh.

"Can you lie back?" he asked. "Just relax? If you fall asleep, that's fine with me. Would mean I'm good at this."

"Oh, you're good at it," she said, her voice sleepy syrup. "But, as we haven't squeaked the bed yet, I'd best keep an eye on you."

"Yes, you probably should," he said gently, and added, "In the morning, darling." He kept rolling his hands, pushing the oil into her flesh.

"Yes," she breathed, sinking into her pillow, closing her eyes.

When she reached to feel for him, to give him a grateful pat, he noted her wedding ring and lifted her left hand. "May I?"

"Mm-huh," she said blearily, eyes still closed. "Just put it where I'll find it. Don't lose it ... like we nearly did."

He slipped the ring off and placed it in a porcelain ashtray on the nightstand, next to the open bottle of Sloan's Liniment. Then he kissed the rosy, straight scar across her thin wrist.

She liked that he did those things she could never do.

Neva contracted polio in 1894, during her first and only visit to New York City. Her father and Reverend Sanders were there, over from Walla Walla, Washington, both serving as ambassadors for the Seventh-day Adventist Church, seeking to procure donations for the newly formed Walla Walla College. Believing it would be a wonderful experience for his eldest daughter, Nevada, he brought her along. She was nineteen, fidgety, and in windswept love with William Haywood, a thirty-two-year-old rising star in the labor movement—and importantly, a man her socialist father liked. But, at the time of their New York visit, and unbeknown to anyone, a noxious, poliomyelitis epidemic was pushing through the city's crowded, elevated railcars. Neva began feeling lethargic on the three-day trip home.

After a few months and a period of improved health, she and Bill married and moved to Denver. Their daughter Vernie came nine months later. A year later, Henrietta. But by then, Neva's leg was failing her, as was Bill. He was convinced she had fallen victim to a plot against him, a poisoning by the New York-based Mine Owners Association. He became progressively hostile, sardonic, if not furious, at her oft-strained expressions, her huffs of discomfort, her grinding immobility—just as he was ascending to the Federation's oak-paneled offices. She was thus overjoyed when her young sister, Winnie, moved in with them, helping attend to her as her life in an invalid chair commenced.

But rumors mounted and doctors echoed them: poliomyelitis was transmittable, and children were particularly at risk. Within days of that news reaching the *Denver Post*, Neva saw women hustle their children from her path, their vituperative glares scolding her: How dare you come near my babies! A few weeks later, Bill arranged for Vernie and Henrietta to be placed in a special wing of St. Vincent's Orphanage in northwest Denver, a wing funded by the Seventh-day Adventists with money donated by the Federation. (Two years later, they would be moved to the St. Agnes School for Girls, a class-floored Episcopal boarding school, also in Denver.)

As St. Vincent's was an orphanage, Neva was not allowed there. At the time, she agreed with the rule—no one feared her girls contracting polio more than she did. That meant she and Bill also feared them coming home, even for short periods—the one exception being Christmas week. So, Neva wrote them. And she phoned them—once telephones was installed on both ends. She tried. But she couldn't maintain it. Finally her spirit broke, and then imploded—culminating in a hot bath and wrist slit one evening when Bill and Winnie were away. By happenstance, grace, luck, or divine intervention, George Pennington stopped by the Park Hill Heights house that night and found her.

In the aftermath of her "little doing," as Bill called it, aching disquiet hung like mildewed heirloom linens, corrupt and manifest, yet impossible to discard. A smell to be borne. Bill attempted a more caring posture, but it was a false flag. He stayed home more, even played pinochle with the sisters, but his advances towards young Winnie amplified: more flowers, dresses, jewelry, lingering shoulder rubs. But Neva couldn't entertain the idea of divorce. What would that life be? With the disease? She would be alone, unwanted, would never see her daughters again, and her next "little doing" would surely not fail.

But if she could allow things, then she could live this life, a new life of sorts. And not just any life, but a life of significance at the center of what mattered. Soon her daughters would be old enough to rejoin them. Bill would allow it. She need only be patient. And this new life meant Winnie would stay near. They could laugh and stay close. And here Neva had money, could travel, and had her refuge in Park Hill Heights. But to have this life, she had to release her antipathy toward it, had to accept it. All of it. She had to value it to the point of protecting it—had to defend it, even encourage it. Thus, when her sister came to her with disclosures and concerns regarding Bill's intimacies, Neva didn't blink: Winnie should allow it. She knew Winnie anxiously attempted to hide her affections for Bill, that Winnie's protestations were masquerading petitions for permission. Why deny them both what they wanted, only to lose everything she needed? Let them be, Neva thought. The affront was necessary for this life. A price for continued admission. As distasteful an elixir as ever there was. But by releasing herself from the fight, she found an accompanying release from the shame. Besides, she had George, didn't she? This life was a good life. Good enough, she told herself.

The setting sun lit the castle-shaped butte rising over Castle Rock, Colorado. Far below it, Haywood's Packard stood empty at a hitching rail on Perry Street. Posted on either side of the car, sluggish horses sniffed at the front wheels and lamps. The Federation guard filled a chair on a long, covered porch, over which the building's gabled face boasted the word HOTEL in green paint. The guard minded one of horses that kept trying to nibble the car's fender. "Shoo! Stop that," he said in a soft voice. "That's not for you."

Inside, the local doctor sweat in a lobby chair, staring up at Haywood's inflamed face while the giant poured humiliation down on him. Claus watched from a nearby leather couch; while at a small bar ten feet away, Captain Swain chomped an unlit cigar. At the hotel's desk, a gaunt clerk screened himself behind an even skinnier flower arrangement.

Haywood clicked his tongue. "Captain Swain, have I been clear with this scum Englishman?"

"I'd say you have," said Swain.

"Yes, Your Excellency," begged the doctor, his London accent trembling. "All medical procedures for union men I am to bill to the Federation. I am fully informed now."

"This is beyond that, doctor," growled Haywood. "I love a good reason to automobile on such a brumal day. Hell, any day. But you were warned. You were telegraphed. You were told. And then I hear last month about a boy, the young son of a labor man"—he thumped the doctor in the chest—"one of *my* men. I hear his boy, nine years of age, lost a foot—crushed by a cart at your employer's mine here. He carried his boy to you, and you refused him. Refused any of your services because the boy's father is in my union. In your goddamned self-righteousness, you doomed his boy to an invalid life. You arrogant—" He grabbed the doctor by the throat and lifted him, then threw him against the wall. "Get up, goddamn you," he shouted. Behind him, Claus growled.

As the doctor stood, he cut a plaintive glance at Captain Swain. "Sir, if your friend—"

"Yes, Captain," barked Haywood. "Advise me. What should I do with this pissant, this lapdog of some Chicago trust? Most likely, he's on the Pinkerton take as well. This sorry discharge of an infected whore. Leaves a young boy to suffer. A boy who shouldn't have even been in that goddamned mine!" Again Haywood knocked the man down, only to watch him stagger to his feet again. "What say you, Captain?"

Swain was acutely aware this was a test of their new relationship—in fact it was the reason he'd been brought on this short trip. An insufficient answer would indicate feebleness, while too aggressive would signal carelessness. He removed the cigar from his teeth and shrugged.

Miffed, Haywood asked, "Do I look like a murderer?"

Swain saw Haywood's red glower, his massive frame, his sleeves pushed up from balled fists, sweaty brow, dead eye looming over the frightened doctor. "Of course not," lied Swain. "The boy is lame and can't be mended. His leg could've been saved had this doctor been of good character, not the meater he is."

"Right," snarled Haywood. "The boy's same age I lost my eye."

"Then, I suppose ..." Strolling toward the doctor, Swain reached under his coat and withdrew a small automatic pistol.

"Wait," said Haywood, holding up a hand.

"Thank you," cried the mortified doctor. "Indeed, that would not have been necessary." He watched as Haywood picked up Claus, walked across the lobby, opened the main door, and placed the dog on the porch.

"He doesn't like gunfire," said Haywood, returning.

"No, no, wait now!" plead the Englishman.

Swain walked forward and, casual-as-you-please, blasted a hole in the doctor's knee. The man screamed and collapsed to the large green-and-gold Persian rug, clasping his leg, blood coursing through his fingers as he scrambled to tie a tourniquet with his belt.

Haywood screwed his face into a satisfied grin. "Yes, that seems fitting." He turned and held the front door for Claus. The dog scampered in and back to the couch while scrutinizing the man on the floor. Haywood approached the now-blanched and round-eyed desk clerk. "We'll need two rooms. And you'll invoice the—"

"The Western Federation, yes, good," breathed the little man.

While the doctor's moans echoed through the wood-paneled lobby, Haywood gave the hotelman a one-eyed wink. "And bill us the expense of that rug. And for a doctor to come for the—doctor."

"Very well," acknowledged the clerk, rotating the guest book for Haywood to sign. But Haywood stepped back, indicating Swain should sign it. Swain did so, signing a fictitious name.

"No, *you*, Captain Swain," murmured Haywood.

Swain smudged the false name and signed: Thiel Agency.

"That's not the same, exactly," observed Haywood. "But it'll do. That pistol of yours, may I see it?"

"Of course." Swain drew the small, nickel, .25 caliber with the swirling letters FN engraved in the black grip plates. He laid it on the counter.

Haywood picked it up. "An automatic?"

"Yep," replied Swain. "The FN. Belgian. There's also a Colt automatic. Maybe a Browning too."

"I've never ..." Haywood marveled. "I've never seen one."

The clerk was also interested, cautiously. "How does it work?"

Swain released the clip. "Bullets are stored in the handle. Feed from the top." He snapped it back in.

"Truly?"

"Top slides." He half-demonstrated, then released it. "Pulls up a new one. Then another. Like a repeater. This top action does it. One pull of the trigger makes it—"

"Automatic," whispered the wide-eyed clerk.

"That's marvelous," gushed Haywood. The doctor's moans had faded. "Where did you come by such a wonder?"

"One of my brothers," replied Swain. "He's a seafarer." Glancing up, he added, "ISU," indicating his brother was in the International Seaman's Union of America, to which Haywood gave an approving nod. Swain continued, "Gave it to me last fall, in San Francisco."

"Could he get more?" Haywood scrutinized the detective.

Swain chuckled. "Well, I'd be lying if I said so. Reckon he lifted this one from a passenger. You wanna buy one?"

"One? No, I want a thousand," laughed the big man. "But I'll begin with this one. How much to part with it?"

Swain glanced at the clerk who was riveted by the men's conversation. Behind Haywood and Swain, the doctor had passed out.

A pensive, obligatory smile came to Swain's face, his eyebrows rising. "You must have it, Mr. Haywood. It'd be my honor."

"Are you certain?" beamed Haywood, taking the pistol in his large hands, ignoring Swain's anguish at giving up the treasure. "You're most generous." He lifted the gun to inspect it, opening the slide, the barrel pointed toward Swain.

"There's a bullet chambered there, already," said Swain nervously. "There in the top part."

"Yes, I see that."

★

– 19 –

MONDAY
January 14, 1907

Harry Orchard was pliant, naked, sprawled sideways on his back, on his Saratoga Hotel bed, his broad, sweaty white belly quivering, a glistening pig down which ran a line of hair from man-breasted chest to small cock—though at this time it didn't reach that far, but merged into the nodding brown hair of the prostitute slurping away. She looked up, wiped her mouth with the back of her hand while receiving a groan from Orchard.

"Ten cents extra, honey, if ya don't warn me first."

"That's fine," he groused. "Godsakes woman, don't stop."

She resumed, and he touched her hair, imagining it belonged to Carla, his Italian beauty downstairs. With that image, his toes curled, and he began a nasally, high-pitched dog whimper before falling pantingly silent. She stood, both indolent breasts slumped over her corset, then spit into the porcelain basin on the washstand.

"There's two extra nickels ... right there," he said, flopping a hand toward the washstand. "Leave the others."

"Thank you, honey," she said. Seeing five silver nickels on the stand, she scooped up two of them. After confirming Orchard's eyes were closed, she considered stealing the other three—her hand hovering over them. But then she noticed a white substance covering the nickels, stuck to them in places. She compared them to the two she'd already paid herself. All were covered in a powdery substance that was also scattered around the back of the basin. She was about to rinse the five coins in the basin's water but changed her mind, considering what she had just spit there. Instead, she placed them all in her bag, dressed herself, and left as Orchard's snore settled in.

Two blocks east, at the Idanha Hotel, McParland dined at his claimed table on the mezzanine above the back of the dining room. He had chosen the location and positioned both the table and his chair strategically. While eating, he could observe who moved through the hotel, who ate below him, and who entered the hallway leading to his office and adjoining bedroom. In addition, he set the other chairs such that whoever sat with him could only focus on him or the papered wall behind him, not the comings and goings of others. To further seal it, he had two gunhands on duty while he was at the table: one stationed in a chair at the foot of the stairs, and one at the top—their purpose being less for protection than for providing a barrier to anyone seeking to intrude upon his conversations or thoughts. The gunman at the top of the stairs massaged a black rosary, the beads clicking against the wood arms of his chair.

McParland had just finished his cherry pie when Jack Garrett, the disheveled Operative 21, burst into the hotel, Carla Capone in tow, then headed toward the hall for McParland's office. Jack was in his average-man attire, and she was in her ruddy, Saratoga waitress uniform.

"I'm up here!" boomed McParland.

"Yes, Sir," replied Jack, removing his hat and heading to the stairs. When Jack and Carla arrived at the table, McParland stood.

"Miss Capone," said McParland, his hand extended. "I'm Chief Detective McParland."

"Yes, I know, of course," she demurred, smiling, providing her hand. "The famous detective and friend of Sherlock Holmes. I'm flattered you know my name."

Don't be, thought Jack. He would have been surprised had McParland not already known the name of this waitress from another hotel. But he couldn't fault her for not realizing the scope of McParland's knowledge—she being a neophyte in this man's world of spies, detectives, and investigations. What did she know of it? Nothing, of course.

Jack had met Carla two days prior on Main Street when she had come to him, saying she had something to share, if only he was a

Pinkerton. They had talked on the other side of the street, but she had said little—only that she'd seen some shifty characters in the Saratoga. That was it. Who hadn't seen shifty characters in Boise? They were everywhere. Then she walked away, and that was that.

Since then, Jack had tried to produce the resolve to saunter into the Saratoga and speak to Carla again. He hadn't quite managed before the exquisite girl once again found him, this time telling him the most extraordinary thing. So he hurried her to the chief—who might scold him later, saying he had unnecessarily compromised his operative cover by escorting her in there—but Jack didn't care. The information she had was worth it. In fact, maybe it'd get Jack out of clandestine work. Maybe he'd be a full agent, even on his way to becoming a detective—all because of Carla and her information. So, he took the chance. Yes, he could've just pointed her into the Idanha—let her go tell Chief McParland on her own. But once in, she would've been scooped up by every man in the room—they'd be appropriating not only this significant break in the case, but her as well. He risked losing her to an assemblage of salivating men, any one of whom she might find attractive in their Pinkerton crispness, recent baths, and shaved chins. And, of course, Jack wanted the glory of introducing her to the Great Detective.

"May we sit, Sir?" Jack asked.

"Please do," said McParland.

Back at the Saratoga Hotel, Orchard remained on his bed, snoring, naked, his penis shriveled, the room's lace curtain allowing in the evening gloom.

Outside Orchard's door, which bore the brass numbers 312, and down the hall, the passenger elevator rattled to a stop. The middle-aged black driver levered open the iron door, nodding to his fare who stepped through. As the lift rose behind him, the Pinkerton, Wade Farrington, took a breath, noting the empty hallway. He then drew his Colt .32 revolver and walked cautiously to room 312. There he listened to the sonorous gurgles within and found the door locked. After holstering his pistol, he withdrew a locksmith's set of skeleton keys on a round fob, holding them close to prevent jingling. In that moment, the elevator's bell tinged. Then came a clank, and out stepped the prostitute who had been with Orchard. She turned down the hall in Farrington's direction, but stopped short upon seeing him. He put away his picking keys and walked to the elevator, passing her with a tip of the hat.

Before pressing the summoning buzzer, he glanced back and saw her place something at the foot of door 312. She then hurried away, disappearing through the far stairwell door. Farrington returned to the 312 door and picked up three silver nickels from the floor. All three were covered in a white, granular, almost pasty material. Unable to make sense of them, he started to replace them, but then changed his mind and pocketed them.

On the mezzanine at the Idanha, Carla knew precisely what she was doing. These men, these paper dolls, were but toys for folding, painting, clothing, unclothing, setting afire. And that included Chief Detective McParland. He was just another man, wasn't he?

Before leaving Denver, Carla had gone to Winnie to get the specifics of what Mr. Haywood wished Carla to do in Boise. Though she and Winnie weren't close, they nevertheless began that meeting with a few laughs over school-day remembrances and other trivialities. But Carla had felt the nippy chill, the impenetrable wall Winnie had erected around herself and her relationship with Mr. Haywood. It was an openly hidden, screamingly silent secret—her serious devotion not only to the man, but to the worker's cause. When the subject turned to Boise, Winnie assumed an air of superior rank which Carla found aggravating. But it didn't take long before the thrill of the assignment abated that annoyance, and the young women ended their conversation as they began it: feigning to be the best of friends.

Carla had three tasks in Boise: First, she was to keep an eye on Harry Orchard—to always know his general whereabouts, including to report if he left town. Second, when requested, she was to secrete some "things" into Orchard's hotel room—the "things" would be delivered to her with instructions attached. And third, she was to attempt to persuade two Pinkertons to spy for the Federation. Carla was comfortable with the first and second of the three assignments—they seemed easy enough. But the last one worried her, though she wasn't sure why. After all, she knew men. She could handle them. But she'd never deceived a man, at least not so blatantly. Yet, she was asking *them* to be deceptive, not her. Still, it muddled her mind and scared her. And it was out of that fear, she later reasoned, that she had panicked and done the silly paper-baby thing on the train.

It didn't take long, though, before she was happy it had happened. The foolishness of it, the near loss of the entire, exciting mission injected cold resolve in her veins, firmed her spine, and narrowed her vision to only the things she could do, what she could control. Not what might ensue. Not what others may think of her. Not what was right or wrong or the damage it might cause. Moreover, she affirmed herself to embrace her sexuality, to employ it, to use it for the cause of the Federation, for any retribution she might bring for the killing of her father and brother.

Within two days of her arrival in October of the previous year, she began her dance with Orchard. And within two weeks, she began sleeping with a Pinkerton operative named Wade Farrington, known as Operative 42 by the Pinks. By Christmas, she had Wade converted. Now the double agent was working covertly for the Federation. She then handed him over to direct communication with Mr. Haywood and thought that was the end of it. But Wade expected their sex to continue, something she was managing, she told herself. At least he was fun, always looking for chancy places for them to meet. But what Carla hadn't considered, much less knew how to control, was his growing fixation on her—fast becoming possession with menacing undertones.

Then came the bombing of the governor. Following that, the cryptic PARIS IN SPRING telegram from Winnie which put Carla into predetermined action. As part of that action, she was to bring Harry Orchard to the attention of McParland at a time to be triggered by a telephone call. As she waited for that call, an idea came to her: she still had another Pinkerton to recruit, something she looked forward to accomplishing, hoping it might give her an acceptable excuse for distancing herself from Wade Farrington.

Surely Wade wouldn't argue with an order that seemed to come from Mr. Haywood. She began looking for her second conquest.

The tall young Pinkerton, Jack Garrett, was easy to find. In fact, Carla had noticed him several times since the bombing, making "finding him" unnecessary. Of course, his peculiar hat—a flat blacky, as Winnie had called it—aided in identifying him. But Carla thought she could've spotted him by his square shoulders and rugged face. Winnie hadn't mentioned those.

What Winnie had told Carla was that Federation guards in Denver had begun to suspect Jack as a possible Pink spy, rather than the Federation man he pretended to be. In fact, had Jack stayed in Denver, he might've been hurt badly. Or even killed. In Boise, any doubts about Jack being a Pinkerton had been erased. He'd been seen close with the Pinkertons, even examining Governor Steunenberg's yard with Chief Detective McParland. Now, under the new plan that Carla was making happen, Jack would be recruited as a double agent, just as the loner Wade had been. Jack the Pinkerton would be helping the Federation, not spying on it.

First, she wanted to test Jack, to toy with him, to tease him, to learn what she could. Thus, two days earlier, she had crossed Main Street from the Saratoga and flirted with him, let him chase after her—even planted the idea that she was someone he could count on, that she wanted to help him. She figured that once she received the telephone call telling her to give up Orchard, she would have the perfect person to take her inside Pinkerton operations. The added benefit was that Jack would be grateful to her; and thus, perhaps, he'd be open to recruitment. Or so went her plan. But she hadn't counted on the tingling flush she felt when she was near Jack, as she was at that moment, standing at McParland's table, waiting as Jack pulled her chair.

"Miss Capone," Jack began, "is a waitress at the Saratoga."

"Of course," said McParland. "How do you like it there?"

"They're decent to me," Carla replied, sitting.

Jack took his seat. "She has a report about a man there who—"

McParland raised a finger. "If you will, let her tell me."

"Oh, I'm not sure it was anything," she said, her voice prim.

"Don't be nervous, dear," said McParland. "Just tell me what you told Agent Garrett—whatever got him to bring you up here."

Jack remained quiet, watching.

"This is quite new to me," she began. "What with the awful murder of— And the crowds and armed men."

"Aye," offered McParland. "It can be a bit overwhelming."

Carla gave a contrite smile—theatrics sold by it being expected. "There's a man who— I'm not sure, of course, but he might be someone ... you know ... involved."

McParland silently counted to four. "All right. Who is he?"

"Mr. Orchard. A guest at the Saratoga for some time."

"How long?"

"Oh, I don't know. Well before Christmas." She paused for another question, but, getting none, she continued, "He's been behaving queerly. Especially the night of the murder."

"How so?"

"With the poor governor, as you know ... well, everyone has been most upset. We felt the explosion all the way from Caldwell. Then, when it was learned what had happened, people in the Saratoga were crying and the like. But this man came in that evening full of lightness. You might say, happy."

"Is he usually happy? Is that the kind of man he is?"

"He's a sheep seller. I don't know if that'd make him so."

"Some sheep sellers are happy, I think," McParland said, drawing a wide-eyed shrug from her. "How do you know his profession?"

"He told me. He's often sought my company."

McParland looked at Jack. "Can't fault the man for that."

"No. I'd expect—" began Jack.

"Did he speak about the bombing?" McParland continued.

"No, Sir. But he gave the image of a man who—I'm sorry to say—seemed pleased it had happened."

McParland let silence come, then asked, "Orchard, you say?"

"Yes, Sir."

"Thank you, Miss Capone." He sat back and considered her, watching her eyes flit to Jack, then back to him. "Do you know what room he's staying in?"

"Three-twelve," she replied.

With the pick-lock keys failing him, Pinkerton operative and Federation spy, Wade Farrington, was frustrated. He had to kill the man inside room 312 before Carla's tip drew McParland there. That was his order, relayed from, he assumed, Mr. Haywood. He was to kill the governor's assassin, and he had to do it right then. Running out of time, he stepped back and considered booting open the hotel room's door. He pocketed the keys and again drew his pistol. Then he noticed the snoring had stopped. Might the killer have awakened, heard the lock attempts, and prepared himself with a sawed-off 10-gauge? Farrington tried to ease his shuddering gun hand. Perhaps the man had already fled through his window, leaving a bomb to be triggered by the opening of the door. Farrington would be dead before he knew what happened. He eased forward and placed his ear to the door. Nothing. Just then, another guest opened a different door to the hall, causing Farrington to jump, hide his pistol, and make for the stairwell.

McParland hurried into the Saratoga with Jack and three other Pinkertons trailing closely. The four in tow carried shotguns. Passing the passenger elevator, McParland considered the baggage elevator but instead headed to the internal stairwell and began walking up. On the second-floor landing, the posse going up met Farrington coming down.

"What are you doing here?" inquired McParland in a hushed voice. He noted Farrington's face flashing disappointment upon seeing them.

"I was here," stuttered Farrington, blanching noticeably. "Followed someone here, up here. He seemed suspicious."

"Who?"

"Not sure, but you don't—"

"Where? Where is he?"

Farrington skipped a beat, then said, "Room three-twelve."

McParland's chin cocked to one side. "You don't say. We're here for the same man. Why are you coming down?"

"He went in his room, and I thought—"

"Is he armed?"

"I don't know."

"Are you?"

"Yes, Sir."

McParland moved by. "Good. Come with us."

"Yes, Sir," muttered Farrington, turning around.

Jack studied Farrington. Something didn't feel right.

At room 312, Farrington moved up to advise caution. But before he could, McParland motioned him to kick open the door.

Farrington pointed at himself, as if to ask, Me?

McParland nodded.

"Maybe we should knock first," Farrington whispered, only to get a grizzled glare from behind the detective's round glasses. The other men were preparing to rush in. Farrington stood for a moment while the imagined threats within the room flooded his mind. He inhaled, blew it through pursed lips, and then, with one explosive kick, burst open the door. But there was no booby-trapped explosion. No shotgun blast from within.

McParland entered promptly, led by his Colt .45 revolver which he pointed at the instantly awake Harry Orchard, cowering on the far side of the bed, having leapt there upon the door flying wide. Farrington entered next, pistol in hand, followed by Jack with a shotgun. The other three remained in the doorway and hall.

"Mr. Orchard?" McParland asked.

"Yes. No," squeaked Orchard, still hiding.

"Get yourself dressed, Mr. Orchard," snapped McParland.

Muttering under his breath, Orchard stood and complied.

McParland surveyed the room, honing in on a small, brown glass bottle in a corner. He picked it up, flinched from the smell of it, and handed it to Jack who likewise sniffed and winced.

"Sulfuric acid," McParland said as he used his foot to open a carpenter's bag beside the bottle. He froze. A low growl of "hmmm" came from behind the mustache. Leaning over, he reached into the bag and withdrew a roll of fishing line. "I was right. Fishing line." He looked at Orchard. "It's more reliable in the snow than string. Isn't that right?"

"Snow? I fish with it."

McParland nodded vaguely. "You came to Boise, mid-winter, to go fishing, did ya? You don't look the sort. Not to me you don't."

"I'm a sheep man in commerce. And I fish. I was tying flies."

"No, Mr. Orchard, I don't think any of that's true."

"It is."

"No. I'll tell you what it *is*—it's incongruous," said McParland. "Do you know that word? Incongruous?" Orchard looked down. "Means out of place. Something that just doesn't fit."

Jack picked up a flyer from the windowsill. "Federation," he said, handing it to McParland.

McParland read a line from it aloud: "'*Soulless corporations located in a foreign state who treat workers like machines*.' Bunch of socialist horseshit, Mr. Orchard." He then tossed Jack a set of handcuffs. "You found the man, you cuff him."

"Yes, Sir," Jack said, beaming on the inside, firm on the out.

McParland was at the washstand, examining the sticky powder that appeared to have been spilled behind the basin. He smoothed a finger through it, sniffed it, ground it between his thumb and middle finger. "Plaster of Paris."

"That ain't—" protested Orchard. "I didn't put that there."

"This is your room, is it not?"

"Yeah."

"Why is plaster of Paris in your room? More incongruity, Mr. Orchard. So you're a sculptor t'boot? Besides being a fishing sheep shagger, of course."

"Dice," implored Orchard. "I made a pair of loaded dice."

McParland tilted his head back as if encountering a bad smell. "Loaded dice, ya say?"

"Yeah."

"Weighted?"

"Yeah."

"Where are they, these dice? Let's have a look at em."

"I gave em— They took em from me."

"Oh, they did, did they?"

"Yeah. Cheatin bastards."

"Cheatin bastards," McParland said loudly. "Yes, that's what they are. I hate cheatin bastards."

"I hate em too."

"I bet you do," said McParland, turning around. "Plaster, acid, fishing line, all right here. You made the bomb right here, right in this room, didn't you?"

"No," said Orchard.

"A little nanty-narking, cheating at craps on your way to fish?"

"No. I mean, yes."

"That's enough. No need to lie about the acid. I'm sure you've got some excuse. What's your given name, Mr. Orchard?"

Orchard shrugged, looking away.

"Come now. I think it's Harry. I've heard of a Harry Orchard, henchman for the Federation. But I thought he was just a rumor. A myth—bigger than life. I didn't realize he was a snively little liar. Guess I should've, though. It's Harry, right? No, now, your real name is Albert Horsley. Isn't that so?"

Orchard's mouth gaped slightly, already answering the question before it produced words. "Might be," he said.

"But you prefer Harry Orchard?"

Orchard nodded.

"In that case, Mr. Orchard ..." McParland counted to four silently before finishing, "I arrest you for the assassination of Governor Steunenberg."

"That ain't right," said Orchard.

"No, it most certainly *ain't*," said McParland. He picked up Orchard's brown coat, the one with the bullet hole in the back, and placed it around the man's shoulders. "State pen's a might cold."

"Then give me my bear one," exclaimed Orchard.

"No, that one will do."

"I want—"

"Shit in one hand, wish in the other, Mr. Orchard. See which one fills up first." McParland smirked. "No, I don't want you entirely comfortable." He paused, looking at the bear coat, remembering the governor's wife and daughter said the pretend salesman was wearing a long fur coat. This must be the one. He would leave it with the man—let him wear it—see who else recognized it. "Then again, we don't want you freezing to death before we get to hang you." McParland motioned with his hand, and Farrington put the larger coat over Orchard's shoulders. McParland then picked up Orchard's dirty bowler hat to place it on the man's round head.

"No, just leave that," said Orchard, as if afraid of the thing. "I don't want it. It's not mine. There's lice in it."

McParland stopped. "This isn't your hat?"

"No."

"Looks like it's yours," he said, turning it over to look inside.

"No. I found it, but it don't fit me now."

"Now? All of a sudden? It is a bit worn," mused McParland, considering the grime on it. Then he set it down. He looked at Farrington. "Collect all this and bring it to my office."

"The hat too?" asked Farrington.

"Aye."

As Farrington and another agent gathered the items, McParland observed Orchard's eyes skittering back to the bowler. Then, noticing Jack was observing the same thing, the chief gave a faint snort of approval. "You should be pleased with yourself, Agent Garrett. This was good."

★

– 20 –

TUESDAY
January 15, 1907

"Goddamnit!" shouted Haywood. He stood in his Denver office the next morning, one of his men standing before him—the one who had just delivered the telegraph sparking this torrent. "Go up and get Winnie. Get her down here."

"Now, Sir?"

"Yes, now. And find Mr. Darrow. He's back from Chicago, I think." Haywood glanced at the tall clock. "Tell him to be here in an hour, at eleven. But Winnie, get her now."

"Sir," replied the man, already halfway gone.

Fifteen minutes later, Winnie entered to see Haywood's broad back as he stared out the window. "Darling," she said, gliding in under a rushed-up pompadour, wearing a dark-pink skirt and a white taffeta-silk waistshirt. "What's the rush?"

"That girl, your friend, she failed us."

"Oh no." Winnie moved closer. "Was Carla found out?"

"No," Haywood muttered, "but it didn't go as I instructed."

She slowly slid an arm around him, resting her head on his back. "I'm sorry."

He moved away. "You said she's reliable, that she'd see it done."

Using her tone of disarmament, she asked, "What's the big trouble, Bear?"

"The man's been arrested! Alive! Goddamnit!"

"What man?"

"Harry Orchard. The one that—"

"Who arrested him?"

"Scum Pinkerton—McParland. Should've killed him here in Denver." His chin fell. "It's all shit now. I'll hang. My God, they're going to kill me, Win."

"Nonsense," she tried. She hated outbursts of weakness from him. That wasn't their arrangement. She was in this for her sister, and for herself. His part was to be Big Bill Haywood, providing them protection, power, and a future without want. Not that her love for him wasn't sincere—it was, she believed—but in this moment, she wasn't acting on it. Rather, she needed to enclose his bad spirits, manage him to an easier mind before Neva (who was in the suites above them) heard him shouting through the floor. If Neva became anxious again, severely anxious, well ... Winnie would not let that happen. "I'm sure you'll find a way through this. You always do." She kissed his neck.

"I don't know."

"Orchard can still be reached, I would imagine. Isn't that so?"

Haywood shook his head. "They've got him in the Idaho State Penitentiary. Not some county jailhouse."

Winnie poured two whiskeys from the glass decanter and handed him one. "You said Carla failed. How? Did she place the things in his room? The plaster I sent her?"

"Yes. I believe so." Haywood groused, taking his glass to the tufted blue settee.

Winnie moved to a chair. "And she alerted the Pinks?"

"Yes."

"But they arrested him?"

"Our man didn't get him. The one she recruited, Farrington. Maybe he wasn't with us after all. If that's the case, then—"

"Then he needs—"

"You go. You can get into that prison. No one knows you there."

"Detective McParland knows me."

"Don't call him that!" Haywood burst. "He's a pulp copper at best. A traitor against the Irish, *his* people. Against everyone."

She slid from her chair to kneel between his legs, laying one cheek on his thigh, the loose bits of her golden hair across his lap, her hand sliding up. "Let's—"

"No," he huffed, moving her hand. "Get up."

She did. Though she felt blistered by the rejection, she didn't allow a clue of it in her eyes. Instead, she returned to her chair, positioning herself on the leading edge so she could still touch his knee. "What can I do?" she cooed.

"I don't need a poke, Win. I need a dead man in Boise."

"Let's start with this, and go from there."

When Clarence Darrow arrived, Haywood's walnut clock struck eleven and Winnie had just left, leaving behind a heady waft of lilac perfume and a big man remarkably calmer. Haywood passed the telegraph to Darrow and watched the lawyer examine it. He knew Darrow didn't just ingest the words, didn't just absorb the implications of the message—Darrow was processing chess moves far ahead. Nothing could surprise this short, solemn man, this orator second only to Shakespeare—had Shakespeare given closing arguments. Of all the trophies Haywood had collected, few compared to having the famed attorney, Clarence Darrow, as his personal counsel. In fact, pressed to rank his most prized treasures, he would begin with the admiration of his men, then having Darrow, then Winnie, and then the Packard. Maybe the Packard, and then Winnie. Oh, and of course Neva and the children would be up there too, somewhere. The Federation had a flotilla of attorneys—multiples in all the western mining states—but there was only one Clarence Darrow. Haywood recalled joking that he wished, just once, to be tried for something awful so he could hear Clarence Darrow give a closing argument in his defense—to hear the man speak about him, to praise him with the eloquence of the gods. What a thing that would be. It might happen now, Haywood thought gloomily, awaiting Darrow's response to the telegraph.

"Don't worry yourself," said Darrow, pocketing the paper.

"Don't worry?"

"I wouldn't."

"You wouldn't?"

"No, I wouldn't." Darrow poured himself a drink.

Haywood laughed. "My attorney, who doesn't drink, says—"

Darrow shrugged a refutation. "I've returned to her of late."

"My attorney who *rarely* drinks, whose counsel is to not worry about being hanged—is having a scotch at a quarter past eleven."

Darrow took a drink and set the glass down. "That's correct."

Haywood blew a deep sigh. "Very well. Tell me. A witness— No, not just a witness, the murderer himself— The man I ordered—"

Darrow raised a hand. "Bill, I don't want—"

"You're going to hear it this time, Counselor. It's all privileged."

"Enhh—probably."

"Hell's pisser," exclaimed Haywood. "Probably privileged?"

"It's moderately clear, yes. Concerning what you tell me. But, Bill, don't tell me about anything you might yet do. What might be coming."

"What's the difference?"

"Old Annesley case. Long time ago. Irish, but—" Darrow waved a hand in surrender. "Fine, say what you're going to say."

Haywood grimaced.

"Go ahead," said Darrow. "I'd never repeat anything anyway."

"Orchard's a dull lamp," Haywood began, "but at least he's skilled with explosives."

Darrow held his eyes closed for a moment. "I understand."

"Now McParland will get him singing, and—"

"Ok, so they have him in custody," Darrow interjected. "Now they'll appoint a special prosecutor."

Haywood nodded. "Senator Borah."

"I know him," sniffed Darrow. "He's, well, he's—"

"Formidable?"

"Perhaps. Newly elected Republican senator of that same state. Good on his feet. Good orator. Could be convincing."

Haywood rubbed his head. "But I shouldn't worry?"

"I never underestimate an opponent. Neither do you."

"Uh-huh."

"Do you think Orchard will give a confession?" asked Darrow.

"I don't know. What do you think?"

"I don't know the man."

Haywood shook his head. "I don't either. Not really."

"Detective McParland will put the man to a painful endurance."

"Not detective."

"What?"

"McParland is no detective," said Haywood.

"A rose by another name," said Darrow.

Haywood looked away, grousing, "A dead rose."

"Bill, now you stop right there. This is not—"

"I know. I know."

"I need your word."

"Fine. Right. He won't be touched."

Darrow studied Haywood for a moment, then continued, "It's best we plan on Orchard breaking. What does he know?"

"My God, Clarence. What does that man *not* know?"

"Any evidence? Is he good at covering his tracks?"

"Thought so," said Haywood. "I wouldn't have tasked him—"

"Wait, wait." Darrow flapped a hand in the air. "His name is Orchard?" He saw Haywood's cautious nod. "How did he receive his orders? Your read-and-burn method? On your paper?" He pointed to the blank, creamy paper on Haywood's desk.

"Yeah. Burned it there." Haywood pointed to the ashtray holding three crunched cigar stubs in a dune of ash.

"Anyone here at the time, other than you two?"

"No." Haywood prickled at feeling on Darrow's witness stand.

"And you're sure he burned it?"

"Now, goddamnit Clarence, it was well executed."

"I'm trying to keep *you* from being well executed," Darrow replied, parrying and riposting in one move. "What might McParland know?"

"I wanted it clear: Orchard was the one and only one—"

"But not able to talk," Darrow grumbled. "Now they have him."

"Now they have him."

"Why does McParland think Orchard's the right man?"

"Some bomb-making things—bottle of acid, plaster—were in his room."

"Anything that might tie those things to the Federation?"

"No. Nothing. She said nothing WFM was there."

"She?"

Haywood took a breath. "One of our people there in Boise. She planted the things and put McParland onto Orchard's trail. But, one of our *other* people failed to silence Orchard before ... before McParland got Orchard. So, here we are."

"Alright," whispered Darrow. "Who was it? The one who put the things in his room and told McParland? I'll need to know."

"Carla Capone."

"Miss Capone? You have her involved in this? My secretary?"

"Your last one, yes. I have my people do a number of things."

"Alright," Darrow said in half resignation. "Carla. Hmmm."

"Why the ponder? What about her?"

"Just a coincidence, I suppose. I hope. Did she tell you about seeing Orchard in an alley here?"

"No."

"I told her to tell you."

"What was he doing?"

"As I recall, she saw him not long before she left. Last fall. He was putting a note in his hat brim." Darrow pointed at the small stack of yellowish paper on Haywood's desk. "Same as that."

"Last fall?"

"Yes."

Haywood stared at the floor, shaking his head. "Goddamnit."

"Not sure they can use it," said Darrow. "Can't prove handwriting. But if it's still there and McParland hasn't found it—"

"I'll get Farrington to look into it."

Darrow tried to buck up his client. "No good worrying much."

"There you go again, saying that."

"Yes, for a few reasons. First, and this is the most important, Idaho cannot come get you here and take you there. They can't extradite you from Colorado without evidence that you were in Idaho at the time of the ... event. That's first and foremost."

Haywood sucked his bottom lip. "Can't they try me here?"

"No, they cannot try you here for a crime that occurred there."

"I wasn't in Idaho. I haven't been there since I was fifteen or so. No, I was there about ninety-eight, briefly, but not recently."

"Good. Stay put here in Colorado for a good stretch."

"I will. And the other reason I shouldn't worry?"

"I don't think we need an additional ace in our hand, but we've got one," Darrow said. "Let's make the assumption they get you there. Not a valid assumption, but let's make it. And then let's assume they put you on trial—"

"Alright, but—"

"In a conspiracy case, as this would be, Idaho statutes require more than one corroborating witness in order to reach a death-penalty verdict. It takes two to hang one, so they say."

"So even if Orchard talks, he'll be only one witness."

"That's right," said Darrow.

"But that's only as good as whatever judge they put on this," said Haywood. "He might not care about the law. Might say one witness is enough."

"That's not going to happen. But, say it did, then the appellate courts would step in."

"Good."

Darrow leaned forward. "It does beg the next question though: Could there be a second witness?"

"No. He worked alone."

Darrow twitched again, hearing his client speak so candidly of orchestrating the killing. It was as if Bill had merely sent the man to the coop for eggs.

Haywood continued, "But what if a second man makes up some story—says he was in the room here with Orchard, or some shit?"

Darrow shook his head. "That'd be hearsay, Bill. Keep your boots on the ground. Stay in Colorado. Stay in Denver. Don't get anywhere near a border. I know how much you like that Oldsmobile," he added.

"Packard! It's not a goddamned tin-bucket Oldsmobile!"

"My apologies—Packard." Darrow knew the make of Haywood's automobile, but he needed to jolt a change of subject—he needed a gulp of cleaner air.

"Told you before, those Oldsmobiles—four-wheeled bicycles—are no better than Wintons."

"Wasn't a Winton the first to drive the continent?"

"Clarence, you son of a bitch," Haywood sneered. "You're just trying to get my goat." He walked to a corner containing a number of rifles and shotguns. "A Winton, by God—is that what you have?"

"No automobile for me. What need would I have for such a machine? You have me on the train half my life. I need to walk in-between—keep my blood going."

Haywood picked up the rifle he'd been given in Park City and brought it to Darrow, who stood and took it. "Have you seen one of these?" asked Haywood.

"Army?"

"Yes, Springfield Armory. M1903. A beautiful weapon. Locals gave it to me." Haywood took it back, rocked open the bolt action, then slammed it closed. A sharp, metallic clink filled the room.

Then he pointed it toward the window, as if aiming at the building beyond. "I have a fella figuring how to attach a scope to it. Then, in the right hands ... Get Orchard in the street, and ..."

Darrow pulled in a deep breath. "I need to be getting back."

Something else had come to Haywood's mind. He hurried to his desk, laying the Springfield there, and pulled open one of the drawers. From within, he extracted the small FM automatic pistol that he'd been "given" by Captain Swain. "And look at this!" He handed it to Darrow. "Look at that. An automatic pistol. Have you ever ... Look here." He took the pistol back, hurried to the window and raised the sash, filling the room with a gust of winter air. "The bullets go here, and ..." He rocked open the slide. "And move up here." He released the slide and fired four times in quick succession out the window and over the roof of the building across Fifteenth Street.

Darrow jumped at the bangs. "Don't! Bill, that's—"

"I was awarded it last week. It's a fine thing. Made in Belgium. Federation chapter down in Castle Rock awarded it to me."

"Jesus, Bill," said Darrow. "Close that window, will you?"

★

– 21 –

WEDNESDAY
January 16, 1907

The next day, George was at his modest desk in his office at the Federation headquarters, thirty feet down the hall from Haywood's office. Neva was in her invalid chair, nearby.

"Winnie told me," said Neva.

"What did she say?" asked George.

Neva glanced toward the outer office before whispering across the desk. "That he's worried. A man named Orchard, I think, killed the governor of ... what, Wyoming?"

"Idaho," George said softly.

"Oh yes, it was near Boise."

"Yes."

She sighed and adjusted her gray Chesterfield jacket. It was too long for easy wear in her chair. "Bill's worried. I'm not sure why, though I might guess."

"Well, for one thing ..." George watched someone pass his door, then glanced out his window to the bright day. "I need some sun. City Park?"

Neva's eyes shined. "Definitely."

He donned his coat and hat and began pushing her chair the short distance to the elevator. On the way, they passed two secretaries. "I'm taking Mrs. Haywood to the park," he said to one. "I'll be back in an hour or so."

"All right, Mr. Pennington," she replied.

George whispered to Neva, "Let's take the tram."

"You'll help me get on?" Neva asked.

"The elevator car? Of course. Here, I'll hold this feather-ball you call a hat." He pressed the down button. "But for the tram, I've got a lasso."

"Lasso?" she asked.

The car arrived, and the operator, a lanky, elderly black man in tan livery, opened the door and clanged the cage wide. George rolled Neva in. “Yes, I’m going to tie you to the tram. Let it pull you. Much easier for me.”

She laughed. “Oh no.”

“You’ll enjoy it,” he said. “Ground please, Lester.”

Neva smiled up at George. “You’ll enjoy watching it drag me.”

“That’s true.”

Moments later, they were aboard a streetcar—she in a seat, him standing. The invalid chair was in the aisle beside her. She glanced up. He was wearing the round-top homburg hat and midnight-blue jacket that she liked. He was not an objectively handsome man: thin face, narrow brown eyes, no mustache, considerable balding. But to her, he was fine. And in that hat and jacket, he was dapper. They passed St. Luke’s Hospital and Unity Church, and then switched to the Route 20 trolley at Trinity Methodist Church, passing the Central Presbyterian Church and St. Joseph’s Hospital before disembarking at Mercy Hospital. They crossed Seventeenth Street and entered City Park. As it was a chilly January day, few others were out walking, and only an occasional bicyclist rattled by. For the most part, they had the walking paths to themselves.

“Should we go see Mr. Bryan?” she asked.

“Ol’ Billy Bryan is hibernating, don’t you think?”

“Yes, probably. Do bears hibernate in a cage? In a zoo?”

“I’m not sure,” George replied as he managed her over an icy patch. “Let’s see how the museum’s coming along.”

“All right,” she said.

He pushed her quietly, the wheels growling over the brick walk. They needed to talk. They would talk. But for the moment, this was all. It was enough.

Pulling a deep breath, she felt the chilly air charge her lungs. On the exhale, her breath fogged white about her face like a gossamer wedding veil. She smiled, listening to the birds, spotting a few quarreling blue jays. This was peace: George close behind, his breathing, the way he lifted her scarf against the breeze, his funny little remarks about the squirrels venturing near, him teasing them.

When they rounded the partially frozen Ferril Lake, with its brigade of Canada geese, a granite building stood ahead, partially covered in scaffolding. The barricade fence bore a sign:

Grand Opening 1908
COLORADO MUSEUM OF NATURAL HISTORY

"Looks the same as last time we were here," she observed. "Weather's held them back, I guess."

"I'm sure you're right," said George, rolling her toward a bench. There he sat and pulled her chair close.

She saw something bubbling within him. "Is Bill in trouble?"

"I think so."

"The thing in Boise?"

George shook his head. "No. I don't know. Maybe. We'll see about that. But right now it's the money. The missing money."

"From the Federation?"

"Yes."

"How much?"

He regarded her, biting his lip. "At first I thought it was different, something less. But it's about sixty thousand dollars."

"Sixty thousand dollars! You must be joking."

"I'm not. I wouldn't. Not about this."

"What's going to happen? Who knows about this?"

"Not many. Just me ... and two others. I think."

"How could he have taken sixty thousand dollars?"

"It's ... uhmm ... yeah."

"Where would he put it?"

"It's not in cash, but in the value of things."

She noted his questioning eyes. "No!"

He nodded. "Your Park Hill home, I'm thinking. And his motorcar. Among other items, other expenses."

"My house?"

"The Federation pays for the suites downtown. It's part of his salary. But the house ... I'm not sure. And like I said, there's the Packard, or whatever it is. And there must've been a thousand dollars spent on dresses and jewelry for Winnie, just last year."

Neva shook her head. "The president is entitled—"

"No, dear. He's entitled to his salary. And the Federation pays his expenses, for travel and such. But our money comes from our members, mostly miners. They pay my wage just as they pay his. I'm responsible to them, our members, first—before Bill."

"I'm sure you'll figure this out, and he'll give it back, if he took it. Maybe someone else did. Have you thought of that?"

"Yes. I've been working on this for months. We know the Pinkertons have infiltrated us, at places, confounded our funds some. But not this. Not like this."

"The Pinkertons," she said with a grimace. "Don't put it past that evil McParland man to do something like this."

"I don't." His squint and tone sharpened. "I'm good at what I do. You know that, don't you?"

She stared across the park.

"Nev?"

"Yes ... of course, dear. It's just a big bite to swallow."

"Was I wrong to tell you?"

"Of course not," she said, still distant. "Thank you."

"I won't take the blame for this."

"What?" She considered him. "Why would you? You dear man, who'd think—" She studied his eyes. "Bill?"

"If this gets caught in the wind— If it gets away from me— If the members find out— It could be bad. Very bad. And we both know Bill won't say 'My apologies fellas, here's your money back.'"

"He'll blame the Pinks. Where the blame probably should be."

"He'll blame *me*, Nev. He'll blame me."

Her eyes glassed. "I would never let that happen. Not to you."

"You couldn't prevent it."

"I'd tell. I'd tell everyone."

"It would appear as you protecting me, not him, which would ”

"I would be!"

"—which would lead to a scandal about ... a number of things. We wouldn't want that."

"Hell's bells, George. This is really terrible."

"I know."

"What *can* we do?"

"The truth will set you free, but ... with Bill, maybe not."

"I'd kill him. I truly think I would. His dung—sorry, but that's what it is—shouldn't get put on you."

"I'm probably already covered in it. I just don't know it yet."

Detective McParland was correct: the Idaho State Penitentiary, a little over a mile southeast of the capital building, was so cold it had teeth. It was also noisy—its stone and steel ossature capturing the shouts, cries, bellows, and loud ramblings of the over three hundred inmates—garbling them, then bawling them back in some mashed-up roar of human despair, timorous bravado that flooded the hallways, reverberating among the phalanxed tiers of cells, pushing out across the courtyards only to echo back again. Perhaps noisiest was death row, the third tier of the cellhouse closest to the administration building and adjacent to the hanging yard. It was inhabited by seven men awaiting execution—plus one more, the only one who'd yet to be convicted, or even tried: Harry Orchard.

McParland had selected that particular death row cell for Orchard, replacing the two wood bunkbeds with a chair and one narrow steel bed. He left the plumbing as it was: a bucket. Though he claimed he did it for the prisoner's protection, it was quite the opposite. Through the grated door, beyond an eight-foot gap of open air, was a high window giving Orchard not only a view of the gallows, but of the nearby hills beyond. Thus far, the intimidation of the gallows had failed. Orchard had maintained his story of selling sheep, winter fishing, and cheating with dice.

"Look here, ol boy, I've made my own set of loaded dice," said McParland, his voice rolling in and out of his Irish brogue. He was sitting in the chair in Orchard's cell, his hat perched atop his cane that leaned against the steel-latticed door. "Want to see em?"

Orchard sat motionless on the bed, bear coat draping his shoulders, a week's growth of beard under his sunken eyes. "No."

"Come, Harry, ya said ya've got a pair. Though, so far, I've reason to doubt it." McParland's mustache curled at his own humor. Seeing it was lost on Orchard, he continued, "You make loaded dice. Ya say you do. I wonder if you think my men can make a set as good as yours." McParland pulled two dice from his vest pocket and presented them to Orchard. "They made these."

Orchard ignored the dice but grumbled, "Why do you got me in this cell? I ain't done nothing. We could talk downstairs at least."

"I assure you, I hate the stink of this place worse than you," said McParland, squinting, pulling his face away as if the stench had assumed a looming, visible form. "But I'm too concerned for your safety to move you. You should be as well. You may be mad, but you're not stupid. Once Haywood learns I have you ... Wooo, what that man will do. He already knows you're here, I'd wager."

Orchard looked away. "Don't know the man to see him."

McParland silently counted to four, then again offered his prisoner the dice. "My man any good?"

Orchard took them, assessed them swiftly, and handed them back. "They're hinky. They'd be spotted."

"Spotted?" McParland chuckled, noting the dots on the dice.

"First toss, they'd be seen for what they are."

"Ya might have me there. Some things are *just* what they seem, and nothing more." He held the dice in one hand, letting them clink dully against each other. With the other hand he smoothed his mustache while looking directly into Orchard's eyes. "But see there, Mr. Orchard, ya're not as stupid as you'd have me believe. You can spot a bad effort to cheat. Same as I can spot a liar—someone set on hiding the truth. To obfuscate, as it were."

"Don't know bout that."

"Aye, but ya do."

"Those dice ain't been cast right—'sall I'm sayin."

"Nah, you've been *sayin* plenty. Except so far, it's all been a sack of shite-n-lies. You're no better than these dice." McParland considered them, his temper rising. "Godforsaken liar."

"Ain't lying—ones I make are better. Get me the makings, I'll show you."

When McParland spoke again, it began as a whisper and grew. "Not one damned word from your bloody mouth carries even the ring of truth. Not one word. You're lying about making dice. You're lying about who you are. Lying about what you did. You're an assassin! You were hired by William Haywood to come up here and murder the governor—to blow him up. You'll lie for Haywood, but why you'd die for him, I don't know. He's the devil. He's a demon from the pages of Revelations, and I think you know it. No, I *know* you know it. In fact, you probably know it better than I do. I've spent three years in Denver, tracking that son of a bitch. And, aye,

I've seen you there many times in that span. I know him. I know what he's capable of, and so do you." McParland took to gesturing with his cane, sometimes poking it toward the prisoner.

"Leave me be," muttered Orchard.

"I know who you are, Mr. Orchard. You're a man at least ... I think. I want to believe so, I do. But I don't know. Time will tell. But I do know William Haywood is a demon walking the face of this earth. He needs to be removed from this world, shot down like a diseased dog. And yet you sit in here, in this fetid cell, day after day, playing the fool—lying for him!"

"No, I ain't."

McParland stood, his gaze on Orchard, his mind sharpening, honing, preparing to debone the man. "You're in here, speaking nonsense, while he has men in this town, perhaps already in this prison, who'd cut your throat fast as wish ya good morning. Yet you continue to lie for him. This farce. You sit here and lie. You know what you did. And you damn well know who ya did it for. You stalked Governor Steunenberg like a panther on a goat. You set your bomb. You had your man, Steve Adams, go talk to the governor. He wore this coat, for godsakes!" McParland jabbed at the bear coat around Orchard's shoulders.

"Ain't true."

"You had Adams go get Frank Steunenberg out of his house, out to that gate. Only the governor went out the back door, so you had to wait till nightfall. Or maybe you planned that too." McParland returned to the bench, sat, and let his volume settle. "But you got him, didn't ya? Aye, you earned Haywood's blood money. How much did he pay you? How much? You blew up that man in front of his children. Blew glass in the face of his wife. They were still picking it out a week after. And you watched him die, didn't you? You saw it all from those hedges sixty-six feet away. You yanked that fishing line, pulling the cork from that bottle of acid, and you saw him die. Then you ran. A coward. You ran off, leaving that man in pieces on his yard. His young children to see. And you did it for Haywood. Why, I ask you? In the perverted name of that damnable union? Some obligation I cannot fathom? Or did you do it just for the money? Or just for the special delight of seeing a man dismembered in a second"—he snapped his fingers—"by your own hand? Was that it?"

"Don't know what you're going on about."

McParland took a few breaths before summing up softly, "Whatever your reasons for the murder, you've no reason to protect Haywood now. You killed the governor. And you know it to be God's truth. Aye, I've grown weary of you, Sir."

"Fine! I'm weary of you!" Orchard erupted. "All you Pink bastards. But you can't make me be somebody I ain't. You can't make me say I did something I ain't done."

McParland continued to rattle the dice in his fist. "Yeah, these dice are liars too. And rotten liars at that—just like you. Made of nothing. Nothing! Only good for doing harm. They aren't just lying about what they are, like you are, but they do a shite job of it—like you do!" With that, McParland hurled the dice hard at Orchard's head. One hit the man in the face, ripping a small cut along his cheek bone. The other flew straight into the cell's stone wall where it exploded, fragments ricocheting through a plaster poof.

Orchard clasped his cheek, recoiling. "Jesus Christ, Detective!"

Alerted by the clatter, a guard appeared at the door. "Everything alright here, Sir?"

"Aye," replied McParland. He regarded a shard of the shattered dice near his right boot. Noticing the guard was still there, he added, "Leave us be." He picked up the piece, considered it, then touched it to his tongue.

"Damn you," said Orchard, wiping blood from his face with his dirty handkerchief.

McParland set the chip back on the floor, stood and ground it under his heel. Then he sat again and pinched the powder, thumb to middle finger, feeling its texture. He returned his gaze to Orchard. "If I was you, Harry, I'd tell me the truth right away," he said, his voice having returned to a solemn brogue. "Mr. Haywood's men are already here." He opened his plaster-dusted hand toward Orchard. "They gave ya up to me. Which means they made a mistake. They intended you to die before you could tell the truth. I know that now. So be assured, they're sore about this going haywire."

Orchard shook his head.

"Definitely," McParland continued. "So, if they were intent on killing you before ... well, they're certainly set on it now. Like I said, Haywood might already have a man in this prison. Maybe that guard out here. Maybe the one that comes with your dinner tonight. He might poison it. Or maybe they'll wait till we transfer you next. One thing's for certain, they're already here in Boise. I assure you." He then used his cane to point through the door toward the far window. "Maybe a marksman is taking a position on that hill—right now, as we speak."

"You don't know that," muttered Orchard.

McParland kept looking toward the hills. "It'd be a difficult shot, I agree." Turning back, he continued, "But it won't be difficult next time you're in the street. I'll tell you what, I'm going to transfer you, walk you over to the Ada County Jail, unless you tell me true. By God I will." He wiped at his nose and again smoothed his mustache. "But if you give me your confession, and tell me true? I'll have it written just as you say it, and you sign it. Then I'll keep you safe. But lie to me more—"

"You're full of shit," Orchard said softly.

"Am I? Alright, Mr. Orchard. How many blocks do you figure it is from here to the county jail? What do you think? And how many sharpshooters does Haywood already have in town? He just needs one." He held up a straight finger. "He just needs one."

Orchard remained silent.

"You think on it. I'll be back tomorrow, perhaps the next day, to walk you to the county jail. But if you wise up and want to talk before then, let a guard know. Deal?" Getting no answer, McParland donned his hat and left.

★

– 22 –

THURSDAY
January 17, 1907

That afternoon, Wade Farrington strolled up the steps of Boise's new Carnegie Public Library on Washington Street and pulled open the thick wood-and-glass doors. Inside, his steps resounded as he crossed the marble entrance, and then onto the wood floor to a central position where he could consider his surroundings. It was silent, save only a conversation drifting from a distant, unseen office. He moved further, past the unattended front desk, through shafts of sunlight slanting across books, by a number of wood tables surrounded by chairs under suspended electric lamps, and alongside bookshelves and oak filing cabinets. Seeing the broad stairwell, he progressed up to the second floor and down a corridor at the end of twenty-four tall rows of shelves, glancing down each row as he passed. At the end of the second-to-last row he stopped, turned, tipped his hat and grinned at the dark-haired splendor standing there, perusing a book from under a pheasant-quilled hat.

Carla responded with a smile that unleashed her dimples, their power devastating to the truly weaker sex. They moved toward each other, embraced, plunging into a boiling kiss that soon engulfed them. His hand slipped under her plaid frock coat, then down her back. She snorted a laugh when he began gathering her skirt, lifting in from behind. "You can't undress me here," she whispered playfully.

"Where can we go?" he breathed, his voice more air than tone. "A week is too long. Shame on you. I don't like being teased." He kissed her again, his tongue finding hers as he placed her hand against his trouser front, solid against her palm. "I need you—*now*," he insisted, pulling away to peer around the end of the shelves. Seeing it vacant, he returned to her.

"No one?" she asked.

He shook his head and they stood for a moment, hearing only the clops of hooves and the laughter of a child outside.

"I need to talk to you first," she said. "Mr. Haywood is upset."

"I know, I know. I didn't get Orchard before we—they—the Pinkertons got him," Farrington replied. "Tell Big Bill I did what he asked. I tried. But I ain't getting myself killed on account of nobody." He pulled her close. "Kiss me again and let's—"

"He wants you to do something else. He sent a rifle."

"A rifle?"

"Yes. Come by my room tonight."

"I'm to shoot Orchard?"

Carla blinked. "Something else. Mr. Orchard has a hat that—"

"All that can wait," he said. "This first, then I'll do whatever you need me to. Whatever he told you. Swear. I haven't been able to think about anything but you. Don't torment me longer."

She paused, sniffed a quick breath and considered him. "Ok," she said with a sigh, slipping to her knees. She carefully removed her plumed hat and placed it on a row of books within the shelves.

Seconds later, he was muttering, "Oh God," his eyes fluttering.

When Carla had him as she wished, she stood, turned and braced herself against the nearest shelf, pressing back against him. She needed this to be done with, regardless of how good it felt. He was too volatile. Too possessive. She couldn't trust him. But she needed him to do one more thing. Actually, two more things. Her heart wound up, her face heating. But then that other Pinkerton, Jack Garrett, came to her mind. Maybe she shouldn't do this. Maybe— She felt her skirt rise, her slip lift, her drawers fall, and cool air waft her rear.

Farrington's mind flooded. He could think of nothing else. No longer checking that anyone might discover them—he didn't care. Not thinking about the Pinkertons—he didn't care. Not a concern for selling his loyalty for this amazing body, this extraordinary girl. He saw her hat on the shelf. What did she say about Orchard's hat? Did she mean that bowler they found in Orchard's room? The one he'd been instructed to collect and bring to McParland's office? His mind shouted: *Don't think about that!*

Carla covered her mouth with the palm of one hand, her other against the shelves, bracing with each thrust. She felt his hands grasp her hips, his strong fingers digging in. Suddenly her outstretched hand slipped, shoving books through the shelf to where they crashed on the other side, tumbling her hat as well. She laughed. "Look what you made me do."

The commotion not only pulled them apart, but it returned his attention to her hat. "What was that you said?" he muttered. "About Orchard's hat?"

She sat on the floor, her back to the shelf, undergarments at her ankles, skirt scantly covering the rest. "So we're talking? *Now?*"

"No, but ..."

She smiled. "There's a piece of paper in the band. Get rid of it."

"The hat?"

"The paper. Or both if you want. But the paper is what I was told." She slipped her underdrawers from around one of her shoes and laid herself fully on the floor.

Detective McParland was in his office on the first floor of the Idanha Hotel, with Jack standing beside him. On the poplar-planked table before them were a few papers, the fishing line, the acid bottle, the WFM flyer found in Orchard's room, a small tin holding the plaster found there, the shard of plaster found at the bomb site, and a shard of the dice broken in Orchard's cell. Alongside those items: a map sketched on a large piece of butcher's paper showed Governor Steunenberg's house and street, the location of the bomb, where the fence and gate would've been, the path of the trigger line, and a stick-figure of a man standing on the far side of a row of poorly drawn hedges—the name Harry Orchard written beneath it. "This is all we have, Agent Garrett. What does it tell you?"

Jack had noticed the chief referring to him lately as Agent Garrett. Was it just a substitute moniker, or did it carry meaning? Only now, when they were alone in the chief's office, did it seem right to ask. "Not Twenty-One, Sir?"

"I can't risk you undercover. Besides, is there anyone left who doesn't know you're a Pinkerton?"

Jack squinted, unsure if that was an observation in his favor or against. "No, Sir," he replied, bracing himself.

"So get yourself out of those cowpoke duds. You're an agent."

"Aye, Sir," beamed Jack, exhaling.

"Go over to The Golden Rule. The department store just up Main. See Mr. Anderson there. He'll get you correctly togged."

"Yes, Sir."

"He'll charge the Pinkerton account." They heard a knock at the door, and McParland invited the person in—a hotel clerk who said, "Mr. McParland, there's a telephone call from a Reverend Sanders, at the front desk."

"Can he not call this one?" asked McParland, pointing to the wood telephone box on the wall.

"No, Sir. Some wiring has become fouled, crossed as I understand it. It's being worked on. Please accept our apologies."

"That's fine." Then to Jack: "I'll be back in a moment," and left.

Jack took a seat on a couch to wait but eventually grew restless and returned to the table to examine the map, then studied the few books and other items on McParland's shelves.

The door banged open and McParland quick-stepped to the table. "Where's his hat?"

"His hat?"

"Did you find Forty-Two—Agent Farrington?"

"Not yet," said Jack, disappointed that McParland referred to Forty-Two as an agent too. "We're looking for him."

"He brought all this," McParland groused, "but where's Orchard's hat? I want that damned hat."

"The one he said wasn't his?" Jack saw his boss's glance. "Yes of course, Orchard was lying about it."

"Aye. I knew it. I knew it. Mother Mary, I knew it. Certainly he was a lying. I wondered why he said it wasn't his. Thank the Lord we kept it, didn't leave it with him." McParland looked hurriedly about the room, then stopped. "But why didn't Farrington bring it over? Everything else is here."

"Maybe he left it—thought it wasn't Orchard's."

"Get it," barked the chief. "Find Agent Farrington and get it."

"Yes, Sir. If I may ask, what's important about it?"

McParland was calming now. "According to that reverend I just spoke with, Orchard had something hidden in it awhile back—

some note of paper. Something from Haywood. Any luck, it's still there, and whatever's on it is written in Haywood's hand."

"All right," said Jack, picking up his own hat.

McParland moved to the mantel to pack his pipe. He nodded at the table. "Before you go—what do all those things tell you?"

Jack stared at the items, but nothing came to mind that hadn't already been said. His thoughts were swimming about Orchard's hat. He had to focus. He revisited each item aloud. "The fishing line: he used it to pull a cork from a vial of this acid, detonating the bomb." He pointed to the nearly empty bottle that still reeked of sulfur. "A flyer from the WFM, connecting Orchard to them. This plaster chunk—a piece from what held the bomb together in the snow. And some plaster powder from his room."

McParland struck a match across the hearth and lit his pipe. Aromatic blue vapor enveloped the man. "That's just the surface of the story, son."

Jack's face lifted at hearing the chief's use of the word "son." What did that mean? *It means you need to figure this out, dummy*, he scolded himself.

"What's the new item there?" pressed McParland.

"This," said Jack, pointing at the additional plaster shard.

"Aye, a piece of the loaded dice we made. Compare the plasters."

Jack pinched some collected from Orchard's room.

"Taste them."

Jack put his tongue to the powdery room plaster, then the shard from the site, then the dice sliver. "They're not the same. Well, these two are," Jack said, pointing at the site shard and the dice sliver. "But the powder is more bitter, I guess."

"Correct."

"This one's plaster of Paris," Jack said, holding the bomb shard.

"They're all plaster of Paris, just two different kinds. We obtained ours from the mercantile here. It's construction plaster. The sort a bomb maker would use if he was familiar with mining—construction and dynamite. Same as we found at the site."

"And this?" Jack pointed to the powder collected from Orchard's room.

"That," McParland began as he touched the powder, "is a type of physician's plaster. It's used for setting bones. Feel how fine the grain is? It wouldn't work for bomb construction. Not very well. Different strengths and set times. Wouldn't work for dice either. Would fall apart."

Jack stared, his mind growling with informational digestion. "So he wasn't making dice ... but not a bomb either?"

"Not from that stuff." McParland shook his head. "When Orchard first saw the powder, when I pointed it out, he seemed surprised. Do you recall? And I think he was, truly. He knew he hadn't put there. A man will often reveal himself in the first instance of revelation."

Jack picked up the acid bottle. "Was this his?"

"Might be. Probably not. The fishing line was his. It was deep in his bag, and he gave no reaction when I brought it out. So, someone wants us to have no doubt it was Orchard. They spilled some plaster around the backside of his washbasin—only they used the wrong kind. Somewhere there is a half jar of surgeon's plaster. Somewhere in this town. I assure you."

"Then Orchard may not be our man, I mean, if—"

"Oh, he's our man, most certainly. The fact they wanted us to find him, to know it was him, only makes it more certain. They want us confident it was him. Why?"

Jack paused, then spoke the only thing that seemed to make sense. "So we'd stop looking."

"Exactly. I might make a detective of you yet. So we wouldn't look for anyone else. Maybe to give time for someone else to get away. But then they'd want to kill Orchard before he could talk to us. Before he was arrested."

"My ... All right," mumbled Jack.

"How do you know Miss Capone, the flower who brought us Orchard's name?"

"I don't know her. Not really."

"You were clearly taken by her charms. If I wasn't married, and was thirty years younger ... Regardless, I think we witnessed a bit of performance."

"She came to me, said she knew I was a Pinkerton," said Jack. "A couple days later, she came back, telling me about a suspicious man. So I brought her to you."

"She's one of Haywood's girls, I think."

"How do you know?"

"Get old as me, doing this," began McParland, "and some things will seem to magically appear—they reveal themselves to you. You'll just know." He tamped his pipe again. "Find out who she talks with, socializes and trades with—whose bed she's in."

"Yes, Sir," replied Jack. He turned and sneezed.

"Bless you. The smoke?"

"I don't think so. Perhaps the plaster dust."

"Just don't get sick, son. I need you."

"No, Sir, I won't." Jack beamed. "May I ask ... when I introduced her to you, you already knew her name—I think."

"That's good that you noticed. I'd heard her name before, just hadn't placed it with her face. A few months ago, our men saw her on a train out of Denver, coming here. She was stooging carrying a baby, but it was just a bundle of newspapers. They wired me about her, gave me her name, but I didn't think much on it—a girl not wishing the attention of men while traveling. That is, until you introduced her to me." He took another considered puff on his pipe. "If you can't see your missteps, then your enemy has you, and then ... Well then, you're no good to anyone. Especially when you're gathering information."

"I'll investigate her, Sir, but why would she tell me anything?"

"Because if I'm right, that she's with the Federation, then she'll try to turn you, make you a spy for Haywood."

"What?" Jack's heart raced at the insinuation.

"She flirted with you, got you to trust her—"

"I don't trust her," he snapped.

"She told you about Orchard, so you ushered her into the Idanha, direct to me. Right?"

"Yes, Sir, but—"

"You trusted her."

Jack looked at the floor. His future with the Pinkertons seemed to be swinging like a pendulum from one moment to the next.

"It's all right. In fact, it's good in this instance."

"Ok," muttered Jack, feeling his fate arc back again.

McParland continued, "She's setting her claws in you. So let her. She's coming for you. Mark my words. Next, she'll tell you how good the Federation is—how bad we are—how much she admires you. She may offer you her body."

"I'd never let—"

"Come now! Let's be honest men."

"I mean, I would never spy—"

"I know. That's precisely why you *will*."

"I will? I should?"

"Aye, I want you as a double, Jack. Outwardly, you're a Pinkerton. While to them, you're a Federation spy. But, in truth, you're a spy for me. And only me. Almost a triple agent. I was your age when I was a triple, inside the Molly Maguires. Did you know that?"

"Yes, Sir, I did. But how should I—"

"Just be yourself. You're a Pinkerton letting himself spy for Haywood. You won't give him any useful information, of course, and you'll tell me everything you learn."

"Of course, Sir."

"Most importantly, tell no one. No one. I'm your *only* contact in this. No one else. Carry on with your work as an agent—not an operative, as I said. No more 'Twenty-One.' Go see Mr. Anderson and get yourself dressed correctly."

"Yes, Sir."

"While you're at it, keep your eye on Agent Farrington."

"For Orchard's hat?"

"That too. See if he has it. Get it to me." McParland paused, took a deep breath, then clamped his pipe as he spoke. "But I'll wager it's long gone."

"Agent Farrington destroyed it?"

McParland was pacing. "If Haywood intended to kill Orchard before we could get there"—he removed the pipe and gestured with it—"then the man sent would've already been in the Saratoga when we were there. Or at least coming quick. Maybe someone on staff there, like Miss Capone."

"She doesn't strike me as the murdering sort, I wouldn't say," said Jack, choosing his words in ones and twos like deli selections.

McParland peered at Jack. "If you underestimate her, you may well lose your life. Don't do it." He shook his head. "No, her job was to tell us about Orchard, not to kill him. She was here at the Idanha when we ran to the Saratoga. Remember?"

"Yes, of course, Sir."

"But the one sent to kill Haywood, he—or *she*—might also have been on the Saratoga staff, or was a guest, or someone who just walked in. Someone out of place perhaps. So, who'd we find skulking down the stairwell that night?"

"Agent Farrington."

"Precisely. He said he'd found Orchard suspicious and followed him. But Orchard hadn't been out in a while. So, how had Farrington just followed him there? No, Farrington being there was too coincidental. And coincidences are fictions of the mind, Agent Garrett. Never accept them in the manner they present themselves. Don't be fooled into seeing them as simply curiosities or odd events. Anything that seems a coincidence should be an alarm in your ear, a foghorn in the night. Always."

"Aye, Sir," Jack said. "You first suspected him that night?"

"First? A few days ago, when he was in this office. But, yes, that night too. As did you."

Jack's brows lifted quickly. It was still an adjustment, realizing the chief apparently had mind-reading skills. It was like trying to grow accustomed to a talking dog—startling no matter how many times it says hello. "Yes," Jack said, "Something wasn't right about Forty-Two already being there."

"There was something awry, all right," said McParland. "Saw it in his eyes. Heard it between his words."

"Between—"

"Tune your ears to the spaces, son. A man will tell you more *between* his words, than with the words themselves. Listen to spaces and watch his eyes. Watch where a man looks between his sentences, when he thinks you aren't looking. Look then."

"Only a man?"

McParland gave a snorty laugh. "If you figure how to read women ... Well, then hell, enlighten us all, will ya?"

★

– 23 –

FRIDAY
February 8, 1907

After exiting the Southern Pacific's San Francisco depot on Townsend Street, Steve Adams walked a half block northwest along Third Street before halting and removing his earthy-green plaid cap, dumbfounded by what he saw. The city lay in ruins ten months after it had been crushed by an earthquake mother and then eaten by her fire spawn. As far as he could see ahead, and over to his right, and over to his left, was nothingness where once had been a growing American metropolis, a western gateway to the eastern world. Where blocks upon blocks of 28,000 buildings had stood, now was a hilly wasteland of brick and stone skeletons, the sooted bones of what few dead buildings remained. And between those ruins was scraped earth, latticed by dirty streets of wagons, cranes, and work crews moving toward and from huge mounds of debris, three stories tall in places, wagoning the refuse by type to the shoreline where it expanded the city that had once been. Adams resumed walking, and by the time he passed Brannon Street and approached Bryan Street, he had forgotten about the Pinkertons trailing him since Ogden.

But the two Pinkertons had equally forgotten about Adams, at least for the moment—both having fallen into slack-jawed stupor, disoriented by the unfathomably barren hills where 3,000 men, women, and children had so recently perished. They ambled apart, moving through the cluttered vacancy.

Adams turned at what appeared to have been an intersection of streets and entered a makeshift storage yard containing a knot of men, their baritone rumblings directed at a scene before them: three men attempting to start a massive, crawler-tracked steam tractor, its canopy bearing a sign:

HOLT'S CATERPILLAR

"What's it do?" Adams asked a spectator.

"Railed it in yesterday," came the reply.

"Over from Stockton," said another.

Adams frowned at it. "What's that belt around the wheels? That don't look proper."

"A track," added the first. "Rolls on it."

The second grinned. "Assuming old Holt can get her running."

Seeing a Pinkerton nearing, Adams tucked his short frame deeper into the throng, his mind snapping back to his mission: getting to the intersection of Franklin and Grove Streets to kill a man. After the Pinkerton passed, Adams sought directions, which in turn sparked a debate as to whether or not all the homes on Franklin Street had burned. The Pinkerton circled back and Adams knelt, urging one of the men to draw a dirt map to Franklin. Just then Holt's Caterpillar belched and barked to steaming life, drawing cheers and jeers from the men. That drew the Pinkerton even closer, though now his attention was likewise on the loud machine come alive. Unseen by the Pinkerton, Adams's small eyes locked on the agent, hand grasping the hilt of his knife.

The Pinkerton continued on, unaware that he had been within six feet of Adams. In turn, Adams slipped away. And no one in that crowd of men—men working in the long aftermath of one of nature's most deadly rampages—knew that one of the most deadly humans had been shoulder-to-shoulder among them.

★

– 24 –

SUNDAY
February 10, 1907

Winnie was already at a table in Denver's Columbine Café when someone held the door open for her sister. Supported by her new green crutches, Neva entered wearing a blue coat with velvet cuffs and collar. Winnie gave a slight wave to show herself, though Neva had already seen her.

"Hello, Sissy," said Winnie, once Neva had hobbled to the table.

"Can you get my chair?"

"Sure." Winnie stood, leaning Neva's crutches against the wall.

"It's good to see you, Mrs. Haywood," said the waiter, taking Neva's coat to hang next to Winnie's. "It is oddly warm. Can you believe this is February?"

"Yes, it is, Pete," replied Neva. "My irises are already popping up. Poor things are so confused." After settling into her seat, straightening her flounce skirt, setting her napkin, receiving her menu, and waiting for the waiter to leave, she looked at Winnie and sighed. "Whew. After all that, I'm going to have to stay the rest of the day."

"Those are from George?" Winnie nodded at the crutches.

"Un-huh. He's such a dear."

"Did Bear say anything?"

Neva lowered her menu and gave Winnie a smile—but like anything that doesn't fit, it pinched. "No, *Bill* didn't say anything. He didn't notice, of course. Just as well. But look at this," she said, touching the Irish lace insert of Winnie's waistshirt. "I like the stitching there—eyelets with tatting. That's wonderful. Did Bill let you order it from Eaton's?"

"I saw it in McCall's," Winnie said flatly before adding, "Yes."

"Well, it's lovely. You deserve those things. You're so pretty in them. I'm glad he appreciates what you do for him."

Winnie looked down, lifting her menu. "Same old things," she observed. "Hmm, a trout roll sandwich. That's new."

Neva looked at the food being delivered to three women at the next table, and then leaned to Winnie, mouthing, "Tongue sandwich. Disgusting."

"Oh, I don't know," Winnie said with a wink. "If it's done right, the tongue sandwich can be quite nice."

"Well then, good for them," Neva whispered, snickering. Then her laugh grew and soon Winnie got the chortles and both sisters were covering their faces with their menus.

Having just recovered when the waiter returned, Winnie asked, "How's your tongue sandwich?"

When he replied, "Oh, it's quite nice, Miss," they again fell into giggles and had to ask him to come back.

Eventually, they managed to order, and forty minutes later were finishing their meals: Neva had lamb stew with green peas. Winnie, the trout sandwich and string beans.

"Has Bill said more about the problem in Boise?" asked Neva.

"He and Mr. Darrow were talking about it some. Why?"

"I feel for him. So many want to bring him down."

"I suppose that goes with leading the union," said Winnie.

"Yes, but with the money matter, and the bombings, I'm just —"

"What money matter?"

Neva hesitated. "I'm sure it's nothing. Maybe it's nothing."

"George has you worried again."

"Why do you say that?" Neva snapped. "Why do you immediately think George is—" She saw Winnie's crooked-cheek expression of disbelief. "Fine. Yes, George said some money is missing."

"Federation money?" asked Winne. "George is the treasurer. Isn't he responsible for—"

"Not if he didn't take it."

"I thought a treasurer protects the treasure."

Neva dabbed her lips with her napkin. "He can't control what Bill does."

"He said Bill took it?"

Neva nodded and took another bite.

Winnie stared at Neva. "Why would George say that?"

"Because, Sissy, he thinks it's true."

"But it's not. Right?"

Neva shrugged. "He wouldn't tell me if he didn't believe it."

"Come now," Winnie retorted. "We're talking about George—the man who's been trying to get you to leave Bill for, what, the last two years?"

"He loves me," said Neva.

"He said that?"

"No, but ... I know he does."

"He wants you to run off with him."

Neva snorted a chuckle. "We won't be *running* anywhere."

"I'm serious," said Winnie. "He knows you won't divorce. So, unless Bill is gone ... or something. Maybe that's why he's accusing Bill of stealing so—"

"Embezzled. That's what they call it."

"They? Who else knows?"

"I don't know. If it gets out, I'm worried for George. And Bill."

They sat in their thoughts until Winnie asked, "So, he's in love with you?"

"George? Yes, the dear man."

"If he didn't say so, how do you know?"

Neva sank her gaze into Winnie. "You say Bill loves you, so—"

"Un-huh."

"So how do you know? He's never told you, I'm certain."

Winnie wobbled her head. "Well ..."

"What?" Neva studied Winnie. "Bill said he loves you?"

Winnie shrugged.

"And you believed him?" Neva's voice was growing louder.

Winnie closed her eyes, then opened them toward the remnants on her plate. "He was probably drunk."

Neva stared across the dining room, then flung her napkin on her plate. "I need to go." She scooted her chair back noisily. "Hand me my crutches."

"Sissy," Winnie implored. "I'm sorry I said that."

"I'm late. I need to go."

"Don't leave like this. I didn't mean—"

The waiter appeared. "May I be of assistance?"

Neva turned to him and snarled, "Her *lover* will pay the check."

Though his hat was the same, Jack was otherwise dressed in Pinkertonian habiliments—white shirt and dark coat—as he stood inside the doors of the Idanha Hotel. He moved to a front window to better observe the street. He felt chilled by the irony: now that he was openly a Pinkerton, like the many men in the lobby behind him, his work was more clandestine than ever before. He was to follow Carla Capone, as he was doing presently, and allow himself to be recruited over to the Federation, allow them to draw him in, place their trust in him—a trust that, if broken, if discovered false, would lead to coyotes dragging his flesh through the snow-dusted sagebrush beyond town.

"Agent Garrett," said Farrington flatly.

Jack turned with a start. "Yes, Forty-Two. I wasn't expecting—"

"Agent Farrington," he said. "Same as you."

Jack noted Farrington's clothes. "Yes, I heard—"

"Or maybe we're still spies," needled Farrington.

Jack clenched. "I'm not." He saw Orchard's bowler hat in Farrington's hand. "Thank you for bringing that. I'll get it to the chief." In the same moment that he took the hat, Carla stepped from a carriage in front of the hotel, arriving just when Jack had expected her. From inside, both men took notice, yet pretended otherwise—a flicker of united uncertainty. "That's the girl who told us about Harry Orchard," Jack offered.

"Who is she?" asked Farrington, dissembling. "She's a sight."

Before Jack could answer, Carla was inside, floating up to the two Pinkertons. She was dressed in a somewhat manly style: a dark coat over a white, box-cut waistshirt with black bow tie. Long, narrow, tobacco-brown poplin skirt. Side-laced ankle boots. Broad-brimmed felt hat adorned with a wide black ribbon. Her focus was on Jack who was failing to blink—his mouth stricken dry. "Agent Garrett," she began. "Good afternoon."

Jack recovered. "Yes, Miss Capone. To you as well. Cold out."

"At least, as you can see, I didn't wear a straw hat."

"As you wish," he replied nonsensically. His mind was too allure-fissured to make use of her quip. He turned to Farrington, then back to Carla. "May I introduce Agent Farrington."

Farrington nodded, replying, "Miss Capone. It's a pleasure to meet you. What brings you to Boise in these troubling times?"

"She brought Harry Orchard to us," said Jack.

"Yes, you told me that, just moments ago," said Farrington, triggering Jack's glare. "Only I had no clue the bearer was so extraordinary. Don't you think, Agent Garrett?"

Jack didn't reply.

"I assure you, Miss Capone," continued Farrington, "in the retelling of your heroics, I wouldn't have overlooked such an extraordinary detail."

"Very kind of you, Mr. Famenton," she said, her melody rippling the air, her eyes narrowing.

"It's Farrington," he corrected. "At your service."

"She works at the Saratoga," Jack interjected.

"No more, I'm afraid," she said.

"You're gone from there?" Farrington asked with as much alarm as question, failing to conceal his tonal shift.

She wrinkled her nose. "They're not keen on serving girls blabbing about their guests."

"They gave you the boot?" asked Jack, frowning. "Just for reporting Orchard?"

"Yes, I'm afraid someone let it be known—after his arrest. You knocked a door down, after all," she said to Jack, a touch of admiration in her voice.

"Actually," Farrington interjected, "I kicked that door down."

Carla hummed a "Mmph" but kept her attention on Jack.

"Will you be staying in town?" Jack asked her.

"Yes, if the Idanha will have me. I've come to inquire," she said, unaware that it was Jack who had arranged her Idanha interview.

Farrington frowned. "Is that wise? With the commotion in town, and this place being a central hub, filled with gunhands, spies, and us Pinkertons, I'd caution—"

"I'll be perfectly all right," she retorted.

Jack smiled. "Miss Capone, if you'll be dining this evening, I would be honored—"

"I do plan to eat, Agent Garrett."

"Leave the lady be," barked Farrington.

"If you tomcats are quite done," she cooed, "this bird must fly."

"My apologies," offered Jack, though she was already ten steps toward the front desk.

For a moment, the two Pinkertons loitered in her wake, until Farrington went after her. Jack watched them exchange whispers, with one obvious glance back at him. He glared at Farrington, his mind sharpening knives.

By the time Carla had disappeared into an office, and Farrington had returned, Jack had steeled himself. "Let's get a drink," he said and began for the bar.

Farrington moved behind him, chuckling. "A drink? Only two types of Pinkertons could drink alcohol openly: undercover operatives and Chief Detective McParland, and the chief's imbibing was rare.

At the bar, Jack ordered, "Two sarsaparillas, if you will." He flipped the bowler and examined its inner band, then the lining, but found nothing. "Damn."

"What are you looking for?"

"Orchard put something in here."

"Yeah?" said Farrington, his voice rising. "Don't know anything about that."

Jack heard the pitch change and looked him in the eyes. Two glasses of root beer were delivered. Jack took a sip. "Funny thing, the chief's sure it was in there—that night. That's why Orchard was so distressed, not wanting us to think it was his. Remember? But if the chief's right, then where did it go?" Jack saw Farrington's face redden, his eyes blink and lower until Jack asked, "Did it just fall out?"

"I never saw a note in it, and nothing fell out."

"A note? Why do you think it was a note?"

"You said—"

"No, I didn't—"

"What else would be in there?"

"A greenback?" retorted Jack. "Maybe a ticket to the opera?"

Farrington jabbed a finger in Jack's chest. "Best step back, if—"

Jack leaned closer and whispered, "You read it, didn't you? Then you destroyed it. What was on it?"

"I don't know—"

"You're working for Haywood now? Is that it?"

"You're a goddamn liar," Farrington barked, standing.

"Gonna take a swing at me, Agent Farrington?" asked Jack, also standing, squaring himself with the slightly shorter man. "Do it. Confirm what I'm saying's true. But make it count, because then it'll be my turn—and that'll be the last thing you'll remember."

Farrington snorted, then spit on the floor. His shoes began a shuffling retreat that seemed as unconscious as deliberate—an untethered boat washing out to sea.

Jack sneered. "I'm not paying for your sarsaparilla."

Farrington removed a coin from his pocket and tossed it on the bar where it went into a tight spin. When it stopped, Farrington was gone. Jack looked at his empty glass, then at Farrington's full one, and then at the coin: a silver V nickel. Then he saw white specks on the dark oak bar where the coin had been spinning. He wet his finger and dabbed at the faint residue, feeling it and touching it to his tongue. "Bitter. Physician's plaster. I'll be damned."

On that day's wintry night, on a hill immediately beyond the Idaho State Penitentiary, a lone man dismounted from his horse. His breath steamed in the moonlight, his gloved hands chambering a round into an M1903 Springfield rifle that had a thin scope elevated over its iron sights. He braced its barrel in the crook of tree limbs, aiming it across the high stone walls, across the hanging yard, and through the dark windows of the three-story cellhouse. He waited. Soon a bright light appeared on the first floor—a guard within carrying two lit kerosene lanterns, both suspended beneath one hand. They swayed with the guard's pace as he strolled the rows. After the light vanished, it soon reappeared on the second floor, where it again moved along the rows of cells. Beginning to shiver, the gunman set down the gun to rub his hands together, and then resumed his aim. The light moved along the third row. The gunman's breathing slowed.

Inside, Harry Orchard was not asleep, though his eyes were closed. He could hear distant snoring, and then dull footsteps as the night guard slowly approached, moving along death row, checking the cells. Orchard opened his eyes when the guard's boots stopped at his door, the amber light of two lanterns flooding his cell.

"Detective McParland said you might want a book."

Orchard sat up, seeing the guard unlocking the cell door. A book slid in, and the guard placed one of the lanterns on the interior floor, before retreating and clanging the door locked again.

"You leavin that lantern?"

"The detective figured you'd need it to read," replied the guard as he turned to walk away. Over his shoulder he snarked, "Set a fire—you'll be first to burn."

Orchard placed the lamp on the chair and leaned close, grumbling at the low level of kerosene in the glass reservoir. He then picked up the worn book, its spine frayed and cracked, and read the gold letters embossed on its red cloth cover: *The Hound of the Baskervilles*, by Conan Doyle.

Seeing the bright, interior light had split into two softer ones—one moving again, the other stationary—the gunman trained his scope on the unmoving lantern. It was not a clear image, but a fuzzy glow in the scope's narrow glass. Once his breath calmed, he slid the crosshairs to the right, onto what he thought was Orchard's illuminated, round face. A difficult shot in daytime. Pure luck at night.

Orchard had just flipped the book's front pages of when the lantern exploded, fuel splattering, glass shattering, fire erupting against the back wall, running across the floor. He screamed, leaping clear of the conflagration, and grabbed a shoe, walloping the blaze uselessly. Then he tried to use the book but dropped it as it too began to burn. Next, he pitched his wool blanket over the flames, and grabbed his brown coat—the one with the bullet hole in the back—and threw it and swore. Finally, he hurled his bucket of piss and shit onto the smoldering coat while coughing and shouting, his wild shadow flailing across the orange-lit, steel-latticed door.

★

– 25 –

WEDNESDAY
February 13, 1907

Carla carried a tray of dishes toward the back of the Idanha Hotel's restaurant. The only real difference between Idanha work from Saratoga work was that her uniform here was blue instead of red. Of course, she was surrounded by Pinkertons here—Pinks, thugs of the mine owners, enemies of the workers—yet they didn't seem malevolent to her. In fact, the Pinkertons were pleasant enough. All in all polite, as she saw it, especially compared to the ruffians and strays who wandered into the Saratoga. Pinkerton temperance went a long way, even if it hurt her tips.

As she arrived in the rear galley, she saw Wade Farrington leaning against a wash basin, positioned so as to not be seen by others. "Hello," she offered, a chill coursing her spine. He was an exception to Pinkerton gentlemanliness.

"Why are you working here?" he snapped.

"Why are *you* here?" She looked at the cooks and porters busy in the adjacent kitchen. "You must go."

"No. I'm a Pinkerton. We run this hotel now. Didn't you know?"

"Come," she demanded, pulling him into the dry-storage closet thick with the aroma of spices and cleaning supplies. She shut the door and switched on the electric light bulb hanging from the ceiling. "What do you want?"

"Brought my girl a Valentine," he said, presenting a red card bearing pink, printed flowers.

She swatted it away. "I can't take that, Wade," she exclaimed, though she kept her voice hushed. "I can't have something from you. What are you trying to do?"

"Don't be like that. Tomorrow's Valentine's. I just wanted—"

"I know what day it is."

"I want you to know how I feel. I—"

"Stop this nonsense. We had some fun, but ... But that's it."

His jaw flexed. With his right hand, he grabbed her by her crotch and held her hard, almost lifting her. "You like public places, so how about you get to your knees here and give me *my* Valentine?"

She grabbed his wrist, digging her fingernails into his skin, and pulled his hand away. "Don't touch me! I'm not your doll to fuck."

"Well, what if I say you are? What'll you do? Hmm? Scream? Do it. I'll tell McParland who you *really* are. Think I won't? I bet you think I won't." He drew close to her face. "No, no, you're a lying, Federation spy. You'll be in prison with—"

"*I'm* a Federation spy?" She pushed him back. "But you're not?" She could see this was taking a moment to register. "Go on, Wade—tell McParland. Let's see how fast he figures you in this."

Farrington shook his head, then picked the card up from the floor. "I'm sorry. Read it, please," he said, attempting to give it to her again. She crossed her arms in refusal. "I started this wrong," he continued. "Listen to me, darling. You and I are meant to be together. You know that. And you know I ... I care about—"

She narrowed her eyes. "Oh, do you?"

"Yeah," he grinned, misreading her completely. "I'm gonna lift that dress and remind you all about it."

She grabbed a cleaver and brandished it. "Just try. Just try."

He inhaled noisily through his nose, nodding as he exhaled. "Garrett said something, didn't he? What'd that goat fucker say?"

"Jack didn't—"

"Jack, is it? You spreading your legs for him now?"

"Don't talk to me anymore. You need to—"

"But you have to work with me. With our—"

"I don't *have* to do anything. I'll report you to Denver."

"No ... now ... I risked my life for you. You can't—"

"Risked? You risked it?"

"Yeah, I did. I risked my career. I risked my life for—"

"You risked your life," she repeated in bemusement, thrusting the blade into the air between them, her eyes fixed on his. "If that's true, then the risk just got a little higher. Yeah? So leave me be. Or Mr. Haywood will—"

The storage closet's door opened, and a Mexican prep-cook entered. He stopped. Taking in the pair, seeing the raised cleaver in her hand, he asked, "Everything alright here, Miss Capone?"

"Yes, Sammy. Gracias," said Carla. "Just deciding how to best carve up a Pink hog."

The cook shrugged. "Save his ears. I'll take em to my dogs."

She snorted with a grin.

Farrington glared at the man, then pushed by him to leave, the Valentine still in his hand. "Step aside. Goddamned beaner."

The warden's office, on the second floor of the penitentiary's administration building, burst with cigar and pipe smoke and the *click, click, click* of an Underwood in action, its ribbon having been twice replaced. At a large pine table sat Detective McParland, Senator Borah, Agent Jack Garrett, a woman from the First National Bank of Idaho brought in to serve as stenographer, and Harry Orchard—three hours into his confession. No one else had been allowed.

"Wasn't like you say it was," Orchard protested, using his lit cigar as a small baton.

McParland raised his hands in mock surrender. "All right, Mr. Orchard. As you wish. It's your confession, not mine." He sucked on his pipe.

"Mine neither," mused Borah, standing to crank the window.

"Senator!" cried McParland at the burst of cold air.

"I hoped for real air," said Borah, waving at the smoke before closing the window. "This man's story is stifling enough."

Convinced that Haywood had ordered him killed two nights prior—and not just shot at, but almost burned alive—Orchard hadn't just agreed to confess, but had demanded he be given the opportunity. Now the mood was heavy. The confession had been long. He had laid out the details of the bombing of Governor Steunenberg, and the murders of at least fifty-three other people, most by bombs made, implemented, and triggered by his own hand; and uncountable other deaths at the hands of accomplices with whom he had cooperated—old sins casting long shadows—including the dynamiting of the Bunker Hill Mine the year prior. It was on that last point that Detective McParland was now focused.

"You said the superintendent of the Bunker—he got away, and Mr. Haywood was unhappy about that, correct?"

"That's right. Don't know how he got out alive. We had him locked in the Pullman. He lost a hand. What I was told anyhow."

"And Mr. Haywood instructed the other man, Steve Adams, to go find the super and kill him?"

"No, we'd been told to kill him there. Him and any other sombitch on that platform, but—"

"No, now, let's get this straight. You said that, when you were in Denver, *later*—that you were ordered by Mr. Haywood to kill Adams, after Adams finished killing the Bunker super. Right?"

"Yep."

McParland blinked a few times. "That's a devil's lot of killing to keep sorted."

"You're tellin me!" exclaimed Orchard. "Cept when I seen Adams here, when I got here, he hadn't gone to kill that fella yet. So, I got him to help me with the governor. Reasoned I'd find Adams after he lit out for the super."

"You used Adams, truth be told," said McParland, "to try to get me off your scent. You got him to go to the governor's house and get himself seen. Then seen again on a train, a little after you popped that bomb. That right?"

Orchard nodded. "About the size of it."

McParland exchanged a weary head shake with Borah, then looked again at Orchard. "So Adams is headed to kill that man?"

"Damnifino."

"But you reckon so."

"Reckon lots of things."

"Reckon you know his name?"

"Steve Adams? Yeah, though I thought it was Addis at first, when he killed those others in Wallace, on our way to the Bunker."

"All right. All right. Wait. I want to come back to that, but I'm asking about the name of the superintendent of the Bunker Hill Mine. Do you know *his* name? The one Adams has gone after?"

"No, Sir."

McParland turned to Jack and spoke quietly. "Find that super's name and where he is. He'll be somewhere in San Francisco, or nearby. We followed Adams there but lost him. So let's focus on the super. We'll surveil him and get Adams coming. Might even save the super's life."

"Yes, Sir," said Jack. "Now?"

"When we're done here."

Senator Borah leaned into the back of his chair, staring at Orchard. "Back a few months, you killed some railroad men up in Missoula, then you killed an owner's man in Wallace, here in Idaho. Then, of course, all of that carnage at the Bunker Hill Mine. That got everybody upset, especially my friend Governor Steunenberg. Even President Roosevelt. Which, of course, led to all those arrests. Arrests that angered labor, and Mr. Haywood in particular, because he'd helped pay for the governor's election. And that, in turn, led to you assassinating the man. Do I have all that right?" Borah waited for a reply, but none came. "Is that right, Mr. Orchard? And you were at the center of all of it?"

"I didn't kill them conductor fellas in Missoula. Don't know who did. And them Wallace ones was Addis. I mean Adams."

"Oh, now," Borah protested. "You're just splitting hairs—"

"Maybe," groused Orchard. "But you missed what came first."

"First?"

"Yeah, the mistreatin—the killin—of thousands of miners, over the years," said Orchard. "You politicians—horse asses, the lot of you—so eager to overlook why these awful things get started firstly. Why it figures a man might take up arms. Might wire some dynamite. You never gnaw on that."

"Maybe," said McParland, flipping his hand to rejoin the conversation. "But that's for the law—"

"Ain't no law to it, Detective," said Orchard. "Where was the law for the widows of the Stratton men?"

"The Stratton?" asked Borah.

"Stratton Mine, a year or so back," McParland explained. "Cripple Creek, Colorado."

"Oh, yes," muttered the senator.

McParland motioned to Orchard. "What does that little mine in Colorado have to do with all this other? It was a terrible accident, but I don't—"

"What's it have to do?" Orchard looked at the detective incredulously. "Everything, Detective. Everything's got everything to do with everything else! Law did nothing for em at the Stratton. Those were Wobblies who fell to their deaths, good Federation men.

Thirty some odd. Stratton owners done nothing for them—the law less. Even Haywood's lawyer, that fancy fellow from Chicago—"

"Mr. Darrow," Borah offered.

"Yeah, him," said Orchard. "He didn't get em nothing."

McParland narrowed his eyes at Orchard. "As I recall, that trial was going on the same day as you bombed the Bunker."

"Maybe. I'm just saying everyone was angry about it all—all of it, all the killing of miners. Still are. Real angry. And Mr. Haywood had to do something. No, I didn't look happy on killing em, all them at the Bunker or any others. Or the governor. But something had to be done, and I was the man chosen to do it."

"You did something, all right," snarked McParland.

Borah leaned and whispered with McParland. Then McParland nodded, and Borah stood and said, "Mrs. Nelson, I thank you, but at this time I think we're done with the recording of the confession." As she gathered her coat, he continued, "Thank you. I have no doubt we'll be in need of your services again." After she left, Borah resumed his seat at the table and began thumbing through the sixty-four typed pages beside the machine. "You're a despicable human being, Mr. Orchard. You must know that about yourself."

Orchard gave no response, keeping his gaze on the table.

Borah continued, "I'm hard pressed not to have vile regard for all humanity, sitting across from the likes of you—knowing such is possible by the hand of one man—one otherwise quite unremarkable man."

Still Orchard refused to look at him.

McParland nodded in agreement. "I've seen so much. But this ..." He waited to see if Borah had more to add, but, hearing nothing, he sighed and spoke directly to Orchard. "You said you were chosen to do it, that Haywood ordered you to do these things."

"That's right."

"How so?"

"What do you mean, how so?"

"How so? How'd he communicate with you? How'd you know what he wanted from you? Did he say it? Did he write it down?"

"I told you—"

"No, you didn't. You didn't tell me."

Orchard cleared his throat and drank from a glass of water.

"You don't want to tell me this?" McParland asked wryly. "You've listed out all these horrors," he said, touching the papers, "and attributed most of them to Mr. Haywood. But on this question, as to *how* you were ordered, you balk? Now that's interesting. Why is that, I wonder?"

"He'd just let me know."

"How, damnit?" McParland pounded the table. "Why are you still protecting the man who tried to shoot you last night?"

Orchard mumbled. "Maybe that was you—Old Necessity."

"What did you say?" asked Borah.

"Speak up," instructed McParland.

Orchard looked at McParland. "After all this time in here with you, I'm beginning to think, maybe it was *you*. You don't follow the law—not really. So, coulda easily been you who had me shot at. Just to scare the life from me. Got me to confess today."

"You think so, do ya?" asked McParland through a chuckle.

"Yeah, I think that's the way it is."

"Why would I risk killing you, Senator Borah's lead witness?"

"There's only one man," said Borah, joining again. "Only one who'd gain from you being dead, and that's Mr. Haywood."

"That's correct," said McParland. He then squinted at the prisoner. "Old Necessity? I haven't heard that in a while."

Borah looked perplexed. "What's that: Old Necessity?"

McParland nodded at Orchard. "Tell him."

Orchard looked at Borah. "You know that sayin: necessity knows no law? So that's what they call him." He titled his head toward McParland. "Old Necessity."

"Isn't that a fine thing?" huffed McParland. "A murderous, misanthrope cur such as yourself, Mr. Orchard, saying that I don't follow the law. Ah well ... The point is, you're still lying for that son of a bitch in Denver. So, let's be done. Answer my question: How'd Haywood give you his orders? Tell me, or I swear to God, I'll make that shot easier for them next time. You understand me?"

Orchard hesitated before saying, "He'd write it down."

"He wrote it down?"

"Yeah, then he'd burn it. He's got special paper only he uses."

McParland's eyes tightened. "A yellowish paper?"

"Yep," replied Orchard, lifting his nose.

"Did he ever *not* burn it? Did you keep any of those orders?"

Orchard held his gaze steady. "You already know that."

Borah tilted. "What does he mean?"

Orchard grinned. "Tell him what you found in my hat."

McParland elevated a brow at Jack. Then he took a deep breath and returned his gaze to Orchard. "The orders from Haywood?"

"You saw it."

"Was that in his hand or yours?"

"His."

McParland let his chin fall a fraction, then stood and kicked one of the chairs, making it skitter and crash across the small room.

Everything fell silent for a bit until Senator Borah looked at Orchard and asked, "You said Adams killed someone else up in Wallace, before you blew up the Bunker Hill?"

"Yeah—couple of em. He shot the owners' man in a saloon there. Said he'd seen that fella's name on one of Big Bill's lists."

"And the other?" asked Borah.

Orchard took his time before replying. "Adams cut the throat of a deputy who came after us. I wished he hadn't done that un."

"But the first one, in the saloon, that one was fine by you?" McParland growled, sitting again. "But not the second one, the deputy. What difference is a single life to a man like you?"

"The deputy was just a boy." A shudder came from Orchard. "Looked like my boy. He didn't have nothin to do with me and Addis. I mean Adams."

McParland stopped on that, then blew a sigh through his nose, making his mustache flicker. "This Adams—he'll have something to say about Haywood and his orders?"

"Doubt it. Doubt he'll say anything. Doesn't matter, though. You'll never find him—least not alive."

"Because Haywood had a kill order on him," said McParland. "Aye, you told us. But you're in here. And I'm sure you'll be sorry to learn this, Harry, but your killing days are done. There's only one person left you're going to help kill—and that's William Haywood."

"Somebody else will get Adams."

"Who?"

"Adams."

"No, who's gonna kill Adams? You have names of any of these other animals like yourself?""

"Not real names."

"Not real names. Of course."

"They'd be dead time you caught up to em. Same with Adams."

"We got you, didn't we?"

Orchard took a beat. "Yep."

"Have to give the Pinkertons some credit," Borah tried.

"Even if you found Adams," continued Orchard, "he'd never confess—not like I just done."

"Oh yeah? Why not?"

"Fella like that don't know the difference tween life and death."

"We'll see," grumbled McParland.

"No, no—he's mad." Orchard fluttered his hand. "His senses are left him."

"But you?" asked Borah. "You're *not* mad?"

"Me?" Orchard winced, wounded. "Of course not."

★

– 26 –

MONDAY
February 25, 1907

"I'm done for, Neva," Haywood said softly.

"Nonsense," she replied. They were in the back seat of a carriage drawn by two gray Walkers. Her invalid chair was strapped to the rear quarter. The sky was clear, causing bright blue to reflect with little suns in the melt-pools of Arapahoe Street, a brick road lined with snow mounds. In front of Haywood, a hulking guard leaned on his shotgun barrel up from the floorboard. In front of Neva, the coach driver presented his middle finger to a passing automobile driver who was squeezing the vehicle's condescending bulb-honker—sounding like a young foghorn going by. Neva snickered at the vulgar gesture, then pulled close the fox collar of her coat. Pleased to ride on Bill's good-eye side, she glanced at him, admiring how his new coat fit square to his shoulders—not always an easy task due to the thickness of his chest.

"I've given everything for labor," he said. "Everything. What more must I do?"

"No one can blame you. You weren't in Boise when—"

"You don't know what you're talking about. The federal government will never let me rest. Not Congress nor Roosevelt. And not that goddamned Senator Borah. They're all spineless puppets of their corporate lords—their overlords. Morgan and Rockefeller and every other one of those sons-a-bitches. And they've got the Pinkertons as their private army."

She patted his arm. It was a tired refrain. "I know, but—"

"That McParland should be dead. Plain and simple. He gives no accounting to the laws of man, of nature, the rights of an individual, the man who works—"

"That's true," she whispered as an intended balm.

"And now they have the goddamned nerve, after all I've given, the goddamned gall of Borah and McParland to scare one of my good men, Harry Orchard, into making a false confession. Accusing me of the whole ... goddamned thing." His words faded as they skittered off to catch up with his thoughts now miles away.

"I understand," she said. Though it was best to let him fume, she loathed the ease with which he cursed in front of her.

When he resumed, his words came just above a whisper. "They'll see me hanged, Neva. If they can, they will."

When the carriage came to a stop in front of the Pioneer Building, Clarence Darrow was standing there. Neva noted the attorney's dreary derby and plodding suit. The man was certainly consistent in his attire, she thought. Haywood climbed down and scooped Neva in his arms before plopping her in her invalid chair, which the driver had set right. The guard stood watchful.

"Tell him something good, Mr. Darrow," Neva implored. "He's inconsolable."

"I don't need consolation!" Haywood shouted, moving ahead of her, leaving the driver and Darrow to lift the chair, with her in it, up the short flight of steps. Inside, Darrow rolled Neva past a door to the Gassell Saloon and on to the elevator where Haywood waited impatiently. The elevator operator clanked the gate closed, followed by the door, before levering the car into a squeaky ascent. Haywood snarled at Darrow, "You need to do something. Get this under control and bury Orchard."

Neva saw Darrow nod toward the elevator operator's narrow back, silently asking Haywood to be quiet.

"I don't give a good goddamn," barked Haywood. "Not now."

Once they had risen past the second floor (the Federation headquarters) to the third floor (the Haywood suites) and exited the lift, Darrow stood in the foyer and spoke quietly to Haywood. "I told you—there's little risk to you in this."

Neva angled her chair back toward the lift operator. "There's luggage to be brought up, Lester. If you please."

"Yes, Mrs. Haywood," came the muffled reply behind the door as it clattered closed.

She watched Haywood and Darrow walk into the drawing room. "You're staying here, Bill? I thought you were going down to your office."

"No. I'm better guarded up here," Haywood retorted.

That made no sense, but there was no point questioning it. She sat for a moment alone in the foyer until Winnie appeared from the kitchen. They exchanged unspoken greetings, and then Winnie wheeled Neva down the hall to the lavatory.

In the drawing room, Darrow lit a cigarette. "Orchard is just one witness. They need two."

"He's on death row in the Idaho pen," said Haywood.

"I know. Though I imagine that's McParland's doing."

When Winnie seemed to materialize in their midst, Darrow caught himself fixing on her. He snapped his look away. But the lithe woman was irresistible: the perky way she tilted her chin, the feminine lilt in her voice.

"May I have one of those?" she asked, indicating his cigarette.

"Certainly, Miss," he said. He pulled a tin from his pocket and popped it open.

"Are these the Marlboro ones?" she asked, taking one.

"What did you expect? Ogdens?" He withdrew some matches, though he wondered that her smile might not ignite the cigarette.

"Ogdens? Not from you, Mr. Darrow." She cupped his hands as he eased a lit match to her.

"Besides," he added, "these are better for you."

"They're not," said Winnie, grinning.

"Sure," Darrow said with a wink. "They're stronger, more potent, so they make you tougher. Survival of the fittest."

"Are you two done?" fussed Haywood.

Darrow anticipated Winnie would take the cue and leave the room; but instead, she took a seat on the settee, crossing her legs at the knees, letting a bare foot dangle and bobble like a fishing lure. Darrow inhaled, returning his attention to his melancholy client. "The government of Idaho cannot extradite you from Colorado," he said. "Not for a crime that occurred in Boise while you were in Denver. The Colorado Supreme Court would never allow it."

"You think so?" Haywood sniped.

"Granted the governor here might, but not the justices. Certainly not Goddard," he added, referring to the Chief Justice of the Colorado Supreme Court. "That man would rather eat his firstborn than betray such a central legal principle as *habeas corpus*."

"You're not a naive man, Clarence," said Haywood, pouring himself a whiskey from a crystal carafe. "But when have you ever witnessed the Colorado Supreme Court aligning with the laboring man? When? When did they ever see things the way of the union?"

"I'm not certain—"

"When they arrested me for writing on a Colorado flag? Then?" Haywood continued. "Or when thousands of men were crushed, fell, blown-up, gassed to death in Colorado mines only to have those goddamned justices turn into blind crones?" He took a drink.

"You need to take my counsel on this, Bill. Justice Goddard is not that sort of man. You're safe here. Keep your men posted, if it makes you feel more secure. Hell, post a battalion of hired guns. But there's nothing else to be done at this point."

"Nothing?" Haywood smoldered. "What about their witness?"

"They'll need two witnesses before they can seat a jury."

"Someone shot at Harry in the pen—probably with a Springfield like I showed you in my office. Missed by a hair—but lit his cell on fire. Hit a lantern."

"Thus his confession," Darrow muttered, thoughts swirling.

"Well, the man *I* sent to kill Harry didn't do it. I know that. So maybe—" Haywood looked at Winnie. "What do you think, Win? Maybe ol' Clarence here has his own gunmen up in Boise?"

"Oh, I couldn't imagine that from the dashing Mr. Darrow," she said, a little too precociously.

"Don't be ridiculous," muttered Darrow. "I'm not—"

"Ridiculous?" Haywood snarled. "Don't go putting on airs with me, Clarence. Highfalutin, like you've got clean boots. Don't do it. You represent men who do what must be done against their oppressors." Now he was in Darrow's face. "They'll do what's right to hold onto liberty and dignity—for the common worker, the true red-blooded American. Your client, the man standing right in front of you, is the defender of tens of thousands of men, women and children—and if some need die in that cause, even by my own goddamned hand, then those are the wages of liberty." After easing his thunder, he added, "You're no better than me. No better."

Darrow stood, his jaw tense, his playful thoughts of Winnie having evaporated during Haywood's exhortation. "Yes, I'm just a man. As are you. As we will ever be." He was sick of Haywood.

This case would be the end of it. He wouldn't subject himself to this patronizing any further. And this case, if there was to be a case, had better get him to Washington, DC, arguing before the Supreme Court.

"That's goddamned right, you are—just a man. Just another, like the rest of us, doing what you must. You use a law book, I use rallies and bullets. And yes, bombs, Clarence, when required. But mostly—to get things as I want them, to see justice done—I use people's opinions, their thoughts. Same as you do."

Darrow nodded, feeling another ache disembarking into his skull. "For now, Bill, I recommend you do nothing. There's—"

"Don't tell me there's nothing to be done. Don't tell me I'm supposed to just sit here like a staked goat, waiting to be fed to the lion. I *am* the goddamned lion! I won't sit around hoping my lawyer's love of the law is accurate. That somehow an American court is going to protect me. They *made* Orchard confess—that feeble-minded, goddamned rat. Our man should've killed him when he could, in the hotel there. But no—now *your* courts, your judges, your law, with their dishonorable, mercenary Pinkerton guns—they're doing whatever they goddamned-well please. While I'm here with my thumb up my ass." Haywood caught his breath before continuing, "You think now, for the first time in the history of this country, that the courts are going to side with the working man and not a corporation?"

Darrow had retreated into his own strategic thoughts. "McParland must've hired someone to shoot at him."

"Are you not listening to me, Clarence?"

"But they didn't kill him—they didn't want that, of course," Darrow continued. "They found themselves a marksman to shoot just near enough to make him think it was one of your men come to kill him. Scared him right into the confessional."

"As I said—there's your law for you. There's your justice," bellowed Haywood. "If I did something like that, it'd be an outright hanging offense. But under the cloak of law? No—those devils."

"I have to agree with you," said Darrow.

Winnie spoke up. "What do we do?"

Darrow exhaled loudly. "They have one witness. Just one. They need two."

"No saying they won't find Adams too," said Haywood.

"Adams?" asked Darrow. "Who is—"

"Steve Adams," said Haywood. "He was there too, in Boise. Maggot of a man. But, as with maggots, he's good at what he does. Orchard wasn't to get Adams involved—but he did. And that might give them their second witness."

"How do you know—"

"I thought Adams was already gone on from Idaho. Gone on to finish another matter. But he was still there."

"All right," Darrow tried again. "But how do you know he—"

"Orchard said it in his confession."

Darrow's brow knotted. "You've seen the confession already?"

Haywood shrugged.

"You had someone in the room?" pressed Darrow.

Haywood gave a single nod.

"In the prison?"

"The stenographer," said Haywood. "Her son's at the Silver Reef Mine, in Utah. She's a Federation mother."

"All right," began Darrow, his head rocking in disbelief. "Adams is the key then. They'll be out to arrest him. Where is he? Can he be convinced to not—"

"Convince him?" said Haywood.

"You know—"

"Yes, Mr. Darrow, I do."

"We have to get him," Winnie interjected, "before they do."

"We need to follow the law, Miss Minor," Darrow said, giving her a dismissive wave. He considered her. Why was she so engaged in this? Did Neva know?

"No, Mr. Darrow," she said, tapping ash from her cigarette, her voice now surprisingly unyielding. "We need to help Bill kill that man Adams. That's what you and I need to do. The worker's struggle is greater than the life of any one man, or woman, including you and me. And it's far more important than the life of a man like Steve Adams ... whoever he is."

Darrow shook his head. "No, dear. I'll lawfully defend my client, Mr. Haywood, but that's *all*."

Haywood slapped him on the back. "In for a penny, in for a pound, old man."

"In for a pound," echoed Winnie, clicking her tongue.

Darrow scolded himself for having ever found her attractive. She was a siren. A dangerous coquette to be sure.

Jack chewed his lunch—chicken-salad sandwich with beans and a glass of tea—while glancing to the side, watching as his waitress, Carla, approached in her Idanha-blue uniform.

Passing behind him, she brushed a finger across the back of his neck, just above his high collar, giving him a jolt. "Is there anything else I can get for you, Agent Garrett?" she asked.

"Oh, no, Miss Capone, no," he stuttered, still tingling from her unexpected touch. As she moved on, he called to her, "Yes, actually. If you don't mind."

"Yes?" She brought a warm smile back. "Call me Carla."

"Alright, then I'm Jack." He stood, beaming, but didn't offer his hand, not wanting to seem too eager to touch her—though that was anything but the truth.

"Ok, Jack."

He took an audible breath and said, "I've been asked to acquire a large chalkboard."

"A chalkboard?"

"Yes. For the chief. A double-sided one. Do you know what I mean?" Though he managed the question without trouble, his mind was on her hazel eyes—they were speckled with green, giving them the color of a forest floor.

"I believe so," she answered. "Sure."

"All I've found so far are some primary slates. But they're small," he said, pantomiming the corners of a foot-square slate.

"Un-huh," Carla quipped. "I attended school."

"Of course. I was just ... I thought ..." His words staggered and swayed like a newborn fawn trying to find its legs. "I wondered—"

"If I might know where to find a large one?"

"Yes," he said cheerfully, but then saw her brows lift. "Oh! Yes, certainly. You wouldn't know. You're as new here as me ... as I am."

"How about a school?" she asked, charmed by his floundering.

"The big ones are all attached to walls. I visited some yesterday."

"You didn't have a crowbar?" She gave a wry grin.

"The little kids took it from me," he replied, thankful for her taking them onto what was far firmer ground for him: the battlefield of wit. "Bunch of smelly little bastards, you ask me."

"Oh, they are! Especially *en masse*. You poor dear."

"I'm glad you understand," he said with a chuckle.

"You know, there's a college in Caldwell, out near ... where the governor—"

"There is? Do you think—"

"Maybe. We won't know till we look tomorrow."

"We? I don't—" He caught himself. "Alright, that'd be good."

Carla pursed her lips coyly. "Yes, it will." As she moved toward another table, she added, "I'll see you here tomorrow—Jack."

Due to Haywood's six-foot-three frame under the low ceilings of the Pioneer suites, when he ran his arms into his night shirt, he had to lean forward lest he smack his hand against the ceiling. Neva was already in bed. "It must be difficult," she observed, "being so tall ... and with the eye."

"How long have you watched me? You're just noticing this?" he asked, sounding more disapproving than disappointed.

"You look like a giraffe putting on his night clothes," she said, grinning at her own description. But seeing Bill's stony face, she let her smile slide away.

He finished buttoning his night shirt and sat upright on her side of the bed. "It's you who's the stalwart. What, with the ..." He gave a hesitant pat to the covers where he assumed her left leg was. Then he pulled away quickly, as if in the instant of feeling the squish of her limb, his hand might fall lame. "I'll take rapping my head into low limbs any day, rather than ... you know." He leaned, kissing her on the forehead.

"Will you stay tonight?" she whispered.

"Is that what you want?"

"It is, husband."

He moved around the bed and slid under the covers, easing against her. "As you command. Wherever you wish me to be."

She gave a small frown. "Be here only if you want to."

"I do," he said blankly, looking at the ceiling.

Neva did the same. "Winnie will have to warm her own bed."

"Sleeper car."

"What?"

"Sleeper car. She left for—"

"She's gone?"

"Yes, I needed her—"

"So that's why you're in our bed?"

"No. Not at all. That had nothing—"

She rolled her back to him. "Shut off your lamp."

He did, leaving them in near darkness. "I'd be here regardless."

"No, you wouldn't. Where did you send her?"

"Salt Lake City."

"Why?"

"Giving a man a message."

"Who?"

"Why do you ask?"

Silence.

He continued, "A man named Swain. That doesn't mean anything to you, so I don't know why you ask."

"You couldn't go?" asked Neva. "Or send one of your men?"

"I can't leave the state."

"Right."

"And I can't chance one of them being a Pink."

"You don't trust them? None of your men? Only my sister?"

"Things are tense right now."

"My, you're observant."

"I meant with my work."

"You couldn't send a telegraph, rather than send her?"

"We can't write the, uhmm, message."

She sat up in the gloom. "Oh, I understand now. So who's the Swain fellow gonna kill for you?"

Silence.

"Who this time?" she pressed.

Haywood turned his lamp back on. "Why are you asking this?"

"I'm angry at you. Shut that off. I don't want to see your eye."

He did, then whispered, "I would've been here, regardless."

"You shouldn't have done that—with that governor."

"I'm not talking about that," said Haywood. "Not with you."

"Oh? What would you rather talk about? That you told Winnie you love her? Go on, you choose: Which do you want to talk about? You blowing up a governor, or you saying nonsense to my sister?"

A long silence devoured the blackness, removing any remaining comfort in the void.

"I wasn't in Idaho when it happened, and they can't take me there. And they need two witnesses to say I ordered it. They've got one, but he's selling them a dog."

"The Orchard man?"

"Yep."

"Hell's bells, Bill. Lying or not, it's still a confession."

"Maybe."

Neva inhaled and blew it out noisily. "So, they won't get the other confession, from the other man, because of whatever Winnie's going to tell Swain to do?"

"We'll see."

"So you made my sister an accomplice to murder."

"I didn't. She's fine. I wouldn't do—"

"Thank God you're in love with her. I'd hate to see the trouble you'd get her in if you weren't!" The covers shifted, and then came the soft *thump-thump* of the invalid chair being dragged sideways across the rug for positioning. The bedsprings squeaked and rose, the chair clattered, and the wheels began rolling.

"Where are you going?" Haywood grumbled, unable to see her.

"Her room. You stay here."

"Oh, I thought you might be going to the Metropole."

The bedroom door slammed with such a concussive report that a framed portrait fell in the hall, shattering the darkness.

★

– 27 –

TUESDAY
February 26, 1907

In a San Francisco market near the Ingleside Racetrack, Steve Adams was next in line. He fidgeted, adjusted his cap, asked the time from the man behind him, and examined the bottle of Coca Cola in his hand. The woman ahead of him was in a protracted conversation with the clerk, causing agitation in the queue. Adams listened to their discussion. In the aftermath of the city's devastation, an explosion of rats and other vermin had caused a run on strychnine. In fact, this store was almost out. When it was his turn, Adams set the bottle of Coca Cola on the counter and said, "This and one them last bottles of strychnine you were gabbing about. Rat problems."

Three weeks earlier, after fully shaking the Pinkertons from his tail, Adams found what remained of the intersection of Franklin and Grove Streets. The home of the brother of James Branson (the one-handed superintendent of the Bunker Hill Mine) had indeed burned down. The next day, Adams made his way into the temporary government building on Washington Street, just past Nob Hill. There he stood in line for two hours before getting an opportunity to flip through the public records regarding the earthquake and fires: ledgers of damage claims, of recovery, of debris removal; a book that listed thousands of names of the dead (or in many cases just descriptions of remains along with any unique features) along with the location where each body or body part had been found; and another book that cataloged the names and destinations of the living who had been displaced.

Thirty minutes later, he walked to a home on Faxon Street—which was between Lake View Avenue and Holloway Avenue as best as he understood from a city map he stole from a street vendor. For the next two weeks, he pretended to be a hobo, and, from across Faxon, he observed the comings and goings at the house—a woman and two children mostly. Never a man. In fact, Adams began to think Branson might have stashed his family in the house before he left San Francisco himself. Then, two days before Adams was going to move on, he spotted Branson entering the home. The time had come. The next day, Adams went to a gambling den outside the gates to a nearby racetrack, won thirty-five cents, and took his winnings to a nearby market for another Coca Cola. It was there that he bought the strychnine.

Before sunrise the next day, Adams slipped out of his boarding house and returned to hide in his observation nest on Faxon. At 7:10 that morning, he heard the approaching clip-clop and steel-banded wheels-on-brick he was anticipating. Then he watched a big, bay horse turning a four-wheeled milk wagon from Holloway onto Faxon and draw to a stop. After unloading wood crates (each containing twelve white bottles) onto a hand cart, the driver proceeded door to door, placing one or two bottles of milk on most of the porches along Faxon, including two on the Branson porch. After the wagon left, it took only twenty seconds for Adams to cross the street, empty the contents of the strychnine bottle into one of the milk bottles on the Branson's porch, and walk away, guzzling from the other bottle, excess milk dripping from his chin.

Late in the afternoon of the same day, Carla and Jack exited a train in Caldwell, twenty-seven miles west of the Boise depot. There they hired a coach to take them out to a cold, sagebrush expanse where a lone wood sign read:

COLLEGE OF IDAHO

Suspended beneath it and creaking in the breeze, a smaller sign announced:

Sterry Hall
Opening This Fall

The campus consisted of two large buildings and their companion multi-stall outhouses. From one, Sterry Hall, almost hidden behind its construction scaffolding, came muffled voices, hammer blows, and the grinding growls of handsaws. As the two approached the other building, Finney Hall, young men began exiting the central, column-flanked door. Jack and Carla stood aside, observing the college boys.

Three hundred yards away, a palomino's breath fogged as it snorted and pawed at the near-frozen ground. From astride it, Agent Farrington took aim with an M1903 Springfield rifle with a makeshift scope, his cloudy breath swirling around his finger as it hovered over the trigger. Giving up on the scope, he tried the iron sights, leveling on Jack and Carla as they entered Finney Hall.

Inside, Jack inquired at the front office. Then he and Carla were ushered to meet the dean, a diminutive fellow in a striped suit and loose tie. After shaking Jack's hand, the terrier of a man was off: "Yes, yes, I spoke with Mr. McParland on the telephone. Did you know? Yes, I imagine you did. Did you? We are excited to help."

"Thank you, Sir," offered Jack. The three were standing—Jack and Carla still coated and scarved. "Yes, I arranged for Chief McParland to telephone you."

"Whatever I can do to assist the State in this sickening matter."

"Thank you."

"Anything the College of Idaho may do to come in aid of the State," the dean said again. If he'd had a tail, it would've been swishing in a blur.

"Just the chalkboard," said Jack.

"An awful thing," sputtered the dean. "Holy crow, what a thing."

"Yes."

"We heard the bomb here. You know, we are only a half mile away. It rattled our windows. Scared us under our desks."

Jack squinted. "You had classes that night, over the holidays?"

The dean stopped. "Well, no. It is just an idiom. But we heard it at our homes."

Carla spoke from the doorway: "Where could we—"

"To think, a bomb," said the diminutive dean, interrupting Carla. "Such a horrible way to be assassinated."

Frowning at the dismissal, Carla pressed a new point. "Would being stabbed or shot have been preferable?"

"Miss Capone," Jack snapped under his breath.

"Or squashing him with a paver?" she muttered, enjoying that she'd stolen the little man's attention after he'd refused to politely give it to her.

The dean's eyes tightened. "Who might you be, young lady?"

"My apologies for not ..." said Jack. "This is Miss Capone."

Though Carla offered her hand, the dean turned as if he'd not seen it. "Capone?" he asked. "I knew a Capone. Italian man, of course." He looked at her squarely. "He arrived in Colorado back in eighty-five, as I recall. Was he a relation of yours?"

"No—no, Sir." Her tone was dampened, her features blanched.

"I knew him in Fort Collins. He and his family had come west. Sheep, I think it was. Good man. Nice family. He had a son and young daughter."

"I don't know him!" Carla blurted, her words a whip's crack.

"I apologize, Miss." The dean gave a disingenuous nod.

"Please excuse me." She withdrew to the foyer.

The dean looked at Jack. "What was the nature of that?"

Jack shook his head, his temperature rising at the man's frigidity.

"I shouldn't be surprised," continued the dean. "She must've known the family."

"Maybe so," said Jack, glancing into the foyer, finding it empty. When his attention returned to the dean, any remnants of supplication had been stripped away. "I need to get the chalkboard to the depot in time for the 6:30 to Boise."

"How old are you?"

"Twenty-seven."

"You seem like a bright fellow. Agent Garrett, you said?"

"That's correct," he replied with a touch of asperity.

"I assume you completed all your advanced schooling," continued the dean. "I'd be happy to receive your application to this college—were you so inclined. Would you like to seek a profession? You're beyond the usual age, of course, but we—"

"I just need a chalkboard, and a wagon to carry it to the depot."

"Then you're in luck, young man. I have six boards in storage. They're over in Sterry, the building being constructed. And, you may use one of the contractor's rigs to transport them."

"Thank you, Sir." He shook the dean's hand and turned to leave.

"The boards are in storage until that hall opens next term."

"Not a problem," said Jack. "This will be done in a month."

"You may take one, or two if you need, for the State's business."

Jack was out the door now. "Thank you."

The dean lifted his voice to be heard out in the foyer. "Anything I can do for the cause of justice!"

The low sun stretched gold carpeting across the alkaline prairie and up the western walls of the buildings. The Sterry scaffolding was quiet now—carpenters, masons, and electricians were coming out in ones and twos, heading for their horses and wagons. Carla hadn't spoken since the dean's office, and Jack didn't know what to say, so an uncomfortable stillness existed between them as they watched two carpenters load the disassembled parts of a large, rolling chalkboard onto a nearby wagon. Jack thanked and tipped the men and turned, assuming he and Carla would also climb aboard the wagon. But, once again, she was gone. Walking under the scaffolding, he entered the skeletal building, feeling a nip of wind moving through. "Carla?" he asked the emptiness.

Behind the outhouse that accompanied Finney Hall, Farrington's palomino stood idle and alone, its flaxen tail drooping, its saddle bearing the rifle, its reins loose-tied to a post.

Jack found Carla standing on the third floor of Sterry Hall, among its barren-framed walls and stairways. "We should go," he suggested, approaching her, seeing her look away, out to the chilly, burning sunset. He touched the center of her back and whispered, "I'm sorry for whatever is troubling you."

"You're kind," she said, turning, flashing a tearful smile.

"If I am, it's because of you, I guess," he managed to say, presenting his handkerchief and admiring as she dabbed her wet eyes, blushing cheeks and perky nose, before returning it to him.

"Thank you," she said.

He pocketed the cloth. "Anytime." She closed the distance between them until her head was resting on his chest. Above her, the corners of his mouth flickered to a small grin. He felt her warmth, her lightness against him. He could smell the fragrance of her hair. He wrapped his arms slowly around her.

"The man the dean asked about," she began in a strangled voice. "He was my father." Jack pulled back to see her face. She continued, "He and my brother were killed in Colorado. Did you hear about the Stratton Mine?"

"Yes," he replied gently. "The lift collapsed."

She moved to a bare window casing and sat, her booted feet dangling in the air. As he joined her, she said, "I never saw them again."

He frowned. "Were they never recovered?"

"The company wouldn't bring them up for proper burial on account they were union. But the Federation did. Mr. Haywood insisted. But I didn't get there in time—not for their funerals." She blinked slowly and took an even-longer breath. "I tried," she said, her voice so slight he had to reach for it.

He put his arm around shoulders. "I'm so sorry."

"You being a Pinkerton, I should tell you: I joined the Federation after that. I've been doing what I can to help the cause."

Jack nodded. "I would've done the same, I imagine."

On the far side of that third floor, across the stands, subflooring, and studding, Farrington was sitting—bit, scowl and strain—watching the forms of Jack and Carla against the distant purple oranges of day's end. Too far to hear more than occasional sounds, he whiskey-imagined their words to be cruelly passionate—and all about him—laughing at what a fool he was to think she might desire him. The longer he scrutinized them, the graver his fixation became, the stronger an invisible bond seemed to form between him and them, stretching the distance of that unfinished floor. The more their lips moved, the more he drank from his bottle. The tighter their silhouettes merged, the tighter he gripped his revolver.

"At first I worked for Clarence Darrow, Mr. Haywood's attorney," Carla was saying. "He'd tried to get justice for the men who died in the Stratton, but nothing came of it. Not a cent."

"That's awful," Jack whispered.

"It wasn't Mr. Darrow's fault," she said. "He's brilliant."

"That's what they say."

"Have you met him?"

"No. I've read about him. I'd like to meet him someday."

"I'd be happy to introduce you."

"Thank you," he said, unsure if she was sincere.

The last of the day dissolved through deep mauve and into black. Far below their boots, a horse stood patiently harnessed to the wagon bearing the chalkboard. Carla took Jack's hand. "You seem like a good man."

His eyebrows peaked, his mind sloshing in the feel of her fingertips. "I'm glad you think so," he muttered.

She pivoted to face him. "But I don't understand any man who'd turn his back on his brother—on decent, working men. Good Americans. I could never love a man like that." She studied his eyes. "Don't tell me I'm wrong about you. Say you agree, Jack. You must. You can't think the mine owners are right—that they should have everything, every advantage, including the courts and the law, all the politicians, while workers and their families suffer and starve. It's just not right. You see that, don't you?"

"I do," he offered. "It's not fair."

Her eyes smiled and her nose wrinkled. Her dimples drew him in further. She began anew, "You could help make things better."

"I'm not sure about that."

"Where are you from?" she asked.

"All over."

"You know open country," she said. "You're not from a city."

"How do you figure?" He saw her glance up at his hat—his black, broad-brimmed range hat with dingy silver stars on each side. "Fair enough," he said with a slight chuckle.

"The hat is one thing, but ... It's more about how you go about things—what you say." She sucked her bottom lip under her teeth, then let it go. "How you treat people ... like me."

"I appreciate that." He scratched one of his eyebrows though it didn't itch. "Of course I agree about the injustice—what reasonable fella wouldn't? Nobody should have to die to make a poor man's living. But I'm a Pinkerton—always wanted to be." He paused. "Alright, maybe not always, but I'm proud to be one now. And I want to stay one. I plan to be a detective as soon as I can. And you can say what you will, but the Pinkertons do a lot of good. A few bad apples, sure. Of course there's some in the Federation too, I imagine. Actually, there's some real rotten ones in the Federation. I know that for certain. And so do you."

She ignored that and pushed on. "It's the cause that matters, Jack. Something has to be done to change things. So I do what I can, what they ask of me. But not for any one person. And if the cause could better use my help elsewhere, I'd move on. Truth is, I don't like what they sent me here to do. But ... I'll not say any more about that." She saw his nod of understanding. "Let me ask you: Can you be a Pinkerton and still help workers?"

"What do you mean?"

"Can you, being a Pinkerton," she began with a plaintive smile, "protect one man? One poor family? Not just the owners of mines or banks? Or trains?"

"Of course," he replied.

"Then I say, be a Pinkerton. Do what you think is best for them. Become a detective or whatever you wish. But help me at the same time. Help me. Help me fight for men like my father and brother. Why can't you do both?"

Jack pulled in a deep, cold breath. The chief had instructed him to go along with this, to let her believe he was flipping sides. But now, sitting with her, listening to her, feeling his heart pounding in his neck, he wanted to say yes—yes, he would help her—but for *his* reasons, not because of McParland's plan. He knew she was right—not just about her cause, but about him. He didn't think the companies who hired the Pinkertons were always right—far from it. He knew what it was to be poor, to be desperate—far better than she could guess. So her question loomed: Could he do good for workers and still be a loyal Pinkerton? At what point would the ruse become real? At what point might the illusion take form? How should he proceed? In which direction? He felt as if he was stuck in the scrub briar of a foreign land—his compass points spinning—thorns ripping at his legs. He had to go with his gut. His heart. So he took a breath, looked at her directly and said, "Alright."

"Alright?" she repeated.

"Yes. I'll help you." He saw a glistening in her eye and, for a flash second, thought he just might love her.

She turned on her hundred-candle smile, leaned and kissed him. He slipped his hand under her hair and pulled her close, feeling her warm nape in his palm, her lips accepting his, the taste of her tongue, the rub of her nose against his own, her tears on his cheekbones. Overcome, they crumpled back to the subfloor, prone, mouths together, breaths mixed in that blissful throe.

"*Goddamn whore!*" Farrington shouted, twenty feet away, his pistol aimed unsteadily.

They both leapt to their feet. "Wade!" she shouted.

"Agent Farrington!" yelled Jack. It faintly registered on him that she'd called the man by his first name.

Farrington approached, gun up. "I should've known."

"Agent ..." Jack began, his thoughts spinning: *Is he undercover? No, the man's a traitor, but—*

"Backstabbing bitch," Farrington said, whiskey swaying him.

"That's enough!" barked Jack.

"And *you*—" Farrington turned his aim. "Think you're so smart."

"What?"

"But you're not, are you?"

Jack started to reach under his jacket, but then remembered he was unarmed. "I know all about you, Forty-Two, Wade Farrington. You've been working for Bill Haywood."

"*She's* his spy. Caught red handed. That cunt right there. Or are you too thick to know it? Just looking to cock her?"

"Shut your mouth!" Jack yelled.

"Hate to disappoint you, but everybody's already been there."

"Goddamn you." Jack started to rush Farrington but was drawn short by the pistol in his face. "I know who she is," said Jack.

"You think so?" asked Farrington. "You know she's Haywood's?"

"I do," said Jack.

"So are *you*!" Carla yelled at Farrington.

"I'll kill you," he snarled at her. "I will."

"What are you doing here?" she asked.

"Followed you two."

"Yeah? Why's that?" asked Jack.

"Chief doesn't trust you fraternizing with the enemy."

"Seems you're the enemy," said Jack, his eyes scanning without moving, searching for some sort of weapon, some advantage.

"Yes, he is," she said. "A jealous schoolboy."

Farrington moved his aim back to Carla, chuckling. "No, now I see it. You're a double. You're a Pink spying on Haywood. Turncoating on everyone."

"You're talking about you, or me?" asked Carla. "I'm confused."

Jack shook his head. "Put the gun down."

Farrington ignored him, his fury rising. "Both of you. I should shoot both of you. Right here. No one would know different. They'd never know it was me. Just two dead spies for Haywood and McParland. And you, bitch, you'd get what you deserve."

Seeing Carla clasp a scrap of wood behind her back, Jack spoke loudly, pulling Farrington's attention. "Maybe I'm wrong, Forty-Two. I don't think you have the *wood* to be a Wobbly spy." He hoped Carla noticed that he was giving her an opportunity.

Farrington spun toward Jack, scoffing, "I'm *Agent* Farrington, not Forty-Two. Besides, what do you know? You don't know me."

"You're no murderer, that's for sure. I—"

Wheeling the board through the air like a bat, Carla smacked Farrington's head. He collapsed and pulled the trigger on the way down, the bullet ripping through a wall stud. Jack was on Farrington immediately, pounding his face. The pistol came loose, and a moment later both men found themselves looking into its barrel, the grip in Carla's shaking hands. "Get up, Wade," she demanded.

Jack stood first. "I'd do what she says."

Farrington rose, his face bloody. "Wop bitch. What are you gonna do?"

"Turn you in," she replied. "But"—she tilted her head in mock contemplation—"would that be to the Pinks or to the Federation?

Mr. McParland will hang you. Mr. Haywood will shoot you. What do you think, Jack?"

"I'll take him to Chief Mc—"

"Goddamn you!" Farrington bellowed, rushing her. She pulled the trigger. The .44 caliber bullet shredded his chest. He buckled, falling off the partial subflooring, down through the second floor, to the first floor where he crashed with a walloping thump. Then came silence, save the ringing from the crack of the gun.

Carla turned, trembling, gun pointed down. "Oh no! Oh God. I shot him! Oh no," she exclaimed, her voice shrill and scared.

"It's alright," said Jack, taking the pistol from her and peering over the construction barrier to see Farrington's body far below.

"I killed him," she said, collapsing to the floor.

Jack came to her. "It'll be alright."

"Will you help me?"

"Of course." His mind was flying into action. "Don't worry."

★

– 28 –

WEDNESDAY
February 27, 1907

"What's this?" asked Neva, opening a thick, red leather-bound ledger book. She sat in a cane-back chair, her disheveled blonde tresses draping her bare shoulders and the top of her lace-trimmed camisole. The book was in front of her, lying on a marble-topped vanity that supported a beveled mirror bearing her morning image. A supply of correspondence paper was also on the vanity, each adorned with a bronze lithograph of a tall, narrow building, below which was printed: The Metropole Hotel, Denver, Colorado. George was in his BVD undershorts and undershirt, standing at the window seat, overlooking the low roofs and high floors beyond.

He glanced at her. "The accounts. The last two years."

"Federation books?"

"A copy of them."

"A copy?" she mused. "That must have been a lot of work, to make a copy like this." She flipped the green-lined pages bursting with hand-written entries. "I don't know how to read this."

"Please keep it in a safe place. You don't need to understand it."

"Why am I keeping it?" She plopped the cover closed.

"Insurance, I suppose. If he thinks I'm on his scent, he's likely to fire me. Then he'll either try to change the books, or keep them and blame me. Either way, that copy is my proof, my exoneration, as it were."

"I won't lose you," she said, trying to sound certain.

"That's right, darling, you won't."

"You know what I mean." She sniffed. "I can't let that happen. Those people—they blindly believe anything he says. Just anything. It's frightening."

"I have the truth. We can—"

"The truth?" she asked, her voice pinching as she regarded George through the mirror. She turned to him. "The truth—from the treasurer who's having an affair with the president's wife? That man is going to be believed? Him saying the husband is stealing money? The truth won't matter to those people, George."

He rubbed his almost bald head, causing wisps of hair to stand in static protest.

Neva looked back to the mirror and lifted her chin, examining it. "He needs to go ... away."

"Maybe it's me who should go."

"No, don't say that! Don't ever say that to me again."

"All right," he groused, watching her in the mirror.

After a long moment, she whispered, "He's a monstrous man."

"Did something happen?" he asked, seeing a further darkness in her expression. "Something else?"

"What do you mean?"

"What happened?" he persisted, moving to the window seat.

She gave a resigned huff. "How do you always know?"

"I know you." He shrugged. "You watch the birds; I watch you."

"What happens when you stop?"

"I won't."

"No?"

"No," he said. "What's going on? Something new happened."

She leaned close to her image, applying cream with her fingertips. She glanced at him, and then back into the mirror. The Bible verse, *That which is crooked cannot be made straight,* came to her mind. She looked again at George, his absorbing eyes formidable. He would wait her out. She would have to say it. Finally, she stiffened, murmuring, "He told her he loves her."

George rubbed an eye, sniffed, and squinted. "What of it?"

"He shouldn't have."

"Why not?" He stood, his jawline becoming visible through his pink cheeks. "Why does it matter what that man, that monstrous man as you call him, says to that dodgy girl?"

"My sister."

"I don't get it," he huffed, going into motion.

"Stop pacing."

He turned around, pinning her with his gaze.

"Please," she added. "Please stop pacing like that."

He sat on the bed. "She's your sister, of course. But you must see this is a difficult situation. Difficult is hardly the word for it."

Neva twisted in her chair to face him, her arm draped across its back. "I know," she whispered, compelling herself to be gentler.

"It's very hard for me," he added.

She gave a strained smile. "What do *you* want, darling?"

He held his gaze on her. "You. To be with you. Just you. Just you and me. Imagine what that'd be: a life together—just you and me. Not Bill. Not Winnie. I mean not—not Winnie like this." He scooted closer to her and took her hand. "That's what I want."

With the pad of her thumb, she wiped a tear from her eye, and then one from his cheek. "Me too. I want that too."

"So, how can we?"

"I don't know."

George sighed. "As you said, he needs to go away."

Neva didn't blink. "If they find him guilty, in Boise, then—"

"They'll hang him." His eyebrows rose as he shook his head.

"He did it, you know. He—" When he looked at her, she completed the thought. "He had that governor murdered."

"You know that?"

"I know it."

"Did he say that?"

She shrugged. "I just know it."

George lay back on the bed and examined the tin-tiled ceiling. "We can't make a difference in that."

"I was thinking of talking to that detective."

"James McParland?" He sat up. "You can't, darling. If you were seen, it would— I don't know, but you can't."

"What else is there?" She glanced at the ledger book.

He saw where she was looking. "Maybe. I don't know. I could take it to the union directly—to the thirty or so local chapters." Both sat quietly until George spoke again. "I wonder what Bill would do, if they turned on him—the chapter presidents."

"He'd take me and the girls to Chicago. And Winnie, of course."

"I don't think so. There'd be no place he could go—not in the United States. Least not any union city."

"He loves Russia. I don't know why he doesn't just ..." A vision landed in her mind: Bill at the railing on a departing ship—not waiving.

"I don't think so," said George.

"The Federation could ban him. But the Socialist wouldn't."

"Our socialists?" he asked. "In America? No, Debs wouldn't take Bill. Both of them can't fit under one red flag."

Neva screwed up her lips in thought. "Would that man—Trotty something—would he want him?"

"Trotty? In Russia? That's not his name, but I know who you mean. No, probably not. I don't know." His mind drifted. "Trotsky, that's his name. This whole matter is speculation. I could try to foment a rebellion against Bill, to drive him out of office. But, as you said, is not likely." George paused, exhaling hard. "Regardless, you're not going to Russia."

"No! I certainly would not ... no ... and you know why?"

"You don't like those poofy fur hats?"

"No, I like those fine," she said with a smile. "No." She lifted his hand to kiss it. "It's because you wouldn't be there. That's why."

★

– 29 –

FRIDAY
March 1, 1907

On the first day of March 1907, Agent Farrington's rigid body was fished from the frigid Boise River, a tributary of the Snake River, now a brawling flow of new snowmelt. By noon, the body was packed in ice, loaded on a train, and was bound for burial in Anderson, Indiana.

Four days earlier, someone had noticed a lone palomino near the college. The shivering horse seemed abandoned, though it was tacked and carrying an oddly scoped M1903 Springfield rifle. Informed of the mystery, McParland arrived and took possession of both horse and rifle, and found blood on the first floor of the building under construction. Connecting the origin of his new chalkboard with the location of the blood, he questioned Jack.

Jack recounted the events, including where he and Carla had ditched Farrington alongside the river. It was an accurate retelling, though he claimed to have pulled the trigger, not Carla—a deviation McParland seemed to accept, if not fully believe. Certain that the chief would send a Pinkerton to retrieve the body, Jack was surprised when a passerby discovered it four days later, simply floating by.

Now Jack was in McParland's office, along with three other agents, each in their almost-matching Pinkerton attire, each holding a drawing of Steve Adams. One of them, Iain Lennox, a massive Scotsman whom Jack had never seen before, was talking with the chief about having won a caber-tossing match—something Jack knew nothing about. The other two were the Polk brothers whom Jack recognized from his early Pinkerton days in St. Louis. As they hadn't been subsequently posted in Denver, Jack didn't really know them—though one, Peter Polk, had been with him in the governor's bloody, snowy yard two months earlier.

McParland stood before the large green chalkboard now covered in white words, symbols, and lines. At the top were three names in capital letters: HAYWOOD at the very top, with scratchy white marks down to ORCHARD and ADAMS. "These two," McParland said, pointing to the lower two names, "are who we need in order to get *him*." He tapped the chalk hard on the name HAYWOOD. "Thanks to Agent Garrett, we have this one," he said, drawing an X through ORCHARD. Pivoting, he motioned to the drawings in the men's hands. "So now, you four, go bring me this vermin." Rotating back to the board, he drew an angry circle around ADAMS.

"Aye, Chief," they replied together.

"We lost him in San Francisco," McParland continued. "But maybe he's still there. On Haywood's orders, this Adams fellow is tracking a man named James Branson, one of our client's men. Adams has gone there to kill the man. Your first order of business is to capture Adams—but do what you can to save Branson. The Federation already took the man's hand, up at Bunker Hill, so maybe you can save his life." After seeing Jack nod, the chief detective skated his gaze across the other three. "Agent Garrett is in command on this. Meet up with our two agents there in San Francisco. They lost Adams, but you can not. You must do better. That'll make you six. He'll only be one. Bring him to Silver City—the Silver City here in Idaho. I'll get him from you there. But do *not* bring me a corpse. Bring him alive. Understood?"

As the four acknowledged the order, Jack noticed the M1903 rifle on McParland's desk.

"Take that with you," McParland said quietly to Jack. "That scope's daffy, but the gun's good." He turned to address the room. "Gentlemen, Adams is a mad dog, a thoughtless, ruthless killer like none you've ever encountered or will again, God willing. So keep yourselves armed, your weapons loaded. Travel light and fast. Operate incognito, under cover. Do what you must. Stay vigilant for one another. Stay ready. Protect each other. Avoid local law. And do not—under any circumstances—kill Adams. He's as a vile a son of a bitch as ever was, but he's *our* son of a bitch. He belongs to us now. He's the witness we must have. So I need him alive."

Confirmation all around.

"That brings me to Captain Swain. He'll be there—watch for him. He's in Mr. Haywood's employ, so he means to kill Adams before the rat can testify. I don't care for Swain, but he's fast and accurate. He's smart. He used to be one of us. He knows how we work." McParland lowered his chin for a moment, letting a thought move by, as if letting a train pass. Then he smoothed his mustache, and resumed, "Don't underestimate him. Swain knows that country better than any of you ever will. And if Swain gets to Adams—and Adams doesn't kill him first, which is possible—then Adams will vanish. He'll rot out in the desert or up in the Sierra Nevadas. We'll never find him. Do *not* let that happen. Would any of you know Swain if you saw him? Would you, Agent Garrett?"

"I believe so," Jack lied. He'd just been put in charge—the last thing he wanted was to now admit ignorance.

"Good," continued McParland. "You've been given as many of the details as we know about Steve Adams. It's all written on the back of those drawings."

The four flipped their papers with concurrent crinkles.

"Names. Addresses. Relations. The code terms to use. And the telephone numbers to reach me, though best you telegraph." McParland watched the young men peruse the information. "Go then," he said. "Give me daily reports. Be smart. Be careful. I want all of you coming home to your mommas—as well as your girlfriends, or your sheep"—they laughed—"all safe and sound."

"Aye, Chief," said the Polks and Iain as they departed.

Jack stayed back. "May I ask—"

"Yes?" McParland lit his pipe.

"Seeing how, last month, you had assigned me to infiltrate—"

"What of it?"

"Well, Sir, you're sending me after Adams before I can—"

"And?"

"I can't rightly do both things in two places."

McParland palmed the air. "Last month you weren't a murderer."

The word froze Jack. "No, Sir. Understood."

"Speaking of killers, we'll keep Miss Capone here. We'll keep an eye on her. But it's best you get out of Boise for a while."

"Yes, Sir."

"Now, that may be why I'm sending you, but it's not why I'm giving you operational command."

Jack's brow furrowed. "Sir?"

"You've got a solid head on you, superior instincts. And that piece of bad business with Farrington—I was impressed with how you handled it. How you protected Miss Capone."

"Thank you, Sir."

"Command means you're responsible not just in the aftermath, protecting your team. But in the moment. And before the moment. In fact, long before the moment ever comes. Do you understand what I'm saying?"

"Yes, Sir."

McParland jabbed his pipe toward the chalkboard. "This is how you might become a detective—leading this campaign to get Adams. Aye, others have far more seniority than you. And they'll be hot at me when you go." After a considered puff, he continued, "But mark me, Jack, there'll always be men with more seniority or less seniority. Better at this, worse at that. Taller, shorter, dumber, smarter. You name it." He lifted a bushy eyebrow, shoved the pipe into one side of his mouth and spoke from the other. "*Quod optima sui oportet quod.*" He removed his pipe. "Be the best self you have to be. Require that of yourself. It's all I require of you."

"I'll try, Sir," Jack said, then saw McParland's eyes narrow slightly. "I *will*, Sir."

"I know. you will." McParland turned his back. "Stay safe, son."

"Aye, Chief."

– 30 –

SATURDAY
March 2, 1907

The next day, as the train carrying the San Francisco-bound Pinkertons bore from the Boise station—steam swelling, wheels screeching, engine snorting—Carla observed from under the hood of her cape, two-deep on the platform. Twenty minutes later, she was in the Western Union office on Main Street, watching a clerk key her message:

> To: W. Minor, Gassell Saloon, Denver, Colorado
> From: CC, Boise, Idaho
> MY LOVE LEFT FOR SF TODAY TO SEE A.
> PRAY HE TRAVELS SAFE.
> MOST IMPORTANT TO US.

What she didn't know was that Senator Borah had persuaded the Western Union Telegraph Company to install a stand-alone wire from the roof of that telegraph office, across Tenth Street, and into the Idanha Hotel where a receiving machine typed out Carla's message. A Pinkerton clerk then took the intercepted telegraph up to the mezzanine and delivered it to the frumpily dressed Detective McParland sitting at his usual table. McParland read it and handed it to his lunch guest, the flawlessly dressed Senator Borah. "Should I send it on?" the clerk asked, unsure to which man he should address the question.

Once Borah looked up from reading it, McParland asked, "So, what do you think, William?"

Borah waggled his head and gave a slight whistle, then looked at the clerk. "Thank you, Douglas, we'll let you know." After the man departed, Borah set the telegram down and cut another bite from his steak. "'A' is Adams I guess. Her 'love' is your agent?"

"Aye. Jack Garrett."

Borah continued, "'Pray he travels safe.' 'He' is Jack or Adams?"

"Jack," replied McParland.

"'Safe.' She hopes he's protected by the Federation. From whom? From the Federation themselves?"

"Uh-huh," McParland mused as Borah chewed. "She's worried about him. They've tumbled into Cupid's bear pit."

"When did Cupid dig a bear pit?"

McParland grinned. "Now, Senator, I imagine you've installed a special ladder, just for you to get out."

Borah chuckled. "That's true."

McParland resumed examining the telegram. "I'd hoped she was obliged to report to Haywood, on our hunt for Adams."

Borah frowned. "Why would Haywood protect a Pinkerton?"

McParland nodded, swallowing his bite. "Two reasons, I hope. One—and it's uncertain—is maybe Haywood likes her, wants to please her, if she pleads on Jack's behalf. And two—and this is what I'm most counting on—she's signaling that Jack's one of them now. That he's their new inside man, after Farrington."

Borah's eyes widened. "Are you saying—"

"He's not *really*, but I told him to make em think it. She took the bait and here she's telling Haywood." McParland picked up the message. "'Most important to *us*.' I wish she'd been more clear."

Borah cocked his chin. "You knew you'd be sending him after Adams, and they might try to kill him. So you put him with Carla?" He laughed. "So you're Cupid. The damn bear pit is yours."

McParland smiled. "Nah, she found him. I just saw an opportunity and took it. I added the double-agent bit as a backup to help protect him—to increase the odds he gets Adams. And maybe we'll get some useful intelligence from it. The young man is cloaked by love and a lie, but doesn't know it."

"The puppet-master." Borah grinned. "I agree, her message could've been more direct. I doubt Haywood will see more than the Adams part. He might still have his thugs go after your boys."

"I doubt it. He sent Swain to get Adams," said McParland. "And Swain knows the hell I'd rain down on him if he hurt a Pinkerton. He'd have to run to China. They've got more to worry about from Adams than from Swain."

"Captain Swain?" asked Borah. "Thiel Agency out of Spokane?" He saw McParland nod. "I know him. He's a piece of work." Borah glanced down to the floor level of the restaurant, then motioned McParland to do the same. Carla was below them, having just begun her waitressing shift. "My God, she's a beauty," Borah murmured. "A Federation spy?"

"A reluctant one, according to Jack."

"Why didn't she telephone her Haywood contact, W Minor?"

"W—Winnifred—Minor is Winnie, Haywood's sister-in-law."

Borah nodded. "All right, but why—"

"And Haywood's mistress."

"His wife's *sister*?" The senator stared at the detective. "Wait a damn minute. What? Does his wife know?"

"Oh aye, she does. You see, Mrs. William Haywood—Nevada Jane Haywood—Neva—is polio stricken, and her sister Winnie takes care of her. So, better her husband beds Winnie than some street whore. Or worse, someone he might leave Neva for."

Incredulous, Borah looked again at Carla below. "So, who is she to the sister-mistress-Winnie?"

"Carlotta Capone and Winnie are best friends, as I understand it," said McParland. "Or they were, in Spokane or Walla Walla, a few years ago. But this new relationship has been *forged in the worker's struggle!*" McParland held his fist high in mockery. "Winnie got involved in the Federation because of her sister. But now Winnie has become a zealot socialist. As for our pretty dago down there, Miss Capone, her father and brother were killed in the Stratton collapse. So she helps the union, however she can."

Just then, Borah caught Carla's eye, and she flashed a grin up at the box-jawed senator. He bowed his head, giving her his best devil-may-care smile. Turning back, he asked McParland, "So, why do you let her work here, around your operation?"

"To keep an eye on her," replied McParland. "And from what I can tell, she's not a radical. She's just a grieving, angry daughter."

Borah held the telegram. "So, what should we do with this?"

"If it doesn't arrive, it might expose our wire diversion."

"No, no," said Borah. "I can't have it known I arranged that." He chuckled. "I was just sworn into office, for godsakes."

"Tell you what," McParland said. "Let's send it, but with a couple of edits." He motioned the nearest guard. "Get Douglas back. Tell him to bring a pen." The man hurried down the mezzanine stairs. McParland looked at Borah. "We'll just push the dates and make it a bit more clear about Jack."

Borah wiped his mouth, then placed the napkin on his empty plate. "You didn't say—why didn't Miss Capone telephone her friend, the mistress, Winnie?"

"Well, it seems that Mr. Haywood thinks we are listening to all telephone conversations, in or out of his Denver homes and offices, even his attorney's office." McParland gave a fast wink.

Borah dipped his nose, silently asking, Are they?

"Bell is a Pinkerton client," McParland replied.

"But he doesn't suspect telegrams?"

"I guess not. Though, of course Western Union is a client too."

When the telegraph clerk returned to the table, he set down a Conklin dip pen and opened a small ink jar. McParland took up the pen. "Douglas, my good man," he began, "have this resent, but with these changes." In the first line, MY LOVE LEFT FOR SF TODAY TO VISIT A, McParland marked through LEFT and wrote *leaves*, and he changed TODAY to *next week*. Then he marked through the last line, MOST IMPORTANT TO US, and wrote *Most Important. One of Us.* He showed it to Borah, getting the senator's nod, then handed it to the clerk.

"Yes, Sir," said the clerk, leaving with the paper, pen, and ink.

With lunch finished, the men stood. McParland asked, "Monday? We're meeting with Judge Wood?"

"Yes. Ten o'clock," replied Borah, watching the detective attempt to smooth his chaotic mustache. "Are you ever gonna finish eating that squirrel?"

McParland chuckled. "Never."

They shook hands. "I must get going," said Borah. "Oh, I meant to ask: Your wife, Mary—is she coming here?"

"Nah, her cluck of Red Rook ladies are in Denver. They play and gab most afternoons. So we write and talk on the telephone."

"Well, the next time you talk to her, give her my regards."

"God no. If she thought the dashing new senator from Idaho knew her name, she'd faint right there in her kitchen."

★

– 31 –

SUNDAY
March 3, 1907

Jack was asleep under his hat in the second-class sleeping car when the Southern Pacific train belled and squeaked to a night stop in San Francisco. As expected, the other two Pinkerton agents met the disembarking four. They divided up, carrying the bags and shotguns to various coaches waiting in the dark. Jack carried the scoped M1903 Springfield rifle slung over his shoulder. An hour later, the six were sitting around a table at the back of the Old Ship Saloon on Pacific Street while a peeved barkeep brought them root beers and Coca Cola. Their Pinkerton togs were gone, replaced with average coats and trousers.

On the train, Jack had become familiar with the three *en route* with him, each about his age: the two Polk brothers (Pete and Stan), and Iain Lennox, the giant Scot who talked about flying as if it was equivalent to bedding the most beautiful woman in the world. After Jack shared a non-Pinkerton flask that Iain had brought, squinting as Iain described something called aerodynamics, Jack decided they were friends. Now Iain sat to Jack's right, smoking a pipe and curling his Rs as the Pinkerton strategy was bunted about. "You've got that all turned wrong there," said Iain in his thick Scottish accent.

"Not John Branson, James Branson," added Pete Polk. "James."

"I heard you. I know," said one of the two agents who had already been in San Francisco for weeks, having lost Adams in the burned-out streets. "But I would've seen a James Branson in the register, seeing how he'd be listed below John."

"Above John," groused Stan, the other Polk brother.

"We'll go check. Iain and I will," Jack said. He focused on the brothers. "What do you Polks want to do?"

Stan glanced at Pete. "We'll cover the saloons, whorehouses, boarding houses, hotels, whorehouses, and gambling establishments. For starters."

"You said whorehouses twice," said Iain.

"That's right," quipped Stan. "There's two of us."

"All that 'for starters'?" Jack asked, smiling. "I suggest you start at the edge of the burned part and work—"

"A grid?" said Pete with a snap of sarcasm.

"Right," said Jack. "A grid." He turned his attention to the original Pinkertons. "You two stand watch at the station. Starting tonight. One always awake. *Always*."

"Damnation," said one of them.

"There's no place to lie down," said the other.

"Why the hell you telling us what we gotta do?" asked the first. "You let them two choose." He pointed at the Polks.

"I know your thinkin, Jack," Iain mocked. "If the Polk brothers see the killer Adams, they won't piss their britches, or be fool stupid enough t' lose him, like these two Nancys did."

Jack nodded at the first two Pinkertons. "Like he said."

That night, Carla was in the dark, on her back, in her Idanha Hotel bed, wearing only her camisole, her hair tied back loosely. She thought of Jack. Where was he that very minute? What might it be like to sleep with him? To feel his arms around her—his chest over her. To smell him. What did he enjoy? Was he circumcised? She shook her head. She should sleep. She rolled on her side, snuggling the covers closer to her neck. She had the breakfast shift at 6:30 the next morning. Her mind drifted. Why was she staying in Boise? Her original assignment was done. Orchard was arrested. Both of her spy recruits were gone, and the Pinkertons would never let her convert another. In fact, she didn't want to do it again. Should she go back to Denver? No. For what? For lecherous Big Bill Haywood? Disgusting. No. She was done with spying. She was done with all of it. When Jack returned, she would admit that she had been instructed to recruit him. But she didn't want it that way between them. Not now. Yes, he had agreed to help her—but he should only do it if he wished to, not because he felt coerced by her. Would he be angry? Could she take that chance? What they had would weather that—right? They had something, didn't they? Of course they did. She could feel it. Just as she could feel she was finished with the Federation. She had planted evidence in a man's room, had given her body to a man she didn't like, and— She tried to keep herself from finishing the thought, but couldn't: she had killed that man. The image of Wade erupted in her mind. She bit her lip, sealing her eyes tighter. She heard the gunshot, saw the blood. She threw the blankets back and sat up. She needed Jack. She would stay in Boise and wait for him to return. He would come back. He had to come back.

★

– 32 –

MONDAY
March 4, 1907

The next morning, Jack and Iain left their boarding house wearing shoulder-holstered pistols under their coats. Outside, they were immediately struck by the sights of widespread destruction that daylight revealed. After breakfast, they stood in line, riffled through the city record books for Branson's address, and by 10:30 were turning the corner from Holloway onto Faxon. There they saw a San Francisco policeman wearing a midnight-blue long coat and black hat standing at the gate to the Branson home, gesturing to a small crowd who had come to whisper and point.

"Move along, gentlemen," said the bear-faced policeman as they approached.

"I'm Pinkerton Agent Garrett. This is Agent Lennox. May I—"

"Doesn't matter who you are," said the policeman.

"Right. But may we inquire about the occupants of this house?"

The man considered the two and blew a sigh. "The Bransons?"

"Aye, Sir," said Iain, adjusting his big bowler.

"Dead. All of them," he murmured, gesturing toward the black crepe draping the picket fence.

For a moment Jack was stunned. "In the fire?"

"What?" asked the policeman.

"They died in the earthquake and fire?" repeated Jack, still not comprehending.

"That was last year, Sherlock."

"Of course."

"They were murdered," the officer continued. "The man, his wife, his two children. Someone poisoned their milk last week. Discovered a couple of days ago. Crying shame."

Iain began walking away. When Jack caught up, Iain softly mumbled, "Adams got him. And not just him, his whole family. Damnit, Jack. Damnit."

"Yeah," was all Jack could say for the next twenty paces. Then he stopped. "He might not be gone. He might've stayed."

"We should tell those policemen," said Iain, heeling around.

Jack trailed after him, back toward the house. "I know. I know, Iain, we need to—but we can't."

Iain recoiled. "Why the bloody hell not?"

"If the whole city plus us six—and Captain Swain too, probably—are all looking for Adams, then one of two things is going to happen: either Adams will turn up dead, because either Swain or the coppers will kill him. Or Adams runs, disappears into the mountains or jumps on a ship. Meaning we'd never find him. That's what I'd do, jump on a ship."

Calmer now, Iain said, "Aye. You're right. I wish you weren't."

Jack nodded. "We'd best keep our eyes open. Might get lucky."

Iain looked toward the house where another policeman had joined the first. "They've got to be told soon, though."

"They do. And they will. As soon as we have the dog in chains, back in Boise. Then I imagine Chief will send a wire."

Senator Borah and Detective McParland climbed the granite steps to the Ada County Courthouse in Boise, entered through the towering, weather-worn double doors, and proceeded through the corridor to a polished oak door bearing a sign reading: Judge Freemont Wood – Idaho 3rd Judicial District. They entered, and Borah spoke to a secretary there. "Judge Wood, please."

She rose, blushing at the striking man. "Yes, Senator, this way." She led them into the judicial chambers. Dimly lit through dingy windows, it was a den of books and furniture smelling of cigars and consequences. The judge was in his shirt sleeves, shuffling papers.

"Your Honor," began Borah.

Wood looked up, revealing warm green eyes and a disciplined mustache, his bald head swept by gray hairs. "William Borah! No, Senator Borah—you're sworn in now."

"Yes, Your Honor, I am."

"Good. I was gratified by your election. A good Republican—just what these outlaw parts need." The judge then looked at

McParland. "Jim, how's your hip today?" It was a simple question, ostensibly pleasant and sincere, but it was packed with subtext. It was the first maneuver in an ancient, choreographed dance among men who seek to control an impending conversation. By calling him "Jim," rather than "Chief Detective McParland" (or even "James"), and by inquiring about McParland's physical weakness—and doing so on the heels of flattering Senator Borah—Judge Wood was claiming an elevated station, placing himself on par with a US Senator. In that one phrase, Wood said the important men in the commencing conversation were going to be the senator and himself, not the Pinkerton.

McParland heard every unspoken word and replied, "Never been better, Monty," referring to the judge by his name-among-friends. Though the riposte wouldn't upend the hierarchy, it just might gain him parity.

McParland and Borah took seats in front of the judge's cluttered desk and settled in. "Thank you for sending Mr. Orchard's confession. What a thing," said Judge Wood. "He is a damnable sort. I think the worst I've ever seen." McParland and Borah nodded but stayed silent. "You want to set his trial? Margie will clear my docket. You just tell her when. *Voir dire* might be a badger, but I'll get you through it. Does he have an attorney yet?"

"Not yet," said Borah. "There was a fellow who came. The Federation sent him from Walla Walla, I believe. But he left without taking the matter."

"We don't want to hang Orchard," McParland began. "Not yet."

"So who are we going to hang?" Wood asked.

"William Haywood," said Borah.

The judge's eyes widened, his high forehead furrowing. "I assure you, gentlemen, no one wants to see Big Bill in my courtroom more than I do. Even better, swinging out at the pen. But you'd need a few things first."

McParland took a noisy breath. "Aye, another witness."

"To hang him, that's correct," said Wood. "But you'd have to get him into my courtroom first." He peered at Borah. "And to get him here, you'd need what?" He reached an impatient hand toward Borah, waggling his fingers like a headmaster impatiently asking a pupil to hand over some contraband.

"Extradition," said Borah, his jaw clenching at the condescending gesture.

"Precisely. He's not in Idaho, I'd imagine."

McParland frowned. "No. But you wouldn't—"

Judge Wood flicked a hand up, interrupting McParland. "It's a simple test: Was Mr. Haywood within the State of Idaho at the time of the governor's assassination?"

Borah shook his head almost imperceptibly. McParland sat lock still.

Wood fixed on Borah. "Then how, Counselor, may I be of assistance to the State in its prosecution of Mr. Haywood?"

Borah glanced away, inhaling fully through his nose.

The judge turned to McParland. "One of you goosecaps needs to say something, otherwise let's go to lunch."

"If the man," began McParland, "let's say, stood in handcuffs before your bench, how concerned would you be with the *means* by which he got there?"

Borah raised his brow in confederacy with the detective's question. "Hypothetically, of course," he said. "Please consider the question as a mere curiosity on the State's part."

"You're an officer of the court," said Wood, "and a United States Senator."

"That's true, Your Honor."

"Bound and sworn to uphold and defend the Constitution."

Borah's face burned. "Of course."

McParland sat forward in his chair. "We've got to end that man's terror. We must. You and I've talked on this, Monty."

Wood squinted at the disclosure of a private conversation.

McParland continued, "I don't know another way. I've had that man and his operations under my nose for years. Mostly in Denver. He has that whole state bought and paid for—sheriffs, judges, even contingents on the army posts. And who he doesn't have pocketed, like the Colorado governor and the chief justice, they're powerless in effect, other than occasional slaps. As you know, Haywood has tens of thousands of armed men across the western states—including here in Idaho. It's unsustainable, and this is our best chance in years—perhaps the only chance we'll ever get—to stop him before he orders another bomb, another assassination."

Borah joined in. "If nothing is done now—now that he's responsible for a state governor's assassination—then I fear, Your Honor, that he'll be unstoppable."

Wood glanced at the politician. "He might kill a senator next."

"Or another judge," said Borah, his gaze fixed. "He's a disease on this country. There's no one—no threat, no man or group—more contrary to the Constitution which, as you said, you and I both swore to uphold."

The judge sat for a moment before rising abruptly. "Gentlemen, my stomach's telling me we're late for lunch. Wouldn't you agree?"

Borah and McParland got to their feet and exchanged glances.

After donning his coat and hat, Judge Wood squeezed Borah's shoulder. "For *any* defendant brought before my bench, I'm responsible for the conduct of a fair trial inside my court under the laws of criminal procedure for the State of Idaho. But that's *all*."

"Thank you," said McParland, catching the judge's meaning.

"Of course," resumed the judge, "it'll all be for naught if you don't present a second witness." He stopped in the courthouse's main hall. "Haywood's attorney is Clarence Darrow?"

"Yes, Your Honor," said Borah.

Wood widened his eyes at the senator. "You've got the grit and gristle to wrestle that tiger? He's a heavyweight."

"We'll see."

"He'll bring a circus to town," said Wood. "And Mr. Darrow will run the *habeas corpus* claim straight to the Supreme Court, squealing all the way. And he'll win, most likely, as you know—ending everything right there. That'd be an embarrassment for a fresh-faced senator. So don't start down this path unless you're ready for that outcome. I won't let you back out on account of your reputation. If you start this fire, you'll have to see it through."

"Of course. That's the only way," replied Borah.

Wood turned to McParland. "And Jim, for the Pinkertons to get Big Bill here *alive*, you'll need the Union Pacific. General Dodge."

Bracing at the instruction, the detective counted to four, then said, "We're meeting with him tomorrow, Monty."

"As you should, gimpy," said Wood, noting McParland's cane. He turned on a heel to resume his pace. "Now keep up. Let's eat!"

A week earlier, a postcard arrived at the Haywood's Park Hill house. The card bore a painting of a city-block-long, six-story, massive red-brick building with large windows connected by bands of limestone and topped by two-story flagpoles bearing twenty-foot American flags. Its ground floor was adorned with awning-covered doors and 650 linear feet of display windows running along a wide street illustrated with horse-drawn coaches, passing trolleys, a few automobiles, and a slew of happy white people. The card read:

Announcing the Grand Emporium Expansion of

THE DENVER DRY GOODS CO.

The Largest Store in the Central West
400 Feet Long; Seven Acres Floor Area;
1,200 Employees; A $2,500,000 Stock.
15th to 16th on California Street
Denver, Colorado

Now Winnie and Neva were approaching the Denver Dry Goods elevators, having just finished lunch in the 2,000-seat Tea Room on the top floor. Both wore tailored jackets over white blouses, but Neva's skirt was mossy and pleated, while Winnie's was crimson and snug. Their deep-crowned hats rode on their stacked hair like two ships on stormy blonde seas. Wheeling Neva's invalid chair into the elevator, Winnie asked, "Where first?"

"Corsets. First and last," said Neva. She might've heard Winnie snicker, but Neva's mind was a mile and two months away—on a similar moment when George had rolled her onto the elevator in the Pioneer Building. He never left her mind, was always there, like the lovely hum of a song that never goes away.

On the wall behind the five other women in the descending elevator, a sign announced that "Stetsons, Saddles, and Everything Else" were available in the Stockman's Room on the north end of the second floor. Another sign eagerly encouraged patrons to stroll the brand new, 400-foot main aisle on the first floor.

"I want to get George a Stetson," said Neva, her eyes on the Stockman sign.

Winnie replied, “Us first—then them.”

Neva nodded as the attendant announced, “Fourth floor. Ladies wear.”

Lined with mahogany paneling below leaded-glass clerestory windows, the women’s floor seemed to stretch beyond comprehension. They stared into the distance, absorbing the store’s expanded new space: from undergarments to ball gowns, from pockets to ostrich hats. Everything was there. And it was abuzz with employees, all featly dressed and responding to tinkling bells summoning them to where they were most needed.

“Well, this does it—they’ve won. I’m never going back to Daniels and Fisher,” said Winnie, referring to the department store two blocks away that boasted a twenty-one-story clock tower.

“Or May’s,” added Neva.

“Or May’s,” echoed Winnie.

“From a spool of thread to a thousand-dollar dress.”

“They have a thousand-dollar dress here?” asked Winnie, her voice up an octave at the thought.

Neva nodded. “Read it in the Post.”

“I think I need a new pair of gloves just to shop here. Bill has an account?”

“Yes, but ”

“What?” asked Winnie.

“He does,” Neva said, then inhaled fully. Women were shuffling by them like torrents of water around river boulders. Neva looked up from her chair. “If you’re waiting for me to suddenly start walking, this would be the place that miracle would happen. But until then, either I start rolling or you push.” No response. “Winnie!” snapped Neva, seeing her sister lost in shopper’s reverie. “Let’s go. Corsets. Thousand-dollar dress. Then down to two for a Stetson.”

“The dress first,” said Winnie, recovering.

At the far end of the floor, about a hundred people, mostly women, were in various states and statuses relative to the processes of the couture dress department: selecting, making, and purchasing. About a third were customers and their accompaniments—some in chairs, some lounging on settees, some standing on stools as seamstresses flowed about them, pinning and chalking, measuring their waists, their hem lengths, and their spending money. Strolling among the throng were a few imperious head dressmakers with long, white sticks with which they identified points for improvement, fit, amplification, or embellishment. In the center of this activity, in a tall glass case, stood a headless mannequin wearing the $1,000 evening dress of golden silk with oak-leaf embroidery and a three-foot train. Neva rolled herself close and read the placard: "G. Giuseffi, Limited. $1,150."

"That's it?" quipped Winnie. "I saw that pattern in McCall's."

"Un-huh," said Neva.

An hour later they had made it barely one hundred feet to the lingerie department and its array of shelves and display tables presenting perfectly formed stacks of corsets of all sorts and makes. Winnie examined a long white one. "Oh my, look at this," she said, bringing it to Neva. "It's twelve dollars."

"Truly?" Neva took it, admiring the ribbons. "It's satin, for a wedding dress." She handed it back.

"Suitable for a bridal trousseaux," read Winnie.

"These sateen ones are fine. I need short. For this chair."

"Or just not wear one. Like that boned under-bodice that—"

"That again?" Neva glowered. "I'm not dead. And I *can* stand."

"I don't think Bill would care—"

"No, he wouldn't," retorted Neva. "You keep looking at those bridal ones. Maybe one comes with a husband of your own."

Yet another hour passed before they were down on the second floor, ensconced in the smell of leather and wool, and bathed in baritone voices punctuated by summoning bells and the occasional hiss from steam-forms shaping hat brims and crowns. Neva compared two Stetsons. "I think I like this one," she said to the clerk.

"The Galena. Excellent choice, Mrs. Haywood."

Neva looked at the man. "Uhmm, yes."

"I sold your husband a beaver Victor two weeks ago. Size seven and seven-eighths."

"Is that big?"

"Yes, our biggest. But no worries, Ma'am, we can stretch this Galena same as we did his Victor."

"No, no need." She paused. "Can you give me a minute?"

"Yes, of course."

She rolled to Winnie who was trying on derbies in a mirror. "I need your help."

"What is it?" asked Winnie.

"He thinks the hat's for Bill, but George's head isn't so fat."

"You're afraid Bill might find out?"

"Foo!" Neva squinted. "How many dresses does he buy you?"

Winnie glanced away.

Neva continued, "I just don't want that clerk thinking things. So come over and let's say it's for someone you know."

"Alright."

It wasn't until they were browsing the ground floor—housewares, with its carpets, silverware, electric lamps, embossed trunks, landscape paintings, dining tables, and porcelain busts—that Neva gathered the nerve to say what she felt she had to: "Things are going to change, Sissy."

"What?"

Neva held the wheels of her chair. "Things are going to change."

"What do you mean?" Winnie moved in front of Neva.

Neva fumbled with their claim tickets. "You know, change."

"What are you talking about? When?"

"Probably soon. This year."

"The Boise matter?"

"That, yes. And financial problems are getting worse."

Winnie sat on the edge of a leather Morris chair bearing the price of $12.85. "It will be fine, Sissy. You'll see."

Neva wagged her head slowly. "No. It won't."

"He can't be guilty because they won't have two witnesses. That's what Mr. Darrow said. So—"

"But he *is* guilty," said Neva. "Doesn't that matter to you?"

Winne stared for two seconds. "What about us?"

"We'll be all right. In fact, we'll be better than all right."

"I thought they can't make him go to Idaho."

"But if they do—" Neva began, then switched course. "Regardless of whatever happens there, he also stole money from the union. Sixty thousand dollars. Maybe more. I won't let George take the blame for it, for what Bill did. And I gained from it too—the house. You and I both did. I can't let George get hurt—even be blamed. It would ruin him. I won't."

Seeing the tears in Neva's eyes, Winnie's eyes glistened too. "No, I know you can't. George is a sweet man."

Neva gave a reflective smile and a little nod. "Thank you for saying that. He really is." She reached and wiped a tear from Winnie's cheek. "Bill made his own bed. He told them to murder that man, and he stole the money." Neva spoke as if the words tasted foul. "He is a devil, to be sure. So, you and I have to look out for each other. As we always have. We have to stay away from whatever storm is coming for him." She dipped her petite chin. "I want to get the girls home. I don't think I'm contagious. And I want you to have your own life. And I want George ... I want George to be safe."

Winnie sighed. "What do we do?"

"Don't do anything. Other than stop helping Bill. And stop helping your friend, Carla. It's Carla, right?" When Winnie nodded, Neva continued, "In fact, if you give a hoot for her, maybe she should know what's what—that Bill's not who she thinks he is—that this isn't going to end like she may wish."

"Alright." Winnie blinked several times, her eyelashes like flags of surrender. She sniffed. "I think I knew this was coming. Something like this."

"I'm sure you did, because you're smart."

Winnie brightened and touched Neva's shoulder. "Thank you."

"If the storm doesn't wash him over the edge, he might need a push. I don't see any other way to protect the girls, you, George, the people I love, and myself, from him—from what he's become."

"But this is ok?" Winnie nodded at the claim tickets.

"Yes," Neva said with a minute smile. "Especially the Stetson."

★

– 33 –

TUESDAY
March 5, 1907

A six-foot-one, seventy-six-year-old man, sporting an even-more-ample mustache than McParland's, entered the Idanha Hotel at precisely 2:00 on the afternoon of Tuesday, March 5, 1907, flanked by three men in close formation. Wearing a black hat and a red-black checkered jacket over striped trousers, he strode through the lobby toward McParland and Borah who stood in clear anticipation of his arrival.

"General Grenville Dodge," said Senator Borah, shaking the older man's hand. I am William Borah, and I believe you know Chief Detective James McParland with the Pinkerton—"

"Yes, yes, Senator."

McParland extended his hand. "A pleasure to see you again, General. It's been a number of years."

"Yes, yes," the man said, shaking McParland's hand.

Borah's ebullience showed. "A *G-A-R* hero. Grand Army of the Republic. I've heard of your leadership with Sherman."

"Grant," Dodge grumbled without eye contact. "Some with Sherman, I suppose."

"General Dodge is a pioneer of US Army intelligence," McParland said to Borah. He turned back to their guest. "I'm a student of yours, Sir."

"No, no," said Dodge. "You're the great detective. I'm just an old general."

Borah added, "And president of Union Pacific Railroad. We're grateful you would join us today."

Moments later they were in McParland's office. "What we're going to discuss," commenced the detective, "must remain a tightly held secret, the details known only to the three of us." He indicated toward the men accompanying Dodge.

With a nudge of his head, Dodge instructed his men to leave.

Once the door closed, McParland lit his pipe and the other two lit cigars, each settling deep into wingback chairs. Behind McParland, a sheet had been hung across a section of the wall. "I hear Butch and Sundance ran into trouble in Argentina," said McParland.

"I read that," said Borah. "Someday—"

"They better think twice about returning," grumbled Dodge.

"Cassidy's too smart to come back," said McParland. "He won't venture north of the equator after what we did to them."

"To *them*?" said Dodge.

"To the Wild Bunch. To their men," McParland corrected himself. "Never got a solid feeling for Sundance's smarts. But Cassidy—all brains. That nickelodeon got him wrong."

"Oh, but what a thing, the flicker," said Borah. "When I was in Washington, I saw—"

"What?" Dodge fumed. "That dung heap, *The Great Train Robbery*? Great train robbery, my ass. Nothing great about it. That goddamned motion picture made a farce of the Northern Pacific. I should sue them. I'd be in my rights. A perversion of the truth. Ridiculous fellas all made up. A puff of smoke to open one of my safes. And those costumes. Milksops. The silliness. Not one of my trains would be— I mean, damn, you could see they weren't even on a real goddamned train. You saw that, didn't you?"

Borah nodded, taken aback by the general's outburst. "I didn't think it was a real train, General Dodge, but I suppose—"

"Charlatans!" said Dodge, stamping a period on his invective.

After a moment of silence between the three, Borah eased them on. "Jim, you were saying—Cassidy, brains?"

"Aye, brains," said McParland, looking primarily at Borah. "Cassidy came barreling out of Telluride, after the San Miguel bank job, and I was tasked to catch him. I was superintendent for Colorado at the time. And Allan Pinkerton's son, Robert, ran the Western Division. General Dodge knows this. In any case, we were on the narrow gauge in a jiff, quick around to Grand Junction."

Borah nodded, already engrossed in the detective's story. Dodge was nonplussed, his expression more toleration than interest.

McParland continued, "We knew they'd be high-tailing it up from Telluride, heading to Brown's Park, so of course they'd have to go through the Junction area, and their horses would slow on the slopes, making it a hard two days from Telluride. That meant they'd get new mounts in Junction. So, we got to Junction first—by rail in one day. Charlie Siringo was my second-in-command. We talked to liverymen there. They said none of the Wild Bunch had come through. Of course, Charlie and I were a might pleased with ourselves, having gotten ahead of em. I posted men there in Junction and took Charlie and the rest south to come at em head on. We were gonna catch ol' Butch and Sundance by surprise. But no more than an hour south of Junction, we heard they'd already come through, going north—the day before! Oh, I was a mad hornet, I tell ya. I'd been sold a dog. We turned back to Junction and there got the truth: The night before, Butch and Sundance had ridden right by Junction at a full gallop. Didn't stop. Aye, they'd been there all right, but they hadn't switched horses there. We'd missed them by six hours. They were long gone to Browns Park, then on up to Hole-in-the-Wall. Disappeared. Not my finest wire to Mr. Pinkerton."

"I didn't know you ran that posse," said Borah admiringly.

"Aye, it was me. But I was out-matched by—"

"Yes, yes, he stationed horses," said Dodge in bored resolve.

"Precisely, General," said McParland. "Butch Cassidy—first bank robber to plan a getaway across three states. Allies and sympathizers all along the way—all prepared, fielding fresh horses, with food mind you, all ready and waiting for em. Planned it out months before he entered that bank. No stopping at towns like Junction—provisioned only out where we didn't expect."

General Dodge lifted an eyebrow and turned his wet cigar between his lips. "So, you're impressed with that whore's son." He spanned his hands as if to say, What of it? Then he grumbled, "The man robbed more from my trains than anyone ever did. We're not pleased they slipped away."

"I understand," said McParland. "As you've been quoted: Even the most loathed enemy can teach tactics." He stood and pulled the cloth from the wall, revealing a large map of the western states. Drawn clearly on it was the railroad going north from Denver to Cheyenne, Wyoming, and then west across the entirety of Wyoming and up into Idaho, ending in Boise. Along the route were a number of red dots and brass pushpins in tiny towns like Greeley, Colorado and Green River, Wyoming.

Dodge stood and studied the map. He pointed at the brass pins and gave an erudite snort. "Unexpected stations. Not horses like Cassidy did, but coal, water and engines."

McParland nodded. "They're my Cassidy stations."

"And for those, General Dodge," said Borah, "the State of Idaho has a special request of the Union Pacific."

"Yes, yes, I see."

★

– 34 –

WEDNESDAY
March 6, 1907

To the rising sounds of a large crowd singing the Star-Spangled Banner, Jack entered the Ingleside Racetrack, Iain close behind, both of them sliding and shouldering through the small crowd and past the main gate with its red-and-white sign:

CHARITY AUTOMOBILE RACE
Benefiting the San Francisco Relief
and Red Cross Funds Corporation

They entered the three-story club house where, at the lightly attended betting windows, they turned and surveyed the big room full of people. Most stood in lines leading to tables managed by women wearing Red Cross arm bands. Iain nudged Jack and said, "Over there," having spotted Pete Polk near the back of a newsstand. As Jack and Iain approached, Pete gave a head tilt toward the door he was holding wide. Inside, the three Pinkerton agents ascended the building's unadorned back stairs.

As they climbed, Jack asked, "What are they betting on? Isn't bookmaking—"

"Automobiles," replied Pete. "It's for charity. The track closed to horse racing last year. The infield is a refugee camp. You'll see."

Re-entering sunlight atop the building, they saw Stan Polk there, alone, kneeling behind a short wall that ran along the edge of the roof. The M1903 rifle was leaning beside him, absent the scope. Also nearby were three shotguns. Stan motioned them to join him and they did. Squatting, peering over the wall and down to their left, they saw four autos abreast at the starting line. Just infield of the cars was a raised white platform on which stood an announcer, bullhorn to his face, addressing the crowd: "*... so much gratitude and appreciation for your generosity today. Your kindness and* *open hearts will never be forgotten. Because of you, our city on a hill will rise again, and so many lives will be restored."*

Jack surveyed the grandstands. It was a sea of brown and black fedoras, homburgs, caps, bowlers, and derbies, interspersed with floral pockets of bursting color—broad-brimmed women's hats spewing feathers—as if a flock of exotic birds had been shot down over the men.

"Our first race will be an easy one, folks—an amateur race—some local heroes, men you know, going up against a racing champion. But the second and third races will be at full speed, with trained drivers. No one will want to miss them!"

In the infield, Jack saw less-bedecked crowds just inside the track's white railing. And behind those people: a sea of gray-white canvas tents dotted with makeshift small buildings and privies.

"Waving both the starting and winning flags today, the man who made today happen, the founder of the Committee of Fifty, and your leader during these challenging months—the Honorable Mayor of San Francisco, Eugene Schmitz!" Big applause.

"Look there," said Stan, handing Jack a pair of binoculars and pointing down slightly to their right. "See the 15/16 pole?"

"But you came for a motor race!" The crowd cheered. *"So, let's meet the first race drivers and their cars."*

Jack used the binoculars but didn't see the pole. He then glanced back at the M1903 rifle. "Where's the scope?"

Stan pointed at the black tube lying behind the shotguns. "I took it off. It's dog shit," he said.

Jack nodded and resumed peering through the binoculars.

"First and foremost, we're honored to have the Mercedes ninety-horse-power automobile that was driven to victory by Willy Vanderbilt at Daytona Beach, Florida, only a few weeks ago—at a top speed of ninety-three miles per hour!" Cheers.

"Who am I going to see by the pole?" asked Jack. "Swain?"

"No," said Pete, kneeling. "Still no hide or hair of that man."

Jack frowned. "Then who? Adams?" Seeing Stan's nod, Jack's eyebrows shot up. He looked again, but still couldn't find the pole.

"Just think, that one machine is ninety horses running this track! Today it'll be driven by Mr. Thomas Kirkland." The driver waved to the cheering crowd.

"Try without the specs," said Stan.

"Daring their luck against the professional driver are three of your San Francisco sons—all members of the Committee of Fifty." Cheers.

"Right there," said Iain, pointing over the rail.

Following Iain's pointed finger, Jack saw a white pole erected alongside the interior rail. It was painted with the marking: 15/16. "I see it," said Jack.

"Alright," said Stan. "Now go right—I mean left—about two deep against the rail. See that man?"

"Which one?"

"Wearing a cap."

"That narrows it down," grumbled Jack.

"Plaid. Sorta green," Stan added quickly.

Looking again, Jack thought he saw him. He pulled the binoculars up and found the man: a sharp nose protruding from under a dingy green cap. Then the man turned, revealing his face in full. Fumbling, Jack unfolded the drawing of Steve Adams. They were the same. "My God, Polk boys—you found him."

"Been living out there," said Pete. "Took one of those tents."

As the race began, Iain yelled over the growl of the automobiles and the crowd. "So what do we do next?"

"Tell the two at the depot?" asked Stan. "Bring em here?"

Jack heard their questions but was still fixed on Adams, who in turn appeared mesmerized by the cars roaring through the first turn at over thirty miles an hour. Jack felt a coolness ripple through his body. They had found Adams. They had found him. Steve Adams. Right down there. "We need to make a plan," said Jack. "That dog might run."

When McParland arrived at tiny Corral, Idaho—traveling east from Boise for an hour by train, and then a half-day north by horse—he was more than aching; he was angry. The gall of Charlie Siringo, the hired gun and on-again-off-again Pinkerton, to make McParland go so far to meet him.

A self-promoting Texas cowhand, Charles Siringo had been recommended to McParland's employ in 1898 by the famous US

Marshall Pat Garrett. Siringo had then worked for McParland out of the Denver office, tracking a number of outlaws, including Butch Cassidy and Sundance. In addition, Siringo had infiltrated the Federation on occasion, as McParland assigned. But when Siringo became convinced Haywood had him marked for killing, he disappeared. Thus, years later, after McParland finally got word to him, this clump of dirt was where Siringo insisted they meet.

McParland found the sun-furrowed, middle-aged man in the only saloon still standing in Corral. On his way in, McParland scrutinized an unexpected sight: an open-seater automobile parked at the saloon's hitching rail.

"Charlie," said McParland once inside. He removed his hat and pulled a chair up to Siringo's table, on which was a half-bottle of whiskey, a glass, and a nickel-finished Colt .45 with a cherry-red grip. Seeing Siringo's hat hanging on a high-backed chair nearby, McParland hung his there too.

"Well, looky here," snorted Siringo. "If it ain't Old Necessity himself." His matted, ashy-brown hair bore a permanent hat crease.

"Pretty gun," quipped McParland, noting the grip.

"Yep."

The detective peered at Siringo. "Why this place?"

"No railroad here."

"That's a problem?"

Siringo shrugged. "I'm careful 'sall."

McParland signaled the lone barkeep. "Another glass."

Siringo squinted. "Don't like being near you none neither."

McParland shook his head. "Came to hire you, not kill you."

"You flatter your damn self. You couldn't hire *nor* kill me."

"Then why'd you agree to meet?"

"Last time I signed on with you, it nearly put me under."

"But it didn't."

"Answer's no."

"You haven't heard—"

"No."

"Put no in a telegram. Hell, try a tele*phon*e for godsakes."

"I've used em," said Siringo.

"I got a saddle-sore ass just so you can say no to my face?"

"Your face looks saddle-sore too."

McParland laughed. "So—just no?"

"The great detective figures sumtun. Shot the brown, Jimmy."

After thirty seconds of silence and stares, save the gurgle of poured whiskey, the creak of chairs, and the bartender's chatter out the back door, McParland asked, "All right. All right. So what can I do for *you*, Charlie?"

"You wanna help me? Good, cause you owe me." Siringo reached into a saddle bag, then slid a book across the table.

McParland picked it up and read the cover aloud. "*A Cowboy Detective*, by Charles Siringo." He thumbed the pages. "Aye. I heard about this. You know the old man won't—"

"But as his favorite prat-o-gee, you can get him to allow it. We know that's so. Old Man Pinkerton's got a ripe hatred for me."

"He just wants things kept private, Charlie. Private eye?"

Siringo pointed at the book. "Took two years to write that. It'll sell like hotcakes. Like my other. But he's got all the publishers shut against me."

"How'd you get this one printed?"

"Done it before he knew nothing bout it."

McParland took a breath. "I'll try, if and when you help me."

"Swore I'd never. Not again." Siringo drained his glass, filled it, and drank again. "You rode a horse here? Ain't the eighteen-hunderds no more."

McParland gave a nasally chuckle and pointed to the front of the saloon. "The legendary cowboy, Charlie Siringo, hung up his spurs for an automobile?"

Siringo slung a dusty boot onto a chair, showing that a battered spur was strapped to it.

McParland smiled. "You wear em driving?"

"Even mechanical nags gotta know who's boss. Especially Priscilla out there." After returning his boot to the floor, he asked, "So, Jimmy ... who needs killing?"

"Haywood."

"Haywood?" Siringo's forehead scrunched. "The man hisself?"

"The man hisself."

"My God. What'd he finally do to get roped?"

"He's not roped yet," groused McParland.

"What'd he do?"

"Assassinated the governor here."

"Heard about that."

"I need your help getting him."

"I'd like to, that's for damn sure. But one step in Denver and I'd be blown full of holes. I'd be that cheese with the holes in it. What's it called?"

"I'm not asking you—"

"He's got the sheriff and all his pissant deputies, night and day."

"You asked who needs killing, but I'm not asking you to do it."

"That's too bad," muttered Siringo, his words whiskey laced. He refilled his glass and lifted it. "A toast! Somebody, someday, somewhere should kill that sombitch." As he pitched back to down the drink, he lost his balance only to catch himself against the wall.

"Devil's water ain't so sweet," recited McParland.

"Sweet enough, by God."

McParland waited till Siringo had his chair settled. "I need your help to get Haywood hanged. But you won't need that gun. It's useless."

"No gun's never useless."

"Tits on a boar," said McParland. "I don't want you shooting—"

"Boar's tits!" Siringo laughed. "Alright, no shooting. So, whadya want from me? Want me to vote eight times for some mine owner's candidate, like you had me do for— Who was that fella? Oh, I remember." He grinned broadly. "Yeah, it was the governor of Colorado, wasn't it? Back in '98, I think."

McParland's eyes grew hard. "We're not talking old business."

"Says's who? Old business," the cowboy muttered, waggling a finger. "Someone's always getting killed riding with you."

"I need a plaster-cased bomb. I'll give you the design."

Siringo's voice dropped to a gravelly octave. "You're gonna—"

"It needs to be real, but it won't be used."

"That all?"

"And I need you to take a train to Denver—about a month on."

Siringo shook his head. "I'd get seen. People know me."

"Aye, they do. One hundred dollars—one bomb, one train ride."

"Where to where?"

"Cheyenne to Denver, then down to Fort Worth."

"I'll be killed in Denver."

"No, you won't."

Siringo paused. "You'll get the old man square on my book?"

"I'll talk to him."

"Priscilla's got to come too."

"Who?" asked McParland.

"My motorcar. I told you."

McParland sighed. "I'll get her to you, wherever you end up."

"If you get me killed, I wanna be buried in her."

The detective squinted. "Your automobile?"

"Yeah. Now, you just said—"

"Alright, Charlie. Alright then."

"Alright then," echoed Siringo with a resigned shrug.

The detective peered over his eyeglasses. "You can't be drunk."

"Says the Mick. No, I'll be sober as a judge."

McParland smiled. "Aye. That's what worries me."

The plan was for Jack, Iain, and Pete to spread out across the infield as the second race got underway. Then they would advance on Adams from three directions, corralling him against the inside rail where it curved at the first turn. Stan would remain on top of the clubhouse as their spotter, signaling the three below. His job was to keep sight of Adams and occasionally point at him. If he could no longer see Adams, he was to cross his arms across his chest until he found him again. That way, the other three need only look up at Stan to get a bearing on their target. Once the three were close and had Adams in sight themselves, they would take up positions and stay put. Then, after the fourth and last race, as Adams moved back deeper into the infield, they would tackle and cuff him, using the crowd to disguise their final approach. That was the plan.

⟡

The three on the ground worked their way behind the grandstands and around the outside rail, out of sight of the first turn where Adams seemed set to remain for the duration of the races. Each carried a shotgun close to his leg, pointed down. As they reached the third turn, they crossed the track when it was clear. Then, once on the infield, they fanned out, heading for Adams in the far corner. Pete moved along the backside rail, Iain along the front side, and Jack diagonally through the refugee tent-city in the middle.

But things went wrong rapidly. When they looked up at Stan, they saw one arm crossed over his chest, the other holding binoculars to his face. Had he lost sight of Adams, or not? Seeing the half-signal, both Jack and Iain slowed, unsure if they might run into the killer. But Pete, having read his brother's signal differently, kept moving swiftly along the backside. When he reached the midpoint of the track, he passed within three feet of Adams—recognizing him immediately—and stumbled into two girls as he came to a stop. One of the girls fell, then yelled as Pete pivoted, pulling his shotgun toward Adams who turned at the commotion, saw the shotgun and drew his pistol. Already within touching distance, Pete kept his shotgun spinning, grabbed it by the double barrels and whipped its butt into Adams's jaw, smashing him against the rail, the pistol flying onto the track. By then the cars were roaring by, down the back straightaway, just feet from the pressing, cheering crowd. Only a few noticed the brutal fight in their midst. Pete again spun the shotgun—this time to fire it—but Adams was on him, leaning into him, Bowie knife in hand, arm shaking as Pete tried to shove the blade away. Pete threw an elbow into Adams's face and turned the knife back.

From above the clubhouse, Stan noticed a commotion on the far side of the infield and began searching the area with his binoculars. (He had, in fact, lost sight of Adams, and was unaware that their target had moved to the backside rail.) When he saw Pete and Adams entangled, he began shouting, but it was no use. He resorted to firing the rifle into the air, but few noticed—other than to presume he was a drunk enjoying the race. His shooting did draw Jack's and Iain's attention, but neither comprehended its meaning—until they saw Stan pointing urgently toward the far side of the track. At that, they both turned and ran, pushing through the crowd.

When Pete saw a chance, he landed another blow to Adams's jaw, dazing the killer for a second. But Pete didn't follow through quickly enough. Adams wheeled, slamming Pete over the railing, landing both men on the dirt track. Looking up, they saw cars rounding the second turn, accelerating onto the back straight, directly toward them. Panicking, Pete tried to roll under the railing but, in doing so, he abandoned his guard. Adams saw it and buried the knife deep in Pete's side. As Pete gasped, Adams leapt the railing just as the front wheel of a speeding Fiat crushed Pete's head, splattering blood and jerking the wheels left, sending the car through the railing at seventy miles an hour where it missed the crowd but plowed through two refugee tents, rolling twice and flipping once, killing both the driver and his assistant instantly.

The infield that had been sheltering refugees of ruin was now a panorama of wreckage—spectators scattering, frantic outcries and confusion, black smoke billowing skyward over an inverted racecar and shredded tents. Against the stampede, the wide-eyed young Pinkertons kept shoving, shouldering and pushing their way toward the tragedy.

Meanwhile, Steve Adams had vanished.

★

– 35 –

FRIDAY
March 8, 1907

"Yes, I'm on my way," Neva shouted, rolling herself with eagerness from her bedroom in the Pioneer suites, her wheels growling down the dark hall's long, wooden planks, past the wash closet and Winnie's room, past the small hall to the drawing room and the dining room beyond, before turning at the foyer where she beamed to her black-suited guest. "Reverend Sanders. Oh, Reverend, you don't know how good it does my heart to see you."

"Neva, thank you for accepting my request." He took her uplifted hand. "You're looking well."

"Then you've gone blind," she demurred in false humility. She knew she looked better than she had in months. It was due to George, of course, but who could say. She did like the silk waistshirt she wore, particularly the pointed yolks, but that wasn't something the reverend would notice.

"I see quite well," he said with a flat smile.

She turned toward the parlor. "Come, we've much to discuss."

"Yes, thank you." He began to place his hands on her invalid chair, to roll her, but she was already in motion.

A storm was rolling into Denver, cutting the afternoon light from the windows to a dusky gray, leaving the fireplace to provide most of the room's illumination. Neva pointed for him to sit on a couch before the glowing mantel. "Harriet," she said to a servant in the shadows, "bring the tea?"

"Yes, Ma'am. Shall I put on the lights?"

"No, the reverend is not a friend of electricity." She pivoted to Sanders. "Sit, won't you?" She patted the couch. "You arrived today from Walla Walla?"

"Yes. I'm no friend of trains either, necessities they may be."

"But can you imagine taking a coach? My father used to wagon from Walla Walla to Salt Lake, to trade. I went with him once. What a fool thing." She refocused. "You were here last Fall?"

"Yes, in October. I came to see Mr. Darrow on the Fort Collins land matter. I called on you, but you were unwell. It was kind of you to arrange for him to handle the particulars. It's God's earth, but it takes lawyers to parcel it up."

"I'm pleased he was of service."

"I've yet to see the deeds, but I don't doubt he—"

"He gets distracted by Bill's business."

The reverend took the tea when presented, thanked the servant, and stared into the fire. "May I ask, is your husband home?"

"He's in his office." She blew across her tea. "Or elsewhere."

"And Winnifred?"

Neva tensed. "No, Winnie isn't here."

"Good." Sanders nodded. "What I must discuss is delicate."

"Then perhaps you should've written."

"I couldn't. I needed to speak with you—directly."

Neva fell silent. On alert. Like seeing a pan fall from the stove, she knew where it was going and hoped to dodge the burn.

"We, your church family, Seventh-day Adventists, we are enormously grateful for the contributions you and your husband have made to Walla Walla."

"Made by me. Me. Bill would end it, but I've persuaded him of the importance of giving for the cause of our Lord."

"As I said, our gratitude is abundant." He blew a sigh through his nose. "But ... the funds come from the Western Federation of Miners. And controversies—great ones, mind you have arisen around that source. So, whether or not I, or anyone, may sympathize with labor causes, it's simply—"

"Those are separate matters."

"I wish they were, but events have caused the college trustees, as well as the majority of our senior deacons, to reconsider."

"No one made you take our money. No one forced you." Neva snipped with an ingénue's air.

"True, very true. But that was before new matters came to light." Seeing her eyebrows rise, he continued, "It's come to our attention that some of the monies that you, graciously of course, have forwarded to the college, originated as monies Bill received from the union in violation of union rules. Further, his dealings with socialist leaders, Mr. Debs in particular, are quite objectionable to church tenets. And that's before the matter in Boise."

"The matter in Boise?"

"Yes." He stirred his tea, arranging his thoughts in the swirl, then took a sip and said, "Are you aware that a man, a Mr. Orchard, has confessed—both to the assassination and that your husband ordered it?"

It was her turn to sip.

He continued, "As I understand it, Bill will be tried in Boise."

She shook her head. "Mr. Darrow says they can't do that."

"But if they do—if they bring Bill to trial—then you'll want to remain unblemished, free from the stain of such an enormous scandal. You and your daughters. Whether he's found guilty or not, the matter will ruin him. And I'm sorry to put this in words, but if Bill's found guilty, he'll be hanged."

"I know that," she said, her voice level.

Sanders took a moment. "All right."

"If you don't want my money," Neva began haughtily, "after all that I've given to the church ... I ..." She fixed her gaze on the blue tips of the flames—evanescence that was never there. "Bill will be pleased," she said, her voice having fallen soft. "He'll buy more automobiles or something. But you can do good with it."

"I'm sorry, but we cannot continue. Not in good conscience."

"I love my church, Reverend. My faith, my girls. I love Winnie and—" She swallowed George's name. "They're all I have ... all that's mine."

Sanders touched her arm. "You're my sister in Christ. That's why I came this distance to speak with you about it." He paused. "And about *you*."

"About me?"

"How you're living in this world, and for the next. The indignity you suffer with your husband ... and your sister."

She was prepared to lash out at the man's presumptuousness, his callous intrusion into such a private matter, but the indignation wouldn't come. Maybe it was the surprise of it all. She had not suspected this was the intention of his visit—to talk about the "arrangement" with Winnie. And to now hear it said aloud, the audacity of a secluded truth put plainly before her, was a detonation in her heart. Even with George, the subject was nitroglycerin, not to be handled carelessly or bluntly. Here was this stranger, this representative of God, daring to speak aloud her sin. A sob rose from her throat and exited her nose. Then another. She sniffed, clamping her jaws, attempting not to dissolve. This man knew what she had fortressed away for years—murky secrets in frigid rooms she willed to stay locked. Not only did he know the contents of those rooms, but he had brought the key. When he gave her his handkerchief, she wiped her cheek and said the only words that dared to emerge. "I'm sorry."

"I'm not here to judge you, Neva. I have no right."

She nodded.

"God gave us marriage as a holy sacrament—a divine gift for one man and one woman. Only your covenant with God, your faith, is greater than the pledge you made to your husband ... and the pledge he made you. The Bible teaches us that to stray from the marriage bed is sin." Holding eye contact with her, he touched her invalid chair. "My sister in Christ, there is no condition or cause, infirmity or ache, that would excuse what your husband is doing—forcing you to accept polygamy." He paused, and then added, "And we're well aware of God's judgment against the Mormons for that wicked practice."

Neva returned her gaze to the flickers and pops of the fireplace.

"I believe I know why you've permitted it," he said.

"I had no choice," she whispered. "For myself and my girls."

"This is a vile thing he's placed on you. But it's a test."

"Polio?"

"No, I don't mean the burden that God has—"

"Yes. My burden."

"I meant the situation with your sister. That's the vile situation your husband, not God, has placed on you."

"But, like this"—she tapped her chair—"I didn't have a choice with Bill. Nor did Winnie."

"Come now, both of you had a choice. *Have* a choice. All three of you do. And I'm sorry to say this, but it is of cruel regard that your sister encourages the sin. Staining your family."

"You don't understand," Neva retorted. "While Bill is my husband, if I refuse this arrangement, I'll lose my sister. And my girls will be sent to a boarding school far away—Vermont. So, I won't. You cannot ask that of me."

"I don't ask it. God does."

"God asks it of me? God? He put me in this chair! He might take me home soon, leaving my girls orphans, essentially. Who is He to give me instructions on my marriage, telling me to lose everything, to be alone? No, Reverend!" She banged her invalid chair. "This ... this chair is my right to refuse!"

Sanders bobbed his head. "God loves you, Neva. And your girls. And your church loves you and them. You'll never be alone, and they'll never go unattended. Bring them to Walla Walla. Winnifred too, if she wishes. Work at the College, perhaps—help others while you still have life and your wonderful spirit. Yes, this mysterious disease has befallen you, but none of us can count his days. I don't know that I'll survive the trip back on that speeding train," he added with an unrequited chuckle. "Who can know what Jesus may ordain for our lives, before we are to join Him in his heavenly sanctuary." He touched her hand as she began to cry. "But, Neva, don't be tempted by what appears as power or privilege, only to lose your soul—just to remain close to William Haywood, who—and I believe you must know this—is consumed in the devil's work: evilness, cruelty, greed, avarice. And he displays the foulest disrespect for you, not just as a woman but as a child of God."

As Neva fell into full sobs, the reverend put both arms around her shoulders. Once a little calmer, she said, "I'm petrified—scared to my core. He would never let us go. With his thousands of loyal men, no one is beyond his reach."

"I think you know," Sanders whispered, "he actually *would* let you go—and your girls, as you said. It's a painful thought, but perhaps best accepted."

"I hate him," she muttered. "I'm not supposed to, but I do."

"Then don't enable his hedonism. Nor ignore his crimes."

"His crimes ..." She gathered herself, wiping away the tears.

"Mrs. Steunenberg—the widow of the governor who was murdered—she's an Adventist. When I went to Boise to pray with her, I heard about a Pinkerton detective named McParland who is working with the special prosecutor, Senator Borah. So, I telephoned the detective. Over the course of a few conversations, he told me a number of things, including about Winnifred and your husband. I told him what I could, but it wasn't much."

"What do you mean, you told the detective things? About me?"

"Oh no, not at all. About their case against Bill. I relayed something I'd overheard in Mr. Darrow's office. The woman there, Mr. Darrow's secretary, I believe, said Mr. Orchard—that awful fellow who confessed—carried secret notes in his hat." Reverend Sanders chuckled at himself. "That's quite pathetic, that that's all I had to offer." He smiled at Neva who was still forlorn. "But nothing about you, dear, except that you're a good Christian woman. And I suggested that you might— Well, that you might see your way to helping them."

"Helping who?" she asked. "The Pinkertons?"

"Yes."

Neva shook her head in depressed amusement. "I must confess, I've been thinking the same. To protect the people I love from Bill's activities—his work. I'd even considered calling on that same detective. God help me, but I have."

"I'm so pleased to hear that," said Reverend Sanders, pulling a letter from his pocket. "He gave me this note to pass on to you."

"Detective McParland?"

"Yes, the same," he said. "My goodness, this is exciting, Neva. Can you feel it? To see God's divine will. I know it's frightening, to be tested like this. But it's good for our souls, from time to time. This is your time. Just as the Holy Spirit wrote in Matthew 14:22: Jesus asked Peter onto the stormy Sea of Galilee. You too, Neva, are asked to trust."

She opened the letter and began to read.

A couple of weeks earlier, while Captain Swain was visiting his ailing mother in Salt Lake City, two messages came to him from Denver. The first was delivered in person by Winnie, Haywood's mistress. It was Haywood's instructions: Swain was to go to San Francisco within a week, find Adams and permanently deny him the capacity to testify in Boise. Swain was not to be assuaged by Adams's attested loyalty to the Federation, nor accept any promise that Adams would lie under oath.

Then, as Swain was preparing to leave Salt Lake, the second message arrived. It was a telegram cryptically advising Swain that Adams and the Pinkertons wouldn't be in San Francisco for yet another week, and that he was to avoid injury to P-JG. Thankful for the extra time, he stayed with his mother for three more days. Considering the P-JG part, Swain had no idea who that meant, other than guessing the P meant Pinkerton. And as he had no intention of injuring *any* Pinkerton, he put it aside in his mind.

When he finally did arrive in San Francisco, he quickly learned about the burned city's most recent tragedies: the Branson family poisoning, and a recent crash at the Ingleside Racetrack where a driver, his assistant, and one spectator had died. The poisoning confirmed Adams's presence a few days earlier, as Swain knew Branson had been Adams's target. That meant Swain had been given bad information and arrived too late.

But had Adams then left the Bay? Curiously, witnesses said the Ingleside crash was caused by a fight alongside the back rail, and the dead spectator had been stabbed just before the automobile hit him. When Captain Swain investigated, he learned the corpse was wagoned away by three men showing Pinkerton credentials. So, not only had Adams already been there, Adams had killed a Pinkerton. Might it have been JG? Swain hoped not. If it was, Haywood might blame Swain. Blamed for a killing he hadn't done—even though he'd come for that very purpose, to kill a man.

Though Swain avoided the memory of shooting the doctor in Castle Rock—violence he'd done for Haywood—at least the doctor had lived. But now he was tracking a man for the sole purpose of taking his life. He was reminded of a similar mission twenty years earlier, tracking Geronimo through the Sierra Madre mountains of northern Mexico. There he had orders to bring the outlaw Apache back "dead or alive." But for this client, the mission objective was "dead and disappeared."

Before arriving in San Francisco, Swain's heart and head had wrestled what he should do. But then he arrived late and a depression of foolishness and ineptitude came over him—he was tired of being a step behind. Only a renewed, locked, and focused resolve could lift Swain's melancholy. But as it did, so too did it silently evaporate the ethical dilemma.

One thing was probable: Adams was on the run. But in which direction? If Adams went west, to sea, then the pursuit was over and Swain would have failed. He could see it clearly, like cascading dominoes—even though Adams would still not be in Boise to testify, Swain wouldn't get the credit. Nor would Haywood admit fault in the error of the timing. That would mean Swain wouldn't be hired further by the union, likely spelling the end to Swain's career.

Considering that, he decided to have an alternate hunch. He chose to believe Adams fled east, back to familiar territory. Probably to Sacramento, and then into the Sierra Nevadas—perhaps thinking its played-out mines were safe from Pinkertons. If so, then that was good—Swain knew well the high Sierras. Or maybe Adams would travel further east, into Nevada—land scarce of Pinkertons. Or, better yet, on to Utah, where the Mormons would just as soon shoot a Pinkerton as tell him the time. So, as he left San Francisco on an east-bound California Special, Captain Swain's mind was fixed on murder, without a twinge of moral conflict.

★

– 36 –

SATURDAY
March 9, 1907

General Dodge, president of Union Pacific Railroad, was standing in one of his private Pullman rail cars as it rumbled toward Cheyenne, Wyoming, the train having taken water and coal, and changed engines in Pocatello, Idaho. His bushy white mustache was suspended above a map of the West, a giant cloud floating high over the Rockies. "How do you know this, Detective?" he asked.

"Someone in Denver," replied McParland, sitting on a nearby velvet couch, one hand grasping the knob of his cane, the other smoothing his own obdurate mustache.

Dodge frowned. "You must have high regard for their accuracy, them knowing precisely where Haywood will be."

"I do."

"Any other source giving you the same information?"

"Perhaps."

"Detective, your entire operation—and my attachment of the resources of Union Pacific, its reputation and my men, thousands of dollars in costs, and lost revenue of greater sums—all pivots on one piece of information from one person?"

"We're already *en route*, General," snapped McParland, unfamiliar with the sting of having his decisions second-guessed.

"Hmmph." Dodge's eyes narrowed. "We'll be suspending rail operations across the eastern front range and the heart of our west-bound traffic while you conduct this operation, which may get some innocent people shot, or some run over as you speed back through these towns. I have some experience with this."

McParland used his cane to lever himself to his feet. "You and I, and Senator Borah and others, have discussed the risks, have we not?" He turned and addressed a group of men at the far end of the car: four Pinkertons playing cards with Charles Siringo. "Charlie, might I get one of those cigars you brought?"

Siringo stood and carried a scowl and a cigar to the detective.

McParland cut, licked, and lit the cigar. Then, adopting a convivial tone, he said, "I'm glad you're enjoying General Dodge's whiskey, Charlie, but I advise you not to forget—those other men are sober. You may lose your shirt."

"Nah, the more I drink, the more I can read a man, see the cards he's holding. Fat lady's gonna sing for em." Siringo turned to General Dodge. "You and I don't know each other, Sir."

"You'd best go back," said McParland, puffing blue smoke.

"Name's Siringo."

"Yes, yes," Dodge said. "I've heard some about you."

"Some true, some not, I reckon."

"As with me," chuckled Dodge.

Siringo stepped closer. "It's no secret I don't give two shits of a regard for my old employer." He motioned toward McParland.

McParland shook his head. "Charlie and I are old friends."

"Time was, I near got myself killed in his employ," Siringo continued. "Even so, if he says his Denver spy is gold, then he's gold—or she is." He winked, adding, "Old Necessity's got a few ladies working for him."

McParland winced for several reasons, starting with Siringo's use of the less-than-flattering appellation. Also, he hadn't realized Siringo had been listening to their earlier conversation. And most galling was Siringo's remark that the detective's source might be a woman. Not that it would surprise General Dodge, but it was much too revelatory of the truth for McParland's comfort.

"Might be skinning the fish, ears first," said Dodge. "We'll see."

"Suppose we will," said Siringo, moving through the cigar cloud, returning to the poker game. "Alright, you lily-livered Pink sassies, hand me your money!"

The two older men stepped from earshot of Siringo and the others. "What's his role in this?" asked Dodge.

"He supplied an important ... prop ... for our upcoming theatrics," said McParland. "Plus, he's my ghost hare. He's a pariah to the Federation. Known to want revenge on Haywood."

"What for?" asked Dodge, looking down the car at Siringo.

"This. That. Everything between," said McParland.

"So his presence in Denver will be known quickly," said Dodge.

"Aye. Then, before we run north, he'll be seen southbound."

"You think he'll pull Haywood's men?"

"Some of them, I hope. If not, then at least it'll get them talking that direction—once they realize Haywood is gone."

Dodge nodded. "You're dusting the air with him."

"Aye," said the detective. "Dusting the air."

"Might get the man killed."

"We'll guard him down to Pueblo, then put him onto an A.T. to Texas."

Dodge nodded faintly, his thoughts having turned elsewhere. "Right after you leave Denver, all rail operations will resume."

"As we've agreed," said McParland.

"Meaning," Dodge continued, "within an hour, a hundred armed Federation men will be on the next train north—coming right behind you."

"I know," said McParland. "But the ones behind us won't concern me near as much as the ones that'll be ahead. According to Senator Borah, every sheriff from Denver to Boise will get a telegram ordering them to board us with a *habeas corpus* warrant."

"I don't want you shooting up my train—or getting it derailed."

"Our Cassidy stations will work," McParland said, uneasy with the older man's recitation of the railroad's rules for this operation. He moved to the table and looked at the map spread there. It bore a series of inked dots, numbered one to eleven, beginning on the railroad just north of Denver and continuing up to Cheyenne, and then northwest to Boise. The dots were in what appeared to be remote locations, similar to where the brass pins had been in McParland's wall map at the Idanha Hotel. He rolled his cigar on the edge of a dish, depositing a plug's worth of ash.

"We were in the middle of Georgia," began the general, now standing on the other side of the table. "We sped forty miles where the Rebs were thickest, running full bore—like a cat on fire. General Sherman ordered us not to stop and we didn't. Ran right past three depots. Killed at least one person—a woman who didn't expect us to come roaring past. That was three depots across forty miles." He knuckle-thumped the map. "Here you've got over nine hundred miles and, what's that, about seventy depots of one sort or another—all of which you must avoid slowing near, must assume are hostile to your endeavor."

"Aye."

"If anyone gets killed, or if some judge raises a fuss," Dodge said, rubbing his forehead with the back of his thumb, "Union Pacific will deny allowing it. We won't know anything about it."

"Mn-huh."

"So if some lawman gets you stopped, you let him board."

"I understand."

"And you'll have to turn Haywood over."

"As agreed."

Dodge pressed on. "The engine crew will be required to stop if they believe the track's compromised, if the train might derail. You understand, correct?"

"Aye," groused McParland. Tired of feeling interrogated, he pivoted to take the lead. "Are you confident you'll have the stations set by Thursday? Water, coal, and engines?"

Dodge's aged eyes knifed the detective. "Precisely."

McParland pressed on. "Just to be clear, once you have everything in place—Thursday, hopefully—you'll have a telegram sent to Mr. Cecil White at the Oxford Hotel, there in Denver. Aye? The name won't refer to an actual person, of course."

Dodge nodded slowly. "It will be Thursday."

"Your message will be ... ?" He lifted an anticipatory eyebrow.

"About cattle business."

"Aye, setting my operation in motion Thursday evening. I remind you, we must roll from the Union Station the moment Haywood is on board, and no later than Thursday midnight."

Dodge gave an irked sigh and scratched at his ear.

McParland peered over his glasses. "That's the only way we'll be in Idaho before the sun rises Friday."

"Yes, yes," said Dodge, his tone terse.

They fell silent. Both were leaning on the table, reviewing the map. And though their thoughts drifted elsewhere, their heads barely moved. Two prodigious mustache clouds floating over the mountains. One gray and stormy. One snowy and aloof.

★

– 37 –

MONDAY
March 11, 1907

Neva once again stood in the expansive Stockman's Room of the Denver Dry Goods department store, only this time she was with George. They were near the counter. She watched him talk with the milliner steam-shaping the Galena-style Stetson she'd given him. After it was formed to George's preferences, he put it on and came to sit near her, though not so close as to set any tongues wagging.

"It's very handsome on you," she said.

"Thank you for it. It was very thoughtful of you to remember my birthday." He then lowered his voice. "But the truth is, it'd look better on you—with nothing else."

She smirked. "That's true. Come. Sit closer."

He did, hesitantly. "Why are you so comfortable with this?"

She spoke softly. "I tell you now, George, I'll never share a house with Bill again. Never again."

"What happened?"

"Actually, it will happen soon." Her eyes sparkled as she leaned toward him. "I know you won't speak of it. I didn't even tell Winnie. No one. But I just have to tell you."

He shook his head. "What? What's going to happen?"

"You're going to faint," she said, her voice light.

"I doubt that." He grinned, happy to see her so effervescent, but alarmed all the same. "All right. So tell me."

"One night this week, they're coming to arrest him."

George gave a stunned grimace. "What?"

"Yes. They're taking him to Boise."

"No. Truly?"

"Un-huh." She smiled. "In the suites. I'm staying at the house. I gave them a map of the suites. It was the most fun. I'm sorry, but it was. I had to tell you."

"Darling, what did you do?"

Hearing his icy pitch, she frowned. "Well, hell's bells, George, I did what I told you I would do—what I might do. I found a way to help you."

"I need to understand. What exactly did you do? Who's coming for him?"

She lowered her nose, giving a look that told him the answer.

"Pinkertons? McParland?" He inhaled and held it. "Oh my."

"After they're gone, I'm having the locks changed. Everything will change."

"Ok. Ok," George muttered, his mind racing. "If Bill's arrested, I'll be president *pro tempore*—I believe. The Federation holds the lease on your suites. Oh, this could be really unfortunate."

"Unfortunate?" snapped Neva.

"Yes. Maybe. Especially if Detective McParland isn't successful. Or what if Bill gets loose before Boise?"

She froze. "Could that happen?"

"What do they have that might show you helped them?"

"I mailed him a drawing of the third floor, our suites."

"Is that all?"

"That's all that's written. The other, we just said."

"What other?"

"What I received for helping. What I got for you."

"You talked to the Pinkertons about me? Neva!"

"Don't raise your voice. Don't ever raise your voice to me."

He recovered. "I'm sorry. I just—"

"He agreed that if—"

"Who agreed?"

"Detective McParland. He said if any embezzlement investigation arises, you'll not be a suspect. You did nothing improper."

"You talked about the embezzlement? With the Pinkertons?" He lowered his voice to a grumble. "Who brought that up?"

"I did, I think. But he knew all about it."

George blinked a few times and shook his head as if to get her words, now afloat in his mind, to settle into some sequence of sense. "You— You, the wife of the president of the Western Federation of Miners, met with the chief detective of the Pinkertons?"

"No. We talked on telephones."

"You dear woman. I know you were trying to help, but if this goes wrong, if they don't get him to Boise, if they don't convict him, he'll come after me, and maybe you."

"Then they must succeed, mustn't they," she said—jaw tight, nose up, chin resolute.

He exhaled loudly and stood. Giving her a sallow smile, he began rolling her toward the elevators. "You didn't tell Winnie?"

"No."

"Yeah," George muttered, "I wouldn't trust her either."

It was not until Colorado Supreme Court Chief Justice Luther Goddard left his Seventeenth Street office and walked three blocks to an intersection just beyond Denver's Oxford Hotel that a white-shirted Pinkerton approached. With a polite gesture, the man motioned for the justice to step inside the hotel. Goddard obliged and, upon entering, found the well-appointed parlor vacant, the bellman's stand barren. The man motioned him further. Past the registration desk, they entered a small office where Detective McParland was half sitting on a dilapidated desk, pipe smoke swirling up past his mustache and nose.

"Good afternoon, Your Honor," offered McParland, bracing himself on his cane as he stood. "How are you on this fine day?"

The bowler-hatted justice hesitated before shaking McParland's hand. "That was a silly piece of writing: you with Sherlock Holmes."

"I couldn't agree more. Aye. I was as surprised as anyone by that. I'm not sure it was a compliment," McParland said, lying. Of course it was a compliment. He was delighted Sir Arthur Conan Doyle had written a "fictional" character named "Pinkerton Detective James McParland" into a recent Sherlock Holmes novel.

"Humph," the justice replied. "Doyle made a mockery of Holmes's genius. I'll not read his tripe again." Once the Pinkerton escort was gone, Goddard continued, "What is your need of me? State your business, James."

"It's a sensitive matter," replied McParland. "Urgent, in fact."

Goddard rubbed his nose and took a seat. "You're back here in Denver intent on arresting William Haywood, I presume."

McParland sat in the chair nearest the justice. "It troubles me, Your Honor, that you know that. We've maintained—"

"My dog could work out what you're doing, Detective, scuttling around with secret meetings like this—right as you've ginned things up against the man."

"I haven't ginned anything. I—"

"You've come to capture him." The justice drummed his fingers on the desk. "Then what? Take him out of the state? To Idaho? I presume you'll transport him through Wyoming first."

McParland hesitated, blinked a few times, and finally nodded.

"I cannot let that happen, you understand. And Mr. Haywood should be made aware—"

"You are famed for your integrity and independence," said McParland. "You wouldn't alert the defendant about—"

Goddard stiffened his neck. "But he is *not* a defendant, is he?"

"Not yet, but secrecy is of the order here, and—"

"Who will be the special prosecutor? The much-too-daring-for-his-own-good Senator Borah?"

"Yes, Your—"

"Then why is he not here seeking this irregular—and *ipso facto* improper—request? An officer of the court should submit this."

"As it isn't a legal matter, as such, I thought—"

"Not a legal matter?" snorted Goddard. "Not a legal matter? So, why are you bothering the chief justice of the Colorado Supreme Court with it—with this non-legal matter? Why am I being hustled aside by a Pinkerton of all things?"

McParland took a breath. "It's not a legal matter *exactly*, but—"

"I see nothing legal in kidnapping a man under the color of the State—for any purpose. It would be illegal on its face. *Contra legem prima facie*. You are overzealous, Detective—blind to your weakness. Your friend Sherlock would see that."

"My weakness?"

"One can hardly blame you. Your entire profession is wrapped in the inquest of others' deceptions such that you cannot see your own contrivances. I know you. You're a clandestine and deceitful sort. Perhaps that's what is necessary, what must be done to find success within all the lies and inquiry—to create your own. To catch the deceiver, you must deceive. Is that it?"

"Haywood is to stand trial in Boise. That's what is necessary."

"Necessary for whom?"

"For justice," tried McParland.

"Justice? That's rich coming from a glorified gunhand."

McParland narrowed his gaze. "I meant no offense."

"Well, I did," quipped Goddard. "William Haywood is a full citizen of the United States, is he not?"

"Aye."

"And he is a citizen of the State of Colorado?"

"I believe so."

"Do you have any evidence indicating he was in Idaho on the date of the assassination?"

"No, Sir."

"And yet you presume you can waltz in, seize the man, and transport him across state lines?"

"It's necessary, I believe—"

"*You* believe. But you're not an attorney, are you? You're not—"

"I represent—"

"You represent nothing, Mr. McParland."

"We *will* be taking Mr. Haywood."

"Then you *will* be arrested for kidnapping and contempt of court. And the Pinkertons will—"

"I'm confident that won't happen."

Justice Goddard exhaled through his nose, frowning at McParland who returned the glare, unblinking. "This is a judicial matter, to be handled by officers of the court. Trained attorneys. The Idaho judge handling this, as well as Senator Borah, should've explained to you how this must work—if it is to work at all." He paused again, as if examining the impassivity of the detective before him. "You cannot extradite a Colorado citizen, legally or otherwise, without securing the governor's signature." He rubbed his chin. "And to get that, you need me."

"I'm here, Your Honor." McParland had let this "man of the law" bellow and stamp, condescend and insult—but now he felt things turning. Perhaps his patience would begin to reap its rewards. He had two cards yet to play: a king and an ace. He tried the king first. "As a brother in the Benev—"

"Benevolent Order?" Justice Goddard snapped. "You and I have not strained to force a friendship where none exists. Let us not feign such familiarities now. Robert Pinkerton and his bootlickers have repeatedly circumscribed the laws of this state, and he is now attempting, for the purposes of doing what he deems necessary, to conduct one of the most severe violations of *habeas corpus* and prosecutorial fraud that I have yet to witness. And by your hand, *Detective*," he said, spitting the title as if it was coated in shit.

So much for the king, thought McParland. He wanted to interject that not only was this plan happening "by his hand," but it was entirely his idea—not that of Robert Pinkerton. Though yes, Senator Borah had assisted. And General Dodge.

Goddard was going on, though now quieter. "I can commiserate with your desire in this matter. No doubt Mr. Haywood carries some culpability and most likely should hang. But your actions will only set him free from prosecution for years, if not decades. I harbor no allegiance to any cause in this state, other than upholding its laws. That notwithstanding, I'm sympathetic to the governor's alliance with the mine owners, and his dogged defense against the Federation's socialist demands for the eight-hour day. But that will not persuade me to fly against my conscious and my distaste for the thuggery of the Pinkerton Agency in this state."

McParland gave a dissembling smile. "I regret the Agency has earned your low esteem."

"It's the secrecy. Robert Pinkerton operates with impunity—like a private army for hire. It is unconstitutional."

Alright, that's enough—time for the ace. "We're a detective agency," said McParland, dropping all supplicative pretense. "We gather intelligence for our clients—in this case the State of Idaho."

"Unless you have some 'intelligence' that—"

"Governor Steunenberg was on a list of several public officials who were to be assassinated."

The chief justice peered at McParland. "A list? In whose hand? William Haywood's?"

"We believe so. Our witness, Mr. Orchard, saw that list, and told us its contents." McParland withdrew a sharply creased piece of paper from his jacket's inside pocket, unfolded it, and began to read: *"There were three others on the list I saw. All were to be killed."*

Goddard pointed at the paper. "Is that it? Is that the list?"

"It's a transcription of Orchard's confession. Shall I continue?"

"If you wish."

McParland counted to four before resuming. *"After Governor Steunenberg, the Idaho man, I was to kill two others. Actually, one other. Steve Adams was to kill one of them.* Here I asked how he knew about the other two, and he said: *Mr. Haywood wrote me a list. The governor of Colorado—he was for Adams to shoot, I think, and Justice Goddard, a judge there—he was for me to handle. I don't know why for sure. I guess because them two had oppressed the Federation some."* The detective paused for effect, meeting Goddard's wide eyes before continuing. "Next I asked Mr. Orchard by what means he was to have handled—assassinated—you." He scanned the paper, finding his place. *"Mr. Haywood wanted me to use a bomb. So, I set one at the judge's house. One like Steunenberg's ten-pounder that had worked so admirably."*

"What?" Goddard stammered. "What are you telling me?"

I'm playing my ace, you pompous blowhard, thought McParland. Instead, he said, "I'm doing my duty, Your Honor. Alerting you to this distressing information that the Pinkerton Agency obtained—obtained by whatever means we deemed necessary. There's more, if you wish to hear it."

Justice Goddard nodded.

"When I asked him about the bomb at your house, he said, and I quote: *I planted it by his gate, same as the other, but it must've been faulty because it never exploded when I went to pull on it. My guess is the acid didn't uncork properly."*

"Are you telling me— Goddamnit! There was a bomb in front of my house?" The justice got to his feet. "*My* house?"

"Aye. It would appear so. I don't know if it's still there, but—"

"It's still there?" Goddard shouted.

McParland raised his shaggy eyebrows. "It may be. What we know is that Haywood ordered Orchard, a known assassin, to build it and place it there, intending to kill you with it. And, according to this confession, Orchard tried."

"I must get home."

"Be careful. Don't dig it up," said McParland, standing.

Goddard was wide eyed. "You do it. Send someone. Now!"

"I have men on the way to your house."

"You do?"

"Aye. They may have already arrived. For your protection—in case Orchard was telling the truth."

The justice was shaking, moving to leave.

McParland continued calmly, "When you get there, they can look for the bomb. And disarm it, if you wish."

"If I wish?" Goddard growled, running to the hotel's front door. "Of course they should disarm the goddamned thing!"

McParland walked behind him, stopping just inside the wood-and-glass doors. "Of course," he whispered as he watched the justice hurry aboard a waiting hansom cab driven by a Pinkerton. Then McParland went to the registration desk, took the telephone, clicked the hook, and told the operator, "Connect me to Justice Goddard's home." After a moment, he said, "It's me. His wife and kids are still upstairs? (*pause*) Aye, he's on his way—fifteen minutes. (*pause*) No, Charlie Siringo made it. Now, mind you, he's the fellow you bested in poker—so when you dig it back up, it could still kill you. (*pause and a smile*) Good. (*pause*) The dirt's stamped, looks worn? (*pause*) No, don't go out there again. She might see you. (*pause*) Aye, when it's signed, bring it to me."

He hung up and pulled his fob chain to study his watch. It was 2:25 in the afternoon. By his estimation, by 5:30 he would have Chief Justice Goddard's signature on an ostensibly illegal order to extradite William Haywood from Colorado to Idaho on charges of capital murder—a murder which occurred when Haywood was not in Idaho, and for which the prosecution had only one of the two required witnesses. *Contra legem prima facie*, indeed.

McParland had the signed order by 4:45.

– 38 –

THURSDAY
March 14, 1907

9:30 a.m.—A telegram was sent to Cecil White at Denver's Oxford Hotel, reading:

> 200 BEEF SHORTHORNS
> $36 PER. TODAY.

6:00 p.m.—A cadre of Federation men shouted at Charles Siringo when he strolled into the Gassell Saloon on the first floor of the Pioneer Building. When one approached, suggesting the "god-damned Pink traitor" was ill-advised to be there, Siringo replied by placing his red-handled revolver on the bar. The man walked away, and a bit of hooting commenced from afar. After finishing his drink, and another, Siringo left. Outside, a Federation guard spat at him as he hailed a cab. Siringo loudly declared to the driver that his destination was the depot as he was bound for Texas. "Good riddance, rat," growled the Federation man. At the depot, Siringo boarded the 7:15 Colorado Central to Pueblo.

11:15 p.m.—All was dark, other than what was illuminated by the moonlight when it emerged from behind fast clouds—cold light brushing a timid glow across the stone façades of Denver's downtown buildings. Everything was in place. From inside the black window of a barbershop, McParland leaned on his cane and studied the Pioneer Building across Fifteenth Street—its street-front empty save two guards standing firm and one lonely whore shuffling by. From what he could see of the first floor, the Gassell Saloon hosted two sleeping drunks and a table of undercover Pinkerton operatives in a mock-heated card game. They were under orders to drink (in moderation) tonight, lest they be suspected of not being the new-in-town union lackeys they were impersonating. McParland looked at the second floor—the headquarters of the Western Federation of Miners, and specifically Haywood's office. He saw no life there behind its gloomy windows. On the third floor, one window gave light from the Haywood suites, while further up, the fourth and fifth floors were as dark as the second. The roof, he knew, bore a lone Federation guard who was probably drunk and thus away from the edge lest he stumble.

McParland stepped out through the barbershop's front door—quietly, as the door's overhead bell had been muffled with a bit of cloth. Both of the guards flanking the entrance to the Pioneer Building observed McParland, but they did nothing—they being Pinkertons pretending to be Federation (the originals having been stealthily hauled off at gunpoint minutes earlier). McParland heard an operative step from the store behind him, and then he saw a female figure pull the curtains across the third-floor's lit window.

"His wife's in there?" breathed the operative.

"No," whispered McParland, checking his pocket-watch.

"Who's in there with him?"

McParland motioned to the operative's shotgun. "Loaded?"

"Yes, Sir."

"Check again."

On the opposite side of the Pioneer, away from view of McParland or anyone on Fifteenth Street, three other Pinkertons were busy, each having been chosen for his mountaineering experience. One had already scaled the back side of the building, tied a rope to a chimney and draped it down to the alley five stories below. Once the other two had soundlessly ascended, all three squatted in a murky corner. Then one whistled to draw the attention of the Federation guard who was leaning against the far roof-access door. The man approached, his rifle aimed at the mysterious sound. As he disappeared into the corner's darkness, a muted thump and thud were followed by two of the Pinkertons emerging into the moonlight and moving quickly toward that same door. One confirmed the door was unlocked while the other lit a match to check his own pocket-watch.

At the same time, in the saloon far below, one of the card players also checked his watch. He then rose, declaring it was time for him to go home, and exited the building onto Fifteenth

Street. Seeing the man coming out, McParland crossed the street, passed between the two Pinkertons masquerading as Federation guards, entered the building, and approached the elevator. Before the elevator arrived, two of the once-card-players stood alongside the chief, shotguns at their sides. McParland drew his pistol from his shoulder holster. His left hand held a piece of paper bearing Neva's drawn layout of the third floor. The elevator bell rang, and, from inside, one of the roof Pinkertons opened the door and cage. McParland spoke as he and the two from the saloon stepped in. "Only his mistress is with him. Not his wife, kids, or any of the staff." The elevator began ascending. "Remember: fast and loud. Hesitate and he'll have you. Most importantly, whatever happens, do *not* kill him."

Inside one of the third-floor bedrooms, two electric lanterns washed the room in dull gold. Haywood sat on the bed, waiting. Though his coat and tie were draped over a blue-upholstered chair, he was otherwise dressed—including wearing his shoulder holster containing his Browning .38 revolver. His Colt .45 was on the nearby cabinet, while the FN automatic was in the inner pocket of the coat on the chair. He inhaled a long breath of contentment, then blew it out slowly, beaming a smile toward the wooden divider-screen behind which Winnie undressed.

He was glad Neva had gone to their Park Hill home. He always had more fun with his mistress when his wife wasn't in the next room. He craved Winnie, and she truly loved him, he told himself. She was more than his *objet de fantaisie*. She was a partner with him in his work. She chose to be involved, to risk herself. She gave a brilliance and illumination that he wanted, that he needed, that he deserved. Winnie was necessary. Neva could never be necessary. Winnie was his, and he was devoted to her. Yes, she made him cover his dead eye, but— *Oh damn,* he thought, scrambling to slip his eye patch over his head. Just then, Winnie's lithe silhouette stepped from behind the screen. She dropped her silk shift, liberating her naked curves. What red-blooded American man wouldn't prefer this young, supple wonder over an aging, diseased wife?

"Bear," Winnie said with a feline growl. "You're still dressed."

"Yes ... Oh, yes," Haywood muttered, kicking off his boots and pulling at his belt. Then his shoulder holster thudded to the floor. Soon his big frame floundered and flailed—shirt landing over the holster, then his undershirt, and then trousers and drawers—revealing himself to her.

Having giggled at his flourishes and flops, she approached with a beguiling smile. "That's better," she cooed.

Haywood pulled her against him and turned her, easing her back toward the bed where she collapsed, her arms around his neck, him atop, kissing her lips, and then her slender neck, moving toward her breasts, her bellybutton, her—

Winnie screamed at the explosion of noise. Both thought the bed had fallen, but in the same instant saw the blast had come from shoulders smashing the hallway door from its hinges, crashing it to the floor inside—eight feet from where Haywood scrambled toward the Colt on the cabinet.

"Stop, Bill! I'll shoot ya!" shouted McParland, pistol extended. With his other hand, he stuffed Neva's floorplan drawing into his coat pocket.

Haywood froze, his naked ass pointed toward the five men standing on or near the collapsed door. He then plopped back on the bed where Winnie peeked wide-eyed from under a hastily yanked sheet. "What do you think you're doing?" asked Haywood, removing his eye patch but leaving his legs apart, airing his shrinking manhood.

"*Big* Bill?" McParland mocked. Then he looked at Winnie. "You're Winnifred Minor, are you not?"

"Don't speak to her," barked Haywood.

Winnie scowled silently.

"Get his gun," said McParland. A Pinkerton came around the bed, toward the cabinet, averting his gaze as much from the nakedness as from the dead eye. Once the Colt revolver was secured, McParland said, "Search the room. Get dressed Mr. Haywood. You have a long trip ahead." He picked up Winnie's shift from the floor and tossed it to her. "You too."

Haywood's jaw clenched as he stood, beginning to dress. "You're a sorry son of a bitch, Jim."

"An honor ya think so," said McParland, leaning into his brogue.

As Haywood retrieved his pile of clothes, his hand found the strap of his shoulder holster that held the .38 revolver. But McParland saw it too. "Bill, I don't want to shoot you, but I will." Haywood released the strap and McParland continued, "Actually, that's not true. I'd be more than happy to shoot you. Aye, but all in good time." Then to one of the operatives he said, "Get that holster. And search his coat and the rest of the room. No telling the other guns in here."

McParland moved closer to Winnie who had put on her shift while still under the sheet. "You're his wife's kid sister," he said, shaking his head.

Winnie's face flushed as she stood, her figure clearly visible beneath the clingy, white silk. "What of it?" she said.

"You're a perversion of all that's good. Both of you."

"That's not your business," snapped Haywood, noting other Pinkerton eyes were absorbing Winnie where she stood.

Winnie glared. "If I scream, a hundred union men will come."

"If you truly believe that, lassy," McParland said, "then, by all means, go ahead."

"No, dear," said Haywood. "They've no doubt killed all—"

"We've killed no one," said the detective as he holstered his pistol. "There are laws in this land, Bill, and by God, I lawfully follow them. I'm not of your foul breed."

"Lawful, you say? Kidnapping me without permission from the Colorado Supreme Court? You imbecile. I have the best lawyer in the world. I despise the law, don't abide it, but I know it, and I know you can't—"

"Now, now," McParland said, raising a hand to hush the big man. In his other hand was the FN automatic pistol that one of the Pinkertons had found in Haywood's coat."

"That's not yours," growled Haywood.

The detective marveled at it, turning it, pulling back the slide, aiming it at a wall. Then he slipped it into his coat pocket.

"Law?" exclaimed Haywood. "Goddamned thief! You're stealing my property. How is that you 'following the law?'"

Still silent, McParland produced from his coat the court order signed by Justice Goddard. As he did, Neva's floorplan tumbled to the floor, landing partially open. McParland briefly held Goddard's order for Haywood to read, then he retrieved the drawing.

"Where did you get that map?"

"Don't ya recognize your wife's handwriting?" asked McParland.

"Goddamn you!" Haywood thundered. "All of you."

McParland withdrew a set of handcuffs, his mustache flitting as he suppressed a grin, logging this pinnacle moment into his memory. "Time to abide by the law."

"Abide? To hell with your *law*. It's infernally corrupt. I'm not a law-abiding citizen."

"Aye, agreed."

"Why should I be?"

"Hands," said McParland.

"The law?" fumed Haywood while being cuffed. "What law? Your law?"

"Save your outrage for the judge, Bill."

As Haywood began to walk, he leaned towards Winnie. "They'll try to get me to Boise," he whispered. "Get word to Swain. Tell—"

"Oh aye, Miss Minor," said McParland with a derisive chuckle. "Go tell Captain Swain. That is, if you can find him *again*. Remember when, only a few weeks ago, you went to Salt Lake City and delivered Mr. Haywood's instructions to Captain Swain? You told him to go kill Steve Adams—remember? A word of warning: you'd better pray Swain's not successful in that endeavor, in killing Adams—or so help me God, I'll be back for *you*, an accomplice to murder." Then he poked his cane in Haywood's direction. "And how about your wife? No message to be delivered to *her*?" He returned to Winnie. "In truth, there's no need to tell your sister, dear." He waved the map. "She knew about this days ago. She made this possible."

"What?" blurted Winnie.

"Don't listen to the bogtrotter," growled Haywood. "As soon as they walk me out, send word to Swain and Clarence—"

"No, she won't be communicating with anyone till later tomorrow, at the soonest." McParland motioned to an operative who began handcuffing Winnie. "Aye, Mr. Haywood, it seems your wife, the poor woman, is all too happy to see you gone."

"You're a yellow—" Haywood was silenced by a gag being tied around his head.

"Stay quiet," said McParland. "Otherwise we'll club you and carry you out. Nod if you understand."

Haywood dipped his nose.

McParland looked at the operative who had finished handcuffing Winnie. "If she makes a noise, gag her too." He slapped Haywood on the back. "Alright, let's go." They left for the stairwell in a formation of two operatives in the lead, then Haywood, and then McParland, followed by one more operative. Soon they were exiting the back of the building and climbing into a waiting coach with blacked-out windows.

For five days, an unremarkable Union Pacific train had been sitting in a railyard ten miles north of Denver, curtains closed, sentries set, and no one allowed near. During those days, Union Pacific completed its logistical work, and McParland and his men conducted their operations in Denver, including orchestrating the dummy bomb at Chief Justice Goddard's home. Then, on Thursday, Dodge's telegraph was received at the Oxford Hotel, and the short train eased into Denver's Union Station while all other rail traffic stopped.

Named the McParland Special by the Pinkertons, the train was comprised of an engine, a tender, a passenger car, a Pullman, and a caboose. The engine, a Sterling Single 4-2-2, had the usual compliment of engineer, brakeman, and boilerman—plus an extra boilerman and a heavily armed Pinkerton guard. The tender, immediately behind the engine, had a custom-built, high-capacity water tank and coal bin. The passenger car carried eighteen men: three hired gunhands (with unique knowledge of certain sheriffs and other potential troublemakers along the route); two Union Pacific representatives (armed with letters signed by General Dodge for the purpose of mollifying any concerns among fellow employees along the line); nine Pinkertons (two of whom were dedicated to operating the telegraph during stops); and four soldiers from the newly formed Colorado National Guard. The federal soldiers were only permitted to act defensively, and only if the train was under direct or imminent attack. In that scenario, they were authorized to operate two Gatling guns mounted in the windows on either side of that passenger car; and to fire, if needed, the latest technology in warfare: a .30 caliber Maxim Machine Gun still crated in the middle of the floor. The Pullman state car, behind the passenger car, carried McParland and the prisoner, plus two cooks, a small kitchen, and a compliment of four Pinkerton guards. Finally, the caboose contained four more Pinkertons, two more contracted gunhands, supplies, and an arsenal of additional weapons.

By midnight, Haywood was aboard the McParland Special. He was reclined on a tufted couch in the Pullman, eyes closed, left wrist handcuffed to the wall.

Nearby, McParland paced anxiously. Why were they not underway? He left through the Pullman's forward door, crossed the covered coupling, and entered the passenger car just ahead. There he found the two Union Pacific representatives sitting on facing benches. As he approached, they saw him and began to rise. "Keep your seats," McParland said, sliding in beside one. "For godsakes, why are we not moving?"

"There's a logging flatcar on the track, just beyond the switch."

"What? Why is it there?"

"We aren't certain, but when the other traffic was shut down this evening, the yard crew just left it sitting there ... apparently."

"That's unacceptable. We had an agreement: the track is to be clear, and we're to leave before midnight."

"Yes, Sir, but we were just told, and—"

"Well, lads, go move it," instructed McParland.

"They will, Sir, the moment they arrive."

"They? Who is they?"

"The railyard crew."

McParland peered over his glasses and growled, "When?"

"Their shift begins at six-thirty."

"In the morning?"

"Yes, Sir, in the morning."

"Are you men mad?" McParland's face was reddening. "Get out there this instant. Clear that car!"

"We can't, Sir."

"Move it right now, or I'll have my men move it."

The Union Pacific men froze, then one mumbled, "It's loaded with timber. It'll take a pusher."

"A pusher?"

"Yes, Sir, from the switching yard."

McParland shook his head, stopped, then angrily scratched an eyebrow. "What does that require, to get a pusher?"

"We'd have to wake some yardies and a foreman. A lineman too. They'd ask a bunch of questions. Mr. Dodge told us to wait."

"This is re-goddamn-diculous," shouted McParland, bringing the whole car's complement of men to silence. "We're sitting here, right out in the open. The great prize is in our possession. We have him. Do you two not understand that? He's in the next car for godsakes! It's the middle of the night. We have the cover of darkness. Do you understand?"

"Yes, Sir."

"The only thing separating us from certain death, from this train being stormed by a thousand angry, armed Federation fellows, is that they're all still sleeping. Do you know that?"

"Yes, Sir, but—"

"They have no idea we've taken their man. Not *yet*! But when they cotton to it, the very last place this train should be is right in the middle of the goddamned Denver station! We need to be long gone, moving a hundred miles an hour across the prairie."

"I don't think this one goes that fast," said one of the men.

"What would you like us to do?" asked the other.

McParland thought for a long moment, then huffed and lowered his chin. When he did finally speak, it was with a soft, resigned voice. "If we get the men and equipment necessary to move it, we risk waking the wolves too. We can't do that. So, gentlemen, be sure they clear it first thing when they come on duty in the morning. The very *first* thing they do."

"Yes, Sir."

"And the second it's on a siding, I want us passing on our way."

The Union Pacific men acknowledged.

McParland stood and walked back to the Pullman where its four Pinkerton guards were playing cards. Haywood was asleep.

"Unchain him," said McParland. "He knows I'll kill him if tries to escape. Leave the cuff. Just unhook the chain from it."

As one guard walked to unchain the prisoner, another asked, "Are we moving soon, Chief?"

"Not for a few hours," McParland grumbled. "Pass the word to all the men: we're delayed here. It'll be a dangerous night. Those on post must stay vigilant. Everyone else needs to get their sleep. We'll have to make our run in full daylight. We'll need every man at his best. And tonight, absolutely no one may exit the train for any reason, other than one of us Pinkertons on watch. And if anyone attempts to board the train, bring them to me."

"Yes, Sir."

As one of the operatives left to spread the word, another spoke up. "Should we send a runner to Twenty-Nine, watching that woman? Tell him to hold off releasing her?"

McParland scrunched his eyes so tightly that they exploded into ripples of deep wrinkles across his face. He had forgotten about Winnie. "Damnit. Damnit. Damnit. Aye, slip off now. Stay unseen, but get yourself to the Pioneer. Tell Twenty-Nine to hold Miss Minor till mid-afternoon. He'll need to keep her especially quiet. In the morning, people will begin arriving at the Federation headquarters just below him. In fact, you stay there with him, help him, then you both come north on Saturday."

The man repeated the details and left.

When McParland sat on the couch opposite Haywood, he saw the prisoner's eye was open. "I have you," McParland whispered.

Haywood rolled away, muttering, "Ah, but can you keep me?"

"Mmmph," McParland snorted, his gaze set on Haywood's back. Here was his twelve-point buck. Now to get it home and gut it.

The Park Hill Heights home was silent, save for the ticks and tocks of two clocks battling for the correct time: a little, mahogany mantelpiece in the drawing room and its foe, the London longcase standing sentinel by the dining room door. Neva was in the fire-painted dark, listening to the time quarrel, half into a bottle of red wine and wondering where Bill was—wishing George was there. She pulled her knitted shawl tighter at her shoulders and rolled herself close to the crackling, popping fire. Her hair having come loose, little gold aggravators tickled her cheeks till she flicked them away. Did Bill know she had betrayed him? No, don't think that, she tried feebly, her thoughts acquiescing to the Cabernet. How could it be? Was it treachery? She hadn't done much, just drawn a map of their suites and where the guards would be. But the years of it. Of it all. The humiliations with Winnie. The stony estrangements. The bouts of anger. Him sending their daughters away. Not touching her. Telling her she was diseased. All of it. Her defenses were in shambles. Eroded. The relentless trickle having gouged a canyon through her self-worth. She downed the balance from her glass, refilled it, drank almost a fourth again, and then peered at the fire through the glass's luminous crystal. Iridescence in shades of red. "Tiger," she said aloud, surprised by the sound of her own voice. "Tiger burn bright." The first swell-tide of alcohol washed through her, and her eyes doubled in weight. Bill will be furious, hurt—and right to feel that way. Would he hit her? He hadn't—not ever. But this was different. "Maybe," she whispered. She had helped the hated Pinks, of all people. She had talked on the telephone with Detective McParland, and she had talked about Bill. She told them things. Another swallow. Would Bill hate her? He should. A swallow again. But it was just a map. And she'd told them when Bill would be in the suites. That's all. And she removed herself from the suites. That wasn't illicit. And she didn't tell Winnie. That was bad. Winnie would be furious. Sissy might never talk to her again. Another slow drink, this time with the trailing need to wipe her lips on the blanket. They would've captured him somehow, regardless. Right? "Of course," she declared to the fire, her eyes wide. The mine owners and their dogs had been after Bill for years. Sooner or later they were bound to have gotten lucky—to get him. Her map had only made the arrest quick. And safer. Bill should thank her, the bastard. Had he fought back? Hopefully not. God, what if he did and Winnie got hurt? No, no, she moaned silently, shaking her head like a rag doll, then holding it steady for another drink. She was being silly. She felt the alcohol's warmth in her forehead. They wouldn't hurt Winnie. The Detective Pinkerton man had assured her. *Winnie will be safe*, he'd said. "No harm," Neva muttered aloud. They were in her house. It was just the suites, not this place. Not here. Not her perfect home. She took a large gulp, imagining them in the halls of the suites. Then she topped her glass. Her silly map hadn't changed the outcome. They wouldn't have hinged the whole arrest on her saying where Bill would be, and at what time. She wasn't responsible. Of course not, she argued, closing her eyes. They could've learned that without her. They didn't *need* her. No one needed her. Maybe. Bill couldn't be mad. Everything would be ok. She'd wait till George came—till he told her Bill was in Boise. "Sweet, sweet ... darwing Geore," she said faintly, failing to enunciate. It would be fine—it would be good—they would be—together—soon. But maybe she should go to Boise, be a good wife. Pretend. Bill will never know what she did. The alcohol put her thoughts at sea, the waves pulling at her. She didn't mind Bill's eye. Winnie didn't like his eye, but she didn't mind. Didn't that matter? Why hadn't that mattered? Did she matter? She should try harder. Bill would see. She'd be the woman he relied on. His rock. See him through this. Whatever this was going to be. Because she had betrayed him. She would've been a good wife had he been kinder. Had she not gotten sick. Had he loved her. She slipped out of gear, rolling toward sleep, faintly aware that her wine-soaked musings—her hopes—were folly. The big grandfather clock across the house chimed 1:00 in the morning. Almost a minute later, a single bell dinged from the mantel, high above where Neva now slept.

– 39 –

FRIDAY
March 15, 1907

That Friday morning, as the sun escaped from the forever horizon, climbing over the plains of eastern Colorado, it illumined the front range of the Rocky Mountains in dull pinks and spring blues, and brought the metropolis of Denver to life. There, yawning travelers coming to the depot for boarding were met with signs declaring that all trains were delayed due to track damage. What they didn't know was that one train had already left. By 6:45, the timber flatbed had been cleared. By 7:00, the McParland Special was gone.

In the Pioneer Building suites, Winnie was asleep in her bed while one of the Pinkerton guards sat drowsily in a nearby chair, facing her, pistol in hand. The other guard was near the elevator, reading a book that he held open across the shotgun in his lap.

In the Park Hill home, Neva was stretched on the drawing-room couch, deep in the grip of a gossamer dream, riding a pale unicorn up from a mine shaft and then out beyond the reach of the trees.

The train's fat shadow tore north, a jagged blade scything the plains, clacking and roaring, whipping at the upstart greens, yellows and early reds. A black notch in the budding grassland, running at a staggering speed. Inside the Pullman car, Haywood was reading a day-old newspaper and sipping coffee, trying to appear oblivious to McParland who, in his shirt sleeves, was pacing and then pausing to peer past the curtains and out at the passing prairie.

The Sterling Single 4-2-2 engine, chosen for its swiftness (so as to get the McParland Special to the Colorado border in record time), accelerated to seventy-five miles per hour and held there as planned, with stretches reaching eighty to ninety. To maintain that pace, the boilerman shoveled ten pounds of coal every fifteen seconds—thus the need for an additional boilerman to spell the first, and the larger capacity tender.

The plan was working well, yet there were hundreds of miles to go; and if at any point along the way, McParland was presented with a valid *habeas corpus* order, he would be obligated to turn Haywood over. Therefore, under no circumstance should they allow the boarding of some labor-friendly sheriff alerted by a Federation telegram. That meant that, for the entire route, as they approached each town, whether it had its own depot or was just a jerkwater (meaning it offered only a water tank), the McParland Special maintained its speed—its whistle wailing from a half mile out, its bell clanging mercilessly as it thundered past each platform, rattling the station's windows, startling anyone there.

But the Special still needed servicing, so all water and coal intake, and the three planned engine changes, would occur at one of McParland's eleven strategically mapped remote stops (his Cassidy stations), each having been constructed for this one purpose. That morning's first two Cassidys (both in Colorado) had gone flawlessly. At 9:12, the train crossed into Wyoming, and McParland allowed himself to breathe.

On that same Friday morning, Clarence Darrow arrived in Chicago on a train from St. Louis where he had held meetings with three clients. Travel weary, he hired a motorized cab to take him home. Finding the house empty, he left his luggage and hailed a horse-drawn cab to Marshall Fields. He needed more shirts and undergarments. On the way, he thought about where he would go next, after the department store. He would go to Hull House, the Chicago settlement house and social reform institution that he and Ruby frequented and supported. Comprised of multiple, tightly clustered brick buildings, Hull House's several dining and drawing rooms, libraries and living quarters attracted intelligent, reform-minded thinkers, artists, writers, and activists—Chicago locals and travelers alike—all seeking refuge from the mundane, all sharing a drive for intellectual curiosity and progressive change. Wakes and weddings were conducted there, holiday and birthday parties as well. It had its secrets, but didn't hold them well, especially among its members. (He knew Ruby was planning a surprise party for him there when he turned fifty in a month.) Though Darrow loved the place for all it provided him socially and cerebrally, he treasured it for a personal reason: Hull House was where, in 1903, he had first met Ruby, an alluring, free-thinking journalist whose unflagging intelligence came with such icy wit and sizzling charm that his nerves had yet to settle.

At the third Cassidy station—just shy of Cheyenne, Wyoming—the boilermen had the McParland Special's tender refilled with water and coal in just under fifteen minutes. The train then hurried back to speed. It was 10:05 when they boomed past the Cheyenne depot at forty miles per hour, the maximum possible due to the curves there—too slow for McParland's liking but still too fast for anyone to jump aboard. Looking out a window as they rolled through, McParland saw a platoon of armed men on the platform, shotguns and rifles in hand. One brandished a red flag. McParland's pulse quickened. Those men had hoped to stop the train. Word was out—already. The union was awake, angry, and gunning for them.

It was early afternoon by the time Darrow hung his hat and set down his Marshall Fields' parcel in the front parlor of Hull House. A huddle of women was there, laughing about something that had occurred during their suffrage-march meeting which had just ended. One acknowledged Darrow, her face revealing a touch of surprise. He kept moving. In the main kitchen, he found Jane Addams, one of Hull House's founders, discussing menus with her staff. Though she was about Darrow's age, Jane was mother to them all, with empathic strength, impenitent compassion, and bright eyes that missed nothing.

"Hello, Jane," he said.

She turned. "Oh, hello, Clarence. I'm glad you're here. Are you familiar with a breakfast dish called cream of wheat?"

"No, I don't believe I am. Have you seen Ruby today?"

"Yes, she interviewed Mr. Wrigley in the green drawing room. But that was this morning."

"Thank you, dear," said Darrow.

He walked through the main building, exited the rear, crossed a small path and entered another building, intent on passing through it to access yet a third building which included the green drawing room. But moving through the second building, he stopped at the sound of feminine laughter followed by distant talking. One of the voices was Ruby's. He climbed the stairs and came to the partially open door of one of the many guest quarters. He eased it open and saw Ruby and another woman at the vanity within. Neither woman saw him. Ruby, in a camisole, stood braiding the sitting woman's auburn tresses. In the vanity's mirror, Darrow saw the other woman's bare breasts perked above her loose corset. When Ruby leaned and cupped the woman's breasts, the woman looked up, meeting his wife's lips in a kiss. Then Ruby saw him in the mirror and straightened, turning to him. The other woman covered herself with a robe.

Darrow's face was blank. He didn't speak.

Nor did Ruby, though she wore a pensive smile.

The other woman bit her bottom lip.

Darrow began a slow nod. "I just got back."

"Hi, dear," Ruby said. Smiling, she came and embraced him, kissing his cheek.

He let her, but gave nothing back.

She turned. "This is Rebecca Tarleton. A visiting resident."

Darrow dipped his chin once. "Rebecca."

The young woman stood, clutching the robe across her chest.

"Rebecca, this is my husband, Clarence."

"Hello," she said. "I'm honored. I heard you speak at the University of Michigan last year and—" She glanced around self-consciously. "I'm sorry if—"

"No, no," said Darrow. "It's— I'll let you two resume what you were ... well ..." He turned to go.

Ruby came after him in the hall. "Clarence," she beckoned, her voice bearing a tone of exasperation. "Clarence, please. Don't be like that. We're just having a bit of fun. It's harmless."

He stopped and regarded her. "I know."

Downstairs, the front door flew open and someone entered.

Ruby kissed Darrow's lips and said softly, "Darling, I'm yours. I'll show you tonight. Will you be home in—"

"Mr. Darrow?" came a man's voice from below.

Darrow kept eye contact with Ruby while he replied loudly, "Upstairs."

Ruby clasped Darrow's hand. "Clarence, darling."

He kissed her, and then pivoted to the man now at the top of the stairs.

Ruby retreated into the bedroom.

The man approached. "Mr. Darrow?"

"Yes."

"Western Union. The ladies in the other building said you—"

"Yes. I'll take it. Thank you."

The messenger handed a telegram to Darrow, received a few coins in gratuity, and left.

Darrow opened the envelope and removed the message.

Ruby reappeared in the doorframe of the guest room.

The telegram was from an unknown source and addressed to Darrow at either his house or at Hull House:

> PINKS TOOK BILL LAST NIGHT.
> TRAIN TO BOISE.

Darrow drew a heavy breath. It had begun.

"Is everything all right?" asked Ruby.

"I must go."

"Not because of this," she said, motioning toward the bedroom. "Surely."

"No. No, dear." He offered a smile. "You know, we've discussed— I must go. I'm not sure for how long."

"Back to Denver?"

"Boise." He rubbed his nose absentmindedly, thinking about the immediate concern between them. "I'll say again what I've long said: I want you happy, dear. Though yes, of course, so long as I'm your only *man*."

She tilted her face toward him, her eyes cheery. "My darling, you are. You do know that. You must." As she began to kiss him, he pressed into her, taking over the kiss, making it his to give. When he let up, she whispered with a breathless grin, "Maybe I should come to Boise too."

"I wish you would. I'll telephone," he said. "We may have to celebrate my birthday there."

Her eyes smiled. "Be safe."

"You too," he said.

After retrieving his yet-unopened luggage from his house, Darrow urged the carriage driver to hurry for the Chicago train station. Once there, he bought a ticket to Boise, checked his luggage, and walked a block to the main Western Union Telegraph office. Within thirty minutes, telegraph machines all along the railroad from Denver to Cheyenne to Green River to Boise were bursting to life, furiously clicking the same message:

> ALERT TO ALL LAW ENFORCEMENT!
> WILLIAM HAYWOOD KIDNAPPED.
> ON TRAIN PASSING YOUR LOCATION SOON.
> BOARD WITH HABEAS CORPUS ORDER.
> REMOVE HOSTAGE. FORCE IF NECESSARY.
> MSG DARROW ESQ AT BOISE IDANHA HOTEL.

Unknown to Darrow, his was the fifth-such telegram to go down the line that day.

The first big test of McParland's pre-stationed system occurred near Buford, Wyoming, where the engine was to be replaced by a Shay 122 geared to maintain speed through the Medicine Bow inclines. During that long stop, all Pinkertons, soldiers, and gunhands were wide awake and alert. This was also the first opportunity to splice into the telegraph lines and learn what was being said about them. Those intercepted telegrams were then brought to the chief detective. Several were alerts about Haywood, including the one from Darrow. They were expected, yet unsettling all the same. What most alarmed McParland was the message he was holding. He had Lieutenant Larson, the officer of the National Guardsmen, summoned to the Pullman, and handed him the telegram.

Larson read it aloud, quietly: "*Green River bridge targeted by Sheriff Wilkins and posse. Knows your ETA. Sheriff's brother on board.*" He looked up at the detective. "Someone's trying to warn us?"

"Looks that way—if it's true. Might be a ruse, trying to scare us into stopping." McParland turned and addressed one of his Pinkerton guards. "Escort Mr. Haywood to the caboose and hold him there until I instruct otherwise."

"Trouble, Detective?" said Haywood as he was led away.

McParland studied the map while others read the telegram. "How far to that bridge?" he asked no one in particular.

"Looks about two hundred miles," offered the officer.

"Damn. Gives them plenty of time. Who's the brother?"

Larson paused. "Maybe a gunhand you added?"

McParland looked a guard returning from the caboose. "Those five we brought on, the gunhands. Any named Wilkins?"

"Yes, Sir. Should I get him?"

McParland blew a sigh. "No. Where is he now?"

"Helping with the new engine, I believe."

"Alright." He turned to another guard. "Place yourself near him—the man Wilkins. Watch him, but don't let on."

With an "Aye, Chief," the man left the car.

"We cleared those men," said another Pinkerton. "Wilkins knows the Green River area. Swore his allegiance—"

"Aye, he knows it, that's for certain," McParland said. He looked at Larson. "They won't blow the bridge. They mean to take Haywood, not to kill him. And I suppose that Sheriff Wilkins up ahead doesn't want to kill his brother—the Wilkins we've got. But one can never know."

"Our Wilkins might try to stop the engine," said Larson.

"Maybe," mused McParland, again holding the telegram. "But they wouldn't be able to count on that. The sheriff will force the stop. Ours has already done his part in their scheme—he got word sent ahead. Somehow. During the quarantine maybe. Regardless, he'll wait till they stop us, and the attack begins, then he'll turn sides. Sure as spit, he will. We can't let it get to that point. We need to convince his brother, the sheriff, that he's too late. Somehow." McParland closed his eyes, his mind shifting into its highest gear, envisioning the possible maneuvers. "If we telegram that the onboard brother has been found out, they'll just go forward with their plan and blow the track. No change for them. In fact, they'll feel more empowered to do so—to rescue the brother too. Same if we put the brother off the train. He'll telegram ahead. No, our Wilkins stays." He walked to the window, pulled the curtain aside, and watched men working on the engine. Is that him?" He pointed at a man next to the Pinkerton whom McParland had sent out.

Larson was also looking. "I believe so."

"We must keep moving, on schedule and on pace. So, what message can we send to delay them blowing the track?"

"That we're delayed?" offered Larson.

The detective nodded, chewing on the man's suggestion. "Aye. Their timing is critical to them. That's their weakness. They won't want to blow it too early. That would give us time to get Haywood off the train miles before." He looked at the map and pointed to Laramie, a town between them and Green River. "They'll have someone wire when we go through. They'll calculate from there."

"Maybe cut the line after Laramie?"

The detective continued inspecting the map. "That wouldn't matter. They'll wire ahead soon as they see us coming into Laramie. Or they'll have someone else wire on, from further ahead."

"If he blows the track, that's a federal crime," said Larson.

McParland considered that for a moment. "The Federation hasn't shied from federal crimes. But a sheriff, a lawman? Perhaps you've a got a point, Lieutenant."

"Do I?" asked Larson. "And what point is that?"

"The sheriff down the line—he'd rather hit us at one of our make-shift stations, when we're already stopped. Better than having Union Pacific collecting repair costs from his county. Yeah, if the brother knows our stations, he'll hit us at one of them. But we don't have a Cassidy station at Green River. So, why Green River?"

"Maybe he doesn't know."

"Maybe," mused McParland. "But if he thinks we plan to stop there, then he'll attack us there." He touched his mustache. "I tell you what, while we're stopped and tapped in, let's send a message up the line—something urgent and open, something they'll intercept. Let's ask for a push engine to be ready for us." He placed his finger on the map. "Right here, a couple of miles this side of the Green River. We'll say: 'Will wait at siderail for replacement. Urgent.'" McParland sucked air through his teeth. "I guarantee, thinking we'll stop there, they'll set up on us there."

Larson inhaled. "Alright. And we will ... what?"

The mustache curled. "We have a Maxim Machine Gun."

Lieutenant Larson nodded, slightly bemused. "Yes, Sir."

"After we've cleared that last tunnel"—again he pointed to the map—"just here, at Bitter Creek, get it up-top the engine cab."

"It's very heavy."

"You'll have to do it while we're rolling fast. We won't be stopping again until we're across the Green."

"Alright. We'll find a way," Larson said, looking at his boots.

"Good. That's our motto: Whatever it takes."

Two hours later, as the McParland Special approached the Green River, everyone on board was tense. McParland and Lieutenant Larson were in the engine cab, angling from the side windows, binoculars to their faces, surveying the tracks ahead. As the train entered a bend, Larson yelled over the engine's roar, "Up there! Men on the track!"

McParland found them in his binoculars: three men leaning by the track. "Bastards are wiring it. Well, they're too late."

The engineer shouted, "If they're blowing it, I have to stop."

"No, Sir!" yelled McParland. "No! You keep this train moving. They're too late. They only want to make us stop, not blow us up. They won't risk killing their man."

"You don't know that," bawled the engineer. "You said they wouldn't blow it at all!" Behind him the boilermen were frozen, locked on the argument.

McParland shouted, "Speed! Goddamnit! Keep shoveling!"

The train neared the band of men a half mile ahead and visible. They were scrambling from the track, unspooling a wire as they stumbled and ran. When the engineer reached for the throttle levers to bleed steam, he saw the end of a shotgun. "I said, no," growled McParland.

The bombers, now a quarter mile away and nearing quickly, were in the sage, righting a plunger box.

"My God, man!" yelled the engineer. "We must stop!"

McParland slapped his hand three times on the outside of the cab. Immediately, automatic gunfire erupted overhead—concussive, deafening metallic cracks rattling the roof, drowning the engine's roar—hot shell casings raining past Larson's window. The would-be saboteurs disappeared in a storm of dirt. Then the train thundered over the bundle of dynamite and McParland leaned out to see up over the cab, giving a thumbs-up to the two National Guardsmen up there, both sitting next to the Maxim Machine Gun. Back inside the cab, Larson and the two boilermen were chuckling nervously, stunned at what had just happened. The engineer sat on his raised chair, his face ashen, staring blankly at McParland.

Hours later, after switching engines yet again, they passed a border sign for the State of Idaho—the word "State" bearing evidence of an effort to change it to "Republic." McParland toasted with his men in the Pullman.

"Give me a glass, and I'll join you," said Haywood.

McParland turned, eyebrows peaked. "Sporting of you."

After an extra glass of champagne was brought, Haywood lifted it toward the detective. "To your unexpected success."

"It required some casualties, from your side," said McParland.

"Did it?"

"You had your people stir up agitators. A few tried to stop us."

"*I* did?" asked Haywood. "I've been right here." He reached for a cigar and received McParland's reticent nod.

"You're responsible, all the same."

"They weren't the first to die for the worker's cause."

"Nor the last," added McParland.

Haywood squared on the detective. "Your men up there—What was that but an illegal firing squad? You slaughtered them. No trial. In the name of the law? Come now." He lit his cigar.

"If they'd blown the track, might've killed us all. You as well."

"So, you did as you believed necessary. Like this kidnapping."

"I'm executing an extradition order and warrant, signed by the chief justice of Colorado," said McParland, packing his pipe. "I showed it to you last night." He then lit the bowl.

"What that must have cost."

"Not as much as you wish it had."

Haywood flapped his hand. "Maybe not the Colorado one, but the U.S. Supreme Court will send me back."

"Oh? You have friends on the high court?" parried McParland.

"The law is the law. You'll see."

"The law is the law," repeated McParland, pondering the phrase. "You did what you did. I'm doing what I'm doing. The damn lawyers will do what they will."

Haywood tilted his glass toward McParland. "Damn lawyers."

McParland scoffed, glass raised. "At least you have a good one."

"He's a potency," said Haywood. "Have you heard him in court?"

"No, but I'm looking forward to it." McParland smiled.

Haywood shrugged. "He's certainly expensive."

"I wonder if your miners know."

"Know what?" asked Haywood.

"That their hard-earned dues pay for you to be defended by the most expensive attorney in the nation."

"Who do you mean?" blurted Haywood. "My men? Men who voluntarily pay those dues? Men whose lives I've bettered tenfold? Whose friends and sons I've paid to bury? Those men? Yes, they know, Jim, and they want no different. They *want* me defended by Clarence Darrow."

McParland sat back in his chair, pleased at Haywood's defensive response. "Then ... bravo, Bill. We'll just have to see."

Haywood blew a blue cloud into the space between them, then held two fingers toward the detective. "You need two witnesses."

"I have one already."

"Perhaps. If Harry's alive come trial."

"Why wouldn't he be?"

Haywood shrugged. "You tried once already. Maybe you'll do it again. But next time, maybe your man won't miss."

That landed on McParland—the knowledge, the betrayal. "Nothing of the sort," he said in a quiet monotone that shouted his disdain.

"It was risky, but it worked," Haywood continued. "Scared the piss out of Harry, obviously."

"What did you think of his confession?"

"The imaginations of an imbecile," groused Haywood. "Harry Orchard is nothing. And his made-up theories mean nothing. There's not a word of truth in him. No jury will ever believe him. You've put all your chips on him, the simpleton, meaning you've got yourself good and rightly fucked, Detective."

McParland reflexively lifted his forehead's gray bushes. "You're worried," he observed. "As you should be."

"I assure you, Jim, your days are less than mine," said Haywood, shaking his head. "You must realize, you'll never relax, never enjoy your life again, never retire into the comfort of your final years. Not after this. Regardless of what does or doesn't happen to me in Boise, thousands of good men—truly thousands—are ready to wreak my revenge. You can bet on it."

McParland snorted a stoic chuckle. "You know, Mr. Haywood, it's unfortunate I'm not a wagering man. My wife, Mary, fine woman, she has a six-gabled house picked out for us. Six gables, can you believe it?" He took a draw from his pipe and continued, "If I were to wager, it'd be on you hanging. And if I did, then my old girl Mary would get her house—all six gables. My, my, what these women want." He paused, counting to four before sinking his poisoned knife. "What does your wife want? Winnie, right? Oh, pardon me—Neva is your wife. Neva's the one who telephoned me. Mailed me a map she drew of your floors there in the Pioneer. Even marked where you post your guards each night. I hadn't asked for that—seeing how we already knew it—but it was thoughtful of her. I think she hopes to see you dead more than any of the rest of us do. Like I said: My, my ... what these women want."

Haywood tried to bore his dead eye into the detective, but he couldn't sustain it. Rather, he glanced away, spluttering, looking as if he had been knocked from his feet by a horse.

★

– 40 –

SATURDAY
March 16, 1907

Carla stood in the Boise depot. It was 1:15 a.m., and the night's drizzle coursed a chill through the station, encircling the people, slipping among them like a whispered premonition, sulking the place in. She was pensive and alert, standing under the electric lamps in an unremarkable coat and lesser hat, hoping to remain unnoticed. The crowd was murmuring, the air draped in anxiety, prickling with anticipation. The train would arrive soon, carrying the enemy/hero of the people. The telegraph office had been deluged with the news, and it seemed half of Boise had awakened to be there, to see the Federation prisoner/torchbearer, Big Bill Haywood, and the venerated/loathed Pinkerton who captured him, Chief Detective James McParland.

She too was juxtaposed—gloomily elated, feeling little but aware of everything, free strands in a tight braid of disheveled hair. She had grown disgusted by Bill Haywood, yet she still found him enigmatic, even mesmerizing. She wished she didn't, but she did. Now, with Jack's departure, she had decided to be done with it all—to walk away from the Federation, to refuse any further requests. But then came news of Haywood's arrest, of his being transported to Boise. He was coming to where she was, to where she had played a conspirator's part. How small or large, she wasn't sure. Certainly she had interfered, had helped muddy the investigation of an assassination. And she had recruited at least one agent, so far, to double-cross the Pinkertons. No denial would be worth the admission. She had acted for Haywood—no, for her father and brother. In the shadows of that light, she judged herself—for her deceptions, for giving her body to Wade Farrington, for the lies she told. Even for killing Wade. In an instant, she felt the gun's grip, the kick, the blood, the crash, the crack—the staggering incessancy of that singular, horrid moment. The crushing liberation of it all.

The Capone family arrived at Ellis Island in 1881, after voyaging from Catania, Sicily. During the crossing, Carla's would-have-been-older sister died. The next year, in a tiny bedroom of a crowded red-brick building in the Mulberry Bend area of lower Manhattan, Carlotta Angelica Capone was born, joining her two older brothers. Hers would be the last birth in the family—primarily because of her father's struggles to provide. According to her mother, it was due to his Slavic looks that New York's Italian labor force had not welcomed him. He tried his hand as a fishmonger—only to be run out by the Irish. Then as a carpenter—but was dissuaded by the Orthodox Russians. Eventually he did join his fellow Italians in Brooklyn as a stevedore. Then Carla's paternal uncle arrived in Brooklyn from Sicily, and soon she and her brothers had cousins to play with, kids with names such as Franky, Vincenzo, Ermina, Umberto, and Alphonse Capone.

That was where the story of her immediate family went thin. One day they left New York. That's all she knew. They boarded a train to St. Louis where they lived for a year, during which time tuberculosis took one of her brothers. They next moved to Denver, then up to Fort Collins for nine months, and then down to the Cripple Creek mining community where her father heard work was plentiful at the Victor Gold Mine. Most mornings, her father and remaining brother would trudge to the mine, with Carla's mother watching them go. Carla could still hear her mother praying, and calling to them, admonishing them to be safe—and, beneath that, the soft clicking of her mother's rough hands thumbing a rosary. Twelve hours later, her mother would watch, pray and thumb the rosary again, awaiting their return. Her mother's daily recitation of the same prayers and admonitions reminded Carla of a sorceress casting a spell of protection on the men. But not a good witch, like Glinda of Oz. No, her mother knew plenty of curses too, including a few special ones she saved for Carla.

After a wage uprising, her father shifted to the nearby Stratton Independence Mine, also a gold mine, and joined the Western Federation of Miners, alongside Irishmen, Russians, Germans, Poles, even blacks, and he told Carla that though the work was grueling, he had never felt so welcome. She loved those stories, seeing him happy. She remembered his praises of the Federation and its rising leader, Big Bill Haywood, the man who fought more than any other for eight-hour work days, against child labor, and who made it possible for her parents to afford a house, food at fair prices, and even a doctor's services. A particular memory was the afternoon in a market when her mother slapped a woman who had mouthed something derogatory about the Federation. Thankfully a clerk pulled her mother away before any real damage occurred. That night, when Carla told her father about it, he laughed so hard that she worried he might laugh himself ill.

A few years later, after the Federation blew up the Cripple Creek depot in revenge for strike breakers, her father fell silent about Haywood. But Carla never felt he had changed his opinion of the labor union's leader, only that he wouldn't talk about him. Then, hearing a fellow named Captain Swain of the Thiel Detective Agency sought miners to become investigative agents, her father quietly moved the family to Spokane, Washington. But that promised work was short-lived for reasons she never understood.

She was in her teens by then, enjoying life, with multiple boyfriends, attending school, and running with an unpredictable girl named Winnie Minor. Then her father announced they were returning to Cripple Creek, Colorado, as he had been offered a foreman position back at the Stratton. Carla refused to go, hoping that might persuade her father to stay. But it didn't. Instead, he and her brother left, while she and her mother stayed in Spokane. Months passed. Her mother grew remote. Her friend Winnie moved to Denver to live with Winnie's polio-stricken sister, Neva. Carla turned to smuggled alcohol and sinful boys.

Then came the blackest memory, the blackest day, the blackest telegram: the Stratton lift had collapsed, killing fifteen, including her father and brother. Carla was distraught, flattened, pierced by guilt. Her mother screamed at her: Carla was to blame. Of course she was. Had her mother been there, at the Stratton that morning, she would have seen the pair off with prayers, preventing this tragedy. But they had not been there. Why? Because of Carla's selfish need to stay in Spokane, that was why. Carla then screamed at her mother—screams that had yet to end. What had her mother done that angered God so much that He wouldn't answer her mother's prayers for protection unless her mother was physically there, watching the men go? No, Carla had shouted, the fault was all her mother's—for being such a hateful witch, hated by God.

They traveled by rail, miserable and numb—a laconic passage to retrieve their men. Upon arrival in Cripple Creek, they learned that the mine's owners had refused anyone entrance to the Stratton. The corpses were to stay where they had fallen, in the water, over a thousand feet below. In response, a force of thirty-seven armed Federation men rode in, demanding access to the destroyed shaft. If demanding wasn't sufficient, Haywood had ordered them to use force, to do whatever they must to gain access and recover the bodies. Carla left her mother and joined the crowds, her heart pounding with pride at the union's strength. But then twenty-one armed Pinkertons, along with a cadre of Colorado National Guard soldiers with three Gatling machine guns, arrived. That was it. No one was getting in. The dead would stay where they lay.

Carla and her mother returned to Spokane, empty. A week later they learned that political pressure had forced the owners to allow the Federation men to enter. Infuriated with the owners' callousness, Haywood had ordered that only the bodies of union men should be recovered and buried. If the owners wished to get the non-union men out, they could. But Haywood knew they wouldn't. The non-union men would remain deep in the wreckage of their master's doing.

Upon learning what had occurred, that the bodies had been buried, Carla's mother imploded. Yet again, she had not been there, had not prayed over the bodies of her husband and son. And she never would. But this time the blame was not cast upon Carla, but rather upon everyone, everything, all creation. And this time, for the first time, Carla cared. But it was too late. Her mother exiled herself from the world, refusing to speak. Then, two weeks later, Carla came home to find her mother gone. She later learned (from a Spokane ticket agent) that her mother had left for good. She had gone back to New York. No letter. No explanation. No goodbye. Carla was alone.

Next came the rage and guilt, and Carla reached for the salves she knew: sex, spirits, and self-pity—usually all at once. But nothing worked for long. Nothing was enough. She wallowed and then sank, spun stories and drank, and found herself spiraling downward.

She knew she needed traction—something her father had told her: *When you're slipping Squirrel, find traction. If you can't find it, make it.* After a few months, she did. She steeled her mind, gritted her teeth, and required herself to stand. She would fight back. She would join the army of the labor union. She would revenge her father and brother. She would forget her mother.

So she moved to Denver where Winnie introduced her to Haywood—leading to her pledging herself to the Federation. Then she worked for the Federation's attorney, Clarence Darrow—a man she greatly admired—the man who had fought for her father and brother in court. Then came her reassignment to Boise, which eventually led to this moment at this depot on this night, awaiting what would come next.

She held her small hands in tight fists as the train's whistle screeched, bell clanging, steam blowing from its cylinders as the engine rolled past and stopped. Four soldiers disembarked, taking positions along the edge of the wet platform, facing the crowd, rifles angling across their chests in both hands. Then came a few men from the front car, and then a few more. And that was all. The truth set in: Haywood and McParland were not on board. She turned and hurried out, stepping into the dark drizzle.

In fact, the McParland Special had stopped at the last of the Cassidy stations, located five miles east of Boise. There, McParland, Haywood, and many of the men disembarked in the rain to waiting horse-drawn coaches. The purpose of this remote transfer was to confound any vigilante rescue attempt that may be lying in wait at the Boise depot, and to facilitate a safe, uneventful transfer of the prisoner to his new home. Fifteen minutes later, as the train was screeching to a stop in front of Carla, muddy hooves and wheels were slowing at the main gate of the Idaho State Penitentiary. McParland stepped down from one of the coaches, followed by Haywood—wrists shackled, ankles hobble-chained.

★

– 41 –

SUNDAY
March 17, 1907

Jack and Iain were on horseback, riding with a guide into the Sierra Nevada Mountain Range. They were following an idea based one quarter on tip, three quarters on guess. Stan Polk had left California a week prior, taking his brother's body home to Cleveland. McParland had wired, instructing the two vanguard Pinkertons (the two who had arrived in San Francisco ahead of Jack, Iain, and the Polk brothers) to keep watch at the bay's depots and docks until they received word that Adams had been caught. That left Jack and Iain in the wilderness, pursuing a phantom.

The tip they were following originated from a dusky, uncombed woman who had spent two tanked-up nights with Adams in the Sacramento whorehouse where Jack and Iain had tracked him (after chasing a series of aggravatingly vaporous sightings). Apparently, Adams had prattled on to the prostitute about how he was the only sombitch still standing who knew the whereabouts of a thousand dollars of gold buried in the gut of a dead Chinaman. Though she thought Adams cracked—another empty man repeating an empty story about never-to-be-found treasure—she had given him a couple of free goes on the chance he might be the one person who spoke true. But all she got were more crabs to make merry with her others, and something about the gut-rich coolie dying in a blue tent. When she had laughed at Adams, saying "who'd ever heard of no blue tent," he had struck her. That's all she knew.

At first, Jack dismissed the story. Finding Adams seemed an impossible task. He envisioned Carla and wanted to be with her, to watch her, to listen to her talk, imagining kissing her lips. He should write her, he thought. No, he couldn't. He didn't really know her. Was she who he imagined? He had told her he was going to San Francisco, but not why he was going. Not exactly. What if she learned he was tracking Haywood's man, Steve Adams? Might she have reported it? If so, Haywood might've sent someone to kill Jack. Thoughts of death brought Pete's body to mind. Carla might have heard about Jack's botched plan at the track—how it had gotten Pete killed. Would she care that guilt was suffocating him? Maybe he should write to her. No, he couldn't.

Iain had fastened himself to the idea that Adams was *en route* for the gold in the Chinaman. Somehow. Somewhere. So, what the hell, thought Jack. As Iain pointed out, they had nothing else, no other leads. Absolutely nothing. So they made inquiries around Sacramento, talking with saloon patrons, work gangs, barbershop customers, railyard crews, a few policemen, but no one recognized the story, or took meaning from "blue tent." That is until Jack took the question to a group of Chinese men who had resettled their families just beyond the city. (He didn't mention the vessel in which the gold was supposedly buried.) An elderly Mandarin spoke up. He had worked a claim near a place by that name not far from there, up in the Sierra Nevadas.

So, Jack and Iain took the Southern Pacific into the mountains, disembarking at the tiny stop of Alta. There they hired a guide with horses and began a day's ride into the high Sierras—following a thirty-year-old map—heading to a dot called Blue Tent.

"When?" asked Neva.

"Nine o'clock," said George.

Winnie smiled. "I'm going to Boise on Wednesday, I believe."

"I'm not sure I want to go at all," said Neva.

The three of them were in the parlor of the Pioneer Building suites: Winnie on a chair, George and Neva sitting near each other on one of the settees, but not so close as to touch. The evening meal done, each sorted their thoughts, tabulating the day. The ladies hadn't changed for dinner as only George had joined them—thus they were in their day dresses. While George would have said Neva's dress was yellow and Winnie's was purple, the sisters knew the details.

"Perhaps I should get on," said George. "Dinner was splendid."

"Oh, don't," insisted Neva. "Not yet. I'll ride with you to the station. You still have an hour, no?"

He checked his pocket-watch. "Yes. An hour."

"Well, I'll leave you two," said Winnie. "I must go anyway."

Neva turned. "Go where, Sissy?"

"A worker's gathering."

"The Socialist Party is making a lot of noise about Bill," George said toward a wall of books.

"As they should," chirped Winnie. "Oh, I didn't tell you. I wrote to Mr. Debs, asking him to come to Boise on behalf of Bill. He should, don't you agree?"

George shook his head. "You know how Bill feels about Debs."

Neva winced. "You invited him to testify? To Bill's character?"

"Someone has to speak *for* him," snapped Winnie. "You won't."

"No, I won't," said Neva, glancing at George.

"What did Debs say?" asked George.

"He will!" Winnie's nose scrunched as she grinned. "It's terrific."

George frowned.

"He'll raise an army of fifty-thousand workers," gushed Winnie, "and lead them to Idaho to liberate Bill. By force if required."

"Jesus," said George.

"Don't," Neva said softly, placing a hand on George's arm.

"Pardon me—yes, dear. But that's ridiculous, don't you think?"

"It is not," protested Winnie. "Mr. Debs is going to lead this country to a socialist revolution. He and Bill. And since Bill is running for governor on the Socialist Party ticket. Yes. Can't you see it? This will be the century of the people, the workers."

Neva shook her head. "Sissy, you read a great amount of—"

"It's all going to happen," said Winnie. Her tone had turned sharp. "You'll see. You always think I'm silly."

"He's run on that ticket before," George began.

"And what will he do, campaign from prison?" asked Neva.

"He wouldn't have to, if it wasn't for ... you," Winnie erupted, getting to her feet, her eyes knives.

"Sissy!"

"That's not true," said George. "You know that's not true."

"I have to go," declared Winnie. She put on her hat and adjusted it in the foyer mirror. "Bill will come home soon. You'll see. He and Mr. Debs will change everything. And I'm going to help them." She turned to Neva. "And your precious George will help too."

"No," said George, "but I'll see you in Boise by week's end."

"I suppose you will then," snarked Winnie.

"Have a nice evening, Sissy," Neva jabbed.

Winnie paused as if to retort, but only muttered, "Bye," before slamming the entrance door behind her.

George walked back to Neva, leaned down and kissed her forehead, and then took Winnie's seat.

"She is insufferable," fumed Neva. "Infuriating. Trying to blame me. She—" Seeing the docility in George's brown eyes, she wrestled her tone to something more hospitable. "Why are you sitting there? Come be here, beside me."

George took a deep breath and blew it out through his nose. "I need to talk with you."

Neva's eyes widened. "What is it?"

"I've called a meeting of the locals. A special meeting."

"The money?"

He nodded. "Do you still have the record book I gave you?"

"Yes. Of course."

"Good."

"What will they do?"

"I'm not sure."

Neva's eyes narrowed. "They'd better not try to blame you, or they'll hear from me."

George put on a small smile. "They shouldn't, but—"

"Does Bill know about the meeting?"

George nodded.

"Yes, I suppose so," said Neva. "But they'll see you're the one bringing the embezzlement to them—that you're not to blame."

"I don't know. If I was to blame, how would my actions look different? They might say I waited till Bill was taken, then blamed him behind his back."

"That's not right."

"It's how it could look. And now they might think I'm working with the Pinks. Which of course could be dangerous."

"Why in the world would they think that?" asked Neva.

He frowned at her. "Uhmm ... the deal you cut with them? With Detective McParland of all people. You gave him the floorplan of this place, trading on his promise not to investigate me. Right?"

Neva didn't answer.

"Right?"

"No."

"What?"

"I'm sorry, but I didn't. I lied. I'm sorry."

"You didn't talk to McParland about me? You said—"

"I know. I thought to make that bargain, for you, but only after I'd already talked to him. After I left. I so wished I'd made that deal. I was mad at myself for just giving him what he wanted without getting anything in return. I was so mad."

"Oh my, dear. No, no. That's good. I'm relieved. That's good."

"You've always been so kind to me," she whispered tearfully.

"It's all right. You wanted to make me happy. But what makes me happy is that you didn't. A devil's bargain like that would've been picked up by a Federation spy, and it would've made the chapters think I'd turned on them. Or, worse, they might think I'm a spy. That might've gotten me killed."

"I'm sorry." She took his handkerchief for her eyes. "But wasn't I a fool to not get *something* in the bargain?"

"Not everything needs to be a trade, dear. Some things are what they are, all that they need to be. And that's enough. You thought helping them with Bill was right, so it was enough."

She nodded and sniffed.

George moved to sit beside her on the settee, then wrapped her in his arms. "You have a golden heart. But you should've been honest with me."

She remained in thought. "How can we protect you from being blamed for Bill's stealing? If the government gets involved, Bill will blame you. And if Bill is ... gone, you'll be the only one left."

"Perhaps in a few weeks, after I've met with the local chapters, then maybe an arrangement can be made. But, dear, only after you and I have discussed it. All right? We'll talk about it in Boise."

"I don't want to go to Boise."

"I know. But Darrow will insist."

"I hate that you're going now."

"It's all right. You'll come. We'll endure the circus together."

She took his face into her small hands and kissed him deeply.

★

– 42 –

MONDAY
March 18, 1907

Jack and Iain stood still, studying the non-existent mining town of Blue Tent, California. Before them, in a concave meadow of early spring grasses, rusted mining equipment lay scattered—angular, thick, iron pieces, abandoned machinery the color of dried blood—protruding from where life reemerged, wisps of yellow buttercups bobbing in the cold breeze, beside snow pockets hiding from the sun under the limbs of stalwart pines and budding oaks.

"Ain't no chink bodies out there," said a hump-shouldered old miner with tobacco teeth—the only person they'd found who could tell them about the place. He might've qualified as a local, had he not lived nine miles away, merely passing along when they encountered him. (Their guide had turned back well before this meadow.) "Heared me the same tale, but it's a fool—" The man stopped talking and began moving into the meadow. "You two's already gone a diggin?"

"No, we just arrived," said Jack. They followed the old man toward the remnants of a conveyor's flywheel and axle. Just beyond the dead machinery, they saw what had the man's attention: a dozen or more holes, thirty or forty feet between them, spread across the lower portion of the field.

"Well, if it ain't you," said the old-timer, "then somebody's been a badger out here, searching for your stuffed Chinaman."

"Wasn't us," said Iain.

Jack walked around a hole and kicked its mound. "This was dug in the last day or two."

"No siree," said the man, waddling toward Jack. "Rained the Furies last night. That's fresh. Reckon the feller's here somewheres."

Jack turned to Iain, alarm in his eyes. "Then we're sittin Indians. Let's go." Once both remounted, they galloped from the meadow.

"Alright den," mumbled the man, still standing amid the holes.

Under dense trees, the horses picked across fallen trunks and up through crusty snowbanks as they climbed. When Jack reined in at a boulder outcrop, Iain stopped too. "We could be in his sights right this bloody instant," Iain exclaimed, twisting, creaking the leather of his saddle.

Jack looked below the canopy to the meadow beyond. "No, he's not out here. We didn't need to run off like that."

"How do ya figure? Could be a bad coincidence."

"No such thing as coincidences—good or bad. No, Adams wouldn't have known we were coming. We'd have surprised him."

Iain groused, "So, he's not here because we aren't dead?"

"About the size of it. We shouldn't have ridden up on the place without scouting it first."

"But he *was* here," said Iain. "Dug for his gold."

"Somebody did. Maybe it was him." Jack frowned. "That guide of ours—he said he hadn't seen Adams, but then he turned back early. What if, instead of going back, he crosscut us and came ahead to dig for himself. Or to help Adams?"

"Help Adams? The bastard has no friends and less money."

"I don't know," said Jack. "We probably shouldn't assume that."

Both paused a moment in their own thoughts while their horses hooved at the mountain foliage, snuffling for something to eat. "I bet he's already back in Alta, or on up in Truckee, on the main line," said Iain. "Probably there waiting on the next train."

Jack sniffed. "Or maybe he's already halfway across Nevada."

"Maybe so," said Iain.

"Or he might've followed the Yuba River further north."

"Or an aeroplane came along and scooped him up," said Iain.

Jack snorted a laugh. "Let's get back down to the rail and see what we can figure."

"Lead on," said Iain, turning his horse to follow. As they moved off, Iain asked, "What did you mean, there's no coincidences?"

"Yeah. Chief said that."

"That motorcar hitting Pete, right when he was fighting—"

"Just the way it happened," Jack said quietly.

"Seems like a damned coincidence to me."

Clarence Darrow arrived in Boise at 10:15 on the morning of that same day. By noon he had requisitioned the meeting rooms on the first floor of the Saratoga Hotel for Federation business and leased six bedrooms (including one for himself) indefinitely. By 2:00, he had couches, chairs, and tables brought into one of the rooms—the one he designated as his office. George arrived at 4:50 and sat on one of the couches, listening to the Federation's lawyer.

"We need twenty trustworthy men handy with rifles. Chain lightning on the draw."

George frowned. "Are you planning a gunfight?"

"No," said Darrow. "But what, I'm not sure."

"We're not busting him out," said George.

Darrow gave George a curious scowl. "Of course not."

"Captain Swain can get you more men."

"I'm not sure what he can do," said Darrow.

"All right. Well, you have the ten I brought with me."

"Good, so ten more please."

"Like I said, let's see if Swain can get them." George sat forward, watching Darrow. "So, you're in charge here?"

"On trial matters," Darrow said. "Union concerns are yours, George. But then again, anyone who thinks Bill isn't in command from his jail cell— Well, they don't know him, do they?"

George drummed his fingers on the leather arm of the couch. "Probably true. But the money needs to come through me."

Darrow nodded. "I just need to supervise our legal strategy."

"Of course," George replied.

"Speaking of men," Darrow began. "I'd appreciate it if you made us three lists." He took a seat opposite George. "List A: those we absolutely trust."

"Absolutely?" George shook his head. "I only know one."

Darrow chuckled. "All right, that we trust for the most part. Granted, it'll still be a short list. Then list B: Any Pinkerton, and anyone else working for the prosecution, or cooperating with them. And C: those here in Boise who are associated with all this, in some form or fashion, but we don't know which list, A or B, to put them on yet."

"All right," said George. "The unknowns."

"And your men all need be vetted and armed to the teeth. Bill wants them guarding this hotel around the clock."

"You've been to see him today?"

Darrow ignored the question. "No one gets into this building who's on List B without an escort. And have your men double check everyone on List A at least once every three days. Assign some to watch others. Boise is the prosecution's territory, so that makes it the Pinkerton's. And that snake McParland has this city thick with spies. Not only do they occupy the high ground, they've had months to prepare."

"The high ground?"

"Judge Wood is theirs."

George nodded.

"And McParland's a crook. Borah too. Senator, my ass," scoffed Darrow. "They kidnapped Bill in gross violation of all legality. As unconstitutional as it gets. And now you and I are here, having to prepare on their battlefield. I don't like it." After a beat, he asked, "Why didn't Mrs. Haywood come with you?"

"I'm not sure when she's coming."

"But she will, right?"

"I believe so," said George. "They've had a discordant episode."

"A discordant episode?"

"A falling out. Did you know?"

"To some degree. What matters to me is that she's here. And if this goes to trial, that she's sitting on the front row, right behind him. And she'll need to testify on his behalf."

George inhaled. "I'm sure you'll discuss that with her."

"Right now, I need talk to Swain about those additional men. Where is he?"

"Bill sent him to San Francisco weeks ago—after Adams."

Darrow stared at George until the full meaning of that sentence set in. He closed his eyes and shook his head. "If Adams is never seen again, then—"

"I didn't say that."

"I don't want to know about it," barked Darrow. "But, as the Federation's attorney, I'm telling you, if Swain succeeds, then the Federation must immediately sever all ties with him."

"Should we recall him?"

"That's management's decision," Darrow said, nodding once at George. "But if you want my counsel, I'd say let Captain Swain be. See what happens. Meanwhile, we still need the additional men, so I suggest you wire Thiel headquarters in Spokane. See if they can send us some smart men to work undercover. Men who know this area." Darrow looked out the window. "It won't be long before we're in *voir dire*, picking a jury from among these people. So I'll need to know everything about them. And about this judge too."

"We already have one spy here," said George. "Miss Carla Capone—who you know."

"Yes. She was my secretary. She's clever, but she's known to McParland too. She can be useful, but not as a spy for us any more. Besides, she killed our actual spy, Farrington, right?"

"I've been assured it was self-defense," said George.

"Maybe so. Maybe not. It doesn't matter," murmured Darrow, lighting his pipe. "That must've been difficult though. She's a good egg. I know who her father was." Placing two fingers over the pipe's lit tobacco, he sucked the flame, making sure the bowl fully ignited. "Can you find her?"

"I imagine so," said George. "She works at the Idanha Hotel."

"At the Idanha?" Darrow chuckled. "I'll be. Right in the den of snakes. Well, I'd like to speak with her. Tonight if possible. But first, I'm heading to see Bill."

After Darrow entered the Idaho State Penitentiary through its imposing, double oak doors, a three-toothed guard ushered him through the building, out the rear, across the high-stone-walled yard, into the first building on the right under a sign reading CELL HOUSE TWO, and then inside, through the noise of men and their cages. Finally they came to an empty cell on the first floor.

"This is his?" barked Darrow. "Where is he?"

"Told to bring ya here." The guard gave an indignant glance.

"Is this a joke, young man? Where is my client?"

"The prisoner was moved."

"So, why in God's name am I standing here!" Darrow fumed.

"No reason yellin. I was t'get you brung here. 'N here y'are."

"Yes. Here I am." Darrow took a breath. "Where did they move him? Can you tell me that?"

"Judge Wood ordered him moved," replied the guard.

"That's not what I asked. I asked, where— *Where* is my client?"

"Listen, city law, don't be gettin all cocked-up at me."

Darrow checked himself. "I apologize. I'm not—"

"I know how to deal with your high-flutin sort."

"Yes. I know. You're just doing your—"

"Been working fifteen damn years here! Every sort of vermin, I seen em. They raise their voice only on pain of a beatin."

"Alright, but could you—"

"Ya hearin me?"

Darrow gave a grimace that he hoped appeared more of a smile, then added a slight nod. "Yes. So ... where is he?"

"Your man's in the courthouse jail. Sheriff's office."

Darrow turned and walked quickly toward the front building, muttering to himself, "Mary and Joseph, I swear."

★

– 43 –

WEDNESDAY
March 20, 1907

They entered the Lone Star Saloon in Truckee, California, at 11:15 at night, after two arduous days. During their ride down from Blue Tent, Iain's horse broke its leg and had to be shot. They camped there, and then continued on foot the next day, leading Jack's horse to Alta. That afternoon, when they returned Jack's horse to the guide, they found the man pacing, worried. Though his agitation put to rest their theory that he might have helped Adams, it raised new concerns.

"You boys wanted by the law?"

"No," replied Jack.

"Should we be?" quipped Iain.

"A man asked after you. Said you were accomplices to a murder."

"Accomplices?"

"A detective, he said. Was eyeballin for your man, Adams. I told him true—I don't know Adams. Then he asked on two fellers with your particulars."

Jack stepped forward. "What did you tell him?"

"I don't talk about nobody. That's what I said. But, you boys best keep movin. He looked to mean you some harm."

"Did you get the man's name?"

"Left this trade-card." He presented a small card printed with:

Captain Wilson Swain
Chief Detective, Northeast Manager
THIEL DETECTIVE SERVICE CO.
Spokane, Wash.

Jack shook his head as he considered the card. "I've never heard of the man, so I don't reckon he's looking for us. Probably just a ... coincidence." The word stuck in Jack's throat like a fishbone—he had to cough to dislodge it. He handed the card to Iain. "What do you think?"

"Aye. Coincidence," said Iain, cutting his eyes at Jack before returning the card to the guide. "Don't know him. Though I've heard of the Thiel Agency. Bunch of penny dobbers, ya ask me."

"Did he say where he was heading?" asked Jack.

"No. But he inquired on the best card game in Truckee."

Jack scratched an ear. "Did he?"

"You told him the tables at the Silver Mine, I bet," said Iain.

"To hell with that place. Fella get hisself killed there," said the guide. "No, told him the Lone Star."

"Oh, aye," said Iain, elbowing Jack. "The Lone Star."

"Yes ... right ... the Lone Star," replied Jack.

The Lone Star Saloon was full of life, even at 11:15 at night. Jack and Iain chose a table apart from the whooperups over at the poker and blackjack tables. They ordered beers, and soon Jack was laughing under the brim of his black hat.

"What's got ya?" asked Iain.

"The Silver Mine? You'd never heard of this town, I'd wager."

Iain chuckled. "Had to get him to tell us the real place he sent Swain to. And every one of these jerkwater, flea-bit towns has a Silver Mine Saloon."

"That's true," said Jack, still grinning. "But, you could've just asked him *directly*." Jack attempted a brogue: "What saloon did ya say that fella went off to?'"

"What accent was that?"

"Scottish."

"The hell it was."

Jack laughed. "Well, you got us here. That's all that matters." Still chuckling, Jack could tell Iain wasn't seeing the humor in this, so he let it go, muttering, "Just funny to me."

They scanned the room. "How are we gonna know?"

"Know what?" asked Jack.

"Who's Captain Swain? You ever seen him?"

"Nope," Jack replied.

"Didn't you tell Chief you had?"

"I thought—"

"Guess I'll go ask them fellas," said Iain, starting to rise.

"Hold on," Jack blurted. "Adams might be here in Truckee. No need to tip our hand just yet."

"I don't think he is. And Swain *needs* to meet me," said Iain, standing. His towering frame seemed to fill that end of the room.

"He needs to?"

Iain looked down at Jack. "Any fella goin round saying I'm a murder accomplice—well, that's a fella who needs to meet me." He strolled toward the nearest table of men gambling.

"Damnit," Jack muttered, standing to follow. On the way, he touched his coat, confirming his revolver was beneath.

"Gentlemen," Iain asked, his brogue applied liberally. "My humble apology for interrupting yar game there, Yar Majesties."

The band of five men, ranging from middle-grizzled to heavy-grizzled, stopped talking, demonstrably unamused as they looked up at the Gaelic giant. Jack stood a bit behind and to the side of Iain—not so close as to be brought into the conversation, but close enough to react if needed.

"You see, I'm looking for a fella named Captain Swain. Calls himself a detective, but I don't figure he's more than a mutton-shuntin, blaggard copper, you ask me."

Four of the men gave Iain variations of a head shake. Iain looked at the fifth who had resumed studying his cards. "You heard of him?" he asked, moving closer to the man. "The name Swain ring a bell to you?"

Without lifting his eyes from his palm-spread cards, the man said, "No. But I want nothing to do with no goddamned detectives—Pinkertons or others."

"Pinkertons, you say?" Iain's eyebrows lifted, his fists forming. "I didn't ask you bout—"

"Damn Pinks!" Jack interjected quickly. "You're right about that, Sir." Then to Iain: "Let's not trouble these men any more."

Iain moved to the next table. "You men heard who I was asking on, over there? Come think of it—" Iain lifted his head and shouted to the room, "Pardon me, all you fine gentlemen and ladies, if ya kindly will."

Jack figured it was due to Iain's size, and the bravado of the interruption, that caused the room to fall silent. Not a single person challenged Iain to shut up.

Iain continued, "My friend here and I have been traveling. We're a bit road weary, so I'll just ask the lot of you, instead of one table at a time. Any you know a man named Captain Swain? Calls himself a chief detective?"

A rumbling of noes came from a few, while the rest let their juddering heads answer. Chairs creaked and scooted, and soon the room was back at its games. Iain and Jack returned to their table.

"A noble effort," said Jack as they sat down.

"I saw him," came a Scandinavian accent behind them. They turned to see a white-haired man, one of the blackjack dealers, having abandoned his table on the far side of the room.

"You know him?" asked Jack. "Captain Swain?"

"I don't wise know the man, but he was at my table some hours ago. Heard the name, Swain, as I recall. One of those ridiculous patch mustaches?"

"I don't know," said Jack.

"Chief detectives all have ridiculous mustaches," said Iain, giving a conclusive nod. "It's required."

Jack snorted a laugh. "Did he say he's staying in town tonight?"

"Think so."

"Hans, get back here!" came shouts from the blackjack table adrift without its helmsman.

The dealer added, "He asked on another man."

"Steve Adams?" asked Jack.

"That's right."

Jack nodded. "Any luck? Had anyone heard of Adams?"

"One of my other players ..." He pointed to a man across the room. "That gentlemen, in the black vest. He was at my table then. No, not him." He scanned more faces. "I don't see him here."

"We're gonna deal for you, Hans, if you don't move your fat ass!"

"What was said about Adams?" asked Iain.

"They talked on a man named Lloyd. Last name: Lilly, or Lillard. Yeah, Lloyd Lillard. One of em said it sounded like Lizard."

"Lilly-livered Lloyd?" asked Iain, pretending he knew the name.

Jack squinted. "What about Lloyd Lillard?"

"The man's squatting in a castle near Austin."

"Say again?" asked Iain.

"Something like a castle. Stokes, I think. Said the Lloyd fella had a son named Stephen Adams. No, a nephew—his sister's boy. That's what got em talking. The Swain fella said he'd go there."

"Austin, Texas?" asked Jack.

"No, Nevada," said the dealer. "Austin, Nevada. East of here."

"That's terrific," said Jack, shaking the man's hand. "Anything else you can recall?"

The man thought for a second. "No, don't think so."

"We appreciate you telling us," said Jack, shaking the man's hand. "Best you get back to your table, Hans. Again, thank you."

After the man left earshot, Jack looked at Iain. "We need a map." They approached the bar. "Excuse me, keep," Jack asked the barman. "Do you have a map of this area?"

"Sure."

"And Nevada," added Iain.

The man turned to look in a cabinet. "Same one." He produced a map and unrolled it on the bar. "California, Nevada, Oregon, and some of Utah."

"May I?" Jack asked. He weighted the corners with shot glasses.

"Don't spill nothing on it," said the barman, walking away.

Iain scoured the map, muttering, "East ... right there." His stout index finger covered a spot near the middle of Nevada.

"Can't see," said Jack. Iain lifted his finger, revealing Austin, Nevada. "Southern Pacific up to, what's that, Battle Mountain?" asked Jack. "Then that spur to Austin. I think that's all desert."

"How do we beat Swain there?" asked Iain. "If we don't get ahead of him—" he clicked his tongue "—we'll find one of em dead for sure. And the other, long gone."

"We've gotta get there first," said Jack, signaling the bartender.

"Yeah?"

Jack put a silver dollar on the bar. "Thank you for the use of your map. We've got one more question, then we'll leave you be."

The man pocketed the dollar.

"The train that comes through here—" Jack began.

"The Overland Limited," said the barman.

"When's the next one?"

"East?"

"Yes, east to Reno."

"9:20 in the morning. Same as came today."

"That's the next one?"

"Un-huh," replied the man.

Jack looked at Iain. "Swain will be on it too."

"That's no way to beat him," Iain groused.

"Yeah, we'll think of something."

"Darrow will get this to the Supreme Court within a month, tops," said Senator Borah, standing in McParland's office on the first floor of the Idanha Hotel. "But ... it'll be all right for us."

McParland, the only other person in the room, creaked his chair forward, taking another bite of his sandwich. He chewed, watching the senator. Once he swallowed, he said, "I got him here. The rest is up to you."

Borah sniffed and shook his head, eyes on McParland. "That was masterful work, Jim. If you could bring that kind of wizardry to the courtroom, I'd find myself out of work. Hell, come to Washington—let's make a few of *those* fellows disappear."

"That's the problem with doing something so brazen—the next time they'd all see me coming. Same as after the Molly Maguires. I can't go undercover anymore."

"You were what, twenty-five then, sneaking around with that Hibernian gang? About the age of that agent, Pat Garrett junior, you had in here."

"Jack Garrett? Aye."

"Well, I hate to disappoint you, but you're a long-toothed old mule, my friend," said Borah with a bemused smile. "That's what would give you away—not because you've done it before."

McParland grinned, his mustache stretching wide. "Maybe so." After a moment, he continued, "As I said, I got the fish in the boat, so you better clean and cook it before it flops back in the river."

"Do I appear worried?"

"Not at all—which worries me," said McParland. "I can tell you this: Haywood will not leave Idaho alive."

"I imagine not," said Borah.

"What will Darrow say to the Supreme Court?"

"He's always wanted to go there. I suppose all of us lawyers do. Any lawyer who says otherwise is either a tin bit, or he's lying. So now that Clarence has this, he'll make a show of it. He'll spin yarns for days—grind the old justices down." Borah took a seat and selected a cigar from the humidor on the table. "He'll claim unlawful extradition, violation of due cause hearings and the *habeas corpus* rule." He clipped the end of the cigar with a cutter. "To cinch it, he'll claim it was state-authorized kidnapping."

"Any of that incorrect?"

Borah gave a half laugh. "It's all accurate. But it won't matter."

"No?"

"Nope." Borah struck a match and lit his cigar.

McParland frowned. "You have tricks up your sleeve, Senator?"

Borah nodded, considering the older man. "You're the Great Detective. What do you think? Why am I not worried about the Supreme Court sending Haywood back to Denver?"

"Should I speculate?"

"Sure. I'd enjoy seeing your detective wheels spin."

McParland gave a pinched smile, peering over his glasses. "You'll give me honest answers? Is that possible for a politician?"

Borah grinned. "Sure. Why not? Tell you what, I'll give you ten yes-no questions. See what you can do with that. But, I gotta warn you, you'll not figure this one."

"What if I do? Shall we wager?"

Borah looked at his cigar before answering. "Two dollars to you for each unused question, out of the ten. Or two to me for each question you need above ten, until you cry uncle."

"Accepted," said McParland. He studied Borah for a minute before speaking. "First question: Does your solution involve President Roosevelt?"

"Yes," replied Borah with a slender grin.

"All right," said McParland. "Number two: When you were in Washington last, a few months ago, being sworn in, did you meet his daughter, Alice—the troublemaker?"

Humor and blood slid from Borah's face simultaneously. "Uhmm—"

"So, yes." McParland stood, his pipe extended like a baton. "Shall I explain?"

"Shut the goddamned door first," growled Borah.

McParland did. "Before you went, I'm sure you read about Alice threatening to publicly embarrass her stepmother. That was when we were planning the extradition. And I think you knew, right then, that this would likely go to the Supreme Court—meaning you would eventually need Roosevelt's help. But he'd not look kindly on being asked to weigh in. He'd probably refuse you outright. So, especially with you being a junior Senator, you'd need something more robust, shall we say.

Your wife went with you to Washington, and no doubt attended the Senator's Ball after the swearing in. And I'm sure Alice was there too, with her father." McParland grinned at the anguish that had formed on Borah's face. "At some point, you found an opportunity to woo Alice, lift her skirts and give her the bully punch. Only you needed it seen by a staff member, but not by your wife. My guess is you paid a man to walk in on you. Coat closet, probably. But if I'm wrong on that detail, that doesn't mean I lose this."

Borah muttered, "My God," and buried his face in his hands.

"The next day, your hired man got word filtered back to the White House that the president's rowdy daughter was corrupted by a certain married senator—and during the ball, steps from her father. When Darrow gets this to the Supreme Court, you'll be there to argue it, and while you're there, you'll pay a visit to the White House. And Justice Fuller will get a telephone call from Teddy soon thereafter."

"Goddamnit, Jim."

"I'm sure I have a few things not exactly right, but close enough. You don't need to confirm it, but you do owe me sixteen dollars."

"All right," whispered Borah, nodding.

"Tell you what, double or nothing. You guess how I figured that, and I'll take nothing. But get it wrong and it's thirty-two to me."

"No. No. I have no idea. None. And, frankly, I'm not sure I want to know. But I'll pay you another two just to tell me."

"Sorry, Senator, I can't do that."

"So the double-or-nothing was already lost?"

"Aye. You'd never have guessed."

"You're a dangerous man."

"Me? Nah, I'm just an old detective. But you, bravo! Darrow will be mighty disappointed on his first go at the Supreme Court."

"That he will," murmured Borah, still stunned—the lit cigar dangling between his fingers, ashes ready to drop, his face a bundle of embarrassment, anger, and wonder at what had just been done to him.

"Ah, don't fret yourself, Senator. You just shagged the president's daughter for this case. You didn't plant a live bomb in the front yard of a chief justice—like I did in Denver."

"How's that— What?"

★

– 44 –

THURSDAY
March 21, 1907

Jack Garrett turned twenty-seven as the Overland Limited glided him across Nevada's alkaline desert—warm sunlight bathing him through the window. The steady rumble lulled his eyes closed, his mind kneading, mulling, gnawing the images it made. In a waking dream he flowed from thought to thought to thought along the long straight stretches of that endless desert, while the memories and moments oozed through the wood walls of the train car, seeping up through its grumbling floorboards.

He was heading to capture a merciless killer. Not to bring him to justice, but to bring him to testify against the killer's master. Had Haywood ever killed anyone—by his own hand? Should it matter? Murderers like Orchard and Adams had a choice, didn't they? They stepped forward to pull their straw. They chose to act. Maybe they enjoyed it. Or they feared reprisal if they failed. Did they fear death? Can Death fear itself? No, they must like it. No sanity there. Killers from the cradle. The devil's agents on earth.

How often had his mother admonished him about Satan's disciples? Her boy was to keep a guarded heart and a steady eye against them—those demons who would harm him, who would bring him to do harm. She'd said it so often and with such fire, that he began to suspect her truth lay elsewhere: that her greatest fear was that he was one of those demons. Just as his father had been.

His father's name was Charlie Bowdre. Jack saw a tintype of him once, but all he remembered was a bandoleer of bullets and the details of a distinctive hat: black, wide-brimmed, round-crowned, flat-topped, probably beaver. Stars on each side. Through the years, he had picked up a few of the stories. His father spent most of his life in New Mexico, around the town of Lincoln, where he fell in with Billy the Kid. In the seventies, they killed a number of men in the Lincoln County War and got US Marshal Pat Garrett on their trail. So they tore out to Fort Sumner. There they hid and rustled some, along with other members of Billy's gang. And there Charlie got a prostitute pregnant, only to bolt again, hiding out in a Stinking Springs farmhouse. When Marshal Garrett and a posse of twenty rode up on that house, the firing started—bullets flying like a plague of locusts, so the story went. When Charlie got shot in the chest, Billy shoved him out the front door, telling him to kill Garrett first, then he could die. But his father met a hail of bullets, dying before his face found dirt. He was put in a hole in the fort's old military graveyard.

Five months later, Jack was born in a boarding house just outside Fort Sumner, and was given the name, Leslie Bowdre. A year later, Pat Garrett killed Billy the Kid and buried him next to Jack's father. Around that time, Jack's mother found Jesus and swapped her boy's last name to Garrett—not to honor the man who'd killed the boy's father, but in the clenched hope that the great lawman's surname might serve as a talisman: repelling bad while forevermore reminding her boy of the godly man she expected him to be. Only then could she have peace.

At eighteen, Jack began his quest. It was more her quest for him, but he convinced himself it was his. In Texas, he sought to join the Rangers, but that ended in a Jack County bar fight where a man died. He had nothing to do with the killing, but when the dead man's friends fingered him as the shooter, Leslie Garrett was a wanted man. He crossed the Red River and began a two-year drunken drift through the Indian reservations of Oklahoma Territory. During those years, he found the hat that he still wore, added the stars, and dreamed of his tintype father.

When he finally pushed north, arriving in Abilene, Kansas on his twentieth birthday, a new century was underway. But what promise it held seemed quickly lost when he learned his mother was dead from galloping fever. Dismayed at himself, ashamed for his betrayal of all he had promised her, he changed his first name to the Texas county where he had first lost his way.

Self-reborn, Jack Garrett rode to Denver, hell bent for leather. There he went straightaway to the Opera Building and pledged himself to the Pinkertons. Chief Detective McParland wasn't there that day, but Jack met him soon enough. McParland transferred him to St. Louis to train as an agent, and three years later, Jack was back in Colorado as the spy, Operative 21.

He wasn't sure if McParland knew his birth name—that his father had been a no-good killer, an outlaw with Billy the Kid. Probably the old detective did. Jack didn't much care either way. He was no more Leslie Bowdre than he was Leslie Garrett. He wasn't an outlaw and never would be. He was no killer from the cradle. He knew he was no agent of the devil. Just as he knew his mother was finally at peace. Oh, that she might see him now. Him a Pinkerton Agent, set to do right. How proud she would be.

Rousing, he adjusted his hat and peered lazily through the window at the passing world in its shades of creams, browns, and distant blues. Returning his focus to within the car, he saw Iain across the aisle, sleeping long-wise on a bench. Finally, he looked forward, through a window, across a passageway, and through another window, to a black blotch in the car ahead. He knew it was the pinched crown of Captain Swain's dark gray homburg.

His thoughts settled up there on Swain. The Thiel detective seemed as calm as can be, with murder on his mind. An execution, really. Jack knew himself: he was no killer. But could he kill a man if need be? Sure. He thought so. But then had to shake off the image of Wade Farrington lying dead. Was any sane man comfortable killing another? Was Captain Swain sane? Adams deserved death for what he'd done—no doubt about that. But by whose hand should that end come?

At 12:15 that afternoon, when Jack and Iain stepped from the train in Battle Mountain, Nevada, they were flummoxed, alone in the rickety depot, certain they'd made a grave error.

"Where is he?" asked Jack.

Iain looked around. "Didn't get off, I guess."

"Damnit," Jack murmured. "Swain stayed on the train. So Adams isn't here, and we're two idiots in the middle of the desert."

"I wish you weren't right, but— Wait." Iain pointed through one of the depot's windows. Outside, Captain Swain was talking with a man wearing a sombrero, standing by a wagon hitched to two horses.

"Son of a bitch," whispered Jack. "Tell me if he's coming." He walked to the closed ticket booth and tapped its wood shutters.

"What you want?" asked eyes through the slats.

"Two tickets to Austin."

"Nevada?"

"Yes. Quickly please."

"No quickly to it," replied the man as he opened the window.

Jack saw the attendant was gaunt, cheeks hollow and dark. "How much for—"

"Three dollars. Six for two."

After glancing at Iain, who was still focused beyond the window, Jack paid the thin man. "When's the next one?"

"Don't rightly know," said the man, handing Jack the tickets.

"What?"

"No silver in Austin for fifteen years. Thus wise, Nevada Central Short Line don't run till— Well, till it does. Nobody living down that way much. Least not the sort to ride the train regular. You got your Jensons, they're there. Stokes is gone. There's the Canter widow. And old man Pritchard. No, he died—"

"How about a guess?" asked Jack. "Next train to Austin?"

"Nevada?"

Jack stared at the man.

"Next week, best I'd tell you."

"Jack," said Iain, approaching. "He's gone."

Jack turned. "Where'd he go?"

"I think he hired one of that man's horses. Rode off on it."

"Damnit." Jack held the tickets toward the agent. "Then I need my money back. We can't wait till next week."

"No refunds."

"How do you figure? I just—"

"They're used."

"Used for what?" asked Iain, now standing beside Jack.

"For the train, of course," said the attendant. "You thick?"

"What did ya say there, slim?" asked Iain, his voice deepening.

"Never mind," said Jack. "I'll keep them. How many miles do you think it is to Austin— *Nevada?*"

"Hundred. Maybe ninety on a good day."

Iain cocked his head at the man. "How do ya figure that?"

"Don't ask him," said Jack. "Just— Don't ask." He walked toward the main door. "Let's go." Once out of the building and down the rickety steps, with their bags slung over their shoulders and a shotgun and a rifle in their hands, the two Pinkertons walked toward the nearest structure, a church, and proceeded to its far side. There Jack surveyed the area, noting two barely standing buildings across from the church: a saloon bearing the name, THE KING'S ARMS; and a mercantile of some sort, its sign appearing to have long fallen away.

"The Austin train won't be till next week," said Jack. "Swain must have known that. So, now he's gone on ahead, on that Mexican's horse."

"He might've seen me," said Iain. "I think he probably knew we were in there."

"Not hard to figure. We three were the only ones dumb enough to get off in this ... place."

"Do you think he spotted us in Truckee?"

"I don't know," huffed Jack. "But he knows we're on him now."

"So, let's find a couple of horses and get after him."

Jack looked around. "Alright. See any?"

They walked to the middle of the dirt street. There was nobody around. But then, following the sound of a sonorous gurgle, they entered the building with the fallen sign. Inside, it appeared to be a general store. Though the shelves were almost barren of food, there were a few sacks of flour and sugar, tins of black beans, along with boots, hats, ammo, tobacco, and hard candy. Beyond the expected, the shelves and cases also bore a dusty menagerie of glass insulators, fishing gigs, oil lamps, beads, porcelain inkwells, a stuffed parrot, brass spittoons, a red fly-pulley, tin boxes, wood spools, a flintlock pistol, and what appeared to be a string of scalps. The detritus and entritus of lost and discovered life, amassed and accreted over decades. Behind the counter of this walk-in cabinet of curiosities, an old-timer had collapsed in a chair with only his snore rising. "Hello there, Sir," began Iain. The man rumbled himself awake and looked up.

"Where is everybody?" asked Jack.

The man stood and toddled around to the back of the counter. "Good sirs, what's your poison?" he asked, his aging voice carrying an effeminate, English cadence.

"No thank you. You serve liquor?" asked Jack. "I thought—"

"I most certainly do. This is a saloon. The King's Arms."

"Oh, I didn't—"

"Nothing for me either," said Iain.

"No?" asked the proprietor, clearly disappointed. "So why interrupt my scandalous dream?"

"Where are all the town's people?" asked Iain.

"Who else must there be?" replied the Englishman.

Iain stared at him.

"Do you have water?" Jack asked.

"Fire?"

"Just water."

"Costs the same, I'm afraid."

"Alright."

Two grimy glasses containing water bearing a sheen were placed next to the dusty brass register. "There you are."

"That's water?" asked Iain.

"Near enough," said the man.

Jack swirled his glass. "Anybody here have horses to lend us?"

"Oh, no. I'm afraid not."

"No?" asked Iain. "Just *no*, English?"

"No."

"We saw a fellow leasing a horse at the depot," said Jack.

The old man nodded. "Hector. Yes. He said he'd be letting a horse this morning. A gentleman wired him for it."

Jack absorbed that for a moment, and then shook his head, giving an almost silent, defeated laugh. "Swain— He knew there would be no train. So he telegraphed ahead for the only horse."

"But the Mexican fella had two horses," said Iain. He looked at the proprietor. "But he leased only one of them."

"Yes," replied the Englishman. "Of course. How else could he have gone home?"

"Where does Hector live?" asked Jack.

"I wouldn't know, now would I?"

Iain grunted at the wizened man's London accent.

The man peaked an eyebrow. "Perhaps a place called Stone House, a day west. But I couldn't be certain."

"No, I don't reckon you could, at your age," said Iain.

Jack glared at Iain, then extended a hand toward the man. "My name's Jack Garrett. I'm a Pinkerton agent. And this irritating Scot is Agent Iain Lennox."

The man shook Jack's hand, then Iain's. "Sir Edmund Rowan, at your service. I'm not actually a Sir, but I should have been ... my friend used to say."

"You'd claim that, wouldn't ya?" groused Iain.

"We're tracking a killer," said Jack. "And we could use your help, Sir Rowan."

"Thank you. Propriety left with the silver, I'm afraid."

Jack continued, "Maybe you can assist us. We need a few things, and some information."

"I make it my *trade* to help others, especially when requested by a handsome law man."

"Excellent," said Jack, placing a silver dollar on the counter. "I have a question for you."

"We're not the law though," said Iain.

"How's that?" asked Sir Rowan.

"You said he's a law man, but—"

"It's fine," Jack said, frowning at Iain.

Sir Rowan pressed on. "So how may I be of service?"

"If you needed to get to Austin quickly— And by Austin, I mean Austin, Nevada."

"Is there another?"

Jack blinked slowly. "Say you couldn't wait for the train. Next week as I hear it. You needed to get there soon—faster than one horse could take you, which I figure is about three days, two in a hurry. How would you do it?"

Sir Rowan took the dollar and pondered the question, letting silence extend beyond his turn to speak.

Iain said, "Do you understand what he's asking ya, m'lord?"

Sir Rowan nodded. "I do, Jacobite. Do you?"

Jack pulled Iain aside and spoke lowly. "Can you leave off the Scottish Revolution, just for a time?"

Iain shrugged and took a step back.

Jack returned to Sir Rowan. "I apologize. Any ideas?"

"You can walk, ride a horse, take the train, or a motor-carriage. Unless you've got one of those flying contraptions, an aeroplane."

"Aye, an aeroplane!" Iain said, becoming instantly animated.

"Oh, no," began Jack.

"That would be the way," declared Iain. "If we flew there. That'd be the bollocks. We'd be there in an hour, if we—"

"Not now—" Jack shook his head and looked again at Sir Rowan. "You were saying—there's no way to get to Austin quicker than three days?"

"I said a motor-carriage. They can go thirty miles in an hour. Some almost a hundred on a hard road."

"Yes, Sir. Ok, I'll ask: Is there an automobile in this town?"

Sir Rowan raised one eyebrow and rubbed the white hairs erupting from his chin. "Only one. Mine."

"Yours?" Iain frowned. "You have an automobile?"

"You find that surprising?" asked Sir Rowan.

"Aye, I do," said Iain.

"Better than any horse. It never kicks or bites. It bucks a bit. It does that."

"And fuel?" asked Jack. "Do you have—?"

"Young man, would you ask a man if he has grain for his horse?"

Thirty minutes later, behind the store, the Pinkertons were getting driving instructions, with Iain standing by, laughing each time Jack ground the gearbox from neutral to the go gear.

"If you can't manage better," yelled Sir Rowan, unamused, "then I'm afraid only the big, annoying fellow can drive. I'd truly prefer otherwise."

"I'll get it, I'll get it," cried Jack, puttering the car forward. As he did, the back of the car came into Iain's view. Attached there was a small board with painted words:

SIR ROWAN - FARRIER - BM1.

Iain motioned toward it. "What's that?"

"That's my boot sign for my horse services. Isn't it clever? And it has the number of my telephone on it. BM1. Number one in Battle Mountain."

"How many telephones are there, here?"

"One."

"Oh," said Iain, watching Jack attempt to turn the automobile around at the end of the street. "You're a farrier, too?"

"I am."

Iain grinned. "An English farrier of two horses in a one-telephone, one-automobile desert town."

"Other horses come through. Jackasses too."

"They won't if those things take over," said Iain, pointing toward the Oldsmobile.

"That's the irony of the sign, don't you see? It being on *my* auto," Sir Rowan giggled. "The farrier's auto. Do you understand?"

"Not really." Iain kept his gaze on the automobile. It was almost back to them, but Jack had no intention of stopping—or perhaps he couldn't. In any case, Jack drove past Iain and Sir Rowan, cackling joyfully from behind the wheel.

The automobile was Oldsmobile Model N, the Touring Runabout sort. It was green with yellow pinstripes and white rubber tires. Its steering wheel was in front of the right, front seat, and under both front seats was a seven-horse-power engine. On the front was a hooded box, the "French sort," containing the machine's water, gas, and batteries. There was no windshield, but two matching pairs of goggles were provided.

Sir Rowan was all too happy to tell its story. It had been abandoned the same year it was made, 1904, when the owner attempted to drive it from San Francisco to New York. But that journey came to an abrupt and noisy halt near Battle Mountain when the crankshaft bolts sheared away. The man took the next train back to Sacramento, pledging he would return for his precious wiz wagon. But he never did.

At that time, the local blacksmith, a seventy-eight-year-old Civil War veteran—whom Sir Rowan referred to as "my dear friend" and "the kindest man you could ever know if you were lucky enough to live so long"—kept the automobile covered in a shed. As the months passed, the blacksmith learned to repair and drive the machine; and when he died (eight months and six days ago), he bequeathed the vehicle and his farrier business to the Englishman who owned the mercantile and saloon, Sir Edmond Rowan, the blacksmith's partner and fellow Confederate.

By 2:00, Jack had mastered the brake, clutch, and fuel pedals, and got the Oldsmobile putt-putting along steadily. So they loaded it for the journey to Austin. With the "farrier" sign removed, a rear cargo platform had been rigged to hold bags, guns, food, extra water and fuel, a block and tackle, a hundred feet of hemp rope, a hand pump, and extra tubes for the tires. Sir Rowan then gave them final instructions: under no circumstances should they attempt to go across open country. In fact, they should never leave the railroad's right-of-way at all. They paid him three hundred dollars—almost all the money they had left—a price based on Sir Rowan's prediction that he would soon be coming, on Hector's other horse, to recover his machine, or what was left of it.

As instructed, they followed the railroad right of way—smoothed from decades of slow wagon, cattle, and sheep traffic. After passing a water station at Dillon, Nevada, an hour into the journey, the thrill of motoring began to fade. They settled in to watching the road ahead, bracing themselves for each jolt and bump. Encountering no one on the road, they saw only occasional cowpunchers on yellow splotches of grass in the shimmering distance.

In the second hour, as the sun poured itself on them, Iain began a lecture on the peculiarities of aerodynamics.

"It makes no sense," said Jack. "I don't think you know what you're gummin on about. They're wings—they have to flap."

Iain grew frustrated. "It's about the flow of the air. A bird flaps to make air go over its wings. Stop, stop!" he exclaimed, pointing at a hawk. Jack slowed and stopped, but kept the engine idling. "See? He only flaps to maintain speed, to keep air moving over him. Or he can float, just glide, if the air's already moving. Or if he's coming down. I'm telling you, it's the moving air."

"Humph." Jack scrunched his mouth in consideration. "Alright. Well, I'm going to stick to these things," he said, patting the steering wheel as he got the Oldsmobile moving again. "I'm going to get one. Just watch. You can go kill yourself flowing air over your wings. But I'm getting one of these."

"Fine. Stay down here. But I'll be up there, going three times as fast."

"Hey, Iain," Jack said, putting on a presumptive air, "I'll wager you don't know why automobiles go. It's because of the Earth?" He pointed to the passing sands. "See? It's because the ground is flowing under the wheels!"

"Actually, sheep-bugger, you're sort of right."

"Damnit," Jack said with a laugh. "I give up."

After another hour of rolling past pitiful efforts at community, places with names like Walters and Clarks, whose signs were their biggest feature, they saw him: a figure on horseback, on their road, a good mile ahead in the early-evening orange. Iain, who was driving at the time, eased the car to a stop. "Is that him?" he asked.

Jack switched his goggles for binoculars. "Must be."

"Thought we'd have seen him sooner."

"He's on a mission," said Jack.

"He might kill that horse."

"Nah." Again through the binoculars. "He's walking it."

"Do you think he knows we're back here?"

"He's not looking, but I bet so. He probably heard the engine."

"So, what do we do?" asked Iain. "Just drive by him?"

"What else can we do? He'll probably stop later, for the night."

"He might shoot us."

Jack had been thinking the same. Not only might Swain kill Adams, but he might try to kill them too. All to cover his tracks. If their bodies were found, which was unlikely, it'd be reasoned that Adams had killed them. "He might try," said Jack. "Tonight, we can pass him close by and take our chances. Or go wide around."

Iain looked at a nearby hill. "Let's walk up there and see about going wide around. Sounds better to me."

"I agree," said Jack, grabbing their map.

In the purple pink light of day's end, the Oldsmobile clattered slowly across rolling hills of gold-lit sagebrush, far from the railroad. No doubt about it, Jack and Iain were breaking Sir Rowan's no-off-road rule. They stopped to refill water and fuel at a providential ranch house, twice more to replace tire tubes, and three times for Jack to crawl underneath to clean dust from the two carburetors. Just after dark they encountered a deep washout that sank them almost past the wheels, but the block, tackle, and rope resolved it. By 11:30 that night, moving in the glow of the accomplice moon, and by the yellow flood from the acetylene lantern fronting the machine, they again found the railroad with its wagon-road easement. Soon they were three quarters the way to Austin, with Captain Swain snoozing somewhere far behind.

– 45 –

FRIDAY
March 22, 1907

By 4:15 in the morning, Jack and Iain were just west of Austin. The moon had deserted, leaving the stars to their void, flickering the chorus of an ancient phrase. But the men didn't see it. They were fast asleep under the chassis of their machine.

At first light they were groggy, eating cold biscuits, discussing their hastily devised plan for capturing Steve Adams—assuming he was indeed inside the building beyond the next hill: Stokes Castle. Slender and three stories tall, made of granite blocks, it was a veritable fortress with sweeping views of all approaches—save one: the hill immediately behind it. Built by a wealthy mine owner named Stokes, it was intended as his family's home in the wilds of Nevada, its thick walls meant to protect them from the riff-raff of the unclean, the foul, the common. But Stokes had visited it only once, back in the nineties. Now it was abandoned, welcoming lonely trespassers who found its multiple floors and cool, stone walls irresistible. The most recent squatter was Lloyd Lillard, uncle of Steve Adams. Though they didn't know for certain, Jack and Iain presumed both uncle and nephew were in the house and armed.

By the time the sun had fully risen, they were prone on the hill adjacent to the tall house, rifle, shotgun, and two revolvers in their hands. They figured the earliest Swain could arrive would be around noon. Thus, for the morning at least, Adams was theirs—if they could get him. The plan was simple: wait until he went to the privy—located between the house and the hill—and then run down and attack him. The artless nature of the plan was bothersome, but neither could think of anything better. Surely Adams would need to piss or take a shit, but would he go to the outhouse to do it? They hoped his morning coffee was strong.

On that day, far away in Boise, Carla watched from a two-horse carriage as freshly arriving passengers streamed from the depot. Her eyes danced over them. Today, finally, a friend would arrive. Someone would be in Boise whom she could enjoy, someone to help distract her heart and mind from her daily wondering about Jack, questions that seemed to fill her chest with each breath. What did it mean that he hadn't written? She had no claim on him. They'd been together very little, actually. Their longest encounter was the trip out to the college where ... where she had killed her prior lover, and Jack took the blame for it. If that didn't mean they were fated for each other, what did? But why would he not write her? Had something happened? Was he dead? No. Banish the thought.

Her eyes locked on Winnie, then approaching. "There she is," Carla whispered to herself. She threw open the coach door and was out, her dark, Gibson-piled hair bouncing beneath her velveta hat. Within eight steps, she embraced her friend. "Winnie! I'm overjoyed to see you!"

"Carla," said Winnie, recoiling. "My goodness, I thought I was being attacked by the Pinks again."

"What? Silly, it's me. Turn, turn, let me see you."

Winnie gave a perfunctory pivot, her travel-wrinkled skirt whishing. "It was a long trip, Carla. May we—"

"You look stunning. I want— Yes, of course. You must be tired."

"You heard about Bill?"

"Of course. It's terrible. He'll be so happy you're here."

"Yes." Winnie motioned the bellman toward her bags.

"This is for us," Carla said, pointing at a coach and driver. "Saratoga, please."

"Yes, Miss," replied the driver.

During the short ride, Carla was a blur of information, pointing out the courthouse, the Idanha Hotel, the telegraph office, directions to the Caldwell home of the dead governor, and then the Saratoga Hotel as they approached it. The horses came to a stop, and the driver was out of the box helping two bellmen unload Winnie's luggage. The women stayed in the coach.

"You've had some trouble here," said Winnie with a squinty smile, like a dog proudly revealing it had dug up another's bone.

Carla blinked. "You heard about that?"

"Mr. Farrington was ours. His death was a loss to us."

"He would've killed me."

"You did what you had to ... I suppose."

The driver stood at the door. "Ladies?"

"A moment," said Winnie.

"Yes, Miss."

Winnie looked again at Carla. "Do you have another in mind?"

"Another?"

"Another Pink to spy for us."

Carla shifted in her seat, her thoughts heating, wondering who Winnie meant by "us." This wasn't the happy reunion Carla had expected. Rather, the message was clear: Winnie was in charge—at least in charge of Carla. But Winnie had been through an ordeal too, hadn't she? Winnie had been there in Denver when Haywood was arrested. It must have been awful, Carla reasoned, but a mile better than killing a man. She had done that, killed, but was still being pleasant. "Yes, I have another Pink. Maybe."

"Maybe?"

"He fancies me, and agrees with our—the Federation's cause."

"The cause of the worker?"

Carla frowned at the forced expression. "Yes. That."

"His name?"

"Agent Garrett. An operative, I believe. Or he was. Now Jack's a full agent." A wave of guilt hit her. Why was she telling Winnie this? Hadn't she decided to keep Jack out of things. Why try to impress Winnie?

"Jack?" asked Winnie, noting the use of the man's first name.

"What can I say?"

"A great deal, apparently."

"No. I don't know."

The driver gave another tap outside the door and spoke loudly. "Ladies, if you could. I must—"

"This is Federation business," Winnie snapped. "Leave us be."

"As you wish," grumbled the deep voice. "I'll need to add it to your fare."

Winnie resumed with Carla. “Is he here, in Boise?”

Carla shook her head. “He’s been gone for a few weeks. I said that in my telegram. I told you.”

“Of course! Jack Garrett. PJG.”

“PJG?”

“Yes! Pinkerton Jack Garrett, right? Your ‘love’ who went to San Francisco.”

“Well, ‘love’ is a bit ... I was being ... What do you mean, PJG?”

A smirk moved across Winnie’s lips. “He must be handsome.”

“Uh-huh,” Carla murmured and smiled. “But he’s not for you.”

Winnie gave a fake chuckle. “Then, who did you leave for me?”

Carla’s brow furrowed. “You’re with Mr. Haywood, right?”

“I’m not *with* Bill, of course,” said Winnie. “And a revolution is not just one man.”

“All right,” said Carla, thinking: *Nor one woman.*

“Besides, Mr. Darrow has barred me from visiting Bill. He said it would look poorly to jurors. I plan to anyway. Meanwhile, I have some time, and I have this.” She waved a hand over her body.

Carla rallied herself. “Perhaps the special prosecutor?”

“Senator Borah?”

“He’s handsome,” offered Carla. “A senator. And *their* attorney.”

“He knows who I am.”

“The sweeter the challenge.” Carla knew Winnie would never bed Senator Borah, but after today’s treatment by this one-time friend, it was a delicious thought, imagining this socialist slut attempting the feat. Even the arrogance to consider it—to think she, Winnie, the defendant’s mistress, could win the bed of the prosecution’s lead attorney. Hubris at its finest.

“I’d have to ask Bill,” said Winnie.

Carla blinked, now more confused. She snapped open the coach door. “Let’s get you settled here.”

Outside, at the back corner of the coach, hidden from any window, the driver had been listening. He jumped at the sound of the door latch and moved to the other side.

They smelled the bodies near Stokes Castle before they realized they had been looking at them all morning: three men, piled one atop the other. The top one's throat appeared cut.

"Jesus Christ," whispered Iain. "His uncle?"

"Probably not," said Jack. "I imagine that swine family sticks together." He examined a quartz rock in the dirt nearby and collected his thoughts. "Maybe it was this: Adams got here a couple days ago, but his uncle wasn't here, only those three unlucky souls." After another long breath, Jack continued, "There's something good though, about them being down there dead like that."

"Yeah? What's that?"

"We know Adams is in there."

"Or was recently."

"Yes," said Jack with a snort. "Or he was. Like bones outside a bear cave."

Iain pulled the rifle up and took aim at the back door. "One bullet, right through the sombitch's head."

"Somebody will. Someday. But not us."

"We're just the unlucky bastards who have to keep him alive."

"Mn-huh."

Iain slid on his back a few feet out of sight, to a place he might let himself sleep.

Time inched by. Jack rubbed his eyes and nose. He wanted coffee. "Come on, muck snipe," he whispered, staring at the door. "Come take a shit." At that moment, seemingly conjured by Jack's words, the rear door opened, and Steve Adams stepped out. He was naked, his body pale white, his arms and head turned brownish red by the sun, his blonde hair matted to one side. Jack scuffled his boot at Iain, and soon both were watching Adams piss on the pile of dead men.

"I'll be damned," said Iain. "Let me shoot—"

"Shhh."

Adams stretched lazily, looked around a little, and then started back to the house. Then he turned, walked to the outhouse, opened its squeaky door, and entered.

"Let's go," whispered Jack.

Leaving the long guns, they descended the hillside, careful not to slide, each with his pistol out and rope coiled over his shoulder. Soon they were approaching the little building from opposite sides. When each was about ten feet away, Jack raised a hand. Both stopped and holstered their guns. A fart came from within the gray-wood building. Using his upheld fingers, Jack counted: one, two, three, and then they both rushed the shed.

From inside, the sound of approaching boots alerted Adams. He had just grasped a knife hidden there when the door burst open. Iain was first in, going low, grabbing Adams by the feet, yanking him out. Adams flailed, thrashing, yelling, being dragged naked by his ankles across dirt and rock. "Sombitch!" he hollered, swinging the knife, wriggling to get himself up.

Jack ran near Adams's head, trying to lasso the man's arms.

Iain slowed, but it gave Adams better purchase on the ground.

"Keep going!" shouted Jack.

"Well, get him!" Iain yelled back, resuming the pace.

"I'm gonna kill you both!" managed Adams.

Jack got the rope around Adams's left arm and cinched it tight.

Iain slowed again, now running out of dragging room.

"Go back! Go back!" shouted Jack.

Iain turned, pulling Adams the way they came. Suddenly, Adams's exposed crotch slammed into a cactus and he screamed. Iain held Adams's ankles high, giving all the desert creatures a clear view of the man's needle-laden balls and bloody ass. Adams cried in pain, still wildly swinging the knife, trying to cut one of Iain's legs. Jack pulled at the rope, and Adams sliced at it, but missed and cut his own left arm. Blood squirted. The knife tumbled loose. Within seconds, Iain had tied Adams's ankles, and Jack had both of Adams's arms tied above the man's head. "Damn you!" screamed Adams, incapacitated.

"Gotta stop that blood!" Iain shouted.

Jack tied a tourniquet high on Adams's left arm.

"What a wee pecker," said Iain. "Look at those thorns— God in heaven, that must hurt."

"Is your uncle in there?" asked Jack.

Adams shook his head. He remained scrunched and bent from the cinched ropes—a red and white squeeze-box in the dirt.

"Go get him some clothes," said Jack. "But watch for the uncle." After Iain went inside, pistol drawn, Jack stood over Adams. "You're a mongrel— A murdering cur."

"Better'n a cocksuckin Pink. I'll gut you, like I did that un at the track."

Jack tsked. "Shouldn't say that."

"Heard about it, did you? Yeah, that was me did it. He—"

Jack kicked Adams in the back.

"Goddamnit." Adams groaned, gasping for air before lying still.

"I warned you."

Iain returned carrying trousers, a shirt, and boots.

"No boots," said Jack. "If he gets loose, he'll die in the desert."

"Nah," said Adams. "I'll kill y'all and have myself two pair."

Iain knelt beside him, then hit him, strappy fist to scrawny face. "We've miles to go," said Iain. "You'll get there alive—don't worry—but just by a fuckin hair."

Jack looked at Iain. "You want to get the auto, or should I?"

Thirty minutes later, the Oldsmobile was on a bluff overlooking the tiny town of Austin tucked in hills a mile away. Most of the baggage and equipment was on the floorboard, and Iain's legs were kicked up over it, stretching onto the walnut dash. He puffed a cigar and looked up at Jack standing in the driver's seat, surveying the town through his binoculars. The skinny form of Adams could be seen within burlap bags bound tightly to the rear cargo platform, bare feet sticking out one end, blonde hair the other. From inside came a polemic of muffled insults, like a faraway dog in an unrelenting fit of barking.

"There he goes," said Jack, seeing Captain Swain riding toward Stokes Castle. Jack hopped back into the seat and coaxed the automobile to life. "To the road!"

"To the road!" echoed Iain. He looked behind him. "It's gonna get bumpy, ratbag. Hang on!"

In Boise, the black candlestick phone on McParland's desk trilled, but the room was empty. The rings continued. Then the door flew open and McParland entered, cane first, picked up the device and snatched the earpiece from the brass hook. "Yes?" He listened for a bit, then smiled. "Very well. Thank you for letting me know." He hung up, set the phone down, hung his hat and coat, and returned to the open door and leaned into the hall of the Idanha Hotel. Only his legs and backside were still inside the room. "Tommy? Come here, Tommy."

From the hall came indistinguishable words from the clerk.

"Go get me Senator Borah, will you?" McParland could be heard asking. "He's in the lobby, I believe. Thank you." A pause, and then, "What? Ok. Sure. Come in." McParland backed into his office, followed by the Saratoga coach driver. McParland motioned the man to sit, but the man didn't. "What can I do for you?"

"Well, Sir ..."

"Have you something to tell me?"

"If your coins are heavy enough."

"They will be for good information. What do you have?"

Borah entered. "What is it? Who's this?"

McParland waved off the senator. "Go ahead, Mister."

"I'd rather not say."

McParland sighed. "Just tell me the nature of what you have. I'll get you paid if it's useful."

Borah sat on the table's edge, watching the man cut his eyes between the senator and the detective.

"Don't worry about him," said McParland. "But get on with it."

"I drove two women to the Saratoga. They were talking about Mr. Haywood. Sounded like one of them had killed a Pinkerton man, and she was working over another. Something about GJP. Or PJG, I think." The driver paused.

Borah widened his eyes at McParland.

McParland appeared nonplussed.

The man continued, "Said the other should be setting her ways on a man for the prosecution. A lawyer. She meant to bed him."

"I imagine she did," said McParland. "Was the name Borah?"

"That'd be correct," said the driver.

"The one who was to bed this Borah fellow," McParland asked, glancing at Senator Borah, "do you recall her name?"

"Winnie," replied the man.

"And the other girl was Carla, perhaps?"

The man nodded. "That's it. That's correct."

"Anything else?" asked McParland.

"One's staying at the Saratoga. I brought the other here."

"Hmm," sounded McParland, his arms crossed before him.

"That's worth something to you, ain't it?" asked the driver.

Borah approached the man. "What do you think it's worth?"

The man glanced at his feet. "Maybe two bucks?"

McParland squinted. "How long have you been driving here?"

"Nine years."

Borah looked at McParland. "What do you say?"

"He's underestimating his value," said McParland. "I think we should pay this man five dollars for this morsel of knowledge, and another five every time he brings us something this good again."

"Truly?" The driver reached eagerly for McParland's hand. "Name's Jenkins."

McParland shook his hand. "We're going to call you Smith."

Borah gave him five silver dollars. "Thank you, Mr. Smith."

"Thank you, sirs. I'll see what else I can gather for you."

"Go about your business as usual," instructed McParland. "Watch and listen. Listen and watch. Same as you did. And if you know any others who are reliable, who might want to make a few dollars—send them to me. Tell them to go to the front desk and say they're a friend of Mr. Smith."

"Yes, Sir. Thank you," said the driver, letting himself out.

After he was gone, McParland stepped into the hall after him. From inside the office, Borah could hear the detective say, "Mr. Smith, before you go. Just so we're clear: my Pinkerton men are everywhere, from the man shoveling your horse's shit here in Boise, to barkeeps in Colorado backcountry, to cowpunchers in Kansas, to coat-check boys in Washington, DC."

Borah's heart fumbled a few beats.

McParland kept talking in the hall. "I've got quite the spider's web. I catch a lot of flies. So, if I hear you've also been selling information down at the Saratoga—well, there'll be a reckoning."

"Yes, Sir," came the voice of the driver.

McParland re-entered the office, walked past Borah, and began preparing his pipe. "Cigar, Senator?"

"Yes. All right."

"My God," said McParland, opening his tobacco pouch. "Haywood's whoring out the sister. Well ... fine, we'll use her. We'll feed them skunked-up information—straight through her."

Borah blinked a few times before realizing what McParland was saying. "Hold on there," Borah began. "You think I should go along with this?" He clicked his tongue. "I have a reputation to—"

"Your reputation, aye." McParland chuckled. "When you're ready for something to tell Winnie, let me know."

"Nah," said Borah. "No more coat checks for me. Not with you anywhere around."

★

– 46 –

SATURDAY
March 23, 1907

"This is a right lally cooler, Bill," said Darrow, stepping into the spacious jail cell set in the corner of the courthouse offices of the Ada County Sheriff. He walked to the window and looked through the bars to the street below.

In his shirtsleeves and vest, Haywood sat on a cane-backed wooden chair, reading a newspaper spread across a table. His shoes were polished, his hair combed tight. His suit coat hung at the end of his bunk. Without looking up, he asked, "What was your delay?"

Darrow raised his brow at the insinuation. "They've been playing hide and seek with your whereabouts."

Haywood continued his paper perusal. "Bested you." He flipped a page. "Yet again."

Darrow exhaled and looked around, then walked to the cell door. A young deputy saw him approach and let him out. Haywood looked up, watching his attorney leave, but made no effort to stop him. A moment later, Darrow returned from another office in the courthouse, carrying a chair. He re-entered the cell, placed the chair facing Haywood, and sat down. "I suspect this will be a long conversation, and I'm not sitting on your bed." He then turned to the deputy. "You need to leave. I'll be having a private, confidential conversation with my client. Lock me in here and go."

The man nodded, locked the cell door, and left the outer office.

"You're upset, Bill," Darrow began. "As am I."

"*You* are?" thundered Haywood. "Were *you* dragged from your bed in the middle of the night? Were you kidnapped, handcuffed, hauled a thousand miles from your home, out of your state and thrown in jail? Did your attorney swear those exact same events would *never* happen? That they couldn't? Tell me, Clarence, is that what happened to you? Is that why *you* are upset?"

Darrow took a long breath. "In a manner of speaking, yes. I'm outraged by that same series of events."

Haywood turned away, then got to his feet and shoved the table aside so he could stand at the window unimpeded. "You said they couldn't do this."

"I said they couldn't do it lawfully."

"They *are* the goddamned law! So, what they do is lawful. You should understand that better than I do, Counselor. Your law and their law are two different things."

"I understand," was all Darrow felt he could say.

The big man's head slumped. "Get Claus. I want him in here."

"Who's Claus?"

"My dog."

"Oh, yes. All right."

"Is Winnie here?"

"I think so."

"And Neva?"

"No."

Haywood looked away. "She turned on me."

Darrow sniffed. "It could appear that way."

"It's Pennington. Goddamned George Pennington. He turned her against me. Or her preacher did."

"I don't know about that. George is here, helping me."

"You'd better watch him."

"I will."

"I've given her everything."

"I imagine so," said Darrow quietly.

"I haven't given Winnie half what I've given Neva. But Winnie didn't betray me. Neva's the mother of my children, for godsakes." After a pause, he grumbled, "I don't want them here."

"Who?"

"My children."

"As you wish, but—"

"Especially not if ... if they hang me."

"They're not going to hang you."

Haywood turned, dead eye first. "How do you know? How does the great Clarence Darrow know that? You know they won't hang me like you knew they wouldn't kidnap me? Wouldn't violate all my rights and drag me here? Is that how you know they won't hang me?"

Darrow didn't answer.

"Can't clam you up, most days. Now you've got nothing to say."

"I have an answer, Bill, but I don't think you want to hear it."

Haywood sat sideways in his chair. "I'm listening."

Darrow dragged his bottom lip under his teeth, gathering his thoughts. "All right, the truth. The truth is: though they have the actual power to hang you, they do not have the legal power to do so. And they cannot hold you here—not without being in open violation of the Constitution. And they cannot find you guilty of a hanging offense without two separate, first-account witnesses. Two. They cannot. I know, all that and a nickel won't buy a dead horse. But it's all I have to work with: the law. I sent a petition to the Supreme Court, arguing for your immediate release. A man can not be extradited without evidence of—"

"But, they did." Haywood picked up the newspaper.

"The Supreme Court will reverse that. It violates—"

"Have you read about that Russian fellow, Trotsky?"

"Sure. The socialist revolutionary."

"Yeah," said Haywood, finding a specific article in the paper. "Lead the workers— The Bolsheviks, they call themselves."

"Yes."

"Amazing victory," said Haywood. "Got the first constitution in Russian history. I bet you didn't know that."

"I did."

"Thousands of strong-hearted workers, good men, died fighting for a constitution, a two-bit piece of paper. Fighting that goddamned czar. People like us. Like any American worker. Like the men of the Federation. Union men. Those men and women. Women too. Even some children." He punched a finger at the newspaper. "They armed themselves and marched in the streets. And they won, by God. But it wasn't enough, was it?" Haywood looked again at the article. "That was in 1905. Then their constitution last year. And now ... Here it says they think over a thousand Bolsheviks—Russian civilians, workers—have been executed this year. In 1907. Just two years since their uprising. One year since their constitution. Men and women, lined up and shot, or hanged. Without fair trials. And you know why? I hate to blame that Trotsky fellow, but he didn't go far enough. He stopped short of the final mile. You can't do that. He left the czar in power and didn't put enough teeth in their new laws. So what's it worth, their constitution? Their ink is barely dry and it's already not worth a goddamned thing."

"American courts will honor the American Constitution," said Darrow. "They have for a hundred years, and I have no doubt they will in this matter."

"Only one way forward for those poor, brave Russians," Haywood continued, laying the paper aside. "Full on war. It will happen. Mark me. They need to drag the czar out and hang him. Him and that Rasputin fellow. They shouldn't 'apply their constitution.' It's too late for that. No 'fair-trial' bullshit. If the czar won't honor it, Trotsky shouldn't. I should write him."

"Write him?" asked Darrow.

"Yes. Perhaps."

"No, Bill. Absolutely not. If the prosecution reads a letter from you to Trotsky—"

"I could help him."

"Oh? How's that?"

Haywood glanced to be sure the outer office was empty, and then spoke softly. "You know exactly what I'd advise him. To do what I've done. I've taken our tyrants into the streets and executed them. I've bombed the trains and concentrators of the corporations and capitalist owners—any of them who would see a good man die for a dollar. And I've killed our political puppets, right at their homes. By God, Clarence, if this country's companies, and our capitalist *lords*, and our governments ... if they won't follow the American Constitution: I ask you, why the hell should I?"

Darrow sighed uncomfortably. "This is where we are. They have you here, illegally. I have petitioned the Supreme Court to send you home. So, if—"

"They won't."

"*If* the Supreme Court allows them to keep you here," Darrow continued, "and this matter goes to trial, you'll still walk out a free man. Either Harry Orchard will retract his confession—or otherwise decide not to testify against you in court. Or if he doesn't change his testimony, but they fail to find Steve Adams. Same result. Or if they do find Adams, but he won't testify against you.

Or if Adams gives a written testimony but contradicts it on the stand. And even if both Orchard and Adams testify against you in court, then I still get to have my crack at the jury—the central reason you hired me. And, we still have the Jew."

"Oh yes, the Jew," said Haywood. "At least he's a Russian Jew."

"Why does that matter?"

"They're the best Jews."

Darrow frowned and pressed on. "The point is, they have many hurdles ahead. This is still weighted in our favor."

Haywood picked a small piece of loose concrete from the wall. "Have you talked with Harry Orchard?"

"Not yet."

"Why not? Isn't he—"

"The judge hasn't let me. But he will."

Haywood shook his head. "The judge won't let my lawyer talk to my accuser. Don't I have a right—"

"Yes, you do. He'll let me."

"You must get Harry, that son of a bitch, to change his mind."

"I'll try."

"If he doesn't change his mind, I'll remove it—his whole goddamned head. You tell him that."

"I won't say that."

"Maybe you should take a cyanide tablet to him. Tell Harry to do the right thing, for his union brothers."

"I know you're worried, but you *will* leave Idaho a free man."

"You're blowing sunshine up my ass, but I'll take it."

"I'm not."

"Any news from Captain Swain?"

"No. The last telegram came from Truckee, in California. On the Central Line, up—"

"I know where it is," said Haywood. "Across from Reno. Near that big lake ... Tahoe."

"Yes. He then headed into Nevada on the man's trail. He said there are two Pinkertons also looking for Adams."

Haywood rubbed his head and glanced away. "Yeah, I know they're out there too. All right."

McParland was in his Idanha office, staring at the black phone before him. His right hand was poised midair, a flared cobra eager for the shiny black rat to flinch. But nothing happened. He snatched the receiver and toggled the brass hook three times. "Yes. McParland, that's me," he said into the cone-shaped piece. "Where's my telephone call? [pause] Robert Pinkerton. The Pinkerton Detective Agency. Chicago. [pause] You were going to put the call through, directly to this phone, but so far— [pause] All right. Did she leave you a note before she left? [pause] No, it's fine. Do you know— [pause] When you get that call, please— [pause] Yes, thank you." He hung up and the cobra flared again.

Telephone calls with his boss, Robert Pinkerton—calls like the one he was awaiting at the moment—had become more frequent. Mr. Pinkerton was nervous with all the national attention the case was receiving, and he was particularly unhappy about the abduction. But McParland knew Mr. Pinkerton's mood would lighten if the extradition stuck. So long as the Supreme Court didn't order Haywood released, everything would be fine. But if it did, well, that would be the end of McParland's career—to bring that kind of embarrassment on The Agency That Never Sleeps.

The Pinkertons were ascendant. Their logo—the single, open eye—had generated a new moniker for a detective: Private Eye. They were coast to coast, even international, serving nations, states, corporations, banks, and wealthy industrialists alike. They were the agency that all others aspired to become. In fact, most every other successful detective agency had been started by an ex-Pinkerton—like the Thiel Detective Agency and its chief detective, Captain Swain.

At this point, any failure of this case would be catastrophic to the agency, and couldn't be saved by McParland's fame. Here in the twilight of his career, McParland had risked everything. The papers were already churning about his capture of the governor's bomber, Harry Orchard. And they were filled with excited words about how that same Great Detective, the one-and-only partner of Sherlock Holmes, had captured William "Big Bill" Haywood. Unlike the socialist papers that screamed KIDNAPPED! in massive letters, the national papers had withheld judgment, for now. But they would turn, fast as their fingers on a typewriter, if the Supreme Court upheld Darrow's petition and released Haywood. This trial would either increase McParland's fame, or destroy his name. One or the other.

The phone rang, and he grabbed it. "Hello."

Through the earpiece, he heard Robert Pinkerton ask: *How are you?*

"This side of the dirt," replied McParland.

Good. Keep it that way.

"Lord willing and the creeks don't rise."

I'm reading some things that have me concerned.

"I know."

We can't have the coat unraveling.

McParland knew what Mr. Pinkerton meant: we can't have the Supreme Court undoing Haywood's arrest. McParland responded, "I have good reason to believe it'll stay intact."

How strong is that belief?

McParland paused, shrugging to himself, but said, "Strong."

Should we meet?

"I'm best on site," replied McParland, knowing Mr. Pinkerton meant McParland coming to Chicago, not the other way around.

Ok, old chap.

"Aye, Sir." When Mr. Pinkerton said, "Ok, old chap," McParland knew it meant the topic was concluded—at least for this call.

What else? Any news from your boys? Where are they?

Both McParland and Mr. Pinkerton knew to use prearranged codes for this topic, in case the telephone line was tapped. In fact, coded communications were usually sent by telegram, just to be sure no one accidentally revealed too much in a verbal conversation. But Mr. Pinkerton asked the question, so an answer was expected. Unrelated city names had been assigned as the code words. "Cincinnati" meant that Agent Garrett and the other Pinkertons had not found Adams. "Louisville" meant the men knew where Adams was and were following him. Thus, for weeks, McParland had been getting telegrams from Jack that simply read:

COLD IN LOUISVILLE.

"Atlanta" meant they had captured Adams alive. And "Richmond" represented an actual place: Silver City, Idaho, sixty miles down the BN&O narrow gauge from Boise. It was in Silver City ("Richmond") where McParland was to meet Agents Garrett and Lennox and take custody of Adams. McParland picked up a telegram from his desk. It read:

> From: Undeclared
> To: James McParland, Idanha Hotel, Boise, Idaho
> ATLANTA YESTERDAY.
> RICHMOND THURSDAY 28.

"They were in Atlanta a few days ago," McParland said flatly.

The phone line was silent, then came: *And, Richmond?*

"Soon."

– 47 –

MONDAY
March 23, 1907

When Neva arrived in Boise, almost two weeks after George and Winnie had, she felt like the ghost of Marley, an unseen scourge. The people knew she was there, of course. They were talking about her. But in passing, they fixed their gazes ahead, neither greeting nor dismissing. Though she was familiar with being observed obliquely, it was the absence of feigned supplication that gave her unease. And yet, it was its own form of comfort: Without presenting insincere displays, the people freed Neva to pretend she was invisible, at least in the wake of their passing. But she knew better. They were aware that the well-dressed woman in the invalid chair was the wife of the accused assassin boss, Big Bill Haywood. Had she known what he had done? How could she not have? Was she an enemy of the people, or a hero? Was she the proud wife of the leader of the workers' revolution? Or was she the lame wife of a murderous socialist who was sleeping with her sister?

But those questions of her relationship with Bill and his crimes were secondary in Neva's mind. What concerned her most was the one question that floated by in insidious whispers: Was she contagious? Nationwide, this fear was on the decline. New press accounts were reporting it rare for someone to contract polio from everyday proximity. Nevertheless, many chose to avoid the chance, however slight. But even that was not what worried Neva most. Rather, it was the emotionally charged fears regarding children and polio. In the crucible of scrutiny that was Boise that year, what Neva craved most were her girls. But they remained quarantined from her, hundreds of miles away.

On Neva's second day there, George arranged to meet her at the front of the Saratoga, where they were staying in separate rooms.

Wearing the Stetson she had given him, he flung wide the small door of a two-horse sedan and helped her through it. She fought off guilt for feeling so happy. The day was beautiful. Her leg wasn't aching. She was with George. She wore a linen skirt and matching jacket with Irish lace, along with kidskin gloves. (She had ordered the ensemble from Eaton's, and it arrived the day before she left Denver.) Yes, of course she was there for the murder trial of her powerful, vulgar husband—to be seen as supportive—but this was a beautiful day and she was with her wonderful man.

After George and the driver strapped her invalid chair to the back, George stepped into the carriage beside her.

The driver climbed aboard, told the horses to walk on, then asked, "Where to, Sir?"

"The state capitol," replied George.

"Where they're building it? Or where they're meeting?"

"The one they're building."

"Very well, Sir," said the driver. "That's only a few blocks."

"Another building under construction?" Neva asked George.

"Yes, I want to see it. Don't you?"

"Not particularly. But I'm happy to ride with you."

"Thank you."

"Why do you like seeing things being built?"

"What do you mean?"

"In Denver, the museum? And the depot before that?"

"I suppose I do. Everywhere, new buildings are going up."

"True," said Neva, noting they were passing an office building under construction. "Must we stop here ?" She flicked a smile.

"Not like those. It's the big, stone ones that interest me. Government buildings. Like the museum. I'm not sure why. Maybe it's the permanence—the future permanence—knowing they'll be around a hundred years. Long after I'm gone. It's something—seeing them being built. To be able to say, I saw it when it had no roof, when it was just a foundation."

She placed her hand over his. As they continued looking out, she began tracing the softness between his knuckles. He winked at her. Another city block moved by with the sounds of the harness's soft jangle, the clopping of hooves, the soft grinding of wheels. Then George spoke. "I met with them."

"Who?"

He glanced at the driver's back and leaned closer to her. "The meeting I set up. The union's local chapters."

She nodded, her brow rising. "What did they say?"

He drew a finger across his throat and mouthed silently: Bill.

"What?"

"No, I mean removal ... depending."

"Depending?"

He waggled his head slowly. "Well ... if it's necessary."

"Is it not?"

"I mean, depending on how things go ... here."

"Oh." She slowly blinked, looking away, and then back at George. "And what did they say about you?"

He shrugged and nodded. "It'll be all right."

"Are you sure?"

He inhaled, then said "Yes" at the end of a sigh.

She shook her head. "I have an idea, to make sure you're safe."

Ignoring her statement, George asked, "Will you visit him?"

"I must, right?"

"I would think so."

She closed her eyes, exhaling through her nose. "This week."

"Good. It'll be fine."

"I don't know ... After what I did, I—"

"He has bigger fish to fry."

The driver pulled the horses to a stop. "Here you are."

"Thank you," said George.

As the driver opened the door, George asked, "How much?"

"You came from the Saratoga. So, no charge."

"No?"

"Nope," said the man, and pointed at himself. "Teamster."

"Ah. Good man. You're very kind."

After unhooking Neva's invalid chair, George helped her into it and pointed her toward the big, stone capitol building under construction. Behind her, more clattering came from the coach. When she looked to her right, she saw George grinning from his own invalid chair. "Want to race?" he asked.

Speechless, Neva nodded, her eyes flooding with happy tears.

"How can you say that, Your Honor?" asked Darrow. He was in Judge Wood's chambers, sitting erect in an oak guest chair, its back bowed and seat bowled from decades of nervous wear.

"I just said it," barked the judge from across his desk. "That's how." Though his narrow head was bald in the center, it was curtained with black hair in need of a trim.

"Harry Orchard is the principal witness against my client. I must be allowed to question him."

Borah sat mute in the matching guest chair, watching the exchange, forcing a stern expression just to keep from smiling.

"Oh? Must you?" asked Wood with an imperious tilt to his nose.

"Yes, Your Honor. I don't need to explain it's a constitutional right for the accused to confront his accuser. And in this matter, that's Orchard, the State's *only* witness."

The judge's mustache twitched as he peered at Darrow. "The U.S. Constitution?"

Darrow frowned. "That would be the one."

"Nah, to hell with the Constitution. We're not following the Constitution."

Darrow blinked, and blinked some more.

Borah's frown was now in earnest.

Darrow spoke again. "Can you clarify that, Your Honor?"

"It doesn't fully apply. Your client assassinated the governor—"

"I'm being played the fool, surely, Your Honor," said Darrow. "My client is shuttled about like a bean in a shell game, and now—"

"I like that," said Judge Wood. "Bean in a shell game."

"And before that, my client was feloniously kidnapped by the prosecution and hauled here, into Idaho, without any respect for *habeas corpus*. And now, this? No consideration for the Constitution? Can a fair trial not be had in this state? Is Idaho so frontier that the presumption of innocence has yet to reach it?"

Wood narrowed his gaze to slits through his nose-clipped spectacles. "This is my home, Mr. Darrow. You're on thin ice."

"Ice? That would be an improvement. I thought I was already drowning, what with the abandonment of the Constitution."

"What say you, Senator?" asked the judge.

Borah shrugged. "I don't know how else to say it, Your Honor: The defendant is the leader of a vast horde, thousands of thugs and killers who are set on destroying that same constitution, so—"

"That's not true," said Darrow. "You can't—"

"Let him finish," barked the judge.

"It's costing the State significant resources just to pay for the company of National Guard soldiers out on the courthouse lawn," said Borah. "They're out there keeping the Western Federation of Miners from storming this building, killing us all, and absconding with the defendant."

"That's not a full company—" began Darrow before Judge Wood raised his hand.

"I'm not surprised you know that, Clarence," said Borah. "Your Honor, I'm sure Haywood's men have surveyed the soldiers. They know their exact count and where each is posted."

"That's not what I said."

"My point is, Your Honor," Borah pressed on, "the threat of the Federation attempting to rescue the accused is as great as the threat that they might kill one of our witnesses."

"No one is going to hurt your *only* witness," muttered Darrow.

"I don't think it's prudent, Your Honor, to allow Mr. Darrow, a representative of that same horde, to have access to the witness."

"This is insane, with all due respect," Darrow said. "What do you think, William? I'm going to kill Harry Orchard? With my bare hands?" Darrow readdressed the judge. "Is that where we are? Is that where we're going with this? Does this predicate the shenanigans and un-constitutional maneuvering to come, against my client?"

"There'll be no shenanigans in my courtroom, Mr. Darrow. You may be a big, Chicago lawyer—"

"America's lawyer for the damned," Borah injected. "So the papers say."

"Then Mr. Haywood has the right one," quipped Wood.

"The jury will decide this," fumed Darrow. "And any irregularities will go to appeal. On that you may be assured."

"Appeal as you wish, as with your petition to the Supreme Court," said the judge.

"On that matter, I'll be seeking a stay pending—"

"Nah, Mr. Darrow. We'll carry on, at least through *voir dire*. The longer I postpone this trial, the greater chance your client turns my county blood-red."

Darrow took a breath. Nothing about this was right, but he couldn't leave empty handed. "I'll proceed as you instruct, of course. In fact, if we aren't going to hold for the Supreme Court's ruling as to the rightfulness of the extradition, which of course would cause the State's case to collapse, then I'll call ready tomorrow."

"While we have the one witness?" asked Borah with a squint.

Darrow addressed Judge Wood. "They need to scrounge up a second witness, so, let's trade: The court can give them more time to buy another false confession. Meanwhile, let me meet with the one and only witness they think they have. Otherwise, yes, let's *voir dire* tomorrow."

"You mean the man your client shot at," grumbled Wood.

"No, Your Honor. Neither my client nor the Federation did that. It was the State. McParland's men, to be specific, hoping to scare Orchard into a confession."

"That's ludicrous," said Borah.

"What evidence can you offer that it wasn't a Federation man?"

"You wish me to prove the negative?"

Wood shrugged.

"Quite simple, Your Honor. As the special prosecutor here has implied, if the Federation took a shot at Mr. Orchard, Mr. Orchard would be dead."

The judge began to chuckle. "That's a hell of a reason."

"Just let my client have his constitutional right to— Just let me talk to Orchard. Please. See if he stands by his confession. The Pinkertons can search me, post men all around me. But let me talk with the man."

The judge pondered for a moment.

"They will kill him, Your Honor," said Borah. "I don't know how, but—"

"Me?" asked Darrow. "You think *I* am going to kill the man?"

Borah held up a finger. "I'll say this, then leave it there: If Mr. Orchard ends up dead, the next man to die will be Mr. Darrow."

"My God!" Darrow exclaimed. "Senator, are you threatening to kill me? Right here in front of the judge?"

Judge Wood appeared bemused. "Fair question, Senator."

Borah took a deep breath. "If Mr. Haywood, or any representative of Mr. Haywood, or any of the Federation's army of killers, assassinates Mr. Orchard, then there will be a blood, I'm afraid. That's all I am seeking to avoid."

"The Federation's army?" Darrow's face reddened. "What do you mean? They are private citizens defending their rights. You are confusing them with the Pinkertons, the State's private police."

Borah shook his head. "Governor Steunenberg was well loved."

The judge leaned on his elbows, clasping his hands together. "Let's keep this civil, shall we? All right, Mr. Darrow, you can interview their witness. But only the once."

"Yes, Your Honor. Thank you."

Judge Wood continued, "As you said, Mr. Darrow, they only have the one. If a second witness is attained, then I'll consider the same for him. Have your meeting, Mr. Darrow. Do it soon."

"Thank you, Your Honor."

The judge turned to Borah. "I assume you'll have the State's witness guarded for the duration that Mr. Darrow is with him?"

"Yes, Your Honor."

"Good. And don't threaten to kill anyone in front of me again. Or, if you do, be ready to pull your barker on the spot."

"Yes, Your Honor."

"You're a bloomin United States Senator. I voted for you twice, for christsakes."

"Thank you," chuckled Borah.

"Oh, well ... that's terrific," Darrow groused, standing.

Darrow and Borah walked out of the Ada County Courthouse. On the wide granite steps, they saw approximately twenty National Guard soldiers ringing the place. "A company?" Darrow scoffed.

"With the ones inside, and out at the pen, there might be."

"Uh-huh," said Darrow. He looked at Borah directly. "That threat to kill me, that was just to get him to approve my access?"

"Nope." Borah started to leave. "Walking?"

Darrow stood for a second. "I'm going back in to talk with my client. That's allowed in your State of Idaho—right, Senator?"

"Night, Counselor," said Borah, descending the wide steps.

"Good night," Darrow replied, watching him go.

★

– 48 –

TUESDAY
March 26, 1907

"See that window?" Orchard asked, shielding the sun from his eyes with one hand. The other was extended, pointing at the high windows of his prison building. "Don't rightly think you can see it from down here, but sure as shit it's there. Bullet hole in one of them panes."

"I don't doubt you, Mr. Orchard," said Darrow, not attempting to see it. The armed guards encircling them were watching Darrow's every move. He was forbidden to get closer than three feet to Orchard, and certainly wasn't allowed to touch the man. They stood in a small field, surrounded by the prison's high stone walls and cell block buildings, on top of which were a number of additional guards, each with a rifle. Beside Darrow and Orchard was the penitentiary's gallows platform, about eight feet off the ground. Darrow noted that, as it was missing its overhead structure and beam, it appeared as an innocuous, wooden stage set in a well-trod field—as if one might expect a repertoire of Shakespeare to occur there. He envisioned *Hamlet*—the play's the thing. Or no, *Titus Andronicus*. This was a stage for a bloodbath.

Orchard turned halfway around and pointed to the hills beyond the walls. "Your fella shot at me from up there."

"Perhaps the shooter was up there," began Darrow, "but you don't know who hired him. I think he was a Pinkerton, trying to scare you into that false confession you gave. But Detective McParland didn't count on you being as smart as you are. I think your gut tells you it was one of them—maybe even one of these men standing here. You never know." Darrow pointed at the guards surrounding them. "But, Mr. Orchard, whoever shot at you, it wasn't one of your labor brothers."

"Don't rightly know. Seen a lot in my days with Mr. Haywood."

"That's right—you don't know. Hell, I don't either."

"Since I seen that kill list Mr. Haywood had, with my name on it, I figured—"

"You can't be certain who was up there."

"Guess not."

"So, how about you stop saying it was a Federation man who shot at you? Since, as you said, you don't know."

"Yeah." Orchard walked to the wide, wooden steps leading up to the gallows stage and sat down.

Darrow stood near him, leaning on the rough-hewn handrail. "I was told you were smart, and I see that's true. And not just smart, but you have an honorable heart. I heard you've found the Lord since you've been in here."

"Yeah."

"Born again. Walk in His love, and He shall light your way."

Orchard looked up at the lawyer. "You came to get me to recant my confession. Want me to say I made it up."

"No, that's not what I want."

"Ain't it?"

"Just the truth. The truth will set you free, right?"

"Told the truth. Most true thing I ever said. This *free* to you?"

"Well—"

"Truth will set me free," scoffed Orchard. "Nah, you know what I think? I think that's one of the biggest lies there ever was. Truth never set a man free."

"You know," began Darrow, "I've read what you said. A few times through. And I've got nothing to say about all those other things you claim you did. But I take exception to one part. You say you planned and constructed the bomb, the one you planted at the governor's house, and you set it off."

"Uh-huh."

"And those things are for *you* to say, because those are all things *you* did. Only you can say them for sure. But you go on to guess a number of other things. Just like today, just now, when you were guessing who shot at you that night."

"I don't think so."

"Mr. Haywood never told you to kill the governor, did he?"

"He wrote it down."

"And you have that paper?"

"No."

"But you kept a piece of paper from Mr. Haywood's office."

Orchard stopped blinking. "Might've."

"You did. And you hid it in the brim of your hat."

"Yeah."

"Where's that hat?"

"Pinks took it."

"But there was nothing on that paper, right? You just took a blank piece, so you could write something on it if you needed to, maybe to gain some upper hand over Mr. Haywood at a later date. Like an insurance policy."

"No, it said—"

"You're guessing again. Don't do that. Don't bear false witness. You read that in the Good Book, didn't you? A man shouldn't bear false witness against another. It's one of the Ten Commandments, is it not?" He saw Orchard nod. "Means you can't guess. You aren't certain what Mr. Haywood said about Governor Steunenberg—if he said anything at all."

"That ain't right."

"All I'm asking is for you to tell the truth about what *you* did. That's your right. But you can't say what was in the heart of another man. You can't say what Mr. Haywood was thinking. You've found Jesus in here, and that's commendable, but He didn't make you telepathic, did He?"

"Telepathic?"

"You can't read other people's minds, can you?"

"No."

"Then all I'm asking you is take back those parts of your confession where you speak about what you imagine transpired in Mr. Haywood's heart. What you guess were his intentions. You may have misunderstood. Do you ever misunderstand things others say? I know I do."

"Maybe."

"Of course you do. So just tell the truth. That's all I'm asking. And the truth is: you don't know for certain that Mr. Haywood asked anything of you."

"Yeah, I do. He wrote the words Steunenberg and bomb."

"Steunenberg and bomb?"

"Yeah."

"I feel for you," said Darrow, nodding. "Detective McParland has got you all confused. But if you remember it right, you'll remember that *you* wrote that. You stole the blank paper from Mr. Haywood, and you wrote those words. The truth, Mr. Orchard."

"I told the truth."

"You wrote it on that paper, tucked it in your hat, and now the Pinks have it. Do you know why McParland hasn't shown it to you? Hasn't asked you to confirm it?"

"No."

"Because it's either blank, or it's written in your hand."

"No it ain't." Orchard stared, then shook his head at Darrow. "You're a famous lawyer. Everybody knows that. Heck, I wish you was my lawyer. Anybody who's got you as their lawyer, they're gonna walk free. You've got wizard's way with words."

"I don't do spells," Darrow tried. "I just tell the truth."

"What I'm saying is—because he's got you representin him, everybody knows Big Bill ain't gonna swing up there." He glanced up at the trapdoor platform.

"I wish it was that certain, Harry, but—"

"I agreed to my punishment: life in prison. Haywood'll walk."

Darrow frowned. "Your false testimony won't help his—"

"See, Sir, that's just the thing, it ain't false. I'm gonna do what I figure I gotta. And you're gonna do what you figure you gotta. Me telling the truth—him ordering me to kill the governor—well it won't matter none. I don't know why you're here fussing over me, wanting me to lie for him. He ain't gonna hang."

Darrow's fists tightened. "All right. Say I represented you—"

"You're offering?"

"One never knows."

"I've hurt a bunch of people, Mr. Darrow. Ok, I'll say it true: I've killed a bunch. I'm a fallen sinner. Why would you want me out? I'd just hurt more. Might even hurt you."

"I don't think you would."

"No? Why's that? Because you think I'm changed? Or cause if I was to step one foot out of here, a Federation bullet would find me— Like that!" He snapped his fingers. "Yeah, that's why you're sure I'd never hurt nobody again."

"I didn't say—"

"Yeah, you didn't. Didn't say either way."

"Can we move off this point? I seem to have upset you."

"Don't matter nonewise. Rubber lips on a woodpecker. I already confessed. Judge already sentenced me. None of you was around. And I'm all right with it. Me and the Lord got eternity together. After this trial, they'll send me to Leavenworth or someplace, and the Lord and I will get to know one another for a few years. Maybe I won't have to burn." Orchard stood fully and stretched. He turned to Darrow. "Tell me if this ain't right: they gotta get someone else to agree with me, to say the same thing about Big Bill. Ain't that right?"

"That's right."

"Well, the only fella I know who can do that without lying is Steve Adams. He saw that note. I showed him it. And he might've talked to Big Bill about the governor. He's the only one. That's another reason I figure Mr. Haywood will be all right."

"Why is that? You don't think Mr. Adams will testify?"

"Nah, they've probably already killed him."

"The Federation?"

"Yeah. Or that sheriff up north has hanged him."

Darrow squinted. "Who?"

"Fellow in here's been talking bout a sheriff from up near the Bunker Mine. He's been on the hunt for a man named Addis for cuttin his boy's throat. Well, I know all about that. I was with Addis. That was Steve Adams. He and Addis are one and the same."

Darrow frowned. "He's the same man?"

"Know it so. Way I figure, bout now there's bits of Adams getting shit out of a couple of buzzards somewhere over Utah. Figure Big Bill sent someone to kill him. Hell, I was supposed to kill him. And I would've too, had McParland not caught me first."

"Ok, Mr. Orchard." Darrow was deep in thought.

Orchard shrugged, then lifted his voice: "Guard, you can take me back." He regarded Darrow. "No skin off me. I just tell it true." As the guards ushered him away, he turned. "Maybe you can keep that commandment too, Mr. Darrow."

The Duck Valley Indian Reservation, home of both Shoshone and Paiute Indians, straddled Nevada and Idaho, taking an unwanted piece from each. It was desolate, a hundred miles from anywhere else—an endless expanse of bulging hills covered in sagebrush and grass. At its center was Owyhee, which was no more than a creaky windmill over a livestock tank next to a poorly made school for forgotten Indian children. Two horses, one roan, one dun, were drinking from the tank, snuffing as they did. "Nobody in there," announced Iain loudly, stepping from the school house. He looked up at the windmill and whistled sharply. "What do you see? Are we about to get scalped?"

"Nope," Jack yelled down from his perch near the top of the tower. He had been surveying the horizon through binoculars. "Nothing and nobody." From up there, he could see the two horses below him, as well as the wagon to which they were hitched. His attention turned to resonant grunts rising from the wagon bed, from under a convulsing, deep-red, canvas cover. "Damnit. Don't let him tear that up," Jack shouted, descending. Seeing Iain nearing the wagon, Jack added, "Wait. Wait. Let me get down first."

Once both were at the wagon, Jack drew his pistol, and Iain aimed his shotgun at the squirming mass. "Cut it out, asshole," Jack demanded. The red canvas stopped moving, and then erupted again, as if boiling blood. Using the barrel of his gun, Iain lifted the edge. There they saw the top of Adams's head, his greasy, dirt-yellow hair, his mouth gagged, hands tied to his belt buckle, feet toward the driver's box. One of his legs, having come unchained from the wagon floor, attacked the cover.

"Hey! Shite-eater!" barked Iain. "You can either lay still while we fix ya, or I can hit ya bout the head for a bit. Which ya rather?"

Jack chuckled. "Iain, I swear—"

"I beg ya, keep kicking. I'll go fetch a rock."

Adams lay still.

Jack walked around to the side of the wagon, lifted the canvas, and re-wrapped the chains. "You need to piss?" he asked their captive. Seeing Adams nod, Jack said, "Go ahead," and tightened the cover in place.

Other than one more tube change and a search for fuel, the plucky Oldsmobile had given them no trouble on the drive from Austin back up to Battle Mountain, where they had arrived three days earlier. After returning the car to the much-relieved Sir Rowan, they moved Adams inside The King's Arms and chained him to a post. Then they took turns sleeping. (Ten more dollars had not only purchased Sir Rowan's silence, but also the use of his mercantile saloon.)

The next morning, Jack had roused the dullard ticket agent and sent the ATLANTA and RICHMOND telegram to McParland. Back in the saloon, they had spread a map and made a plan. To reduce the chance of running into Captain Swain, or any other Thiel or Federation man, they would not put Adams on any trains. It didn't matter anyway as there was no rail between Battle Mountain, Nevada, and their destination: Silver City, Idaho (code-named "Richmond"), a hundred and fifty miles or so north. Based on Sir Rowan's descriptions of the terrain, and figuring a two-horse wagon, it would be a week's journey to Silver City. But where to find the wagon team? And, more critically, how to conceal their route out of Battle Mountain?

First, Jack bought three tickets eastbound, and talked loudly while a couple of drifters were in the depot, being careful to mention Ogden, Utah, a few times. When the Southern Pacific train arrived from Reno, Jack boarded, only to climb off the far side, unseen. He then returned to Sir Rowan's store and guarded Adams, while Iain walked to the depot and did the same thing: publicly getting on the train before slipping off just as the wheels began to turn. Meanwhile, Sir Rowan used the third ticket, but stayed on the train. Two short stops east, he got off, leased a wagon and two horses, and drove it back to Battle Mountain.

During their long day waiting for Sir Rowan's return, Jack and Iain took alternating posts: one watching Adams, the other watching the tiny Battle Mountain depot. As expected, Captain Swain arrived on horseback and began asking grumbling questions about three men who may have been there. The ticket agent reported to Swain that, yes, he had sold three tickets east to a man of Jack's description. One of the drifters confirmed, saying he had seen the three get on the train. No, they hadn't mentioned Boise, best he remembered, but one of them talked about Ogden. So, Swain boarded the next train to Utah.

Now, three days later, Jack and Iain were facing north in the driver's box of their lurching wagon, keeping it at a keen clip. Due to this ancient, nomadic trail's north-south orientation—between the distant Rockies to the east, and the Cascades to the west, coursing through an area void of arable land, navigable rivers, or natural wonders—there was perhaps no traversable path in the United States more remote, more untouched by modern civilization, more ideal to be transporting such a wanted prisoner—a man like the one covered by the red tarpaulin behind them—their prize groaning through each jostle and jolt.

Far behind them, the Owyhee windmill slid from the Earth. To their right, a herd of antelope kept the wagon in steady contemplation. While to their left, the sky began to catch fire, throwing its glow across the rolling hills of pink-flowering sagebrush, gooseberry, bitterbrush, patches of yellow balsamroot, and the blooms of Indian blankets that matched the orange above.

Iain gazed up in wonder as the vast sky streaked with color.

Jack looked ahead, lost in warm thoughts of Carla.

★

– 49 –

THURSDAY
March 28, 1907

"It's *The Jungle*," Haywood replied to Neva's question about what he was reading. "By Upton Sinclair." He faced the cover toward her briefly.

"What's it about?" she asked from a chair outside his cell. They were alone. She wore her midnight-blue wool coat and a demure hat. It was perhaps too late in the season for a thick coat, but it made her feel sheltered, bundled there in that cold office, talking to her cold husband through cold, steel bars.

"Animal slaughter," he said, sitting on his chair inside the cell. He was in his shirt sleeves, his suspenders loose.

"Oh. Sounds interesting," she said without having heard him.

He cocked his dead eye. "It's of no interest to you, Nevada."

"No," she admitted, glancing away toward her green crutches on the floor beside her chair. "Nevada? Not Neva?"

"Would you prefer Collaborator? Traitor?"

"I'm sorry. I just couldn't— I just can't."

Just above a whisper, he said, "You gave the goddamned Pinks a map to our offices, to our home." He took a noisy breath. "It was that preacher, wasn't it? After all I did for him."

She heard the frightful faintness in his voice. He was not enraged, as she thought he would be—as perhaps she wished he was. His rage she could understand. She had dealt with it for years. She could ball up and hide from it. But this, this sinister calmness, bore a chill she didn't know.

"That preacher's an ungrateful charlatan," he continued, his tone even and deliberate. "Seventh Day bullshit."

"Not our home."

"What?"

"You said I gave them a map to our home, but I didn't."

"You know what I meant. The suites in the Pioneer."

"That was never my home," she said, then looked at him squarely. "I'm not responsible for them arresting you, Bill."

"You helped. And you didn't warn me, when you could have."

"I didn't know."

"Don't lie to me!" he thundered.

There it was. She relaxed, slightly. "I didn't come to be yelled at," she said—though perhaps she had.

"What did you expect? Huh? What?" His voice stayed loud. "They have me here. They'll hang me. I may not live for more than another month or two, Neva. I might die! Don't you care?"

"Of course I do. But you've—"

"Your husband just told you that he's going to die. How can you be so cruel?"

"*Cruel?* Me?" She found her anger. "It's because of *your* cruelness that I did what I did. It's because of you that so many innocent people died and—"

"Innocent?"

"—so much money was stolen." She inhaled sharply. She wasn't supposed to have said that.

"I didn't kill anyone. And I didn't steal any money. Is that what they're saying? Is that what that ass Borah is claiming, that I—"

"It's just a rumor. Apparently money is missing from—"

"Then that's your fellow's problem."

"Who?"

"Are you going to play ignorant with me?"

"George has nothing to do with anything."

"He's the union's treasurer. Any missing money is his—"

"I'm not talking about that. I don't want to. I don't, Bill." After a pause, she added, "Some local chapters have questions. That's all I've heard."

"Oh? Nah, they love me."

"Are you sure?"

The question caught him for a moment, then he said, "Of course. They know I protect them. And the ones who don't love me, they fear me—as they should. They know I'll do what I must to protect myself and the Federation."

She looked at him. There was his admission. At least to her, that was it. She had managed to keeps the waves of repulsion topping and collapsing far out at sea, but now the Earth had shifted, things were different—now those waves were here, ripping into her shore. She looked deeper. His wide face. The missing eye. The shoulders slumped in a jail cell, his thick neck likely to be hanged. Hated by thousands—perhaps more than the thousands who loved him. This was not a champion. Not a powerful man. But a weak man. How had she never seen it before? Reverend Sanders was right. George was right. Even Detective McParland was right, at least partially. This was not a father. Not a husband. But a deserter. A brutal coward who knew only to save himself at all costs. Loyal to no one. Not even to the members of the Federation, unless they were unflinchingly loyal to him first. And even then, he would betray them. A black-hearted man in love with one thing—power. She sat straighter in her chair. "You need to know, Bill. Whatever happens at the trial, I'll not stay married to you."

"Alright, that's fine," he said as flatly as if agreeing to the asparagus chicken.

She stared at him. Why no tears? she wondered. Not from him—that wasn't surprising. But why none from her? Because she was right, she told herself. She didn't love him. She loved George. She needed her daughters home. She needed to enjoy what life she had left. And at that moment, she needed to leave this place. She needed to be done with Bill forever. She picked up her crutches and stood. "Mr. Darrow asked me to testify on your behalf."

He came to the bars. "Why? You don't know about— Oh, about my character. What I've done for labor."

"That's right. Your character."

"Good. That'll be good. Do as Darrow tells you."

She stared at him, snorted in disgust and turned away.

"You will, right?"

She pivoted on a crutch. "You actually believe I would."

"Of course you will. You're my wife!"

"On paper, perhaps. But it repulses me. Every fiber in me."

"Goddamnit! Look around! This isn't about *you*, you selfish woman. You child. And it's not about *us*. It's about thousands of men, the workers, their families. It's about justice and revolution. This is not about you, but it *is* your obligation. You're called—"

"No, Bill. It's about *you*. It's about a man you had killed in front of his children and his wife. It's my decision, whether or not I'll testify about your *character*. You really want me to? Think hard on it. That decision definitely is about me. And about God and my eternity. And happiness. Yes, it's about happiness. To the devil with you, Bill Haywood." She spun and crutched to the outer door.

"Neva. Neva. Come back. Let's—"

She kept moving, not turning.

"Go then, damn you! Go to your thieving adulterer!"

After managing to close the door behind her, she leaned on the wall in the courthouse hall, listening as he kept bawling. *"You can't judge me! You can't testify for me! I won't allow it! Who do you think you are, Nevada Jane Minor? A broken hag! A disease-filled, chatter-mag cripple! An adulterer! You're nobody!"*

Neva saw others in the hall were hearing Bill, their eyes critiquing her. She resumed moving to the lift, swinging her left leg between her green crutches, tears burning down her cheeks. She knew what she now had to do—for George, for herself. As the elevator's doors closed, she clenched her eyes shut and whispered, "That's enough! I'll never speak to you again. Never."

"It's not required, Ma'am," said the lift operator. "Just point at the number you want."

"Oh, not *you*. Yes. I'm sorry," she breathed, wiping away what remained of her salty streaks. "One please. To the street."

McParland tried to sleep on the BN&O narrow gauge but found it impossible, the anticipation too consuming. He had been sick with the sweats the past two days, and though the nausea was lifting, his body remained wracked with exhaustion. Still, nothing could keep him from being there, on that train, winding through the chalky hills, valleys of pinon and juniper, and then rising again into the mountains. He opened his eyes to the wood ceiling of the car. Then came a whistle from the engine and he sat up, looking out the window toward the front. They were approaching a small mining town. Senator Borah rose from his bench on the other side and slid into the one behind McParland. He too examined the cluster of homes and mine shacks outside. Then came the bell and the blow of steam and the train crawled to a stop beside a platform over which swayed a green sign painted with white letters:

SILVER CITY, IDAHO

McParland heard his men on the roof of the train car, and saw others stepping onto the platform. Pinkertons were also taking positions among the trees across the track and turntable. The town appeared deserted, but he knew better. Somewhere in that ramshackle cluster of buildings were two Pinkerton agents and a prisoner. And this was a remote mining town, thick with Federation men and their sympathizers. If a battle was to be had, if Pinkertons were to be slaughtered, this was the ideal location. There was only one narrow gauge track coming in. Wilderness for miles. Nowhere for a non-union man to hide. In some ways McParland regretted his decision to make this the hand-off point, but it was the last place someone would expect it.

The door to the ticket shed opened, and three men stepped onto the platform, each carrying either a rifle or a shotgun, and all wearing silver badges: a sheriff and two deputies.

"Damnit," said McParland, donning his hat and moving to the door of the passenger car. Borah came up behind him. "Stay put, Senator, please," said McParland. "Let me see about this." Stepping out, McParland saw Pinkertons, including those on top of the train, taking aim at the lawmen on the platform. "Lower you weapons, gentlemen," he yelled at his men. They did, and he walked to the sheriff. "James McParland," he said, offering his hand.

Without accepting the gesture, the sheriff spit tobacco to one side. "State your business, Pink."

McParland stared at the man and counted four seconds before speaking. "I'm an agent of the State of Idaho, and I've come to take custody of a prisoner."

"Oh yeah? What prisoner would that be?"

"You know, Sheriff." He was reminded why he hated these petty, small-town sheriffs who bore no loyalty to any cause greater than their own—each playing god of their own worthless patch of dirt.

The sheriff shook his head. "Don't think I do."

"Must we do this waltz?" McParland said. He gestured toward the floor of the rail platform where they stood. "Got a dance floor right here. That what you like to do round here? You wanna dance with me, Nancy?" McParland swayed a few waltz steps.

The sheriff didn't budge. "I don't think you heard me, old man."

"Oh, but I did. As you observed, I'm a bit lanky in the tooth. But, that means that in my long career, I've dealt with more puffed-up little shits like you than I can count." He took a beat and said, "And I'm feeling quite sickly today. So, let's dispense with all ... this. Whatever this is." He felt his head swimming. He needed to sit down. "You know who I've come for, and you're going to hand him over, along with my two men."

"I don't—"

"Shut your trap. You know who the prisoner is. And the way I figure, you've already wired Denver, setting off the alarm. I bet Captain Swain and a good size posse are headed this way. Right?"

No answer.

"Yeah, I'm right. But they won't get here in time, because I control the one pissant railroad coming in. It's just you and these two sniveling cowards"—he indicated the men flanking the sheriff—"against my whole company ready to gun you down. But they won't have to. You'll just step aside and let me have who I came for. Then I can go home and rest."

"You think so?"

"I do. In fact, if you had any balls—if you really believed in the Wobbly cause—well, you would've already killed my men, burned their bodies, and hid that excrement, Adams, off in these hills."

The sheriff looked away, wiped his nose, and kicked at the wood floor planks. "How do I know you're authorized?"

"Good question. At least now you're acting like a lawman." McParland turned toward the train and said, "Senator? Can you join us?" As Borah stepped out, McParland turned to the sheriff. "My I present the United States Senator for the State of Idaho."

Borah smiled broadly, spreading his arms in a "let's be reasonable" gesture.

The sheriff's eyes widened.

"I'd appreciate your cooperation," Borah said as he approached.

"Yes, Sir," said the sheriff, shaking the senator's extended hand. "It's good to meet you."

McParland raised his eyebrows at the sheriff and gestured toward the shed. "So, let's go. Don't make me bring President Roosevelt off that train."

The sheriff's eyes widened again toward the passenger car's door, before he realized McParland wasn't serious. He looked at his deputies. "Go get em." After they left, the sheriff turned back and saw McParland's bushy mustache raised over a haughty smile.

McParland turned and began surveying the mountains around them. As he did, he softly sang:

Red is the rose by yonder garden grows.
And fair is the lily of the valley.
Clear is the water that flows from the Boyne.
But my love is fairer than any.

The sheriff continued watching McParland and Borah. The only sounds, besides McParland's quiet lyrics, came from the engine's steam, a few men clearing their throats, adjusting their rifles, and a chorus of mating calls from the valley's bird populace.

"Nice little town you have here," said Borah.

"Thank you, Senator. I hope you'll return sometime. The missus would like to meet you also."

"Your wife? Well, in that case, perhaps I will."

The sheriff frowned and McParland grinned at Borah.

Footsteps and the shuffle of chains, then Iain and his shotgun appeared through the door and onto the platform. His face bore a black eye. Behind him came Steve Adams, bound at the wrists and wearing a walking chain between his ankles. Then came Jack and his rifle. Other Pinkertons escorted Adams onto the train. McParland grinned at Iain and Jack, slapping them on the back. "Thank you, gentlemen. I'm mightily impressed. Well done."

"Thank you, Sir," said Jack, boarding the train, noting that McParland appeared ill. Behind him, Iain pivoted, walked up to the sheriff and hit him square in the face, sending the man onto his back with a broken nose.

As Iain got on the train, Jack nodded at him. Then Jack spoke to McParland. "Sombitch deserved it."

"No doubt," chuckled McParland, sitting on a bench across from Jack. "Are you well?"

"I am, Chief."

"Good. I was worried." McParland pulled a handkerchief and blew his nose.

"How are you?" asked Jack.

"Good. Good. Just got a little bug."

Iain started to sit beside Jack, but McParland stopped him. "Agent Lennox, could you give Agent Garrett and me a minute?"

"Yes, Sir," said Iain before moving to a further bench.

McParland leaned toward Jack. "When we get to Boise ... I don't want anyone knowing you're in town, not for a few days. So, you and Agent Lennox find a boarding house in Caldwell or someplace, till I give word."

"May I ask why?"

"If you're in Boise, people will ask questions. It's well known you went to get Adams. So, if they see you, they'll figure he's in the pen. Federation boys will be chomping to kill him. Of course we'll have him protected, but all the same. So, let's delay word getting out until I get his written confession." He saw Jack's disappointment. "Just a few days, Romeo. Then you can go see Miss Capone—and resume what we discussed before you left."

Jack nodded, unable to hide a smile.

"Agent Lennox," McParland said loudly. "Come back. We have a train ride ahead and I want to hear you-two's stories. But sit on that other side, by Jack. Don't want either of you catching this."

★

– 50 –

SATURDAY
March 30, 1907

Darrow sat on a crushed-velvet couch in the middle of the Saratoga Hotel lobby. It had been raining most of the day and into the evening, the chill cutting through him. He hoped he was not getting ill, but his clammy forehead and palms said otherwise. Some flu had been going around Boise, and he hoped he wasn't next. He let his gaze drift to the empty couch facing him. His usually well-combed hair was mussed forward. His hat was beside him. He groaned. They had Adams—damnit to hell. Word had come from a union-loyal guard out at the penitentiary. Apparently, in the dead of Thursday night, McParland had secreted Adams into a solitary cell somewhere on the pen's grounds. If only he had the Pinkertons working for him, not that damn Captain Swain. Just then, two slender hands and their bare wrists slid across his shoulders and onto his shirt, slipping down his chest. He crooked a half smile, taking one of the warm hands into his, and breathed deep, inhaling the perfumed air.

"Don't worry, Counselor," Winnie whispered closely. She slumped over the back of the couch, draping his right shoulder, her golden Medusa curls about his ear.

He closed his eyes as her breath tickled him. "My dear, you're balm to the soul." He kissed her hand. "Have you seen Bill?"

She came around the couch and plopped beside him. "I have."

As she leaned into him, he noticed the bodice of her pink-lavender dress was loose, the lace insert missing, her firm breasts barely covered. "Did you tell him?" he asked.

"Yes," and then a sigh. "They gave us privacy. I, uhmm ... Well, I pleased him, hoping it would help."

"But it didn't."

"No."

"He has reason to be worried."

Winnie pulled back with a glare. "You can't say that."

"I'm sorry, dear. I—"

"You must find a way."

"I'm working on it."

"You'll win this for Bill, the union, and the workers' struggle."

"Yeah ... maybe not for all that. But I'm here for Bill. I see you've taken to reading *The People*."

"Yes. I joined the Socialist Party. You should too."

"My dear, I'm quite familiar with it, but it isn't right for me. But my wife, on the other hand, she's a comrade like you."

"I'd like to meet her. Will she be coming?"

Darrow glanced at her. "I believe so."

"Good." Her expression darkened. "What will you do now?"

Darrow looked at this vixen. This young woman. Her sexuality, her smell, the way she moved, presenting herself as available for all carnal pleasures, for ravishing. She was intoxicating. Ruby would find her irresistible. He scolded himself for dropping his guard. There was only one mistress he afforded himself: Lady Justice. It was a ludicrous adage, he knew. In fact, it was embarrassingly silly, so he never said it aloud. But he believed it all the same—had it pasted to the inside of his forehead. There it helped him put his mind right in times of need. As in this instance: Winnie asking about his plans. No, he wouldn't reveal them. Not to her, not to anyone. But, since Haywood's attitude lifted and fell on the crest of her tide, Darrow needed her to remain optimistic. "We have two significant things in our favor. First, the Supreme Court agreed to an expedited ruling on my petition for his release, because of the kidnapping. And I have high confidence they will—"

"You're going to Washington?"

"No," said Darrow. "They're only accepting written briefs on this." It was a frustrating fact—bitter in his foul-mood stew. This case would not be the one to give him his first argument before the Supreme Court. Perhaps that was why he was feeling so ill.

"Did they say when?"

"A month maybe. Judge Wood will push us to trial now that Adams is here. We'll pick a jury in two or three weeks."

"That soon?"

He nodded. "I'll need your help. And Miss Capone's. She's recruited another Pinkerton?"

"Yes. And fallen in love with him."

"That's good."

"Maybe. What's the second thing? You said—"

"Yes, the second reason for hope— Well, it's not entirely certain that the mad dog, Adams, will testify against Bill."

Winnie pulled herself close and whispered, "Maybe he'll not live that long. He *is* a murderer, after all."

As her breasts were pressed against his arm and shoulder, and her breath was in his ear, it took a moment before he could say, "No, dear."

She pulled away. "Bill said once, 'where there's a will, there's a kill.' So...you never know."

Darrow shook his head. "I'll go see Adams tomorrow, if the judge allows me." He saw her eyes brighten. "Maybe I can convince him of what's in his best interest—for after the trial."

"Meaning, what might happen to him?"

"We'll see," he said, scolding himself for having revealed even that much of his plan.

★

– 51 –

SUNDAY
March 31, 1907

It was still raining as Jack entered the Idaho State Penitentiary through a small, rear gate guarded by four Pinkertons—one of whom gave him a lantern. He then went into the walled compound, using the lantern to pick a path through the mud. He walked past the building holding the death-row inmates (including Harry Orchard, still in his burned cell), across the execution yard, past two other cell blocks, to a small structure tucked in the far corner—a building called Siberia. There, the most troublesome prisoners were sent, put in tiny, isolated cells where their in-prison offenses could be punished though the deprivation of light, exercise, talking, and sometimes food, or even water. There too the instruments of persuasion were brought to bear: whips, pipes, ceiling mounts for hanging inmates by their feet for hours at a stretch. Siberia was a place for wrestling with sins—those of the wayward prisoners and of the guards alike.

As Jack stepped inside the building, he heard a sickening gurgling and thrashing noise, followed by the sound of a metal bucket clattering to the floor. Tracking the sounds, he entered a back room where his lantern joined the lights of several others, all illuminating Steve Adams who was tied to a table, a cloth over his drenched face, coughing water up through the fabric. Two men whom Jack didn't recognize stood next to Adams's head. McParland, standing to one side in his shirt sleeves, directed the proceedings. He looked at Jack and asked, "What did you find out?"

Jack approached, glancing at Adams.

"He'll be all right," said McParland, still looking peaked. "He got thirsty while deciding to sign a confession."

"I met with Senator Borah," said Jack. "He said the judge won't let Darrow talk to him." He motioned toward Adams.

"Mmph," McParland grunted, pleased. He stepped over and jerked the soaked cloth from Adams's face. "You hear that, Stevie?"

Adams's bloodshot eyes glared up at the detective.

"The good judge is worried about your health," McParland said. "He's not going to let Bill's men get to you. Not even the attorney. Doesn't want anyone hurting you."

Adams coughed at Jack, recognizing him. "You're a dead—"

McParland slapped Adams lightly on the forehead. "None of that. Behave yourself. I know you're scared of him, but—"

"Ain't scared of nobody," sputtered Adams.

"Well, you should be. I'd be. He might jam another cactus up your skinny arse." McParland looked again at Jack. "We're about done. By morning, he'll either sign or be dead." He gave Jack a wink. "Besides, I hear word's already out that he's here. So, unless you hear from me otherwise, you can go back to the Idanha tomorrow around noon. And go see Miss Capone."

"Aye ... Chief," muttered Jack. He was still stunned by the scene, wary of its meaning, bothered by McParland seeming to enjoy the dark doings there.

McParland gestured for him to leave, and as Jack walked out of Siberia, he heard the detective saying, "Harry Orchard already told us these things. So it's your turn, Stevie. Then we'll all go home."

★

– 52 –

MONDAY
April 1, 1907

Mid-afternoon of the next day, the first of April, the Idanha Hotel's restaurant stood almost empty, even with all the bustle and tension of late. During that gap between the lunch horde and the dinner gathering, only two cooks and a waitress were on duty. Today, Carla was that waitress, and she busied herself by preparing dinner-service napkins. Each setting required a charger plate capped by a cloth napkin—white linen with piping the same shade of blue as her uniform—folded into a precise *fleur-de-lis* held in place with a shiny brass ring. The large room was quiet, save for the distant sound of people talking in the lobby, automobile engines outside, the occasional dings from the elevator, and small sounds from her only diners: an elderly couple at table sixteen.

As she made her way around the seventy-five tables on the main floor, folding each napkin, sliding on the rings, she came upon a round, six-top that she'd already done, but at which all of the brass rings were missing. Without their rings, each napkin had expanded its folds, losing its flower shape. She looked around. No one was there but her and the couple at the faraway table. She sighed, pulled six brass rings from her apron and proceeded to fix the settings, making her way around the table. As she returned to where she'd begun, she felt the presence of someone else and looked up. Across the table was Jack, wearing his flat black hat, holding his hands up, fingers spread, each bearing a brass napkin ring. And between his hands: his striking face and broad grin.

"Jack!" she exclaimed, beaming. "You're a scoundrel. Do you know that?"

He came to her, hands still raised. "Yes, Miss Capone, I do."

She held open her apron pocket and he turned his hands, letting the rings fall into it, and then stepped back. They stood a few feet from each other, eyes swimming in the other's mind. She cocked her head. "You didn't write."

"I couldn't. But I thought about you."

"Did you?" Her lips pursed between blushing dimples.

"Mn-huh," he hummed

"I heard you were in town, but you didn't come."

He sighed. "I wasn't allowed, until now."

"Is that true?"

"It is. Can't be too careful."

"Can't you?"

His grin widened then faded. "I knew what you were doing."

"Oh yeah?" She moved some stray hairs behind her ear.

"Recruiting me to spy for the Federation," he said.

"You wanted me to."

He paused, and then chuckled at her knowing that.

She continued, "Once Pink, always Pink."

"I'll need us to keep it up."

She eased back, leaning against a table. "I imagine we can."

"For our bosses to think so."

"I don't mind," she said. "Use me ... if needs must."

He smirked, stepping forward. "Needs must."

"The Federation thinks I'm still with them," she began. "But ... I'm loyal to myself now. To what I choose. To whom I choose."

"To whom— That right?"

"Yeah," she breathed. "There's a fella."

"There always is."

"He's got blue eyes like a sled dog."

"Oh— So he's handsome."

"He wears a weird hat."

Jack laughed. "Nooo."

"He's been gone a month, but he didn't write me, so—"

"Bastard."

"And now he's just standing there."

He grabbed her, embracing her, kissing her deeply.

It wasn't till Darrow's face was fluffed white with lather that he noticed the gunhands. He figured he was being tracked, but he hadn't—not until that moment—spotted the men set to the task. But there they were, in the mirror behind the fat barber, across Boise's Main Street, loitering, watching the barbershop a bit too long. He'd seen them before, but previously gave them no mind—just two more men with gunslinger strides: gun hand held close to their body. The town was thick with their sort. He lifted his chin to give the barber access to his neck.

For weeks, news of the pending murder trial of America's most powerful and deadly union leader had filled newspapers and imaginations from coast to coast, even as far as London and Moscow. And, as a lion-kill draws hyenas, the showdown in Boise was a magnet for a certain type of human male—the violence opportunist. Such a man didn't come bearing some ideological flag. Rather he was a loner, a cowhand, a failed outlaw, a nomad. Not the sort to draw affinity with either organized labor or the monied class. He wanted in the new century what he'd missed in the last: the adrenaline rush of possible death. Or at least a story his grandchildren might repeat. He hadn't seen battle—hadn't participated in the Civil, Indian, or the Spanish-American War. But now, maybe he could finally attain what he saw as the ultimate masculine insignia: to have risked his life for a righteous cause. Better still, to have killed a man righteously, no matter the cause. So, each of that sort packed his best gun and trickled into Boise, one by one. Within hours of arriving, each had signed his allegiance at either the House of Idanha or the House of Saratoga, in trade for room, board, and a chance at glory. Darrow figured a few signed on at both hotels. Perhaps more than a few.

The shave complete, the barber turned his attention to Darrow's hair. Usually the haircut would come first, but Darrow preferred the other order.

He was primarily concerned about a small subset of those transient excitement-seekers. All who came hoping for action—the risk of death, the opportunity to kill—would be going home disappointed, the cold truth having revealed itself: Though judicial procedures thrive on animus, they are contra-designed for the spilling of blood. Some of those men would be angry, feeling cheated by fate, convinced they'd been abandoned by the gods of both man and war. And perhaps one of them, seeking to rectify that cosmic unfairness, wanting to take his due before he left, might spark the keg himself, self-fulfilling his opportunity for violence.

Of course, it could also be sparked by a rank-and-file Pinkerton or Federation man. Among those two groups, which one would more likely produce a radical desperado? The more Darrow thought about it, the less he could decide. Both the owners and the unionists carried a nature of banded honor, seeded with insecurities, exercised as vigilantism. Both justified killing as the consequence of the necessary. Both defied what they deemed to be corrupt government. Both judged the judicial system to be unjust. And both fought either capitalists or socialists whom they perceived to be a threat to their individualism, to their mythological freedoms as Americans.

He let the big man brush the hair from his body and accepted a splash of aftershave. When the barber asked the famous lawyer to accept the services free of charge, Darrow thanked him, but paid.

Walking back to the Saratoga, feeling the breeze tingle his smooth jaw and the back of his neck, Darrow noted that the two Pinkertons—or mercenary gunhands in the employ of the Pinkertons—were still following him. He needed more men of his own—a man or two to follow McParland, one for Borah, some tasked to identify spies and to help investigate potential jurors. And, he conceded, he needed a guard for his own protection. He had already assigned the ten George brought, mostly for clerical tasks. So, he would get his spies from Captain Swain.

Captain Swain had slunk back into Boise the day before, tail between his legs, but brazen enough to seek payment for his failed efforts. From his cell, Haywood had fumed, shouting demands for Swain to be refused, if not worse. The goddamned audacity of the flea-bit maggot. After all, not only was Steve Adams still breathing; Adams was out at the pen under Pinkerton control, probably signing a confession at that very moment!

Nevertheless, George paid Swain. He and Darrow had discussed it, and made the decision themselves. The way they saw it, Swain had tried. He was one man bested by a team of Pinkertons. And privately, they were relieved Adams was still alive. What would the alternative have made Darrow and George, but accomplices of sorts? And, to cap off their decision, they'd learned that, on his way back, Swain had stopped in Salt Lake City to bury his mother. He might be a dull knife, but he was their dull knife—the only one they had. They needed him to stay, to fight on with them. So they paid him, and said nothing more about it.

Before Darrow could reach his make-shift office in the Saratoga, he saw Swain in the hall, hat in hand, talking somberly with Winnie. Seeing the attorney, Swain looked up and withdrew a folded piece of paper from his pocket.

Darrow saw it and stopped six feet away. "I'll be damned."

Swain nodded, and Winnie sighed loudly.

"To be expected," said Darrow, coming closer to take the paper. He unfolded it and read the title aloud: *"The Confession of Steven Adams."* He glanced up and then back at the paper. "Does he say—" He read silently, biting his bottom lip, then read aloud again. *"Mr. Haywood told me that if I didn't think Harry Orchard could kill the governor, that I was to do it. After, I was to then kill Orchard."* He shook his head. "Damn. And Judge Wood won't let me talk to this man. Not even across a room." He regarded Winnie, noting tears in her eyes. He wanted to tell her something positive, but nothing came to mind.

"The Supreme Court might still release him?" asked Swain.

Darrow shook his head. "Hell, at this rate, they'll not only deny my writ, they'll convict him while they're at it." He started to go inside, but then looked at Winnie. "Are you joining us?"

"No, I'm due to meet with ... my friend."

Darrow glanced at Swain and then back to Winnie. "Captain Swain needs to know about Miss Capone."

"Ok," she said.

Darrow turned to Swain. "The friend she's referring to is a young woman named Carla Capone. Carla used to be my secretary, for a short spell. Now she's made some inroads with McParland's operation. But I'm fairly sure McParland's onto her. He must know she killed their man Farrington, a spy for us. Winnie can give you the details, or you can get them from Carla directly."

"Carla has a new Pink," added Winnie, her tone subdued.

"Yes," said Darrow. "Agent Jack Garrett."

"Him?" Swain shook his head. "PJG. Pinkerton Jack Garrett. That sneaky son of a bitch is—"

"He got lucky," said Darrow. "Meanwhile, we live to fight another day. Speaking of that ..." He turned to Winnie. "Tell Carla I want to talk with Jack. Tomorrow. Someplace away from here."

"With the Pinkerton agent?" asked Winnie.

"Yes. Thank you, dear." Once Winnie was gone, Darrow entered his office with Swain close behind. Inside, he saw eight men sitting in chairs at the end of the room. "Are these them?"

"Yes," said Swain.

Darrow hung his hat and coat before addressing the men. "Gentlemen, I'm Clarence Darrow, Mr. Haywood's attorney. I understand Captain Swain has hired you to help us."

A smattering of agreement.

"First, let me ask you," Darrow said, "how many of you are current members of the Western Federation of Miners?" When none raised their hand, Darrow continued. "Good. I obviously have great admiration for the Federation ..." He sat on the edge of a table. "But this matter stirs the hearts of Federation men. I need men without personal vendettas or agendas. Without a cause of their own, if you understand. All right, clearly you've sworn to secrecy on your honor as gentlemen regarding anything you see or hear while working for us?"

Again, agreements all around.

"Good. Take no offense if information given you is limited, and if many of your questions go unanswered. This town is a leaky sieve, so I share only what I must with whom I must. But that doesn't apply in reverse. Any and all information you gather, from any source—about the Pinkertons, Detective McParland specifically, anything regarding Senator Borah, Judge Wood, or any of the members of the jury pool, or anyone who visits or otherwise communicates with any of those people—should be reported quickly to Captain Swain. He'll then communicate with me. Do what you can, but by no means—and I need you to all hear me clearly—by no means are you authorized to directly or indirectly act in a manner that is illegal, or which might be reasonably construed as illegal. Do you understand me on this?"

A chorus of "Yes, Sirs."

"Actually, I want confirmation from each of you individually." Darrow pointed at each man, getting a "yes" or "agreed" from each in turn. He then continued, "If you break this agreement, I'll see you charged with the offense. If this is not clearly and fully understood and agreed to, then you should take your leave now."

Silence. No movement.

"You'll be paid—handsomely. Money enough to keep you in bullets and boots, anyhow." Darrow received a nod from Captain Swain. "Alright— We need our people protected, theirs tracked, and we need to know who's following whom. We can't avoid them if we don't know who they are. To begin, McParland's men heeled me here from the barbershop just now, and I imagine they're out there in the lobby. So, I need one of you assigned to me. And I'm sure there are Pinks on George Pennington. He's the acting president of the Federation while Mr. Haywood is ... detained. Mr. Pennington is in Boise for the duration, but he has a very large union to run. So, he won't be directly involved in what we're doing. Nevertheless, we need a man guarding him. After all, he pays our wages."

Murmurs all around.

"And they're probably following Winnie Minor. She's ... she's also working for us. Well, Captain Swain will assign you out and give you further details. Any questions?"

No one spoke.

"Alright gentlemen, get to it."

★

– 53 –

TUESDAY
April 2, 1907

McParland and Borah both stood from their dinner table in the Idanha. Due to the limitations of their guest, they weren't at their usual place on the mezzanine, but were on the main floor near the back. They watched as a guard rolled Neva to them. Borah pulled a chair, making a space for her.

"Good evening, Mrs. Haywood," said McParland.

"Good evening, Detective," she replied, noting the sharp contrast in the level of wrinkles in the two men's suits.

"May I introduce Senator Borah," said McParland.

"My pleasure," said Borah.

"Yes, mine as well," she said, then added, "Could you keep that chair? Just help me into it?"

"Yes, Ma'am. Of course," said Borah. Due to the pleats of her dress, it took a few tries for him to get his hands under her knees.

"Don't be shy, Senator," she said wryly. She could have done it on her own, using her right leg and a steady arm, but the square-jawed man with the warm hands didn't need to know that. Besides, she liked starting this meeting with the senator serving her.

Borah managed her into the chair, then scooted it to the table. "All good?"

"Yes. All good. Thank you."

"Thank you for coming, Mrs. Haywood," began McParland, taking his seat.

"This must be a difficult time for you," said Borah, also sitting. "But please know, we're duty bound to proceed in accord with the law." Seeing her green eyes narrow at him, he stopped.

"Senator. Detective," she said, "thank you for agreeing to meet with me. But I'm not here to plead for my husband."

The men blinked, sniffed, adjusted their napkins.

"You're surprised?" she asked.

Borah bobbed his head. "We're aware there's discord between you and your husband, what with ..." His voice trailed off.

"My sister?"

"Perhaps ... yes," said Borah softly. "And with the Federation, regarding some financial irregularities."

She shook her head. "My reasons are my own."

McParland leaned forward. "You don't agree, Mrs. Haywood? That your husband has embezzled a large—"

"What difference is it to you?" she shot back. "If you're successful in this trial, then—that matter will be resolved. If you're not, then the Federation will square things with Bill. Surely you know, they'll never allow you to scrutinize union books."

"Perhaps not," began McParland. "But our bank clients will—"

She lifted a gloved hand. "The money issue has nothing to do with this awful thing with the governor."

"You're right, it doesn't," said Borah. "But some banks have been holding union deposits, and if there *are* irregularities, they'll look to the union. Specifically to the affairs of its treasurer."

"How dare you! George's *affairs?*" She glared at Borah. "His affairs, Senator? I was hoping to like you." She glanced at her menu then back at him "You mean George's relationship with me?"

"My goodness, no," he protested. "Not at all."

"Oh, I see." She shook her head. "So, we *won't* be speaking our minds directly. Personal matters being what they are: *personal.*" She absently studied her menu, then was back at Borah. "The temerity to question *my* relationships. *You*, Senator? I read the papers."

"My apologies," began Borah, visibly shaken. "I concur. That's uhmm ... That would be for the best, for all involved."

Neva could taste her own disgust. Her tolerance was gone for this sort, these hypocrites, these powerfully weak men—the likes of her husband and this senator. As the bile bubbled up, it dissolved her guilt, her shame, her acceptance—even for having enjoyed the senator lifting her. She leveled on him. "While we are *not* discussing the unspeakable, I'll say this: I expect my sister will attempt to ... to be with you. And you her, I'm sure. So I'll tell you now: I won't have it. You'll both be using each other, perverting everything to the embarrassment of us all."

Borah bristled. “Ma’am, I’ve never met your sister, and I’ve no intention of doing so.”

“I’m warning you,” Neva said, taking a breath. “I’ll go directly to the press. I love my sister, but I’ll do what I must. This whole thing is a moral travesty, and that would only make it worse.”

“I agree,” Borah replied flatly.

McParland said nothing.

She stared at Borah another moment, then took up her menu.

In the cold silence, McParland cleared his throat and asked, “Shall we order?”

“No,” Neva blurted, setting the menu aside, her face reddening further. “I’m afraid I’ve made a mistake. I came here to talk about my husband, but—” She looked at Borah, willing herself not to cry. “George is a dear friend. That’s all. And that’s more than you deserve to know.”

Borah saw her wet eyes and softened. “You have my apologies, Mrs. Haywood, if it seemed—”

“And mine as well,” said McParland. “This is an awkward, uncomfortable situation. Especially for you, Ma’am, I’m sure.” He adjusted his glasses, counting to four. “Might we begin anew?”

Neva took a drink of water and dabbed her napkin to her lips. Once she’d gathered her thoughts and settled her heart, she glanced about the dining room, reassuring herself that no one else could hear. (Though she saw a waitress watching their table, Neva didn’t know Carla to recognize her.) Finally, she addressed McParland. “All right. As you know, Mr. Darrow would like me to testify on my husband’s behalf. Apparently, I might be persuasive to the jury. I’m to speak of his generosity to the miners and their families, and such.”

“I wouldn’t worry,” Borah tried. “It’s common for a wife—”

“But you aren’t going to do that,” McParland interrupted, his gray eyes fixed on her.

“No,” she said, tilting a nod to the detective’s intuitive skills.

“For your private reasons,” said Borah.

“Yes, but allow me to clarify,” she said. “I *might* not testify for him ... were my personal concerns assuaged.”

Borah bounced a glance at the detective, then back at Neva. “I think I understand,” he said slowly. “Please tell me if I’m wrong, but ... what if I could assure you that, regardless of the outcome of this case, there'll be no inquiry into or against Mr. Pennington? Not on this matter, nor on any union money concerns."

Neva's eyes brightened ever so slightly. "Well, Senator, of course I don't speak for Mr. Pennington."

"No, of course not."

"But," she continued, "were you to insist, then I would accept that guarantee on his behalf."

"Good," said Borah, "Then I insist."

Neva continued. "And all monies previously donated to Walla Walla College?"

"No inquiries," said Borah.

"You can give that assurance?"

"Yes, Ma'am, I can."

She looked at McParland. "And if the banks instruct the Pinkertons to harass the college? Or to come after George? Will you be kidnapping him as well?"

McParland winced. "You're a smart woman, Mrs. Haywood. You know I can't speak for Robert Pinkerton. So any assurances I gave you would— Well, I just won't give you any. But, the United States Senator here has that power. And he has the ear of the president. So, if he says George won't be implicated, and your donations will remain in place, then that's how it'll be."

Neva relaxed. "Then, I'll put my faith in you, Senator Borah— and your word as the gentleman I'll choose to believe you are ... that you can be. I'll not give any testimony." She lifted her menu. "Let's eat, shall we? What's the specialty here at the Idanha?"

"He's over there?" Darrow asked, walking on the shore of the swollen Boise River, about a mile from the center of the town. Captain Swain's lantern swayed in the dark, alternating their path between the visible and the unseen.

"Crossing is here," said Swain, indicating a rope-drawn ferry.

Darrow frowned at the flowing water. "When I said far from town, I didn't mean this."

"I don't know what to tell you," said Swain, "except he's over there." He motioned to the far side of the river. "No one will see who you're talking with, that's for sure."

Darrow stepped onto the platform. "If I don't drown first."

Twenty feet away, deep in the impenetrable blackness, Iain huddled close to the ground, crouching his big frame within a wooded declivity, listening, watching the faintly illuminated men.

"Take a seat there," said Swain, handing the lantern to Darrow. He then murmured, "I must say, I don't trust Garrett."

Darrow matched Swain's whisper. "I'm not sure I do either."

"He might be an imposter—not really a double. McParland does that. He ran me as such, once."

"He's a sly one. You'll wait here?"

Swain nodded and, staying on the near shore, began pulling the rope hand over hand. The pulleys squeaked, the platform moved, and Darrow and his lamp eased into the darkness, cross-cutting the cold rush of snowmelt water.

When he reached the other side, he stepped onto the ground and waved the lantern to signal Swain. The creaking stopped. He listened, and then inquired of the dark, "Mr. Garrett?"

"Mr. Darrow," came Jack's voice. "Up here."

Darrow lifted the lantern and began up the incline. At the top, he shook Jack's hand. "I appreciate you meeting me."

"The pleasure is mine," said Jack. "It's an honor." He motioned into a stand of woods. Once there, they sat on downed trunks. "I realize you don't trust my intentions."

Darrow chuckled. "That's about the sum of it." Darrow knew that whether or not Jack was a true double agent, Jack would still need to take something back to McParland. Thus, Darrow planned a series of innocuous revelations—to say things that sounded secret, but were of little consequence. A breaking twig gave Darrow a start. "Who's—"

"Mr. Darrow," said Carla, approaching.

During the prior night, much had become clear for Carla and Jack. In the hazy afterglow of their shared passions, they had talked for hours, exploring the common threads of their entanglement. In the end, they affirmed a pact founded on a shared opinion: Haywood was a pig and most likely a murderer, so to hell with him. She would help Jack do what he must for the Pinkertons and the prosecution, but only just. Nothing to harm the Federation as a whole. Perhaps it was contrition, an act of expiation for her cumulative surrenders: allowing herself to be Haywood's pawn with Orchard, for giving her body to Wade, for killing him. She shuddered off such inviable self-examinations. She would simply do what she could to help Jack. The rest must remain where it was and what it was. So, when Winnie came to her seeking this clandestine meeting between Jack and Mr. Darrow, Carla agreed but affected uncertainty in arranging it. And here, in the night-shadowed grove with Darrow, they would pretend a distance existed between them—though she'd cautioned Jack that Darrow might see through it. She had laughed when Jack replied, "Then try not to touch me."

Darrow stood at her approach. "Miss Capone. I hoped you'd be here." She offered her hand, and he helped her find a place to sit. With the lantern on the ground in the middle of them, their faces and hands seemed disembodied specters floating in the dark. "So let's get some things in the open," began Darrow. "You, Mr. Garrett, are Agent Jack Garrett, a six-year Pinkerton man. You have no ties to the Federation. No union family. And you have been, until now, quite loyal to Detective McParland. Am I right so far?"

"Yes."

"And Miss Capone, of course I'm familiar with your connection with the Federation. But to keep things in the open, you've made some efforts to win the trust of Detective McParland by identifying Mr. Orchard. And Carla, if I may, I know you planted the plaster of Paris, at Bill's request, to assure Orchard received the blame—but, my dear, you used the wrong type of plaster."

"I didn't."

"I'm sorry, but you did. McParland knows it. Right, Jack?"

"Yeah, that's right," said Jack.

Darrow nodded toward Carla. "I don't think it changed things any. I did wonder why though, if you were true to the Federation, why you betrayed Mr. Orchard? Why not help him escape?"

"I didn't—"

"I figured it out," Darrow pressed. "Orchard was supposed to be killed before he could be arrested."

"I didn't know that," Carla protested. "Not at the time. Or I wouldn't have—"

"I know, dear," said Darrow. He paused a moment before resuming. "I've met a number of killers. Heard their schemes. This seemed sloppy—to not get Orchard and plant the plaster at that same time. Assuming the plaster was needed at all. Regardless, I don't doubt your loyalty, Carla. But, and you'll have to pardon me, I'm not so confident about the Pinkertons you recruit. Wade Farrington was— Well, I'm sorry it ended as it did."

"I'm still shaken by it," said Carla.

"I imagine you would be. And now you've recruited Mr. Garrett here. The young man who bested Captain Swain." Darrow cleared his throat. "The man who may have hurt our case more than any other. If you wanted to help us, Jack, why didn't you let Swain get Adams?"

"He was going to kill him."

"Yes," mused Darrow. "That he was."

"Besides," Jack continued, "if I hadn't done my best, I wouldn't have the chief's confidence. And I'd be no use to you now." The words of deceit felt mushy in his mouth—the foul taste not hidden by a seasoning of truth.

"So, what use can you be now, to us?"

"Surely, having a man inside their group is helpful," said Carla.

"Maybe," said Darrow. "This case is stacked against us."

"What do you need?" asked Jack.

"Well, of course, for Orchard or Adams to not testify against my client. Failing that, a sympathetic jury."

"Maybe I can help with the jury," said Jack.

Darrow thought for a moment. "I talked with Orchard. He won't change his testimony. But I don't know about Adams. They won't let me see him. Won't let anyone from our side. I'd ask that you talk to him for us, but, as you're the one who brought him in— Well, that obviously isn't going to happen."

"No."

"Do you know anyone Adams trusts? Any family?"

"We heard he had an uncle, but that's all."

"Oh yeah?"

"A man named Lillard. He was supposed to be holed up in the place where we caught Adams—a house, or a building or something, called Stokes Castle, just west of Austin, Nevada. But we didn't see him there. Unless Uncle Lillard was one of the men Adams killed clearing the place. We asked him about it, but he never said."

"Hmmm," murmured Darrow, his mind twitching, making a note to ask Swain about Lillard. "All right," he continued. "Maybe you can help with the jury. Obviously I need men who look favorably on Mr. Haywood. Or at least ones who dislike the Pinkertons."

"I don't know people here, but most don't seem to like us."

Carla addressed Jack. "Could you find out who Senator Borah picks for the jury?"

Darrow gave an emollient smile. "We'll all know who he picks, dear. But you have a good point." He looked at Jack. "If you could tell me who Borah favors, who he wants on the jury and who he doesn't, that'd be helpful."

"I can get that, I think." Jack glanced at Carla. "I can try."

"Good."

"What can I do?" asked Carla.

"Keep your eye on this man," Darrow said, tilting his head toward Jack. Then he eased a smile.

Across the river, Captain Swain sat on a boulder, smoking a cigar, waiting for Darrow to signal him to pull the ferry back. And nearby, Iain was still prone in the dark, watching Swain.

– 54 –

FRIDAY
April 12, 1907

It had been nine months since Sheriff Angus Sutherland, protectorate of Wallace and the Coeur d'Alene Mining District in far-northern Idaho, had the worst day of his life—all on account of two worthless men. Since then, he'd been on a singular mission—to track and kill them. At least one of them. Not arrest. There would be no trial, no rope. The killers began that horrible day by murdering a company man in a Wallace saloon. They ended it, ten miles up the track where they bombed the Bunker Hill Silver Mine and Concentrator, killing twenty-six. But it was the murder between those two events that most haunted Sutherland. Just off the Wallace station platform, just across the tracks, one of the killers slit the throat of Sutherland's son and deputy, Frankie, leaving the boy to die in the grass.

In the interim, Sutherland had learned little. Of course, he knew what everyone knew: the anarchist/socialist/terrorist attacks that day at the Bunker were conducted on behalf of the Western Federation of Miners, and undoubtedly on orders of its leader, Big Bill Haywood. That had led Governor Steunenberg to impose martial law and mass incarcerations across the state, which in turn led to the Federation assassinating the governor. But Sutherland wasn't shotgunning for the whole lot of them—not the Federation or even Haywood. Most of Sutherland's family were union, as were most of the men in his mountainous county, home of the Coeur d'Alene Mining District. In fact, he hated the Pinkertons worse than about anybody—those pretend lawmen with little respect for an actual badge. Regardless, this fury was different, persistent, singularly channeled on one animal—a man named Addis, the one who murdered his son.

Knowing Addis was hired by Federation men, Sheriff Sutherland's search took him south to Denver, into the mouth of the union, and then back up to Cheyenne, and over to Salt

Lake City. But no one knew Addis. At least, no one said they did. Defeated, Sutherland went home. A month later, he buried his wife. She'd been kicked by a horse. Despondent, crushed by failure and loss, he retired his badge and rolled himself into a blanket of whiskey solace.

Then, on the twelfth of April, he read in the Spokane newspaper that a man named Steve Adams had been caught by a pair of Pinkertons and was held in the Idaho State Penitentiary, down in Boise. Reportedly, Adams said he would testify against William Haywood regarding the assassination of Governor Steunenberg. Sutherland took passing interest until one sentence cracked him sober: *Mr. Adams is a suspect in numerous murders and acts of terrorism, including the bombing of the Bunker Hill Silver Mine and Concentrator last year.* "Adams—Addis," Sutherland breathed, then repeated it louder, "Adams—Addis. Addis—Adams." An hour later he reclaimed his badge from the mayor, reloaded his guns, and rode south for Boise.

On Monday, the eighth of April, Judge Wood's clerk released to Darrow and Borah the names of two hundred and forty-nine potential jurors from which twelve would be selected for the trial of William D. Haywood, scheduled to commence in one month, on May 9. Both camps went to work immediately, and similarly. For both, the lists were alphabetized and mapped, and loyal men were assigned to canvas each candidate, to discover all that could be known about each potential juror's church, family, politics, and feelings regarding the case, miners, mine owners, labor unions (specifically the Western Federation of Miners), Governor Steunenberg, and the governor's actions against the Federation. It didn't take long for those two hundred and forty-nine men to know they were targeted, and many started avoiding being approached by anyone. To counter that, Darrow's men often posed as encyclopedia salesmen, and Borah's posed as insurance salesmen. Both groups had their canvassers work in pairs, so they could give matching testimony in court against a potential juror if he expressed an unfavorable, pre-formed opinion about the case.

Borah had the power of the Pinkerton Agency at his disposal—professional and disciplined agents, including the canvassing team of Agents Jack Garrett and Iain Lennox. Plus, Borah knew he had a key, secret advantage: he knew Jack was spying for him from inside the defense's camp.

Darrow had Captain Swain and his ragtag collection of men—not nearly as efficient as the Pinkertons, but they knew Idaho far better than the Pinkertons did. Plus, Darrow thought he had a key, secret advantage: he thought Jack was spying for him from inside the prosecution's camp.

On the third day of canvassing, Jack and Iain rode out to a sheep ranch five miles from Boise, intending to talk with a man on the potential juror list—the ranch foreman, O. V. Sebern. Both were wearing their Pinkerton regimentals. On the way, Jack noticed Iain was not only unusually quiet, but kept pulling his horse into a pace behind Jack, thus eliminating the possibility of a conversation. Finally, Jack had had enough. He pulled his horse to one side and stopped. As Iain passed, eyes forward, Jack asked playfully, "Why so blue? Betty laugh at your wee pecker?" He spurred to come alongside Iain. "That's gotta be humiliating, especially for a big fella like you."

"Go bugger yourself," Iain muttered without a hint of teasing.

The blow landed. "What?" Jack pushed his horse into Iain's.

"You heard me, traitor."

"Traitor?"

"Maybe I should just shoot ya."

"You dumb Scot," chuckled Jack. "What are you talking about?"

Iain stopped his horse. From the shadow of his hat, he leveled a glare at Jack. "Can I trust you?"

"Of course," said Jack.

"Then you need to be straight with me."

"Alright."

"I'm gonna ask you something. You tell me the truth, and we're gonna ride on, good as a daisy. But you lie—" He set his shotgun across his lap.

The air stopped—dried up in an instant. Jack reached under his jacket, drew his pistol, and held it near the pommel of his saddle. "What's your question? It'd better be a good one."

Iain hesitated. "Did you meet secretly with their attorney, that Darrow fellow, and with Captain Swain?"

Jack's eyelids narrowed. "You've asked me a question I can't answer. At least not yes or no."

"Just answer the bloody question!"

"Honestly? Yes and no."

Iain raised the shotgun toward Jack. "That ain't honest."

Jack aimed his pistol. "It actually is. Are you gonna kill me because you don't understand my answer?"

"It can't be yes and no."

"I met with one of them, but not the other."

"Alright, damnit, I mean the lawyer," said Iain.

"Clarence Darrow? Yes, I met with him."

Iain snorted at the vague answer.

"As long as we've got these things pointing at each other," said Jack, "why were you following me? Chief tell you to?"

"No. Told me to follow Swain. He and Darrow were going out to meet someone. Sounded like it might've been you."

"It was." Jack holstered his pistol. "Square?"

"I don't know."

"While you decide, point that scattergun elsewhere."

"Why were you talking to Darrow?"

Jack raised his hand. "As you know, there's some things Chief's told us to keep under our hats—and that's one of em." He spurred his horse to a cantor and yelled back, "If you're still gonna shoot me, you'd better catch up!"

With little else to do in Boise, Neva opened a Haywood account at the city's largest department store, The Golden Rule. Though it couldn't hold a candle to what Denver had to offer, the sisters nevertheless enjoyed themselves there, strolling the aisles for hours.

Being on Main Street and near the Idanha, the store often teamed with Pinkertons. But Neva had lost all care in that regard.

In fact, she barely noticed them. She wasn't sure when it had happened—when the anxiety, the caution, even the hatred for the Pinkertons had dissipated, dissolving from her heart. One day it was there, the next it was gone. Perhaps the deciding moment came in her elevator-pledge to never speak to Bill again. Perhaps it was her arrangement with Senator Borah—the one for George. Or had she begun to soften earlier? Maybe at the opera when George told her about the embezzlement. Was that when the anger began to slide? When Bill began to slide? Or something else? Perhaps it was that day George gave her the crutches. Or when they danced on Christmas Eve. Or when he got his own invalid chair. Was that when had she fallen in love with George?

Her sister had changed too, Neva had noticed. When Neva demanded Winnie avoid any appearance of scandal with Senator Borah, Winnie had seemed generally hurt by the implication. Even more surprising: gone was Winnie's fervent hand-wringing about Bill. In fact, in their last two outings to The Golden Rule, neither Bill nor the trial had been mentioned once. Winnie had shifted passions. She was expanding her young-twenties hauteur to the fullness of the worker's cause, to the Socialist Party and its infamous leader, Eugene Debs. Neva had even heard Winnie use the word "communism," and had seen her with a book called *The Communist Manifesto*. Though Neva didn't see the allure, she understood what it meant: Winnie would be moving on soon, and that would have to be all right. Somehow.

At the Eight Wire Ranch, O. V. Sebern sat on his porch, ready for the jury scouts. "Insurance or 'cyclopedia?" he shouted as they dismounted.

"Neither," Iain replied.

"Mr. Sebern?" asked Jack.

"That's me. So which ball club are you two playing for?"

"The prosecution," said Jack, coming up the porch steps.

"In that case," said Sebern, "you're going to be disappointed."

"Why's that?" asked Iain.

"You boys wanna sit?"

"Sure. Thank you." They sat in chairs on the wide porch. "So, no one's been out to canvas you yet?" asked Jack. "I mean from the defense—the encyclopedia boys?"

"Nope, you're the first. Heard there was a list and that I'm on it. Knew somebody'd be coming. Heard you boys were giving things. Little woman and I need some life insurance and thought we'd look at one of them book sets too."

"I'm sorry, Sir," said Jack. "Some potential jurymen are hiding from being questioned, so some of our sort pretend to be selling things. But not us."

"Well, don't that make me a fool."

"Not at all," said Iain.

Jack leaned forward in his chair. "You said we'd be disappointed in what you have to say. Because we're with the prosecution?"

"Yeah. You're working for Senator Borah. Is that right?"

"Yes, Sir," replied Jack.

"I voted for him. Seems good enough ... for a politician."

"Have you already formed an opinion about this case?"

"You can't use me if I have, right?"

"Maybe not," said Iain.

Sebern put a dab of tobacco in his cheek. "I hate those damned Wobblies, those union boys. And Haywood—I'd string him up from that tree there, if I got half a chance. He's responsible for blowing a bunch of good men to their maker, up in Bunker Hill last year. He and his murdering thugs. No need for a trial. Steunenberg—he was alright for a Democrat. He got one thing right: throwing all those labor lowlife's in jail, and everyone who did business with em. Shouldn't of brought in the blackies to guard em though."

Iain and Jack sat slack-jawed for a moment. Then Jack joked, "So, I take it, Mr. Sebern, you have no opinion on this case?"

Sebern registered a faint smile. "Said you'd be disappointed. I know what I know. That's the Lord's truth. I'm a Christian man, you understand."

Jack bobbed his head. "Of course you are, but—"

"Nothing wrong with *not* sayin everything you know," said Iain. "Maybe keep your sauce box closed." Iain and Jack exchanged a look, acknowledging their squabble on the road there.

"Silence isn't truth, son," said Sebern.

"Truth," Jack repeated. "Does Haywood deserve the truth?"

Sebern took a moment, clearly considering Jack's question, then said, "I suppose you're right. Can't see as how I'd be obligated to be honest with an agent of Satan."

"Amen," said Iain, drawing a frown from Jack.

Jack clapped his hands once and said, "Good. Tomorrow or the next day, two others are going to come see you."

"From Haywood's lawyer?" Sebern spit off the porch..

"That's right," said Iain.

Jack sat straighter. "How about telling them you've been out here tending your sheep, paying no mind to the papers. You've got no opinion on the Federation. You don't know much about mining for that matter. You only want a fair trial for Mr. Haywood. Just like for any man."

"And say 'innocent till proven guilty,'" added Iain.

Sebern smiled and gave a conclusive cluck. "God's work."

"Yes, God's work," said Jack.

★

– 55 –

MONDAY
April 15, 1907

Sheriff Sutherland trotted his horse through the middle of Boise toward the Idanha Hotel. Earlier that day, at the Idaho State Penitentiary, the warden briefed him on the status of things in the strained city: two hotels, two opposing forces, jury selection is underway and no one is trusted. And yes, Steve Adams is there in the penitentiary, but no, Sheriff Sutherland can't see him. By order of Judge Wood, no one gets to see Adams other than family—of which there are none—and other than Chief Detective McParland and the special prosecutor, Senator Borah. Those two can be found at the Idanha Hotel, but don't expect much assistance. Why not? Because they now have two witnesses with two confessions, meaning the accused will hang. So they aren't about to risk losing one of those witnesses. And yes, by "losing" he means one of them getting killed by some over-eager sheriff who rides in with his own ax to grind. Simply put, the sheriff shouldn't get his hopes up.

As Sutherland passed the Saratoga Hotel and approached the Idanha, he noted a team of men on ladders installing additional wires to the telegraph office. Below them, armed men lingered on the front walks, peering at him from under low brims, squinting silent questions: Are you with the State or the Federation? Are you a threat? Are you a spy? He was already anxious to leave.

Dismounting in front of the Idanha, he adjusted the sheriff star on his coat, making it conspicuous, sparking snickers from two Pinkerton guards manning the hotel door. Inside, past further guards, two of whom were Jack and Iain, Sutherland approached the front desk. "I'm Sheriff Sutherland," he declared to the short clerk there. "I'm here to see Detective McParland."

"You're the Wallace sheriff?" said the clerk.

His eyebrows peaked. "The warden said I was coming?"

"Yes, Sir. He telephoned."

"Telephoned ... yes," grumbled the sheriff, giving the device a look that could've knocked a bird from the sky.

"Detective McParland isn't here."

Sutherland growled his displeasure. "Where is he?"

"He isn't here."

"You said that."

"Yes," said the clerk. "I've been told—"

"Mister, my ass is weary from a long ride out of the mountains, all to come down to this piss-hole city to exercise my warrant and collect a man who murdered my son. I'm in no right humor but to get a goddamned straight answer from you."

Iain loomed forward. "The man told ya: the chief isn't here."

Sutherland turned and looked up at Iain, considering him. He then eased back the flap of his coat, revealing his holstered pistol. "My business is none of yours, you big Mick."

Iain clenched his fists. "I'm not Irish, you dumb—"

Jack placed a hand on Iain's shoulder.

"You'd best get," said Iain, though it was unclear who he meant: Sutherland or Jack.

"He's a sheriff," Jack said calmly. "Let him be."

"He's on Pinkerton ground and ought to respect—"

"What's that? Pinkerton ground?" Sutherland surveyed the lobby and scoffed. "Look at you boys, cocking around like you're something. Show me a real badge, any of you. Which of you has sworn for the defense of the public? Any of you police? A marshal or a sheriff? A deputy?" No one responded. "Any of you put your hand on the Bible and made an oath to defend the Constitution?"

"We've all done that," said Jack, slipping in front of Iain.

Sutherland wasn't listening. "A company of ne'er-do-wells. You come into towns like mine, spread lies, get people hurt, and—"

"Let's go," said Jack, taking Sutherland's arm to turn him.

Sutherland slammed a fist against Jack's chest. "Don't touch me, boy!"

Jack recovered his stance, then huffed a sigh. "Tell you what, Sheriff. How about I escort you to Chief Detective McParland?"

Iain spoke lowly. "He said not to—"

"I know," said Jack. He walked toward the door then turned back to Sutherland. "Will you come with me, Sheriff?"

They walked silently for two blocks before stopping in front of a building bearing a faded sign:

MORTON AND SON GUNSMITHING

"Wait here, please," said Jack. He entered the store, causing the door's bell to dingle.

From the front walk, Sutherland could see Jack inside, talking with McParland—the two were standing by a wood counter which held a Winchester rifle with its sights removed. "No, now—" said Sutherland, pushing the door open, making the bell ring again. "Are you McParland?" he asked, moving quickly toward them.

"Sheriff Sutherland," said McParland. "You were told at the penitentiary, and at—"

"Look here," Sutherland said, "I don't give a good goddamn about the lies you told your boys to say."

McParland gave a disingenuous smile. The men were similar in appearance and age. Both barrel chested with big, square, impressive heads. Both fully gray and announced by profuse mustaches below steady eyes. "What can I do for you?" asked McParland.

Jack knew that small-town sheriffs like this one were the type who most annoyed McParland. Like that sheriff in Silver City, Idaho who caught Jack and Iain, along with Adams. Though they were all thrown in jail, the Pinkertons were treated worse—especially Iain who wouldn't stop guessing the physical attributes of the sheriff's wife. Then the BN&O rolled in bearing McParland, Borah, and a small army, and the matter ended without much trouble. But there Jack saw first-hand McParland's bitterness toward these sorts. Like this sheriff, sauntering in from yet another mining town, carrying his inscrutability like a weapon, a cudgel carved from ... What did he say? The murder of his son?

Sutherland closed his eyes and sighed noisily at McParland. "You know who I'm here for."

Jack noticed Iain peering through the gunsmith's window, apparently having followed them.

McParland pointed at the Winchester. "I like a solid repeater like this one. Don't you? Terrific weapon."

"I'm gonna take Addis," groused Sutherland, "and hang him."

"I'm sorry, Sheriff, but you can't have him. As you were told."

"Then I'll wait till you're done with him."

McParland squinted. "He's confessed to aiding in the assassination of the governor, on orders of the accused. Once he repeats that in court, he'll start a life sentence for it. That's the deal he cut with the special prosecutor."

"He needs to answer for what he did up in my town."

"No one's getting near him till he gives that testimony."

"If this isn't some prime chicanery. The way I heard it, he didn't have a direct hand in that bomb here. But he slaughtered my son in cold blood, in broad daylight ... by his own hand." Sutherland's voice cracked.

McParland paused to let the man gather himself, then said, "Fine, Sheriff, try him. Hang him. *After* I'm done with him."

Sutherland shook his head. "Sure as shit, Addis will get his throat cut in prison, or he'll escape. So, no I—"

"You keep calling him Addis," McParland interrupted. "My prisoner is Steve Adams."

"Same fella, goddamnit! And I ain't gonna let him be jailed comfy for something the mine owners probably did themselves, under the protection of the likes of you."

"Sir!" McParland snapped. "I've heard enough! I'm truly sorry for the death of your son. But that man there"—he motioned to Jack—"and that one outside"—he indicated Iain who still had his face to the glass—"tracked Steve Adams across two thousand miles, risking their lives. Damn near lost them. Just to bring that son of a whore back here alive. Now he's confessed—in writing—meaning the end of Mr. Haywood and the outlaw hoodlums of the Federation, the greatest threat to this country since the war. I'll not risk that on your behalf. So, maybe he is 'Addis,' the one who killed your boy—nothing blacker—but he's killed maybe a hundred others, one way or another. In just the last few months, he killed a family in San Francisco, including two young children, a daughter and a son. Poisoned their milk. Then he killed one of my Pinkerton men there—the son of parents in Indiana. Then he killed several other men in Nevada—each a boy of someone. That was until we stopped him. You didn't stop him. Those two men did." McParland paused and scratched the back of his head. "I know that bitter taste in your mouth, Sheriff. But you can't have Steve Adams, or Addis, until he's given his confession in court. Then you can have him and hang him, on behalf of your boy, and the many others he's taken from this world. You don't like that—I don't blame you. But that's the way it is. And you coming down here insulting my men and the Pinkerton organization— Well, you're trying my patience."

Jack was as impressed by McParland's argument as he was by the implacable, almost bemused, expression on the sheriff's face—one of subtle curiosity, giving away nothing.

"Very well, Detective," said Sutherland, extending his hand. "We'll see how it goes."

McParland shook his hand. "Aye, that we will."

After Sutherland left, Jack asked, "Should I follow him?"

"No, he's beaten. Leave him be." McParland picked up the Winchester. "He'll go back north where he's god."

Without any Pinkertons trailing him, Sheriff Sutherland walked unobserved from the gunsmith back to his horse at the Idanha Hotel. Then he rode it two blocks and tied it at the Saratoga Hotel. Inside, he navigated the defense's gunhands. Though these had rougher appearances than the Pinkerton guards—these were unshaven and smelled a bit—they gave companionable greetings, even when he refused to surrender his firearm. One even commented on the pleasant April weather as he showed Sutherland to a chair to await Darrow's return from the courthouse—which occurred forty-five minutes later. Then Sutherland was ushered into Darrow's office, and the door was closed.

After thirty minutes, the door opened, and Darrow asked the first guard he found to fetch Captain Swain. After ten more minutes, Captain Swain entered the office, and the door was again closed.

Inside, Darrow and Sutherland were in the sitting area.

"Captain Swain," Darrow began, "do you know Sheriff Sutherland from Wallace, up near Coeur d'Alene?"

"We've not met, but I know who you are," said Swain, shaking his hand. "I grew up in Spokane. My father traded in Coeur d'Alene and on over to Wallace. Your father was a wheelwright?"

"Yes."

"Captain," began Darrow, "the sheriff has a warrant for Steve Adams. Can you tell him about Adams's uncle?"

"Sure. His name's Lloyd Lillard," said Swain. "I found him passed out where the Pinkertons got Adams—in a odd building out in the middle of Nevada."

"Did Lillard seem fond of his nephew?" asked Darrow.

"Seemed so. Maybe. Why?"

"I'd like us to help the sheriff execute his warrant on Adams, for murdering the sheriff's son."

"Your son?" Swain as Sutherland. "My condolences. That's awful. Truly awful. But Adams is already locked away for the rest of his life."

"Maybe not," said Darrow. "I think we and the sheriff can help each other by getting Adams up to Wallace, after he's done here."

Swain's brow furrowed. "How does that help us?"

"If Adams believes he's to be tried and will likely hang up there, we'll have some leverage."

"How so?"

"Suppose he thinks we'll help him escape on his way to Wallace?" said Darrow. "That is, if he changes his tune here."

"He won't escape though," grumbled Sutherland.

"No, I imagine not," said Swain.

Darrow continued. "So, we need to get that message to him: That he's going next to Wallace, what will happen to him there, and our proposal."

Swain nodded, now understanding. "And Judge Wood will only let family see him."

"That's right. So, what do you think? Might the uncle still be there, where you found him?"

"Maybe," said Swain. He then blew a sigh and shook his head. "Alright, I'll go try to get him. But damn gentlemen, it's a long trek to get there."

★

– 56 –

THURSDAY
April 18, 1907

Jack awoke in the pale light of early day, feeling her touch, but didn't open his eyes. If he stayed put, maybe Carla would continue for a while—her small, warm fingertip, moving along the curve of his chin, over its square end, and up to the crease midway to his bottom lip, where she seemed to measure the fold, and then up to his lip, tracing across it. He hadn't shaved in two days, but she didn't seem to mind. He felt tempted to playfully bite at her finger, to scare her, making her yelp and laugh. But that would end this, so he remained still, trying his best to not reveal himself as awake. She lingered on his bottom lip, feeling its roughness. He sensed her warmth, the smell of her closeness, and then felt her kiss just that lip. She pulled back, her finger resuming its tour, its journey of exploration. On to his left cheek bone and the stubble beneath it. She stopped and moved to the other cheek, and he could feel her comparing each side's hair growth. He heard her whisper, "Hmm," but wasn't sure what to make of it. Maybe she was noticing the area on his left jaw line, about the size of a nickel, where no hair grew. She traced his ears. He hoped they weren't dirty. Then his eyebrows. She smoothed them with the pad of her finger, and then traced his hairline around his forehead before touching the bridge of his nose. Then each eye. She gave a sunny laugh, and he knew she could tell he was awake—his flinch having given him away. He grinned, but kept his eyes closed, lifting his mouth to find hers, feeling her tongue between his lips. When he tried to press back, she murmured, "No," and held his mouth with her fingers, running her tongue along his teeth. He chuckled and opened his eyes.

"You ruined my work," she whispered. "I was seeing how old you were."

"You're checking my teeth, like a horse?"

"Exactly."

He laughed. "I've fallen for a gypsy circus freak."

"Fallen, have you?"

"You missed the gypsy circus freak part."

She slid her body on top of him, straddling him, but keeping her breast against his chest. Feeling himself hard against her, he moaned.

"Back to your teeth," she said.

He snorted a laugh. "I might have bad breath."

"Gypsy freaks don't mind. I like it when you let me do whatever I want to you."

"It'll be my turn next."

"Good."

Thirty minutes later, having made love, she was nestled in his arms, his mouth near her ear. "Will you go to court this morning?" he whispered. "Watch them picking the jury?"

"Must we talk about ..." she began, then added, "Mn-huh."

"Please tell Darrow that the sheep rancher, O. V. Sebern, is union. Died in the wool for Haywood."

"Ok, darling, I'll tell him. Now ... hush."

Late that afternoon, Clarence Darrow walked from the Saratoga, jogged across Main Street, turning on Twelfth Street, and then hurried another half block to the US Post Office where he burst in. "Where is it?"

"Here, Mr. Darrow," said the clerk.

Darrow pushed past two customers, reached across the counter, and grabbed a large, tan envelope that the clerk was holding out for him. After moving to a corner of the lobby, he started to tear into the package, but stopped. It was addressed to him, care of that same post office, from the clerk of the United States Supreme Court, Washington, DC. He ripped it open, removed a sheaf of white papers, and, leaning on his shoulder by a window, began reading. It wasn't long before he closed his eyes and shook his head. "Shit," he muttered. Clutching the papers and envelope in one hand, he used the other to push past people entering. Once back in the sunlight, he walked to the Saratoga where he had the bellman summon a taxi. Darrow instructed the driver, "Courthouse.

Quickly, if you will." In the coach, he read the papers again, this time more carefully, though with no less disgust. In the courthouse, he took the stairs to the third floor and entered the sheriff's office. "I need to see my client," he said. The deputy led him into the inner room containing the jail cell in one corner. "Leave us be," Darrow instructed the deputy.

In the cell, Haywood looked up from his newspaper and considered his attorney who was dragging a chair to just outside the bars. "Clarence," said Haywood. "You don't look happy."

Taking a seat, Darrow drew a deep breath and grimaced.

Haywood saw the papers. "Supreme Court?"

Darrow nodded.

"Well, the sorry sons of bitches. Complete denial?"

"Eight to one."

"Miserable swine. Only one had the balls to uphold the Constitution?"

"That's right."

"What did they say?"

"I'm sorry, Bill."

"Just tell me, what was their reasoning?"

Darrow sighed loudly, flipping the papers. "They upheld the State's arguments. They say: '*the accused*'"— he glanced at Haywood—"'*may not receive asylum in any state from another.*'"

"I wasn't asylumed in Colorado, goddamnit! I live there!" After a pause, he motioned Darrow to continue.

Darrow read silently for a moment, and then said, "Basically, they're saying that once the accused is physically in the jurisdiction of the state where he's been accused of a crime, then he must stay there and stand trial." He read some more. "They say the method by which the accused was brought to that state doesn't matter. Once he's there, he's there."

"That's how they said it?"

"No, I was summarizing. The accused, uhmm ... '*is not excused from answering to the state whose laws he has violated because violence has been done to him in bringing him within the state.*'"

"That's wrong, Clarence. These states, these corporations, with their private armies, with no oversight, no protections for the people they're supposed to serve. They do whatever they goddamned-well please."

Darrow nodded. "Compete violation of the Constitution."

"Bunch of skunks. It's because it's me. That's why."

"Probably."

"And what did that son of a bitch Roosevelt have to say? I bet he's behind this. He and Borah are bastards of the first order."

"To my knowledge, he didn't—"

"Oh, I'm sure he put is bully thumb on the goddamned scales."

Darrow shrugged and looked down.

"What did the one *smart* one say? McKenna, was it?"

"Yes, Justice McKenna dissented." Darrow flipped and scanned. "He wrote, '*Kidnapping is a crime, pure and simple. All of the officers of the state are supposed to be on guard against it. But how is it when the law becomes a kidnapper? When the officers of the law, using its forms and exerting its power, become abductors?*' He's right."

"Goddamned right, he's right. But right won't save my neck."

"It's rough. It sure is."

"Two witnesses ready to testify, and now the Supreme Court is letting the Pinkerton kidnapping stand. Everything you said would never happen. If this isn't being 'sold down the river,' I don't know what is."

Darrow pulled a deep breath, pursed his lips and blew slowly, intentionally, as if to flicker an invisible candle, but not extinguish it. "I have a plan in action that might— Well ... I'll just say, I'm not done, Bill. Not by a mile."

Silence spanned between them until Haywood finally spoke. "Anything good you can tell me?"

"I'm optimistic about the jury."

"Optimistic. I guess that's something," said Haywood.

"You recall the rancher, Mr. Sebern, this afternoon?"

"Yeah—why the hell did you take him?"

"For one thing," murmured Darrow, "we were out of peremptory challenges. But I wanted him anyway."

"Why? He's no friend to us."

Darrow shook his head. "He was just putting on. He *wanted* to get chosen by Borah. Truth is, he's full-bent for labor."

"I doubt that. A rancher? "

"I have it on good word," said Darrow.

Haywood squinted his good eye. "Your spy said Sebern is favorable to us, but Sebern told Borah the opposite? Somebody's double-crossing somebody, either Sebern or your spy."

"If I thought it was my spy, I wouldn't—"

"I've seen men who could deceive the devil himself."

"Me too." Darrow sniffed, looking at Haywood. "But advantage is of no use unless it's seized. Besides, my spy was recruited by one of your people."

"Who?"

"Miss Capone. They're sharing a bed."

"Jesus. Carla Capone? Lucky him."

Darrow stood to leave. "Borah needs all twelve, but we only need one. And Sebern may well be our one. So ... that's something."

Haywood puffed his cheeks and exhaled. "That and a jitney nickel, Clarence. A goddamned jitney nickel."

★

– 57 –

FRIDAY
May 3, 1907

Darrow was in his Saratoga Hotel office, writing and re-writing his opening argument, when Captain Swain knuckle-rapped the door frame and entered.

"You're back," said Darrow.

"I am. We arrived this morning."

"And?"

"Rode the train with me."

"Good. Where is he?"

"The Occidental. No ties to us."

"Good. He knows when to go?"

Swain nodded at his pocket-watch. "Guard's changing at two."

"All right," said Darrow, examining his own watch.

Swain leaned on a chair. "My God, that skinny, deaf man stinks."

"That bad?"

"Death's head on a mop stick. I felt for the people in our car," Swain said, walking to the window. "And he's near deaf entire. Worst train ride I ever took. Trial starts in a week?"

"Yes. Next Thursday. We can't have any surprises. We know where all their people are?"

"Briefed an hour ago. All here. McParland, Borah, all of em."

"You got them off your trail, right? When you went?"

"They followed me to Pendleton, Oregon, then I doubled back, right on down to Ogden. My man who stayed back said they rode that train all the way up to Spokane before they realized I'd vanished." Swain chuckled to himself.

Darrow shook his head. "They're still following me here."

"Yeah. The same two, plus one more now."

"We need a solid plan for when I slip out. It'll have to go even smoother than yours did."

"I've got some ideas—things we learned watching them track me. I'll tell you when it's nailed down." After a beat, Swain asked, "How's Mr. Haywood?"

"Good as expected," said Darrow. "They have two on me?"

"Yes."

"Get him off of me for the afternoon."

"All right. Any particular reason? Are you going to see Lillard?"

"No," Darrow said abruptly. "How many are on you, since you're back?"

"Two."

"And on Miss Minor?" Darrow asked.

"One. Winnie just goes from here to the courthouse to visit him, and otherwise she's with Mrs. Haywood."

"And Mrs. Haywood? They're watching her?"

"I don't think so."

"And Miss Capone?"

"Nobody."

"Nobody?"

"No. They don't have anybody on her."

"Not on Carla Capone? Why not?"

Swain clicked his tongue. "I don't know."

"You don't find that curious?"

"Guess they don't think she's of value anymore."

"How would they know that? Why not track her? They know she's loyal to the union. Hell, she killed one of their men. You don't think that's crooked?"

"Maybe. But they know she's with Jack Garrett, so, maybe they think he's watching her for them?"

"I don't know. He's not always with her." Darrow calculated aloud. "Who do they track? Us, right? Our people. And the jurors."

"That's right."

"And who do they not track?"

"Their own people. And everybody else."

"Exactly," said Darrow.

"But Haywood sent Carla here," tried Swain.

"Yes, but ... if she's actually working for McParland ... then they wouldn't waste a man to follow her."

"I bet it's 'cause she's with Jack."

"I don't know. Feels wrong."

"You can't see wolves in every cupboard."

"No," said Darrow, disquiet fogging the room.

"Tomorrow morning then," said Swain. "Eight o'clock?"

"Yes," replied Darrow.

Swain brightened. "That juror you got while I was gone—Mr. Severeen—heard he'll be our ringer."

"Sebern," Darrow corrected.

"Should I double-check him?"

"Too late for that."

Swain touched his mustache. "Who was your source on him?"

Darrow lifted his eyebrows and gave a slight shake of his head. "Carla. She was told by Jack, her turned-Pinkerton."

"Hmm," murmured Swain.

Darrow sighed. "Sebern's already been selected and sat, and I open in the morning. So, that's that."

"Yeah ... guess that's that," said Captain Swain.

Two hours later, a gaunt man worn by weather, whiskey, and the quest for worth, strolled out the front doors of the Occidental Hotel. He was following a map given him by Clarence Darrow, who had just come to see him, entering and leaving the Occidental by way of the alley.

Wearing a dirt-gray coat torn at the arms, over-sized brown britches, and a twice-crushed bowler, the man now crossed the Ninth Street bridge over the Boise River and strolled to Main Street. There he glanced left at the Idanha Hotel one block up, turned right and walked nine blocks to where Main Street became Warm Springs Avenue. After another mile, he turned left on Penitentiary Road, and a short walk later stopped in front of the heavy prison gate. He found the pedestrian door and entered. Inside, he addressed the pinch-faced guard who didn't look up from the desk. "Come t' see my nephew. Name's Lloyd Lillard."

"Oh, have you?" mocked the guard, still writing in a ledger book. He looked up and paused at the sight of the skeleton before him. "So, Ichabod, who's your nephew?" When Lillard cupped his ear, the guard repeated louder, "Your nephew—what's his name?"

"Steve Adams."

The guard flagged a palm. "No, that fella ain't allowed visitors."

"I's the only family he got."

"He has family? Wouldn't have figured. 'Cept, the resemblance. But, it don't matter no how—no visitors. Alive or dead ones."

Lillard missed the insult, his ears having been damaged decades prior in a tunneling blast. "Fella give me this from the judge," he said, presenting a paper.

The guard unfolded and read it, considered Lillard, looked at the clock, and then back to Lillard. "I gotta telephone the judge."

"How's that?"

The guard pantomimed using a telephone. "The judge."

"What's that?" asked Lillard, pointing at the guard's gesture.

"A telephone. Never you mind." The guard shook his head then shouted to be heard: "I'll talk to the judge!"

"Ain't stoppin you, is I?"

"Telephone's in the warden's office," the guard mumbled to himself, standing. He then left with the note. Lillard couldn't hear the phone chatter in the next room. The guard returned and again spoke loudly. "You'll need to be searched, Mr. Lillard. Can't take nothing in. And you can't touch him. Just talk."

Lillard frowned and nodded.

The guard sighed, unsure if he'd been heard. "Ok, let's go."

★

– 58 –

THURSDAY
May 9, 1907

When the case of the State of Idaho versus William D. Haywood began, on May 9, 1907, Boise was a city on silent edge, as if holding its collective breath. There had always been threats of violence upon both camps. The Idanha Hotel had received nine bomb threats over the prior five months; the Saratoga, twenty-two. But since the jury had been selected, new rumors abounded: planned assassinations of Orchard or Adams—or both. Supposedly, riflemen were on the roofs, aiming for Haywood's attorney, Clarence Darrow, or at the special prosecutor, Senator Borah—or both. And some said hidden bombs were planted beneath the floorboards, set to kill Judge Wood or Haywood—or both.

The courthouse lawn played host to the chaos—a flurry of anxious humanity. The bulk were the curious and general intriguers. There were also hundreds of union men, including many with their wives and children, standing in solidarity with Haywood, the man who had stood with them in their darkest days and coldest nights. Further out, at the edges, stood the civilized and moneyed, including mine owners and their representatives. Though privately they were rooting for revenge, payback for Haywood's damage to their body corporate, collectively and publicly they feigned to be inconvenienced by the whole affair, as if trying Haywood was a nuisance, judicial resources being best spent elsewhere. Why not just hang the man and be done with it? At least Senator Borah was one of them, so watching him eviscerate the cyclops scoundrel would be entertaining. They had that.

Also present were over fifty leading reporters, the vast majority being men with press badges in the bands of their bowlers or homburgs, each representing either a newswire (including Associated Press and Reuters), or a major city daily, or a magazine. Eight new telegraph wires had been erected for just this event, running from the Western Union offices on Main Street to the makeshift press room on the second floor of the courthouse. That morning, those lines were humming with phrases such as: *"The eyes of the civilized world are on these great proceedings."—"A most determined struggle between labor unions and capital."—"One of the great court cases in the annals of the American judiciary."—"Destined to be the greatest trial of modern time."*

Inside, the halls were not as crowded as the outside masses would seem to indicate. Rather, Judge Wood had ordered the Ada County Sheriff's office to guard the granite building's main doors, limiting access to only those with direct business in the matter, and their select attendants. As a result, only a hundred people or so filled the courtroom's gallery and the outside passageways—plus the reporters, who came and went from the courtroom to the telegraph machines on the second floor, and occasionally outside to a row of provisional privies along the edge of the courthouse lawn.

In the courtroom, Neva sat at the left end of a long bench at the front of the gallery, just behind Haywood. Her invalid chair was beside her. For the trial days, she chose not to wear a hat and to keep her look plain: waistshirts, skirts, jackets, on mixed and matched rotation. No dresses. No significant jewelry. Nothing to draw attention. (She told Winnie to do the same.) She had hoped her agreement to attend the trial would allow her the choice of where to sit—the back of the gallery being her preference. But Darrow wouldn't allow it, saying that if she sat anywhere other than directly behind her husband, it would doom him. Though that tempted her all the more toward the back, she sat where she was instructed, staring at the broad shoulders of Bill's coat, contemplating his straight, brown hair. The jailhouse barber had cut the bottom at a small slant, leaving the left lower than the right. She wished she could fix it. A voice shouted within her: Why? She was done with him. Done. After what he'd screamed at her upstairs the other night. Calling her crippled. She hated him. She renewed her vow never to speak to him. That was in her power. Her choice. The one thing. Even if he turned around right then and there and asked her something, she wouldn't speak. What would she do? She would just look away, she told herself. Pretend not to have heard him. But, of course, he wouldn't turn. In fact, he didn't seem aware of her presence at all.

To Bill's right sat Darrow, also at the defense table, dressed in a black, three-piece sack suit with a dark tie. He was doing his job, but why did he have to be so good at it? He should've let her sit in the back. Or not come at all. Further right, across a narrow gap, the prosecution's table bore the well-carved Senator Borah, sitting orthodox and composed, along with two assistants. Borah was as fetching as ever. She remembered him lifting her from her invalid chair when they met—the evening she made her deal not to testify in trade of protecting George. To her left was the empty jury box. And around Bill's left shoulder she could see the empty witness box. Around his right shoulder stood the judge's bench, also empty. And in front of the bench was the stenographer at his table, straightening a stack of extra ribbons beside a brand-new invention—the Ward Ireland stenotype machine. George, always fascinated by the latest contraption, had said one was to be used in this trial. Beyond remembering that, she gave it no mind.

She heard shuffling and looked back over her right shoulder. Several men were entering, moving down the center aisle. Guessing they were Pinkertons, she wasn't surprised when they slid into the front two benches behind Borah. More people were entering, including Carla Capone. Neva didn't know what to think of her. Rumors were, Carla had dropped her loyalty to the Federation. But no one seemed to know anything to support that notion. More likely, it was just that she'd once been an outspoken supporter, but now wasn't. It wouldn't mean anything in most situations. But it rang bells in an organization as melancholic and angst-riddled as the Federation.

But hadn't she, the wife of the labor union's president, done much the same? Others were saying she no longer defended her husband—which was true—but they didn't know that for certain. Just a few months ago, she would've set them straight. But now she found herself numb to it all. Neva watched Carla slide into a row on the other side of the center aisle, near the middle of the gallery; then noted an affectionate glance between Carla and a tall Pinkerton on their second row—a young man with extraordinary, sky-colored eyes.

Then came more people, and in their lead was Winnie, her hair done up, wearing the diamond earrings Bill gave her for Christmas. Neva kept her frown facing forward as Winnie slid in to her right. *Some socialist you are, Sissy,* Neva fumed silently—then remembered they were called Bolsheviks. She looked again at Bill's crooked haircut. Her Bolshevik-yet-capitalist sister would never fix that—wouldn't even think to do so. She envied Winnie that freedom of mind. Then she smelled George and all her angry thoughts seemed to evaporate, like stink overwhelmed by a fragrant candle. She turned. He'd slid in behind her. Good. Moments later, with the gallery full and settled, the bailiff ordered everyone to stand. The jury filed in, taking seats in their long box. Neva studied their faces. Do the right thing, she silently implored.

Darrow also watched the jurors, contemplating them one by one, wondering what they were thinking. He had made as good of choices as he could, he assured himself. The cattle rancher—said he'd been working his place most days over the past weeks, thus he didn't know much about the matter and thought any man should get a fair trial, union or not. The real estate man, and the two in construction—all solid. They would be fair. Then there were the other cattleman. And the horse rancher. And Darrow's silent ringer, or so he hoped: the sheep rancher, O. V. Sebern—a devout labor union man. Then the owner of a mercantile, and—

Darrow stopped and returned to Sebern. What was that look? The older man was watching Haywood, almost studying him. Jurors in criminal cases were loath to look directly at the accused. Or if they did, it was quick—just a glance, then away. No eye contact, no connection, no risk of inadvertently communicating hope, or receiving a nonverbal plea. But Sebern had walked in, sat down, and begun studying the accused. And he seemed to be doing so with narrow-eyed contempt. Then those eyes shifted, softened, and he gave the smallest of nods. Who was that for? Darrow turned to his right and back, just in time to catch Jack glancing from Sebern to Darrow, and then a hasty pivot forward. What could that look have meant? Did they know each other? Had something transpired between them? But he knew the answers before he asked the questions. Just as he knew it was all a futile exercise at that point, just a palliative habit—examining puzzles his gut had already solved, like writing already-completed tasks on a to-do list just for the satisfaction of marking them off. Only there was no satisfaction here.

In that moment of seeing such a little thing, he saw it all. He knew he'd been manipulated, and how it'd been done. Agent Jack Garrett had never been a double. Garrett was a Pinkerton, and only a Pinkerton—then and now. McParland had run Garrett at him, just as both Haywood and Swain had warned, posing Garrett as sympathetic to the union cause. And that meant Carla had also betrayed Darrow. Her lover and confidant had fooled him into allowing Sebern into the jury box. Not just that, but Darrow had proactively picked the man. He'd sought out and chosen Sebern, for godsakes! Borah must have rejoiced when he did that. It meant Sebern would vote guilty, regardless. He saw Carla sitting on the prosecution side, like at a divided wedding—not an accidental placement at all. Of course she knew Jack was not a real double agent. But when did she learn that? Had she always been betraying the Federation? Betraying him?

He could never admit this to Haywood—no damned way. And he had to hope Haywood never learned of it from some other source. If Haywood wasn't hanged at the end of this, the man could seriously damage Darrow's reputation. But if he did hang, and the Federation thought their leader's death was due to Darrow betraying them—throwing the case by putting a guilty vote on the jury—they might kill him. He felt the blood fleeing his face. His secret plan *had* to work. It was all he had left now.

After Judge Wood entered, draped in his black robe, the trial commenced. Borah rose to give his opening statement for the State. He began with a spirited discussion of the positive qualities of organized labor activity: fair wages, limited work hours, child-labor laws, safer conditions. And he allowed that the Western Federation of Miners, and indeed the defendant himself, William Haywood, the union's president, were central to those advancements for the working American. But no amount of virtue, no degree of good intentions, could possibly absolve such an individual from the heinous act of murder. He leaned further into the distinction between the union and the man. The Western Federation of Miners is not on trial here. Labor unions are not on trial. And this shouldn't be considered a referendum on the Socialist Party. Likewise, nor were the mine owners on trial. And certainly not Governor Steunenberg. The only one on trial was a solitary man, William Haywood, who ordered the murder of—

"Objection!" Darrow stood. "Argumentative, Your Honor."

"Overruled."

"But, Your Honor, saying my client ordered any such thing is not within the bounds of the proposed evidence, which Senator Borah is limited by the rules of procedure to be—"

Judge Wood peered over his small round glasses. "Mr. Darrow, I said your objection is overruled."

"Yes, Your Honor."

Borah continued, diving back into the assassination of Governor Steunenberg. He hadn't gone beyond, "the fishing line laid by Harry Orchard," before Darrow was on his feet again.

"Objection, Your Honor."

"Basis?"

"Argumentative. The senator is not outlining specific evidence he can later present, he is straying into his suppositions as to the imagined use of what he hopes this jury will believe to be evidence."

Borah interjected, "The evidence will be the testimony of Mr. Harry Orchard, Your Honor."

"The objection is sustained, Mr. Borah," said Wood, to Darrow's surprise. "You may re-phase." Darrow knew Judge Wood thought it more proper to refer to Borah as Mr. Borah, not Senator Borah, during the trial. But Darrow had no intention of letting this jury forget that this was David versus Goliath, that the special prosecutor was not just some attorney appointed for the State of Idaho. No, Borah was a sitting United States Senator, and as such he represented the oppression of a national government a continent away that had come to this remote state, to this small city, to lecture these local men.

Borah resumed his walk-through of the bombing, only to be interrupted by Darrow's objections fifteen more times. Darrow was just warming up. When Borah turned to the testimonies of Harry Orchard and Steve Adams, how they directly inculpated Haywood, Darrow grew relentless.

"Objection, Your Honor," Darrow said, shrugging an apology to the jury. "The government's special prosecutor seems to think this is the floor of the United States Senate where he can say anything he wants without the bother of truth. Understandable, as he is a politician, but this is a court of law."

Borah snapped, "Your Honor! I'm making my opening statement under Idaho's rules of procedure. But Mr. Darrow wants to turn my time into a conversation, apparently. Not even that, but a grandstanding debate. Anything to obscure the evidentiary facts from the good men of this jury."

"Oh, now," said Darrow, "the *good men of this jury* understand what they're listening to—a politician's sales pitch." Keeping his eyes fixed on Borah, Darrow added, "And not just the *good men* on the jury, but the others too." Chuckles went through the jury box and rippled across the gallery.

Judge Wood banged his gavel. "Mr. Borah, you will continue. And Mr. Darrow, you will resume your chair."

"Yes, Your Honor," said Darrow. Once seated, he asked, "For the record, Your Honor, was my objection sustained?"

"No, Mr. Darrow. Most emphatically not."

"To preserve my objection, may I know if it was overruled?"

Judge Wood scowled at Darrow. "It was."

"Thank you, Your Honor." Then to Borah: "My apologies, Senator. Please continue."

Borah hesitated, then began again. Only this time, his argument was truncated and moved in fits and spurts. Darrow's bite had set its venom.

After Borah concluded his opening, Judge Wood motioned toward the defense table. Darrow rose and declared, "The defense elects to not give an opening statement at this point, but rather to do so at the commencement of the defense's case in prime."

While Judge Wood was accepting that declaration, the central gallery doors creaked open and a tousled man shuffled in. Fully bearded, with no hat, he wore a soiled deerskin coat that, by its askew appearance, must have been the first its maker ever attempted. In his hands, both of which were muddy or perhaps bloody, he carried a package wrapped in sackcloth. Before anything could register, two deputies rushed in behind him, tackling him to the floor, kicking the package back into hallway, while the word "bomb" cracker-popped through the room. Some in the gallery flung themselves to the floor, others pushed to the outer walls, while others streamed from the room, stumbling directly over the package and into the hall like bats at dusk.

But the only explosion was that instant conflagration of scrambling, shoving and shouting. Guards removed the man. People settled back in. It was over. Judge Wood brought the room to order and called for a ten-minute recess. During that time, they learned the man was a sheepherder come to town for the day, only to wander into the center of the town's focus, sniffing out the hub-bub. In the package: dirty overalls destined for an in-town laundry woman for their monthly cleaning.

★

– 59 –

FRIDAY
May 10, 1907

Knowing his first big witness would be Harry Orchard, Senator Borah began by calling a smattering of people to testify about the bomb and the bomber. One group witnessed the explosion—some from a distance, some from next door to the Steunenberg home. Others had observed Orchard acting shiftily before the bombing, including seeing him surveilling the house with binoculars. And one had seen him leaving the Saratoga Hotel the morning of the explosion. Borah then called McParland, who walked the jury through the evidence in Orchard's room, most importantly the fishing line, bottle of acid, and the plaster of Paris.

Then it was Darrow's turn—his time to cross-examine McParland. His primary objective was to confuse the jury by painting all the minutia of the State's evidence in a cloud of doubt, while impugning McParland's judgment in the process. He began by staying in his chair for the initial questions—a clear statement to the jury that the famous Clarence Darrow was not impressed by the famous Chief Detective McParland, and neither should they be. "Mr. McParland ... I would call you Detective McParland, as Senator Borah did, but that might imply some title granted by a government authority. It might imply some level of assumed responsibility on behalf of the public."

"As you wish," said McParland, his brogue resolute in the silent courtroom.

"I thank you for that, because I know you pride yourself not only on the detective title that the Pinkerton Agency has bestowed upon you, but 'chief detective,' no less."

McParland didn't respond.

"Even Sherlock Holmes has been investigating you—I mean *with* you, I heard."

Laughter flowed in the courtroom and Judge Wood's chair squeaked. "Do you have a question for the witness?"

"Many, Your Honor." Then to McParland: "As you know, I'm not allowed to ask you about how you kidnapped Mr. Haywood."

"Objection!" shouted Borah.

"Sustained. Counselors approach." When Borah and Darrow were up to the edge of the bench, Wood said, "Mr. Darrow, you've been clearly instructed on this."

"Yes, Your Honor," said Darrow, leaving his voice just loud enough to be heard by the jury. "My purpose was to acknowledge it to the witness. I thought he might be confused as to why I didn't immediately address the controversy about illegally capturing—"

"There will be no more on that matter," barked Wood. "The Supreme Court gave its answer. Clearly."

"Clearly," echoed Borah.

Darrow looked at Borah. "Clearly."

Wood ordered them to step back, and Darrow walked to McParland. "Let's talk about the items you claim to have found in Mr. Orchard's room at the Saratoga Hotel. You said it was a fishing line, a bottle of acid, and some plaster, correct?"

"Correct. Among other things."

"The fishing line. What did Mr. Orchard say, when you were in his room, as to why he had it?"

"Said he'd been fishing."

"Fishing—with fishing line?" (*a few chuckles from the gallery*)

"Yes."

"Is that unusual? Fishing with fishing line?" (*more laughter*)

"That's not what he had it for, I don't believe."

"And the acid?"

"He tried to claim it wasn't his."

"Tried to claim? Or he *did* claim?"

"He claimed."

"And the plaster of Paris?"

"He said he'd made loaded dice."

Darrow nodded. "To cheat with? That sort of dice?"

"I suppose."

"Well, are there any other reasons to make a pair of loaded dice, other than to cheat?" (*chuckles*)

"Objection," said Borah. "Asking for a speculation on a matter not relevant—"

"Sustained."

Darrow turned imperiously toward McParland, refusing even a flicker of defeat. "Loaded dice? That's what Mr. Orchard said?"

"Yes."

"How did he say that, about the dice? I mean, did he have to think first?"

"I don't remember."

"But you didn't believe him, isn't that right?"

"That's right."

"Why is that? What did you think the plaster was for?"

"To bind a bomb to its trigger. Done in mining, sometimes."

"*Sometimes*," said Darrow, walking to the prosecution's table. There he lifted a small jar containing white power, and then brought it to the witness stand. "This plaster is what you found in Mr. Orchard's room?"

"I believe so."

"No, Sir. A moment ago, when you were talking with your friend, Senator Borah, you two agreed that this was *indeed* the plaster found in that room."

"Yes."

"To your knowledge, are there different types of plaster?"

"Yes."

"Like what?"

"Kind like that." He motioned to the jar. "Used in mining."

Seeing apprehension form in McParland's eyes, Darrow pressed his advantage. "Are there other types?"

"Yes."

"How about medical plaster, for the setting of broken bones?"

McParland hesitated before replying, "That too."

"But this, it wouldn't be that soft, powdery, medical sort," said Darrow, holding up the jar. "That sort wouldn't be suitable for binding a bomb together. So this must be construction plaster, the kind an experienced bomb maker would use. I mean, if it is what you claim it is. Isn't that correct?"

McParland didn't answer.

"Isn't that correct, Mr. McParland? This must be construction plaster if it was used for a bomb?"

"I would suppose," was McParland's muttered response.

Darrow opened the jar and handed it to McParland. "If you will, Sir, please put a small amount here." He pointed to the witness box's rail in front of McParland. The detective did as instructed, tapping a small amount of white power on the oak rail.

"Thank you. That's perfect. So, if that plaster, there in front of you, was medical plaster, not bomb-making plaster, would that surprise you?"

When McParland froze on the question, Darrow knew he had him—the detective was already aware that it wasn't bomb-making plaster. "I'll rephrase. You know this is too soft to be—"

"Mr. Orchard said he used it for a bomb—"

"Your Honor, that is hearsay," said Darrow. "The witness—"

"You're on cross, Counselor. I'll allow it."

"All right, Your Honor." He looked at McParland, and then at the powder on the rail. "In your opinion, as a man investigating this matter, not as a construction or mining expert, if this is soft, medical plaster, then it wouldn't be suitable for bomb construction. Is that right?"

"That's my belief, but I don't—"

"All right. Thank you, Mr. McParland." Darrow looked at the plaster on the rail. "I guess we should put that back. Will you?"

McParland pinched at the white plaster, but it slipped through his fingers.

"Apologies," said Darrow, taking the bottle from McParland. "That looks difficult. Let me." Using his fingers, Darrow brushed the powder into a small cloud of white that drifted to the floor. "My goodness, that sure is soft plaster," said Darrow. He returned the lid to the bottle and brought it back to Borah's table. "Once out of the bottle—" he said quietly, then clicked his tongue and turned. "Mr. McParland, now let's talk about the bottle of acid you were so certain must've been used for bomb-making."

★

– 60 –

THURSDAY
May 16, 1907

A week later, during a thirty-minute recess, Neva stood in the hallway, looking from the window, leaning on her green crutches that had begun to show evidence of wear. She had stopped using her invalid chair in court, disliking being so low around people who were already looking down on her. She finished the sandwich she had brought and brushed the crumbs from the box pleats on the front of her taffeta waistshirt. Nearing footsteps drew her attention. She turned with modest indifference until she saw George standing there.

"How are you, m'dear?" he asked.

With a faraway smile, she lifted her shoulders and let them fall.

"That well?"

"I'm afraid this'll take longer than two weeks, George."

"I believe you're right," he said, placing his hand on her back.

She kept her gaze beyond the window, but her mind zeroed on his hand, the warmth, the meaning. Outside and three stories down, the crowd had nearly doubled since the first day of the trial. News accounts had attracted many travelers who decided to delay their east or west-bound journeys for a day, just to say they'd been there, that they'd seen her villainous husband—and his beautiful, spry, young mistress. Maybe that's what they thought—the godless wags. And there were more of them than usual today. It was probably, she thought, due to rumors that the State would call its chief witness that afternoon.

As if reading her mind, George said, "Orchard's next."

She nodded.

He moved closer, and his woody scent became evident to her. "Why Bill hasn't killed him yet, I don't know," he said.

"He's not on the stand *yet*," she quipped dryly.

George stepped back, giving her room to turn her crutches.

Facing him, she straightened his blood-red bow tie and took his hand. "I love how you smell, George. I don't think I've ever told you that."

"No, you haven't."

"And—"

"Yes?"

"I love you, George."

He grinned. "Miss Hobble has her humor. That's good."

Her eyes glistened at him.

"You're serious?" he whispered.

She crutched past him. "And what if I was?"

"Not just how I smell?"

"Nope. Not just that."

The trial was underway again with Neva sitting in her place behind her husband's back, with George directly behind her. With what she'd said in the hall, she knew she'd set George's world on fire—hopefully the good kind of blaze. Tempted to look back, she imagined he'd flash her a smile. She couldn't smell him, not with all the other people. A shame, she thought, and then grinned to herself, imagining crawling backwards over her bench. If only the jury were not right there, the closest only a few feet away. Even if they were further, how would that look, the wife of the accused snuggling with another man right there in the courtroom? She would have laughed at the vision, but the truth was not funny—she was no one's wife. Not really. Certainly not wife to the murdering, thieving man in front of her. She was not his. Not anymore.

Glancing again at the twelve jurymen, she saw they were focused on the next witness. Neva scooted slightly left to see Harry Orchard being sworn in. She knew Harry Orchard. More accurately, she'd seen him before, in Denver. A version of him. Not this version. That man had been a balding, fat-faced louse, a reprobate. This man didn't seem so dangerous. This Mr. Orchard was neatly trimmed, wearing a tweed suit, bearing a tight mustache, eyes open. He reminded her of a Sunday-school teacher. Well rested—that's what came to her mind. Yes, this version of Mr. Orchard seemed well rested. A cold-hearted bomber? Of course he was, but one had to strain to see it.

As did every other person in the packed courtroom, Neva listened intently to each word of Orchard's testimony. Borah moved him through his particulars: forty years of age; born in Ontario, Canada; came to America ten years ago. Since then, he'd worked at six mines, a mucker and mule wrangler at first, but found a penchant for dynamite—for managing the explosions, if one could manage such a thing. He joined the Western Federation of Miners at the silver mine in Burke, Idaho. What led him to do that? He attended a rally—maybe in 1902—where the president of the Federation spoke, calling men to take up the cause, to do whatever was necessary. That man's name? Big Bill. Yes, Mr. Haywood. Yes, the defendant, William Haywood. Yes, the man sitting right there.

After helping others blow up the Vindicator Mine in Colorado, Orchard gave himself over to a new career: union killer. Yes, he'd designed the Vindicator bomb. He'd been paid $500. He'd killed two people with it. Then came a string of bombs, though some hadn't gone off as planned. In 1904, he was assigned to the team who dynamited the depot at Independence, Colorado, high in the wilderness. Not going to say who the other bombers were. How many died? Thirteen, all non-union. Yes, there were also some failures. Mr. Haywood ordered him to assassinate the governor of Colorado, two Colorado Supreme Court Justices, and the president of a mining company. Why the governor and justices? Mr. Haywood wanted to strike fear in the heart of any politician who might consider crossing the Federation. None of those bombs had been successful. Mr. Haywood got a might angry at those failures. Yes, one of those bombs had gone off accidentally and killed a bystander. Yes, an innocent man.

As far as Governor Steunenberg, the governor of Idaho—yes, Mr. Haywood had ordered him to do it, and specifically by bombing. Yes, it was Mr. Haywood, the accused, who'd ordered him. Mr. Haywood said Steunenberg had lived too long. Orchard was to get $900 plus a ranch near Fort Collins, Colorado. No, Haywood hadn't said the dollar amount at the time he gave the kill order, but Orchard knew it, from prior conversations with the man. Yes, since he'd been in the Idaho State Penitentiary, he'd come to realize that he wouldn't be getting the money, or the ranch.

Why kill Steunenberg? Not certain—but figured because the governor jailed all those labor boys in Idaho, without trials, after the Bunker Hill bombing. Yes, he'd done the Bunker Hill bombing too. He'd lit that fuse himself. They'd hijacked a Northern Pacific train out of Missoula. Others had packed it with dynamite, on Orchard's orders. He didn't know the names of those men. Took it up to Wallace where another man killed someone, and then on up to the Bunker Hill. The other man? Fella named Steve Adams, went by Addis then. Same one as helped him kill Steunenberg. Yes, he thought Haywood had ordered Steve Adams to help Orchard kill the governor.

Sheriff Sutherland, who for days had been sitting discreetly in the back row, rose and walked out.

During the second day of Orchard's mesmeric testimony, a whirlwind blew into the courtroom, upstaging him like none other could: the famed actress, Ethel Barrymore. When the courtroom fell to buzzes of wonder, Judge Wood suspended testimony and greeted the twenty-eight-year-old splendor to his courtroom. She wore a traveling outfit, more Victoria bicycle than common train: an amber silk jacket flared at the hips over striped breeches, with a straw boatman's hat, cream gloves, and matching Oxfords. She apologized for the unfortunate disruption, said she was in Boise with her touring theatrical company. Don't mind her. Do continue. She'd thought to just pop into the courtroom to see what all the fuss was about. Oh yes, they were on the return leg of their western tour of *Captain Jinks of the Horse Marines* (the same one Neva, George, and Winnie had seen in Denver the prior January) and hoped all would come. Then, with a dramatic flourish, she declared the witness seemed the picture of niceness, but that man—she pointed at Haywood—"frightens me half to death." The room laughed, applauding as she exited stage center through the main doors. Haywood appeared flattered, if anything.

Darrow—enraged that Judge Wood not only allowed Miss Barrymore's interruption, but her statement about Orchard and Haywood—launched into a cross-examinatory onslaught of

Orchard: twenty-seven hours of blistering attacks and insults. Darrow parsed every word of Orchard's testimony, levering the sentences open like cracked lobsters, pulling out morsels of lies and fleshy disgusts to feed to the jury one bite at a time. He painted a picture using Orchard's own blood and shit: beyond being America's most prolific murderer, Orchard had abandoned his family, become a bigamist, a drunkard, a liar, thief, whoremonger, gambler, and cheat.

At one point, Darrow leaned close and said, "What we know, Mr. Orchard, is that you carry no sympathy for your victims, no remorse for your sins."

"Not true. I'm born again in Jesus Christ," Orchard declared. "My sins are forgiven."

"Forgiven!? You sit here and tell us that you—" Darrow checked himself. "Yes, so you say. For the God-fearing, decent among us, rebirth in the Savior is a transformation of the soul, a beautiful ascension to the family of Christ. But for you, no, I think it's all a ruse. All a lie. You don't have a care in your heart for the lives you've taken. You're just on that stand to say whatever you can to save your own neck. Isn't that right?"

"No. I'm going to prison for the rest of my days for what I done. I'm telling the truth of it all because this here is when I can. And because I've gotten right with the Lord."

"But you've not 'gotten right' with your fellow man," said Darrow. "That would take a hanging."

"I don't know about that."

"You knew that if you created this imaginary story about Mr. Haywood, you'd escape the noose, correct?"

"I reckon I'll receive what I deserve." Tears began streaming down Orchard's cheeks.

"Answer my question, Mr. Orchard. Isn't it true that you'll not be executed for your murders, because of this wild yarn you're spinning today?"

"That's true ... not that it's a yarn. But I won't hang."

"I understand your tears. It must weigh on you. You thought you could bring peace to your soul by having someone else hanged in your stead, didn't you?"

"No, Sir. No, Sir. I'd no thought of getting out of it, not by laying it on nobody else. I just began to think about the unnatural monster I'd been. That's why the waterworks. That's why."

Two hours later, Darrow moved Orchard to the subject of Steve Adams. "You lied earlier, didn't you, Mr. Orchard, when you said you believed Mr. Haywood instructed Steve Adams to commit the same act of murder as you. To kill the governor. Isn't that right?"

"I didn't lie."

"You have no knowledge of that, isn't that right?"

"I think—"

"I'm not asking you what you think. I'm asking what you know. What you directly witnessed. Not what you guess. But the truth of what you *know*. Not suppositions—like you thinking Mr. Haywood gave some such order or another to Mr. Adams. You don't even *believe* that! You said Adams is an idiot, a simpleton. Mr. Haywood didn't give you or Adams any such orders, did he?"

"He gave me orders."

"Well, as we've already made clear to this jury, you have no evidence, do you? No mysterious piece of paper that you supposedly kept. Where? In the band of your hat, you said? You're just saying these things to save your skin, are you not? Just making them up as you sit there. Right? And you think Senator Borah needs a second witness to testify similar to you, all so the wrong man might hang for your crimes. Isn't that correct?"

"Which question am I to answer?"

"Oh, go ahead, give this jury your best lie to any of them." Before Orchard could speak, Darrow continued, "I think you know that when that Adams fellow is sitting right there in that chair, that he won't agree with you—so you're scared. Because when he tells us the truth, that he had no orders to assist you in any way, that your lies will be made clear. You know that, don't you? You'll be on your own, alone with your sins, before God, exposed for the lying murderer that you are."

"Ask Adams then," said Orchard, worn down but not defeated.

"Oh, I will. I hope you're ready for that."

"I hope *you* are," Orchard murmured under his breath.

A *Collier's* reporter would write that Orchard had been *"the most remarkable witness that ever appeared in an American court of justice."*

That evening, over dinner and found Sherry, both Borah and McParland were worried. Especially Borah. Why would Darrow talk on and on about Adams, their hidden-away witness? Saying Adams's yet-to-be-heard story might differ from Orchard's. What nerve. They already had Adams's confession. What game was Darrow playing? What gave the great orator such confidence to even mention Adams by name, much less seed the idea that Adams's upcoming testimony might not align with Orchard's? This was especially perplexing as an easier, far-less risky option had been available to Darrow: Say nothing. Then, on Monday, work with whatever Adams said when he took the stand. But by presenting the idea now, that Adams's yet-unheard testimony might not match Orchard's current testimony, Darrow seemed to be setting himself a lethal trap: If he was wrong, then Adams's testimony would only ring louder, amplifying its damage to Haywood. After their dinner, they returned to the penitentiary and spoke to Adams, getting confirmation that his upcoming testimony in court would indeed match what he'd said in writing. Yes, Adams assured them, it'd be the same: Haywood ordered him to help Orchard kill the governor.

The prosecution team also discussed Darrow's wife, Ruby, who had been in the gallery for most of her husband's scorched-earth, cross-examination of Orchard. McParland had seen her when she arrived a few days earlier, and both he and Borah met her soon thereafter. Had she affected Darrow's behavior? Was Darrow feeling cocky in front of his wife? Showing off? Surely such a courtroom ace would never showboat for his wife, and, by so doing, risk so much for his client. A virtuoso conductor doesn't embellish the crescendos in Beethoven's "Ode to Joy" simply because the conductor's wife is in the audience.

Then their conversation turned to the accused. Haywood had appeared in fine spirits throughout Orchard's marathon testimony—adding to Borah's stress. Haywood was an unrepentant denialist. His canine stoicism, in the face of damning odds, carried weight to the uninitiated. Might that include the jurymen who surely expected some element of despair on the man's face? McParland weighed in: Borah should not let Haywood's calm deportment bother him. It further evidenced Haywood's moral vacancy. Nothing more.

⟡

That night, surrounded by three guards, Darrow and Ruby took a walk. Neither mentioned her friend at Chicago's Hull House. They returned to their room in the Saratoga Hotel and cranked the windows slightly, letting in the perfect amount of chilly spring air.

⟡

At the Idanha Hotel, George had slipped into Neva's room, where they discussed little, but said plenty, him holding her all night, whispering that he loved her too.

⟡

In the sheriff's jail cell, Haywood shuddered, tugging at his blanket, lost in the hinterlands of sleep, traipsing through a fogged-out landscape where pockets of dark trees sapped blood and bore noose-shaped fruit.

⟡

At the Occidental Hotel, Lloyd Lillard enjoyed his second night on clean sheets. Well, they were, before the prostitute arrived, courtesy of Captain Swain.

⟡

Back at the Idanha, the Gordian knot in Borah's stomach kept him tossing, rolling his mind on the rocks of scattered slumber.

★

– 61 –

MONDAY
May 20, 1907

The next Monday morning, the rattle of hobbling chains being removed indicated Steve Adams was in the court's anteroom. Then a deputy entered, followed by Adams, and then another deputy. As Adams made his way to the witness stand, his freshly provided brown suit and slender black tie slumped against his thin frame, a sail luffing in an absent wind. He was sworn in, and, for the first time in his life, prepared to actually tell the truth, or at least tell of truth's shadow.

Before rising from his chair, Borah studied Darrow's placid face, and then Haywood's. Something felt wrong. Over Sunday's break in the trial, the dispiritedness in Haywood's expression seemed to have caught a virus of calm. Worse yet, Darrow seemed to have caught it as well—a too-easy smile, a secret knowing, a dangerous indifference—all spinning Borah's stomach. Borah stood, approached Adams, got him to say his name, and asked, "Where are you from, Mr. Adams?"

"The Idaho State Penitentiary." (*chuckles in the courtroom*)

"I meant, before that."

"Austin, Nevada. You know, where your Pinks attacked me."

"You attacked *them*," barked Borah. "And in San Francisco. There you killed a Pinkerton man, and an entire family."

"Ah, you don't know. Hoe your'n row."

"How's that?" began Borah.

"One murder at a time, Mr. Borah," said Judge Wood. "How about you stay with just the governor? For now. Then ... we'll see."

Borah agreed. Harry Orchard had talked openly in court about his many other killings because they were part of his sixty-four-page written testimony. But Adams's written testimony was a third of one page and only said that Haywood ordered Adams to participate with Orchard in the bombing of Governor Steunenberg.

"Why do you think you were arrested," asked Borah. "Why are you here, Mr. Adams?"

"Cause those deputies pulled me from my cell. I'd eht only a bit of my biscuit." (*chuckles, but Wood ignored them as he was smiling too*)

Frustrated, Borah decided to go to the point directly. "Are you familiar with the bombing of the governor of Idaho, Governor Steunenberg, last Christmas?"

"Heard bout it."

"To be exact, Mr. Adams, you more than heard about it. You were ordered to participate in the assassination. Isn't that right?"

Adams's eyes disappeared into slits, which, along with his long, crooked nose, and half-slung mouth, gave him the look of a confused stork. "Don't right reckon I know what you're talkin bout."

"What?" Borah froze. "What did you say, Mr. Adams?"

"Ain't sure what—"

"No, Mr. Adams, you know precisely what I'm referring to. You were ordered by the defendant, Mr. Haywood"—Borah pointed at Haywood—"to assist a man by the name of Harry Orchard in causing the death of Governor Steunenberg. Isn't that true?"

"Don't know that man," Adams said, appearing to be pondering Haywood. "He ordered me to do *what?*"

"You know damn well!" Borah boomed, cheeks flushing.

Darrow got to his feet. "Objection, Your Honor. The State is badgering its own witness. This poor man—"

Senator Borah wheeled on Darrow. "Goddamn you, Clarence." (*gasps in the gallery*)

Judge Wood pounded his gavel. "Mr. Borah! Senator! I'll not have such language in my courtroom. Especially not against another officer of the court."

"Yes, Your Honor," huffed Borah. He grabbed a piece of paper from his table and turned to Adams. "Permission to treat the witness as hostile, Your Honor?"

"Yes, I would imagine so," said Wood.

"Mr. Adams," Borah pounced, handing him the paper. "I'm handing you your own written statement, which you gave, under oath, freely, no more than six weeks past. Do you recognize this?"

"Yeah."

"That *is* your testimony, is it not?"

"That's my mark, but I didn't write them words on that part."

"But you did sign it?"

"Guess so. Looks that way."

"Read the second to last sentence, Mr. Adams."

"Last one?"

"Second to—" Borah took the paper and placed his finger on a line. "That one."

Adams stared quietly at the paper.

"Out loud, Sir!"

"Can't rightly, can I?"

"Why not?"

"Can't read." (*more chuckles*)

"Then what were you just— All right, Mr. Adams. I was there, was I not? I was there when you signed your attestation to this statement. At that time, you said it was true and correct."

Darrow objected. "Your Honor, is Senator Borah now giving his own personal testimony? Regardless, this man is obviously not certain what Senator Borah is trying to get him to say."

"I'm not *trying* to get him to say anything," Borah protested.

Adams clucked his tongue and said, "Hell you ain't."

"Mr. Adams," said Judge Wood. "You've sworn to tell the truth on pain of being charged with perjury. Therefore, I'll ask you, do you see the defendant, sitting before you?"

"The one-eyed feller?"

Judge Wood hesitated. "Yes ... that would be the one."

Haywood gave a docile, flat smile accompanied by a deep sigh, as if watching someone else's mildly amusing, petulant child in need of a good ass kicking.

"I see him," said Adams.

Judge Wood continued, "Did he ever, at any time, give you any orders of any kind, written or verbal, to do anything?"

"Well, Mister Judge, like I told this tall feller here," Adams said, motioning toward Borah, "I don't know ol' one-eye there. He never told me to do nothin."

"Hell, I'll read it for you," said Borah. "You put your mark in agreement to the following statement: *'Mr. Haywood told me to lend a hand, and that if I didn't think Harry Orchard could do the thing through, then I was to do it. Either way, after the governor was dead, I was to kill*

Harry.' That's what you signed, Mr. Adams, agreeing that it was a true and accurate account of your testimony, given on the first of April of this year. Isn't that right?"

"April fool's day?" asked Adams.

Borah was flabbergasted.

Darrow held his composure, refusing to reveal anything.

Adams looked at the judge, then at Haywood, and back at Borah. "I didn't say nothin like that. Didn't agree to it, neither."

"Why then, Mr. Adams, did you sign this statement?" asked Borah, his nose twitching, neck reddening.

"'Cause that Pink there"—Adams pointed at McParland—"told me I had to, or he'd drown me more."

Judge Wood tilted down toward Adams. "I don't know what game you're playing here, Mr. Adams, but I won't have it. You're under oath, Sir. Just as you were when you signed that paper. Have you been asked to change your testimony in this case?"

"No, Sir."

Wood continued, "Has anyone approached you with a reward or a threat of any sort in an effort to induce you to give the testimony you are giving here today—saying that you don't know Mr. Haywood?"

"No, Sir."

Wood looked at the special prosecutor who'd already collapsed in his chair. "Any more questions, Mr. Borah?"

Borah shook his head. "No, Your Honor."

Judge Wood looked at Darrow.

Darrow shrugged. "No questions."

"Well," began the judge, "in that case, you're excused as a witness, Mr. Adams, and remanded to the custody of—"

"Your Honor?" asked Sheriff Sutherland, standing with the deputies who had escorted Adams in. His badge was clearly visible.

"Yes? You are?"

"Angus Sutherland, Shoshone County Sheriff, up in Wallace."

"I'm familiar."

"I've got a warrant—sworn arraignment and writ—for that man, Mr. Steven Adams. To my knowledge, mine is prior to any claim by any other court or law enforcement agency. Therefore, I ask that he be remanded to my custody."

Judge Wood waved Sutherland forward and examined the papers. "You swear to this, Sheriff?"

"Yes, Your Honor."

Wood then looked at the two Ada County deputies. "Deputies, has your office received any other warrants for this man?"

"Not as of yet, Your Honor."

"All right, then he's yours, Sheriff Sutherland."

"Thank you, Your Honor," said Sutherland.

The deputies handcuffed Adams, and the group exited through the anteroom.

Soon thereafter, Darrow and Borah were at the bench, whispering with Judge Wood. Borah had announced the State rested, followed by Darrow announcing the defense ready. But first, Darrow had requested a directed verdict from the judge.

"No, Mr. Darrow," said Wood. "I don't see it."

"Your Honor," insisted Darrow, "as the Idaho criminal code requires, in a capital murder case such as this, seeking the accused to be held culpable as an accessory, the State must produce no less than two corroborating witnesses as to their central claim. But the State rested having failed to produce two such witnesses."

Borah protested. "Maybe Mr. Darrow has not been paying attention, but we presented a host of witnesses—"

"Not to their case in prime," said Darrow. "Not to the linkage of Mr. Haywood in such a manner as to warrant any capital charge."

"We presented—"

"All you gave this jury was Mr. Orchard, Senator," scowled Darrow. "That's all. And that's only one." He lifted a single finger.

Judge Wood cocked his head and shook it. "No, Mr. Darrow, I'm thoroughly satisfied the case should be submitted to the jury."

"Your Honor, the code is clear," said Darrow.

"That's my ruling. The motion for a directed verdict is denied. Counsel will step back."

As the two attorneys returned to their tables, Wood gaveled the day to a close, saying the trial would commence the next morning when the defense would begin its case.

From the time Adams took the stand, Haywood had been relaxed, but now his face appeared ashen. The deputies cuffed him and led him from the courtroom.

That evening, Darrow sat on a chair in Haywood's locked cell, watching his client who sat on the bed crosswise, reclining against the back wall, eating his dinner of fried chicken off a tin plate. They were silent. Darrow glanced to his left, through the cell's floor-to-ceiling bars and into the sheriff's office. A deputy stood there, leaning over a desk, his back to Darrow.

"I can't talk with my client till you clear out," said Darrow.

"Yeah, I know," grumbled the deputy, shuffling some papers. "Guess you'll have to wait a moment longer."

"It's been a long day for all of us, so the sooner—"

"Yeah, yeah."

Darrow looked back at Haywood. The big man smacked his lips and sucked his fingers as he devoured the chicken.

"Got a question for you, Mr. Darrow," said the deputy. Darrow looked at the younger man who had turned.

"Uh-huh."

"I've been working for the sheriff's office here for a time. Seen my share of robbers, killers, and rapists come through."

"What's a man's *share* of those?" snarked Darrow.

"What?"

"Go ahead. Especially if it'll lead to you getting out of here."

"Just answer me this," said the deputy, "then I'll go."

"Ok."

"With all them came their lawyers. I seen em all. Some too dumb to climb from a tipped bucket. Some smart, like you."

"Oh, you're talking about the lawyers?"

"Yeah," the deputy continued. "I know some of em. But you came all this way from Chicago to—"

"Let me get you to your question: How can I represent a man if I believe he's guilty?"

Haywood turned, fixing his dead eye on Darrow.

"Yeah, that'd be it," said the deputy. "See, right there—you're smarter than them others, that you knew—"

"His guilt or innocence isn't mine to decide," said Darrow. "That's for the—"

"Deputy," Haywood interrupted, his voice deep and breathy as he wiped his mouth with the back of his hand. "If someday you find yourself on this side of these bars, you'll be glad your lawyer doesn't bother with that question."

Darrow shrugged toward the deputy while motioning toward Haywood, as if to say: *There's your answer.*

The deputy kept his mouth closed.

Haywood continued, "And if you're lucky, you can afford a lawyer as good as Clarence Darrow. Especially when the law itself is corrupt—the judge already siding with the government, the corporate puppets. You know that's who you work for, don't you? I don't mean your sheriff, God rest his soul."

"He was a good man," said the deputy.

Darrow just listened. He knew they were referring to the death two weeks prior of the elderly Ada County Sheriff, leaving this young deputy in uncertain command and out of his depth. Judge Wood said he'd appoint a new sheriff after the trial finished.

Haywood continued, "Who you *actually* work for is who pays your wage—that's the corporations, the mine owners. Might usually be the taxpayers, as it should be, but in this trial, it's fat capitalists, far from here."

"You think so?" asked the deputy.

"I know so. What's your name?" Haywood pressed.

"Billy. Billy Jones."

"What'd your father do, Deputy Jones?"

"Pappy's got a general mercantile, in Cheyenne."

"He's a working man. He answers to himself?"

The deputy nodded. "He started with less than nothing. When my momma died, he brought me out west, from that stinkin city."

"Which city?" asked Haywood. "'Stinkin doesn't narrow it."

The deputy's expression lightened. "New York. I was in britches, but I remember it smelled something awful."

"Now, your pappy's got his own store. An American man, self-made, not the slave to some New York corporation or bank. Not risking his life for their greed."

"That's right."

"But tens of thousands of other men, just like him, also came west for honest work." Haywood stood and moved to the bars. "They had a vision for their lives, same as your pappy had—only they got crushed or gassed in the mines out here, or lost an eye"—he pointed at his own—"for those sons-a-bitches on Wall Street."

Deputy Jones nodded. "School mate of mine died last year."

"He was a miner?"

"Yeah."

"Then you understand. These owners didn't care about your friend. He was just a machine to them. Goddamn em, is what I say. The owners overworked him, abused him, took him for granted. They didn't care whether he lived or died. All they cared about was serving their own purpose—that was it. Your friend was just a cog in the wheel, a body that, once dead, they forgot like so much dirt. That's why I'm dedicated to this fight. Dedicated my life to it. We can never surrender, never stop resisting. Where'd he die?"

"Bunker Hill. At the Concentrator."

Haywood glanced at Darrow, and then back at the deputy. He then asked softly, "A mining accident?"

"No, he was blown to bits when your men bombed the depot."

"Not *his* man," snapped Darrow, indicating Haywood.

The deputy took a moment. "That fella Orchard said he and Adams blew up the Bunker Hill. That means they killed my friend, ain't that right?"

Haywood ignored the question. "You have brothers? Sisters?"

"Got a sister and a brother. They stayed in New York."

"What do they do?"

"Sister's a garment maker."

"Where?"

"Place called Triangle Shirtwaist. Good money, but—"

"Garment makers have a tough go," said Haywood. "Twelve-hour days. They need to better unionize. Where's your brother?"

The deputy hesitated before saying, "He's a banker. Assistant to a vice president of one of them banks."

"In New York?"

The deputy nodded as if admitting to have broken a window.

"What's your pappy think of him?"

"They don't talk."

"That's too bad," said Haywood. "Your brother chose something dishonorable—the business of making money by controlling the earnings of labor. But I know many good men who wear badges like yours. They're honorable because they care who they work for. Judge Wood, the Pinks, their prosecutor, that politician, Senator Borah—they're all paid for by the Mine Owners Association. Including you during all this. Paid out of a New York bank. Maybe the one where your brother works."

The deputy looked at Darrow. "That right?"

Darrow nodded.

"I bet you want to make your pappy proud," said Haywood, "and from what I've seen of you, he should be."

"But your man killed a good number of innocent—"

"Let me ask you, if you decided to open this cell—"

"I ain't gonna—"

"Of course not. But, let's say you were angry at the far-off corporations ruining your life, killing your friends, maybe your family—you might feel powerless to stop them. Might you?"

"Might."

"Say you saw the leader of the Federation standing up against the owners' greed and corruption. Say he was locked up here. You might decide the right thing to do was to let him loose."

The deputy looked around nervously, "I ain't—"

"No, I know. But if you did, would that make you *his man?*"

"No, Sir."

"Then I ask you to stop saying Harry Orchard's *my* man. He chose to do whatever he chose to do. I had nothing to say on it."

The deputy nodded.

Darrow squinted at Haywood, wondering if the man actually believed what he was saying.

"You seem like a good fella," Haywood continued. "They might hang me, or maybe, by some miracle, they might cut me loose. But cither way, your life will go on, Deputy Jones, and you'll have choice upon choice given to you. Remember this conversation. Remember your pappy. Be honorable to yourself, to your country, to the badge you wear. To the citizens, the workers you serve. You understand me?"

"Yes, Sir."

"Now get your coat and go, young man. I'm tired and need to confer with my attorney."

"Yes, Sir," said the deputy, grabbing his coat. He approached the cell and extended his hand between the bars, saying, "Thank you, Sir." After shaking Haywood's hand, he left.

As the outer door closed, Darrow murmured, "Nice speech."

"Wasn't a speech," grumbled Haywood, turning away.

Darrow took a breath. "Denying a directed verdict is standard procedure. It wasn't checkmate, Bill."

"Damn sure sounded like it."

"We have our case."

"What case, Clarence? What case? What would that be? Me taking the stand saying I didn't order the bombing? That was supposed to be our fight *if* they put two witnesses on against me. But here we are, on the walls of the Alamo, even though they've only got one goddamned cannon! One witness. That judge has no intention of following the law."

"It's clear grounds for appeal."

"You know Borah and McParland will hang me before you can get a higher court to step in. Hell, we've already seen what the Supreme Court thinks of this—thinks of me. Any appeal judge will know it too. They'll just say: 'Nah, Borah doesn't need two witnesses.' No, Clarence, they'll protect their own. You know damn well how this'll go. Even though you said otherwise at every turn that got us here."

"Now damnit, Bill, I got Adams to switch stories."

Silence blanketed before Haywood spoke. "That was something," he said, noticeably subdued. "I'll give you that. Only wish it'd make a difference."

"It's not over," said Darrow.

"So— Now what? Now you get sick?"

"Yeah."

"And I'll take the stand once you're back?"

"Probably."

"And you won't tell me why?"

"No. Sorry, Bill."

"All right." Haywood took a big breath. "So, what else? What else can we do?"

"I still have my closing statement."

Haywood snorted. "My life hinges on your talking skills." He shook his head, and then clasped Darrow's shoulder. "Thank God I've got America's Orator."

"That's Bryan."

"What?"

"America's Orator. William Jennings Bryan."

"The hell you say. Not you? What did the *Tribune* call you?"

Darrow took a breath. "America's Lawyer."

"Ah ... well ...to hell with America, I say. You just be *my* lawyer—come last bell. You're all I've got left."

★

– 62 –

TUESDAY
May 21, 1907

The next morning, Judge Wood entered his chambers, removed his coat and hat, and lifted his black robe from its hook behind the door. While he moved toward his desk, a knock resounded behind him. His clerk entered. "We received this about ten minutes ago," the man said, holding out a folded piece of paper.

Wood took it, flipped it open, and read. "Well, I'll be."

"Mn-huh."

"That shoots today," said the judge. "Would be unseemly, the defense attorney vomiting his breakfast on his first witness."

"Or on Senator Borah."

Wood humphed. "Borah might deserve it."

Deputy Jones tapped the door behind the clerk and pushed it further open.

Judge Wood looked up. "No court today, Jones, on account of Mr. Darrow's illness. Tell Senator Borah, of course, but first let the jury go."

"Mr. Darrow is sick?" asked Jones.

"Yes."

"Down a wheezer, or just not up to dick?"

"Who knows," said the judge. "Just ill, I guess."

"Somebody poison him?" Jones pressed. "Hope not."

The judge and the clerk stared at the deputy. "No, Deputy Jones," said the judge. "Is somebody saying that?"

"No, Your Honor," said Jones. "Just with all the things going bad for Mr. Haywood, it made me wonder."

Judge Wood frowned. "Release the jury and tell Borah."

"Yes, Your Honor," said Jones, leaving.

"Where the hell is he?" McParland was pacing his office. "Sick? My Irish ass, he's sick," he growled at Jack and Iain who stood at near-attention. "Find him!"

Jack started to speak. "Men are at the depot, and up the line—"

"There's something afoot here," McParland continued. "Every one of my fibers knows it. And yours should too. He was healthy just last night."

"Looked it," said Iain.

"You sure it was him?"

"I am, Chief."

"Tell me again. He was at the river, near the Ninth Street bridge. Just walking?"

"He and Captain Swain. They crossed, but not at the bridge."

"Where?" McParland asked, referring to a map on his desk.

"There's a ferry rope there," Iain said, pointing. He then glanced at Jack. "Where he crossed before."

Jack glanced at McParland. "I'm not sure—"

"Darrow crossed there?"

Iain frowned, glancing between Jack and McParland. "Yes, Sir."

"Did you hear what they were saying?"

"Swain said something about Chicago, but that's all I—"

"Alright." McParland stared at the map. "Get out there, Agent Lennox. Take some men. See where the tracks lead you."

"Yes, Sir," said Iain, and added, "Agent Garrett may know—"

"Leave that alone," said McParland.

Iain paused. "Aye, Chief"

"Find him ... before too many rumors spread."

"Maybe Darrow got what the sheriff was sick with."

"The sheriff was just at his dizzy age," said McParland. "If Darrow's sick—and I don't think he is—he'll be with his wife."

"His wife?" asked Iain.

"Ruby Hammerstrom," said Jack.

"Aye. A first-rate muckraker." McParland looked at Jack. "Has she checked out of the Saratoga?"

"Aye, Sir." Jack glanced at the upright clock. "A couple of hours ago. Wouldn't talk with anyone. She's still at the depot. Bought a ticket for the 3:45 to Chicago. Should we detain her?"

"Detain her? Agent Garrett, on what grounds do you intend to arrest the wife of the defense attorney?"

"Of course not," said Jack. "Should I go to—"

"No," said McParland. "I'll talk with her."

Boise's depot bustled and hummed—its usual state since the assassination. McParland saw Ruby sitting alone near one wall, reading a book. He adjusted his coat, straightened his vest, and strolled in front of her.

"Mrs. Hammerstrom?"

She looked up and set her book aside. "Yes, Detective?"

He removed his hat. "Ma'am," he said. He looked at her bag on the bench beside her. "May I?"

"If you wish." She moved her bag to the floor.

He sat, placing his hat in his lap, resting both hands on the brass knob of his cane. "I suppose you know why I'm here."

"My husband is ill, Detective. He made that clear. I'm leaving to join him. Other than that, I have nothing to say."

"You're joining him in Chicago?"

"Yes."

McParland looked away, as if studying others in the depot. "Well, that's just not true."

"It is."

"I had men on both of today's trains to Chicago, Ma'am."

"He left last night. You missed him."

"Were that true—first, you would've gone with him, and second, he wouldn't have been seen here in Boise late last night."

Ruby didn't speak.

"Will you at least assure me he's well?"

"No, he's sick."

"I mean, nothing afoul has occurred. You'd tell me, surely."

Ruby gave a small snort. "Afoul? You mean rumors that the Pinkertons killed him."

"Well," said McParland, "of course that's not true. So, if Mr. Darrow is ill, then where is he? Let one of my men confirm."

"*If* he's ill? I don't appreciate— Listen to me, Detective, my husband wants his privacy. Can you not understand that?"

"Aye, but the press are stirring up ideas, saying the trial must end. You're a journalist. Perhaps you can help me." He put on a grandfatherly smile. "Dear, just set minds at ease that no one has been poisoned."

"Poison? You poison the truth every day, at every turn."

McParland's jaw rippled where he clenched it.

"I'm returning to Chicago to be with my husband," she continued. "You and I have finished talking."

"Chicago. Aye. Maybe we should look for him at that socialist bullpen, Hull House."

Ruby looked away.

"As you know, Pinkerton headquarters aren't too far from it. There's no place we don't have access to, in some way. Especially in Chicago."

"This bully tactic won't work on me, Detective. I'm not impressed by, nor afraid of you. Mr. Darrow and I proudly attend events at Hull House, gatherings of people whom you would not begin to understand."

"You're right," said McParland, his brogue emphasized. "I'm just an old Irishman. Not educated beyond a Cork primary school— The nuns tried their best," he said dissembling. "So, no, I wouldn't understand all the bourgeois socialism and hedonism promoted out of Hull House. Maybe you can explain it to me? But start with your unnatural relationship with Miss Rebecca Tarleton."

Ruby's eyes hardened. She blinked, sniffed, glanced away, and then back at McParland. "You may go and rightly fuck yourself, Detective," she said calmly as she stood. She gathered her bag and walked away.

McParland took a deep breath and watched her go, irritated at himself for letting his temper get the best of him.

★

– 63 –

THURSDAY
July 4, 1907

Every several days during the trial's six-week suspension, a telegram arrived in Boise, addressed from Ruby in Chicago to Judge Wood. Each message reported the changing health status of her husband:

MR. DARROW HAS HIGH FEVER.

DOCTOR IS HOPEFUL IT WILL TURN.

MR. DARROW IS BETTER TODAY.

MR. DARROW HAS RELAPSED TO ILLNESS.

HE IS MUCH IMPROVED THIS WEEK.

A small army of Pinkertons, including McParland himself, had fanned out in Chicago, searching for Darrow, but to no avail. They even tried to spot Ruby at one of the telegraph offices, but never did. In one of the telegrams, Ruby said they were not at their home or Hull House—but the Pinkertons already knew that. One thing the telegrams did do was settle the rumors that Darrow had been poisoned. After all, the messages were from his wife. Or were they really? McParland continued to be wracked with anxiety, fearing the famous attorney's body would show up at any moment.

Judge Wood had let the jurymen retire to their homes, but with orders to be ready to return swiftly upon summons.

May turned to June.

Other than nine days in Washington DC, Senator Borah remained at the Idanha Hotel. Isolated in his sheriff's-office cell, Haywood plowed through six more books and engaged in copious correspondence, primarily with the leaders of other labor unions, and with Eugene Debs of the American Socialist Party.

June turned to July.

Then, on Thursday, July 4, in the midst of an Independence Day celebration, Clarence Darrow stepped from a train onto the Boise depot platform. Making his way past its railings festooned in red, white, and blue bunting and banners, Darrow looked well, wearing a new light-wool suit, freshly cut hair, eyes lively and ready. At the taxi stand, he turned to consider a men's acapella group singing a new patriotic song, "America the Beautiful." When someone in the small crowd recognized Darrow, he resumed his progress, hiring a coach to the courthouse. There he declared his readiness to commence the defense's case, and Judge Wood set the trial to resume the following Monday. Deputies were dispatched to the homes of the twelve jurors, and to the prosecution team at the Idanha Hotel.

McParland got the news in Chicago by telegram. From Pinkerton headquarters, he dialed the phone and spoke with the Idanha's front desk attendant.

"Agent Garrett, please. Right away."

After a short wait, Jack came on the line. *This is Agent Garrett.*

"Jack, McParland here. Which train did Darrow arrive on?"

Union Pacific, from Walla Walla.

"From the west?"

Yes, Sir.

"He boarded in Walla Walla?"

We're still interviewing, but that's the earliest any recalled seeing him.

"Damnit." After a moment, he continued, "Swain's still there in Boise?"

Yes, Sir. Might this all be Captain Swain's doing?

"I don't know," McParland muttered, eyes closed. Like a safecracker listening intently to a lock's tumbler, the chief detective let his mind drift through the rack of possibilities, hoping to hear the distinctive, distant click of truth. "Swain lives in Spokane, up from Walla Walla. But he's stayed in Boise?"

The entire time, replied Jack. *Kept himself visible.*

"Anyone else go to Walla Walla?"

Mrs. Haywood did.

"She did?"

On account she's one of those Adventists.

"Right." Another long pause and then, "The governor's wife, Mrs. Steunenberg, she's an Adventist too. Did she also go to Walla Walla?

No, Sir. She left for Los Angeles a few weeks back. Going someplace near there. Hermosa Beach is what the report said.

"Alright, so what did Mrs. Haywood do in Walla Walla?"

I'm not certain. She's been back here a week or more.

"We didn't follow her while she was gone?"

Mrs. Haywood? No, Sir. We heard she was going to Walla Walla College and planned to meet with her preacher, Reverend Sanders, while she was there.

"Maybe she was helping Darrow."

To do what?

"Don't ask me. You find out."

Aye, Chief.

"I'll be there day after tomorrow. The trial is reset?"

Monday morning.

"Alright. Send Agent Lennox up to Walla Walla. Tell him to sniff around. See what he can find. See if Mrs. Haywood was seen with Darrow there, or anything of the sort. And keep talking with those passengers. I want to know where Darrow first boarded that train back to Boise."

Aye, Chief.

★

– 64 –

MONDAY
July 8, 1907

After Judge Wood welcomed Darrow back with platitudes of gratefulness for the attorney's better health, Darrow gave a brief opening statement. Then he called a number of witnesses, each designed to refute some element of Orchard's confession, his actions, his motives, and especially any direct connection between Orchard and Haywood.

Three days later, he called Morris Friedman to the stand. Clean shaven and wearing thick glasses exaggerating his already large eyes, the young man appeared poised and prepared. One reporter would later write that Friedman *"was slow and deliberate in his actions, like the railway conductor who knew the train wouldn't leave without him."* Borah first objected on the grounds of Friedman being a surprise witness, but Darrow successfully beat back that challenge claiming Friedman had only come to Darrow's attention during his illness. Borah's next objection claimed Friedman's testimony should be rendered privileged, as the Pinkerton agency remained in the employ of the State in this matter. But the judge overruled him. So, Friedman swore on the Bible, and Darrow approached.

"Please state your name, Sir."

"Morris Friedman. Miroslav by birth, but Morris will do," he said—his Russian accent thickening his words as they tumbled through his puffy, beet-red lips.

"Mr. Friedman, you were employed, until last October, by the Pinkerton Detective Agency?"

"Of course."

"Is that a yes? You were—"

"Yes."

"How long were you so employed?"

"For the most part of five years, or thereabouts."

"And where did you work, and for whom?"

"In Denver, as stenographer for Chief Detective McParland."

McParland's brow furrowed as he leaned to Jack and whispered, "Maybe that's why Darrow went to Walla Walla—to find this back-stabbing Bolshevik."

"Mr. Friedman was in St. Louis," whispered Jack.

"Alright," said McParland, impressed by the young agent.

Darrow was still talking: "So, what kind of things did you write for him?"

"Correspondences on different matters. Within the agency, for the most part. To Robert Pinkerton and agents in the field."

"And how would you characterize the nature of those correspondences?" asked Darrow, then saw Friedman was confused. "What was the most common subject of those correspondences, to your recollection?"

"Pinkerton operations. I would say. For the most part."

"Objection, Your Honor," Borah said, rising to his feet. "This has no bearing on—"

"Perhaps, but I'll allow it. For now. Let's see where it goes."

Darrow looked at Judge Wood. "Thank you, Your Honor." Then to Friedman: "Operations, you say. Since you were in Denver, working for Detective McParland, would it be correct to say that the majority of those Pinkerton operations were targeted against the Western Federation of Miners?"

"Many." After a thought, he said, "Most, yes."

"All right, can you give us an example of those Pinkerton operations ... against the Federation?"

"Spying. Some of the men were operatives. They infiltrate the Federation. They're numbered—each operative has a number."

"Like Operative 21, for example?" Darrow cut his gaze at Jack.

"Yes," replied Friedman, also glancing at Jack.

Borah was on his feet again. "Your Honor, the internal, private practices of my client are not relevant to—"

"Your client?" burst Darrow. "So the Pinkertons are—"

"No, I meant the agency in the employ of my client, which is of course the State of Idaho."

Wood shook his head. "I think you overruled yourself there, Mr. Borah."

A few chuckles rippled through the gallery.

Borah sighed and sat.

Darrow continued, pleased with how this was going. "Mr. Friedman, for what purpose did these Pinkerton operatives infiltrate the Federation?"

"For the purpose of subverting the Federation's activities. And to report back on those same activities."

"How might an operative do that, subvert union activities?"

"A number of ways. Some as suppliers. Pad their bills."

"They would commit fraud?"

"Yes," said Friedman. "They'd pull money from the Federation."

"And where did that money go?"

"To Pinkerton accounts."

Darrow tightened the knot. "In the five years of such correspondences that you personally read or wrote, could you estimate the amount of dollars taken from the Federation by that means?"

"Something like eighty to one hundred thousand dollars."

Gasps and rumbles came from the gallery.

"Surely that's not correct," said Darrow, feigning surprise. "A hundred thousand dollars stolen by one private organization, the Pinkertons, from another private organization, the Federation? That would be theft, would it not?"

"Objection," fired Borah. "This testimony is about finances? That's prejudicial and irrelevant to this case, Your Honor."

"Counselors approach," said Wood.

Darrow began speaking in a hushed tone the moment he and Borah touched the judge's oak bench. "The State's case pivots entirely on their assertions as to the inner-workings of the Federation, what the Federation's president, my client"—he glanced at Borah—"did or did not say to a third party, Mr. Orchard, who claimed to have been working for the organization in the conduct of a crime perpetrated by that same individual, Mr. Orchard. And those assertions are based in whole on the work of the Pinkerton Detective Agency, which has a long-standing extreme and prejudicial bias against my client and the Federation on matters far outside the State's charge in this case. So, when Senator Borah relied on information provided to him by the Pinkerton Agency, he opened the door for the jury to understand the nature of the relationship between those two organizations—the Pinkertons and the Federation—and specifically between Chief Detective McParland and my client."

Wood's head bobbed as he blinked and his eyebrows rose. He turned to Borah. "I think your objection is overruled, Senator."

Borah clenched. "May I argue in support of my objection?"

"No. Mr. Darrow's said all there is to say on it. More than I want to hear."

"Thank you, Your Honor," said Darrow. He gave a dutiful nod toward the bench and stepped back.

Borah walked away muttering under his breath, "There's more to be said, you two-bit—"

"Counselor," snarled the judge, crooking a finger at Borah, summoning him back. Darrow also returned. Judge Wood leaned toward Borah and spoke louder than was necessary. "I don't give a good goddamn that you're a United States Senator. Not while you're here in *my* courtroom. You will conduct yourself accordingly."

"Yes, Your Honor. My apologies."

Judge Wood continued, "You chose to climb into the ring with this heavyweight boxer"— he motioned toward Darrow—"so take your punches like a man. Sit on your hands if you must, but I intend to let this witness talk."

"Yes, Your Honor." Borah glanced toward the jury as he returned to his seat, hoping they'd missed all that.

"Mr. Friedman," resumed Darrow, "moving along now. You've testified that during your five years with the Pinkerton Agency, you witnessed correspondence from Detective McParland indicating that, over that same time period, as much as one hundred thousand dollars belonging to the Western Federation of Miners had been siphoned into Pinkerton accounts? Is that correct? I mean, is that a correct summary of your testimony today, so far?"

"Yes."

"Very well then," continued Darrow, "in what other ways did the Pinkertons 'subvert Federation activities,' as you called it?"

"They'd cut pay to miners, monies coming though the Federation, just to anger the members against the leadership."

"And by leadership, you mean—"

"Mr. Haywood there, and Mr. Pennington."

"Mr. George Pennington? The Federation's treasurer? The acting president in Mr. Haywood's absence?"

"I don't know about now, of course, but when I was fired, Detective McParland was focused on Mr. Haywood."

Feeling good about this examination, Darrow thought to tidy up any problems that might arise on Borah's cross. He came close to the witness box and spoke in a gentle tone. "One more thing, Mr. Friedman. Why were you fired?" It was a question Darrow hadn't discussed with Friedman, but thought its answer would be harmless: The man was writing a book on the Pinkertons, something Mr. Pinkerton didn't approve of.

Friedman looked spooked for a moment. He frowned and repeated the question, "Why was I fired?"

"Yes, Sir, if you don't mind," Darrow urged. His mind whirled: *Something's wrong. Why is he hesitating?*

"Detective McParland found a manuscript I'm writing."

"A book?"

"Yes, Sir"

"What about? What's your book concerning? The Pinkerton Detective Agency?"

Again Friedman dithered, his eyes locked on Darrow's. Finally, he blew a breath and said, "More than that. I was writing on the embezzlement action—the Pinkerton's work to make it look like Mr. Haywood had stolen more than he already had."

"More than he already—" As soon as Darrow began, he regretted it. "I retract—"

"We knew Mr. Haywood had skimmed thousands from the Federation, but Detective McParland wanted it to look worse, so the papers—"

"Hold a moment, Mr. Friedman," Darrow interrupted. "You don't know if Mr. Haywood had done such a thing."

"I saw Federation ledgers."

"I have to stop you right there," said Darrow, feeling his cheeks flush. He had called Friedman to give evidence against the Pinkertons—revealing the agency's nefarious practices and motivations, how the Pinkertons couldn't be trusted to be the gatherer of the State's evidence. But he'd led this witness right off the path. Now, suddenly, Friedman was introducing evidence that Haywood stole from the union? Embezzlement didn't mean Haywood was guilty of ordering the assassination, of course, but it certainly didn't help his case. Worse yet, the accusation might put Haywood's life in danger—not from the Pinkertons or the government, but from his own labor men. And to tie a big black bow on all this, Darrow couldn't switch to taking Friedman on as a hostile witness, nor could he imply that Friedman was lying—the man was *his* witness after all.

Behind him, Borah was smiling, watching the heavyweight stumble on his own shoe strings.

Darrow continued, slowly, as though easing a horse through fallen timbers. "Would it be correct to say the Pinkertons discussed the *idea* that Mr. Haywood *may have* done such a thing as embezzle, but, as far as you know, there is no direct evidence of such?" He pulled a breath, scolding himself for not better preparing Friedman—for not better preparing himself.

"That's correct."

"All right. Thank you for clarifying ... that point." He stalled again, looking for a pivot back to firmer ground, feeling the juridical parts of his brain scramble for congruence, gasping for the oxygen of a logical argument. "What other actions by the Pinkertons against the Federation were you aware of?"

"All sorts," said Friedman. "The Pinkertons think themselves a secret police force. The one eye—always open and watching."

"The one open eye, yes," mumbled Darrow, his mind not fully re-engaged. *What one eye? Haywood's eye? Oh, yes, the symbol of the Pinkertons—the one eye.* "From your testimony so far, Mr. Friedman, it sounds as if the Pinkertons believe they can do anything they wish. Would you agree?" *There, that was better.*

"Yes."

"Objection," growled Borah. "Leading. Argumentative. This isn't cross-examination or a closing argument."

"Sustained," said Wood. "Mr. Darrow, wrap this up."

"Yes, Your Honor," said Darrow, leaping at the judge's permission to abandon this witness to the wolves. "Thank you, Mr. Friedman. I have no further questions."

Borah stood and said, "Mr. Friedman, thank you for your candor as to the Pinkerton's discovery of possible embezzlement by Mr. Haywood of union funds."

"Objection," blurted Darrow, "that is testimony beyond—"

"Come now, Mr. Darrow," said the judge.

"I would agree with Mr. Darrow, Your Honor," said Borah. "In fact, the State will stipulate that any embezzlement by Mr. Haywood from union coffers is *sui generis* to the facts in question."

Though Darrow winced at the right hook to his jaw, he had to admire Borah's skill at landing it. While making himself appear reasonable and conciliatory, Borah had repeated the embezzlement accusation to the jury, and threw in unnecessary Latin to make it sound even more true.

"Very well," said the judge. "All questions and testimony alleging Mr. Haywood embezzled from the Federation will be struck from the record."

"Thank you, Your Honor," fumed Darrow. Now the judge had repeated it. No matter what the jury thought regarding Haywood's role in the assassination, one thing was now clear to everyone there: Haywood had stolen from the union. But there was little Darrow could do. It was his own outhouse that he'd tipped over.

"So, Mr. Friedman," continued Borah. "I'll ask you directly: Do you have any knowledge or information that might refute the evidence the State has presented in this court, that Mr. Haywood ordered the assassination of the governor of Idaho?"

"No."

Judge Wood shook his head as Darrow rose to object.

Borah turned on his heel. "Very well. No further questions."

Darrow took a breath, unsure how much of that exchange his volatile client had followed. Probably all of it.

– 65 –

TUESDAY
July 23, 1907

The trial was in its third month, counting the recess for Darrow's absence, when, on a hot, ninety-five-degree July day, Darrow called William D. Haywood to the stand. Looking out over the packed room aflutter in hand fans, Big Bill calmly denied every allegation that had been presented by Orchard. Not wearing an eye patch, he was careful to keep his dead eye away from at the jury. In fact, he scooted himself such that even the furthest juror couldn't be jarred by the offending orb. No, he hadn't ordered Mr. Orchard to harm or otherwise do anything regarding anyone, and that included Governor Steunenberg. And no, he had never ordered Mr. Orchard to blow up any mine or depot. Nothing of the sort. Nothing written. Nothing verbal. And no, he had no knowledge of the special yellow paper on which he supposedly wrote orders before burning them. Darrow then took him through the good deeds of the Federation, the lives saved, the widows protected, the children fed and clothed.

When Borah came forward to begin cross-examination, Haywood lifted his head and engaged the special prosecutor with his dead-eyed stare—an unshakable assault on the senator's concentration and confidence. Borah would later shudder in recapping the encounter, saying the man's glare "doubled me up like a jackknife." After an hour, and making no ground against the implacable giant, Borah moved toward his table and began to say, "No further questions," when he pivoted, lifting a finger to the air. "One more question, Mr. Haywood." Staying at the prosecution's table, he raised his voice to be heard by the jury and the gallery alike. "When you were arrested in this matter, where were you?"

Darrow's chair scraped the wood floor as he stood. "Your Honor, I must object. The location of his arrest, which we attest to have been improper at best, is not relevant."

Judge Wood sagged his chin in contemplation, and then raised it and rubbed his neck. "I'll allow it. But, Mr. Borah, I must caution you, if you travel this road too far, I'll have no choice but to allow Mr. Darrow's wish to bring in the procedural questions surrounding the arrest and transportation of the accused."

"I understand, Your Honor," said Borah.

"Then proceed, with that caution."

"Thank you. So, Mr. Haywood, I ask again, where were you at the time of your arrest?"

"At home, in Denver."

"You have two homes, I believe. In which were you that night?"

"My suites in the Pioneer Building."

"And more specifically, in which room were you found?"

Neva turned to look at Winnie four rows back. When the sisters' eyes met, and Winnie saw Neva's tears, Winnie mouthed silently, "I'm sorry," then rose and hurried from the courtroom.

Haywood watched her go, then bounced a look at Neva. Then he turned to Borah. "You asked where I was—when they invaded my house and kidnapped me?"

"In which room were you when you were arrested?"

"None of your goddamned business is where."

Borah looked at the judge. "May the witness be instructed—"

"I'll certainly not," barked Judge Wood. "It's his prerogative not to answer such a question."

"Then I choose not to," said Haywood.

"I'll ask it another way, then," said Borah. "Isn't it true that you were in bed with your wife's sister at the time of the arrest?"

The gallery had to be gaveled to silence and order.

Fixing his gaze on the empty air before him, Haywood flexed his jaw and shook his head, almost imperceptibly.

"So, you're saying it is not true? You might not answer, but you may not lie, Mr. Haywood. So, I'll ask you again, were you not in bed with your wife's sister—in her bedroom?"

Haywood's glare remained, his head now motionless.

"Very well," said Borah. He turned to the jury. "The defendant refuses to answer—thus inviting us to draw what conclusions we will. Are you a Christian, Mr. Haywood?" He pivoted to face the witness chair.

"No. Most certainly not."

Darrow started to stand, but Woods motioned him down.

"No?" pressed Borah. "And why's that?"

"It's nonsense," said Haywood, his fingers now entwined with themselves.

"Including the faith of your wife, the Adventists?"

"Fables and the vagaries, like that old woman's science."

Borah frowned at the unexpected answer. "Do you mean Mary Baker Eddy?"

"Yeah, the blathering bag."

"That's Christian Scientists, right? The Adventists are—"

"Same damn thing, basically."

Neva blanched and looked at her hands in her lap. George handed her a handkerchief across the back of her seat.

"I'm certain the two religions are not the same. But to continue: as a professed atheist, Mr. Haywood, do you nonetheless think it not an outrage of natural law, a corruption, for a man to lie with his wife's sister? To commit such an act of obscene adultery?"

Darrow got to his feet, but it was not necessary.

"All right, Senator," said the judge, intentionally using the title. "Shall I open up the entirety of the arrest?"

"It won't be necessary."

"No? Then this line of questioning is at its end."

"Yes, Your Honor," said Borah. "I have no further questions for the defendant."

Judge Wood looked at Darrow. "Redirect, Mr. Darrow?"

Darrow scratched his eyebrow, took a breath and stood. "No, Your Honor. The defense rests."

Behind Darrow, Neva dabbed her eyes with George's handkerchief, then set her gaze on an angle away from Bill as he stood from the witness box.

– 66 –

WEDNESDAY
July 24, 1907

The time came for Darrow to give his closing argument, to say whatever he could to persuade the jury to save Haywood. In the weeks leading up to this moment, he'd often focused his thoughts on the sheep rancher, O. V. Sebern, the juror who Jack had deceived Darrow into sitting—the juror who undoubtedly would vote to convict, regardless of the evidence, regardless of the two-witness rule. How could he convince *that* man? That man who shouldn't be on this jury in the first place. How could he turn Sebern's vote from guilt to innocence? He rolled the problem around like a Chinese puzzle box, vexed, looking to unlock it, trying to convince himself that it had at least one invariable solution.

Meanwhile a blacker question hissed at him from the procedural gloom. How had he allowed himself to be so manifestly misled? The most treacherous man is the one who moves with grace through his own deception. Jack Garrett did that. Darrow had to respect the young man's skill, the simplicity of his ruse, the elegant prevarication. It had rattled Darrow since he realized it that first day in court. He'd been tricked into putting that spurious Sebern fellow on this jury, a certain ringer for the prosecution—*not* for the defense, as advertised. What a fool, he'd been. It was a far worse error than calling Friedman to the stand. Well, thank God, Haywood didn't know about Sebern. But Carla knew. Of course, she did. She'd carried the lie from Jack to Darrow. But had she known it was a lie when she relayed it? Darrow was unsure. Regardless, surely she knew now. But she wouldn't tell Haywood. Would she? She wasn't allied with the Federation's cause anymore. She'd even stopped coming to court. That did little to allay Darrow's worries, but it was all he had.

He banged his thoughts back to where they belonged: persuading Mr. O. V. Sebern. In fact, as he got to his feet to address the jury, he told himself to be glad Sebern was sitting there in front of him. The man wasn't a villain, he was an opportunity. The man gave him a target, a single person whom Darrow's words must impact, must sway. If he won Sebern, he might win them all. But Sebern wouldn't be convinced by outright denials. Darrow would have to take a serpentine path of his own, a calculated risk. He'd need to concede a few Federation faults and transgressions. Then, once Sebern became convinced of Darrow's reasonableness—once Sebern sensed Darrow understood him, indeed aligned with him in some ways—then Darrow could lead Sebern, and thus the other jurors, out of the darkness of the union's misdeeds, and into the aura of innocence of one man, and then on to the inevitability of a not-guilty verdict. Or so went Darrow's plan.

He began by excoriating Orchard, calling him "the biggest liar that this generation has known." He went further, declaring, "Any man who'd take away the life of a human being, another man, simply on the testimony of an animal of Harry Orchard's low character, would place a stain upon the state of his nativity that all the waters of the great seas could never wash away."

Six hours later, Darrow went for his divergent gambit. "I don't mean to tell this jury that labor organizations do no wrong. I know them too well for that. They do wrong, often, and sometimes brutally. They're sometimes cruel. They're often unjust. They're frequently corrupt." The courtroom seemed to gasp in unison. People whispered, scooted in their benches, then froze. Darrow glanced at Haywood who remained composed. He looked at Neva, behind Haywood. To Darrow, she seemed a flat cut-out, an enduring shell of a woman. He faced the jury again.

"Yes, labor unions can be corrupt. Capable of being unjust. Human. I know that. As do you. But I'm here to say that in a great cause, these labor organizations, despised and weak and outlawed as they generally are, have stood for the poor, they've stood for the weak, they've stood for every human law ever placed upon the statute books. They've stood for human life. They've stood for the father, bound down by his task. They've stood for the wife, threatened to be taken from the home to work by his side. And they've stood for the little child, also taken to work in their places, that the rich could grow richer still. And they've fought for the right of the little one, to give him a little of life, a little comfort while he is young."

Darrow returned to his table to drink from his water glass. As he tipped the glass back, he let his gaze fall across his fingers to the silent gallery beyond. A few women were dabbing their tears. Good, he thought. The time had come. He returned to the jury, looking first at Sebern. "But I don't care how many wrongs they've committed. I truly don't. I don't care how many crimes these weak, rough, rugged, unlettered men who often know no other power but the brute force of their strong right arm, who find themselves bound and confined and impaired whichever way they turn, who look up and worship the god of might as the only god they know. I don't care how often they fail, how many brutalities they're guilty of. I know their cause is just."

An hour later, feeling that he had Sebern, he began to slowly pull the jury in, reeling them toward "not guilty." Even if he couldn't convince them of an alternate motive for Orchard's actions, Darrow needed only plant the seed of doubt regarding Haywood's involvement—to refuse them the safe harbor of "beyond a reasonable doubt." Governor Steunenberg's assassination had clearly been motivated as Orchard had said: in retaliation for the governor wrongfully incarcerating (for a time) all the Federation men in Idaho, after the Bunker Hill attack. But the assassination had not occurred by Haywood's order. No, Orchard had lost a share in a silver mine due to the governor's actions in the wake of Bunker Hill. Thus, Orchard killed the governor, acting alone, and without the assistance of Steve Adams—just as Adams had testified. It was nothing more than personal, spiteful revenge. And Orchard's shameful lie of a "confession" regarding Haywood and the scrap of paper? Harry Orchard would take it to his grave as to why he had given such unconscionable false witness against Bill Haywood. Perhaps Orchard carried some depraved hope for revenge against Haywood, just as he had carried against Governor Steunenberg. No one would ever know.

Finally, in the eleventh hour of his closing, Darrow delivered his summation. "I have known Bill Haywood. I've known him well, and I believe in him. I do believe in him. God knows it would be a sore day to me if he should ascend the scaffold. The sun would not shine, nor would the birds sing on that day, for me. It would be a sad day indeed if any calamity should befall him. I would think of him. I would think of his wife. I would think of his babes. I would think of the great cause that he represents. It would be a sore day for me. But, gentlemen, he and his wife and his children are not my chief concern in this case. If you should decree that he must die, ten thousand men will work down in the mines to send a portion of the proceeds of their labor to take care of that widow and those orphan children, and a million people throughout the length and the breadth of the civilized world will send their messages of kindness and good cheer to comfort them in their bereavement. So, no, it's not for them I plead."

Again, he sipped from his glass. Finishing the water, he motioned to Deputy Jones, who brought a pitcher and refilled it. Darrow stationed himself in front of Sebern and said, "Thank you, Deputy Jones." He looked at the floor, and then surveyed the eyes of the jurors. "Other men have died. Other men have died in the same cause in which Bill Haywood has risked his life. Men strong with devotion. Men who love liberty. Men who love their fellow men. Men who have raised their voices in defense of the poor, in defense of justice. They've made their good fight and have met death on the scaffold, on the rack, in the flame. And they will meet it again and again until the world grows old and gray."

Darrow turned to face Haywood. "Bill Haywood is no better than the rest. He can die, if die he needs. He can die if this jury decrees it." Facing the jury again. "But, oh, gentlemen, don't think for a moment that if you hang him you'll crucify the labor movement of the world. Don't think that you'll kill the hopes and the aspirations and the desires of the weak and the poor." He focused again on Sebern, and then the others. "You men, unless you are anxious for this blood, are you so blind as to believe that liberty will die when he's dead? Do you think there are no other brave hearts, no other strong arms, no other devoted souls who will risk their lives in that great cause which has demanded martyrs in every age of this world? There are others, and these others will come to take Bill Haywood's place. They'll come to carry the banner where he could not carry it. And it is one banner, the same banner. And in that same banner runs the color red, for sacrifice, blood spilt for the most noble struggle. For liberty. For justice. For life."

Pockets of sobs came from the gallery, elsewise crisp with silence. Darrow turned toward the sounds and sniffed. He gave a sad nod toward Winnie who wiped her cheeks, and noted Neva was still stone. He rotated back to the jury. "Gentlemen, it's not for him alone that I speak. I speak for the poor. For the weak. For the weary. For that long line of men who in darkness and despair have borne the labors of the human race. The eyes of the world are upon you, upon you twelve men of Idaho tonight."

He leaned on the rail of the jury box and spoke softly. "Wherever the English language is spoken, or wherever any foreign tongue known to the civilized world is spoken, men are talking and wondering and dreaming about the verdict of you twelve men that I see before me now. If you kill him, your act will be applauded by many. If you should decree Bill Haywood's death, in the great railroad offices of our great cities, men will applaud your names. If you decree his death, amongst the spiders of Wall Street will go up paeans of praise for those twelve men, good and true, who killed Bill Haywood. In every bank in the world, where men hate Bill Haywood because he fights for the poor and against the accursed system upon which the favored live and grow rich and fat, from all those you will receive blessings and unstinted praise."

Darrow paced, took another sip of water, and returned. "But, but, if your verdict should be not guilty, there are those who will reverently bow their heads and thank you, you twelve men, for the life and the character you have saved. Out on the broad prairies where men toil with their hands, out on the wide ocean where men are tossed and buffeted on the waves, through our mills and factories, and down deep under the earth, thousands of men and of women and children, men who labor, men who suffer, women and children weary with care and toil, these men, and these women, and these children will kneel tonight and ask God to guide your judgment. These men and women, and these little children, the poor, the weak, and the suffering of the world, will stretch out their hands to this jury, and implore you to save Bill Haywood's life."

★

– 67 –

THURSDAY
July 25, 1907

For five hours the next afternoon, lasting again till after dark, Senator Borah gave the State's closing argument. He began by saying the trial was not an attack on organized labor, but "simply a trial of a murder." Indeed, the only thing the prosecution sought was justice for his friend, Frank Steunenberg. "Let us never forget that night when he was sent to face his god without a moment's warning, and within sight of his wife and children. It has never left my mind."

Borah then deconstructed and denigrated the Federation and Haywood. He walked the jury through the details of Orchard's "born again" confession. "In it, in his words, I saw divine grace working upon his soul, and through him, to bring justice to one of the worst criminal bands that ever operated in this country." Borah implored the jury to also examine Orchard's actions, what he did and where he went, like his many trips to Denver. "Why? Why always back to Denver? Unless it was to find there the protection and pay of his employer."

Nearing the end, he paused, clutched the witness-stand rail, and stood straight. "In preparing to speak with you tonight, I remembered again the awful thing of December 29, 1906, a night which has taken ten years from the life of some who are in this courtroom now. I felt again its cold and icy chill, faced the drifting snow, and peered at last into the darkness for the sacred spot where last lay the body of my dead friend, and saw true, only too true, the stain of his life's blood upon the whitened earth. I saw Idaho dishonored and disgraced. I saw murder—no, not murder, a thousand times worse than murder. I saw anarchy wave its first bloody triumph in Idaho. And as I thought again, I said, 'Thou living God, can the talents or the arts of counsel un-teach the lessons of that hour?' No, gentlemen, no. Let us not be blinded by the art of oration. Mr. Darrow has that art within him. You heard it yesterday. Last night,

I saw tears throughout this courtroom. What elegant oration. But of what consequence upon the facts in question? None. The facts remain: Mr. Haywood ordered the killing of Frank Steunenberg."

Borah walked to his table for water, returned and regarded the men in the jury box. "Let us be brave. Let us be faithful in this supreme test of trial and duty. If the defendant is entitled to his liberty, let him have it. But, on the other hand, if the evidence in this case discloses the author of this crime, then there's no higher duty to be imposed upon citizens than the faithful discharge of that particular duty. Some of you men have stood the test and trial in the protection of the American flag." He turned and looked at the American flag behind Judge Wood. "You know all too well the meaning of the red stripes in that flag. You don't need a Chicago lawyer to come explain it to you. You know it in your soul. You have served your nation. You *are* this nation." Finally, he softened his voice and said, "But you've never had a duty imposed upon you like this—one which requires more intelligence, more manhood, more courage than that which the people of Idaho assign to you tonight. And now it is time for you to discharge that final duty."

★

– 68 –

FRIDAY
July 26, 1907

It was a beautiful Friday in Boise. The prior evening's rain, during Borah's closing arguments, had cooled the ground and air. Then came the morning's clear skies throwing newness across the long-trampled courthouse lawn.

Inside, once all were seated, Judge Wood gave the jury their instructions. "You must keep forward in your mind that the defendant is presumed innocent. The State of Idaho—the prosecution—had the burden to prove guilt. You may only convict if it is your unanimous verdict that the defendant is guilty of the charges beyond a reasonable doubt. The only other verdict can be where you *all* agree that the defendant is not guilty. You must deliberate until you reach a unanimous verdict, of one or the other. Further, due to the charge against the defendant, you may not reach a guilty verdict unless you believe the prosecution presented corroborating evidence by two or more persons of to the defendant's involvement in the assassination of Governor Steunenberg."

The jury began deliberations at eleven-ten in the morning.

"So I don't hang, the jury needs to hang," mused Haywood.

"That's about the sum of it," said Darrow, sitting next to his client in the spacious cell. Both were leaning against the wall, their chairs' front legs off the floor. Both were in their shirt sleeves. Haywood puffed a cigar. Darrow a cigarette.

"And you say they won't retry me?"

"Yes, I said that, but— My God, Bill, after all this— One missread after another. Bad guess upon worse. How am I to know?"

Haywood nodded. "You've done as best you could."

"I don't know."

"Just to hear you in that closing argument."

"I apologize I had to acknowledge some less favorable things. It was strategic, of course."

"Well, the rest was terrific eloquence."

"Mmph," snorted Darrow. "I suppose we'll see."

Haywood blew a blue cloud across the cell, then followed it with a self-satisfied chortle. "I know where you went, when you were killdeer-ing like you were sick."

"I told you I was going to mock an illness."

"Yes, but you didn't tell me why, or where you'd go."

"No. It was best to—"

"But I figured it out. Where you went. What you did."

"You think so?"

"While you were gone, I had more talks with Deputy Jones in here. They wouldn't let anyone else come see me. We put our minds to it. He's a smart young man."

Darrow smiled. "So, where did I go?"

"You went to Wallace, up north, where they tried Adams for murdering the sheriff's boy. You represented Adams there."

Darrow didn't blink. "Why do you think that?"

"Deputy Jones helped take Adams up there for that sheriff. On the way, seems Adams jabbered about how he wasn't afraid because he was gonna have America's Lawyer representing him."

Darrow shook his head. "That nickname again."

"So that was right?" Haywood absorbed the implications.

"Thank God the deputy didn't tell McParland," said Darrow. "He and Borah would've told Judge Wood, and he, well—"

"No, I won young Deputy Jones over that night you were here. You saw that. So, he kept it to himself. I think he's a little afraid of me." Haywood squinted the dead eye.

Darrow stared blankly into the vacant office beyond the cell. "I'm not sure I did right. Sheriff Sutherland was fireball mad. I can't say I blame him, seeing how I used him for your benefit. He hadn't seen what I was going to do, or he'd never have agreed to it." Darrow rubbed his nose. "He thought we were going to dupe Adams into some hair-brained escape plan. Instead, I got his boy's killer set free."

"No, don't be hard on yourself. You did him a favor."

"Who?"

"That sheriff."

"Why's that?"

"He'll kill Adams himself. Right?"

"Probably."

"That's what I'd do if someone hurt one of my girls. That's justice. Real justice can only be found outside a courthouse. A man has to set things right himself, directly. These goddamned judges and juries, they never get it right."

Darrow doubted Haywood realized that the very vigilantism Haywood advocated might come looking for him—if the union believes Haywood stole from them. But that was a fight for another time. And only if Haywood didn't hang first.

"This jury had better get it right," said Haywood.

"I hope so," murmured Darrow, beginning to be unsure which verdict would be "right." Had he gotten the "right" verdict in Wallace? He closed his eyes, his mind flooding with the absurdity of his client, this murderer, explaining justice, saying he'd kill someone who hurt one of his girls—children the man rarely sees. It was repulsive—Haywood's obscene hypocrisy—reflecting Darrow's own. He shook the thought free, creaked his chair forward, stood, then extinguished his cigarette under his heel. He should get this in the open. "There's another matter, Bill. Those missing funds that the Russian fellow, Friedman, was talking about."

"Why'd you let him say all that nonsense? Not a word of truth to it. You heard what he said: Pinks are inside our accounts, twisting numbers to say I'm thieving. But you know that's not true."

"The leadership came to me," said Darrow, his face hardening.

"You mean George Pennington came to you."

"He did, along with the local labor presidents."

"How many?"

"All of them," said Darrow.

Haywood stood abruptly, but stayed silent for a bit. Then he said, "You represent *me*, Clarence."

"Yes, in *this* case. Otherwise I represent the Federation."

Haywood glowered. "The great Clarence Darrow, America's Lawyer—my savior today, my hangman tomorrow."

"I'm not your savior, nor—"

"That wasn't the point!" thundered Haywood.

Darrow squared with Haywood but spoke calmly. "Nor will I be your hangman. After this jury returns, regardless of the verdict, I'll no longer be your attorney. And, in truth, I'm not sure I'll want to further represent the Federation."

"If you're not mine, you lose the whole union."

"So long as you're its president, that will be—"

"So long as I'm president? What does that mean?"

"I'm just being clear, in case we win tomorrow," said Darrow.

Haywood nodded. "Well, we goddamned-well better."

By nightfall, with no word from the sequestered jury, the saloons, parlors, and hotel lobbies across Boise vibrated with speculations. Those who hadn't heard Darrow's closing argument tended toward Haywood hanging. But for those who'd heard it, a unanimous guilty verdict seemed unfathomable. Many thought it'd be a mistrial, a hung jury—11 to 1, 10 to 2, maybe 9 to 3—in favor of conviction to some, or in favor of acquittal to others. But no one guessed a unanimous verdict of not guilty. Haywood, by popular estimation, would either hang, or he'd be tried again.

★

– 69 –

SUNDAY
July 28, 1907

The jury was nerve-rackingly silent on Saturday. Then, at 6:40 a.m. Sunday morning, Judge Wood was roused from sleep with word that, after deliberating all night, the jury had reached a verdict.

Darrow studied their faces as they entered the courtroom, shuffling into the jury box. As he expected, none would make eye contact with him, or look at Haywood. Then O. V. Sebern glanced at Darrow and seemed to scowl. Darrow leaned close to Haywood. "Bill, old man, you'd better brace yourself for the worst. I'm afraid it's against us. Keep your nerve."

Haywood gave a "Mmph."

Judge Wood began. "Gentlemen of the jury, your service across the dark hours of last night is greatly appreciated. Have you elected a foreman?"

Sebern raised his hand. "Yes, Your Honor. I'm the foreman."

Darrow closed his eyes. *Sebern. Damnit.*

Judge Wood said, "Mr. Foreman, it's my understanding that this jury has reached a verdict. Is that correct?"

"Yes, Your Honor."

"And is the verdict you have reached the opinion of each and every member of this jury?"

"Yes, Your Honor."

"Very well, present your verdict to the clerk."

The clerk took a note from Sebern's hand and brought it to Judge Wood. He looked at it nonplussed and handed it back to the clerk. "The clerk of the court will read the verdict."

The clerk turned to face the gallery. "We the jury in the above entitled cause find the defendant, William D. Haywood, not guilty."

Darrow sat stunned. As did Borah.

Haywood jumped to his feet, laughing and crying at once. As Darrow finally responded, grinning, standing, Haywood shook his hand, and then bear hugged him, lifting Darrow off his feet. Then Haywood turned and rushed the jury box, attempting to shake all of their hands.

Neva stood, gathering her crutches under her arms, then eased herself into the aisle, George close behind. She gave Winnie a grave smile, then made her way up the aisle to the main doors. In the hallway, crowded and loud with reporters and attendees pouring out, George helped Neva to the elevator.

Having walked out just after Neva and George, Winnie shuffled down the courthouse's stairwell, avoiding the elbows and shoulders of the press—some coming up, most barreling down, racing to feed the world the verdict.

At the front of the courtroom, Haywood spun, elated, hoping to find Winnie and Neva—but both were gone. He asked Darrow if he'd seen Winnie, but Darrow hadn't. Darrow pivoted to Senator Borah and shook his hand.

"Clarence," said Borah, his tone brusque. "Congratulations."

Darrow sighed. "Senator."

"Tough battle," said Borah. "I'm surprised, of course."

"Without a second witness—"

"Yes, Steve Adams." Borah shook his head. "How?"

"He changed his mind," Darrow said firmly.

Borah sucked air through his teeth. "Nah, no ... I'll figure out the truth. Then maybe I'll let the Illinois bar know it."

Darrow felt a shimmer of anger and grabbed Borah's arm. "What truth, Senator? It's all vagaries. You know that. Transient facts. You and your private army—" He nodded toward McParland who was approaching. "You did as you pleased. Ran roughshod over the Constitution. Kidnapped a man in the name of the law. Before that, your client imprisoned thousands without trial. And now you want truth?" Borah started to move away, but Darrow pressed, still talking quietly. "You bottle truth like my aunt cans her peaches.

What you can't use here"—he gestured toward the judge's vacant bench—"you hide in your basement or throw to the pigs."

"Be happy with your win, Clarence," Borah admonished.

As McParland was now standing beside Borah, Darrow addressed them both. "You want to know why Adams changed his plea? You want to know why you lost?" Darrow's face was flushed. "No ... no." He turned and started to gather his things.

"Mr. Darrow," began McParland, "we've only begun to look—"

Darrow wheeled on him. "I fought on the battlefield of *your* making, Detective. You defined the high ground. And you dug the low as well. You did that before I got here. So, truth? Facts? I say, do as you please. Follow the strings into the damn woods. See where they take you. Vagaries. That's all you'll find, vagaries of the truth. No matter how far you go. Because, gentlemen, the strings were yours all along." He stared at them, nodded and moved quickly toward the exit. He wanted nothing more to do with them, with all of this. He wanted to leave Boise and never return. And he would. But there was one man he had to speak with first.

At one of the hitching rails along the edge of the courthouse lawn, O. V. Sebern prepared to mount his horse. "Mr. Sebern?" cried Darrow, approaching hurriedly. "Mr. Sebern, if I may?" Darrow offered his hand to the wrinkled rancher.

"Mr. Darrow," said Sebern, shaking the attorney's hand.

"This has been a grueling time for us all."

"Were you not paid?" asked Sebern.

"Yes, I was."

"So—one of us was."

Darrow attempted a smile. "Your service was appreciated."

"Two dollars a day, they gave us. For two months."

"Yes, Sir. I wish they paid jurors more, I do. I know you must be exhausted after your all-night work, and I'm sure you want to get home to your family. But, before you go, may I ask you a question? I promise to be quick."

"If you don't ask me right here, are you planning to come knocking at the ranch? Gonna bother me there?"

"I don't intend to bother you, but ... Would that be better?"

"God no," said Sebern. "Just spill it here, Mr. Darrow."

"Thank you." Darrow sniffed. "Could you share with me how the jury came to its verdict?"

"I'm allowed to do that?"

"Yes, Sir. Now that the trial is done."

Sebern glanced around. "Took us six ballots, one every few hours or so. We started at eight for acquittal, two guilty, and two couldn't decide."

"Am I right that you were one of the two guilty?"

Sebern frowned. "Why would you assume that?"

"You seemed certain of his guilt, at the beginning."

"I was and I still am." He peered at Darrow. "Why select me then, if you knew my mind was made against your client?"

"The Pinkertons had a spy in my— It doesn't matter."

"Mn-huh," grumbled Sebern.

Darrow frowned at the acknowledgment, as if Sebern might have known he'd been used. "You were saying, about the decision?"

"We had to acquit the man."

"Why was that?"

"The State only had the one witness."

Darrow nodded.

"Some were all worked up from your long speech, there at the end. I didn't care how they got to the right decision, just that they did. We couldn't convict the sorry son of a bitch no matter how much he deserved it. Your fancy speech didn't matter to me."

"You convinced the other four?"

"I did. Me and another. Took the night. Couple stubborn assess, they were. I'll tell you straight, Mr. Darrow, I heard you did something to get that other witness, that Adams fella, to change his mind. But I couldn't think on it as I knew nothing about it. The law is the law. And who made the law but us anyhow? If we say it takes two witnesses to hang a man, then by God it oughta take two witnesses. It doesn't matter how much I despise those union vermin—Haywood and his bunch. Or the Pinkertons. Damn em all. They're all corrupt, you ask me. And you, with your smooth talk, saying unions do bad sometimes, like that might justify anything."

Darrow dipped his head. "You noticed that."

"Yeah, sure," scoffed Sebern. "I'm not saying you're no good at what you do, Mister. You are. You got most all the jury going with you. But not me. I wasn't gonna fall for it."

Darrow nodded. "That's fair."

"But I got them others to come round."

"Thank you, Sir."

"Yeah. Well, you have yourself a good day."

"You too," said Darrow.

With that, Mr. O. V. Sebern mounted his horse and rode away.

An hour into McParland supervising the crating of his Idanha Hotel office, his telephone jangled.

"James McParland."

Ah, Jim, said Robert Pinkerton on the other end.

"Mr. Pinkerton," McParland replied, then heard a deep sigh over the line. "We did our best. Whether Senator Borah could pull out a win was—"

I'm not going to sugar coat it. The Tribune *has been unkind of late.*

"I imagine so," said McParland.

Darrow's wife was already riding us rough-shod— Then the verdict.

"Mn-huh, I've read some of it."

That was a serious shelling you bought down on us.

"The men did their best."

I'm sure they did.

"We lost the one in San Francisco. Otherwise—"

Jim, now you know that's not the shelling I'm meaning.

"No. You mean Morris Friedman."

Yeah. How'd that Jew get to say all that rubbish about your work?

"Courtroom procedure is Senator Borah's—"

The senator knows my displeasure. The phone remained silent for a moment, as if the device itself knew what was coming. Finally, Pinkerton resumed, *We need to make some changes.*

"Oh?"

Yeah, I'm afraid so. With the Jew, and then all the other things.

"I had your approval on our—"

Jim, now, we're not going to discuss anything operational.

"Of course not."

How about, instead of heading back to Denver, you come to Chicago for a stretch. We'll bring Mary here too, for you.

"For a stretch," said McParland, feeling his voice crack.

For a stretch. We'll talk.

"I want to first get to the bottom of this matter with Darrow," McParland said, clambering for a slippery lifeline. "Where he went. We need to know how he got Adams to switch—"

No, Jim, I'm telling you to let that go. We got whipped. That's just the way it is. The how of it all doesn't matter right now. That'll sort itself in time. Put Jack Garrett on it, if you want. Let's see what he can do running Denver. He'll make a good detective, from your reports. But, let's you and me have this conversation in person.

McParland felt his throat tightening, his face warming, his career sliding to an end. "I understand, Sir."

Good. And don't worry about a thing. We'll talk over fourteen-year-old Jameson and some fine Partagás. We'll see what's best. Hell, Jim, at some point, a man has to think on retirement. Mary would be thrilled if you were home more.

McParland cleared his throat. "Aye, Sir. Of course, Sir."

★

– 70 –

TUESDAY
July 30, 1907

The Minor sisters were riding next to each other in the first-class passenger car of a Union Pacific train rolling slowly across the Green River bridge, east bound. Though Neva sat nearest the window, only Winnie was focused outside. But once across, Neva also looked out, seeing the waning sun casting its flame over the rocky hills, the tree clusters, and the long Wyoming grasses hurrying along. A mile later, and unknown to them, they passed the site where, four months earlier, the local Sheriff Wilkins and two of his men were machine-gunned to death as they attempted to blow the track and rescue Neva's husband.

"I'll miss you terribly," said Neva.

"We'll see each other," said Winnie. "I'll just be in Chicago ... or Kansas."

"I know, but— You know."

"Yeah," said Winnie. "I can't believe you want to go back to Walla Walla. I don't think I could."

"We'll see. For the time being, I'll stay in Denver. The house is perfect for the girls. And George likes that it's so close to City Park and the new museum."

"George," Winnie mused warmly.

"Yes. George." Neva nodded and flashed a rueful smile.

"I'm happy for you, that you have him, Sissy."

Ten minutes passed before Neva leaned close to Winnie and whispered, "I hope that socialist, Debs, knows what he's getting himself into—bringing on a mustang like you."

Winnie shrugged. "He said they need my spirit, so ..."

After another mile, Neva spoke again. "It was kind of Mrs. Darrow to credential you for Mr. Deb's newspaper."

"Yes. It's called *Appeal to Reason*. I like that." Winnie produced an issue from her satchel.

"Oh, yes," said Neva, scowling at the socialist rag, as if Winnie had proudly pulled a dead rat from her bag.

Twenty-five minutes, two trestles and one tunnel later, Winnie asked, "Are we going to talk about Bill?"

"Must we?"

"I suppose not."

"Good."

"He'll be in Denver?" Winnie asked.

"Tomorrow, I believe."

"I want to see him."

"Do what you will," Neva said dryly.

"But you aren't—"

"I told you, I'll never speak to him again. There must be consequences for what he's said and done. I thought we weren't going to talk about him."

"Yes, all right," Winnie murmured.

"You're a grown woman, Sissy," said Neva. "If you love the man, well, Lord help you, but that's something you need to resolve on your own." She looked out the window before continuing. "I don't love him. I'm not sure I ever did. I'd divorce him if I could." Her mind wandered at the thought. She'd been chewing on the idea of divorce for so long that it'd begun to soften and tear. "But that's neither here nor there. I'm getting the girls back. And George and I will— I'm going to live my life. And so will you."

"What's going to happen to him?" asked Winnie.

"To George? Nothing. He did nothing. There's—"

"No, Sissy, to Bill. What's going to happen to Bill?"

"I don't care."

"But, do you know?"

Neva took a considered breath. "I have a pretty good idea."

"What?" Winnie implored. "What's going to happen?"

Neva sat motionless for a moment before taking one of Winnie's gloved hands into her own. "I'm not saying this to be impolite. I'm not, truly. But I'm not going to tell you what the Federation has in mind for Bill. He stole a great deal of money from them. I know you'd probably tell him and—"

"I wouldn't."

"You probably would, Sissy. So, let's just leave things as they are, shall we? Let's not let that man come between us any more."

Winnie withdrew her hand and looked out the windows on the far side. "So, you won't tell me?"

Neva smiled at her petulant young sister. "No, crock-cratcher, I won't."

Winnie held her face stern for as long as she could before finally her cheeks burst, laughing at the ridiculous memory.

★

– 71 –

WEDNESDAY
July 31, 1907

Three days after the trial ended, Jack and Carla met the train from Spokane. As Iain stepped onto the platform with a bag, Jack shook his hand, and Carla gave a smile. Her dark hair was pompadoured under a narrow-brimmed motoring hat that Jack had bought her that morning.

"What a circus you missed," said Jack.

"Been reading about it," said Iain. "All the way from Spokane."

"You have bags to collect?" asked Carla.

"Just this one."

"Spokane?" asked Jack. "I thought you were in Walla Walla."

"Trail carried me north."

The three were quiet until they approached the depot's curb where horse-drawn coaches were passing. Iain started to hail one. "No, we're taking you," Jack said, grabbing Iain's bag and walking away with it. Carla walked alongside.

Iain followed, curious and bemused. Across the street, he laughed seeing Jack toss the bag onto the rear luggage platform of an open-topped, 1907 Mason Runabout—cherry red with two cream leather seats.

"I'm done with horses!" declared Jack, going around to hold Carla's gloved hand as she stepped aboard.

"Oh, I don't get shotgun?" asked Iain.

Carla turned. "I'd drive, but he wants to show off to you."

"Show off? I've seen his driving. I endured it for two hundred miles. For godsakes, please do drive, Miss Capone."

"Alright, damnit," said Jack, laughing as he got in behind the wheel. "You both have to squeeze your butts into that seat."

Iain climbed aboard, but his big frame was too much to share the seat with Carla, so she moved over and sat on Jack's lap. She turned her head and kissed his cheek, though it was awkward under his hat's wide brim. "You need to take this off or you'll lose it," she said, playfully reaching for it.

He grinned and leaned away from her. "Not so fast."

"If I get lucky," she said, settling against his chest, "it'll just blow away." She fluttered her hand in the air.

"I guess I have to get out and crank?" Iain asked.

"If you will," said Jack.

As Iain did so, he muttered, "Don't run me over."

Minutes later, while crossing the small bridge into the center of town, Jack got Carla's hair in his mouth. She chuckled, tucking the fly-a-ways.

"Can you see where you're goin?" asked Iain.

"Don't worry," Jack replied, smiling. "Carla wants to see the governor's house. Do you want to go with us? Or should we drop you at the Saratoga?"

"No, I'll go," said Iain. "But they probably don't want lurkers."

"It's all right. They're all gone."

After blowing the horn to startle some children, Jack asked, "See? Pretty good driving."

"We're not dead yet," said Iain.

After an hour, they rolled to a stop in front of the boarded-up Steunenberg house—abandoned bleakness among the greens and flowering colors of the neighborhood. Jack killed the engine, and none of them spoke. It fell silent, save for the birds and a slight breeze in the trees. After a minute, Carla and Iain stepped out, followed by Jack. Iain walked ahead, past the collapsed remains of the fence, across the over-grown lawn, and up to the front of the house. For Jack, standing in the street was close enough. Carla joined him and they looked at the house and yard and watched Iain on the front porch.

"That's it?" asked Carla.

"That's it," Jack replied.

"It's so awful."

"Yes, it is." With the snow long gone, the yard was full of grass and weeds. Jack pictured everything: the fence, the children at the window, the man, the bomb. The blood. When Iain returned, Jack asked, "What do you think?"

"It's haunted." Iain leaned against the front of the Runabout and glanced at Jack who was doing the same. "We can't do this with a horse."

Jack smiled and slapped the hood. "Nope, we sure can't."

"Look at us," said Iain, grinning. "Leaning on an automobile."

"So easily amused," Carla said with a grin. "I think I'll get in."

"As you wish," said Jack, "but you'll miss out on the *leaning*."

"You boys go ahead."

After offering his hand to help Carla aboard, Jack rejoined Iain. "What did you find in Spokane? Where Darrow went?"

"I did." Iain bobbed his head.

"Tell me."

"I'll trade you," said Iain. "Information for information."

Jack cut his eyes toward Iain. "What do you want to know?"

"Your meeting with Darrow, that night by the river?"

"I guess I can say now," said Jack. "I was operating like a double, but, in truth, I was a plant. Carla was there." He turned to get her confirmation.

"I set it up," she said, beaming smugly. She scooted back, putting her feet up on the dash.

"She didn't know I wasn't *really* a double," said Jack.

"I suspected," she said.

"It worked out."

"How's that?" asked Iain.

"He got a bad juror on," said Carla.

Iain frowned. "What do you mean?"

"Someone who'd vote guilty," Jack said. When he glanced back at Carla, he saw her skirt flutter up in the breeze, exposing her knees. He gave her a knowing smile, then looked again at Iain. "Mr. Sebern. You remember him—the sheep rancher we went to see."

"Yeah, I do."

"But, it didn't make a difference in the end," Jack continued.

"That's too bad," said Iain.

"Maybe. I don't know. Alright, I told you, so it's your turn. Where'd Darrow go?"

"You're not gonna believe it," said Iain.

"After what we've seen, what *couldn't* I believe?"

"You remember how Adams was figured to be living with his uncle at that castle-looking place in Nevada?" asked Iain. "We didn't see his uncle there, but it turns out he *was* there—on the third floor, three sheets to the wind. When I went in for Adams's clothes, I missed him. But after we left, Captain Swain spoke with the man. Later, after Darrow learned of it, he sent Swain to get ol' Uncle Lillard."

"He went all the way back down there?" asked Jack. "Damn."

"Aye. Brought Lillard here to give Adams a message."

"Which was what?" asked Jack.

"First," said Iain. "you remember that sheriff from north Idaho? Name of Sutherland. He came around inquiring on Adams? Said Adams had murdered his son."

"Yeah," said Jack. "Chief turned him down."

"That was a mistake," said Carla.

Both men turned and looked at her.

"That's right, Lassy" said Iain, clearly impressed.

Jack squinted at her. "You're following this?"

"Of course, darling." She grinned. "I'm always a step ahead."

Jack smiled back. "So, dear, why was it a mistake?"

Carla sat up in the car seat, accepting the challenge. "All right. Iain, tell me if I'm right. Detective McParland didn't help Sheriff Sutherland, but Mr. Darrow did. He agreed to help. Yes, I think he made a deal with Sheriff Sutherland." She thought for a second. "Jack, didn't that sheriff take Adams, right after Adams testified?" She saw Jack nod. "So that was worked out by Mr. Darrow ahead of time. Ok, well ... so why did Adams change his testimony against Mr. Haywood?"

"Are you giving up?" asked Jack.

"No, no," Iain said. "Keep going. You're heading the right way."

Carla scrunched her lips, then continued. "Ok, so ... Adams was in the penitentiary, but Mr. Darrow needed him to change his story. So, Mr. Darrow had the uncle brought here ... to take a message to Adams. But what was the message? Something was offered to Adams." She paused, mulled and continued. "Maybe Mr. Darrow told Adams—through the uncle—that Adams was going to be tried for the murder of boy. Hmmm. I might be stuck."

"You're doing good," said Iain, trying to help her. "So if Adams was going to be tried for the boy's murder, then Adams would likely be hanged. Not a good outcome for him."

"Right—" she began.

Jack joined in. "But ... but if Adams changed his testimony in the Haywood trial, then Mr. Darrow would be sure that Adams—"

"Darrow promised to represent Adams in that other trial!" Carla shouted, trying to beat Jack to the conclusion.

Iain applauded as Carla stood in the Runabout and bowed.

"So, that's where Darrow went, right in the middle of Haywood's trial?" Jack said, dumbfounded.

"Precisely," said Iain.

Jack looked at Carla still up in the car. "How'd you see all that?"

She hopped to the street. "I worked for Mr. Darrow, remember? Everything is a chess to him."

"Bad thing is," said Iain, now somber, "Mr. Darrow did his law magic, and the animal who killed that boy, and Pete, and that family in San Francisco, and a hundred others, I'm sure—he's free again."

They held silent for a moment. Having been carried away in the fun of solving the puzzle, they were shocked by the image it formed. Jack shook his head. "I'm sure Sutherland had no idea he was being played, that Darrow had agreed to come to Adams's defense. That's pretty shitty, you ask me."

"His first job was to win for Mr. Haywood, right?" asked Carla.

"I guess," said Jack. "But still, doesn't sit right."

"No, it doesn't," said Carla, now standing in front of him, leaning her back against his chest. His arms were draped around her waist from behind, their fingers intertwined.

Suddenly Jack shook his head in realization of another detail. "Good Lord. So Darrow pretended to be ill so he could go represent the low-life. Even got his wife to help."

"Aye," said Iain. "He lied to Judge Wood."

For a moment, the three watched two young girls playing hopscotch across the street. The only sounds: the small shoes tapping the chalked walk and the girls' laughter as they leapt their markers. Eventually Jack asked Iain, "What's next for you? Did you get a new assignment?"

"Nah, I'm leaving the Pinkertons," said Iain.

"Is that right?" asked Jack, clearly disappointed.

"Mn-huh. I'm going to Seattle."

"Your father lives there?"

Iain nodded. "A friend of his is starting an aeroplane company. A man named Boeing. He offered me a job."

"What kind of company?" asked Carla.

"Aeroplane," said Jack. "Flying machines."

"Oh my, Iain," she said. "That's exciting."

"Don't ask him how they work," Jack said with a smirk. "He doesn't know."

"I know. The propeller turns," began Carla, "and that blows air over the wings which lift it up, right?"

Iain laughed. "Sort of."

She flashed a winsome smile at Jack. "See? Always a step ahead."

Jack chuckled, then looked at Iain. "I think it's terrific, you and your aeroplanes. So long as you get me a ride in one."

Carla spun. "Never, Jack. You'll never get in one."

"Why?" asked Jack. "You know how they work, so—"

"That doesn't matter one hoot. They're too dangerous. You're not flying." As she turned back, she caught Iain's nod to Jack. "No," she said, waggling her finger at them, as if to mischievous pups.

"So, Miss Capone," Iain began. "Old Jack's going to Chicago. You too?"

"Eventually." Carla glanced up at Jack. "My cousin Al is moving there from Brooklyn. I don't have other family, so"—she squeezed Jack's arm—"we think we'll go, someday."

Jack nodded. "But Denver first."

"Back to Denver, then Chicago?" asked Iain.

Carla beamed. "Mr. Pinkerton asked Jack to run the Denver office. Made him a detective."

Iain pulled away, staring at Jack. "Ya don't say!"

Jack nodded with a self-congratulatory grin. "We'll see."

"You devil," Iain continued.

Carla squeezed Jack's arm. "I'm very proud of him."

Iain pulled a breath. "Good luck to you both, then." He then focused squarely on Jack. "And you, my friend, be safe."

Jack gave a small snort of understanding. "I will. Thank you."

★

– 72 –

THURSDAY
August 8, 1907

As the Denver streetcar squeaked along tracks embedded in Fifteenth Street's red-brick paving, its connectors to the overhead wires crackled with wisps of sparks—the popping consequences of little electric bursts vaporizing as they appeared. From his seat near the back of the streetcar, Jack held a new, brown homburg hat in his lap and gazed indifferently at the passing city. Noting his reflection in the glass, he touched the shield-knot of his black tie, and then looked down at the watch chain connecting his suit's vest pockets. He tugged at the chain, creating a golden smile in its drape. When the trolley stopped at the Mining Exchange Building, a number of people exited while others boarded—those who'd been waiting in the shadow of the building's clock tower with its sentinel—a twelve-foot copper prospector. As the streetcar resumed, sparks sputtered and Jack stood, releasing his seat to a woman in mourning crepe. At Curtis and Sixteenth, he stepped to the street, donned his hat, and walked half a block, arcing around a paint crew before entering the shuttered Tabor Opera House. Inside, he climbed the stairs to the fourth floor. The hallway was empty. Even the chairs once occupied by guards were gone. He entered the unmarked Pinkerton office.

"Good morning, Detective," said a woman.

"Good morning, Margaret," he replied, stopping in front of her desk. He gave an anticipatory nod toward the closed inner door.

"They've been here for about fifteen minutes."

He riffled mail on her desk. "Anything from Mr. Friedman?"

She handed him an opened letter. "Yes. He declined to rejoin us. Says he prefers to write his books."

"Fair enough." Jack nodded. "At least we offered." Glancing again at the closed interior door, he blew a sigh. Then he removed his homburg and brushed a bit of dust from it before hanging it on the stand next to his black hat with the silver stars. A look of surprise came to him as he studied the outer office. "The boxes ... They came for them?"

"Yes, Sir. At half past eight. I told them to take everything you marked yesterday for Detective McParland. And anything else you marked for the Chicago office."

"Good," Jack said softly. He looked again at the closed door to his office. "This will be interesting," he muttered to himself. He turned the handle and entered. Inside, he was greeted by Darrow and George who were standing, apparently having heard him through the door. "Gentlemen," said Jack, shaking their hands.

"Jack, this is George Pennington," began Darrow. "He's been appointed the interim president of the Federation."

"Yes, of course," said Jack, addressing George. "We saw each other at the trial. And the chief and I discussed the arrangement—" He stopped himself and gave a flat smile. "Of course the Pinkertons are aware of you, Mr. Pennington."

"As we're aware of you, Detective Garrett," George replied.

"Gentlemen," Darrow began as he lit a cigarette. "So, that's established—we all know each other. We also know the purpose of this meeting is for the greater good. There's work to be done, an agreement to be reached—one that will serve the interests of the Pinkerton clients, as well as the Federation."

Jack nodded, motioning them to chairs. Once they were seated, he looked at the two older men. They were waiting for him to speak. He was surprised not to feel more nervous. But why should he be nervous? These men came to him, in his new position. They were here, in his office, once the office of the great Chief Detective James McParland—now the office of freshly minted Detective Jack Garrett—a room barren of accoutrements and décor as all of McParland's personal effects and furnishings had been removed, leaving the desktop, tables, and walls bare, save the wooden box telephone by the door. Even the large, green wool rug had belonged to McParland. At least the array of wingback chairs belonged to the Pinkertons, and thus were available for the three men to use that morning, while they negotiated the fate of William Haywood.

Though Billy Bryan peered curiously at Neva's invalid chair, the summer heat kept him recumbent in the shade of an ancient oak looming from just beyond his cage. He was Denver Zoo's only permanent resident, a black bear named in honor of his donor, William Jennings Bryan. There were other furry residents of the zoo, but their permanence was in question—as they consisted of several hundred, fast-multiplying red squirrels that had appended the entirety of City Park as their home, even the adjacent Park Hill Heights neighborhood, including the trees surrounding the Haywoods' house.

Vernie, the eldest Haywood daughter, now thirteen, pivoted her mother's chair to face the bear. Neva smiled. They were quickly joined by Henrietta, ten, who stared wide-eyed at the snoozing Billy Bryan.

"He's so big," said Vernie.

"He'd be even bigger if they let him out," said Henrietta.

"That's not true," Vernie snapped.

"It is so," persisted Henrietta. "In the wild, bears grow bigger and meaner!" She growled at Vernie.

Neva smiled at her youngest. "How do you know that, smarty?"

"The zoo man said it." Henrietta pointed at an attendant addressing a group of visitors.

As Neva noted the zoo attendant, she saw Carla approaching from that same direction.

"Hello," said Carla, offering a pensive smile. "Mrs. Haywood?"

Neva looked at the young beauty. "Miss Capone," she said, making it more of a statement than a greeting.

"Yes, Ma'am. Is this still a good time to talk? Here?"

"Yes, it's fine." Neva looked at her girls. "These are my daughters, Vernie and Henrietta. Girls, this is Miss Carla Capone. She works ... she worked for the union." Neva smiled at Carla. "I'm sure you're employed elsewhere now."

"In truth," Carla replied, "I don't work for anyone."

Neva considered her. "It's a commendable sentiment, dear. But everyone works for someone—even if only for ourselves. And all are answerable to God."

"Yes," replied Carla, glancing aside, hoping the young girls might be dismissed.

Neva saw the unspoken request and sent her girls for ice cream from a vendor alongside the park's lake. She then rolled herself to a bench and indicated Carla should join her."

Carla sat and smoothed her skirt. "Mrs. Haywood—"

"I'm Neva. Just call me Neva."

Carla smiled. "All right."

"Listen," began Neva. "George—Mr. Pennington—asked that I meet you. So, here we are. But you need to understand something: I want nothing further to do with Mr. Haywood—and that includes matters of the Federation. And of course I have no desire to be of benefit to the Pinkertons. So it's best, I believe, for you to save your breath. Let's presume you asked of me whatever you came to ask, and I said, 'no thank you,' and that was that."

Carla lowered her nose slightly. "I know you bear me no fondness, for having betrayed the Federation and Mr. Darrow, but—"

"I have no mind on that account—one way or the other. I don't know the particulars, and don't wish to. Both the Federation and the Pinkertons are corrupt institutions, or they have been. God has opened my eyes to the cruelty and savagery of the man whom I once called husband. I don't care about him or whatever fate befalls him. I care to seek the will of God. And that George be held blameless—that he can conduct the new business of the Federation in peace. The Federation, when serving its members, is a wonder. It can serve labor honorably if it's led by honorable men."

"I agree. My father was a member and—" Carla stopped upon seeing Neva look away. There would be no shared camaraderie here. It was best she get to her point. "The man whom I love, Jack Garrett, now Detective Garrett, runs the Pinkerton office here. He's been tasked by his boss, Mr. Pinkerton, to resolve some outstanding concerns against your husband, but he needs—"

"I heard Detective McParland was fired for what he did."

"Not fired, I don't think. But he did move back to Chicago ... or he is moving back there. I really don't know."

Neva caught herself. "It doesn't matter what those men do."

"No. I suppose not."

"What can I do for your Detective Garrett?"

Carla took a breath, feeling as refreshed as she was intimidated by the direct question. "The union, the Federation, has expelled Mr. Haywood, as you know, but the Pinkertons have other clients, banks in particular, who want to open investigations into the Federation's finances—what Mr. Haywood may have taken, what he may owe."

"That will be a messy matter."

"And all that stirring may get Mr. Pennington's name—"

"No!" Neva pointed at Carla. "The Pinkertons and the government agreed to leave George out of *any* investigations. Any improprieties were entirely Bill's."

"I was told as much. Yes, Ma'am. But I was told it might not be possible—not entirely—to protect Mr. Pennington, as he *was* treasurer during the—"

"He had nothing to do with any of the stolen money."

"I know," Carla said. "They know that too. But forces may still pull George in. And the newspapers, well—"

Neva shook her head, agitated. "You didn't come to tell me this. What is their proposal?"

Carla took a breath. "Russia."

"Russia?"

"Mr. Haywood must go to Russia."

Neva frowned, absorbing the idea, and then smiled. "Russia?"

"Yes," Carla said. "That would end the financial inquiries."

Neva touched her own face, traced the bridge of her nose, and snorted a surrendering chuckle. "That seems silly. Bill will think it's a reward."

"But you wouldn't object?" asked Carla. "They need to know."

"Object? Why would I? Bill is a murdering ogre who's lost his way. A cruel husband and an absent father. Plus, I suppose I could divorce him if he's ... exiled. But he couldn't come back."

"He can't."

"Good." Neva shook away some thoughts, nodded, and gave a resigned smile. "What do they need from me?"

Carla dipped her chin faintly—a feminine salute. "He's living in the Pioneer Building suites, currently?"

"I'd imagine so. I live in my home near here."

"Yes. They'd like you to invite him to that house, your house, at 11:00 tomorrow morning."

"What reason do I give?"

"I don't think it matters, as long as he comes."

"All right, but how does that help?"

"They're going to tell him and send him on his way. But Mr. Pennington doesn't want it happening in the Federation's building."

Neva's eyes narrowed. "What's George's role in this? Why isn't he asking me this himself?"

"He's is meeting with the Pinkertons right now. Along with Mr. Darrow. They thought you'd prefer to appear ... disassociated. As least involved as possible."

Neva gave Carla a conspiratorial nod. "They think we're invisible. Send a woman to talk to a woman and no one will notice."

Carla rolled her eyes. "I know. It's ... well ..."

"Yeah," said Neva. She looked at Carla squarely. "I appreciate you coming." Seeing her girls bounding back loudly with half-eaten ice creams, Neva asked them, "Did you bring any change?" Henrietta handed her a few ice-cream-covered nickels. Neva glanced again at Carla. "I'll do it. You can tell them."

George was pacing Jack's new office. "Sure, the press would lap it up, but I say no. It should be kept quiet—the entirety of our plans for Bill. There's no need for publicity. It'd probably unravel the whole ball of yarn." His eyes met Jack's. "Which wouldn't serve either of our interests."

"Agreed," said Jack. He then noticed Darrow was studying him, setting off a flush of intimidation that tingled his spine. He turned into the wind. "Is there something you want to ask me, Mr. Darrow?"

Darrow smiled broadly and shook his head. "No, son. I'm simply impressed. You outflanked our man finding Adams. You buffaloed me with false information on jury selection. And you brought my once-assistant, Miss Capone, over to your cause. And now, here you sit, in McParland's office. How old are you, son?"

"I'm thirty," Jack lied, adding three and regretting it. He needn't be intimidated. He was a few years older than McParland had been when McParland got his first posting—though McParland's first posting wasn't to lead a whole division. Albeit, this was temporary. Jack pressed down his doubts. He could manage this. He could. He kept his gaze on the lawyer. "Why do you ask?"

Darrow gave a surrendering gesture, palms out. "I'm impressed. That's all. Especially if you can turn your agency from their criminalities."

"That's not what we—" George tried.

"Mmmph," snorted Jack. "Criminalities? Ours? Is that right? Say again how you, on behalf of the Federation"—he glanced at George—"got to that killer to lie under oath."

A knowing half-smile came to Darrow's face, followed by a prolonged nod and a pivot. He clicked his tongue and looked at George. "So, what do you think, George, is the plan acceptable to the Federation?"

George looked at Jack and nodded. "So long as the Pinkertons—meaning their clients, the banks and anyone else—will hold to the bargain. If one or two don't agree later, down the road, and make a public fuss about the money, it'll cast a shadow over the union. And Bill won't be around to answer the charges. That'll leave the Federation bare to meet those financial obligations—something we simply cannot do."

"Our clients will let this matter rest, in perpetuity," said Jack. "Mr. Pinkerton asked me to give you that commitment."

"And if Bill Haywood returns?" asked Darrow, his eyes lost between Jack's and George's chairs, making the intended recipient unclear. As a result, they answered simultaneously: one that Haywood would be arrested, the other that he'd be killed.

– 73 –

FRIDAY
August 9, 1907

On Denver's Bellaire Street, a motorized taxi rumbled to a stop behind a Packard Model S that was parked in front of the Haywood's Park Hill Heights home. From the backseat of the taxi, Haywood studied the Packard. It was his, yet he didn't recall it being there. Of specific curiosity was the steamer trunk tied to the back of it. He then noted other automobiles parked in front of the house, and focused on a man, dressed like a Pinkerton, leaning against a red Runabout just ahead of the Packard.

Having heard the vehicle approach, Jack adjusted his broad-brimmed black hat, stepped away from his Runabout, and turned to squarely face the taxi.

The taxi driver came around and opened the passenger door. Haywood froze while stepping out, his back arched, one polished shoe hovering midair, his eye staring at the house. Two men whom he recognized as Federation were on the wide porch steps, flanking the door, each bearing a sawed-off shotgun. "Wait here," Haywood grumbled at the driver, then finished standing.

Jack moved slightly toward Haywood, and for a moment they considered each other. Haywood stopped walking. He looked at the porch, then back at Jack. He was as perplexed by the Federation men on his porch as he was by the lone Pinkerton in his yard. He vacillated for a moment, almost swaying between the two threats. Like a grizzly surprised by mountain lions to one side and a wolf to the other, he calculated whether to charge or run. After five seconds, he recovered, reassuming his veneer of coarse indignation, and strolled quickly toward the house. As he neared the porch, the guards came down from the steps and stood in front of him.

"Mr. Haywood," said one guard.

"How's your day?" asked Haywood, feigning interest.

"We can't let you enter," said the other guard.

Haywood stopped. The dead eye glared. "What the hell—"

"Sir," one raised his shotgun. "We've got orders to not—"

"Orders? Whose? George Pennington's? That sorry sack of shit." He pulled a Colt .45 revolver from under his coat and held it toward the ground. "Tick tock, time to move," he growled. When they didn't, he stepped back and yelled at the windows. "Neva! Come tell these whores' sons, Tweedledee and Dum, that I'm about to shoot them if they don't move." He looked behind him. "And why is a goddamned Pink on my lawn?"

"Bill!" said George, hurrying out the front door while putting on his Stetson.

"This is my house, George! Get off my porch. And tell—"

"No, Bill," snapped George. "That's not right anymore."

"What in God's name do you think you're doing?" Haywood fumed, raising the pistol, flashing a glare back at Jack, then forward again at George. The guards leveled their double-barrels, clicking the hammers back. "What is this?" Haywood asked, his voice wobbling ever so slightly.

George lifted a hand. "Stop, Bill. Put it down. Otherwise everything will end for you—right now. I don't want that, and you don't either."

Haywood spun, pointing his pistol at Jack, unnerved by Jack's continued advance from his rear. "Get off my property, you shit-eating Pink!"

Jack didn't flinch.

"Put it down, Bill," said George again.

"Yes, put it down, Bill," echoed Jack.

Haywood boiled, turning, snorted a chuckle, and re-holstered his pistol. "Fine. I'll play your game, Georgy. What's all this?"

George whistled over his shoulder, and a tall Federation guard came out onto the porch. All the men, including Haywood, watched the tall guard trot past George, go around Haywood, nod at Jack, and go to the taxi where he paid the driver and told him to scoot. After the vehicle left, the tall guard took up a position behind Haywood, near Jack.

Haywood nodded at the trunk on his Packard. "What's that?"

"All you're allowed to take," replied George.

Haywood pivoted. "What?"

"You stole eighty-five thousand, six hundred and twenty-three dollars and thirty-five cents from the Western Federation of Miners. You received a letter from Mr. Darrow to that effect. As of the date of that letter—today's date—you, William Haywood, are no longer associated with the Federation. You no longer have access to any Federation property, including the offices or the suites in the Pioneer Building. The locks have been changed. That includes that automobile and this house."

"That's my car! And this house isn't Federation property, you half-witted, cuckolding, son of a bitch!" Haywood's face had ripened to shades of panicked red over sweaty white.

"That's correct, this house is not the Federation's," George said calmly. "But I'm barring your entrance all the same—on behalf of Neva and the court. The sheriff offered to come today, but I assured him that these fine union men would uphold the court order."

"What goddamned court? What order?"

"As you know—this morning Neva sued you for divorce." George pulled a piece a paper from his coat pocket. "Here's the court's order restraining you from entering. Signed by none other than the chief justice of the Colorado Supreme Court, Justice Goddard. Imagine that."

"On what grounds? Nevada, goddamnit, roll your ass out here!"

George nodded at the tall guard behind Haywood. Haywood turned and watched the man crank the Packard to start it.

Haywood spun back. "Goddamn you all. I'll kill every one of you!" Just then he saw Vernie rolling Neva onto the porch. Henrietta was just behind. Trailing after them was Claus, Haywood's bulldog. Neva and the girls came to a stop beside George. Claus walked near the top of the steps and plopped down. All stared at Haywood, expressionless. Haywood's eyes filled with angry tears. "Nevada. Neva. Girls. What is this? You can't—"

Neva handed an envelope up to George.

Haywood shouted, "I got your goddamned divorce papers."

George gave the envelope to a guard, who then stepped from the porch and handed it to Haywood. With the tall guard now behind the wheel, the Packard was gurgling and purring. George flashed a sad yet reassuring smile at Neva. Neva touched Vernie's hand and whispered to her. Vernie took Henrietta, and both girls disappeared inside the house. Claus remained where he was—jowls splayed on the porch planks. As Haywood was busy tearing into the envelope and assessing the documents, he hadn't noticed his girls going back in the house. He looked up at the porch, then back at the papers, struggling to make sense of what he had read. "What the hell is this? A steamer to St. Petersburg?"

"That's right," said Jack, coming around Haywood to stand between him and the porch. "Third Class on the SS *Finland*. Red Star Line. New York to a place called Antwerp, then on to St. Petersburg. In Russia."

"I know it's in Russia, you ass."

"Of course you do," said Jack.

"It leaves New York a little over a week from now, on the twentieth," said George. "That's all the Federation will give you."

"As for getting from here to New York," said Jack, "that's a parting gift from the Union Pacific and us Pinks." He nodded toward the papers in Haywood's hands. "There's a letter there to that effect, signed by General Dodge and Mr. Pinkerton."

Haywood looked back to George and Neva. "I'm not going to New York. And I'm sure the hell not going to Russia."

"These men," said George, indicating the guards closest to the porch, "will accompany you until you're on board the SS *Finland*."

"The hell they will."

"It's very generous," said Jack. "Some of us wanted to take you out and shoot you, like a useless horse."

"That's correct," added George. "In fact, Mr. Darrow suggested we throw you down the Stratton Mine shaft."

"Did he?" snarked Jack. "I like that."

"What ... are ... what?" Haywood stuttered, struggling to grasp the tiers of duplicity packed in their words. "The Pinkertons and my attorney are— What?" He fixed on George. "This is madness."

George persisted. "Every one of our local Federation presidents voted for this—voted for you being packed off to Russia. Every single local. It was unanimous. And yes, the Pinks are on board too." He motioned toward Jack and received Jack's nod. "So this is what you get, Bill. This is *all* you get."

Haywood pivoted to Jack, then back to George, then to Jack again, and then to Neva on the porch. "Neva, my darling. Talk some sense into your man George here. You can't want me to go, to leave our daughters and you, and Wi—" He stopped just shy of saying, "Winnie."

She looked away.

His voice tightened. "Is that right, Nevada? You still won't speak to me? Still? Even now?"

"She's pledged not to," said George. "As you know."

Haywood reeled until his gaze settled on the disinterested dog. "You're keeping Claus?" he asked, his voice almost shrill.

"Your deputy sheriff?" quipped George as everyone glanced at Claus. "Take him." Claus wrenched around to lick himself.

Haywood scowled and commanded, "Come, Claus!" The bulldog slowly rose and ambled off the steps toward Haywood. Everyone was silent, watching the dog's short legs moseying toward the glowering man. As Haywood scooped the dog with his left hand, his right bore a finger at George. "You're swine of the lowest order, George Pennington! All this. You're weak—a weak man hiding behind my lame wife." A menacing laugh burrowed out of him as he began to nod. "Yes, yes, isn't this rosy. You're making your move. I see it. I see it *all* now. Scheming, using her, an unfaithful excuse of a woman. And you both conspired with the goddamned Pinks." He wheeled on Jack and was met by a blank stare. "Enemies of the worker—of this nation." Again he drew his revolver and again pointed it at Jack.

Jack methodically drew the FN automatic pistol (the one McParland took off Haywood during the Denver arrest) and aimed at Haywood's face.

Silence—save bird chirps and the chitter of red squirrels.

Haywood squinted at the FN gun. "Is that my automatic?"

Jack might have feigned sarcastic surprise, were he not disgusted beyond mockery. "It's mine. Now."

Haywood began shaking his head, then growled, "I should've bombed the Pinkerton offices. Should've killed all of you *and* your families. You're all—"

"Shut your mouth!" roared Jack, rage hitting the back of his throat, filling his nose and eyes, the heat finding his ears. He moved within feet of Haywood. "You're a two-bit mangy dog, reeking of death. A murderer who escaped the noose only on account of your tricky lawyer. And it's only because of the law, the law you spit on, that we don't gun you down right here. Hell, we should get your daughters back out here and kill you in front of them. Eye for an eye—for what you did to Steunenberg—killin him in front of his kids." He huffed. "And then you had Adams kill a whole family in San Francisco. The man, his wife, and his two children. And he killed a good agent, a man named Pete who—"

"I had no doing in that," tried Haywood.

In a flash, Jack smacked the big man's jaw with the pistol, sending Haywood stumbling but not down. Claus came loose, hit the ground and ran off. "I said shut your goddamn mouth," shouted Jack. "I was there! Best for everyone: we shove a stick of dynamite up your ass and light it."

Haywood stepped toward the street, cocking his revolver as he resumed aiming at Jack.

Jack continued, the automatic still leveled at Haywood's face. "But we won't do that. Not because we can't. Hell, no one would flinch at us killing you here. But we're not your scum sort. And we won't let you escape justice again by corruption of the law. So we're gonna feed you to the Russians." Jack stepped forward, further corralling Haywood toward the idling Packard. "But it's not justice—letting you leave. Far from it. So, by God, please—don't lower your gun, Billy-boy. Make me think you might pull that trigger. With this fancy automatic, I'll have two rounds through your good eye before you hit the ground."

Haywood staggered slightly, as if some of Jack's words had shrapnelled within him, shredding organs—the ruptured bleeding of long-buried despair. His countenance became distorted—first to blankness, then to a frown, and then softening to a stare, followed by slow reformation until his eye closed, chin dipping as if in prayer. The cards had been dealt. His fortune had been told. He murmured, "Russia," and lowered his gun.

"Damn you," said Jack, stepping forward to yank the revolver from Haywood's hand.

"Yes, Russia," said George who had now moved into the yard behind Jack. "I wrote a letter of introduction to Mr. Trotsky. High recommendations and all that. Lies, but we'll let that revolutionary do as he wishes with you. Of course, I have no idea if he'll receive it before you get there, or if he ever will."

Haywood gave a snort. "At least I'll be appreciated."

"Piece of advice," said George, "don't steal from the Bolsheviks."

"You're done in America," said Jack. "Bulletin already dispatched today: any union man sees you after August twentieth, you'll have a high bounty on your head, dead or alive. The Federation"—he nodded toward George—"and we the Pinkertons, have agreed to pay half that reward, whatever it's up to at that time. It starts at fifteen-thousand dollars today."

George motioned toward the guards, and they began ushering Haywood the last distance to the automobile.

Walking backwards, Haywood pointed violently at George, then at Neva on the porch, then at Jack, and then back to George—as if his finger was the tip of a flailing spear. His mouth shaped unheard words, silent invectives. When he touched the car, one of the men opened the door for him to get into a rear seat. He did, but looked forward, keeping the dead-eye toward the house, toward the Pinkertons, toward to the Federation, toward Neva and his girls. Once the guards got in, the Packard drove away, turning from sight at Twenty-Sixth Street.

Approaching Jack, George whistled and Claus ambled back to the porch.

"Sticks in my craw," said Jack. "Letting him go like that."

"Mine too. But let's see what happens," replied George.

"Think he'll try to come back?"

"Probably."

"If he does," said Jack, "he'll be shot."

"I think you made that clear."

"We'll see."

"Yeah," agreed George. "Either way, better days ahead."

Jack smiled and shook George's hand. "Better days, Wobbly."

"Better days, Pink," replied George. He then returned to the porch where he leaned to kiss Neva's wet cheek.

Jack walked to his Runabout and slid behind the wheel.

As Neva wiped her tear and sniffed, something caught her eye. "Look, Cardinal Dedlock is back," she whispered, pointing to the red bird preening beyond the end of the porch.

"He's a handsome devil," said George. "Lady Dedlock must be pleased."

"I would imagine so," she said with a wink.

George held the door wide as he rolled Neva inside.

Behind them, Jack had already driven away.

– 74 –

TUESDAY
August 20, 1907

While the Red Star Line's SS *Finland* was steaming from New York Harbor, rumor had it Steve Adams was on the run. At his mid-June murder trial in Wallace, his attorney had caused quite a stir. Even the judge had fawned like a black-robed ingénue at Clarence Darrow's presence. But Sheriff Sutherland was not impressed. Quite the opposite. He raged at Darrow's duplicity—the audacity of the snake to come defend Adams, the very man Darrow had helped Sutherland arrest.

Still, it would be a simple murder trial, no more than a day or two. Hardly worth seating a jury. The verdict a foregone conclusion. That is, once the circuit judge arrived. And once they obtained a sworn affidavit from Orchard, bearing witness to Adams killing Frankie, the sheriff's boy. At that time, of course, Orchard was cooling his heels in the Idaho Pen while Darrow was away "sick."

At first, Sutherland threatened to wire Judge Wood about Darrow's unwelcome presence in Wallace, hoping Darrow would leave on his own accord, or be recalled to Boise either way leaving Adams without representation—the way it should be for a guilty man, reasoned Sutherland. But that threat ended abruptly after Darrow explained two things: First, Sheriff Sutherland had committed felony perjury when he swore to Judge Wood that he had no knowledge of another warrant for Adams. In fact, Darrow had shown Sutherland a bench warrant for Adams from a San Francisco judge. It pre-dated Sutherland's warrant. Darrow had then destroyed it, assuring Sutherland that it didn't matter. (Sutherland didn't know Darrow had instructed Captain Swain to mock up and send that San Francisco warrant.) Second, exposing the whole arrangement would trigger a mistrial, setting Adams loose—the last thing Sutherland wanted.

So Sutherland kept quiet. He was furious, but he thought he had the matter in hand. He sent a deputy down to Boise to discretely get a statement from Orchard. But the man returned empty handed—Orchard said he hadn't seen Adams near the sheriff's boy. Then the circuit judge was killed by a falling tree, and it took weeks for another to be appointed and arrive. Finally the trial came. But with no witness to the killing, the jury deadlocked and Adams walked free. Then Darrow returned to Boise on July 4th, and Adams disappeared.

At that, Sheriff Sutherland resolved to find and kill Adams by his own means. With the Canadian border so close, he knew where Adams would likely go. But to get there, Adams would need to flank the Cabinet Mountain range, either to the east or the west. He might go west from Wallace, past the destroyed Bunker Hill Mine, on to Coeur d'Alene, and then north to Canada. Or by train east, maybe as far as Missoula, then north through the Flathead Indian Reservation. Unable to search both directions, Sutherland chose east, betting Adams would think the reservation would give him cover. But weeks of searching, including scores of conversations with Flatheads, led to nothing. So, Sutherland returned to Wallace with plans for a tracking expedition into Canada.

His luck changed upon arriving home where an urgent message awaited him. It was from the barkeep at the Eagle Head Saloon there in Wallace: Adams had been spotted in town as recently as a week prior. Sutherland hurried to the Eagle Head and approached the bar. "Clement," he said.

Clement poured Sutherland a drink, then spoke. "He was in here. Had his hat down round his eyes, but I recognized him. He knew I'd seen him cause he hurried out quick enough. But I knew it was him. Same sombitch as at that trial, about your boy. Same one that killed the mine fella, standing right there." He indicated the spot where Adams had shot the Bunker Hill vice president. "You remember. Before he—"

"Yeah," said Sutherland.

"Heard he's been in Pat's livery last few nights."

Sutherland's face tightened to stone. He turned to leave.

"He'll know you're coming," said Clement.

"How?"

"Couple union boys just lit out. Knew you were back."

"Just now?"

"Uh-huh. Ten minutes maybe."

Sutherland looked toward the saloon's front windows. "He won't stay put. He'll be trying to get—" Realizing something, Sutherland left before finishing either the sentence or his drink.

At the nearby Wallace depot, a short Northern Pacific steamer stood hissing as it took on water and a few passengers. Sutherland walked alongside the tracks, looking under each car, between each coupling, and then began the same on the far side—though he avoided looking at the spot where Frankie died. There was no sign of Adams. He heard the conductor bellow, "All aboard for Missoula and points east! All aboard!"

Sutherland ascended the steps and walked the length of the interior, moving through the passenger and cargo cars, checking faces, heading toward the rear. Then he hopped to the ground and climbed aboard the caboose, but found its door locked. He shielded his eyes to peer through the windows but saw nothing—he knew short hauls often pull an empty caboose.

The engineer blew the engine's whistle, the bells rang, and the wheels began to screech and turn, each car successively lurching to life with a loud, steel clang. Sutherland returned to the station's platform and walked with the train as it slowly rolled. Reaching the end of the platform, he stood and watched the remainder of the train move by. Just as the caboose came alongside, the face of Steve Adams momentarily appeared in the caboose's dark window.

"Son of a bitch!" Sutherland shouted. He jumped from the platform and ran along the tracks. As he reached the steps to the caboose, he grabbed the rail and lifted himself aboard. He drew his pistol. Now clear of the station, the train was lazily gaining speed. He approached the door of the caboose. No longer locked, it was swinging open. On the floor, just inside the black interior, he saw the legs and back of a stabbed engineer. Sutherland's nerves prickled. "Adams, you're done," he said, easing inside, pistol first.

In an instant, a knife sliced from the darkness, cutting Sutherland's hand, causing him to drop the pistol and jerk himself back onto the rear deck, blood rushing from the wound. Adams burst onto the deck, knife fast at Sutherland. Immediately they were struggling for control, to stay alive. Sutherland's blood smeared Adams's ferrety smile. Adams's hands were shaking, the knife two inches from the sheriff's ear. Then Sutherland pivoted, spinning, throwing Adams against the railing. For a moment they separated, panting, Sutherland's gray eyes fixed unflinchingly on the killer's face. Then they rushed each other again and Sutherland side-stepped the stab, grabbing Adams's wrist. Holding the knife-wielding hand away, Sutherland began pummeling Adams in the ribs, overpowering him, beating the breath from the man. Finally, the knife came loose, clattering onto the deck. Both men dove for it. The train, now nearing speed, bore into a curve. They strained against the turn. After a few more deftly placed punches, Sutherland had the blade. He held Adams from behind, standing him up, left arm encasing the man, right arm bearing the big knife to the man's scrawny neck.

"This it? Is this the knife?" Sutherland screamed over the clack-clack-clack of the cross-ties, the wind, the anger, the exhaustion, the regret. "You killed my son with this?" When Adams gave a nod, it ended. Sutherland yanked the blade across the man's throat, opening his carotids, and shoved him from the caboose, watching him crash bloodily onto the rail bed. There Adams grew smaller and smaller until dissolving from view behind the train that remained, bearing ahead.

Sutherland collapsed, sliding till sitting, looking through the railing toward the winnowing ground. When he saw he still held the knife in his blood-drenched hand, he flung it—a blur twirling till it fell from the sky, its red blade clanging on the black steel road, a wending wound through the wilderness.

★

EPILOGUE

Within a year, Neva and George had moved to Spokane. Though Neva's health gradually declined, she managed an active life, attended by her daughters and a nurse, and always by George. George left the Federation in 1909 to make a career of building houses—including the home he built for Neva and himself. They were married in a small ceremony on July 10, 1911. In 1921, Neva's health took a difficult turn and she died from polio-related complications. George, Winnie, and her daughters were by her side. She never heard from Bill again.

Winnie Minor remained with the Socialist Party of America for the rest of her life, though with limited activism. She married, had eight children, three of whom fought in World War Two. Of those three, one survived a Japanese prison camp, one was killed in North Africa, and the third was killed on Omaha Beach on D-Day. Winnie died in an automobile accident on Christmas Eve, 1951.

James McParland retired from the Pinkerton Detective Agency in 1908, the same year the Federal Bureau of Investigations (FBI) was formed. McParland spent his remaining years in Denver, alongside his wife, Mary. They had no children, but were visited regularly by many acquaintances, including Jack and Carla. McParland died in 1919, in Denver's Mercy Hospital, just blocks from the Park Hill Heights home that once belonged to the Haywoods.

Harry Orchard was formally convicted of the murder of Governor Steunenberg, but, as had been pre-arranged, his death sentence was commuted to life in prison due to his cooperation in the Haywood trial. He remained in the Idaho State Penitentiary in Boise, working as a prison trustee, raising chickens and growing strawberries. He died there in 1954.

William Haywood arrived in St. Petersburg amid an early blizzard in November of 1907. There he made acquaintance with leaders of the Bolshevik party, including Leon Trotsky. Though he became fluent in Russian, participated in the 1917 Bolshevik revolution and the subsequent civil war, and became a confidant to Vladimir Lenin, his presence never amounted to more than political curiosity and occasional propaganda. In 1924, convinced that the new leader, Joseph Stalin, had poisoned Lenin, Haywood feared for his life and attempted to win an alliance with Stalin. But it was to no avail—he was no longer welcome at the Kremlin. In 1928, abandoned and penniless, he died of a stroke in a dilapidated barn outside of Moscow. Only then did Stalin honor him, interring half of Haywood's ashes in the wall of the Kremlin's necropolis. The other half were shipped to Chicago where they were buried with labor-hero honors near a monument to the 1886 Haymarket rioters—the men who had inspired Haywood's life of radicalism. He never attempted to communicate with Neva or their daughters, nor did he attempt to return to the United States.

Due in no small part to its troubled history under Big Bill Haywood, the Western Federation of Miners (the Federation) changed its name to the International Union of Mine, Mill, and Smelter Workers (the Mine Mill), and ended all forms of sanctioned violence. Over the ensuing decades, the Mine Mill became increasingly active in the American Communist Party and helped form the Congress of Industrial Organizations (the CIO) which later joined the American Federation of Labor (the AFL) to become the AFL-CIO that exists today. Due to the Mine Mill's heavy communist leanings, it was expelled from the CIO in 1950. Thereafter it disbanded slowly until the last remnant of the Federation was gone by 1967.

The Pinkerton Detective Agency disavowed all illegal practices after the trial of William Haywood. Still headquartered in the United States, and still bearing the solitary "private eye" logo, the Pinkerton Agency has continued to grow and works today in over one hundred countries. Its focus remains on corporate risk management and security services.

Clarence Darrow, "America's Lawyer," continued his celebrated legal career, taking on many high-profile defense cases. In 1910, his work took him to Los Angeles where he defended the bombers of the *Los Angeles Times*, only to find himself indicted for jury tampering. When, in 1924, two wealthy, thrill-seeking, Chicago teenagers kidnapped and murdered another teenager, Darrow defended them, successfully keeping them from the noose. Then, in the famous 1925 case of *Tennessee v. John Scopes*, commonly known as the Scopes Monkey Trial, Darrow defended a public-school teacher accused of teaching evolution. William Jennings Bryan, "America's Orator," and famous legal scholar (and donor of the Denver Zoo's first bear), represented the State. Though Darrow lost the case, it nevertheless opened America's national discussion of evolution. His tactics and oral arguments are still studied in law schools across the United States, especially his closing argument in the trial of William "Big Bill" Haywood. Clarence Darrow died in Chicago in 1938.

Iain Lennox became a pilot and worked for William Boeing in Seattle, creating one of the first factory-produced airplanes. In 1910, his work took him to Los Angeles where he participated in America's first Aviation Meet.

Jack Garrett and Carla Capone were married in Chicago in 1908. Soon thereafter, they formed their own independent detective agency. In 1910, their services took them to Los Angeles where the *Los Angeles Times* had been bombed by radical terrorists. There they reconnected with Iain Lennox and once again found themselves in a struggle of wits with Clarence Darrow.

★

AUTHOR'S NOTE

Historians may note that a few of the dates of actual events were adjusted in service of the story, though none significantly. Also, many readers have inquired regarding which characters were real persons and which are fictional. The following characters in this book were real people, and their actions, though dramatized, are depicted close to historically accurate. Those not listed here are amalgams of actual persons, created for dramatic purposes.

William Haywood
Nevada "Neva" Haywood
Winnie Minor
Clarence Darrow
Ruby Hammerstrom
Senator William Borah
Judge Freemont Wood
Governor Frank Steunenberg
James Branson III
Captain W. S. Swain
Chief Justice Luther Goddard
Sheriff Angus Sutherland
James McParland
Robert Pinkerton
Operative 21
Morris Friedman
Charles Siringo
Harry Orchard
Steve Adams
Lloyd Lillard
James Bullock
General Grenville Dodge
Ethel Barrymore

★

ACKNOWLEDGMENTS

I offer my unwavering gratitude and appreciation to you, the reader. Your love of written stories makes this crazy profession have meaning. I write for you.

Special thanks to my team of extraordinary editors (especially Carolyn Marlett and the inimitable Philip Newey); my array of loyal beta readers; my unflagging and ridiculously patient publisher, Lou Aronica; and the late J. Anthony Lukas, Pulitzer-winning author of *Big Trouble*, the seminal non-fiction work on the Haywood trial.

Also, I am indebted and grateful to the many historical, institutional, and governmental organizations that were invaluable to my research for this novel, including:

Ada County Courthouse
AFL-CIO
Boise State University
City of Boise
City of Denver
Found San Francisco
Historic Vehicle Association
History Colorado
History.com
Idaho Architecture Project
Idaho Mining Association
Idaho Museum of Mining and Geology
Idaho State Historical Society
Illinois Labor History Society
Jane Addams Hull-House Museum
Mining History Association
Museum of the American Railroad
National Automobile Museum
National Museum of American History
Nevada Historical Society
Pinkerton Consulting and Investigations

San Francisco Museum and Historical Society
Seventh-day Adventist Church
Smithsonian Institution
Socialist Party USA
State of Colorado–State Archives
Union Pacific Railroad Museum
University of Colorado-Boulder
University of Colorado-Denver
University of Denver Sturm College of Law
University of Idaho
University of Idaho College of Law
University of Texas School of Law
Western Museum of Mining & Industry

And it is with deep love and gratitude that I thank my parents, Robert and Carolyn, and my children, Meredith, Caroline, Kathleen, and Jack, for their unwavering love, uplifting support, and enduring patience. My cup runneth over.

★

ABOUT THE AUTHOR

David Marlett is a historical novelist, award-winning storyteller, Moth story champion, professor of story and law, and an attorney. In 2014, his first historical legal thriller, *Fortunate Son*, was well reviewed and rose to #2 in historical fiction and #3 in literature and fiction in Amazon's rankings. He has been published in a number of magazines and was Managing Editor of *OMNI Magazine*. The father of four, a graduate of Texas Tech University and The University of Texas School of Law, David currently lives in Manhattan Beach, California.

www.davidmarlett.com